RETURN TO EGYPT

THE ORACLE AWAKENS

AMANDA ROMANIA

BOOK 2 OF THE DIVINE ORACLES SERIES

Return to Egypt: The Oracle Awakens
Book Two of the Divine Oracles Series
By Amanda Romania

Published by Flower of Life Press
www.FlowerofLifePress.com

For information about special discounts for bulk order purchases, email support@floweroflifepress.com

Interior Design: Flower of Life Press
Cover Art: Amanda Romania
Editorial services: Jen Kirwan and Erin Puckett

Library of Congress Control Number: Available upon request.

ISBN: 979-8-9987870-9-6

To my Oracle sister and brothers—thank you for remembering your sacred truth, walking the path of devotion, and anchoring ancient wisdom into this world with courage, love, and light.

Prologue

Dear soul friends, I welcome you once again to the story of my ancient past lives and present work in Glastonbury, England, and on to the sacred lands of Egypt.

I invite you to follow the sacred pathway to the temple and through the lives of my soul friends to perhaps also remember who you were and truly are.

My name is Anna Harris, and I was born in North Yorkshire. One year ago, in 2008, I thought I had found my purpose in writing for a magazine and would eventually settle down with a family of my own. However, when I met my tarot teacher and energy healer, Lucinda, a whole world of spiritual arts opened up to me.

When my life suddenly turned as the home I rented flooded and I lost my job, I slid into the dark night of the soul, yet help was at hand. The kind landlord of my workplace handed me a check for a fine sum of money after my then-evil scheming boss had conned me into signing away my life.

If it had not been for the gentle-hearted owner of my flooded home who took me in, a woman called Laura, goodness knows where I would have slept.

Lucinda and Laura helped me start anew and directed me to Glastonbury, a mystical town in southern England. There, I would be nurtured by Emilee, a French woman who owned the Gables guest house. This would become a safe place from which I would venture into the town and encounter many new friends.

Isis, a teacher, high priestess, and my beloved mentor who was awaiting her successor for her Temple known as The Sanctuary Retreat Center; Lucas, a gifted psychic and past-life priest of Egypt, who gave me tarot card wisdom and honest answers; Naomi, an ancient oracle with a torn and tattered past life story; and Alice, a woman of ancient knowledge and a guardian of the Chalice Well, a magical place in the heart chakra of the planet.

There was even Lesley, a gifted priestess and student with whom competition was the focus of her journey. We followed a path towards the highly coveted position of the new high priestess. We had some challenges, to say the least, but she was still a sacred sister.

That year, all of us heard the call of the Tor, the sacred site in central Glastonbury, and over the past few months, we have held the sacred ceremonies, gatherings, and visions to help us all remember our past connections and karmic paths. We have lived the light and shadow, which they say brings balance and healing. Each day brings a new twist and turn. And now, we start our next adventure towards deeper healing and discovery. Thank you for joining us.

CHAPTER 1

Sunday, 21 December 2008
Winter Solstice

I was woken early by some unearthly force, wide awake and alert.

"Anna, it is time," a woman's voice floated into my consciousness.

I looked around and remembered this was normal in Glastonbury. In the eight months I had been here, I had learnt that we did hear voices in our heads and we were not crazy.

This voice I knew, and she was calm and loving. I had no fear or hesitation. I dressed and made myself ready to step into the day.

It was still dark outside as this was the shortest day of the year. I was being called to the Tor, the sacred monument that stood high on a hill in Glastonbury—a place where spiritual energy was strong and magical things happened. This place was known as the Heart Chakra of the world.

It was a few minutes' walk from the Sanctuary, a retreat center where I lived and now worked, using my spiritual gifts and conducting Akashic Record readings.

All was still as I crept downstairs. Thankfully, the central heating had switched itself on, and as I retrieved my scarf and gloves from the warm radiator, I sent out a prayer to my angels, thanking them for taking care of me.

As I glanced in the mirror, I hardly recognised myself.

Such a transformation from a year ago. I smoothed my auburn hair, which Naomi had insisted I have professionally styled and straightened, and even managed to tie it back into something that looked presentable. As I stared at the young woman facing me, I was not sure what had changed, but the Glastonbury lifestyle suited me. My skin was glowing, and my blue eyes had a sparkle. I was lost in my vanity for just a moment. I began to giggle—who would have thought it? Me... no longer afraid of a mirror.

"Anna, where are you? We are waiting," a gentle female voice called to me. She was persistent.

I reminded myself that we had no guests and I was alone, apart from the spirit guides, or as I had come to call them, the druidesses.

"Anna, hurry, we start the climb," the voice was impatient.

"I'm coming, I'm coming," I answered out loud and, with that, pulled on my welly boots, grabbed my coat, and was out the door.

☥

The garden looked picture-perfect, with a sugar-frost coating of ice. It was nearly sunrise, and everything felt magical.

I let myself out of the wooden door in the outside wall and ventured into the street, making haste down the pathway and turning to reach the first gateway that would lead me to the hill on which the stone monument towered. I could see that there were already a few pilgrims making their way to the top, and I could just make out the lanterns lit with their soft amber glow.

I made my way to the second gate and reached the wooden bench where I expected to join the druidesses I had come to see in my visions and dreams. I heard a familiar voice behind me.

"Anna, they are starting." I was surprised. It sounded like a real person.

I turned, and there stood Alice, my friend and dear mentor.

Wrapped in many layers of clothes, you could just see her face and silver wisps of hair. Her pixie-like nose was already rosy pink from the cool morning air. Tiny and petite, she was in frame like a fragile doll, but when she came close to me, I felt her like a towering giant.

"You see them, the druidesses?" I whispered.

"But of course, they often visit me in the Chalice Well gardens." Alice was a guardian of one of the area's most holy and special gardens—a master of sacred ceremony and an Akashic librarian.

She smiled, took my hand, and began leading me towards our starting point.

"Now we go through the portal," she announced.

My vision shifted, and once again, the houses and signs of modern life disappeared, and we were standing in a timeline of 1000 years previous.

"Ladies, will you join us?" A tall woman stood in blue velvet robes with a golden sash. Her hair was long and flowing. Another woman with ebony-black hair stepped up next to us, her skin dark, with a pearlescent glow. They handed Alice and me tall wooden staffs, and I saw us in deep purple robes. Alice looked so much younger, and her eyes were bright and excited.

"Then we begin the solstice climb," the woman in the blue robe announced. Her blue eyes shone brightly, reminding me of my mentor, Isis. I found myself in a procession of women of varying skin and hair colours. Everyone wore jewel-coloured velvet robes, and each carried a staff with emblems and sacred symbols that declared their spiritual lineage. Eight of us in total seemed to float up the pathway.

Alice and I followed silently as we walked the path directly to the top of the hill. The sun was still rising, and I took each step carefully to avoid slipping.

When we reached the top, Alice and I stood together and watched as the sun slowly made its way into the sky, with all shades of yellow and orange shining towards us.

I felt the warmth on my skin and looked around to see that our friends had left, and we were back in the modern world. Other pilgrims were now wandering up the hill to pay homage to this sacred place.

"Alice, you never said you knew the druidesses," I whispered.

She smiled, said nothing, and pointed to a spot beside the monument where we could shelter from the wind.

We huddled together.

"People must think us quite mad," I said.

She leaned into me and whispered. "No, we see the real world." With that, she pulled a flask from her coat pocket and poured two steaming cups of tea into two small plastic cups from her other pocket.

"Always prepared," she said, handing me a cup that I was beyond grateful for.

"Now, let me share a little secret."

Alice had the best secrets, so I snuggled into my coat and scarf and let the steam from the tea warm my face.

She smiled and continued.

"I met the druidesses many years ago when I first came to Glastonbury. It began in my dreams, and then I had a visit one day when I was sitting in the Chalice Well Garden near the Lion's Head Fountain.

"I was only a volunteer there at that time and had been

taking classes with beloved Isis at the Sanctuary. At first, I thought it was a group that had come for a ceremony. They looked so real. They all wore the robes and carried the wooden staffs to identify who they were, and they began to share their stories. They are all druidesses, sometimes known as oracles and priestesses, who have crossed over but, when needed, are called to sacred sites such as this to watch over us. They felt like my soul sisters, and I kept it a secret. I have made this journey every winter solstice ever since, and you, Anna, are the first of our group of friends who has ever shown up."

"Do you think the others see them? Isis, Naomi perhaps, or Lucinda?" I asked.

"If they did, they never said."

"Then why you and me?" I quizzed her.

"I'm not sure," she said, shaking her head, "but I feel something significant is about to happen to our merry group, and they may have a warning for us."

More people were making the journey up the hill, and someone had even begun to play a flute. Alice and I finished our tea, and I was not sure if it was telepathic or not, but we knew it was time to go.

"Now, let's hurry back to my home for some breakfast; it's freezing." Her teeth chattered, and her nose was more blue than pink. As we started our descent, I heard my name and turned with a start.

"Did you hear that, Alice?"

"Hear what?"

"A man's voice call my name."

"No, my dear, it was the wind."

I was not sure, but one thing I did know was that the man's voice gave me greater chills than the icy wind.

☥

Alice's house was next to the Chalice Well. Cozy and simple, it was soon filled with the scents of hot coffee and buttered toast. Alice bustled around in the kitchen. Her house was one of the quaint red brick terraced houses. Built just before the war, they carried all the charm of another time.

As she continued putting more logs onto the fire, I looked at her many pictures on the walls.

"This looks like an old photo, but it looks like you." I pointed to a small image in sepia of five young women.

"Oh, that's from my childhood. I was five; it was taken in 1950." She smiled.

"But who are those two young women? They look familiar."

"Do you want eggs?" She changed the subject and headed for the kitchen.

It was strange, as Alice typically had remarkable hearing. I decided to leave it and was drawn to her bookshelf. Something about this room and its memories made me curious, but I was more interested in the visions of the women on the Tor. I waited until she returned and joined her to eat the eggs she had prepared.

"So, Alice, the six other druidesses, do you know any of them?" I asked.

"Not really, though they do feel familiar. Do you think that also?"

I nodded. "Yes, but I cannot place them and have been trying to find books about them, any of them. Did you notice they all have different symbols on their clothing and staffs?"

She nodded as she munched away.

"I guess in time we'll find out more," I continued. "Do

you think they have a warning?"

Alice put down her cutlery.

"Well, there is a legend that had a prophecy."

Oh, prophecy. I was always ready to hear about those.

"Let me find it here." She stood up and went to the bookshelf.

"Ah, yes, here it is."

It was an old green leather-bound book.

"That looks old," I commented.

"It is. It was only printed a few times and written by one of my mentors," she replied.

"She had had a dream where those Ladies of the Tor came to visit her and told her they would always make themselves available during times of great need. They had a sacred promise to protect the heart chakra of the planet, which is here in Glastonbury, and if evil flowed into town, they would challenge it. They were all initiated as druidesses at the ends of their lives and bound to walk around the Tor every morning at sunrise and then again at sunset to protect the energy."

"How many have you seen over the years?" I asked.

"Oh, many shapes and sizes," she laughed, "but this morning's group felt different."

"Have you met this particular group before?"

"No, I don't think so, I recognised a few of them. But this group seems to belong together, like a club within a club."

"Or a sect within a temple." She looked at the bookshelf as if searching for inspiration.

Alice was a librarian, and while I intuitively knew things through my clairvoyant gifts, Alice could go to any library and pick a random book, and there would be the answers she needed.

As she looked at her books, I reflected on the prophecy.

"But has evil flowed into town," Alice said in a low voice.

My eyes began to look around the room.

"I thought we drove out the evil when we banished Lesley back to London," I said.

"Yes, we did. That poor child." Alice shook her head. "She had such promise."

"The thought was that she could help me also with my work," I continued, "but how could she help as she has conspired against us in all those past lives?"

"Anna, that's very judgmental. You know we have all done dark deeds," she scolded.

"Yes, but I bet she's done more than most."

Alice began to clear the dishes. She was never one to be drawn into drama.

"Wow, it's nearly 9," she said.

"Oh no, then I need to check the Sanctuary for messages. Isis and Naomi may still be in Egypt, but will need the daily report."

"Daily report indeed." I raised my eyebrows and shook my head.

"I was promised Egypt," I said.

"And now I just heard Lucas has joined them," Alice said.

"Aren't I a chosen one? It seems I'm forgotten and doing all the work here with the Akashic readings," I said.

"And don't you have Laura and Lucinda's help at the Sanctuary centre?" She was talking to me like a child.

"Well, yes."

"And didn't I hear Emilee came over last week and helped you prepare all the rooms for guests?"

I began to feel uncomfortable. "But we haven't got guests at the moment. The two bookings we had canceled."

"So you have no guests?"

"No," I shook my head. "Nothing in the diary until maybe March."

Alice looked at me, "That's most strange. But the diary is full for sessions?"

"Oh yes, booked all the way through from the new year, as a matter of fact."

"Okay, well, I have to get ready for work, but maybe I'll call over later," she said. "Now, before you leave, here is some blessed salt and rosemary. And..."

I interrupted her. "And I will put it at the door and do the clearing for the evil spirits."

She smiled and followed me as I went to the hallway.

"This image, I've never seen it before." I pointed to the papyrus. It showed what appeared to be a couple of importance, with children holding their hands up to receive ankh keys.

"It just arrived yesterday from Egypt. I think Isis sent it," said Alice.

"It's Akhenaten and Queen Nefertiti, and they are with their daughters." Alice pointed to the children, who looked beyond happy.

"Where's his son?" I stared into the image, becoming quite dizzy.

"They had no son, well, maybe not then," she replied.

I studied the image closer and could feel a vision coming to me when Alice politely opened the front door, and the draft of the cold, fresh air brought me to my senses.

I raced back to the Sanctuary and was just in time to catch the phone call from my beloved teacher and mentor, Isis.

"Anna, you sound out of breath."

"Oh, Isis, I went to the Tor this morning with Alice and just came from her house. I was admiring the image you sent her."

The phone was silent.

"I sent her no image."

"Yes, you did the Akhenaten one with his children. I nearly had a vision when I looked at it."

Isis was silent, and I could tell she was distracted; she must have forgotten. These older ladies... well, I guess it comes to us all. I began to babble about the day before and the work I had been doing, and was very careful not to mention the Druidesses from the Tor or the man's voice. Perhaps I would solve the mystery before they returned.

"Anna, are you listening?" Isis raised her voice.

"Yes, sorry," I stammered. "Yes, I'll check the plants and have the roof checked for leaks."

Isis could always predict the weather. We said our goodbyes.

☥

The image of Akhenaten from Alice's house lingered in my mind, compelling me to search through our collection of photographs and explore the books available for guests and those in Isis's private library. It seemed that every timeline was there, and many books about his son Tutankhamun, but there was nothing to be seen depicting this image of the King and Queen.

Oh, here was a book with the golden mask of Tutankhamun. They had to be in there. How strange... There were pages removed. I looked in the glossary at the back.

Akhenaten, Nefertiti, and Armana... yes, they were there; however, those pages had been removed and not with care. I ran my hand gently across the page and could sense the anger or even the rage spilling into the book as the pages were ripped out. I carefully placed the book back onto the bookshelf and decided to quiz Isis when she returned home, which should be any day, so it could wait.

A warm breeze surrounded me in the curious place I found myself. Not yet a dream place but not physical either, I was floating in the in-between. The breeze coaxed me forward, whispering comforts to me as we went along. Suddenly, a blinding light pierced through the dark, causing the breeze to swarm around me and ever more pressingly push me forward. The thought crossed my mind that I should be wary of this, and I attempted to grasp at anything that would slow down my path, but found I had no physical form to speak of. I was the wind rushing towards the light, coaxing myself along, telling myself that the light would not harm me. It was at this moment that I reached the light, enveloped by it, or I was it; either way, I felt a peace that I had not felt in my entire existence, could I say life? I couldn't recall a time when I had a life or a body. Had I always been a warm breeze in the dark, waiting for the light to find me? I was so calm, so whole, the universe was syncing up to me and I with it and...

Pain. Searing pain. And darkness... and sand? I felt sand in between my toes and a dampness on my face. Toes? A face? The memories of my previous physical existence came violently crashing into my mind. I shouldn't be here; something was very wrong. As I sat up and opened my eyes, I could see just how wrong it was. Several other people were around me with the same look of horror and confusion I had. We were meant to be somewhere else; I just couldn't remember where.

Farther away from me, I saw two figures arguing, made to look impossibly small by the large pyramids and

Sphinx directly behind them. Squinting, I noticed they were a female and a younger male figure. The woman was dressed in beautiful finery that only someone of the royal line would wear, only I couldn't tell where she was from. She didn't bear the hallmark headdress or ankh that a queen of Egypt would possess, but they looked Egyptian. I could see a scroll in her hand with a symbol I had never seen before. The woman was waving it around in a dramatic fashion. The younger male was similarly dressed in clothing I could not place. I wanted to know what they were talking about. It seemed important, and that strange scroll must also be part of it. Maybe it had something to do with my presence here in the sand. I could hear only words, "We lost the game; we have no more pieces to play." The woman was shaking the younger man. By his composure and age, I assumed he was her son.

As I made a motion to stand, I was brutally thrown down by an unseen force. I tried to get back up but couldn't break free of what was holding me down. I heard the others around me crying out in pain, desperately attempting to break free from whatever was keeping them captive. It became overwhelming to fight against this force, and I felt darkness overtaking me again, only this time it was devoid of warmth and comfort. There was only terror and cold as I succumbed to it.

Monday, 22 December 2008, 1:22 a.m.

I jerked my eyes open to escape the darkness of my dream, only to be confronted with more of it. It took a moment for my eyes to adjust, to realise that I was no longer engulfed in the oppressive blackness I had just experienced but rather in the familiar darkness of my bedroom at the Sanctuary, illuminated only by the faint glow of my alarm clock in the middle of the night. I took a large sigh of relief, feeling far less fearful than I had been. The memory of the dream was quickly fading, and I scrambled to grab the notebook and pen on my bedside table to write down what I had seen.

There was an unfamiliar symbol; *it must be important*, I thought as I flipped the light on and opened my notebook to a new ecru page. The symbol was a beautifully complex design of petals that formed what looked like a flower at first, or was it a plant? It seemed to have 8 points. Perhaps it was even a star, but then it had a line around it as if it were held in a vessel of some sort. I imagined what flowers it could be based on: a pansy, a chrysanthemum, or maybe even a rose. However, none of these flowers seemed to hold a candle to this most sacred of geometry: *Oh no, what else was there? Sand? I think there was sand... and a shadow, a younger man, and a fantastically dressed woman... I felt I knew them; maybe I'd seen them in a history book.* I mused this all to myself. *Oh, and there had been something about a game and losing.* I pondered on this, my pen just tapping the page of my journal.

I knew there was more, but whatever else there was, it could wait. There was a reason that symbol burnt so brightly in my mind's eye. I needed to know what it was, and I couldn't wait another few hours until morning to find out.

I took care to rush quietly down the stairs. I hurried to Isis's office, or I suppose my office, although it didn't really feel that way, as Isis had not moved anything out prior to my occupation of it. As she had told me, what is hers is mine, meaning snooping around was well within my purview. It wasn't as if Isis would be around to question what I was doing.

Isis and Naomi ran off to Egypt at the beginning of December, some three weeks ago, just after I received the strange call from Egypt.

Isis and Naomi said they thought the mystery man had something to do with the Cairo Museum, and they packed and left that evening. Nothing they had said about their reason for leaving me made sense, mainly because they gave no good reason, only that it was imperative that they leave at once. I had offered to join them; after all, Isis had promised to take me to Egypt. However, my offer was swiftly rejected. Naomi had scoffed at this and told me that suggesting such a thing was in poor taste. The look of confusion on my face spurred her on, and she explained that there was no way that I could leave the Sanctuary, as I was to be the new guardian and hold a leadership role. It was my karmic duty to keep watch over it and help any lost people who might be searching for spiritual help. I had thought I was to be the High Priestess, but then the oracle work was calling. There were so many roles and titles, I was not sure who I was supposed to be anymore.

But the thought of them both in Egypt, for some reason, began to really anger me. I could imagine them in the sacred sites. Isis in her glory, standing at the high altar, her white-blonde hair glistening in the sunlight. Her white robes highlighting her gold ankh pendant. I imagined her chanting and leading rituals I felt I should have been part of. Naomi, her counterpart, I imagined all in black. Her signature black bob hair, black sunglasses, and red lipstick cast a definite contrast to Isis. My feelings towards them in that moment were not love and light.

Ha! Some leader I was going to be. I could never reach my full potential if I didn't go to Egypt, and it was frustrating that they were preventing me from doing that. I almost thought that it was intentional on Naomi's part, but Isis had sensed my thoughts and told me that it was a matter of safety for me, that they would be engaged in rituals I had not ever been present for. I argued that the Cairo Museum man had explicitly asked for me personally when he called a few months back, to help with the Amenti Scrolls.

I could still hear his voice.

"Anna Harris, I think you can guide me. I am the keeper of the Scrolls of Amenti and the Sphinx, and we need your help."

"Do you even know what they are?" Isis had inquired calmly.

"Of course," I had replied, "they are relics in the Egyptian Museum."

"Oh, my dear, for an oracle and psychic channel, you still have much to learn," she said, shaking her head and patting my arm sympathetically, "Now, run along; I have a lot to pack still and not a lot of time to do it."

She abruptly ended the conversation and treated me like a child, to boot. I was livid. It wasn't fair! After I had cooled down a bit, I went to speak with her again, only to find her rushing out the door into the waiting car Naomi was driving. So much for clearing our karma before her trip, I thought. Isis and Naomi were gone, and left in their wake, I was confused and hurt.

This interaction really put me in a dark place. How could I ever feel part of the group if they excluded me? Why did they think I was not worthy of being taken on this trip? What if that meant that I was a horrible High Priestess or oracle and would fail everyone? Isis and Naomi must have realised they had made a mistake and had gone to Egypt to secretly search for someone else to wear the crown.

It had only been a few months since I had saved the day

and brought our temple back together. My mind wandered to the image of all of us gathered in a circle at the August 8th ceremony. I was the one who had been shown the past lives of us all. I was the one who had started the healing and knew what to do with the relics; the sacred scrolls and scarabs we had been gathering to help us to reconnect our sacred temple.

I, I... Oh lord, I sounded like a martyr. I was beginning to feel this new role may not be the life path I desired. It was those thoughts that had swirled in my head over the past few weeks while they had been gone that now cast a dark shadow over the Sanctuary. That shadow would apparently not be letting up any time soon as I hadn't heard any real insight from them since they left, just water the plants and check the phones, and it was just a few days before Christmas. *Great. What were they up to*?

I pushed them from my thoughts. Whatever they were up to didn't concern me at the moment; I was deep into my research in the office, poring over centuries-old vintage books, attempting to get a glimpse of that symbol from my dream. Isis might think me a sub-par High Priestess and novice psychic, but my detective skills were excellent, and I was determined to reveal the secret of my dream symbol on my own. This would be a pivotal moment for me, the day that I stopped needing Isis to explain everything, and it would open me up to becoming a fully actualised High Priestess. Surely, that would lead Isis to trust me with more advanced work.

I clung to that notion after the first hour went by, and I found nothing. At the second hour, I was still determined and making careful note of each book I had looked through. By the time the third hour came around, I was exhausted and unsure what to do, so I started frantically rummaging through the room, looking for any item or scrap of paper that might help me. The phone rang as I was precariously perched atop the desk chair, pawing at the items on a shelf too high up for me to see in. It startled me so much that I lost my balance and flailed my arms out in an attempt to grab onto anything that would prevent my fall. I was not so lucky.

I managed to land with a loud thud on the desk, conveniently next to the phone. Looking around, I was thankful that it was made of the same solid oak that all the other furniture in the house was made of. Isis said oak represented strength and stability and was charged with a protective energy that vibrated throughout the Sanctuary. Thankfully, that energy was vibrating in just the right place as it took the full weight of my body while simultaneously preventing any serious injury to me, Anna Harris, the super sleuth who felt much better than she deserved at that moment.

I quickly composed myself and grabbed the phone, answering in the calmest voice I could manage, "Good morning, the Sanctuary in Glastonbury. How can we help?"

"Anna, my dear, how are you?" asked a familiar voice on the other line. It was Lucinda. Hearing her voice always made me feel calmer, as she was such a positive person in my life. She had been the first one to introduce me to the spiritual worlds and had been the person to set me on a journey of discovery and enlightenment. Lucinda had come to join me in Glastonbury but was currently away. She had chosen, unlike Laura, our other Yorkshire friend who had relocated to Glastonbury, to migrate to work in a spa in Bath, a more temperate energy, so that she could have her "winter rest time."

"Anna," Lucinda asked, "what on earth are you getting

yourself into?" Oh, and of course, she was a gifted oracle and psychic.

"Well... I... I was... um," I began to stammer, my previous bravado abandoning me.

"Are you in the office?" she asked.

"Yes." She knew the answer already, but asked me anyway out of respect.

"Are you going through the office looking for something?"

"Yes," I answered sheepishly. *Caught in the act.*

"Well, you know that karma will find you, and Isis will find out," she said in a serious tone, only to break it a moment later with a small bout of laughing.

"Karma has already found me, Lucinda. I was supposed to go on the next Egypt trip, and they left me out again. It's not fair."

"Oh, well, if fair is what you want, you are simply not going to get it, my dear. Nothing is fair in this life, dear one, but patience and compassion certainly help tip the scales in your favour," she responded. *Lord, was this woman half-witch and half-saint?*

"I know, I know. I just wish Isis trusted me. The ceremony was months ago, and I feel like she still doesn't see me as a leader, which means no one does—" Suddenly, the desk creaked as if to say my weight was unwanted and perhaps I should find a chair to sit upon. "Lucinda, hold on, let me just get off this desk." I jumped down from my position, clumsily dropping the phone as I went. "Oh no! Lucinda... just a... ugh... I dropped the phone... oof," I sputtered, frantically dashing for the phone. I then tripped over my own feet and knocked into the bookcase behind the desk. *If anyone had ever doubted that karma existed, they would believe it after witnessing this sorry scene before them,* I mused.

As I picked up the phone, a small red box fell from one of the upper cupboards, narrowly missing my head. The box looked ancient in design, but aside from the slightly rusty hinges and a layer of dust atop it, it was in good condition. It dawned on me that I had seen this box many months ago on the bookshelf behind Isis's desk when I had just begun my spiritual training. I wondered why it had been pushed so far back on the shelf. I had missed it when I was looking earlier. Looking closer, I could see something inscribed on the box, but the dust obscured it.

I was shaken from my thoughts by the voice on the phone, "Anna? Anna, dear, is everything alright? I heard a horrible commotion. Please answer me," Lucinda pleaded with a concern that seemed far greater than the situation warranted. That struck me as odd.

"Oh, Lucinda, sorry, I was sitting on the desk, and when I hopped down, I dropped the phone, and then a red box fell from the upper cupboard and nearly hit my head! Talk about karma! The universe is definitely telling me to stop complaining so much," I laughed. "I feel like I am having my hands slapped. Naomi must have put a curse on this office before she left."

The phone went silent.

"Lucinda? Hello? Lucinda, are you there? Is this your way of getting back at me?" I tried to lighten the mood, which had shifted to one far more serious.

"Yes, yes, I apologise," she said in a slightly detached tone, "and yes, Naomi did weave a spell on the office, but I guess she forgot just how powerful you, our dear sister, can be."

"Who? You mean me? That's a change from the norm."

"Yes, I do." Lucinda's voice then sounded more present. "Now, tell me about this red box."

I sat back in the chair and placed this small red box in front of me. The dust was obscuring the inlaid design on its top, so I brushed it away with the corner of my sleeve. I almost dropped the phone again when I saw what was on top. It was that beautiful interlocking-circle flower symbol, but now the petals looked more like leaves of a plant. Yes, it was the seven leaves with a stalk I had seen in my dream. The sight of it made me gasp.

"Should I open it, Lucinda?" I whispered.

"If you feel you should, but remember what happened with Pandora's box," she said.

Gently, I lifted the lid and peered inside. The box was filled with what looked like old photographs, worn around the edges from being held, and yellowing pieces of paper that denoted their old age. "Oh, this must be from Isis's family," I told Lucinda, "It's like a box my aunt used to have that she collected memories in."

"What kind of memories does this box have, Anna?"

"I'm not sure. I'm guessing just various memories of important events in Isis's life, by the looks of it." I lifted out a picture of Isis with a group of women standing in front of the Great Pyramid. "Oh, Lucinda, here is one of you and her in Egyptian outfits with sparkling headdresses. It has 2005 on the back!" I exclaimed.

"Anna, I don't think you should be in this box." Her voice sounded concerned.

"Oh, Lucinda, don't fuss. This is just the thing that I've been looking for to get answers!" I rummaged around some more and saw a picture of the Titanic and a few other pictures and papers dated long before Isis was born. It must have been a collection of a few generations of her family. As I pushed aside a picture of a handsomely dressed woman in front of the Eiffel Tower, my fingers touched something else.

"Oh, Lucinda, it's a sacred scarab." I took it out to study it.

On my arrival into Glastonbury, Isis had given me the role of studying the set of sacred scarabs and scrolls. There were eight of each, and it was said that when they were all collected, a mighty temple could be created. We were missing at least half of them.

"It's the Protection one."

"Put it back now!" Lucinda was most direct. But I was not paying attention as my eyes fell to another photo. I was startled by a picture of a sinister-looking man with piercing black eyes.

A sudden wave of nausea and dizziness overtook me. I pushed that photo aside to see another four women and four younger girls in a sepia-coloured picture; I turned it to see on the back of the photo that it had been taken during World War II in 1943. My finger brushed against the images, and I instantly regretted it. A sharp pain hit me in the stomach, and I cried out in pain.

"Anna," Lucinda said sternly, "put back those photographs and scarab and close the box right now!"

Something began to feel hot on the back of my neck as my stomach continued to feel as if a thousand tiny knives were stabbing it.

I mustered all my strength, put the box in order, and closed the lid. The pain instantly stopped, but left me winded and unable to catch my breath.

In between pants, I said, "I'm sorry... Lucinda... I closed the box... I closed it."

"Now place it back where you found it." Lucinda's voice was most urgent.

I placed the phone down, like I was on autopilot, climbed onto the desk, praying it would not protest again, placed the box back into the upper cupboard, and gently closed the doors firmly shut. I returned to the phone, but Lucinda was gone for some strange reason. I tried calling her a few times, but it just went to voicemail. A year ago, I would have felt this strange and rude, but now I knew it was just how Lucinda was, and there was always a good reason that would reveal itself in due time.

I looked at the clock and realised it was just past 5 a.m. Wow, where had the time gone? If I hurried, I could get a couple more hours of sleep. I crept back upstairs, not wishing to disturb any other sleeping ghosts or spirits. After my last dream, I was apprehensive about going back to sleep, but I knew I needed to be fresh in the morning. After that strange wave of sickness, I needed all the rest I could get. That rest was precious, considering all of the other nighttime disturbances I generally had.

Over the past few months, I had received several visitors from the spiritual realm. It terrified me the first few times it happened; they were so loud and wouldn't leave me alone. I quickly realised, though, that they were harmless and just wanted to be heard and acknowledged. So, as they would come, I would listen to them talk and record their stories and messages in my notebook. Often, they were relatives of the clients who would be visiting the Sanctuary the next day, so the message would be for them. I developed a sort of spirit memo system for this. While the interruptions to my sleep were often frequent and numerous, I didn't mind. I was helping these spirits and their loved ones find peace. It was precious work that made me feel like my gifts were valued and useful.

I had gone to bed earlier that night, praying that I would enjoy uninterrupted sleep for the first time in months. Of course, the universe had other ideas for me, and

I was interrupted by that nightmare. Hopefully, I could get through the next few hours without another interruption. That was apparently far too much to ask.

I was just about to fall back asleep when a loud banging noise from outside woke me. I could hear the chimes in the meditation courtyard violently crashing into one another, turning their normally calm sounds into loud, eerie screams. I looked out my window and saw just how strong the winds were. Slats from the roof littered the lawn, and the trees were bending so far to one side that it looked as if they might snap. It dawned on me that the banging was probably coming from the wind pounding on an unsecured door or window downstairs. I knew I could not sleep with that banging, so I got up, pulled a warm, plush robe around me, and slipped my feet into my fleece-lined slippers.

I started methodically searching the Sanctuary for the culprit, but couldn't seem to find it. Some gnawing feeling told me that the source was the very office I had just gotten sick in. I cautiously peered into the office and found a mess. Well, mess was an understatement. It looked like every book had been pulled off the shelves and unceremoniously tossed on the floor. The same went for the files. Paper blanketed the floor like a fresh snowfall in winter. The lamps were tossed on their sides, and pieces of broken light bulbs surrounded them. Even the computer had been smashed. I noticed that the window closest to the door was open and quickly went to shut it.

I surveyed the room and knew the most violent winds couldn't have done this kind of damage. Someone must have broken in. Or something, the voice in the back of my head said. My blood ran cold. We must have had burglars who could still be in the house. That terrified me. I knew there was no way someone was hiding in here, and I couldn't risk going to another part of the Sanctuary and getting caught, so I quickly and quietly shut the door and locked myself inside the office. Thank goodness the phone still looked intact and in working order. I had to climb over discarded books and papers and an overturned chair to get to the phone on the desk. They were the only two items in the office that seemed not to have been disturbed. Once I reached the phone, I tried dialling emergency services but could not get through. The strong winds had most likely knocked out a telephone wire, which cut service. The terror was seeping into my bones now, and my vision started to get cloudy. My whole body felt so heavy, as if I had been drugged with some powerful sedative. I froze.

I could see dark shadows moving out of the corner of my eye. They looked humanoid in shape and were circling me like lions do their prey. I swore I could hear one of them laughing—a sinister laugh I had heard before. To anyone on the outside, I must have looked crazy, shouting for them to show themselves. I reached for the large citrine crystal that Isis had on her desk, praying it would be enough to ward them off. I brandished the makeshift weapon, threatening the shadows with it.

The citrine gave them pause enough. However, one shadow slowly floated forward, seemingly unafraid of my crystal. I attempted to back up as it glided towards me, but found myself paralysed with fear. This was everything I had been dreading for months, and it was finally going to happen. As it came upon me, I noticed that it almost took on a feminine form. It seemed amused by me and gave a wicked cackle that I was now all too familiar with. The noise was enough to shake me out of my trance, and I hurled the crystal at the shadow and ran towards the door. There was a large crash, but I kept on. As I turned the knob to release the lock, I took one last look behind me to see if the shadows were pursuing me and saw that they had disappeared. All that was left was a mirror shattered into a thousand pieces, and the citrine crystal cracked in half. I ran over to investigate further, to see if there had been anything else left behind, lest I be blamed for unnecessarily trashing Isis's office.

Bang! Bang! Bang!

I was suddenly awake again. What had just happened? How could I be downstairs in the office one moment and back in my bed another? I checked the clock and found out that I had lost another hour. It was almost 7 in the morning now.

The banging was continuing from the front door. Once again, I got out of bed, pulled my robe around me, and put on my haphazardly placed slippers. We had no clients coming today, *so who would be banging on the door? What if it was someone who was just dropping by for a walk-in reading? Oh no, what if there was still someone in the house?* I pushed those thoughts out of my mind; it had probably been a dream, and I was being paranoid. Just to be safe, I glanced into the office on my way to the door, expecting there to be a mess, but to my surprise, everything was exactly where it was supposed to be; even the mirror looked intact as if it had never been broken, but how strange, on the floor, there were the missing pages ripped from the Egypt book. They looked like the woman and the young man from my dream. The banging continued, and I decided that a small miracle would have to wait. I quickly picked them up and slid them into a drawer.

I went to the front door, opened it, and to my surprise, found Lucinda and Emilee there on the doorstep.

"*Ma chère!*" Emilee gasped and took hold of me, "Are you alright?" She checked my brow, my arms, and my waist as if checking a child for trauma.

"I'm fine, Emilee, I promise!"

While Emilee looked me over, I saw she was still in her satin pajamas, a pale pink fleece dressing gown, and green welly boots, her raven curly hair hidden under an expensive-looking silk scarf. I looked over at Lucinda, who was in her regular eclectic rainbow-coloured clothes but had left in haste, judging by her hair and makeup.

"Whatever is going on, I think it's best we head to the kitchen for some tea," I suggested, motioning towards the kitchen. They silently followed me.

Emilee and I swiftly got to work making the tea. As I put the kettle on, I realised that Lucinda was standing in the doorway. Her vivid, deep golden red hair hung in strands across her face, her green eyes distant. Her normally healthy, freckled face had a grey cast to it. Her clothes were always immaculate, but now, like her whole energy, they felt dishevelled. Emilee saw what I was looking at, and led her slowly into the kitchen, and sat her down. They exchanged worried looks but otherwise ignored each other while the tea was being made. It was most strange to see them act like this. They were usually so chatty and in sync, even finishing each other's sentences. They were soul sisters, you could say, because of how close a bond they shared. But today, you would think they were distant acquaintances by the way they were acting. The mood was incredibly strange and far too sombre for three days before Christmas.

Lucinda sat at the table and continued staring. Emilee joined me at the back of the kitchen and poured the hot water into the pot while I gathered the cups and utensils on the tray. We looked up at the window before us and could see our reflections in it. We both jumped when Wallis jumped up to the window ledge and began to meow. Emilee's feline psychic guardian was a creature who saw through the sacred veils and came to warn us to tread with care. She had come across the gardens between The Gables guest house and the Sanctuary retreat centre. She often did not stray, so I knew this was a powerful situation.

I couldn't stand the silence any longer, so I whispered to Emilee, "What happened? Lucinda called me a few hours ago and then abruptly cut the call off. Now she's here? How did she even get here so quickly, and why does she look like she hasn't slept in days, and why did she not use her house key?"

"I'm not so sure," Emilee spoke in a hushed tone. "I received a call at 6 o'clock, but no one was there, and no message was left. I thought it was an accidental call. Then I heard banging on the walls, and Wallis mewed so loudly that I had to bring her into my bedroom. Thankfully, I had no one at the guest house overnight. Just half an hour after that, Lucinda showed up at my door. I was concerned at her arriving so early, and all she kept saying was your name and that it had returned. That it had found Anna and would soon be upon us. Then she jumped up in a trance and began to make her way towards the Sanctuary, so I figured I should go, too. It was all so quick that we both forgot our keys."

"But what did she mean by 'It has returned?' What or who has returned? You don't think 'it' refers to the Priests of Unal, do you? They haunted my dreams when I first came here, but I thought part of doing that ceremony a few months back was supposed to cleanse us of all that."

I had tried to move them out of my memory. They

were such evil creatures and abominations created from a hidden scroll of Unal, which had been reenacted through the Temple of Edfu and led to one of Naomi and Isis's most prolific past lives in ancient Egypt.

"I do not know, *ma chère.* All I know is that she was very desperate to get here, to you."

"What should we do?"

"Maintenant alors, d'abord, first of all, we give her this," and she pointed to the tea. *"Un instant, s'il vous plaît,"* she whispered as I reached for the cup. She reached into her pocket and pulled out a small golden bottle. "Deux drops, I think, for her," Emilee stated, "And un for you and me." I smiled and held my cup up, also. I followed Emilee to the table with the tea tray. She had been using a lot of French, something she only did when she was anxious. Whatever was going on was most certainly cause for concern.

"I'm sensing a past life reading will need to be done," I stated as I took my seat at the table. This early morning felt so different from all of the others. The air around us was thick, and the mood was morose. The pit in my stomach told me nothing good was going to come from this morning, and it made me ache all the more for those others here present.

☥

Sometimes, when I would wake early in the morning and come downstairs, it was as if I was stepping into another dimension. The Sanctuary was located on the sacred site of the Tor and was once said to have been hidden by the mysteries of the Vale of Avalon. There was an ancient wisdom here stemming from the time of King Arthur, Merlin, and the Druids. It broke down the barrier between realms and allowed for the spiritual and metaphysical to mingle with me. Just last week, I found a mystic medicine woman in ghost form in the living room with a message for her great-great-granddaughter regarding the secret to some of her most potent elixirs. I said a blessing for her, and she disappeared. Not an hour later, the very granddaughter showed up as one of my clients. That was the part of my job that I loved. There was so much to learn from these spiritual beings.

My thoughts returned to the morning before me and the tension in the air that made the prolonged stillness suspicious.

"Lucinda, ma chère, drink your tea, s'il vous plaît?" Emilee touched her arm.

Lucinda flinched at Emilee's touch and absentmindedly brought the cup to her lips and drank. Whatever had been haunting me must have been haunting her. "Lucinda, would you like me to look for you?" I offered, "I am sensing that something from your past has come back to haunt you, and I think the only way to get through it is not to avoid it. What do you say?" Often, she trusted me with the gift of a vision in the early days when I was a novice and had little control over the various past lives of others I was channelling. Alice, my friend from the Chalice Well, would say it was ego run amok and to take baby steps as she would scold me for my pride.

Lucinda took a sip of her hot tea and let out a long, deep sigh. Then she reached out her hand to me and nodded her head. I took her hand, and the psychic connection was made. I took a large gulp of my tea and, in my own special way, opened up the vision to communicate the timeline and oracle insight I was receiving.

"I am seeing back to last night, and I am in the office looking through the red box. Oh, lord, those photos of you all were precious. But now I'm seeing the photo of that uncanny man and his beady eyes."

Lucinda went to pull her hand away, and Emilee tried to stop her, but Lucinda jerked back and stood up abruptly.

"NO!" Lucinda commanded, no longer speaking in hushed terms, "This is not the time. Anna, control yourself!"

I got up from my chair, matching her stance, and said, "Lucinda, clearly you need to resolve some karmic imbalance from your past. Let me help you!"

"No, absolutely not. You are in no condition to be doing any readings right now, especially with that attitude!"

Lucinda was starting to frustrate me now. "My attitude? What attitude? I have been perfectly pleasant to you since you got here!"

Lucinda spoke, "Your attitude last night. You never think before acting and just assume you can do whatever you want because you have a lot of raw talent. You have no discipline and a remarkable lack of consideration for the people around you that you do readings on."

"What?!?!" I yelled angrily, "I have the utmost consideration for the people around me. That's why I'm trying to help you! And for the record, I wouldn't have to keep exploring and doing things on my own if you all would actually teach me and tell me what's going on! You can't blame me for your poor teaching skills!"

Emilee tried to diffuse the situation and stood between us, saying, "Now, Anna, there is no need to say such things; please, Lucinda is your sister!"

"So you are on her side, Em? Really?"

"I'm not on anyone's side—"

Lucinda interrupted her, "Anna, don't bring Emilee into this. The fact of the matter is that you are not in a condition to do readings right now. If you had never opened that box, you would have never released the darkness that now clouds your aura. And if you had listened to me, you would have known that this is what would happen. Had you actually done a regression for me, you would have poisoned me with that darkness, too, and permanently locked in that bad karma for that life!"

Her words hit me like a gut punch, and I instantly felt ashamed, but stubbornly didn't back down, replying sarcastically, "Well, I'm so glad the ever-wise and all-knowing Lucinda was here to stop me!"

Lucinda just shook her head at me, turned to Emilee, and in a kinder voice, asked, "Is there any chance I can stay with you for a few days at the Guesthouse? There is too much darkness here at the Sanctuary, and I think it would be best for me to give Anna some space to sort it out."

Emilee nodded, "Of course. Why don't you go pack a bag from your belongings upstairs while I finish up here?"

"Thank you, old friend. I will be down in five minutes." With that, Lucinda turned and left the room.

As she was cleaning up the tea, Emilee gave me a look. "Anna, she was not wrong, you know."

I rolled my eyes and sat down in a huff, "Yeah, yeah, but why is it I never get to be right?"

"You will have your time in the light, I promise. In fact, I'm counting on you to bring us all into that light with you!" She touched my arm, and I knew she cared deeply but was caught in a dilemma between Lucinda and me.

☥

After Lucinda and Emilee left, I went into the office to see if there was any other evidence of a break-in. I figured that I should at least consider that my encounter last night might have affected me this morning. I found it still in perfect order, except for the torn book pages. Sighing, I sat down at the desk and checked the phone for any messages that I may have missed. There was only one, and it was from Isis, saying: "*Anna, call me the moment you receive this—it's most important.*"

There was a tone of fear in her voice I rarely heard, and it was most strange. However, I was not going to jump just because she said so, especially after she abandoned me in favour of going to Egypt. I scoffed at the thought of Isis visiting the Great Sphinx and exploring all its hidden rooms.

Just then, as if on cue, the office phone rang, and I had no doubt who would be on the other line. So, I begrudgingly grabbed the phone, answering, "Hello, this is the Sanctuary. I'm Anna. How may I help you?"

"Anna," said a stern voice on the phone. It was Isis, how predictable. "Is Lucinda with you?"

"No," I answered flatly.

"Where is she? Is she not at the Sanctuary today?"

"She left to stay at the Gables with Emilee for a few days."

"Why would she do that?"

"Why are you asking me a question you already know the answer to?"

"You found my red box and opened it."

I really had to check that security camera system we pretended to have. "What red box?" I played innocent.

"Anna, you know."

"Well, it fell out, and I looked."

"Lucinda called me in a panic before she left Bath and set off to you. Anna, you know looking at such things awakens the spirits!" she scolded.

"Yes, but Isis, it was only a box with old past lives and only holiday images of Egypt trips. Oh, yes, and the Protection Scarab."

"My dear, this is so much more than that."

"I obviously know that now! The whole night was crazy, there were some shadows—"

Before I could get the words out, her voice rose and cut me off, "Do not finish that sentence. You will conjure them up! I imagine Lucinda warned you of this, and you didn't heed her advice. Can I assume you two got into a fight about it this morning?"

"Isis, she was so rude! There was clearly some sort of karmic healing she needed, and she freaked out when I tried to help her."

"Yes, and for good reason, child. Whatever happened to you last night has clouded your aura and placed a darkness over your head. If you had done a regression, you would have hurt Lucinda."

"But, I di—"

"Anna, stop talking."

I held my breath and listened.

"Now, Anna, listen carefully," her voice softened, "I appreciate how difficult this has been on you, being left out of the loop, but there is a good reason for it. I know you are not in a space to really hear what I'm saying, but I do hope that once some of this darkness has dissipated—and it will—you remember this conversation. Naomi and I will return next week and begin planning the trip to Egypt in March. I promise you that you will be a part of that. Your destiny, my beloved one, will be realised and fulfilled."

"Remember, Anna, you were the one who allowed many of our sacred sisterhood's scrolls and scarabs to return to us."

She sounded like a voiceover for a film trailer.

I had forgotten about how I had been able to collect the scrolls and scarabs connected to the first creation of the divine Temple of Philae. These small, palm-sized pieces of stone with carvings that matched the scrolls were easy for me to match and decipher. No one else seemed to really understand how they worked. But for me, those small postcard-size pieces of papyrus with symbols and strange words made perfect sense. It dawned on me that perhaps I should be here as their guardian and not seeking the glamour of Cairo.

"Now, go cleanse your aura, and then go heal your friendship."

Obediently, I promised as I hung up and headed out of the office towards the stairs. As I ascended, I caught a glimpse of something in the mirror at the foot of the stairs. I could have sworn it was my mother walking behind me. I had not thought about her in months. But here she was like a ghost, with no words, no actions, just an image and a feeling. I went back to the office, sat down, and retrieved the ripped pages of the Tutankhamun book from the drawer, stuck them in a sort of fashion back into the book, and closed it with a prayer.

"It is a warning," I heard a voice that made me shiver, but no one was there.

I rose slowly, lit some incense, and silently left the room. Sometimes, it's best to remove yourself and pray that the incense does its job.

CHAPTER 2

After about twenty minutes of stewing in my room about my conversation with Isis, I decided it didn't serve me to stay at the Sanctuary by myself and continue putting negative energy into this sacred space. So, I followed Isis's advice and quickly got dressed in my favourite denim pants, navy wool jumper, and thick wool socks. I knew today would be cold and wet, as it so often was this time of year. As I made it to the door, I remembered that last week's snowfall had melted, so I opted for my army green parka and slick black wellies. With the addition of a scarf and matching mittens that Laura knitted me, I was out the door. Oh, my goodness, Laura. I missed her gentle counsel at times like this. Her cottage was not far, but I did not wish to burden her with my woes.

The crisp morning air felt good on my hot cheeks, smelling of freshly cut pine and fir. The mist had settled in the courtyard, filtering through only the gentlest of the sun's rays, giving my eyes a moment to adjust. Blackbirds were excitedly chirping on a nearby hawthorn bush, the bright carmine berries perfectly framing the lively pair. Their melodic tweeting was a welcome sound in my ears. I could feel the dark cloud above me dissipating with every step I took farther into this idyllic scene. *Perhaps I should go to the Gables Guesthouse and check on Lucinda.* Having unresolved conflict between us wasn't good for our Christmas plans, auras, or skin, for that matter.

However, just as I was turning toward the Guesthouse, the two blackbirds flew in front of me, getting so close that I had to take a few steps back to avoid them. *I suppose this is a sign, little birds. Great,* I thought, chuckling to myself, *of course it was! I guess you are telling me Lucinda isn't ready, right? Did she send you? It wouldn't surprise me.* So, not being one to ignore a sign from such elegant-looking birds, I instead changed destinations and carried on down the hill to one of my favourite places in Glastonbury: The Chalice Well with its guardian, my friend Alice.

☥

It was before opening hours when I arrived, but as always, I knew that Alice would be around saying good morning to the flowers and trees, blessing the water fountains, and calling on the earth spirits to send peace to the world. Alice was nothing if not a creature of habit, and as long as I didn't disrupt her morning tasks too much, I was welcome to roam the grounds and meditate. After the third time I had taken her up on this edict, she hid a key to the gate for me in a loose stone along the outer wall. Now arriving at the gate, I pulled off one of my mittens and pawed along the wall until I felt the loose stone. It detached from the wall easily, and when I held it upside down over my hand, the old iron key fell into it.

Just then, an icy breeze blew through the walkway, sending a chill down my back. I quickly returned the stone to its place, as I did with my mitten, and put the hood of my parka over my head. As I went to open the gate, I noticed that Alice was standing in front of the main vesica pool, chanting, most likely calling upon the local water spirits to bless those who would come to the sacred garden that day. I knew the old gate was creaky, so I opened and closed it behind me as quietly as I could; I didn't want to disturb her sacred purpose. I crept up the cobblestone path, in awe of the elegant flourishes of her hands and masterful command of the sacred words used for such blessings. When I was a safe distance away, I stopped and stood in silence, feeling my heart fill with love. Ritual with intention and pure heart always made me want to cry. It was a deep remembering in my soul.

Suddenly, Alice stopped and looked straight at me. She must have known I was there the whole time and had probably sensed my presence coming long before I arrived. *Perhaps those birds were sent by her,* I mused to myself. She must have seen me smiling and motioned me to her side with a grin matching mine. Like a child eager to please, I ran to join her.

"Do you need to see my pass?" I joked, "Because you know you need a pass to be in here; the spirits don't like a cheat!" I was mimicking Alice's voice. She was very strict about those sorts of things, which many of us chided her about from time to time.

Alice laughed and said, "No, dear, I do not. You made good time! I was worried the wind might hold you back. It was most disagreeable this morning. It's a good thing; the birds are worthy adversaries!"

"I knew it! I knew you sent those blackbirds!" I exclaimed.

"Now, I have absolutely no idea what you are talking about!" she winked. "Come on, Anna, let's go inside and have some hot cocoa in the meeting room; it is far too cold outside for my ageing bones." She motioned for me to follow her inside the meeting room adjoined to St. Michael's Retreat House. Alice was one of the wisest women I knew, and she was an oracle and priestess in her past lives connected to some of the most famous historical timelines.

As far as I was concerned, she was spiritual royalty, and I always hung on to her every word. Alice opened the meeting room, and we ventured inside.

It was a beautiful room with a circle of nine chairs positioned on top of beautiful blue Persian area rugs, a vaulted ceiling, and plenty of windows to let in light. It was cozy enough for an intimate gathering yet spacious enough to hold all the energy of the spiritual classes it was blessed to host. Most recently, I had attended a healing with crystals workshop. Who would think these beautiful items I had once been using as bookends, door stops, and miscellaneous décor could soothe the soul and clear the mind in such a profound way? However, there would be none today, just Alice and the woman lucky enough to hold her sole attention—me.

"Sit, my dear," she pointed to the chairs. I slowly made my way around the circle, taking care to pick one that felt clear of bad karma from its last occupant. I didn't need to catch some spiritual sickness right before the Christmas break.

As I sat, Alice was over at the kitchen station, pouring hot cocoa into two handmade ceramic mugs emblazoned with the name of the grounds on it. "Would you like me to add some marshmallows to your cup?" she inquired.

"Yes, of course!"

She smiled at my enthusiasm and added several marshmallows to my cup. As she walked over to hand me my cocoa, I could feel the energy in the room shift; something important was in Alice's mind, and she needed to be serious with me.

"So, Isis called me from Cairo this morning," Alice said hesitantly.

"Did she?" I said, not letting on that I knew anything about why she called.

"She said you found the red box."

I shrugged and bit my lip. "More like it found me. It nearly took me out when it fell off the shelf.

"Mmhmm, and what were you doing that led the box to fall?"

"Well, I was looking around the office, which is technically mine, as the guardian in charge of the Sanctuary, but guess what? I found the Scarab of Protection."

"What were you looking for?"

I felt like a child being interrogated by their mother after getting into the cookie jar. Why did no one applaud my new discovery?

"I don't know exactly," I replied, "Answers? I feel like there is still so much that I don't know and even more that Isis is keeping from me. We have so many of the ancient scrolls and scarabs we set out to collect for the temple creation ritual, but we still don't know everything. I just want to figure out what is going on."

"The box of scrolls and scarabs is one of the most powerful gifts we have, thanks to you, Anna. This is the first time in thousands of years that we were able to start truly deciphering them and collecting the ancient wisdom of the priestess temples in Egypt. Until you came along, we simply had bits and pieces of our past that no one was willing to bring together and share. Give it time, and don't be too hard on yourself!"

"I know, but we are still missing many of the pieces. What if they are the key to everything? We don't have unlimited time!" I was getting increasingly exasperated with each sentence, "Isis and Naomi are off on some weird secret trip to Egypt, which means we don't have them if we get into trouble, and we are stronger together. Plus, there is the issue of our sacred eight not technically being complete, which means until then, we can't truly form a powerful sisterhood and a sacred temple again!" I hadn't meant to unload all of this on Alice, but it was nice to say it out loud.

While I was rambling, Alice had been very quiet, taking in my words and carefully considering them. Once I was done, she paused and took a breath before replying, "Anna, why are you suddenly so worried about not having enough time? What is going on that would depend on us having enough time to get the right sacred eight together and for you to finish your learning?"

"They are coming!"

"Who is, my dear?"

"The Priests of Unal!"

"The Priests of Unal?" Alice looked a little confused, with a hint of, was it fear? She pressed on, "Why do you think they are coming? They died off at the ceremony last year when you cleared the past lives. As far as we can tell, they were the only ones ever created and were done so by Naomi over 2000 years ago, and none were made since, none could be made since."

In a panic, I blurted, "T-T-They were in my dreams last night. It's the first time in months, but it was different, and sand, and there was this laugh... oh god, it was awful... then I found the red box, and Lucinda got mad at me... and they were in the office! YES! They were there as shadowy figures, and I thought they were going to kill me—and then I heard that laugh again. So I picked up the citrine crystal and threw it at them, and it broke in half and broke the mirror, and then when I went back the next morning, nothing was broken or out of place, and I was horrible to Lucinda... oh, Lucinda! She is so mad at me, and Isis is disappointed, I can tell... and... and my aura is all dirty and gross, and everything is just going to crap right now."

I started having trouble breathing, "Plus, Christmas... is in... days... and... I... still have... shopping to finish!" I let out the last bit in the longest breath I could muster. Then, I clutched my heart in pain from not being able to take deep breaths. I tried my best to slow my breathing, but to no avail. My hyperventilating got to the point where Alice had to lay me on my back on the floor and do breathing exercises with me. It would seem the events of the last night and morning had finally caught up with me.

☥

Once I had come down from my panic attack and was breathing normally again, Alice helped me up off the floor and back into my chair. She asked if I wanted some more hot cocoa, and I nodded. As Alice handed me my full mug, I gave her a feeble smile, suddenly ashamed of my helplessness and drama. Alice seemed to pick up on this and empathetically patted me on the back before returning to her seat with another cup of cocoa in hand.

I took a big swig from my mug and focused on the pleasant sensation of the warm, chocolaty liquid flowing down and soothing my ragged throat. I made note of the hints of cinnamon and nutmeg in the brew and filed it away to try again at home later.

After one more gulp of my beverage, I spoke, "You know, I really thought that the summer solstice ceremony had been the end of them coming to me."

Alice nodded and considered my words before responding, "The solstice is a convergence of sorts. Several planes of reality blur and reorient themselves before returning to their more natural states. We are both at our most powerful and our most visible. During the summer solstice, at the height of your power, you must have willed the Priests of Unal into a plane that they couldn't reach you from. Remember how you brought the past life of Naomi forward to heal her. You were still relying on your raw talent as an oracle, so you probably didn't realise what you had done. Think of it as a sort of built-in, automatic defence." The ceremony created that day was powerful. And remember, we only had a few of the scrolls and scarabs to work with.

"Yeah, but if that's true, wouldn't my previous banishment of the Priests of Unal keep them from coming back?"

"Well, my dear Anna, the winter solstice was last night, so what do you think?"

"Oh wow, well, I suppose that last night, I was unusually powerful and visible..." I paused momentarily, "but that also means the Priests of Unal were also at their most powerful and visible. Plus, with various planes of reality blurring and thinning, they could more easily come back."

"Very good, Anna!" Alice exclaimed. "Anything else?"

I thought for a second, "Oh, yes! Because I was dreaming about them, they were able to find me and probably found a way to enter our plane that way. They were able to place a darkness over me because of all the plane blurring. But wait, does that mean they are back in a plane where they can't touch me?"

"What does your oracle intuition tell you?"

I closed my eyes, took a deep breath, and listened to what my spirit was telling me before saying, "I will see them again, and it's going to be different this time."

Alice furrowed her brow. "How is it different?" she asked.

"Before, my dreams were all about trying to figure out who the emerald-eyed woman wanted me to find, which turned out to be the key to solving the mystery of why the Temple of Isis fell. That woman turned out to be Cleopatra, who was a mother of mine in a past life, and every time the Priests showed up, she told me not to let them get me. They came close, but I never felt like they consumed my being. The dreams would always end with my vision going dark. This time, I started out in the dark and then was violently pulled back. I couldn't see them, but I knew it was them. The Priests of Unal had me."

"And you think that this means they have some way of harming you in the physical world?"

"Maybe. It isn't a coincidence that they come back on the solstice when Isis isn't around and so aggressively haunt me. I didn't even have a chance to get away. I was just already got. Then, when I awoke, they were able to visit me in shadow form in the office. Now, again, they had the benefits that come with the solstice, but it isn't a good sign. I felt another dark presence among them, one that was far more powerful and sinister. Who—or whatever it was—seemed to be controlling them and helping them in some way. And if this being is as powerful as I think it is, it is only a matter of time before we see these creeps in the flesh."

"Wow, that would be a terribly powerful force to reckon with. Now tell me, dear Priestess of Isis, what can you do to stop it?"

"I'm not sure yet...I think I need to wait and see what my dreams reveal. I need to try my best not to let them get hold of me in my dreams again. I fear that if they can get me in a dream, they can get me in real life, which means they can get the rest of you, too. I will do everything I can to keep them in my dreams and away from you all."

She gave me a sad smile and looked at me in a sympathetic way. "That is just the kind of thinking our

High Priestess needs to be doing. Well done, Anna, truly. I hope this conversation has shown you that you need not doubt yourself, as you are already acting as a leader and wise beyond your years." She sighed, shaking her head, "Unfortunately, that also means your load is heavier for it, my dear. You are correct in your assessment that you alone have the tools to fight them right now. However, I do hope you know that we will do all we can to support our leader!"

I leaned over and squeezed Alice's hand, "Thank you, Alice. I am trying my best to see where I fit in so many titles and roles, but I know I can be vulnerable with you."

She broke free of my grip and waved me off, "Oh, tut, tut, it is I who should thank you for your sacrifice and willingness to put yourself in harm's way for my safety! Please, my dear child, is there anything I can do for you? I am an Alexandrian Librarian, after all!"

I made a big show of thinking about my response. So, I cocked a sly smile her way and pretended to heave an exasperated sigh, "Well, now that you mention it, I have been awfully lonely lately! Tell me, if I become the High Priestess with all the responsibility and power, would that mean I am destined to have no one to share it with?"

Alice smiled and did the thing with her fingers where she muscle-tested them and then began whispering words into thin air. She looked at me and said, "Oh no, someone is already on their way."

"What, like a boyfriend?" I was all ears now.

Alice threw up her hands noncommittally, "I don't know... the vision is fading... I suppose you will have to see!"

We both had a good laugh at our silly antics.

Alice then asked me, "So, do you feel any better?"

I nodded, "Yes, now that you ask, I do! I feel so much lighter, and so does my aura! How did you do that?"

"Oh, I didn't. You did by working through the events of last night and this morning. That, and I may have slipped a little water from the Lion fountain into the brew."

"Ah, ha! I knew there was something special about it!"

"Well, dear, now that your aura is restored, why don't you tell me more about that red box!" she asked

What was it with this silly old rusting evil box?

"Well, I looked through it, and it was full of old tickets to events, pictures from the past 100 years, and holiday snaps. I didn't really think much of it."

"Did you look closely at the faces?"

"Not really. I did see Lucinda, Isis, and a few others who I thought looked familiar. But they were really old, so I can't be sure who they were."

"And tell me, Anna, was there anything else?"

How did she always know? "Y...Yes," I stammered, "A symbol. Here, let me draw it for you." I went over to a side table, grabbed a scrap of paper and a pen, and began drawing the concentric circle design that had petals or leaves with the line around it floating around my head all morning. I decided not to mention the torn pages from the book as I was constantly being told one step at a time, and I suddenly realised the two were related in some way.

She furrowed her brow at the symbol and looked from me to it and back again. "Where did you see this?" she asked. "It was on the box, right?"

"Well, yes, but that's not where I saw it first."

"Where did you see it first?"

"In my dream," I blurted out.

"I am guessing you know what it means?"

I continued to draw the best I could, but then my hand went to automatic as if possessed, adding to the symbol, but when I heard Alice gasp, it looked like a five-year-old child's scribble.

She took the pen from me and began drawing a far more elegant Ankh with an open flower upon it. Rather than the dish holding the symbol, it was covering it like an umbrella.

"Yes, that's it," I gasped.

Her eyes grew wide, and she smiled, "That, my dear, is the Seshat symbol and the Flower of Life that allows access to the universal Akashic field. She's giving you her key and secret. I think that is what the dream meant."

"But why me? Do you know?"

Alice shook her head, "No, Anna, I don't." She looked at me with a slight fear in her eyes.

"I suppose you could channel your Records. It may be from a recent past life."

My heart sank. I hadn't ever been good at channelling my own past lives. The best I had done was when I was channelling my past life with Anne Boleyn and a little bit of my time at the Temple of Isis at Philae right as it fell. However, I resolved to try and do so now that I knew it would have all the answers I needed.

"Alice, I guess that is exactly what I am going to have to do. Will you help me channel?"

"Of course, my dear, it would be an honour. Now, let's prepare, relax, and Anna," she said, "You're safe. Close your eyes."

☥

I am in a city, one like I have never seen before. It seems like it is from another time. It feels like Egypt, but I'm not sure. I feel like I'm floating above, seeing the image but not actually there in reality. I'm an observer.

The buildings are made of limestone and have hieroglyphs that I do not recognise, yet they reach into the sky like our modern-day buildings do. The streets are lined with what look like streetlamps, but they shine a beautiful blue hue. The people walking around seem otherworldly, impossibly beautiful, with navy-sheened raven hair and tan olive skin. They wear crystals of all colours around their necks, set in intricate jewellery of gold and silver. Stone machines whirl down the streets, seemingly being propelled on their own like cars are today. This is strange. I know the city to be of ancient origin, I can feel it. But I do not know where I am.

Suddenly, I hear a rumbling in the distance, and something inside me tells me to panic and to run to high ground, so I run up the nearest hill and wait. Everyone is going about their day as if there hadn't just been an earth-shattering rumble. I am trying to warn them, but they will not listen. I do not know what I am warning them about.

Now, I see what made the sound—a wave is gaining size just a few hundred yards offshore. It is speeding towards the city, its dark waters blocking out the bright, warm sun. I am yelling at everyone to run, but they cannot hear me. It is not until the wave hits the shore that people start to panic.

They go off running in all directions, pushing and shoving each other out of the way. I hear children crying and looking for their parents, but they will not find them. The wave hits the street, and everything gets swept away in one glorious blast. I can't breathe, I can't...

I am violently hurled from my vision and awake on the ground of the meeting room, gasping for air. I look up and see Alice shaking in her chair. I have never seen her look so horrified.

Still attempting to catch my breath, I asked her, "What the hell was that? I have never heard of a city like that before in Egypt, or anywhere, for that matter, being destroyed by a flood."

Alice didn't answer me; instead, she got up and ran out of the room, mumbling about getting a book from her office. As I waited for her to return, I couldn't help but wonder if it had anything to do with my dream last night. Something bad had happened, and the clothing the people were wearing looked like what the two people arguing in my dream had on.

I didn't have much more time to ponder it as Alice had returned with a very old leather-bound book. She gave me an odd look, and I realised I was still on the floor, so I got up and sat back in my seat as she did.

"Well," Alice began, choosing her words carefully, "I have never seen anything like that before, not in all of my lifetimes, but I have read about it."

"Read about it? What was that? Where was that?"

"Here," she said, handing me the ancient book. "This is a hundred-year-old copy of the Emerald Tablets of Thoth. I bookmarked the page. Read it."

I complied and quickly opened the book to see what answers it held. After quickly reading the passage she was talking about, I looked at her curiously. Trying not to be dismissive, I said, "Alice, are you serious? This is about the destruction of Atlantis. Atlantis isn't a real place." I shook my head.

"Oh Anna, after everything you have seen, do you really think Atlantis isn't or wasn't a real place?"

I thought for a moment. She was right; why would this be any less real than everything else I had seen? "Okay, okay," I conceded. "So, Atlantis was probably a real place, but why do you think that what we saw was Atlantis?"

"Did you read the passage? It describes exactly how Atlantis was destroyed and what its people did to deserve it!"

"Yes, okay, yes. But why did we see Atlantis? I was trying to channel one of my last lives. There is no way my last life was in Atlantis thousands of years ago!"

"No, it wasn't. You are right, Anna. I am not sure why you channelled that. Strictly speaking, our oracle cycle didn't start until the creation of the Temple of Isis at Philae, and that was long after Atlantis had disappeared."

"So, I must have gotten my wires crossed then? So what was I channelling?"

Alice looked just as puzzled as I felt, "I am not sure, Anna. Like I said, I've only ever read about Atlantis, and pretty much everything I know is in that book I handed you. All I can say is, I would not ignore what we just saw."

"Oh, I won't. As you said, I suppose it is my job to figure it out."

Alice nodded in agreement, still looking confused at what had just transpired. "Yes, and if I knew more, I could tell you. For right now, why don't you take that book and read through it? Maybe it will stir some other visions. And also take this book." She left her chair, went to the back of the room, and pulled what looked to be a very old book with damaged binding.

"I am not sure how we came to have this book, but I came across it just after the August 8 ceremony. I am not sure why or if it's fact or fiction. It is a story about a young Egyptian queen who was the last ruler of a long line of powerful yet cursed leaders. The failing of her ancestors and how they came to power by signing a sacred contract with someone they called the Scorpion Queen. I had a vision of something dark and hid the book, but my intuition tells me this book may have some answers for you. I've tried to open it many times, but every time, I felt sleepy, a sign for me to leave it alone, but for you, I think it has answers."

I could tell that Alice was unnerved by what we had seen. She was one of the most knowledgeable of all of us, and it irked her when she didn't know as much or more than everyone else, the latter usually being the case. That also worried me. If she didn't know why I was channelling an event that happened before our oracle lifetimes, then chances were that Isis and Naomi, the two people I looked up to more than ever and felt protected by, didn't know either, which meant I was truly on my own.

Chapter 3

The Gables Guesthouse was a quick walk from the Chalice Well, and in this windy weather, I was glad it was the case. As I walked up the pebble drive and saw the shuttered windows and well-kept garden, I smiled, thinking about my first time seeing the place. It had been May, and I had been so taken by the bright flowers and charming exterior of the guesthouse. Over the course of my first few months here, it had been my personal sanctuary, where I did some of my best writing and channelling. Leaving the Yorkshire area was one of the best decisions of my life. Everything was better here in Glastonbury, and the Gables was a reminder of that.

Instead of going through the front door, I decided to go around back, not wanting to run into any of Emilee's guests who may be checking in, or Lucinda for that matter, as I still wasn't quite sure what to say to her. The back door was through her garden and next to her small greenhouse, which always had the most wonderfully fragrant and beautiful plants necessary for her various potions and elixirs. She was also a master at making soaps, creams, and other items with her homemade distilled essential oils. Plus, I figured Emilee could also be a good sounding board for my as-yet-to-be-formulated apology to Lucinda.

True to form, I could see Emilee through the kitchen window, and I tapped lightly on the glass. She looked up from her oven where she was cooking and smiled and waved me to enter. The air was thick with the smell of baking bread mixed with the bundles of lavender hanging on the fireplace mantle and the hickory burning in the hearth. I could see Emilee darting from the frying pan on the stove to a serving tray where she had placed the rest of the breakfast. The tray had baked beans, fried tomatoes and mushrooms, and sausage. When I reached the kitchen table, she was placing the fried eggs on a blue and white floral plate and running back to flip the bread.

She looked up at me and motioned for me to sit, saying, "Oh, Anna, come sit! I just finished the eggs for my hiking guests and need to tend to the bread, *un instant s'il vous plaît.*" She took the fried bread from the stove and placed it in an elegant toast holder. She may have been preparing a full English breakfast, but the presentation was laced with a class and elegance that was distinctly French. I smiled at this—even after all these years, Emilee was still true to herself and her culture. I took a breath to apologise, but she shook her head.

Having arranged everything just so, Emilee picked up the tray and, on her way into the dining room, said, "Oh, and help yourself to coffee. It is hot and fresh, and there is an egg and toast left. I will be back in a moment." She disappeared into the front room, where the guests ate all the delicious breakfast fare. Emilee, a true entrepreneur, had supplemented her income by providing a late breakfast for hikers visiting the Tor. "No beds, no stinky towels to wash, just food and love, all for a special price," she said, winking at me.

I went to the cupboard, grabbed a mug, and poured myself a cup of coffee from the French press on the table. It was just what I needed after being out in the freezing wind. It seemed like today I would be holding court with all of my favourite people while holding a mug. I wasted no time in devouring the delicious leftover breakfast items.

Emilee's reappearance roused me from my thoughts. "Okay, they are all munching away. I can focus on you for a little while," she said, wiping her hands on her apron, unceremoniously removing it, and throwing it over a chair.

She stopped and looked at me with one crooked eyebrow. "Something amusing, *ma chère, soeur*?"

"Oh, no, Em, not really," I said. "I just realised that at every stop of my tour of the countryside this morning involved receiving a hot beverage in a mug."

"*Oui*? And where have you been other than to see your favourite Glastonbury sister: moi?"

"A little birdy... well, a pair of them actually, told me to stop by the Chalice Well and see Alice."

"Ah, I see. And what wisdom did dear old Alice have for you, or rather, what book did she give you?" She pointed at the copy of the *Emerald Tablets of Thoth* that I had placed on the table when I sat down; I had hidden the other in my large coat pocket.

"Well, she gave me some much-needed encouragement about my role within our sisterhood and this book. You see, we had the strangest past life regression—"

I was about to launch into the story when I noticed Lucinda in the doorway. Her body instantly stiffened when she saw me, and her face scrunched into a scowl. I could tell she was debating whether to enter the room or return the way she came. Having realised that there was now a long, awkward silence in the room, Lucinda sighed and walked in, taking great care to calm herself and mask her discomfort.

"Judging by that book, you are looking into something beyond the sisterhood that formed in Philae. Atlantis, perhaps?" Lucinda replied in the most measured tone she could muster. However, an acridness still lay just under the surface.

"I don't know why you are looking into that right now,"

she continued, "when we have more important matters to attend to."

"And what are those, may I ask?" I enquired, anger rising inside me.

"To finish collecting the scrolls and scarabs, to start, and then using them to unite the Sacred Eight and restore balance to the temple, or have you forgotten?"

Why was she still being so rude to me? I do not understand what is bringing all of this on. She knows she is just going to make me upset. What is the point? I thought to myself.

And right on cue, she said, "You are angry with me; I can feel it."

I sighed, "I was. I'm more frustrated than anything else right now, and this morning was not great." I paused and decided to let the words flow. "I know I wasn't kind to you this morning, and it pains me to know that I hurt you. I was a massive bitch, steamrolling you like that. You were correct in your assessment that my aura had been compromised, and I shudder to think about what would have happened had you not stopped me. Please know that I would have never knowingly put you in such terrible danger, Lucinda."

"I know you wouldn't," she replied, "However, your behaviour to 'steamroll,' as you say, is still prevalent, even when your aura is clear. Prior to your ascension as the next High Priestess of Isis, it was more excusable for you to go about reading everyone's past lives because you were excited and didn't have a full grasp on your abilities yet. But if you are to be a High Priestess now, you must start practising more restraint. With your now even more enhanced abilities, you could end up really hurting yourself or someone else if you continue to be so cavalier."

"Logically, I understand that, but I still feel as though I haven't had enough instruction to do that."

"Well, then you need to ask for help and not assume you can do it alone."

"I know! Then, consider this me asking, alright?"

Lucinda considered my words before replying, "I am not sure if it is wise for me to help you with this at this juncture. At least, I don't think I can take an active role in your instruction."

I was dumbfounded, "But why? Lucinda, you were my first teacher. You've known me the longest out of everyone here! And without you, who knows if I would have come here and done all of this!"

Lucinda grabbed my hand and patted it sympathetically, replying, "Yes, and it was a blessing and an honour to be the one to introduce you to this world! However, what you are experiencing is something I never will. If what you said was true, you are seeing past lives beyond the normal oracle cycle and ability, which isn't something I can help you with."

I looked down at our interlocked hands, disappointed, "But if you won't or can't, I suppose, and Isis and Naomi are both gone, who will help me?"

Lucinda smiled sweetly at me, "I will reach out to Isis and see if we can do anything in the interim to help you. The best I can think of until she gets back is for you to meditate and keep yourself as centred and calm as possible."

Emilee piped in just then, "And I will get you some elixirs that will help! You are not alone, *ma chère*. By the way, I sense your aura is returning to a healthy mix of blue, purple, and turquoise. Tell me, how did you get such a wonderful mix of colours?"

I laughed, "Well, let's just say you aren't the only potion master among us!" I winked.

Emilee, in pseudo-incredulity, exclaimed, "Another? You have been cheating on me with another? Who is it?

Who is this," she put up air quotes, "'maestro' of yours?"

In a teasing way, Lucinda said, "Who do you think? The only other woman who could give you a run for your money, who happens to be the guardian of a magical water source."

"You think Alice is that good?" Emilee asked.

"You don't?" Lucinda questioned. "Alice is so respected. Really, Emilee, how often has she instructed you in the sacred rituals and arts?"

Emilee turned beet red at Lucinda's insinuation and made a surprised squeak. She rushed out of the kitchen into her storeroom of potions and elixirs. I looked to Lucinda for an explanation, who was chuckling to herself and shaking her head. I decided that perhaps I should start showing that restraint Lucinda was talking about and let it go.

Instead, I opted to finish my apology to Lucinda, saying, "I promise I will start using more caution and better judgment. It's my hope that I can prove to you that I am worthy of meeting your expectations. I am truly sorry for hurting you this morning, my dear friend."

Lucinda nodded, "Thank you. I appreciate you saying that. There is no doubt in my mind that you will not only meet but surpass my expectations. I forgive you, Anna, as long as you can forgive me for not being more patient, considering your nocturnal experience greatly influenced your temperament."

"Of course!" I paused, "Now, I know that my most recent endeavours aren't something you can help with, but maybe you have some insight into the Sacred Eight and getting the scrolls and scarabs together?"

"As it so happens, Anna, I have been having visions about the Temple of Isis for the last six months and what is to become of us. At first, it was glorious; we were all together, holding hands in Egypt, forming a circle, and bringing balance back to the temples for the first time in thousands of years. All portents pointed to this coming to pass, so I said nothing. Even when your hubris was at its worst right before the Solstice, I knew that would not prevent us from coming together. However, on Portal Day, August 8th, remember the 888, the ceremony did not go as planned."

"Well, everything with Lesley was a bit strange, but we still stood as the Sacred Eight," I interjected.

"No, we stood as *a* sacred eight, not *the* Sacred Eight. Lesley was banished from the circle, and Lucas had to step in. Then, when Isis passed the mantle towards you, we were no longer the Sacred Eight."

"Even if Lesley left the circle," I argued, "she was still technically part of the original Sacred Eight, as Isis was, which we needed to get together to restore balance!"

"Yes, Isis was, but you weren't. That's how the oracle cycle works. She was the original High Priestess, also the teacher and guide of oracles, and was bound to be so in every lifetime until a worthy soul could replace her, and that was you. We thought all had been achieved, that we were free of our past life curses and the sacred contracts that had been binding our souls for thousands of years. However, the only thing that the Portal Day ceremony accomplished was establishing you as her successor. You have done good work freeing some of us from our cursed bondage; you have, but—"

I completed her sentence, "—I haven't actually balanced the temples."

"Correct. Can't you feel it? We are better than we were, but something isn't right. We are missing at least one member of our new Sacred Eight."

"Who? Lesley?" I asked with disgust in my voice, "She was one of the forces working against us!"

"Yes, Lesley," Lucinda nodded, "And one other. With Isis's cycle nearly over, we are going to be one person short. The oracle who served the goddess Renenutet is missing, as well. At first, I thought you were her, but when you ascended to the role of High Priestess, I knew you weren't."

"Then who is?" I paused. "And in truth, Lucinda, I'm not sure this High priestess role is my path."

She looked surprised and then nodded.

"I am not sure either, but we must figure it out soon. There is still a great deal of fear and bad blood that runs through our histories that must be cleared. This task of gathering all eight together is a very delicate matter."

"Can you see now? What do your latest visions say?"

Lucinda sighed, "They aren't very clear, unfortunately. As of right now, it could go either way."

An alarming thought struck me, "Lucinda, that means it could go the wrong way, right?"

Lucinda hesitated, "Yes... I... I think it could. I'm sorry, Anna."

Just then, Emilee came back into the room with a basket full of blue bottles and set them near my book before tending to her cooking. She looked a little shaken up. I realised she had been listening.

"Em?" I asked, "Are you alright? You know that Lucinda and I were only having a laugh with you earlier..."

Emilee let out a breath and turned to face us, replying, "It isn't that. I'm French; I can take a little kidding around. It's just that Lucinda's visions scare me. I always thought it was a given that once you arrived and we had our new High Priestess, everything would be okay. It scares me to think that this is not over yet."

For Emilee's sake, I pressed Lucinda further, "Please, is there anything else you can tell us?"

Lucinda considered her answer for a moment. I could see she was having an internal debate about what to say in light of our most recent words. Finally, after what seemed like an eternity, she responded, "Well, it is resolved, or it isn't... or I suppose it isn't that simple. The visions in which we don't come together only show a few of the temples not being reunited and cleansed. But which temples were they? I think that means something important. We all have to stay vigilant and not let any of our sisters fall to the wayside. The cause is something dark running around our sisterhood that will destroy us, and Anna, I am sorry to say that darkness is concentrated around you."

"Me? What did I do?"

"It isn't what you have done. Something is attaching itself to you and darkening your spirit. You need to be careful, or it will swallow you up. It won't be any of us who prevent the sisterhood from reforming. It will be you."

"It's the Priests of Unal," I gasped.

"Yes," Lucinda shook her head, "You must be diligent not to let them consume you. They were successful once, and we all know how that turned out."

"*Oui*, but that was not Anna's fault. We all played a part last time. The Priests of Unal were just increasing the darkness that had already penetrated us. Now Anna is here to help heal us and keep us in the light."

"Yes, she is, but she cannot absorb the dark in order to do that."

"She will not!" Emilee said, her voice rising, "Anna is strong, and we must trust her. The mistrust is what got us into this mess!"

Lucinda gave Emilee a piercing look and lowered her tone to a harsh whisper, "Do you think I don't know that? But I can't help but be cautious. The Priests of Unal are powerful forces, and Anna is still very new to this! Emilee, you clearly do not understand. Your potions and elixirs are otherworldly, but you have always had limited foresight!"

I was growing weary of them talking about me as if I weren't there, so I piped in, "Anna is right here and can speak for herself. Lucinda, I promise I will temper my ego and put everything I have into balancing the temples. Part of that is stopping us from fighting about it here and now. Emilee is right; if we start to doubt each other, we will never be rid of the curses we set for ourselves. You have every right to be worried, but not trusting me when I have always trusted you? That won't work. Please, Isis and Naomi are already cutting me out; I can't have you doing that, too, and taking Emilee down in the process. If I am to be the one who unites us, I need you to help me. Please do not fight against me!"

Lucinda's face grew pale, and she looked as if I had just hit her. She hadn't expected me to be so forceful, I could tell. Emilee, too, looked shocked, but I could see a quiet appreciation growing in her expression. Lucinda's next words were markedly more measured, as if she had realised what she had said was taken too far.

"Yes, you are my friend, and I lost sight of that. Anna, I am not perfect, and I know you see me as some higher being, but I'm not. I am subject to the same faults as anyone else, in this case, fear. When I was expressing my concerns to Isis the other morning, I sensed her concern, which led me to let fear and doubt in. I am sorry, Annie. Please forgive me?"

Emilee tried to comfort me by rubbing my hands in hers, but I jerked them away.

"We all have been there except you, Anna, and we know the trials..." She stopped mid-sentence. It was true, they had all been to Egypt before and worked together to keep it a secret.

I felt so betrayed. How could they all lie to me? I felt like none of them trusted me. If they couldn't trust me, the cycle would repeat itself, and we would never come together as one united sisterhood.

"Annie," Lucinda said gently, placing her hand comfortingly on my shoulder. "It wasn't that we didn't trust you; we just didn't want to lose you before you could do what you were destined to do. You are more powerful than any of us has ever been at this stage in your development. We know you can do it, but you need to be alive and well to do it. Isis and Naomi are just trying to ensure that."

Emilee gave me a smile and went to hold my hand. This time, I let her. I looked at both of them. I could tell there was no malice in their words and that they were telling me the truth. There was no use in continuing this fight. They both meant well, and it wouldn't do any of us any good if I kept pushing against what they were saying. So, in the interest of peace, I chose to accept what they were saying and move on, all the while worrying that the rest of our sisters really didn't trust me to lead them.

"So," Lucinda enquired, "Can we put this to rest?"

I smiled at them, "Yes, of course."

"Here, here!" Emilee and I cheered, raising our mugs and clinking them with Lucinda's.

Just then, we heard the sound of a plate shattering to the floor.

"Ah, oh no, my guests!" Emilee said, getting up in a hurry and rushing into the other room.

Lucinda and I looked at each other. I knew that we had a difficult road ahead, but for the sake of our Christmas celebration, any bad karma could wait until after the new year to be resolved.

Later, I returned to the Sanctuary, and on the door was a note from Laura: *Much work to do. Isis called me to check on you, but you were out. I will be back soon. Be patient, my dear one; you are braver than you think.*

Great. Me home alone to fight the demons.

Chapter 4

Darkness. Light. Searing Pain. Sand. Why was it always sand? I opened my eyes to the harsh light of the desert and found myself lying in the dirt. My body felt all out of sorts, like my soul had been ripped from it and stuffed back in haphazardly. Instead of sitting up, I just lay there, hoping I could figure out what was going on. I heard the impossible young boy and regal woman fighting. I could hear bits and pieces of the conversation about the scroll and how the woman had not understood it. The boy was warning her to undo what she had done. Their voices faded, so I sat up to see where they had gone.

I saw the glimmering pyramid and Sphinx and was overcome by its beauty. As I scanned the scene, I saw other women in a dazed state, but I recognised some of them. Isis and Naomi were just a few feet away from me, holding each other, sobbing. I tried to get to them, but was too weak to move. Suddenly, I saw two dark shadows form behind them. I yelled out to warn them, but the shadows had already snatched them, all but disappearing into the darkness.

Then, I heard a sinister laugh behind me, which shook me to my core. Out of the corners of my eyes, I saw a shadow and knew it was going to take me. My body was all but paralysed from the waist down, its energy spent from sitting up. The shadow's dark tendrils began to snake around my ankles, pulling my legs out from under me and forcing me to land flat on my stomach. They slowly made their way around my calves, then my thighs, and were tightening around my waist. I was so tired, and the parts of my body held by the shadow felt cold. My eyes fluttered shut, and I resigned myself to let the darkness take me. I was too weak and tired to fight back.

Then, just as the shadow was about to reach my neck, I heard Cleopatra's voice in my head, saying, "Don't let them get you! Run! I can't protect you for very long!" Her words infused me with resolve, and I started to fight back, grabbing at anything on the sand that would give me purchase to get away. I dragged my limp body across the sand, managing to push the shadow back to my waist. Screaming for anyone to help me, I hoped someone else had been lucky enough to escape. Someone must have heard me because I saw a pair of legs in golden sandals standing before me. I grabbed onto their ankles and looked up to see who my saviour was. The regal woman was staring down at me with a confused look in her golden eyes. She seemed familiar, but I could not be sure. One thing I knew was that she was not Cleopatra.

She knew exactly who I was, and her face quickly twisted and contorted into disgust and contempt. Her eyes went from a bright gold to a deep crimson. She shook me from her ankles and kicked me so hard in the face that it sent me over to my other side. As I lay there whimpering, I could feel a searing pain in my nose and felt hot blood trickling out of it and pooling onto the ground beside me. Through my blurred vision, I could see the woman giving me a satisfied grin. She let out a haughty laugh and walked away, leaving me to the shadow nipping at my feet. As my eyes fluttered shut, I felt ice in my veins, then nothing.

Tuesday, 23 December 2008, 3:33 a.m.

I awoke with a start, grateful to be away from that horrible woman. A rush of cold air hit me, sending a chill down my back. Just then, I noticed how cold I was and found myself completely uncovered. I pawed around in the darkness for my blankets, hoping to wrap myself in their warmth, but to no avail. Not wanting to trip on them getting out of bed, I turned on my bedside lamp. As my eyes adjusted to the light, I noticed a crimson stain on my pillowcase. Confused, I looked around and saw another stain on my nightshirt. Panicking, I ran to the bathroom to investigate and screamed at the sight of my reflection in the mirror. There was dark, dried blood crusted around my nose and lighter, wetter streaks down my mouth and chin. My hair was sticking out in ten different directions and also had dried blood in it.

In that moment, I feared that something from my dream really had kicked me, and I frantically checked my nose to make sure it hadn't broken. I sighed with relief when, after cleaning off my face, I found no bruising or swelling. I must have had a nosebleed during my sleep. While I was glad that my nose wasn't broken, it wasn't comforting to think that it had coincided with being kicked in the face during my nightmare. My dreams had always been very vivid, but this was at a whole new level. *What if things continue to escalate?* I thought. *What if next time I take a bad fall or sleepwalk out the door and in front of a car? There is no telling what could happen.*

Those thoughts were enough to keep me from going back to sleep. I considered calling Lucinda; she was still staying at the Gables with Emilee, maybe to warn her and alert her to the danger I saw with Isis and Naomi, but I knew that would only make things worse. Lucinda and I were still on shaky ground, and I didn't need her accusing me of tampering with oracle rituals that I wasn't supposed to. There was no way I would let that happen, and as the High Priestess in waiting, it was my problem alone to solve.

Besides, it was two days before Christmas, and after the last couple of mad, busy months, the last thing any of us need is dealing with my nightmares that fight back.

After I took a bath and laundered my soiled bedsheets, I spent the rest of the early morning tidying up the Sanctuary, performing cleansing rituals, and meditating with the elixirs Emilee had given me. I made it my mission to banish any evil lurking around, whether the spiritual or dirt kind. There was no way that any evil thing was going to ruin Christmas. I wanted to show Lucinda I could be a calming and tempered presence in the household. Which meant that by the time she returned, I had purged the entire place of bad energy. So I lit the incense, put on the Hallelujah Chant music, and made a proper English breakfast to boot.

I was just pulling the kettle off the stove when Laura came in through the front door. She instinctively stopped at the threshold and looked around. I gave her an inquisitive look. She was draped from head to toe in warm cashmere scarves. Always in fine clothes, her ash-coloured hair was cut into a pixie style to frame her small face, which always wore a smile. A twinkle was in her blue, almost lavender eyes.

"Is there something wrong with the doorframe, Laura?" I asked, "Or are you put off by the smell of fried eggs, sausage, and toast?"

Laura shook her head, "No, Anna, not at all. I was just noticing the lack of clutter and ghosts around the place."

"Oh, yes, I was feeling domestic this morning and cleaned up around here. Want me to fix you a plate? I have plenty."

Laura nodded as she came over to me to collect her

breakfast. "Yes, there is no physical or spiritual clutter around here..." she said, her words trailing off as I handed her a plate.

"Well, I figured the place should be free and clear of any negative energy and dust as Christmas descends upon us. Don't you think that is a good idea?"

Laura sat down at the table and responded, "Well, yes, Anna, I do; I just didn't know that you were so concerned with those sorts of things. There wasn't any particular incident that spurred this on, was there?"

"No, of course not," I replied calmly with a wink and joined her at the table. "I am just trying to be the best temple guardian I can be, that's all. If any of the women in our group are ever going to start seeing me as a leader, I need to start acting like one, which means being responsible for keeping up the health of the Sanctuary."

"Hmmm," Laura hummed, eyeing me with a slight degree of suspicion, albeit slightly mockingly, "I think it is wise for you to do so. Good work, Anna."

I smiled with satisfaction and dug into my eggs. Laura seemed to be impressed with my cooking and my new attitude. Now this felt like home. Laura had been my refuge when my home flooded, and I lost my job all within 24 hours. She was a wise lady and made me feel safe. I had loved my few days' stay with her before setting out on my Glastonbury adventure. And having her here sitting at the large oak table where we shared all our sister secrets made the world feel in balance again.

So, we ate the rest of our breakfast in mostly comfortable silence, only breaking it when Laura offered to clean up with me. I was thankful for her offer, as I had a few of Emilee's guests coming over for a channelling session later that day that I needed to prepare for. It was part of the Gables

Guesthouse Glastonbury Christmas Package that she had offered. It included a private tour of the Tor and Chalice Well and a lovely sampling of Emilee's potions and elixirs.

Once everything was set into its proper place, Laura made some fresh tea, checked her watch, and looked at me. "Anna, fetch the scrolls and scarabs, please. I want to share something with you."

I did as instructed and went to the office. From a secret chamber behind the bookcase, I retrieved a very special box where we stored the scrolls and scarabs of our divine temple. I also retrieved the Protection Scarab from the red box.

Each scroll contained wisdom and knowledge, and it was fully activated when it connected with its matching scarab. Originally, there were eight sets, which were used by Isis in one of her past life incarnations in 380 BC to create a temple on Philae Island in Egypt. Well, I suspected it may have had older lineage, but this was as far as we could see in the Akashic Records.

So I came back into the room where Laura had lit a candle and laid out a white linen cloth on the table.

I opened the box and began to lift them all very carefully onto the white linen.

"So here is the Scroll and Scarab of Magic and Prophecy. This is the Scarab of Creation that was left to me by Cleopatra, with its matching scroll. Oh, and the Protection Scarab from Naomi. The Death and Resurrection Scroll from Isis."

I watched as Laura looked a little uncomfortable, but she was the best ghost whisperer we knew.

"This was your Scarab of The Goddess and Fertility." I smiled at her. "And then last but not least, the Scroll and Scarab of Truth and Integrity from Alice."

I began to count them. "That's nine in total."

"And here is one more," whispered Laura, holding her

hand open to reveal a small scarab that she placed next to the Death and Resurrection Scroll.

My eyes felt like they would pop out of my head.

"That's 10! Oh, my goodness."

We both sat motionless, staring at the table.

"Now, Anna, I think you are ready to hear something."

She leaned in closer.

"These are no ordinary pieces or relics. Sometimes, I don't think they even belonged in Egypt. They feel so much older."

"Like Atlantis," I leaned in and whispered.

"Yes," she said.

"Alice mentioned this to me."

"Did she mention the Children of Light?" Laura responded.

"No, I don't think so."

"Well, I have often seen myself in an older timeline with highly evolved souls. I have seen myself leaving and always holding pain in my heart."

"I feel that sorrow, too." I nodded, and as I reached out and took her hand, I caught a vision.

"People leaving and a group being separated. I see the boats and such sorrow."

She pulled her hand away.

"Maybe we can look another time when we're not in such powerful company and I'll share more." She pointed to our treasures. I wanted to know then and there but stopped myself from pushing her.

"Of course," I nodded and began placing the scrolls and scarabs back into the box.

I stood up to leave when she caught my hand.

"You are stronger than you know, girl; trust the ancient ones. They will protect you."

A green glow like an emerald began to appear around her, and I was sure her face had changed. She began to look around the room and chant under her breath something I had never heard. "All will return from the veil" was all she said, and I did not understand.

I know Laura, and I will trust. There is nothing else I can do.

"Now I must fly," she said, standing up abruptly. "I have a ceremony at the Abbey." And before I could hug her, she was out the door.

Once she was gone, I put the box away safely and walked into the front room to arrange the pillows and start the fire. As expected, the relatives of those coming to see me made themselves known, and I took down their messages in my book. As the last of them dissipated into the ether, a large scorpion, about the size of a corgi dog, appeared on the coffee table. It clicked its slick black jowls at me and dangled its stinger dangerously close to my head. Something deep inside me told me that it was not there for any of my clients but for me. I slowly backed away, worried that it was more tangible in form than the other apparitions. With every step back I took, it stepped forward until I felt my back hit the wall opposite it.

The onyx demon took that as an opportunity to rush at me the rest of the way. I closed my eyes and held up my arms, bracing for impact, but it never came. I looked up and saw an ibis diving and pecking at it while a baboon stood in front of me, wrestling the stinger away that was inches from my face. The emerald-green light surrounded them. The scorpion retreated, having been almost completely immobilised. It suddenly vanished, and no sooner had it gone when the ibis flew out the window that I had not previously noticed was open. The baboon followed, pausing to look at me just before it jumped out. We locked eyes, and it was as if we had a telepathic connection in that one moment. I could understand what he was trying to convey to me. He was letting me know that he and the ibis would keep the scorpion from infecting me, at least until Christmas was over.

Thus, the baboon and ibis made good on their promise to me. That night, I slept soundly without any dark shadows, violent women, or nosebleeds. Whoever sent them sent me the best Christmas gift I could have gotten. My nightmare had left me really shaken, and it was comforting to know that someone or something was looking out for me. It gave me a chance to enjoy the festivities and be present in a way that had become increasingly difficult in the last few months. I was absolutely jovial during preparations, to the point where Emilee was worried that I had accidentally taken the wrong potion from her. Not even Isis and Naomi's delayed homecoming would dampen my holiday cheer and good tidings. I prayed they were safe as I hadn't shared my recent vision with anyone.

Wednesday, 24 December 2008, Christmas Eve

On Christmas Eve morning, Alice held a gathering at the Chalice Well for Emilee's guests to help them connect to the spirits around them. Seeing so many women being open to new experiences and coming together in this sacred space filled my heart with hope and joy. We most certainly gained some new members of our sisterhood that day. In fact, Lucinda and I got very close to three women who were visiting from Marseille, France. They had never experienced a British Christmas, and we were happy to show them what one was like. It was hard to return to an empty house that afternoon, but clients had been booking and needed my attention.

As I finished logging them in the diary, I looked around the Sanctuary. With Isis away, there were no celebration decorations and only a few Christmas cards. My first Glastonbury Christmas.

I looked at my phone, but there were no messages except from Laura and Alice. For some reason, my mother came to my mind, and I remembered our Christmases—just us and my aunt growing up.

We had some strange candlelighting rituals. My aunt would bring out the photos of their ancestors in an album—old sepia-toned photos where no one smiled. They would share whispers as I played with my dolls and watched TV. Then, they would bring out a very strange bottle of alcohol with weird writing and toast their lost family. I had never asked about this in my teenage years. But now I was wiser and much more grown up, and I felt a pull to heal and mend the broken bridges.

I picked up my phone and dialled my mum's house number, hoping I could leave a message, but to my surprise, the line went to a disconnected message.

How strange. Oh, well, she must have moved. Perhaps I would see when Laura was next visiting North, and I'd take a trip with her, creating an excuse to visit my mother.

Thursday, 25 December 2008, Christmas Day

The next morning, I got up early, excited to start the Christmas festivities Emilee had planned for us. I had already pulled on my fancy red silk blouse, which Naomi had left for me as a Christmas gift, paired it with my jeans, and was just putting on my coat when, right as I was about to exit, I saw Lucinda walking up the path.

"Merry Christmas," her voice sang out. "I wanted to catch you," she called. "Before you leave, Isis said she sent you an email that she would like you to respond to."

I looked at Lucinda curiously. "An email? Since when does Isis send an email at Christmas? She could call?" I asked.

Lucinda laughed heartily, "I would assume when she had Naomi to focus on."

"Ah, of course. Well, I suppose I should go back to the office and check it then." I changed directions and headed to the office to see what was so pressing that Isis told Lucinda to notify me in person, no less.

When I booted up my laptop, I went to my email to see what was waiting for me. In my inbox, mixed with various Christmas wishes and adverts, was an email from Isis with the simple subject line: *Christmas Call.* I clicked on it, and the message read:

Dear Anna,

I hope you are enjoying your first Christmas in Glastonbury. It pains me not to be there to celebrate with you and the rest of our sisterhood. On that subject, I hear you are doing wonderful things and charming the pants off of Emilee's guests. It fills my heart with pride to know that you are really starting to come into your own and the role set out for you. Please be patient with our sisters; it will take some time for them to adjust, but they will come to see you as the capable leader you are. I know that you found it frustrating that Naomi and I left for Egypt without you and without telling you why. I promise, when the time is right, you will know everything. I hope you trust that my reasons for not involving you stem only from my desire to protect you, not because I think you can't handle what is going on. You are very special, my dear, and our hope for the future.

I need to share a secret. Do you remember when the mystery man called and he said he was the keeper of the Scrolls of Amenti? Well, he is a man I know in Cairo. He is a curator at the Egyptian Museum... a Mr. Imran, but I will not know for sure why he called you until I meet with him. He just returned back to Cairo from New York and called me yesterday to arrange our meeting. I am sending you this message via email because Naomi and I will be hard to reach for the next week or so, and this will be the best way to reach us. However, do expect a call from Lucas tomorrow. He is not coming with us for this next part. I love you and care for you deeply, Anna. Take care of yourself and the others and send them my love. Hopefully, we will be together soon.

Always and forever,
Isis

I smiled at the last part of the message, glad to know she was safe and seemed to be planning to return soon. However, the rest of the message left me with more questions than the answers I had hoped for. Where was she going to be with Naomi where they couldn't call, and why couldn't Lucas go with them? After all, he was one of the first people here to become my friend, and his tarot card readings at his shop were always helpful. I definitely should have checked in with him, perhaps privately. I hoped he would be calling me today or tomorrow, and I could make sure to express my regrets for not reaching out sooner.

Another part of Isis's message stood out to me. She

and Naomi were moving on to the next part. What did that mean? What were they doing that required them to go to a remote location like that? I know Isis said to trust that everything would come out in time and that she was only doing this to protect me, but the way her message was written made me think that she and Naomi were engaging in something really dangerous, which worried me. And why oh why was she meeting the man in the Cairo Museum when he had asked for me? The whole situation just reeked of something bad, and I really hoped the pit in my stomach that had just formed wasn't an omen for things to come. I shook the thought from my head and resolved not to let it ruin my Christmas spirit. Lucas would be calling, and I could interrogate him about it. I could hear Lucinda upstairs and didn't wish to discuss matters with her. With that notion tucked away, I grabbed the gifts for my sisters and sped off to the Gables to help Emilee prepare for the day's festivities.

When I walked into the Gables, I was overwhelmed with the beautiful decorations that adorned every inch of the entry. There were garlands made of fresh forest pine winding around the rail and banister of the stairs. Sprigs of holly and mistletoe hung from every entrance, and lush ruby poinsettias with leaves the size of dinner plates sat on every flat surface. Strings of lights wove in a cross-stitch pattern across the ceiling, giving the appearance of twinkling stars.

As I walked into the sitting room, I was taken by the magnificent sight before me. There was a resplendent fire in the Georgian-era fireplace, and a brightly coloured knit stocking hung on the mantle for each of Emilee's guests. I found my name stitched in gold on a cobalt stocking and smiled at the thought of Emilee taking the time to create a stocking in my favourite colour.

I turned to get a better look at the seven-foot-tall Norway Spruce with impressively full branches in the corner. It had hand-blown glass ornaments in the shape of apples and brightly coloured tissue paper fringe garlands in hues of currant and ochre. In place of traditional string lights were lights in the shape of lit candles. As I approached the tree to deposit my gifts to the large variety of adorned gifts already underneath it, I saw more of Emilee's handiwork: beautifully knit dolls that looked oddly familiar.

Upon closer inspection, I realised that each was meant to represent one of our friends. I recognised the white pantsuit of Naomi, the colourful velvet cape of Alice, the eccentric dress of Lucinda, the warm smile of Laura—even the gold wedding band she wore from her late husband—the silver hair of Isis with her gold ankh pendant, the classic French ensemble of Emilee, and my comfortable jumper and denim combo with a journal in one hand and pen in the other... at least she had given me tidy hair. There was Lucas in his white priest robes with a tarot card in his hand. She even had a doll that looked a little like Lesley, although I couldn't understand why. Then there was one more doll that I didn't recognise. I was so preoccupied with figuring out who she was that I failed to hear Emilee walk into the room.

"Ah, I see you have found my Christmas tree, eh?" Emilee asked, placing a hand on my shoulder. I jumped at her touch. "My apologies, Anna. I did not mean to startle you," she said.

I turned to face her and said, waving my hand, "Oh, don't worry. I have been a little jumpy lately!"

"Well, I hope it has nothing to do with bad dreams! I see you admire my French Christmas tree! It does not matter how long I am out of France; she is still within me!"

"Yes, it is gorgeous, Emilee! I don't know how you got all this together so quickly!"

"Ahh, that is a secret! Perhaps it was the spirits of my ancestors that helped me, perhaps not! No matter how much mulled wine you feed me, I will never tell!"

I laughed; it sounded like she was already indulging. "Well, either way, this place is absolutely magical! I love the stocking you made me and the knit dolls of all of us!"

"Oh, I am so happy! Yes, the dolls are my French tradition!"

"I see one for each of us, but who is this one here?" I pointed to the doll with almond-shaped eyes and long dark hair. "I don't recognise her."

Emilee leaned in and looked closer, "I was hoping you could tell me, *ma chère.*

I furrowed my brow and concentrated hard on the knit doll. She was completely unfamiliar to me. I looked up at Emilee and shrugged, "I'm sorry, Em, I have no idea who she is. Perhaps she will make herself known soon."

"Perhaps, Anna. Well, no matter, there is much to do before the guests arrive downstairs, and I will need your help to get it ready!"

I smiled. Emilee was amazing. She never did anything half-done. It was always perfect, and I was happy to help her achieve this.

☥

Brunch was served in the dining room in spectacular fashion. Trays upon trays of sticky buns and pastries were doled out to the guests, as well as Lucinda and Laura, who had joined us for the day. There was also a beautifully arranged fruit spread, with a watermelon shaped like a swan filled with berries. Mountains of rich, clotted cream and jam were available to heap on the dense, moist scones that were stacked in piles that seemed to go on forever. Smoked salmon canapés with crème fraiche and chives were served as a savoury respite from our otherwise saccharine meal.

I sat with the women from Marseille. They were fascinated with our British customs, like the Christmas crackers and the fact that we exchanged gifts on Christmas Day. We spent the rest of the day swapping stories about France for my tarot card readings. I wasn't the best tarot card reader, but Lucinda and Lucas had taught me enough to get by. All of Emilee's guests were spellbound, and I was sure she would be getting business from them again and more business for the Sanctuary, as well.

☥

As the night drew to a close, following our Christmas feast of roast turkey and sides, after indulging in copious amounts of mulled wine and brandy, donning paper hats, and playing games, most of Emilee's guests had retired. Left by the warmth of the fire were Lucinda, Emilee, Laura, Alice, and myself. We conversed about the past day and other light topics. Looking around at these women filled my heart with love and made me so thankful to be in Glastonbury with them. I thought back to my time in York and chuckled to myself. I had come a long way from being some evil woman's assistant at a local magazine with no prospects and a tiny flat to being in a position with an amazing group of women who were helping me do some of the most important and fulfilling work I had ever done. My flat flooding was the best thing that had ever happened to me.

Suddenly, Laura yawned, "Well, my dears, I am absolutely spent. Emilee, any chance you have an extra room? I don't know if I can make it all the way back to my cottage!"

"Oh, but of course!" Emilee exclaimed, "I will show you upstairs and can perhaps prepare the attic for you. Lucinda will stay in her room. Look, she is already asleep!" She pointed at Lucinda, who was slumped down in her chair, snoring softly.

Laura nodded, "Yes, I think that is best. If she wants to get up from the chair!"

Just then, Lucinda roused, opened one eye and looked around. In a sleep-laden voice, she said, "She does want to get up from this chair and sleep in a bed, thanks!"

We all laughed at this, and Emilee motioned for her to follow, leading Lucinda and Laura to the stairway. Before heading upstairs, Emilee turned to Alice and me. "You two are welcome to stay, as well! I have a pull-out couch in my room if you want!"

I shook my head and said, "You are very sweet, but I think someone should stay at the Sanctuary and watch over it. You take care of our sleepy ladies, though!"

"Alice, what about you?"

Alice waved her hand, "Oh no, you have done more than enough today. Besides, like Anna, I have a sacred space to watch over, and the faeries would miss me dearly."

"Alright, just be safe getting back, and do text me to let me know you are safe!"

I laughed, "Don't worry, Em, I won't let any gnomes or pixies and the like take Alice!"

"Alice is not who I am worried about, Anna. Just be safe!" With that, she was upstairs and off with the others.

At the gate of the Chalice Well, Alice and I turned to each other to bid our goodbyes. It was strange that the others were heading to sleep, and I felt we were heading to work the night shift.

Friday, 26 December 2008, 2:00 p.m., Boxing Day

I was deep into the book Alice had given me at the solstice. *The Emerald Tablets of Thoth* had so many interesting stories, and I felt like I was learning more from this book than I had from anything else I had read recently. I had hidden my other book about the Scorpion Queen under a pile of angel books in my closet. Since the early morning, I had been poring over the book in the office, with the fire going and a large pot of tea to keep me company. Lucinda and Laura, who had arrived back an hour prior, had popped in to tell me they were going out for the day. They wanted to attend a fun festival in town. They asked me to join, but I politely declined and told them I wanted to keep reading.

I was still in my holiday pajamas when I remembered that Isis had said in her email that Lucas would be calling. Suddenly, as if by magic, my phone began to ring.

Oh, Lucas, his face popped into my mind. No, no, no, where is my phone? Practically breaking the teapot as I stood up, I scrambled to the phone and picked it up right before it went to voicemail.

"Hello, hello, Lucas?" I said, out of breath.

"Whoa, there, Anna, are you alright? You weren't scrambling to get to the phone just to talk to little old me, were you?" Lucas's husky voice said on the other end.

"Oh, well, no, I... I suppose, yes, I was. I can't lie to you, my friend, you know that!" Lucas was one of the first people I met in Glastonbury and one of the people I trusted the most to give me good advice when I didn't want to go to any of my sisters. He owned a small store in town where I would get tarot card and psychic readings from him for guidance. The man was always so colourful and flamboyant in his dress, sometimes bearing the bald head and white robes of a priest and other times sporting a purple crushed-velvet suit and matching top hat, complete with white gloves and a walking stick. This avant-garde sense of style came in handy when he was working on Naomi's television programmes and appearances. In fact, he had gained somewhat of a dedicated following all on his own because of it. I smiled at the thought of it all.

"Hello, Anna, are you still there?" he asked.

I must have been in thought longer than I realised. "Oh, I am sorry, Lucas, I am here! I was just thinking about how much I have missed you!"

I heard his deep laugh on the other line, "Well, I have missed you as well, Anna. I hope you aren't getting into too much trouble over there without me!"

"Only a little. But that's not important! How are you? How is Egypt? How are Isis and Naomi? And what in the hell are you all doing over there?"

"Well, first of all, Happy Christmas from Isis, Naomi, and me. Egypt is wonderful! I am currently in Cairo, lounging by the pool at our hotel. I must say, Anna, it sure does beat cold and wet Glastonbury!"

"Are Isis and Naomi with you?"

"Unfortunately, not at the moment. I'm afraid they are off to the pyramids and the Sphinx and left me behind. We met a group that is studying some of the secret tunnels there. It's a fascinating bunch, I must say! There was one very handsome young man that I found especially fascinating and... well, at any rate, they promised to show Isis and Naomi those tunnels, so that is what they are off doing now."

"And you didn't want to go?"

"Not at all, my dear. Listen, I love the heat, but a dry, sandy heat without access to a pool is simply not my style at this point in my life. Besides, I spent thousands of years as a priest in Egypt. I've spent more than enough time in the desert!"

I laughed at this. "Plus, you wouldn't want to ruin your expensive clothes!" I teased.

He chuckled, "You know me so well, darling!"

"There is no chance of you telling me why you are all there, is there?"

"Sorry, chick, that is not something I am at liberty to say."

"Not to be rude here, Lucas, but what can you say? I've been in the dark here for weeks, and I get the sense that something very important is going on! I doubt Isis and Naomi are taking that little side trip just for fun!"

"They are not, and something is. I know, and Isis knows, that you are getting tired of hearing this, but you are just going to have to trust that what is happening is only being done with your best interest at heart and that when it is the right time, you will know what is going on."

I blew air out of my nostrils in frustration. "Yes, but when? When you all get back? When we go to Egypt in a few months? In a few years? In a different lifetime? Come on, Lucas, I know I am still new to everything, but continuing to keep me in the dark isn't going to protect me forever if that's what she thinks she is doing. I know something is wrong. I can feel it. Why won't you all just be honest with me? I can't get ready to protect myself and the others from a threat I don't know about."

I could sense Lucas taking a moment to consider my words. He responded, "I agree, but it isn't my call. Just out of curiosity, what have you been sensing?"

"Well, it all started on the solstice; there was this darkness that overtook me in a way that it hadn't before. My dreams were getting violent, and I woke up with a nosebleed the other day after dreaming I got kicked in the face by some evil woman. The shadows that haunted me months ago are back, and I can't escape them when I dream. I need to know if what Isis and Naomi are doing is causing this or if they are trying to fix it."

"Did you have this dream last night?"

"No, a few days ago, a shadow appeared and tried to take me, but an ibis and baboon came and stopped it. They gave me a few days of protection."

"Yes..." Lucas said, trailing off. "Hopefully that will be enough."

"Enough? Enough for what?"

"Nothing. Look, I will keep this line open. Please call me if you experience any of these dreams again before I return. That is very important, Anna. Do you understand? I need to know the moment you wake up what has happened."

I felt myself getting angry, and it was heard in my voice, "No, you don't. Isis, Naomi, and you all don't think I need to know what is going on. Why would I turn around and tell you everything? It is clear that none of you trust me."

"Anna, that is not true. We know we can trust you. We just can't tell you right now what you want to know."

"Only people who don't trust someone would say that to a person. You are asking me to trust that you, Isis, and Naomi have my best interests at heart and that everything will be revealed when the time is right. There is no right time. There is never a right time to discuss these things. Whatever is happening is happening to me here, in Glastonbury. It didn't start until you all left. That leads me to believe that you all are tinkering with some forces over there that are causing this!"

"I can assure you that we are doing everything possible

to prevent the Priests of Unal from finding you!"

"Finding me? They've found me! They found me months ago when I got here, and again a few days ago! And for the record, I never said the shadows were them!"

"Oh, come on, Anna, what else would they be?"

"I don't know, but it seems like you all knew they were coming back!" I was practically shouting into the phone now, and Lucas's voice was also rising.

"Of course, we knew that! We knew they weren't gone. We knew they could come back, and if they had pierced the veil, it would be all the better if you didn't know what we were doing. If they find a way to contact her, the Priests of Unal will be the least of your worries!"

"Her who? Oh, wait, there's no bloody way. You are going to tell me! You are supposed to be my friend and confidant. All you are doing is speaking in riddles and dodging questions like I am some stranger. I would expect this from Isis but not from you!"

"Don't you think I would tell you if I could? I barely know what they are doing! All I know is I need to be around to help when they get back. Please, be patient, please?"

"I am so tired of hearing that. You know what? Whatever in the hell you are doing, you better hope it works! Because at this rate, if the Priests of Unal come back again, I'm screwed, and it will be all your fault, so I hope you can live with that!" I screamed at him.

Lucas went silent on the other line. I could tell he was still there because I could hear him breathing. At this point, I was so upset that I didn't wait for him to respond, so I hung up instead. I ran over to my computer to send Isis an email. Where did they all get off like that? Knowing that I was going to be stalked by the Priests of Unal and that they were not warning me, never mind that mystery woman

Lucas mentioned.

I angrily typed out a message:

Isis,

I am tired of being kept in the dark. You keep telling me to trust you; in fact, everyone keeps telling me to trust you, but how can I trust you or anyone else when no one will tell me the truth about what is happening? You knew about the Priests of Unal coming back, but you didn't even tell me! How dare you keep something like that from me? What if they had really hurt me or worse, and now it seems another demon, an evil woman, is to follow? Well, guess what, they already found me!

Look, you passed the mantle to me months ago with the intention that I take over for you. You say that I am in charge of the Sanctuary and the future leader of the Sacred Eight, but you still treat me like an ignorant child. No one will ever see me as a leader if you keep getting in my way.

It is your duty to fully prepare me and share all the information I need to know in order to fulfil my role. As such, I demand that you tell me what is going on!

You asked me to trust you, but I don't. It goes both ways, and clearly, you don't trust me. So, here is what I am proposing: either you tell me exactly what is going on, or you don't contact me again. I am done playing these games with you.

—Anna

I hit the send button and closed my laptop. I sat there for a moment, fuming. The fact that she knew that the Priests would come back to hurt me was the final straw. There was no way I would continue to go along with this cat-and-mouse game of getting information out of her. I was to be the Queen Bee now.

My phone began to beep and stopped my stream of thought. I clicked on the text from Lucas: *Now, Anna, beware. There is always a Tower waiting. Remember the Queen's curse: Don't lose your head.* My hand reached up to my neck, and I felt a freezing chill; I saw a vision of a man in brown robes praying at an old stone altar somewhere here in Glastonbury as I could just make out the Abbey. He lit a small candle, pushed a small bundle of papers into his robe, and looked around as if he were in fear of someone watching him. Something dark, and perhaps it was now watching me.

CHAPTER 5

Wednesday, 31 December 2008, 10:51 p.m., New Year's Eve

After my blow-up on Lucas and Isis, I was in self-imposed exile and isolation from the others. I claimed that I had a lot of work to do before the new year, but I didn't. More than anything, I was embarrassed about how I had yelled at Lucas and sent Isis a nasty email. It was well within my right to be upset but not express it as I did. I figured I shouldn't be around the others until I mustered up the courage and humility to apologise to them. Lucinda always knew what was going on with me before I told her, and I didn't need her reading me and making me feel worse about the situation than I already did. She had moved back into the Sanctuary, but we had thankfully managed to avoid each other. By some karmic miracle, I hadn't received any reprimanding message from Naomi, although I suspected that if she could have sent one, she would have. She and Isis were probably up to their necks in sand right now, digging out tunnels or whatever they were doing.

I sighed. It was just an hour or so until the new year, and I was spending it alone in the office with a book I had stopped reading an hour ago and a piece of beans on toast I let get cold and soggy. Fireworks could be heard over the tree line, and if I angled myself the right way, I could see flashes of them off in the distance. I wondered what they looked like up close. Lucinda, Emilee, Laura, and the women we had met from Marseille would all have a great view from the Chalice Well. Alice was leading a midnight meditation group there, and everyone but me had decided to attend.

The thought of all of them getting on like best friends without me made my heart heavy with sadness. *What is wrong with me? I finally have all of these amazing people and the life I have always wanted, and I'm sitting here by myself, wallowing, I thought.* Truly, this bad mood was of my own making, and it would be very easy for me to rid myself of it. Perhaps if I just sent Isis an email apologising and left Lucas a message doing the same, I would feel less guilty about joining my friends for the festivities. So, I got up, resolute in my decision to apologise and go hang out with the other women.

No sooner had I stood when I felt a sharp stabbing pain in my heart. My breaths became shallow, and my arms numb. I panicked, thinking I was having a heart attack, and tried to get to the phone just a few feet away on the desk. Another wave of sharp pain in my chest threw me to the ground, and I struggled to move. My throat started to feel tight, like something was choking me without anything being there, and white-hot pain seared my forehead. I tried to crawl to the desk, but was getting too weak to move. I made it halfway to the desk before I could no longer move. On my back now, I attempted to breathe as deeply as I could, but it was getting more and more difficult. Blackness crept into the corners of my eyes, and I knew that if I didn't do something, I was going to lose consciousness or worse. I felt a weight around my neck. With every last bit of strength, I crawled to the large amethyst geode in the corner, put my hand on it, and cried out to Archangel Michael for protection. Immediately, my symptoms started to subside. My body went cold, and my vision went black.

A warm breeze coaxed me into the brilliant, peace-bringing light. I opened my eyes and found myself, at twilight, standing in a manicured garden outside a large salmon-coloured stone building. There were pieces of statues placed about the grounds and tall palm trees lining the marble path up the steps of the building. This wasn't right. This is not where the light wanted to take me. I looked down and found myself enveloped in petticoats and a floor-length satin gown. Suddenly, a shrieking howl pierced the darkness beyond the garden. Whatever was making that noise seemed to be coming closer. So, rather than wait to discover the source of the noise, I ran up the path and up the stairs into the building.

Once inside, I managed to stumble into a formal celebration taking place in the central hall. It had Egyptian columns three stories high and relics from the temples throughout the main atrium. Scattered throughout were men and women dressed in formal attire similar to mine and jovially conversing amongst themselves. Attendants were making the rounds with goblets of wine and small plates of food.

As I strode down the steps, no one seemed to notice or acknowledge me. I made my way through the crowd and saw a table with a cake fashioned in the shape of the building we were in, with the words "The Egyptian Museum, circa 1901." Ah, I was at what appeared to be the celebration party for the museum opening. Just then, out of the corner of my eye, I saw a flash of white go up the stairs and knew I should follow.

Once up the stairs, I went down a long corridor plated with pinkish marble slabs and columns. What should have been paintings hanging on the walls were instead mirrors that gave one a garish appearance when they looked into them. I saw the flash at the end of the hallway and ran towards it. Just as I rounded the corner, a dark shadow poured out of the mirror closest to my head. Narrowly dodging it, I looked back and saw darkness pouring out of all the mirrors on both sides of me. Having little to no options, I opened the door behind me, falling inside and scrambling to shut it just in time.

Turning around, I took in the contents of the room—or what little contents there were. It was a large, impossibly circular room with dark wood floors and nothing on the black walls. A single chandelier in the centre of the room hung, illuminating the symbol inlaid in gold on the floor. Looking closer, I saw that it was the symbol of connecting concentric circles I had been seeing everywhere. I stepped into the centre of the room and took a deep breath. This symbol meant something, and meditating on top of it might give me further clarity.

Unfortunately, I didn't get the chance. The shadows had gotten in through the space between the door and the floor and were trickling in. They began to take form, and I knew exactly what they were. Each held space in one of the circles, except for the one I was in. They were just standing there, waiting for something. Just then, the light from the chandelier changed and intensified, blasting me with a crimson beam. I heard this maniacal laughter and knew someone was there to take me. My fight-or-flight response kicked in just then, and I bolted for the door, barely making it out before the shadows grabbed me. I ran back down the corridor, all the while hearing the maniacal laughter behind me.

I got to the top of the stairs and, in my haste, tripped over my feet, sending me tumbling all the way down to the landing.

I awoke at the bottom of the stairs, apparently having fallen down them. My body ached, and I was weak from my earlier episode. From where I was, I could see that no more than an hour had passed, and it was just after midnight. The house was cold and dark, and I was still alone.

Something in my bones told me that whatever was going on wasn't over yet, and I needed to prepare. Although shaky, I managed to get up and walk to the kitchen to turn the heat on and check to make sure all of the doors were locked, not that whatever was after me would be deterred by a lock. Then I shuffled back into the office, having grabbed a blanket and restarted the central heating. Looking around, I saw a mess of pillows on the floor and bile in the spot where I had passed out earlier. A sudden dizzy spell came over me and caused me to lie as still as I could on the lounge chair. Cleaning up the bile would have to wait. Just then, I started coughing as a result of my dry throat, but I couldn't get up or risk vomiting whatever I had left in my stomach. I prayed that whatever this was would pass quickly.

After a few minutes, the coughing subsided, but I was still too dizzy to move. My forehead felt hot to the touch, which meant I most likely had a fever. Hopefully, Lucinda would be back soon and could help me. Until then, I decided to surrender to sleep, calling in all the healing angels as I went.

☥

I think I was covered in a dark silk sheet, violet-coloured, but it was hard to tell in the dim light. As my eyes adjusted, I could see that I was surrounded by a hard, translucent case that faintly glowed pink. I could see outlines of shapes moving below me; my encasement seemed to be water, so at least I knew I was above ground. Oh no. What if someone was about to drown me? I began to bang on the ceiling and the sides, screaming at the top of my lungs to let whoever was out there know that I was alive, that I shouldn't drown.

"Please let me out," I screamed, "I'm not dead! Please, someone help me!" Then I began to gasp for breath as water

came over me, and I felt like I had slid into another timeline.

I continued in this way for what seemed like hours until my voice went hoarse. I was going to die in this strange chamber, and there was nothing I could do about it.

Suddenly, a voice from outside screamed, "We need to go, NOW. Grab them, and let's go!"

A mournful wailing pierced my ears. I saw a woman off in the distance crying and beating her chest. She knelt by the seashore, the waves lapping at her waist. I could hear her crying in the distance, saying, "Why did you do this? I just needed more time. They just needed more time. Please, bring them back, please. I beg you, bring them back."

I could see two women speaking on the steps of a strange temple, but their faces were slightly obscured.

"Our time is fast approaching; we must go back."

"Wait, you can't; we need you."

"You will survive. It is only 60 years."

"You say that like it isn't a long time."

"It isn't. Not for you, nor your people."

"My people won't survive 60 years at this rate."

"Yes, they will, as they always do. You are young, my child. You will see. We have gone through over a dozen cycles, and every time, your people are here when we come back."

"I am telling you, it's different. This cycle has been rife with misfortune and tragedy unparalleled. Never before has so much of our population been wiped out by a sickness, one that has no cure and is always fatal. The crystals were supposed to give us enhanced vitality, but they were the cause!"

"They were the cause because your people sought to pervert their use."

"Which happened during your last absence!"

"Yes, as much change usually does. And we have done everything we could have to help fix it."

"Oh, have you? Our population is at an all-time low. We

don't have enough people to tend to the crops, which means basic necessities have drastically gone up in price, leading to famine and starvation for our most vulnerable people. The wealthy have sought to tighten their grip on their resources and refuse to help. They had the Anointed Twelve strip the Elected Twelve of their voting power so that they could avoid paying taxes that would fund programs to help. Then, the poor and the disenfranchised rose up to fight against this injustice, which led to thousands more people dying. Tell me, what have you done to fix all of that?"

"I do not need a history lesson from you, girl. I know, and we have wept many days at our altars for your people. We have searched and searched for a solution, but once someone has thrown themselves out of balance in the way many did, there is no way to come back from that. The best we can do is teach people how to respect the crystals' power and to use it for positive and intellectual advancement instead of as an instrument for destruction. We have spent more time in the Twelve Kingdoms than in any other cycle going around and educating the people with promising results."

"Yes, while these new ways of living are a good step in the right direction, it isn't going to fix the socio-political problems that still plague us."

"No, perhaps not. But you seem to be a very capable leader. After all, you've studied with us your whole life, which gives you a unique store of knowledge to pull from. I suspect that's why the people were content to let you become the Queen of the Twelve after your father."

"Yes, the same people who murdered him do currently favour me. However, their favour is tenuous at best. Then there are the elite who are not fans of my new tax initiative. I've had to enlist the royal guard to take their taxes by force. They might be a small group, but they have the resources necessary to overthrow me, as we've already seen them try twice. All I

am trying to do is save my people, but they are coming for me from both sides. To have you all here with me, as my advisors, actively supporting my rule, would go a long way towards my goal. Please, I beg you, stay. I am only asking you to postpone your ascension for a few years. How much harm could be done because of that?"

"Oh, my dear child, please dry your tears. First of all, you do not need us. In your first few months of rule, you have done so much, including getting the Elected Twelve their voting power back and the Anointed out of the capitol, allowing you to enact sweeping reforms aimed at helping. You genuinely care for your people, and that is what will get you through! Yes, the elites might be upset, but they will fall in line, as is what always happens. Secondly, as much as we would love to stay, we cannot. We must ascend at the same time as the others to ensure continued cosmic alignment. You know that."

"I know that you could stay; you could help more if you wanted to. You could stay and take away the crystals from those who only abuse them. You could ask the Dweller to come out of stasis and force the wealthy to fall in line. You could call upon the Lords of Space-Time to rewrite the last thousand years and eradicate the sickness that started all of this!"

"How dare you speak such blasphemous thoughts! Have we taught you nothing? There is an order to our universe, a way to go about things that prevents its destruction. What you suggest would mean putting your people's survival over the rest of the entire cosmos. We will ascend in thirty days, whether you wish it or not, and in 100 years, we will return to a wonderfully thriving society that I am sure a clever girl like you can make happen."

"And that is your final decision?"

"Yes. We will aid you and the Children of Light in any way we can for the next thirty days, and then you will take it

from there."

"I will, and it will be your ruin."

☥

The pain was unbearable. I felt like my soul was being ripped from my body and crammed back in the wrong way. Nothing felt right. My toes felt like my fingers, my stomach felt like my heart, and I couldn't even say how my head felt. Over and over again, I was violently thrown from myself and pushed back in, all the while hearing someone cackling at my pain. Once they were done with my spiritual torture, they ejected me from my fitful slumber and yanked the sheets off my bed, which I had apparently gotten to at one point. It was the shadows again. They were here, real and in front of me. Ready to start up their attack on my physical form.

First, I was thrown to the floor and dragged by my feet to the other end of the room. Then they picked me up by my ankles and smashed me against the wall, letting me drop onto my head and sort of roll over myself. The shadows hoisted me up by my arms and once more pushed me up the wall and pinned me there, filling up my body with darkness. I started to cry, begging for them to stop. All the negative emotions I had felt over the last few days were amplified one hundred-fold. I cried out to Lucas, begging him to forgive me for being so horrible to him and telling him that it would be his fault if something happened to me. One of the shadows contorted its shape into a gaunt and grey-skinned version of Lucas.

"It isn't my fault," he whispered harshly, *"You were right. It's yours. I'll never forgive you for how horribly you treated me. This only proves that you don't belong with us. There is so much doubt and hate in your heart. It goes against everything the sisterhood stands for. You don't deserve to be the High Priestess. If anyone does, it's Naomi."*

"Yes, I agree. We should have never passed it on to her," a raspy voice said. Another shadow had just materialised and contorted into the form of Isis. *"You are such a disappointment. Is it any mystery why I don't tell you anything?"*

The shadow of Lucas chimed in, *"Not that she knows anything to begin with. If she did, she would have united the temples again and restored balance. Instead, she sits around sulking like a child because mommy won't reward her for her mediocre work."*

"Mediocre is generous. She has had hundreds of lifetimes to figure it out and still has no clue. You are a disgrace to the mantle I have bestowed upon you and dishonour us all with your lack of respect for it. How dare you question my methods? Who are you to think that you know more in the few months you have held the position than I, who has been the High Priestess for thousands of years?"

My sobbing intensified, and I fell to my knees and crawled to the shadow of Isis. "Please, forgive me, I will do anything, forgive me!" I begged.

She smirked, *"Oh, now you ask for forgiveness after that wretched note you sent me? You have done enough for one lifetime, don't you think? Luckily, my friends are here to help ease my pain!"* With a bone-chilling laugh, she and Lucas disappeared with all the other shadows, leaving me a slumped-over mess on the floor.

I looked around, not knowing what she had meant until I felt something on my ankle. Crawling up my leg was a black scorpion the size of a teacup. I screamed and shook it off me, scrambling back to the wall. Just then, I saw dozens more scorpions coming out from under the floorboards and running towards me. Suddenly, hundreds of scorpions were crawling all over me, piercing me with their stingers and filling my veins with poison. Screaming and thrashing, I couldn't get them off of me. Once again, I was plunged into a painful darkness, hoping that this time, I wouldn't come out of it.

☥

Why was I so hot? Ugh, where am I? Oh, right, I should open my eyes. Ah, my lord, why is it so bright? Well, what do you know, I am lying in the sand. Great. Why does my nose hurt so much? Oh, right, I got kicked by that crazy woman. Wait a second, where is she? Where is anybody?

I got up and surveyed the scene around me. To my horror, I saw seven dark spots in the sand around me, knowing they were the women I had been with earlier. I choked back a sob; my sisters were gone. Everyone was gone. Now what do I do?

There wasn't anything left to do. It was over. I wanted to cry, but I had nothing left inside me to do so. It didn't matter if I was here, or in Egypt, or Glastonbury, nor did it matter at what point in time I was at, or if I was asleep or awake. The Priests of Unal, in all of their shadowy horror, were always going to find me and terrorise me. At least right now, here in this sand, despite having lost everyone I love, in whatever lifetime this was, I could rest. Maybe I could even stay here for a while. That woman and the Priests of Unal seemed to be gone, so that means that they might not even return for me. Yeah, I could live out my life here in the desert. I'd be alone but safe. Or maybe not.

Outlined by the red sun, I could see a bird carrying something large, flying towards me. As it approached, I saw that it was an ibis carrying a baboon on its back. They were the same ones I had seen earlier. They landed and walked towards me, settling on either side of me. Their presence calmed me and made me feel safer than I had felt in a long while. The ibis nuzzled my shoulder and let me pet its head and beak. The baboon took my hand and gently stroked it. They both looked at me and then to the dune in the distance. I knew they wanted me to go there.

So, the three of us walked together towards the sand dune and up it in the direction of the sun. Once on top, I could see a large body of water I hadn't noticed during my other times here. There was a large cylindrical dwelling near the water's edge. It was made of the most reflective and glassy obsidian I had ever seen. There was not a blemish on it, and the only indication that it was a building of some sort was the singular three-metre-high door made of gold that faced us. My companions sensed my hesitance to go towards it. The ibis squawked, and the baboon gently nudged me forward. I knew I could trust them; they had once saved me from that giant scorpion, and my gut told me that there wasn't anything they would not do to protect me.

Thus, I made my way down the other side of the dune towards the obsidian structure, finding the door easy to open for the first time in my life. Once inside, I saw the interior was made from the same onyx stone. There were ornate gold torches that illuminated the chamber, which seemed to be the entirety of the building—one giant circular room with nothing else inside. It was grand and ornate but somehow modest and humble as well. I could feel an energy radiating from the walls that was slowly recharging my soul and replenishing my life force. I could feel my sisters' spirits around me and those others who were part of our sacred sisterhood. They were lost but weren't gone, and I knew they'd be back.

I felt a tap on my shoulder and turned around. Standing before me was a woman dressed in a black cape with white robes underneath. The hood she wore obscured her face, but I could tell that she meant me no harm because I was sure we had met before.

"Anna," the woman said, "What you have experienced and seen is something that has been with all of us for lifetimes."

"All of who?" I questioned.

"All of them." The woman gestured around the chamber. Colourful shapes began to emerge from the ether. One formed into the familiar ceremonial garb of a Dendaran priestess. Another wore a short linen toga fastened by a leather belt of Greek origin. Then, another walked by wearing Roman battle armour and carrying the eagle legion standard. More and more people, men and women alike, appeared and disappeared, wearing the clothes of their time and culture. I saw women dressed for King Henry VIII's court and a Zulu chief standing proud. A woman with a pink silk kimono approached us and bowed as a native American woman in an ornate beaded headdress came up beside her to bestow a blessing on us.

All of these people felt familiar, even though they were from every time and place imaginable. Their vestiges would change, but their souls stayed the same. I knew we were all connected by something greater than ourselves.

"I know you have felt very alone lately, Anna," the woman said, "But just look around. Look at all of your brothers and sisters and those in between who are here for you now. They are your fellow oracles brought here to you by the Halls of Amenti."

"How? I don't understand."

"The Halls of Amenti are both a physical and spiritual place. The entrance exists in your plane of existence, but it is also a portal that can take you through to the others and allow others to get through to you."

"Is that how you got here?" I paused and whispered, "And how, you know, they got here?"

"Ah, yes," she nodded, understanding I meant the Priests of Unal. You have been through it with them over the last little while, haven't you? Rest assured, the worst of that has passed. Yes, unfortunately, they stole that ability and can use the portal in limited capacities. Something must have happened

that allowed them access, and they managed to break through into your plane. At the same time, it was what allowed us to be here with you right now and all connect for the first time in a very long time, for however brief a moment it was."

I looked around at all of the beautiful faces that now surrounded me. I was struck by their grace and stature. The oracles here came from everywhere, every time, and were of every shape, size, and background one could imagine. My eyes brimmed with tears, not out of sadness, for once, but out of reverence for those who stood before me and beside me.

I turned to the woman and asked, already knowing the answer, "You can't stay, can you?"

"I am afraid not. But I promise that when the time is right, and you need to call upon us again, we will come; it just might not be in the form you expect."

"You all have corporeal forms on Earth right now, right?"

She smiled and tilted her head, looking at me like I was a clever child who had just figured out how to tie their shoes for the first time. Her head was at such an angle that I could see just her mouth by the torchlight, and her smile was beautiful. "Well, Anna," she cooed, "the portal is closing, and we must get back, and you must go back as well. Your sisters are worried about you." The woman started to turn away from me when I stopped her.

"Wait," I said, "I'm not entirely sure where 'back' is for me, and I'm not really sure where we are now, so I guess, um, you don't happen to know where we are, do you?"

She looked around, removing her hood as she did so. "I'm not sure. This doesn't look like any of the temples from where I'm from." With a gold glint in her eye, she winked at me and disappeared.

At that point, I felt very tired and lay down on the cool stone floor, drifting off into a heavy but peaceful slumber.

Chapter 6

Saturday, 3 January 2009, 9:45 a.m.

The first of my senses to awaken was the sense of smell. A combination of juniper, sage, and oak, most likely from a protection and cleansing ritual that had been performed. The next sense to come back was that of touch. I could feel soft wool blankets on top of my cotton nightshirt and fleece socks on my feet. It was at that point that my hearing decided to join the party, indicating to me that it was a slightly windy day outside, but otherwise, it was very quiet. Lucinda must have returned late from her evening's festivities and decided to sleep in. At that point, my eyes thought it prudent to open, and a flood of morning light burst through them. I groaned. It was too bright and too early for me to be up, or at least I thought it was. I looked over to my bedside table and saw it was just a quarter to ten. Blimey, I feel rough, I thought. Wait, when did I start saying blimey? One thing was for sure. My fifth sense was keen on making itself useful, and my stomach was in fervent agreement. I needed to get up and find some food.

However, I realised very quickly that it was going to be a hard task to accomplish when I sat up and swung my legs over the edge of the bed and tried to walk on them, crashing to the floor like a newborn foal. My second attempt to get up was met with equal struggle as I grabbed my blanket on the bed, failing to grasp the mattress itself for stability and falling again as the blanket pooled around me. By my third attempt, I was on my feet and lumbering from one piece of furniture to another until I got to the door. After I got it open, my confidence grew, and I slowly made my way down the hall and to the top of the staircase without using furniture or a wall for support.

I was still pretty out of it, but I figured that any fog left in my brain from my ordeal would leave once I had toast and beans in my stomach. Yes, that toast and beans were going to get me down the stairs and into the kitchen. It felt like it had been aeons since I had set foot in there, but it had only been last night. Or was it? These things were hard to remember. At any rate, I made it down the stairs and to the kitchen without making too much of a racket, lest I wake my housemate.

Once in the kitchen, I got to work making my breakfast, even managing to remember to put the kettle on as I went. The toast and beans were hastily made as I felt how hungry I was, and I made very quick work of them once I sat down. Still hungry, I decided to make another round and add some cheese to it. I was mid-bite when I heard a commotion outside the kitchen door.

"She's gone," Laura said.

"What do you mean, 'She's gone?'" asked Lucinda, "She has been bedridden for days. There's no way she could have just gotten up and left!"

Bedridden for days? I thought. *That can't be right.*

"Well, maybe she is in the bathroom?" Emilee suggested.

"No, I checked there," said Laura.

"Well, she has to be somewhere!"

"I am sure Anna has not gone far," Emilee said, always the mediator.

"Yes," Laura said, "If anything, she probably got up to find us and is lumbering about upstairs."

"I hope that she is," Lucinda hissed, "Because we are

sworn to protect her, and with Isis and Naomi not responding to messages, we need to be diligent. If something happens to Anna, I would never forgive myself or any of you for that matter." I had never heard Lucinda speak that way to the others, but it warmed my heart to know she cared for me so much.

"Agh, I cannot think under this pressure," Emilee said, "I need some tea. Come, I will make some for us. Laura, you go upstairs and see if Anna is there. We will be in the kitchen calming ourselves down with some relaxing herbal tea."

A moment later, Emilee burst through the door with Lucinda close behind. It took them a moment to spot me, and when they did, both just stood there dumbfounded.

I sheepishly grinned at them and waved. "Morning," I said in the most casual tone I could muster, "How were the fireworks last night?"

Emilee shook her head in disbelief as if I had just told her that the grass was blue and the sky was green. Lucinda eyed me suspiciously and circled the table until she stood opposite me.

"How were the fireworks?" she parroted, "You've been seriously ill for two days, and that's the first thing you think to ask? It's January third!"

"I... I dunno." I paused, getting a sinking feeling in my stomach. Suddenly, my throat went dry.

Emilee must have noticed the change in my expression because she came right over to me and sat beside me, grabbing my hand and gingerly stroking it. "Oh, ma chère!" she said gently, then turned to Lucinda and spoke in a harsher tone, "Lucinda, she does not know. I understand you were very worried, but there is no need to speak to her in that tone!"

Finding my voice, I asked, "Could someone please tell

me what is going on? Did I really lose two days?"

Lucinda sighed and replied, "Yes, Annie. I apologise for being cross with you. We were so worried, that's all. When I got back early on New Year's Day, I found you in the office, passed out. I thought you had just gotten a bit drunk on the sherry and passed out, but when I tried to wake you enough to move you, there was this horrible energy radiating off of your skin. I knew you were sick from nothing of this world. So, I called Laura and Emilee for help. We got you into bed and have been monitoring you ever since."

"*Oui*. I have never seen such a horrible spiritual sickness. You were screaming in your sleep, and nothing we tried made it better or woke you up. I thought we were going to lose you, Anna."

"Wait, I don't understand. Why didn't you just take me to the hospital?"

"We couldn't," replied Laura, who had somehow snuck into the room without me noticing, "You weren't sick from anything natural or earth-born. They wouldn't have been able to do anything."

"Did you call Isis or Naomi or Lucas? Couldn't they have helped?"

"We lost contact with them," said Lucinda, "None of our messages were getting through, and Lucas has still not flown home as far as we know."

"So, we did everything we could to help you and protect you, je promets."

"WELL, YOU DIDN'T DO ENOUGH!" I shouted in a sudden burst of anger, tears forming in the corners of my eyes. Looking at their shocked and hurt faces, I choked back my tears and calmed my tone, saying, "I'm sorry. I... I don't know where that came from. I guess I'm still just a little raw from it all. It was a horrible ordeal and felt like it would never end. Out of curiosity, did I get out of bed at all?"

Emilee and Lucinda looked at each other, seemingly not wanting to answer my question and hoping the other would do so first. In the end, Lucinda was the one who spoke up and said, "Well, we were downstairs when it happened. We were all trying to put together the most effective protection elixir and ritual we could when we heard something."

"What did you hear, exactly?" I asked.

"A crash and crying coming from your room. To be more accurate, several loud crashing noises were heard."

"Yes, but they were over by the time we got there," Laura said, "You were on the floor, and you had—" She cut herself off.

"I had what? Tell me!" I pleaded.

Lucinda explained, "You had bruises on your arms and legs and red marks on your shoulders. Your nose was also bleeding. It looked like somebody had beaten you, but no one else was there."

"I was able to heal most of your injuries with a salve I make, so you should not be in pain now," Emilee said, still stroking my hand gently.

On the brink of crying again, I dared to ask one more question, just holding it in as I did. "Could you make out what I was saying?"

"Not really," Lucinda said, "The wailing had mostly subsided by the time we reached your room. I thought, perhaps, I heard you apologising just before we got there, but I can't be sure. I'm so sorry, Anna. You must have been so scared."

Their words were really sinking in now. I had been in that hell for two days. The Priests of Unal must have actually attacked me in my bedroom. That physical pain I had felt was real. Then I remembered that horrible cackling in the back of my mind that entire time. Something was trying to hurt me, or worse. Whatever it was, it was controlling the Priests of Unal. Suddenly, that extra helping of beans and toast wasn't sitting well in my stomach. I tried to choke back the bile, but to no avail. Luckily, Lucinda was far enough away across the table that it didn't get all over her.

"Anna!" Emilee cried, "Are you okay? What exactly happened to you?"

I looked at Emilee and then at Lucinda and Laura. *How could I tell them what I had gone through? How could they understand?* I didn't even know where to start or how to explain. It was all too overwhelming for me, and I needed to get out of there and away from everyone else.

In a quiet voice, I said, "Excuse me, I need some air." Without another word and tears streaming down my face, I ran to the door, hastily grabbing my boots and duffle coat as I went.

☥

The crisp mid-morning air had done wonders to shake me out of the fog I had been feeling. I finally started to feel more like myself, and the terror I had felt was slowly melting away. Not wanting to go back to the Sanctuary just yet, I decided to head to the Chalice Well and see if I could get some of that healing water to help banish the last of the bad karma that was welled up inside me.

☥

Alice wasn't there when I arrived, by some miracle. The last thing I wanted to do right now was have someone fuss over me and have to explain myself. I settled myself at the edge of the Lion's Head Fountain and watched the iron-rich water spill from the Lion's mouth. The sound of the thin stream of life-giving liquid pouring into the pool was very calming, and its ripples were very peaceful. I stared for a moment, looking at my distorted, reddish reflection and thought about all that had just happened to me. I reached down into the water and then sprinkled it onto my face, feeling the freshness revive me. I thought back to the conversation I had witnessed between two women on the steps of a temple. It dawned on me that they had been talking about Atlantis.

I recalled from the copy of the Emerald Tablets that Alice gave me that the Atlanteans had become the most advanced society in the world at the time, and it all went to their heads. They abused the crystals they were given and were destroyed as a result. I had been listening to their leader's last-ditch effort to save Atlantis. Their Queen was trying to convince the other woman to stay and help them. She kept talking about cycles and needing to leave, but I didn't quite know what she meant by that. I would have to go back and look through my book when I returned.

Then, there was the woman in the black cloak. She had mentioned the Halls of Amenti and how the Priests of Unal used them to get to me. Everything I had read about the Halls of Amenti had indicated that you needed some sort of enlightenment event to enter it and ascend the various planes of existence within it. I didn't understand how the Priests of Unal were able to do this, considering they had perverted and twisted their souls to a degree that it would be impossible to do. But then again, the woman had said that they stole that ability from someone. I needed to know what happened, but I was afraid that attempting to regress back would leave me open to being hurt again. Hopefully, Isis would be home soon, and I could get some much-needed clarity, of course, after I begged for her and Lucas's forgiveness.

I sighed. *Boy, was my mind really wandering today. It must be the pixies whispering in my ear.* Getting up from my spot, I decided I had had enough reflection for the time being and needed to get back to the Sanctuary to try and explain the visions I had seen and experienced to the others. And not forget to write them down. This was a jigsaw to say the least.

☥

It had taken me a while to explain everything to Lucinda, Emilee, Laura, and Alice, who had all been waiting for me when I got back. They let me do most of the talking, only interjecting when they needed something clarified. I could tell that what I had to say shocked them, and they had no clue why I had seen what I had seen. Poor Laura looked like she would pass out from thinking so hard about what I had said. Alice was the first to ask questions when I was done.

"That woman mentioned the Halls of Amenti, and you overheard a conversation between the Queen of Atlantis and someone I would assume was an oracle connected to the Lords of space and time. There was some talk about saving Atlantis right before its destruction. Am I getting that correct?" Alice asked.

"Yes," I replied, "You are the only other person here who knows a lot about Atlantis and the Halls of Amenti. Do you know why I've been seeing visions about them so much lately?"

"It is hard to say. Truth be told, I only know as much as what is contained within the Emerald Tablets and a few old relics I can recall from my time at the Library of Alexandria."

"Relics, what relics?"

"Oh, nothing that significant, really. Just a few broken pieces of pottery and some rusted jewellery I've collected over the years. The only reason we thought it was from Atlantis was that it was made of strange metals that didn't exist in Egypt at the time. There is something significant, though, about you seeing several visions that have to do with Atlantis."

"How so?"

"Atlantis was experiencing unprecedented spiritual imbalance. They were destroyed because their arrogance and abuse of the gifts of the Children of Light threatened to put the whole world out of balance. What happened at the Fall of the Temple of Isis at Philae and what has continued to happen as a result has most likely built up an almost equally as disconcerting imbalance within our sisterhood."

"But we are just a few people," Emilee reasoned, "How is it that the oracles have done what an entire civilisation has done?"

"We, as with the Sacred Eight, less the few who are not here, have had hundreds of lifetimes to resolve the past, get rid of the bad karma, and restore balance to ourselves and the Temples. In case you haven't noticed, we've not done that. Thus, with every lifetime, every reincarnation, that bad karma carries over and builds up," Lucinda explained.

"So, what does that have to do with the Halls of Amenti and Atlantis?" Emilee asked.

Alice took over and explained, "Well, perhaps the Lords of Space-Time or the Children of Light or whoever is trying to send us a message through Anna."

Putting it together, I said, "That message is that we have to restore the temples, resolve all of our past traumas, and come together as a sacred group to prevent another Atlantis-level event from occurring."

Alice nodded, seemingly impressed by my astuteness, and responded, "I think Anna is exactly correct. To add to that, it was a clear message that we must restore everything in this lifetime."

"And that there are forces out there who will seek to stop us from that," I added.

"The Priests of Unal are those forces, *oui?*" Emilee questioned.

"Yes," I answered, "Maybe someone or something else. I don't think they have a lot of autonomy. Remember, Edfu's High Priest controlled them at Philae when they last had physical form."

Emilee's eyes widened, "Do you think that it is him who is preventing this?"

"I'm not sure. The energy behind the Priests of Unal feels different. I think whatever is trying to stop us—stop me—will reveal itself eventually. At least for now, I don't think they will be able to get at us in quite the same way."

"Let's hope so," said Alice, who then turned her attention to Lucinda, "Hey, Lucinda, you've been quiet for a spell over there. What is going on in that head of yours?"

Lucinda took a moment to consider her words and then took a deep breath before saying, "I think I might know how Anna ventured into this Atlantis realm. Give me a second to go grab something from my room."

Lucinda looked at Emilee. "I can share this now, can't I?"

Emilee nodded. We knew this day would come, and I have to say it was a relief.

"Share what?" asked Alice.

"Our secret," said Emilee.

Without giving us time to respond, Lucinda dashed

off, only to return a few minutes later with her red box. She indicated that we should gather around her as she opened the box and took out a few pieces of paper.

Lucinda opened her red box and pulled an image that reminded me of a picture I had seen in the box Isis owned. There, in sepia print, was an image of two women in very fine dress standing on the deck of a ship. I turned it around and read the words: *Titanic April 11, 1912.*

I held up the image. It looked like me and a young woman who I did not know but who felt familiar.

"We drowned, didn't we?" My voice was hushed.

"Yes," said Emilee. "This photo was taken by a professional photographer, the morning of the first passenger sailing. Lucinda was there when you left. She had warned you not to go, but you did not listen. The Atlantic Ocean is a very mysterious place, and your soul essence would have connected back to Atlantis..." Her voice drifted.

"But look, we are in fine dress. How could I have drowned? Those in first class were the first to leave, weren't they?"

Emilee shook her head. "No, Anna, I think you went to save someone."

"Why was I going to America?" I asked, looking around at the others for insight.

They all shook their heads.

Suddenly, we heard a door slam somewhere in the house, and a cold draft came through the house.

"He's here, the monk. The veils are so fine, ladies," said Laura.

"Is it the monk from the Abbey?" I whispered.

Alice looked at me. "The man you heard on the solstice?"

I nodded.

"Richard, it's Richard. I know it is," Emilee announced,

standing up.

She began to whisper to someone in the room. Usually, I would think she was mad, but I also began to feel a familiar presence.

"Anne, is that you?" I looked to the corner of the room. "No, this is I, Queen Katherine."

I could see her plain as day. A petite woman dressed all in black robes, and around her neck, she wore a high collar with an obvious cross upon it. It was as if everyone had disappeared, and it was just her and me.

"I have awaited this a long, long time, and here you are again, oracle." Her accent was strong, maybe Spanish or Italian—as was her will.

"Me? How do you know me?"

"We all knew you. You were famous in your Tudor lifetime. You were in the high courts of France and Spain and then England."

"Katherine of Aragon..." the words fell from my lips.

The woman nodded and held out her hand. "Let me show you."

I had no hesitation; curiosity took over, and I reached over and took it gladly. I was suddenly transported back in time. This type of vision had never happened before to me. It was a whole new way to view history and the Akashic records.

I turned around and saw a long, dark corridor behind me, and I could see my friends in Glastonbury. They all stood like statues. Lucinda and Emilee were talking, Laura was sitting, and Alice was the only one watching me as my physical body appeared to be turned away from them.

"Anna, you are in the astral plane?" she called to me.

"How are you in the Akashic Records?"

My brain was trying so hard to understand, but I let go

of control to see what was in front of me.

Katherine took my hand again. "*Come, dear one, you are very safe.*"

I looked around this room, and it showed the banners and flags of royalty, but nothing looked like the historic English scenes I had seen in history books.

We walked out into beautiful gardens, and there were orange and lemon trees, so I knew we were not in England. "Spain, Espana," I tried my best.

Katherine laughed. "Yes, just watch."

I was taken aback when I saw Isis walking with a very royal-looking woman. Isis looked much younger than I knew her, and the women appeared to be deep in conversation.

"We must protect the holy church. It is the only way we can claim peace."

"I agree, Your Highness, but England is still unstable, and the portals are open again for dark wizards and evil," replied Isis.

"The young prince will be King, but perhaps not for long. His brother also has great karma to clear."

"Then will you go to the English court and advise?"

Isis shook her head, "No, my timeline is very short, but another will come. She will bring great powers of vision. The time of darkness is now here. We have been waiting for this for 1500 years. We cannot change the course of fate."

"You may not, but I can. I have defeated all my enemies, and with your help, my oracle friend secured many of our faith in places of power."

"Yes, Your Highness, but they are weak and will fall to the ego and greed."

The Queen, as I now assumed her to be, looked disappointed.

"Your daughter must go to England," said Isis.

"'No…" the queen said, taken aback.

"She is trained in our ways, Your Highness. She is a true priestess. I have seen her be initiated."

"Against my wishes."

"We cannot fight the will of the Priestesses of Isis. Theirs is a true faith and order, bound to good."

A young girl suddenly ran up to them.

"That's you," I said, looking at Katherine.

She was so young and beautiful, her skin touched by the sunlight and her hair raven black.

Katherine smiled and touched her cheek.

"I had forgotten my youth, so brave and full of courage."

The Queen took the young girl's hand, whispered words to her, and then handed her hand to Isis.

"Make her worthy, my friend."

The image faded, and we were then many years forward, and I could see we were in England, in one of the Royal palaces.

I felt a cold fear as we walked through the corridors and saw many courtiers huddled in corners, whispering and plotting.

We walked into a large chamber of rooms. The curtains were closed, and a strong smell of church incense was burning. I could hear the wailing of a woman and watched as what looked to be a nurse came running out, holding a very still newborn baby.

The nurse looked at me, and I saw it was Emilee. She was sobbing as she handed the infant over to a priest for him to perform a blessing before they began wrapping it in a large muslin cloth.

I followed Emilee back into the chamber and there was Katherine. Other women were around them, but my attention was focused on Katherine, who was obviously distressed. As I soon learnt, fate had not switched in her favour.

"It was a boy, my Queen. He took no breath in this Earthly world. He simply slipped back to the realm of the afterlife."

Katherine was wailing and sobbing.

"How can this be? She wove the spell." I looked to where she was pointing and saw a young version of Lucinda.

Lucinda simply sat looking at the floor, shaking.

Katherine then threw up her hands.

"We are cursed, all of us. My king will not favour this day, and I know he seeks a new life. You have seen this, no?"

She looked at Emilee, who now also looked at the floor.

"But, Your Majesty, you have a beautiful daughter and powerful allies. She can marry into Europe and restore all that we have dreamed of."

"No, the curse is still in place," came a voice from the back of the room.

A very old woman threw a piece of parchment onto the bed.

"Behold, our fates are set. This is a dark age for us all. Save yourselves, and may we meet again in another life." It was Alice, and she quickly disappeared.

"Who was that?" Emilee asked Katharine.

"The Druidess of Glastonbury. She appeared a few days ago, and I knew the birth would be soon. The friends of Avalon are our hope now, and I will write to them today."

"Shall I bring her back for you?" whispered Emilee.

"No, those wise ones, they say, can walk through walls and are invisible," Katherine replied.

"This one," she pointed to Lucinda, "has failed the initiation to be with them." Lucinda was muttering.

"Speak up, woman," Katherine shouted at her.

"I did not fail, Your Majesty. I was misled and cursed by the dark one."

"Your kind have the power to vanquish curses."

Lucinda slowly stood and her eyes, I was sure, had fire in them.

"I will find my path," she said, glaring at Katherine and Emilee.

The room began to swirl, and again, I found myself in another royal court, but this one was full of life, and a great party was taking place.

I could see a young woman who looked straight at me.

"Don't you remember me?" she asked with a wicked smile on her face.

She winked, and I suddenly knew it was Anne—Anne Boleyn.

I looked for Katherine, but she was nowhere to be seen.

"Now pay attention," said Anne. The party shifted, and we were now in a small room.

Lucinda was there, and I could see her whispering to Anne and the others. They were playing with a type of tarot card.

"You see, every time it points to you, High Priestess Anne, you can have the world."

Anne, who was about 14 years old, seemed enchanted.

"But the oracle warned me," she argued.

"She knows nothing about this. She came from the region where they think they know. It is said that those people from the Basque region have special blood and can see the future. She's not one of them, and anyway, where is she now?"

"In Spain, and then I think she will go to Rome."

"Well, then she's not here. I tell you, she's an outcast." I saw Lucinda's eyes flash with black and I looked away.

I found myself back in the kitchen in the Sanctuary.

"Anna, wake up." Lucinda was tapping my arm, and

Emilee was holding out a strong cup of tea.

"I went back to the 1500's."

The women all looked at each other.

"And you saw us..."

"I saw you, Lucinda, Alice, Emilee, and Isis."

"Not you?"

"No, not me in that story, but I was with Katherine of Aragon and saw Anne Boleyn. I think I was an outsider. My only recall to date was when Anne was sent to the Tower of London. I came back to warn her, but by then it was too late."

Another door slammed shut from upstairs in the house, and I felt a presence in the kitchen.

"Who is it?" Lucinda looked very afraid.

Laura spoke; she had been taken over by a spirit. *"It is I, Richard Whiting, the last abbot of the Glastonbury Abbey. I have been held here for over 500 years."*

The room grew cold, and we all became silent. Laura had this faint white glow around her, and I felt a chill all over my body.

"Richard, we acknowledge your presence and ask why it is you are here now," Alice spoke in a low yet strong voice.

"They were dark times, and the energy portals were compromised and closed."

"Can you explain?" Alice responded.

"In 1533, King Henry Tudor broke with the holy church as it was destined to be. A dark force had come to these shores from Rome. They spoke holy words; however, they had been stealing relics and valuable possessions from many churches and holy lands.

"The evil one created curses on the two queens that they would not bear boy sons, and England would have no protection. Vulnerable, the crown would pass to the Holy

Roman church, and they would own the powerful keys to the treasures that had been hidden and protected within the English churches.

"In Glastonbury Abbey, we had many tunnels and would work side by side with the druid priests. They had long been present and were a protected community for thousands of years. I guarded a scroll and scarab connected to the Magic and Prophecy. It had the power to control the energy of alchemy, to be able to summon all the Earth elements and an army that is not of this world. Tools from Atlantis, long forgotten and only known to the descendants of Merlin.

"Queen Katherine knew of this and was told of its power by her mother. She never shared the secret with King Henry and wrote to me many times with cryptic messages in order to communicate with me."

"Why would she protect this?" Alice asked.

"She was one of the priestesses close to the teaching of Isis. She knew the power of the church and tried to manage both sides. Sadly, she was unable to pass the secrets on to her daughter, Mary. Her daughter fell into the web of the Catholic faith, and that faith was so very far from the teachings of Christ.

"Queen Anne also knew of the sacred arts of Isis and its teachings. But she did not listen to the words of The Oracle, your present friend Anna, and listened to others who sought to weave the ancient magic of the druids in order to tip the scales of justice. Anne, however, did pass her learning and wisdom on to a handmaiden who would watch over her daughter, Elizabeth.

"Elizabeth started the quest to try to bring many of the relics back to England; however, her time was short. Henry Tudor had a curse long in his family line. Elizabeth would be the last of his line. The work was lost, and the scroll and scarab

remained hidden for many years until the oracles returned to Glastonbury. In the late 1700's in this house, a secret room was found, and the Scroll and Scarab of Magic and Prophecy were revealed. They began to call to the rest of the set, and when you created your recent ceremony, it sent out a tremor and message. This set was once together in Atlantis, Egypt, and in Jerusalem. They create the gates to the Halls of Amenti. Many rulers have tried to re-create them to bring about a golden age but have failed."

"We failed in the past, did we not, sir?" asked Lucinda with tears on her face.

Laura nodded, and his voice came through with compassion.

"You did, my sister. You helped to bring our sister Anne back to England in the hope she would reveal the relics."

"But I sought them for my own protection." I turned and saw the spirit of Anne standing near the table.

"Richard, I tried to bear him a son and protect you all."

I felt a cold breeze and began to see the Queen pleading with the King and begging for more chances. They had come this far, and he didn't need a son if he had faith. If he helped protect the new faith.

I watched as she moved over and stood behind Laura. Laura lifted her hand to her shoulder.

"Queen Anne is with us now, as is Queen Katherine," she said, her voice coming back to normal.

"They ask if the oracles will help again. This is the time when the Halls of Amenti are open, and the chosen oracle has seen this and will regain her full sight again."

"Who is she?" Alice asked.

"She is with you," replied Laura.

"And what can we do now for you?" I asked softly. My heart told me it might be me, but for once, I curbed my ego.

"Help me and these ladies make our peace in the Akashic Records and journey from this Earth plane that binds us. Mine was a tragic death."

I watched as Queen Anne touched his shoulder.

The words fell from my lips. "She says she is sorry. When Katherine passed, she knew her fate was sealed, and her death would follow. This was in 1536, and you were not warned of the darkness that would follow. Richard, when you were hung, drawn, and quartered, and killed in such an ungodly way upon the Tor, your torment was forever bound to this location and timeline. Anne knew you tried to have Katherine's divorce stopped and had allowed others to curse Katherine many times with the help of another priestess."

I stopped when I saw Lesley flash into my mind. She was there, binding thread around sticks and placing them around the Abbey.

"Much wisdom created the Holy wars of our time," continued Laura now as Richard, *"but now you have the power to bring balance. We are here as a reminder of your past and with a warning. Remember, the scorpion can hide deep within and never show itself until the last moment."*

"I see a vision of you all," I announced. "In Egypt, during an ancient time as priestesses, but you are all leaving on a journey to a new land... the timeline of Akhenaten. You were connected to his daughters. But the golden age was not to be."

"You are a wise young lady. Your sight serves you well, oracle sister," replied Richard.

"But what happens next?" My eager question was perhaps a little too forward.

"We must go," he announced.

"Godspeed, ladies. I give you my leave and blessing."

And suddenly, the room was warm again, and I realised

they had all gone back to the spirit world.

The room was silent. “Anna, what else do you see?” said Emilee.

“Nothing more,” I said. “That was all I could see. I’m sorry.”

Lucinda was crying silently beside me. I turned towards her and gave her a big hug. Whatever issues we had were over. Getting through this together was far more important.

“I didn’t mean to cry,” Lucinda sniffled. “I never realised what happened. What were they trying to do?”

“It is most strange,” said Emilee. “I saw myself there, but I have no memory of it. We were all together.”

“Clearly, a dark force is watching us and has been for over 500 years. I think they summoned the Priests of Unal to get them. I’m wondering if maybe what cursed the Queens and Richard is controlling them.”

“It is possible,” Alice chimed in. “Either way, they are a dangerous entity we need to be on the lookout for, in any form they might take.”

“*Oui,* but I think that is enough diving into the past for today. Anna has only just barely recovered from her illness, and we have greatly upset our dear friend, Lucinda. I think it is best we let them both recover for the evening. Hopefully, we will hear from Isis and Naomi soon, and then we can go from there.”

Alice scrunched her nose in confusion, “Have you not heard from them today still?”

Lucinda shook her head, “No, not since before New Year’s. I got a message saying that they would be back in early January. I assumed that meant any day now. But when I tried to contact them yesterday, I didn’t get a response and Lucas is still MIA.”

“I hope they are alright,” said Laura. But I’m sure

they were probably just in a rush to get back or were on a plane and couldn't respond. I bet you they will all call later tonight!"

"Ever the optimist, Laura," Lucinda cooed, "That is what I love about you. Emilee is right, Anna. You need to lie down and rest, and I will do the same."

Too exhausted to argue, I left the kitchen and went upstairs. Figuring out who this oracle was and how they all forgot why they were together in England would have to wait until later.

CHAPTER 7

Sunday, 4 January 2009, 4:44 a.m.

I awoke to the sound of pans clattering and a familiar smell coming up from the kitchen. At first, I thought I was back in the Gables, but looking around and realising I wasn't, there could only be one explanation: Emilee was here. I looked at the clock and saw that it was only 4:45 in the morning, way too early for her to be rustling around downstairs. So, I quickly got up and put on my robe to see what was happening. Once in the kitchen, I saw not only Emilee but Lucinda, Laura, and Alice all running around the kitchen frantically preparing something.

I yelled out to them in a teasing tone, "Hey, all you silly chickens running around with your heads cut off, what is going on?"

Lucinda stopped what she was doing and said in a very serious voice, "Isis, Naomi, and Lucas will be here within the hour, and Isis is sick."

I froze in my tracks and started to have trouble breathing. It was as if Lucinda's words had punched me in the gut and left me gasping for air.

Laura came up to me and patted me comfortingly on the back, "It will be okay, Anna. Go get dressed and come back downstairs. We didn't want to wake you unnecessarily, but since you are up, you may as well help."

I nodded, hearing most of what Laura was saying. Without delay, I dashed back up the stairs. *They were coming back, and Isis was sick. Was she sick with what I had? Did I somehow give it to her?*

Once in my room and facing the mirror, I realised it wouldn't be a good idea to head back downstairs in the robe and pyjamas I'd been lounging in for days—or in any robe and pyjamas, for that matter. So, I searched my dresser for a clean oversized blouse and leggings. After I got fresh clothes on, I got to work on my hair and face.

My hair was a proper rat's nest that took fifteen minutes to untangle before deciding it didn't want to be worn down anyway. I sighed and placed it in a messy bun atop my head the way Naomi had shown me. Next, I went to cover up the red blotches on my skin with some makeup, a result of sneaking downstairs in the middle of the night to feast on chocolate. I wasn't going to let the best-dressed woman I knew see my chocolate overdose-complexion.

Just as I was doing last looks in my mirror, I heard the front door open. Butterflies furiously fluttered in my stomach in anticipation. Taking another deep breath, I went downstairs, not sure of what I would find.

Everyone was in the sitting room, crowding around the couch, where I could only assume Isis was. It dawned on me that the last thing I had said to her was horrible, and I instantly felt guilty about it. *Did she hate me? Did she even want to see me?* I thought. Emilee saw me lingering and pulled me closer to the group.

"Come on, Anna, you must see Isis," she said, dragging me through the half-circle that had formed around the couch.

When we got to the front, I audibly gasped. Laid on the couch was a gaunt and frail old woman. Her cheeks were sunken in, and her eyes were red and bleary. The woman's skin was pallid in colour and so taut in certain areas you could almost see the outline of her bones. The only recognisable feature left on her was her long silver hair. Isis was a shell of who she had been.

"I don't understand," I said, turning to Lucinda, "She was finc when she left a few weeks ago."

"That is what happens when you are old and get sick," said a familiar voice from the corner. Naomi came out of the shadows just then, which gave me a chance to take in her full appearance. She, too, had been through something rough. Her skin was sunburnt and peeling in several places, and her lips were chapped and cracked at the corners of her mouth. Naomi had several bruises on her face, and her left arm was in a sling.

"What happened?" I asked, the horror evident in my voice.

"Wow, I missed you too," said Naomi dryly, "Wouldn't you know it? I don't actually know. My ever-forthcoming past life mother over there won't tell me."

"You don't remember?"

"No! I don't remember. Please try to pay attention, Anna, my god," Naomi said in a very irritated voice.

"I don't understand. You have all sorts of bumps and bruises on you, and you don't know where you got them from?"

"No, I don't! Don't you think if I knew, I would tell you? Don't you think I want to know who did this to me?" Naomi's voice cracked at the end of her sentence.

Just then, Lucas came sweeping in, saying, "Alright, Naomi, it will all get sorted out. I know you have been through an ordeal. Why don't you go up to your old room and relax? I'm sure Emilee can help draw you a bath with her ever-so-special healing elixirs."

Emilee took that as her cue and collected Naomi, who

at that point was shaking, and left with her to presumably go help Naomi take a bath. Satisfied that Naomi was cared for, Lucas immediately turned his attention to Isis, markedly avoiding eye contact with me. Lucinda approached Lucas and asked him more about what had happened.

"Lucas, Anna is right to raise concerns. How did she lose so much weight in the last few weeks?"

Lucas sighed, "I am not sure. She had been slowing down, but such is the case for any of us older folk. I got to them in Cairo right before Christmas, and Isis informed me that she and Naomi would be taking a trip into the desert with a few archaeologists for a few days and would return late on New Year's Day. In the end, I decided to wait for them. She looked completely fine when she left. Fast forward to New Year's Day, and they still haven't returned or contacted me at all. I notified the university in charge of the expedition, who said that the two women had gotten separated from the group on New Year's Eve, and they had already dispatched a team to search for them. They were only found early yesterday, stranded just outside of Siwa in the desert. I am glad they found them when they did. Otherwise, I don't know what would have happened."

"Why didn't you take them to a hospital in Cairo? Why bring them back here?"

"Well, Lucinda, it was because Naomi insisted. She said that Isis wasn't sick from any earthborn disease; it was something spiritual in nature that needed to be healed here. Naomi insisted she was fine other than the injuries you saw and slight dehydration."

"Did Naomi say when Isis got sick?"

"Naomi said she didn't know for sure. She just remembers waking up in the sand in the morning and finding Isis a little way away, looking like she does now."

"If it's all the same with you, Lucas, I think I will still call Dr. Malcom. Hopefully, he can at least make her more comfortable," said Lucinda.

"Yes, of course. Have him check on Naomi as well. She says her wrist is only sprained, but I think she might be understating her pain so as to get Isis the attention she needs."

"Of course, excuse me." Lucinda left, and with her, Laura and Alice, who were going to put on a kettle and make some breakfast for everyone. That left me with the two people who probably hated me most in the world. I hung my head in shame. They were two wonderful people whom I had needlessly berated in a moment of anger.

"Anna," Lucas called, rousing me from my thoughts, "Isis would like to speak with you."

Before I could turn to thank him, he was at the other end of the room, getting the fire going. So, I slowly approached the sofa, not knowing what Isis was going to say, and prepared for her to let me have it. I knelt down and held her hand.

In a surprisingly solid and normal voice, Isis said, "It's okay. It looks worse than it feels. I suspect after a few days of rest, I shall look a bit less like a corpse."

"I should hope so!"

"And I heard you were sick as well. I'm sorry you had to go through that."

"It's okay, I'm on the mend."

"That you are, my dear."

"Isis, how did we both get sick with the same thing? Is it going to come back? It was so awful, and I—" I cut myself off; I was upsetting myself.

Isis took my hand to calm me down, "No, no, my dear. Although it is curious, you automatically made the connection that our sicknesses were linked. What you got was the indirect hit. I took the brunt of it."

"The brunt of what? Isis, please tell me. I am tired of always asking questions and not getting any answers. I get that whatever you were doing was to protect me, but clearly, it didn't work. If something is coming after us, I need to know everything I can, so I can protect everyone. I don't stand a chance if I am fighting with one arm tied behind my back."

"Anna!" Lucas scolded me, standing up from the chair near the fire, "How dare you speak to Isis like that!"

I looked back and forth between them, "I-I, I'm sorry. I didn't mean..."

"I know you didn't, Anna," said Isis, "And you make a great point, but unfortunately, knowing what you are up against will not help you fight it. You need to come into your full power first. That can only be done in Egypt."

"And what if whatever controls the Priests of Unal gets me before then? They terrorised me, attacking me in the real world. How can you guarantee they won't come back and do it again and finish me off before I make it to Egypt?"

"I promise they won't. They got hurt, too. It will take a while for them to regroup, and when they do, you will be ready."

I sighed in frustration. Even at death's door, Isis was still refusing to tell me what was going on. "Fine. Don't tell me. I will figure it out on my own. I'll leave you to your rest." I left abruptly and locked myself away in the office. She was back, and nothing was different, except now her health was failing. I cried out, angry that I was still being iced out, angry that my mentor was possibly dying, and angry at myself for not being good enough to figure this out on my own.

Evidently, I was not quite over my sickness as I had thought. The excitement of Isis's return had wiped me out, and I spent another three days in bed with a low-grade fever. However, I made the most of my time and carefully read through the Emerald Tablets to see if I could find anything more that would explain what I had seen in my visions. The Scorpion book was now covered by clothes and books, as I was fearful to open it, and even more terrified to hand it back to Alice.

Wednesday, 7 January 2009, 9:03 p.m.

Heading downstairs, I could hear loud sounds coming from the kitchen. I walked into a cosy and downright jovial scene. Lucas and Emilee were busy fussing over something on the stove, the two playfully flirting with one another. Isis was holding court at the top of the table and looking radiant in her signature royal blue scarf. Whatever Dr. Malcom had given her seemed to have put colour back into her cheeks and more meat on her bones. She was conversing excitedly with Lucinda, who was hanging on her every word.

Naomi also seemed much improved; her skin was no longer peeling from sunburn, and the bulk of the bruises on her face were barely visible. Her arm was in a brace, but it looked like the removable kind, so at least it wasn't broken. She was also sitting at the table, listening to the conversation. She was the first to look up and notice me.

"Good evening, Anna," Naomi called. Everyone stopped what they were doing and turned to look at me.

I awkwardly waved, "Evening, everyone. I hope I'm not interrupting anything."

"Not at all," said Isis, "Come sit down. Lucas and Emilee are about to serve breakfast for supper."

I nodded, taking a seat at the table. There were lit candles in the center surrounded by floral decor. Everyone was in an amazing, upbeat mood. For a moment, it made me forget just how messed up things had gotten lately. But that's what tends to happen in families. I smiled to myself. They were a family, my family. In that moment, I was so grateful I had found them and confident that we would get through whatever storms we were weathering.

"Tre bien!" Emilee announced, walking over to the table with a large quiche on an elegant glass stand. "We have done it! The most perfectly flavorful and fluffy little egg dish you have ever tasted!"

Everyone cheered and went about doling out the rest of the food and drink. Isis handed me a plate with some of her delicious vegetables, and I took a heaping spoonful. They were filled with her magic, and I could do with some, as I could with a large slice of quiche and a glass of wine. I successfully obtained the quiche, but when I poured myself a glass of the cabernet Lucas had opened, Isis stopped me.

"No, no darling," she said, "You are still in recovery. Herbal tea and blessed water for you only!"

"Blessed water? Like holy water?"

Isis laughed, "No, like water from the sacred spring that feeds the Chalice Well and, coincidentally, our well out in the back here. You know, the one with the three Knights Templar image on it?"

"Oh, right, of course. I didn't realise the well out there was fed by the same spring."

"That is one of the reasons I created the Sanctuary here. That water carries with it a strange energy that seems to have all sorts of effects on people. Normally, I would be safe rather than sorry, but I have a feeling that this water is just what you need!"

"Good, then pass that water pitcher to Anna!" Emilee ordered, "She needs something in her glass, so the cheer is good."

"Cheers?" I asked, pouring myself some water, "What are we cheering to?"

"Why, to our dear sister Isis, for making such a quick recovery, and to you, who has also healed impressively fast! To Isis and Anna!"

Emilee raised her glass, as everyone else did, mimicking her sentiment. Everyone clinked their glasses with each other and drank. As I took my sip, I caught Isis's eye, and she gave me a sad smile. Something told me that her chances of fully recovering were not great, that she was trying to put on a brave face for everyone else. However, it was no use letting others know about it. It would only make things harder. Instead, we engaged in light conversation and had a wonderful meal.

☥

After the food was gone and the wine drank, we all settled into a comfortable silence. The water from the well had filled me with its chaotic and vibrating energy. I felt more alive and present than I had since Christmas. I remember Isis had said something about ley lines running through here and the Tor, and I wondered if the water from the ancient springs was the physical manifestation of that.

"It is, in a way," Isis answered my thought, "The water carries the energy in a complex labyrinth running beneath the ground. It is very similar to how energy flows throughout the world, even in places where there is no water to be seen."

"Like in Egypt?" I asked.

"Precisely. The Nile was the way to tap into that energy."

Lucas piped in, "Ah, yes, the good old days when you could just throw on a silk robe and walk to the river to do all of your rituals and send off all of your prayers."

Isis smiled, "And have them answered in the form of miracles."

"Yes, my darling, I remember. We danced and sang, and life was very simple."

"Until it wasn't."

The room became very sombre and still. Everyone had that faraway look in their eyes, and Naomi had tears in hers.

Isis shook herself from her thought and said, "Well, well, let's end this evening on a positive note, shall we?"

Isis had us all gather each other's hands and form a little circle around the table. An outsider looking in would think we were saying grace or something, but to those who knew, we were passing energy through each other. Isis ended the energy session by saying, "One heart." Everyone replied the same in unison and let go of each other's hands.

Isis took a deep breath, "Now, Anna, let's you and I go into the living room and catch up."

"Okay!" I got up and went to clear the plates.

"No, we have this," said Naomi, and I saw Lucas beginning to stack the dishes.

I thanked them and followed Isis into the room where all the secrets were revealed: the sitting room. I sat in the small chair, and she took her place on her chair. I was used to giving sessions from her seat, but as with my temple training, I had learnt that my mentor and elder would always hold her place and throne.

"So," she looked at me, gazing deep into my soul and smiled, "Updates, please?"

I was a bit taken aback by her casualness. We both knew

that she was still waning in health despite her improved appearance, and it seemed trivial for her to be asking me about commonplace updates about the day-to-day of my life.

"Well," I started, "Other than catching your second-hand spirit sickness, everything has been pretty quiet around here since you left. I had a few clients and did readings for Emilee's guests. We all celebrated at the Guesthouse with her and her guests. It was absolutely lovely. Then we had a quiet week until New Year's, and I suppose you know what happened after that." I glossed over the part where I yelled at Lucas and sent her a nasty email on Boxing Day.

Isis clicked her tongue. "Hmm, is that all? Any particularly interesting regressions or dreams lately?"

I knew what she was getting at. In addition to being incredibly intuitive, Isis also had a good confidante in Lucinda, who I'm sure had told her what I had been seeing. It irked me that she was asking me to divulge what I had been channelling when she was withholding information. Frankly, even if I was in the sharing mood, there didn't seem to be much point because Isis hadn't been in an explaining mood lately. So instead, I pivoted and asked her about something else.

"Do you know who the eighth member of our sisterhood is? Now that you have retired."

"Just one?"

"Yeah, Lesley is one of the Sacred Eight, is she not?"

"She is... but I fear that she is still not ready to rejoin us. Anna, why are you fixed on this Sacred Eight?"

"Lesley might not have that option," I continued. "We need to come together and restore our temple to its former glory and do it soon."

Isis smiled, "Or the Lords of Space-Time will do to us

what they did to Atlantis?"

"Yes! Wait, did you know that already?"

"I've also read the *Emerald Tablets.* I'm glad that you have been, as well. It provides invaluable insight into our history. Plus, Alice stopped by to give me her thoughts."

"I thought our history started at Philae?" I sighed, "Wait, we are getting off-topic. Do you know who the eighth person is?"

Isis shook her head, "I'm afraid not, dear. And your past lives are a bit of a mystery to the rest of us. You've intersected with some of us a few times, but not nearly as much as we have with each other."

"They are a mystery to me, too. How is it I am this amazing oracle with other people, but I can never look back on my own past?"

"Looking back into our own past traumas is one of the hardest things to do. We block certain parts of it from ourselves in order to protect ourselves. That's why we so often have another oracle helping to guide us along. They are there to keep you from closing off certain parts of your past lives."

"Is there any way we could do that now? I feel like I know so much less than everyone else, and maybe learning more about my past lives will help."

"I would love nothing more, but not tonight. It is late, and I'm very tired from tonight's festivities. Would you be a dear and fetch Naomi for me?"

I could tell Isis was done speaking for the time being, so I went off to go find Naomi so she could help Isis to bed.

I spent the rest of the week catching up on client appointments since we had been closed due to my illness.

I was so busy that I barely got to see Isis and Naomi, and I didn't see Lucas at all. I still hadn't apologised to him, or Isis for that matter, and it was really weighing on me. I resolved to remedy this on Saturday, but as the gods would have it, I was inundated with last-minute appointments from clients, which meant I was also flooded with the spirits of their loved ones, too. With Isis and Naomi back at the Sanctuary, as well, it was a full house indeed.

Sunday, 11 January 2009, 7:45 a.m.

I woke up bright and early. I looked around my room and decided it was time to reset. I pulled all my laundry into piles, changed my bed linen, took a shower, and put on fresh clothes. I was wearing my spa outfit, as Naomi called it—a pair of loose-fitting linen pants and a matching loose-wrap tunic. It was white, and I always felt so special wearing it. I placed my hair up, applied a light makeup, and made my way downstairs.

Naomi was in the office and checking her phone.

"Any appointments?" I asked as I poked my head around the doorway.

She never even looked up, "No, honey, nothing today. Those three ladies from Oxford cancelled late last night."

Well, now, I thought, *what should I do?*

In my head, I could hear a voice.

"Have we heard from Lucas?"

"Anna, I'm not your secretary," Naomi snapped back. I was taken aback by her rudeness.

It was like working with Lesley again when we had been students of the Sanctuary last year, and as that had turned out rather a dramatic episode, I decided to rise above it and ran back to my room to grab my coat and bag and head out.

Heading into town, I could still hear someone's voice in my head. It was Lucas. I was sure it was. I quickened my pace and headed for the high street.

Being Sunday, everywhere was still closed, and as I checked my watch, it would be a while before anything opened. I looked up and down the main road; nothing seemed open, and I was aware of just how cold it was.

"Cup of tea?" I heard a soft female voice behind me.

I turned and remembered the young woman who had waited on me all those months ago when I first reached Glastonbury.

"Yes, but where?" I pointed to everything.

"The Sacred Travelers Cafe, of course," she pointed to the café where I had first met Isis and where Naomi met some of her clients.

It had been a while since I had visited.

"Come on, it's freezing."

She linked my arm and ushered me to the door, where she produced a large set of keys.

"It's an hour before we open, but it's my job to do the Sunday early shift."

She opened the door, and we ventured in.

"I'll turn everything on if you want to boil the kettle." She pointed to the area behind the counter and disappeared into the back room.

I put down my bag and took off my coat. I began to make myself useful with tea making as she lifted out the trays of baked goods and set up the cappuccino machine.

"It's nice to 'ave some company." She smiled and put some teacakes into the toaster, and we made conversation while I helped her set everything up and wipe the tables down, ready for opening.

"Won't the owner mind?' I was conscious they may

walk in at any moment.

"No, this is me mum's business. I have been helping since I was a small girl. I help out at the holidays, but I'll be back at uni next week."

"Uni like university?" I asked.

"Like university, yes, and by the way, my name's Julia."

"Julia, I'm Anna."

"Oh, I know your name; the whole town knows your name."

I wasn't sure what to say.

"What do they say?"

"That you're a witch, and when Isis dies, you will take over running the show."

"The show?"

"Yes, the coven."

"So that's what people think."

"No, Anna, that's what people say."

I began to feel uncomfortable, and the room suddenly became dark. I could see tunnels, and the walls were all made of stone brick.

"You see them, don't you?" Julia asked

"See what?"

"Them spirits."

"Do you?"

"Sometimes when I'm here on my own locking up at night, I hear people crying."

"I don't hear them," I said, shaking my head. "Why would they be here?"

"Many trapped souls are still here, I think, left over from the olden days."

"Has this happened recently?"

"More and more," Her words were serious.

"Boo!" I felt someone behind me grab my waist, and I screamed, and Julia jumped.

"Julia, be an angel and make me some breakfast. I'm starving."

"Oh, Mr. Lucas, you gave us a fright!" she scolded him.

"Go and sit down. I'll bring it over. The coffee is nearly ready. Don't know how to cook that one," she said, pointing at him as he sat down and looked at me with a wicked grin.

"Here's your coffee and tea cake, Anna. If you want tea, sir, you know where it is. Fred will be here soon. He will make you something."

"So, this is where you come for food?" I asked Lucas.

"Nearly every day. I have no time to cook."

Julia overheard us. "Get thee a wife," she called out as she began to give the breakfast order to what looked to be her grandfather, who had just arrived and was putting on an apron in the back.

"Family business," whispered Lucas. "He's as old as the church."

I held back my giggle. "Lucas, you have a wicked sense of humour."

"It's my gift with the ladies," he sighed.

Lucas was most upbeat and playful, and I made light conversation as I was not sure if I should go into the poor Richard hung, drawn, and quartered story or the evil depths of hell trying to devour me one. Worst of all, I feared if I had to broach the subject of our last conversation.

Soon, the comforting smell of toast swept through the café, and Lucas was feasting on his breakfast fare, even sharing a small plate with me. "Here you go," he said, like I was a small child, placing scrambled eggs and some toast in front of me. As he did this, I saw him as a priest but not like I had seen him before—smaller and with a very clear energy, almost like a Buddhist monk.

When we had finished, I was about to launch my

apology, yet he was already paying the bill and ushering me out of the café.

"Anna, I have something to share with you. Now follow me," he said, pointing to his storefront.

"Gossip, Egypt gossip." I was excited.

"No, not really, but I wanted to share something important."

I had to admit I loved to visit with Lucas. He was one of the first people I had met in Glastonbury, and his tarot readings gave great insight, even about the things you no longer wished to hear about in your life.

"Are you working today?"

"No, it's really strange. I had two people cancel, and my girl is still sick and I think avoiding me."

"I cou..."

"No, Anna, you can't come and help. I know you mean well, but your fate line is now set. Your destiny is not behind a shop counter."

I knew he was right, but all the same, I longed to be able just to come in and have no responsibility, play with crystals, and talk to angels.

"It's harder than you think, holding space in a store. It's not like selling shoes or bags."

I nodded. "I can believe you, but sometimes..." he paused to open the door to his magical world.

"Well, you can come do some dusting," he glanced around.

"But I'm to be a high pr...."

Again, he stopped me.

Even High Priestesses had to clean and dust.

"Okay, so what's the gossip?" I followed him to the back room through the velvet curtains where he gave private readings.

"Well, I rather wanted your help on something."

"Me?" My ego was alerted. Helping Lucas was nearly as good as helping Isis or Naomi.

"So, I wanted to show you these." He lifted out a box and opened it, placing it in the center of the desk.

"Oh, wow, more scrolls and scarabs."

"Do you know which ones these are?"

On the desk, he produced three scrolls and a scarab.

"Where did you get these?" I held my hand lightly over the top and closed my eyes.

"Well, remember I was pool lounging in Cairo?"

"Yes, your sunshine vacation," I said sarcastically and smiled.

"Yes, well, I decided to stay and await their return, but I got bored. I was going to take a day trip to Alexandria and was halfway there when I received a call from our agent stating that someone from the Egyptian museum had called them about connecting with Isis."

Apparently, he was someone from her past and remembered her as a girl growing up, and also when she and a friend had visited as teenagers after the war."

"How did he know she was there? Was he the man who called me last year about the Scrolls of Amenti?"

"Yes, I think so, but he would not say more on the phone. What I do know is that I headed back to Cairo, and that's when I lost contact with Isis and Naomi."

"Did you meet the museum man? Do you know if his name was Imran perhaps?" I remembered the email Isis had sent me about a Mr. Imran.

Lucas shook his head.

"I am not sure... it was all so secretive."

"And here is what is also strange. After setting up an appointment with me, he failed to show up and sent a young

American professor to meet me and give me this box."

"Did he know what was in the box?" I asked.

"I'm not sure, as he asked lots of questions. I was also told not to open the box until I reached England, and only then in the presence of Miss Anna. So to answer your question, I think the phone call and this man and the professor were linked. I have to say, a very handsome professor."

That really sparked my interest, and I held my hand over the treasures. Lucas touched my hand, and I began to have my vision.

"Lucas, I see us. We are at the Pyramids, but there are many rooms and tunnels. King Alexander is dead, and a new ruler is to be sent for. He is Greek and does not understand our ways, but they say he is a follower of the great Isis.

"I am all alone, and I have these scrolls and scarabs in boxes on the walls, and I have candles and a hole in the roof. I see you, a kind young man; you bring me food and water. Then you leave but never speak.

"It's a strange life. I feel numb, with no emotions, and it is as if I'm simply a caged pet of some kind to bring messages or counsel.

"Alexander ordered this so.

"He is afraid, as he has visited with others of my kind in Siwa. Yes, Siwa had been my home and we have told him things he thought no one knew, and they also forecast his death.

"He carries a great karma on his head and has fallen from grace. I see Alice now. She was his teacher, and he disrespected her wisdom and that of the Oracles of Alexandria, which sealed his fate.

"But these beautiful pieces remind me of home, my real home. But I don't know where that is.

"Now I'm seeing the new ruler, a respectful man who

wants to learn more. He wishes to be king, and I am his channel. I see his beginning and his end, but I tell him his reign and line will continue for hundreds of years, but I know it will only last 330 years until the great end of time and the time of Pisces to start.

"A time of 2000 years of darkness. He promises to build temples and give resources to save his family and commands me to help him.

"And so it began."

I opened my eyes, and I saw Lucas. I realised then that Lucas was the leading priest of the 33 who went to Philae with the box of scrolls and scarabs to help Isis not only build the temple but to resurrect the Philae Temple. Lucas sat with his mouth open as I told him my vision.

"How have I not seen this? It is a major part of my karmic history," he shook his head.

"Because we had to wait thousands of years, my dear friend." It was Isis behind him.

"Lucas, you really must get an alarm set up." That was Naomi.

Lucas stood up in silence as the two other women sat down. He never said a word, went to the front door, and locked it to ensure the closed sign was obvious.

Naomi leaned across and whispered. "Is this a séance?"

"No, look." I pointed to the treasure on the table. "Where did those come from?" She looked at Lucas, who again was silent.

"My friend sent them." Finally, Isis spoke.

"Imran was the son of a museum curator in the 1950's. We had a great love for each other in this lifetime and in other lives. We were supposed to meet during this last visit to Egypt."

"Your boyfriend?" I could not keep that to myself.

"No, he was my priest, the high priest from Edfu, my love. She looked at Naomi, "Yes, my dear, he was the priest chosen for your past life father and me. This lifetime was, well, let's say, a beautiful connection, but in later years, it was simply friendship. He was also a guardian of these sacred pieces but had written to me that they may be in danger and insisted I visit. He was also a guardian of the Scrolls of Amenti."

"But where was he?" Naomi asked. "I never met him."

"He never made it to us. His assistant, a young professor, met with Lucas."

"The Well of Souls..." the words tumbled from my mouth.

"What did you say?" Isis looked at me.

It was then that Lucas spoke. By now, he was in full trance.

"For thousands of years, Egypt held the energy wisdom of the planet. Those of us, the sons and daughters of Thoth, incarnated to watch over the ancient messages. I was a young priest tasked with bringing a specific group of scrolls and scarabs to you, Isis, and assisting in the formation of your temple here on earth.

"I visited with the Oracle of Siwa, and she wove a great magic upon this group and then called forward a group to follow me up the Nile by land and boat, linking all of these sacred pieces through each of the temples and would-be temple sites.

"We followed a very dangerous path, as there were both thieves and dark energies that were in pursuit, but it was the women of each village who had heard the message, and because as we travelled in groups of three, they were able to give us sanctuary and protection. Finally, we reached the island and our work was completed. We met with the group of

eight women, and this sacred eight formed one of the first true temples to the Light and the true teachings of the Magi. Those were the watchers of Atlantis, the Lords of Space- and Time. They were said to have come from other worlds.

"I see you now, dear Isis, with your friends tuning in to each of these sacred scrolls and scarabs and proclaiming your sacred mission. I watched your sunrise and sunset proclamation and was inspired as the sky fell to the deep rose pink of the divine feminine presence. While no one spoke, I knew we were all connected."

He stopped, and I saw tears fall from his eyes.

"Where did you go next?" but I already knew the answer.

Lucas took a deep breath and bit his lip.

"*We did not,*" he shook his head. "*We were betrayed by a brother. He had been the last to leave our ferry boat and sent a warning to the brothers of darkness about our location. As each boat arrived and set off back to Cairo, we were slaughtered. Picked off in our small groups, as were many of the women who had helped us. No one made it back alive. So even as the temple link was created, a darkness was surrounding it.*"

We all sat in silence. Once, this story had been a celebration of the union of the work of the priest and priestess, but now, it was like a horror story with a sad ending.

"We must heal this," said Isis.

"Now, let's name these pieces we have here and place them with their family."

Naomi lifted the box containing everything we had collected from the Sanctuary so far out of a bag she had and laid it on the table.

"Now, which are these?" Isis asked, pointing to the new pieces.

"I can't tell," said Lucas. "I leave it to the oracles." He pointed at Naomi and me, and I suddenly envisioned us both being at the pyramids and selecting various pieces.

"We were there at the start and the end, it would seem," whispered Naomi.

"Then we should know what to do," I said, sitting up in my chair.

Slowly, we laid them all out into two rows.

"Scrolls at the top and matching scarab underneath."

"So, the Magic and Prophecy are first. It was strange that this set seemed more powerful."

"Then we already have the Creation Scroll and Scarab," and Naomi set them down.

"Ah, this is the Scroll of Protection to match my scarab that seems to have been moving around in a very suspicious way," she announced from the new pile, looking at me.

"Death and Resurrection; that set is already complete."

Isis placed more pieces onto the table. But they seemed out of order.

"They don't look right," said Lucas.

"No, these two go together, I'm sure. I know I have worked with these two. They are from the Records of Life." I put them together.

"Figures," smiled Lucas. "Akashic Records wizard you are, Anna."

"Then that leaves a scroll."

"It's the Goddess Scroll," said Isis. "I know because I think I actually wrote it in a very ancient time. Put it with its matching scarab."

"Oh, and here is the Truth and Integrity we were gifted from Alice," I said, moving them into the picture. "How many now?"

"Fourteen. So that leaves two missing pieces. The Scroll

and Scarab of Light and Shadow," said Naomi.

"Didn't you have one of these?" asked Lucas.

"No," Isis shook her head. "We thought we did. Lesley claimed to have it, but it was fake."

"So those two are still out there."

I suddenly had a very uneasy feeling and saw a dark night and a train station.

"What is it, Anna?"

"It was hidden," I announced. "But it keeps moving, and it's still in Europe. A very evil man tried to steal it. No, two evil men tried to steal it."

"Steal it, my dear? From where?"

"During the war, both wars, evil wars. St. Petersburg, Berlin, Paris, many places... but they are still safe."

"Only one person knows of the secrets in those locations," said Naomi, looking at Isis.

Then they spoke in unison, "The Contessa."

"Then we have no time to lose." I was about to ask or to vision this when Naomi began to bundle up all the scrolls and scarabs with great haste. We said goodbye to Lucas, bundled back into Naomi's car, and sped up the hill to the Sanctuary. My head was buzzing, and one word seemed on repeat... *Siwa.* Isis and Naomi had been lost there, and I felt that it had been my home.

Monday, 12 January 2009, 3:33 a.m.

I woke with a start. Since the recent dream jacking started at the beginning of the year, I had created a ritual next to my bed of a clear crystal and journal in order to collect dreams and release fears. It meant I was a light sleeper; however, it also meant I was not waking up to bruises and high blood pressure.

I looked over to the corner of the room where my cozy chair was. I recalled it was clear, and the clothes I usually left there were in a neat pile on the floor. My room felt calm and peaceful, and the most beautiful scent of lilies floated around me. I felt a presence in the room, seated on the chair.

"Blessings, Anna. My name is Edwina, and I am one of the druid priestesses. I think we have met before," she said as the silhouette of her hair began to define itself in the dim light.

I had noticed her always at the front of the druidesses who walked the Tor, but up to this point, she had not made any contact with me.

"Great changes are coming to this house and to you, my dear."

"I have felt them." I sat up full in my bed and wrapped the quilt around me.

"Can you come closer, please, Anna?"

I nodded and slowly pulled myself and my quilt off the bed, went to the chair, and knelt down.

"Here, I wish to show you something." She held out her slender hand and took mine. The moment we touched hands, I began to vision.

"*I am seeing us walking up the Tor in small groups. But it's not the Tor; it's somewhere else. I'm trying not to look back, and my heart is breaking. There are twelve groups of us: two oracles, eight guardians, a High priest, and a High priestess.*

"*We all know each other, but we don't look alike. But we all feel alike. We are all connected by what looks to be a web of energy. But then it's broken, the thread. And now I'm on the Tor, and I see my friends, the druidesses they are guardians, weaving it each night, but there are only six of them. That's not enough.*"

I came out of my vision.

"As you see, Anna, we try to weave the web that will join to other places, but we can only hold so much. You can help us."

"And Isis and Naomi, they can help; my friends, I'm sure, will help. We are going to Egypt soon and have nearly all the scrolls and scarabs. I'm not sure what this has to do with here, but I'll make it work. I'll call a meeting tomorrow, our first temple meeting. I am sure I can tell the others what they need to do."

"Return to Egypt," the woman spoke very slowly. *"Return and align the gateways of the souls, Anna. This will allow us to free many ghosts from these lands."* Then she was gone.

I scuttled back over to my bed and switched the lamp on. I must prepare for the meeting to be called tomorrow. I wrote down the key points of order, and then, for the first time, I set my alarm to wake early and be fully present.

Monday, 12 January 2009, 7:30 a.m.

When Naomi was here, I always made the effort. She was always styled within an inch of her life and camera-ready. The few times I had seen her in the last couple of days, her dress had been more subdued, albeit still perfectly styled. From what I could tell, she was tending to Isis around the clock, making sure she had everything to recover. However, as I reached the bottom of the stairs, she was the opposite of this. Her makeup was smudged by her eyes as if she had been rubbing them, and her foundation was coming off in places. It was clear that she had slept in her makeup from yesterday. By the look of her wrinkled-up cotton jumpsuit, it also appeared that she had slept in that as well, most likely in a chair, if I had to guess.

"Naomi, what happened?" I asked, dreading her

response.

"It's Isis," she said.

"Where is she?"

"She's in bed upstairs."

"What happened?"

"The illness is getting worse." Naomi broke into sobs. I had never seen her in such a state. I took her by the arm and guided her into the kitchen.

"Now, sit down and take a few deep breaths," I instructed her. For once, I was in my own power and able to hold space.

"Once you've calmed a bit, tell me what we need to do. I'm going to make some coffee. Want some?"

She nodded, so I busied myself making the pot of coffee and gave her a chance to calm down. Out of the corner of my eye, I could see Naomi was just shaking and pulling at her nails repeatedly. For her to ruin her perfect manicure, I knew this must be bad.

After I had finished making the coffee and poured us each a cup, I placed the fresh coffee in front of her and waited.

Naomi picked up the cup and took a long sip before explaining, "She is getting worse. I haven't been able to get her to eat much in the last day since we came back from Lucas's yesterday, and now she can't get herself out of bed at all. She's having trouble breathing, and her whole body radiates with pain. I don't understand. She was a lot better just a few days ago."

Before I could answer her, I heard the doorbell ring. Naomi sniffled once and wiped under her eyes, "Oh, that must be Dr. Malcom; I'll go let him in."

We both went to the door and let Dr. Malcom in. He had been the priestess's doctor for years and understood the unique things we experienced.

"Thank you for coming so quickly, doctor!" Naomi said.

"Of course, Naomi," Dr. Malcom replied, "I am here 24/7 for you all."

"We really appreciate that," I said, holding out my hand to shake his.

Dr. Malcom enthusiastically grasped my hand and shook it, "Ah, Anna, how are you doing? I understand you got a bit of the sickness as well?"

There he stood in his pristine white shirt and tweed jacket. His balding head and round, thick-lensed glasses reminded me of an old professor. But his spirit was that of a warrior just humbled in service of our group.

"I'm alright, Dr. Malcom, thank you for asking. It was a bit rough at first, and then I got better, and then worse, but I'm definitely on the mend now!"

"Glad to hear it! Now, if you'll excuse me, I've got to tend to Isis."

I turned to Naomi, "Is there anything I can do to help?"

"You've done enough. Just get back to whatever you were doing, and I'll fetch you if we need you or if anything changes."

I realised then my big entrance and meeting would have to wait.

☥

My laundry was on, and I was back upstairs cleaning my room and bathroom. I could feel the air lighten. My sacred space felt clean and clear. Throughout the morning, I kept the bedroom door open, hoping that perhaps I would see the Doctor or Naomi come out, but to no avail. The door remained shut, and all was quiet. I decided to head downstairs and be very business-like, make myself productive, and calculate my earnings for the last few weeks.

☥

After another two hours and no sign of either Naomi or the Doctor, I began to get nervous, so I headed upstairs to take a listen as to what was going on. I heard voices on the other side of the door, so I knocked.

"Hello, everyone. I hope I'm not interrupting; I just wanted to see if anyone needed anything." Before I could get all the way in the door, Naomi rushed me out, with Dr. Malcom following closely behind.

"Isis needs her rest, Anna, Naomi whispered harshly, "What are you doing, knocking and disrupting her?"

"I'm sorry, I was getting worried. I hadn't heard anything in hours. I was just trying to help."

Dr. Malcom patted me on the back, "That was very kind of you to do, Anna. However, I'm all finished up. Naomi has a prescription for Isis that should help with the pain."

"Is she going to pull through, doctor?" I asked, dreading the answer.

Dr. Malcom looked at Naomi, who nodded. "Well," he started, "I am not sure. Her vitals are all over the place. Unfortunately, this is going to be a 'wait and see' sort of situation. Remember, Anna, Isis is an older person. Illnesses affect her a lot more. Just don't expect any miracles. I'm sorry."

"Thank you, Dr. Malcom. I'll call you if anything changes," said Naomi, leading him down the hall.

Once he was gone, Naomi turned to me and barked orders at me like I was her personal lackey, ordering, "Call Emilee and tell her to bring over the Thieves bottle, the big one. Tell her to get over here right away!"

I was still trying to process what Dr. Malcom had said and didn't understand what she meant. Naomi, what

Thieves? Does Emilee know?"

Naomi rolled her eyes, "Just go call Emilee and tell her to bring the Thieves. She will know what you mean. I'm running down to the chemist and will be back soon. Leave Isis be. She needs to rest." Naomi turned on her heel quickly and rushed out the door.

Not wanting to find out what Naomi would do if I didn't call Emilee, I set about doing that. Once off the phone, I lumbered into the kitchen, muttering under my breath.

Who did Naomi think she was ordering me around like that? And what in the world did she need a big bottle of Thieves for? Were they little totem dolls or something? I don't know why this isn't making sense this morning.

☥

About twenty minutes after Naomi left, the front door flew open, and Emilee, in a tight-fitting dress of scarlet red and heels, barreled in. Barely stopping to greet me, she dashed up the stairs to Isis's room and shut the door. It really was impressive how that woman could move so well in stiletto shoes. Naomi got back not long after Emilee arrived, and she, too, went upstairs immediately. I decided against going to check in on them lest I feel Naomi's wrath again.

Monday, 12 January 2009, 1:35 p.m.

"She should be fine now," I heard Emilee say.

"Are you sure? I'm so nervous," said Naomi.

I was in the hallway on my way to the office and could hear both Naomi and Emilee talking on the stairs.

"Yes, she just needs to rest, and you need to take charge of your temple. Our precious one was left most vulnerable last night."

"I know what to do. Thank you, Emilee."

Naomi went back into the bedroom, and Emilee came down the stairs. It dawned on me that this could be it for Isis. If she and I had the same sickness, but she had it worse, then she must have been going through the most terrible things. I rounded the corner to meet Emilee at the stairs.

"Emilee," my voice trembled so. Isis was my teacher mentor, and I began to feel a great fear moving through me.

"Anna, she is okay. She will be fine," Emilee assured me. She came towards me and hugged me, and that was when the smell hit me, and I began falling. It wasn't a fainting spell, but my body was going into a space I could not control.

"Naomi!" Emilee shouted up the stairs, and the next thing I remember was them both kneeling over me on the kitchen floor.

"Let's get you back up," Emilee said, gripping my arm and hoisting me up into a chair with Naomi's help.

"What happened to me?" I asked, still confused.

"What did you see?" asked Emilee.

"Not what I saw but what I smelt."

"Ah, the thieves. I was just applying it to Isis."

"I have smelt it before, but I don't know when." I felt myself drifting into a vision but tried to stave it off.

"Do not resist it," said Naomi, "we need to know what happened. It could help Isis."

I nodded, and they helped me up, led me to the living room, and laid me on the sofa. Closing my eyes, I allowed the vision to surface.

"I see Lucas and Isis in a small house with a thatched roof. They are speaking French, and it's around 1345 AD, but I understand them. Lucas mentions that a preacher who claims to be the last Templar Knight is speaking in the square that day and asks if Isis will go with him. Oh, they are brother and

sister! Isis agrees, and they go to the square.

"Now, we are all at the village square. There was a stage of sorts set up, but I think it was left there from an execution. I'm there on a balcony overlooking the square, but far away from Isis and Lucas. I look down and see that I am wearing a fine silk gown and a large pearl necklace. Isis and Lucas are far more plainly dressed and amongst the crowd. They must be peasants, and I am in the nobility for some reason. It doesn't matter; now, the preacher everyone has come to see gets on the platform and speaks.

"He says he has travelled throughout France and warns of a great evil coming. There is a darkness that has been unleashed on our lands. It will infect everyone and turn their souls as black as coal. The preacher warns that if the town does not atone for its sins, the darkness will be upon them, too. He offers his services to everyone, rich or poor, so that the whole town can be spared. A man in the crowd jeers at him. This starts a ripple effect, and everyone heckles the preacher. He responds to them, saying that the curse will fall upon them if they do not listen, and it will be their ruin.

"The people I am sitting with order their guards to seize the man, calling him a heretic. One of the women next to me comments that the noblemen have been on edge since the start of the war. They execute anyone they think threatens France. I ask her if that will happen, and she points back to the square in front of us. The guards have now reached the preacher, and they are forcefully dragging him to the centre of the platform. Another set of guards is bringing up a large pole and fixing it to the platform. They are tying the preacher to it and laying wood all around him.

"Suddenly, they light the pyre and the preacher is screaming. He is telling them that they are killing their only path to salvation. With his last dying breath, he curses us all

before letting out the most horrific scream. Isis buries her face in Lucas's chest, upset by the scene before them. Lucas comforts her and assures her that nothing will come of what was said. They decide to leave the man's burnt corpse in the town square for days to teach everyone a lesson.

"Now, I am being rushed forward. It is a few months later, and I see Isis in her kitchen with another woman. The woman turns around, and I see that she is Emilee. They speak of a black death sweeping throughout their village and leaving very few people untouched. Isis and Emilee have been trying to find the right combination of healing herbs to save the townspeople but haven't had any luck yet.

"I'm watching Isis and Emilee making another potion that they think will work. Oh, that is the smell! It comes from an ancient remedy. I smell vinegar, wormwood, rosemary, sage, clove, marjoram, campanula, angelic, meadowsweet, and camphor. They try it on one sick woman, and it seems to help. So they now make it in large batches outside, using pendulums to check when it is ready. Chanting over the brew, they try their best to revive the sick. I watch them from another balcony, out of the way of the infected and the dead. My family is of noble blood, and we have managed to keep from getting sick.

"It is now a few years later, and the plague has ravaged the community. The streets are mostly empty, and Isis looks as if she has aged thirty years in just five. She is the only one left tending to the sick. Emilee is no longer with her.

"A man on a horse comes riding up to her and gives her a note. She reads it to herself and finds it is from one of Lucas's friends. It tells that he has perished at the Battle of Mello in northern France, and the Jacquerie peasant uprising has been defeated. Isis wails at the news, devastated that her best friend and family have been taken from her.

"Troops from the nobles start pouring into her village, dragging anyone associated with the revolt out of their homes. They also gather all of the healers. Isis is both, and the nobles see her as the leader of the other healer women. All of the others will be executed by hanging later in the week. However, Isis will be killed in a worse way."

"I have to stop," I yelped, not wanting to see Isis perish in 1350's France.

Naomi looked absolutely crestfallen but managed to ask, "Please, Anna, we need to know if she gets out alright."

"No, I just saw it. You don't need to see it."

"Then you need to tell us what happened."

"It doesn't end well. That is all you need to know."

Naomi kept pushing me, "How does it end, Anna?"

I sighed, upset that Naomi kept asking, and at what I had seen, "Fine. You want to know? They forced her to drink the blood of an infected person and left her tied up outside for days until she died of the black plague and exposure. It was awful! Absolutely—" I cut myself off with a sob. What I had seen was horrible, but it was made more horrible by the fact that what I had seen had meant that Isis in our time wasn't going to get better, and the realisation of that was too much for me to take.

CHAPTER 8

Monday, 19 January 2009, 7:43 p.m.

Then came a day that I would remember forever. Having spent much of the week preoccupied with clients and Egypt trip planning, I finally had a free moment tonight. Isis had been tended to all week by Naomi and Emilee in an attempt to heal her, but as far as I knew, nothing was working. She was stable and able to visit with small groups of people for a short time, but I knew this wouldn't last. The other ladies had hope, though, and the last thing I wanted to do was dash it. In between my spare moments, I attempted to visit with Isis. I still hadn't been able to properly apologise to her and wanted to do so before it was too late. Unfortunately, I didn't get the chance because Naomi would always stop me. She would claim that I had come at a bad time and to try later.

I had pushed it out of my mind for the evening, though. As a bit of a comfort for myself after the horrible visions I had seen, I had purchased a few items that I wanted to have for the Egypt trip and was taking some time for myself to try them on. There was a beautiful white linen tunic with white embroidered flowers on it that I was planning on wearing for our temple visits. It matched the silver ankh with inlaid blue lapis that Isis had insisted I wear. The whole ensemble was something to behold, and it inspired me to practice a few of the rituals I would be performing at the temples in a few months in front of the mirror. It was fun to imagine what was going to happen.

Suddenly, I was roused from my fantasy by a loud thud coming from downstairs and the ensuing commotion. I ran down the stairs as fast as I could, sensing that something was very wrong. When I got there, Naomi and Emilee were carrying an unconscious Isis into the front living room. Naomi looked up at me with unshed tears in her eyes. That could only mean one thing: it was time. So, I ran to call Lucinda and the others to the Sanctuary.

Lucinda picked up on the first ring. "I'm on my way, we all are," she said and hung up the phone. Turning my attention back to the living room, I saw that Isis was in her chair, and she could hardly breathe.

When she saw me, she gasped, "Anna, you knew it was time, and you are ready." I looked at her, puzzled. It wasn't until I got a glimpse of myself in the mirror a moment later and saw the looks on Naomi and Emilee's faces that I knew. I was still in my white tunic and wearing the ankh, ready indeed to lead a sacred ritual and last rites for our dear leader. So, I knelt in front of her and took her hand, cold as ice. I smiled at her, and without a word, we both acknowledged what was about to happen. Just then, Lucinda, Alice, and Laura burst through the door, with Lucas and Dr. Malcom following closely behind. The two men immediately went to Isis's side and gently hoisted her, taking her upstairs to the bedroom with Lucinda supervising. Once they were gone, I let out a sob that I hadn't realised I had been holding in.

"*Ma amour,* I am sorry. Naomi and I did all we could," Emilee said, placing her arms around me.

"I know," I sniffled, wiping my eyes, "It is her time."

Naomi huffed, "Well, it shouldn't be!" I saw just how much Naomi had been holding in at that moment. As soon as she had spoken, she crumpled to the floor, heaving and shaking. Laura went over to comfort her, and she waved her off. She continued on like this for a few minutes, wailing and rocking back and forth with her legs to her chest. It was hard to watch her in such a state, absolutely beside herself.

Then, Naomi got really quiet and looked over to Emilee, saying, "It isn't her time. We just need to go back to the Guesthouse and look through your supply for the right elixir. We just weren't using the right one, that's all!" She got up quickly and tried to bring Emilee with her to the door, determined. "C'mon," she continued, "If we hurry, we can get there and back in minutes!" Naomi again tried to get Emilee to come with her, but after the second try, she gave up and went to the doorway.

On the other side, Lucinda appeared, holding up her hands to stop Naomi from leaving. "I'm so sorry, dear," she said, "but it is her time."

"No, I don't accept that," Naomi countered, "Where is Dr. Malcom?"

"He is packing up his things. Naomi, he isn't going to tell you anything different!"

Naomi ran out of the living room just as Dr. Malcom rounded the corner with Lucas.

"Please, Dr. Malcom," she begged, "Tell me Isis is going to be alright?"

Dr. Malcom shook his head and sighed, lightly touching Naomi's shoulder, "I am sorry, Naomi. I've done all I can. Her heart is very weak, and the illness really did a number on her. I've given Lucas some pain medication for when the pain becomes too much for her."

"When what becomes too much? So, take her to a hospital! You are a doctor. You are supposed to save people, not help them pass on!" Naomi pushed Dr. Malcom away from her.

Lucas stepped in and explained, "Naomi, there is

nothing he can do. Moving her to a hospital would only prolong the inevitable. Besides, it is Isis's wish that she stays here and passes on in the Sanctuary. We need to respect her wishes. Naomi, I know this is hard to accept, but you must stay focused and prepare yourself."

Naomi finally seemed to hear what everyone was saying and nodded, "Okay. Thank you, Dr. Malcom. I apologise for getting so rude with you."

"Not to worry, my dear," he responded, "Now, go and be with her. I will keep you all in my thoughts." With that, Dr. Malcom left, leaving the rest of us to figure out what to do next.

Monday, 19 January 2009, 10:01 p.m.

After Dr. Malcom had left, we decided we would all take turns visiting with Isis. Alice and Laura had been first since Lucinda and I had to call and cancel all of the appointments set up for that week at the Sanctuary, and Emilee had to do the same with the guesthouse. It surprised me how calm and professional I sounded making the calls. Everyone else around me was barely holding it together. I supposed that it had something to do with me figuring out what was happening before everyone else.

When the last calls had been made, I made my way into the kitchen, where Emilee was preparing a late supper. She tended to cook when she was upset and knew that a little food was comforting for the soul. Alice and Laura were sitting at the table, talking in hushed tones. Lucinda wasn't with them, so I assumed she was upstairs visiting with Isis. As always, Alice remained stoic, but Laura was still quite shaken. Her cheeks were stained with tears, and her bright blue eyes were wet with more. Despite this, she looked beautiful, as she always did. I heard her say to Alice, "Our lady really is ready to depart. I can't believe it." Then she let out a sob and shuddered. Alice took her into a big hug and held her tight.

Just then, she looked up and caught me watching her. I tried to give Laura the most casual smile I could, but it came out as more of a grimace. She gave me a small grin and nodded to the table, indicating that I should join them. Emilee was done cooking and placing a large pot of pasta covered in marinara and melted cheese on the table.

"I made what you all call 'spag bol.' I figured it would be good for a night like this," Emilee said.

Alice replied, "Thank you, Emilee. I appreciate it. I haven't had much to eat all day, and this looks delicious." She immediately grabbed a plate and silverware, helping herself to a large portion of the pasta.

"Agreed," said Laura, "Thank you!" She did the same and served herself.

Emilee smiled at them and then looked over at me, "Come on, Anna, you must eat."

"I'm not very hungry," I replied.

"You should still eat; you will need it for strength. There is much to prepare for."

I hated this. We were all sitting around waiting for our dear friend to die and eating dinner like it was no big deal. It was all too much for me. I couldn't just keep sitting around waiting. So, I got up and made my way to the door.

"Where are you going?" asked Emilee.

"To my room," I responded, "This is all just a bit much for me right now. I'm sorry."

"Do not be, but please take a cup of tea and some biscuits in case you do get hungry. When it is your turn to see Isis, someone will come and find you."

I nodded, running back to grab the tea and biscuits before dashing out the back and into the garden, hoping the misdirect would give me some much-needed peace.

"You know, you are going to catch a cold or worse, not wearing a coat out here!"

I turned to see where the voice was coming from and found myself in the garden. There, in front of me, was Isis, wearing a white nightgown with gold trim. Her hair was perfectly set in an updo, her cheeks were flush, and her eyes bright. This wasn't the look of a dying woman. She, noticing me staring, smiled at me, laughing heartily.

I shook my head and responded, "But I'm not cold."

"Well, of course not now! You will be, though. Oh well, you'll be fine soon enough." She shrugged and turned back towards the door.

Something dawned on me, "Hey, wait a minute! Why are you out of bed? How are you out of bed? You looked so frail earlier."

Isis turned around and smiled at me, "Well, that was earlier, this is now. Come along, Anna. We don't have much time, and there is much to discuss." She ushered me inside and took me to her office. The house was remarkably quiet, and I didn't hear any commotion in the kitchen or footsteps upstairs. I wondered where everyone was.

"They will join us later," Isis said, reading my mind.

We walked into the office, and I could feel the angels and spirits around us, there to bless our meeting. They were the people of the sun and stars, higher celestial beings who had come to pay their respects to a person who had been a prominent spiritual leader for generations. Isis immediately went over to the desk where her red box was sitting on top and beckoned me over.

"You know, after all of this time, I am still a little afraid

of what comes next. I've felt very alone because of it."

I turned to her, "You aren't alone. I'm here, always."

"Thank you, Anna. Please promise you will stay until the end?"

"Of course, I promise. Whatever are we going to do without you?"

"You will do what you were meant to do: unite your sisters and lead them into a new age of connected and prosperous temples."

"I know. I just feel like there is still so much for me to learn, so much you haven't told me."

"Unfortunately, I won't be able to explain everything. Not now, at least. Anna, you have a future and can work beyond this place and my side. You will persevere. Now," Isis said, gesturing to the red box, "I want you to take this with you. Don't worry, nothing bad will happen. I give you permission to open it."

I nodded and paused, but quickly realised she wanted me to open the box right then. "Oh, you want me to open it right now!"

She chuckled, "Yes, and you are welcome to open it and look inside it as much as you need to after I'm gone. It isn't your red box, but it will still provide you with some of the answers you are looking for. The history of the outgoing High Priestess for the benefit of the new one!"

I opened the box, and on top was a large envelope bound by string. Isis gave me an encouraging smile, so I took it out. Once I had the string undone, I took out the packet of papers that were contained within it. It was Isis's will.

"You'll find something of interest in the section on property and business," she said. "It is your responsibility to keep the temple going and help them all remember. Now, I've left something else for you in there as well."

Turning back to the box, I saw a set of notecards with photographs of temples attached. "What are these?" I asked.

"The others will help you prepare, but you alone must enact the rituals that come to you."

"You are speaking as if we are still going on the trip."

"You all are still going on the trip. My death should not and must not prevent that. Everything you need to lead the trip is right in front of you."

"But what if I have a question? What if I need to talk to you?"

"Then all you need to do is call on me. You are powerful enough to summon me in a vision. Neither I nor anyone else is going to let you fail. The work of the scarabs and scrolls must be completed. Look there, pick up that packet of photographs labelled 'Paris.' That woman there with me is the Contessa. She will be a good place to start for locating the last remaining scarabs and scrolls, she may know more details of your soul path."

I looked at her, hopeful, "That would be wonderful! I know so little about my own past lives and true purpose. I've seen more of Naomi's than mine!" I chuckled, "And so much still seems like a mystery."

Isis pointed to the box, "That's why you have my box. You'll be able to learn more about me through this. Now, come. I've got one last thing to show you."

She led me out of the office and around the corner to a small antechamber just outside the living room. I thought it was storage and hadn't ever bothered to go in there. However, what was inside was anything but. The walls were covered in dark obsidian, and the floor in marble. The room was empty except for a few gold torch stands and a large mass of something in the centre. As we walked farther into the room, the torches lit themselves and revealed the mass was a pink translucent stone—what I could only assume was a ritualistic casket. I looked at Isis, understanding.

"I'm not going to see you in my next earthly life, am I?"

Isis looked around the room and nodded resolutely, "No, I think I'm done with this world for a while. Now that you're here and set to carry on for me, there isn't any reason for me to come back."

"So, this is it? I'll never see you again."

"I didn't say that. You just won't see me in quite the same form again. But I promise we will meet again, and it will be glorious and more wonderful than you can imagine!"

Suddenly, I felt a tugging and looked at Isis, confused, "Isis, what's happening?"

She came up to me and held me tight, explaining, "It is almost time. I just need you to hold on a little bit longer."

"I'll try, I'm here."

"Thank you. Promise me one more thing, Anna?"

"Anything."

"Write about this. I know your goals have shifted since coming here, but that doesn't mean you can't still become the author you've always wanted to be! Tell our stories and spread them far and wide to all those who will read and listen. Promise to write about me as the Isis you knew, just as I was!"

I laughed, "Is that all? Of course, I can. I love you, Isis. I truly thank you for everything."

"Oh, you are most welcome, my dear Anna. I am so glad you found us. I love you, too. Now, I think it is time you get back; I will see you again soon, and at the Well of Souls, our work will be completed."

"Back? I haven't gone anywhere."

Isis gave me a knowing smile, "Then why do you keep feeling a tugging sensation?"

I looked at her with my mouth gaping, not knowing what

to say.

"It's okay, go on back." She coaxed me out the door and in the direction of the garden.

I turned around to look at Isis, "Wait, I never got a chance to say I'm sorry for—"

The door closed abruptly, and the last thing I saw was Isis smiling.

☥

I opened my eyes, finding myself on the bench out in the garden I had been sitting on earlier. Everything was the same, except I was clutching Isis's red box. Wasting no time, I ran back into the Sanctuary and went into the antechamber to find Isis, but it was empty, nothing more than a small dusty room with some old furniture. Confused, I turned around and ran towards the kitchen, hearing voices in it. I saw Alice, Lucinda, Emilee, and Laura all sitting around the table, sipping tea and conversing. Right as I was about to ask what was going on, I heard a scream from upstairs. We all looked at each other and ran to the source of the noise.

It had come from Isis's room. When we arrived, we found Naomi knelt beside Isis's bed, sobbing into the covers. Lucas was patting her on the shoulder, tears silently streaming down his cheeks. Emilee burst into tears, and Laura let out a choked sob behind me. Lucinda's eyes filled with tears, and she covered her mouth. Alice stood still; all the colour had drained from her face. She leaned against the doorframe for support. I went to Lucas and Naomi, taking their hands and kneeling down beside Isis's bed to cry with them. I began to chant and say a prayer that I had never heard before. Naomi, Lucas, and I then stood up, and they began to chant along with me.

When we were finished, I closed the prayer, Lucinda lit some incense, and Laura opened the window. I quickly left after that, dashing to the safety of my bedroom to let out my grief. I held it together just long enough to close the door. A huge sob rose from my chest, and I felt a pain in my soul that I would never forget. Our dear leader, mentor, and protector was gone.

Wednesday, 28 January 2009, 7:30 a.m.

"Come on, Anna, it's time." I heard Naomi say from my doorway.

I sighed, taking one last look at myself in the mirror. The white ceremonial robe I was wearing felt strange to wear to the ceremony, especially because everyone else was wearing colour. I turned and looked at Naomi. She had been a mess after Isis had died, but to her credit, she pulled herself together and looked absolutely stunning in her red silk robes.

She continued, "You look fine, come on. We have to start this at sunrise." Naomi turned and walked towards the stairs. I silently joined her, walking just behind her. As we descended, I could see the others looking at us. They were all very quiet, as one would expect on such a sombre occasion. However, when they noticed me, I could see a shift in their faces. It was as if they were looking at me with expectation in a way they never had. I supposed there was no mistaking it now; I was supposed to be their guide in this process.

As I got to the landing, they parted, allowing me to lead them to the sitting room. Isis was already there, the photo of her face smiling and radiant was in the centre of the room on a table next to a lit candle and white and yellow roses, as had been instructed. Naomi had pointed out that the ceremony was usually done differently, but I assured her that this was what was supposed to happen. She had wanted us to keep Isis there in her casket, but I knew in my heart that this would be difficult for the energy of Isis and may have resulted in her becoming earthbound to help us in grief. When I had explained this to everyone, they were all in unison that the undertakers should take charge of her physical body, and we should take care of the rest.

We all entered the room, single file, with Lucas bringing up the rear and closing the door behind him.

"Come," I said, "Let us gather and form a circle around our friend. It is time for us to send her soul on and to help her reach her destination safely."

Everyone grabbed each other's hands and formed a circle. I looked at each of them one by one. They bowed their heads and closed their eyes, letting themselves succumb to the process, and so I, too, closed my eyes.

I awoke standing in the sand, Naomi by my side. The others were there watching over us, but Naomi and I would be the only ones to guide Isis through the process. We began making our way towards the Great Sphinx, leaving gentle footprints in the sand as we went. Up ahead, I could see her majestic paws stretched out, beckoning us towards her. Right in between them stood an altar, and a woman with long blonde hair turned away from us. She was in ivory robes made of silk and wore a cobalt scarf that billowed out behind her like a cape. As we got near, she turned around and revealed herself to be a young Isis.

She smiled and held out her hands, looking first at me, "Ah, my dear Seshat," and then Naomi, "My dear Nephthys.

I am humbled by your divine presence. Thank you for coming today."

I looked at Naomi, whose appearance had changed. She wore a crimson floor-length gown that hugged her body tightly. It had an embroidered pattern of hawk feathers in gold thread. Atop her flowing raven hair was a headdress shaped like a tiered crown. Her gold and blue lapis necklace shone bright, and I could see my reflection in it. I had changed, too. Looking from her necklace to my own body, I could see I was wearing a similarly cut gown made of leopard, and affixed to my head was a gold crown with a long rod that fanned out into a seven-pointed star; the symbol from my dream was now so clear. We both bobbed our heads at each other and looked back at Isis. This was part of the ceremony, becoming proxies for the goddesses who could guide her on her journey. I would record the passage for the annals and Naomi, as Nephthys, would administer the funeral rites and give the proper lamentations. Isis's soul would only see us as the goddesses and not as who we really were. As was the custom, we played our parts.

"Will you come with me?" she asked. She held out her hands, and we walked towards her.

"Only to the seventh gate," we said together, in voices both our own and not, each grasping an outstretched hand.

She smiled, and I noticed her eyes shone golden. We all turned to the Sphinx, and holding our hands above our heads, began chanting in our sacred language. We called upon Lord Osiris to open the doorway and for Anubis to give us access to the sacred bridge and the boat of everlasting life. An opening at the base of the Sphinx opened with stairs leading down below it. We let go of Isis's hands and coaxed her forward gently.

With us close behind, Isis walked down the limestone steps for what seemed like forever. We finally reached a dark landing that lit up as soon as our feet touched the floor.

Torches lined a long corridor that stretched back as far as the eye could see. Everything was hazy, and I tried to focus and understand the path ahead. Coming into focus just a few feet ahead was an altar with a tall, dark figure atop it, wearing a dark red cloak and a hood obscuring its face. We were at the first gateway.

"Stay close," Isis whispered. I could hear the nerves in her voice.

"Approach," said the hooded figure, waiting for Isis to do so before continuing, "Identify yourself and your companions."

"I am Isis, and these are my guides, Seshat and Nephthys."

The hooded figure nodded, accepting her answer, and turned to Naomi and me. "And do you, Mistress of the House of Books, and you, Lady of the Temple Enclosure, vouch for this soul's identity and take responsibility for the journey ahead of her?"

"We do," Naomi and I said in unison.

"Very well," responded the hooded figure, "Isis, come to me and recite the celestial words that are never spoken."

Isis approached him and spoke in such a hushed tone that I couldn't hear what she was saying. I would have thought she wasn't saying anything at all, but I saw her lips moving. She finished then and stepped back. The hooded figure took a moment to consider her words before responding.

"You may pass," they said before moving to the side to allow us passage.

We bowed as we walked past and went to the next altar. Another hooded figure—the guardians of the gateways—stood waiting for us there.

"What do you bring, my lady, for us from the other world?" they asked.

Isis retrieved a pomegranate and a small loaf of bread from her robe and placed them on the altar. "I bring sustenance to nourish the soul," she said.

The hooded figure inspected the items and said, "You may pass."

We moved to the third gateway's altar; this time, it had an hourglass on it with no sand in it. The guardian approached and turned the hourglass over, silver flecks of sand magically appearing and falling to the bottom.

"How was your time spent?" they asked.

"My time was spent in service of the Temple of Isis. I have devoted all of my lifetimes to restoring the Temples of the gods and have not wavered."

"Is that true?" they asked us.

"Yes, we attest to it," we said again in unison.

The guardian turned to the hourglass, which had sped up and almost completely filled its bottom chamber up with silver sand, and then looked back at us, "If that is so, then you may pass," said the guardian.

With that, we were on our way to the fourth gateway's altar. This one held a dark pink rosebud in a glass jar. As Isis approached it, the rose bloomed, revealing hundreds of petals in various gradations of pink, far more than any earthly rose.

"In order to pass, you must show you had an open heart," the fourth guardian revealed. "Each petal represents a time when you allowed yourself to care for and share love with another soul." He turned to the rose, which now encompassed the entire jar, pointed at one lone dark red petal and looked at Isis: "I see that you have sacrificed a part of yourself for another and broken a law of ours to do so. Do you deny this?"

This made me nervous. I didn't know that Isis had broken a sacred law. If this guardian didn't let her pass, she would be stuck, and us with her for allowing her to lie. Isis didn't seem deterred, though. She stepped forward and again, bent in close to the guardian and whispered something to them that we could not hear. The guardian then touched the jar, causing the red petal to fall.

"You may pass," they said.

At the fifth gateway, there was a simple wooden box on the altar. The guardian came from behind it and said, "In order to continue, you must prove your oracle sight is more than just mere intuition. What is contained within this box?"

Isis closed her eyes and hummed a little to herself. Then she opened her eyes and said, "It contains a key."

The guardian questioned her, "A key, you say? Such a small item for such a large box, are you sure?"

"Yes, I am."

"Describe it to me then."

"It is a gold key about the size of my index finger with jade stones inlaid along its shaft. The actual key has a small ruby on it that acts as part of the mechanism for opening the lock. It is the key to the final gateway, the key to the afterlife."

"Very good," said the guardian, "You may collect your key and pass to the next gateway."

She gently lifted the key out of the box, and we moved on to the sixth gateway. At this altar, the price for passage was steeper.

"You have made it far, Isis. You have passed the tests of the heart and the mind, but you cannot go further until you pass one more test. Perform this test, and you shall pass," said the sixth guardian, handing Isis a small dagger and a piece of white silk.

Isis took the items and placed the white cloth on the altar. She then raised the dagger with her right hand above her head and brought it down to her left palm, slicing it open so that blood would fall out. She let a few drops of blood fall onto the white cloth. As soon as her blood touched the cloth, it began to glow and radiate with its own energy. The guardian took the cloth and turned it over on the altar, allowing it to soak the blood from the cloth. They removed the cloth from the altar and revealed it to be completely free of any stains.

"Your blood is pure, and your offering of self will be with us. You may pass," they said.

As we reached the seventh gate, I saw no hooded guardian but a woman with golden wings stretched out behind her. "My dear sister," she said, "you have been away from us for a long time. We welcome you home with open arms!"

Isis ran to the woman and embraced her, saying, "Hello, Ma'at, it is so wonderful to see you. Here, I have the key." Isis reached into her pocket and pulled out the key.

"Wonderful. You have proven you are ready. Now, I must ask your companions one final time if this is to pass. Seshat, by proxy of Anna, and Nephthys, by proxy of Naomi, do you confirm that our dear sister here is Isis?"

"We do," we said.

"Do you advocate for her entrance into the afterlife?"

"We do."

"Will you help your sister by observing the mourning period correctly and recording her story for subsequent generations?"

"We will."

"Then, dear Isis, there is nothing left to settle. Your memory will be cared for by your companions, and your soul will be cared for by us. It is time for them to go and for you to come with me."

Isis started to walk away from us with Ma'at before turning around to see us one last time. She smiled, recognising who we were, saying, "I love you and will see you again, my dear ladies."

Thursday, 29 January 2009

The ceremony had lasted from sun-up to sundown, and when we had come out of it, we were all exhausted.

From there, the earthly protocols could take over, and we would simply become a group of friends and mourners at a graveside. It seemed Isis had no surviving family.

The following day, we gathered for a simple burial ceremony, and many from the town came to visit and pay respects.

I watched as three women gathered whom I had not seen before and were whispering. I had a strange feeling about them.

"Who are they?" I whispered to Alice.

"Not sure, Anna, but I think I've seen them before."

My mind wandered.

"Past lives, I think, but something more."

I felt a great mistrust going through me, and I looked around the churchyard. My whole body had a psychic chill, as I called it. I was sure I saw Lesley, but her hair was bright red. Same face, wearing a black coat and a wide-brimmed hat. She disappeared behind the church, and as I was in the front of the group, I was unable to run over and check.

My imagination was running overtime, and I returned to my senses. I looked at our small group as we stood together, barely keeping it together. We went through the motions even though we knew in our hearts that Isis was far, far away, flying through the heavens and on a far greater mission.

☥

After the precious day we'd had, we welcomed the simple instructions of the day-to-day, and I postponed all sessions and healing circles.

Everyone agreed it was time to rest, and they planned a large feast to honour Isis after the Will was read. It felt as if we were having a reset break, and each of us sent texts of simple words. I began to think about the future.

It was decided first that there would be a formal Will reading in mid-February with an informal meeting of our group about how we were to proceed with the Sanctuary and the various streams of Isis's spiritual businesses. Then, we would host a celebration of her life. There was, of course, the elephant in the room of who would be in charge. I wondered if we would have a High Priestess crowning ceremony.

What should I wear, and what would I say? My mind was turning loops as I looked online for my perfect outfit.

Also, I wondered if I should open a formal business in my own name like Naomi had. I still had some savings left over. I was in my own world, extending the diary further and further, with "no sessions" marked in large red ink on the business diary. Thus, the Sanctuary became more of a social place for us all to meet.

Wednesday, 11 February 2009

Today was the day we had all been awaiting: the reading of the Will at the Sanctuary. The meeting was set for 2 p.m., and we decided that the kitchen table would be the best place to host everyone.

Lucinda and I laid the table with water glasses and put out cups for tea, and Emilee arrived early with tins of her freshly baked cheese scones and shortbread biscuits. Plenty for us all. We had a celebration dinner planned that evening.

The solicitor who introduced himself as Mr. Haven arrived just before 2 p.m. with his assistant, who introduced herself as Sheila. They seated themselves at the top of the table with a box of files and laid them on the table.

Alice arrived with Laura, followed by Naomi, Emilee, and Lucinda. Lucas came and was followed by the three women I had seen at the funeral. They seated themselves near the solicitor and made conversation with Sheila. They accepted tea but were otherwise silent.

At 2 p.m. sharp, Mr. Haven asked all to sit and read out our names. He referenced the three women in a very formal way. Miss Lever, Miss Thomas, and Miss Blackwell. These ladies seemed too old to be referred to as Miss, and I had the thought that they may be school friends of Isis. They looked the same age.

He then opened up a large file of papers and began to read.

I, Isis Clarissa Johnson, testify this is my living will and testament.

My mind began to drift, and I felt this sick, heavy feeling come over me. I missed what he said next.

To my dear friend and brother Lucas, I leave the mahogany box that contains gifts to all of my dear sisters.

Each gift is named, wrapped, and sealed, and the box is not to be opened until one month before the next trip to Egypt. The gifts and Egypt envelopes are to be given at an appropriate time of his choice.

To Naomi and Anna, I leave my Egypt sacred journey business. They are to continue the work with others. There is a bank account with 44,000 pounds towards the next trip and to settle all outstanding accounts and bills.

My books, sacred art, and crystals are to be shared between Laura, Emilee, and Alice in their Glastonbury homes. All my other personal possessions are to be either auctioned or given to charity.

My cottage will be held in the custody of Lucinda for her to act as a guardian of the Tor. The cottage deed is part of the sacred journey business.

The Sanctuary building and furniture will return to the custody of my silent partners and financiers, Lever, Thomas, and Blackwell. Their names are still on the deeds.

I saw the women look at each other and smile.

"What? I'm sorry?" Naomi interrupted the solicitor. "They own the Sanctuary?" and she pointed to the women.

Fear washed over me; these three strangers were going to take our home.

"Can we stay?" I lowered my tone in respect, hoping they would say, "Of course, we will take care of you and be a great spiritual community."

"No, I'm sorry. We have other plans," one of them spoke directly at me.

"How long do they have?" Emilee was her most diplomatic.

"Till the end of the week, when we take possession."

"But that's only four days. That's not long enough!"

"Well, you will have to make ready."

One of them looked at Lucinda. "You may take all of Isis's possessions, and we will take ownership of what is left. Most of the furniture in this house was paid for by us, so it is only right that it stays."

Lucinda nodded in shock.

"We will be in touch," they spoke directly to Sheila. "Can you take care of the keys and the handover?"

"Yes," the assistant nodded. "I'm hoping, if I may, to help?" She looked at me, and I nodded blankly.

The women then stood, and without even a goodbye, they left.

"They can't do this!" Naomi was in full rage.

"But why?" Alice looked at the solicitor.

"Ladies... and gentlemen, I'm sorry. I know nothing of the details, only the requests. Now, Lucas, here is the box. Ladies, here are the details of the journey business and cottage. You have until next Monday morning, the 16th of February, at 11 a.m. to retrieve all that you wish, and at 12 noon, the locks will be changed, and the property will officially change hands, and the Sanctuary will be closed."

He then left, and we all sat in silence. Sheila hurried out after him, letting us know she would be there Monday for the handover.

Emilee put the kettle on to boil, and Lucinda went into the back storage and brought out a bottle of brandy, placing it on the table.

I found myself still abuzz with energy and shock, so I poured myself a glass of wine and went out into the garden to the bench that I had sat on a few weeks ago, saying my farewell to Isis. It was an unseasonably warm night for February. Considering the monumental loss we had all just experienced, I suspected it was the angels and the other spirits around me doing me a small kindness. The sound of approaching footsteps roused me from my thoughts, and I turned to see Naomi, also carrying a glass of wine.

"It sure is mild out this evening, isn't it?" Naomi said as she stopped in front of me, "Mind if I join you?"

"No, not at all," I replied, moving to the left side of the bench to make room for her.

Naomi sat down and looked at me, "We did the work, Anna. When she asked, we were there, like we promised, always and forever."

"I know."

"Then why do I get the feeling that you aren't at peace

with this?"

"Are you at peace with your mentor and mother from another life leaving this world and now our home to be taken from us?" I asked.

"Peace? Well, no. Of course, I'm going to mourn her and miss her. I'm just barely holding it together right now. As soon as I get up into my room, I'll be bawling my eyes out like everyone else in there is right now."

"But aren't you concerned about what this means for our future as a sisterhood?"

"Sure, but my thoughts and opinions on the subject don't really matter."

"Why not?"

"Because I'm not Isis, and I'm not you. Whatever I think about the situation or however I think we should proceed doesn't factor in."

"What do you think about our situation, Naomi, and how we should proceed?"

Naomi shifted uncomfortably in her seat, "Anna, I don't think it would be helpful for me to say. Not when everyone is still so raw."

I furrowed my brow, "Since when do you care about sparing my feelings? Please, I want you to be honest with me."

Naomi looked away and said, "Okay, if that's what you want. I'm worried that Isis passed the mantle to you too soon. You seem very unsure of yourself a lot of the time and are quick to get frustrated and lash out. We need someone who is confident in their abilities to take charge and can stay calm under pressure. You haven't even been doing this for a year, and you are now expected to run the move of the temple and an Egypt trip when you have not even been before. With everything that is happening, I'm worried that any rookie mistakes could land us all in serious danger."

Her words stirred anger inside of me, and I responded, "You don't think I can do it! You think that you would be a better leader. Isis wouldn't have put me in charge if she didn't think I could handle it!"

Naomi put up her hands in peace, "Whoa, whoa, Anna, calm down. This is why I didn't want to say anything. More to the point, I trust—trusted—Isis, so I trust her judgment. She must know something that I don't about you. Therefore, any doubts I have about your abilities are moot. So, whether I think you are our best choice doesn't matter. If she did, then you must be."

"But to be clear," I asked in a biting tone, "you don't think that I should be in charge?"

"Anna..." Naomi trailed off, "Let's just forget this conversation. You are lost in your High Priestess ego, okay? It isn't productive, nor is it proper to be fighting so close to the end of that ceremony."

"Fine. I'll drop it, but then you need to tell me what really happened when the two of you were in Egypt. I think I have a right to know."

Naomi looked down at her glass and sighed, not meeting my eyes as she spoke, "I can't."

Naomi continued to evade eye contact. "I don't know. I can't remember what happened that night or why we were there in Siwa. But I don't know if I can't remember because I hit my head, or because Isis did something to me to make me forget, or whether it's something else entirely. Any way you cut it, I just can't remember, and before you even think about it, I will not be doing a regression with you, so don't try."

"Unlocking that memory could be the key to figuring out how to rid ourselves of the Priests of Unal and unite the temples, and you don't want to do it because, what, you're scared? You shouldn't be making this my problem. That's selfish."

Naomi stood up in a flash of anger, "Oh, you are one to talk, Anna. That note you sent Isis was pretty selfish. You know what your problem is? You only care about what's happening if it relates to you. You don't really care about me, or the other women, or Lucas, or Isis. You just want to avoid going back to that crap life you had working as some asshole's assistant! Thank God I had the better sense to delete your e-mail before Isis saw it. I only wish I had been around to shield Lucas from your wrath!" With that, she walked off in a huff, leaving me stunned and alone with my thoughts.

How dare she call me selfish! I was killing myself trying to help everyone. She's making things more difficult by refusing to show me what happened. Or maybe Naomi really can't remember. I can't believe she read the message and Isis didn't. Wait, that's a good thing. Isis never saw the horrible things I sent her! But Naomi did, and she hates me for it. What if she is right? Lucinda has accused me of being grand before, too. Maybe I am being selfish. Oh no, I am being absolutely rotten.

My own thoughts and Naomi's words had sunk in. I had gotten upset because she was merely voicing my own concerns. I jumped down her throat for being honest, like I asked, and then berated her for something that was not her fault. What a mess of things I had made. However, there wasn't much more I could do today, so I went back inside to my room and started to write, as had been Isis's last request. I may be technically homeless, but I was open again to the change. It had served me so far, and I prayed my forever home would not be far away.

CHAPTER 9

24 February 2009, 12:00 p.m.

The last month had been rough for our sisterhood. The day of the will reading, we had cancelled the banquet to have a simple meal to celebrate Isis's life, however most were so devastated that they couldn't fully participate. We all thought we could continue and that the Sanctuary Temple would keep us close to her. It was not to be, and once her sacred pieces had been removed, it was like a web had been broken. I took a few books, including the Tutankhamun one where the pages had been removed and the red box, and moved back to Emilee's.

Lucas took the scrolls, scarabs, and some of the older pieces from her collection, such as books on magic, for safekeeping.

Lucas and I went through every room for hidden walls and even under the floors and the attics. I was sure Isis had left more clues for me to find, but sadly, nothing was to be found. Lucas was kind enough to create a small room for me to do readings at his shop in the town, and I created the best space I could. It felt strange to be in the back room of his shop, as if I were hidden away. I also had to face the walk-in tourists who came for the type of reading as if I were a fortune teller at a fairground.

"So you're the shop psychic? Tell me about meself," I heard a man say as he sat down and threw a 5-pound note at me one day. He crossed his arms and stared at me. I could hear his friends laughing in the front shop. To them, we were a freak show and entertainment.

Normally, Lucas would have thrown them out, but he was out for the day, and his assistant Lydia had given me the booking. It was my first reading in the last few days. All my lovely temple priestesses were now visiting the women in the Sanctuary who had proclaimed themselves healers, and I heard they were busy with ceremony and teaching.

"Are you not listening? Tell me about me fortune and fame." His eyes were dark as he mocked me.

"Come on, Joe," one of his friends said as he pulled the curtain back. "She's wasting our drinking time."

The five pounds sat in the middle of the table. With it, I could buy lunch, I thought. It felt as if I had no money, yet suddenly, I became aware that this sensation was an overlay from a past life seeping into my present. Joe pushed back on the chair and reached for his money.

"Waste of space and waste of time," he said as he stood up.

I don't know why, but my inner priestess rose. "She knows you know," I said. "She sees your texts and has you watched."

He sat down and had gone quite pale. "Who's she?"

"Your wife. I don't blame her. Oh, and she's well gone by now, which is why you could not reach her this morning." His eyes grew wide.

"Joe..."

"Shut up," he snapped at his friends.

He stood up and pulled the curtain closed. He stood there just hovering, unsure whether to stay or go.

"Your father's here."

"Where?"

"In the corner from spirit world. He says he is sorry he

left you when he did and that you, young man, are making mistakes in your life. He knows you sold his pocket watch for drinking money."

"Have you got cameras?" he asked, looking around.

"Shall I continue?"

He nodded and came back to his seat with a nervous look.

"So your wife found the money you hid. She's taken your daughter, and by now, they are on the plane back to her parents in, mmmh... let me see, Europe, Spain... ah, yes. Madrid."

"Madrid," he muttered. His jaw literally dropped.

"You only have yourself to blame for this sad path you have chosen, and by the way, your mistress is also sleeping with one of your friends. She's looking for a 'sponsor' for her double life, but as of yet, she's not sure who to pick. Oh, and your blood pressure is seriously high, and you may be in hospital before the month is out. Sad and lonely with regret is your future path. Shall I continue? Or have you had your full five pounds' worth?"

I smiled and stood up. My energy must have been at full force as he seemed to slip from the chair. He was in shock and, I have to say, so was I.

"Now I think you need a strong drink. There is a pub down the street."

He nodded and went out to his friends, who were obviously shocked by his pale complexion.

"How was it?" one of them asked.

"She knows everything," was all he said, and they all turned to look at me.

"No, today's not a great day for you all," I shook my head.

Suddenly, we heard a crash, and we all ran to the door.

"My car!" one of them shouted. A large van had just

rammed the side while a police officer was writing a ticket for illegal parking.

The men ran out, and I had to hold back my emotions as this was a fast karmic message delivery even for me.

"Now, Lydia. What to do with these five pounds..."

"Magic, Anna. Let's do a money ritual!" I had forgotten the witch she was. For the first time in what felt like an age, I had woken to more of my psychic gifts. Perhaps I would not be so direct or cruel, and there was no doubt I needed to work on my craft. But the message was clear: It was time to get myself ready. No more backroom hiding for me.

After that, I made the decision that the others should take some time to themselves in order to heal and that we would all come together in a few weeks' time to plan our next moves. Mostly everyone was on board, except for Laura and Emilee, who looked a little forlorn when I suggested it. Those two were the gentle heart of our group and certainly needed to be around others when they experienced hardship. Frankly, at that time, I couldn't really do that for everyone else. I needed time alone. There was so much that I needed to catch up on, so much I needed to know about our dearly departed before I could go and lead the Egypt trip.

I had sent out an email to everyone to start the excitement for an Egypt trip in the fall, but no one had responded. Not even Naomi. I had tried to call her to set up our formal business, but she was distant and not interested. Her London work had expanded, and I had only heard her voice when she was in a business lounge at Heathrow awaiting a flight to New York. "Anna, it is just not my plan to do this Egypt business. I have to follow my strategy, and I'm about to launch a book and speak at some big events in Florida. You are on your own."

"Did you see the brochure?" I asked her.

"Yes, and it was a copy of one of Isis's old trips. Nothing

new for me."

So that was it. I was not up to the level of Isis, and she was not willing to help me. It was time to create a new plan.

☥

The last three days or so had been spent in my room at the Gables, going through every detail of the ceremonies and rituals that I wanted to perform. It was only just now that I had gotten through them and had moved on to the other contents of Isis's red box. I started sifting through the old photos, beginning with the ones from earlier in this past lifetime. They were mostly pictures from past Egypt trips. I smiled at the picture of a young Isis, similar to the one I had seen during her descent to the afterlife, and Lucinda with teased-out fire-red hair and large circular sunglasses that covered most of her face. Seeing these pictures made me remember, or really consider, that these women had all had full and complicated lives before I showed up, and I hadn't really made the effort to learn about them.

Naomi's words had hurt, but they weren't false. I knew that in order to be a better leader, I had to start looking beyond myself and my own growth in order for us to become whole. After all, we were still down a few members, one of which, much to my dismay, was Lesley. Sure, she had caused a lot of problems in our pasts, but she was still our sister, and we would have to reconcile with her eventually. As to another member to join our group, I was hoping that Isis's box would contain a clue.

So, I continued looking through the photographs, old ticket stubs, and other bric-à-brac that was housed in the tin. I came across a paper package with writing that read, "Paris Autumn/Winter Collection 1970." Intrigued, I carefully unwrapped the package, taking care to unfold the brown paper without ripping it. What I found was a collection of photographs of a fashion show. I'd always fancied myself an admirer of *haute couture.* The photographs did not disappoint.

The women in the photographs were impossibly chic, and their tall, lithe bodies were attached to legs that reached the sky. Each one had a look on their face that told you they didn't have a care in the world and that they were absolutely better than you. Some of them were dressed in impeccably tailored velvet smoking jackets and trousers with light-coloured silk undershirts and wearing floppy bow ties. Other women were dressed smartly in tight pants and thigh-high boots, in sleeveless black mini dresses, an obvious departure for the time. I was completely taken by the beautiful clothes, so much so that I almost missed a younger Isis in the last photograph.

It took a moment for me to figure out what I was looking at. It was Isis, that I was certain, with two other women. The model immediately next to her was in a dark velvet tuxedo; she had a big smile on her face and bright eyes. Moving my eyes to look at the model on the end, I had to do a double-take. The young model, who looked maybe sixteen or seventeen, was tall and statuesque, like the others, but she looked exactly like me. Quickly, I turned the photograph around to see if there was any writing, and sure enough, the back of the photograph said *Francine, Lottie Rousseau, and I after the show.*

I gasped and dropped the photograph. That woman who looked like me was my mother. Her nickname was Lottie, short for Charlotte, and her maiden name was Rousseau. I knew that she had had an interesting life before she met my father, but I didn't realise she was a model. She'd often talked about her days living in Paris and all of the fine things she had experienced, but this was not something she had shared.

Frankly, it wasn't something Isis had shared with me, either. That feeling of uncertainty and distrust was bubbling inside me again. *How could Isis not have told me this? Obviously, I am not close with my mother, but she could have said that she had met her! I would give Isis the benefit of the doubt and say that she just didn't make the connection, but Isis was way shrewder than that. Is my mother somehow connected to all of this? Who else knew about my mother's connection to Isis?*

With that, I was spiralling and had to go get answers. Lucinda was the closest person I could think to ask—I just hoped that she was in a sharing mood.

☥

I grabbed my coat and wandered up the road towards the small winding lane to the cottage. It was so silent as I unlocked the small gate and quietly walked the few steps to the cottage. It was built in the late sixties, a small one-bedroom with a kitchen and bathroom. Just enough for a personal retreat and very simple.

I knocked, but no one answered. I could hear classical music playing, and I knew Lucinda was home.

"Lucinda," I called out.

"In here," she called back.

I found Lucinda sitting on the bed, staring at the pillows. Being careful not to startle her, I knocked gently on the bedroom door. Lucinda quickly roused herself from her daydream and turned to locate the source of the noise.

"Oh," she said, at first looking apologetic but then shifting to a more exasperated tone when she saw it was me. "Anna. It's just you. What do you want?"

"Hey," I said, inching my way into the room cautiously. "Could I ask you a question? It won't take long, I promise."

Lucinda sighed, "Fine, but quickly. I have a few more

cleansing rituals to perform in here today, and I don't want to delay them for too much longer."

"No, yeah, of course. It's just that I was looking through Isis's red box, and I came across a very curious photograph, and I was wondering if you could tell me any more about it?"

"I suppose I can try. But I didn't meet Isis until about six or seven years ago. You would probably have more luck asking Alice if it's older than that."

"I'll ask Alice after this, but I know the two of you really shared a lot, so maybe she told you about this." I handed Lucinda the photograph.

She took a moment to look it over and then turned it over and read the writing on the back. "Oh, that's why she looks familiar," Lucinda said, nodding her head, "This is a picture of the Contessa."

"Yes, but that's not the one I'm asking about," I said a bit impatiently, "But did you see who is next to her on the right?"

Lucinda shrugged, "Someone named Lottie Rousseau? Is that name supposed to be significant?"

I sighed, slightly frustrated that Lucinda was being so obtuse, "Yes, Lucinda. That's the name of my mother. She is the woman in the picture. My mother, Charlotte 'Lottie' Rousseau, now Harris, is in a photograph with Isis in a Paris fashion show."

"There is no need to be terse, Anna. I didn't know that she was your mother."

"Did Isis? Did she ever tell you anything about her or why she was with her? Has this woman ever come to the Sanctuary?"

"Wow, okay, that was a lot of questions at once. Um... let's see... If Isis knew she was your mother, she never told me. Isis and I were close, and she did share a lot about her life with me, but I don't remember her saying anything specific about a Lottie Rousseau. She's told me a lot about the Contessa. That woman is as fearsome as she is fabulous. She was one of Isis's oldest friends.

She stopped from her thoughts and looked at me, "What, Anna?"

"Don't you think it's odd that Isis would keep this from me? That she knew my mother?"

"I don't know. It's entirely possible she didn't make the connection. After all, that photo was taken before your mother got married and had you, right? So, how could Isis know that you would be her daughter? More to the point, you don't know if Isis knew your mother well or if they had just met that day and never saw each other again. It's a strange coincidence, I'll give you that, but unfortunately, I can't help you with any of that because I just don't know. Now, if you are done asking questions, I really need to rest."

Even to Lucinda, it seemed, parts of Isis's life were a mystery. However, our conversation did give me an idea. I hadn't yet gone through that many photographs, and if my mother had been a significant part of Isis's life at that time, there would be more evidence of that. There could also be evidence of my mother's presence at the Sanctuary in the old ledgers and journals we had kept after the move. I knew better than to believe that it was a coincidence, like Lucinda had suggested. As I walked home, I had begun thinking. Who was this Contessa? If she was an old friend, then why had there been nothing from her at Isis's passing or funeral?

Back at the Gables, it was almost midnight when I had finally gotten through all of the photographs from the red box that could contain my mother in them, and any of the journals that coincided with a time my mother could have been travelling. I had found nothing. According to my research, the only recorded instance of my mother and Isis interacting was at that fashion show, and it seemed to be around 1970. That just didn't make sense to me. Everything I had been taught was that nothing in our lives was just happenstance, and yet, I was meant to believe that this was.

Sighing, I looked down at the scattered paperwork. Out loud, I said, "I wish you were around to explain this, Isis. I just want to know how I am connected to all of this beyond my role as the new High Priestess... that dream, I think, has sailed away. Your past was supposed to help me learn about mine, and all I've learned is that you met my mother."

A thought dawned on me just then. Isis had told me that she could be called upon, that I could summon her or channel her to get clarification on things happening around me. So, I went about grounding myself and prepared to call her up. I lit a candle and sat in a chair across it, breathing deeply, closing my eyes, and holding the ankh pendant in my hand to help me.

"Let me use my oracle sight to see beyond and call upon my mentor."

At first, nothing happened. I was just sitting there, but then I felt a rush and flash of light, so I opened my eyes.

I am in the office of the Sanctuary, and things are quiet and still. It feels like it did before when Isis came to me. I get up to look around, hoping to find my mentor. Out of the corner of my eye, I see a flash of white go by the door and hear a high-pitched laugh. So, I get up to go see what it is.

Out in the hallway, I don't see anything, so I peer into the kitchen, which has no sign of life in it. The flash of white goes by the kitchen door, and I go out to follow it in the direction it went. I run to the antechamber, thinking that is where it would go, but nothing is there. Then, I see a white blur moving up the stairs, so I follow. Once up the stairs, I hear the giggling again that seems to be coming from Isis's room, where she spent her last days. When I get in there, however, there is nothing: no furniture, pictures, or anything else to indicate a person lived there. The window is open, and I go to look out. Down in the garden, I see a figure sitting on the bench where I was last time. So, I bound out of the room, down the stairs, and out to the garden. The figure is still sitting on the bench, now joined by the ibis and the baboon.

"Isis?" I call, "Is that you?"

The figure doesn't respond. I can't see its face, but I know that it is a woman dressed in white with long, blonde hair. I call to her again, but again, she does not respond and makes no indication that she hears me. Perhaps I need to get closer. Thus, I come around to the other side of the bench to see the figure's face. The ibis squawks when I come around, which seems to rouse the woman from her thoughts. I can see her face, and it is indeed Isis, younger than I had ever seen her. She looked like she was maybe ten years old, a mere child.

She addresses the bird, "What is it, my friend? Is someone there?"

I walk right up in front of the young Isis and kneel down, trying to make eye contact, and say, "Hello, Isis! It's Anna. You said that I could call on you whenever I needed advice or help. Do you think you could help me out?"

The young Isis looks at me for the first time, her big blue eyes looking confused. She doesn't recognise me.

"Isis," I continue, "I'm Anna Harris. You passed the mantle of Isis on to me."

Isis tilts her head to the side, speaking for the first time, "You aren't the High Priestess of Isis; I am. Don't be silly."

"No, Isis, I am. You were the High Priestess. Please, don't you remember?"

"I am the High Priestess, not you, 'Anna-whatever-your-name-is,' and I don't like you lying about it!"

I am getting frustrated now, "No, Isis, you were. Please, you have to remember. I need you to tell me about my mother, Lottie Rousseau. You met her at the fashion show. Can you tell me about that, please?"

Isis is starting to get upset and is fidgeting in her seat, "You need to stop, I don't know you! I don't like this game anymore!"

"It isn't a game; it happened. I don't know why you are being so difficult!"

Just then, Isis gets up, yelling, "Stop it! Stop it! STOP IT!" and puts her hands to her ears to prevent her from hearing me.

I am about to protest when I feel a strong set of hands on my shoulders, firmly pulling me up and turning me around. It is Ma'at, looking extremely angry. The young Isis, the ibis, and the baboon scurried to her side, Isis hiding behind her cloak.

"What do you think you are doing?" she asked.

"I... I had a few questions to ask Isis. She said I could always call on her." I stuttered out.

"Does this child look like Isis to you?"

"Well, yes. I would assume a younger version?"

"Correct. She doesn't know who you are. Berating her will not suddenly make her available to help you."

"But she said—"

Ma'at cut me off, "Said what? That you could call on her? Did she say that you could pester in the weeks after her death? I don't know how you were able to break through, but you have no business being here."

"Isis has only just entered the afterlife, which can be a traumatic experience for a soul. She needs time to adjust and get reacquainted with everything. You coming in and disturbing that process is not good for her and could prevent

her from fully engaging with the afterlife. I don't care who you think you are or how important you think your reason is for disturbing Isis. You need to leave and not come back."

"What, like ever? Isis said that I could!" Now I am sounding like a child.

"She misspoke. You cannot call upon her during the mourning period. Normally, oracles can't even get through if they try. I will not let that happen again. If you try to come back before Isis is ready, you will be blocked and sent back into one of your more painful regressions as a punishment. Do not try this again and leave now! Do I make myself clear?"

"I... yes. Perfectly."

"Good. Come, my lady, let's leave from here," Ma'at said, turning to Isis and holding out her hand. Isis took it, and they turned to walk away. I could hear Isis asking who I was from a distance and Ma'at telling her to forget about it.

Just like that, I was back in my room, feeling dejected and betrayed. No one had told me about the waiting period. No one had been able to tell me anything. This was the final straw, and all of the emotions I had been feeling for the last week bubbled to the surface and exploded. Hot, angry tears fell from my eyes, and a loud scream erupted from my mouth. I ran to the bed and flung all of the papers on the floor. Picking up the red box, I looked at it before also tossing it to the ground. It hit the floor and bounced, opening and spilling its contents. Then, I grabbed a pillow and screamed into it, having enough presence of mind to know that I should try to keep from waking everyone else up.

It worked well enough, and after I had finished screaming, my throat was sore. I went into the kitchen to grab a glass of water and fix myself a snack. Not a moment later, Emilee was entering the kitchen. She was the last person I wanted to talk to.

Evidently, I was the first person she wanted to speak with, and she came right up to me in a huff and asked, "What is wrong with you? I heard such a noise and came past your room, and the door was open. I went in and found it a mess! Isis's box was on the ground, cast aside like nothing. Have you no respect for her? Thank goodness we have no guests."

"Look, Emilee, I am tired. I've had a long and very disappointing day. I really don't want to discuss this with you right now." I made a move to get up from the kitchen table and walk around her.

She moved into my path, stopping me, and said, "We don't always get what we want. Anna. I can see that you are upset, but desecrating Isis's most sacred possession is not going to make you feel better. It's only going to cause karmic problems for you down the line."

"Isis is the one causing me karmic problems. You know, I thought that when she got back from Egypt, she would explain everything to me. But she didn't, and then she died. Now, I'm finding out things that I definitely should have been told, and I can't even get answers because she's gone and apparently unavailable for a spiritual call right now, even though she said she would be there for me and help me!" As the last of my words left me, the unshed tears fell from my eyes.

Emilee's face softened slightly, but her tone was still stern. "That doesn't give you license to make a mess of her things." She paused and continued, now with a tone that matched her expression. "I can see now how hard it's been on you. I thought the worst was over. I thought that Isis had made a mistake in passing the mantle to you. That greatly upset me because I hated that I was questioning Isis. I won't lie to you and tell you that I am devoid of doubts and worries, as I am only human, but I acknowledge that you are trying your best with what you have. You just need to start going about it without getting so upset when it doesn't work out for you. Time for you to grow up, ma cherie."

I sighed, collecting myself some, "I know. I just feel like it's been one thing after another for the last couple of months that I haven't been able to get through. I'm fighting with one arm tied behind my back, Emilee, and I have no discernible way to untie it. It makes me wonder if Isis always intended that to be the case, that she didn't really want me to succeed. It just feels like she is setting me up to fail."

"Isis lived a long and very storied life, well, many lifetimes, I suppose. She had to do a lot of things to get us to where we are today that weren't always what we would think of as 'karmically sound,' which means she got good at keeping secrets. That is a hard habit to break, even at the end of one's life when there is nothing to lose. However, that doesn't mean that she was trying to hurt you in any way. Isis was a lot of things, but she was never a liar or the type of person to hurt those in her sisterhood. You have the right to be upset and even a little angry, but you can't let it consume you and turn into doubt and hate. So, for the sake of the sisterhood and my sake, please refrain from desecrating Isis's things and speaking ill of her to others."

I simply nodded my head in agreement, too tired to protest any longer. Emilee shook her head in acknowledgment and got out of my way. Immediately, I ran out of there and into my room, letting myself break down and cry. The rest of the night and early into the morning was spent writing, finding myself unable to sleep or do anything else.

Monday, 9 March 2009, 8:30 a.m.

When I arose, it felt like the dark cloud surrounding me had lifted for the first time since Isis's death. I looked at my phone and saw a message from Lucas: *The Benson sisters are booked with you tomorrow. They have a retreat group coming next week, and they wish you to lead the rituals.*

The Benson ladies were very wealthy and lived in Bath. They had been monthly regulars of Isis, and now they wanted me. Perhaps the gods were turning in my favour.

I felt like I had a purpose again. The last few weeks had been spent wandering around aimlessly, reading and researching about various things in Isis's red box that had never really panned out. The writing I had done was disjointed and wasn't coming together in a cohesive story the way I had wanted. Going back to a normal schedule, where my day would be filled with different people with different stories, would keep my mind from wandering to Isis's and my own.

It seemed everyone else shared my feeling of levity. Emilee and Lucinda were excitedly running about the kitchen, getting everything ready, as many of the retreats were returning to us to be held at the Gables. We all weren't really speaking much to each other still, but we could put aside our grievances and quarrels for the sake of our clients. I think getting the chance to help other oracles and priestesses was going to be the best way for us to all reconnect after Isis's death and find a new path forward. Speaking of new paths forward, I had hoped to connect with Naomi now that things had settled, but her schedule prevented me from doing so. I didn't know if she was so busy because she wanted to avoid me or if throwing herself into her work so intensely was her way of dealing with Isis's death. Either way, I would most likely have to wait a few more weeks to see her. At least I had my work to distract me now, and she would have time for me then, I hoped.

☥

That notion that I may be working full speed in the coming week had led me to announce to the rest of the house that I was taking the day off. Lucinda had asked me what I was doing instead, and I told her that I was going to spend the day as a Glastonbury tourist, visiting my favourite shops and cafés while writing in my journal.

So, before she or Lucinda could ask any questions, I ran out the door. As I headed down towards the main street, I heard a voice in my head, Call Lucas, have a reading. I had been embarrassed to contact Lucas after the weird reading with the men. The whole situation had been wretched, and I had asked Lydia to tell Lucas I would be taking readings via phone and did not need my small office. I hadn't even told him myself, which was very sad.

I sat on a bench at the crossroads. Now, calm and centred, I was ready to call his shop and see if he had time for a walk-in today. Normally, I would have rather spoken to Lucas rather than his assistant, but I wanted to surprise him.

Lydia picked up the phone on the second ring, greeting me, and then asking, "And how can I help you today?"

I was a little taken aback by the nice and helpful tone in her voice; she was often indifferent and witch-like.

"Hi, yes, I'm visiting town for the day, and I was wondering if the great Lucas had any available time to do a reading for me?"

"Hold on, let me check," she said, coming back to the phone just a minute later, "Yes, it looks like we have some time available this afternoon. Is there a particular time you were looking to do this?"

"Um, well, sooner rather than later would be great!"

"Okay, well, if you are nearby, we can get you in at 10 a.m. That's in about twenty minutes, so I'm not sure if—"

I cut her off, "That would be perfect!"

"Oh, okay, then I will put you down, Anna."

"But how did you know it was me?" She had improved her psychic gifts.

"Your number shows up on the phone," was her response.

Oh, silly me. "Thank you! Bye!"

We both hung up the phone then. I needed to see Lucas. It was all in service of doing something good, after all. Checking the clock, I knew I still had about ten minutes before I had to leave, so I reviewed some questions I had for the reading that I had been working on in my journal. Hopefully, Lucas would be my hero to help give me direction at this point in my life.

I had originally wanted to ask about my book, my work, the Egypt trip, and my love life, in that order, since those had been the things weighing on me the most as of late. However, once I thought about it, I knew that asking about all of these things would be too much, so I narrowed it down to Egypt and, surprisingly, my love life.

With that, I headed out to Lucas's small gothic shop down a side street. However, it wasn't there. It was gone. In its place was a store that looked similar in layout and content, but everything was painted white and accented with gold, and it had a white sign with gold on the front door. I would have thought Lucas had moved had it not been for the gilt letters spelling out his name on the window.

Stepping inside was like stepping into a parallel world. Everything was the same as it had been the last time I was there, but now the shelves and the walls were painted white, and the floors were made of pale wood planking. The more macabre items had been replaced with their spiritual opposite, and the glass bottles of dark potions had been replaced with ones in varying shades of light rose and amber. What was most surprising of all was the assistant, Lydia, at the counter. I knew that it was the same goth princess of the night that had been there before because of her eyes and face shape, but everything else was different. Her long black hair was now a silver grey, platinum, and her gown was pure white with gold edges. Her manicure, which had been striking with sharp red points, was neat and a delicate pink.

She looked up at me and smiled, "Anna, we missed you and have been waiting for you to drop in. Do you like our makeover we changed last week?"

Then, in what was the most shocking thing of all, she came around the counter and right up to me to give me a hug. I felt like I was in a fairytale.

The assistant pulled away from the hug and said, "Well, now, I will go and get Lucas. Stay here. I will only be a moment."

"Okay," I said, not knowing how else to respond to this uncharacteristically warm

reception. She smiled at me and went off through the back curtain, also now made of white satin.

There I stood in my ripped jeans and jumper, and I felt I was in a temple from another time. Pristine and perfectly staged to be sacred, and here I was, looking like I'd just fallen out of bed to meet angels in heaven. However, I didn't have much time to ruminate on this as Lucas came bursting out of the back.

"Anna!" Lucas called, greeting me with a smile. Lucas had a way to sing my name that pushed all these thoughts from my head. He had a way to make you feel special, and no matter how you looked or felt, nothing could make you feel "less than" when you were around him. It made me emotional. I didn't deserve his kindness.

"Oh, Anna, why do you look so upset?" he asked.

"Because," I explained, my voice thick with emotion, "I'm sorry for bothering you now... I'm ashamed. I left with no notice from doing the readings, and I didn't even contact you. It looks like you are doing really well, and I don't want to make you upset and ruin all of that because I know I tend to do that!"

Lucas stood there in his full orange robe with three sets of prayer beads, looking radiant and healthy, not seeming to be upset at all. He patiently waited for me to finish and closed the distance between the two of us, wrapping me up in a big hug.

"As you can see, this place—myself and Lydia included—has been going through a metamorphosis of sorts. Isis's death gave me the push I needed to leave the past life and goth persona behind and become a being devoted to the light.

"Lydia told me about that reading with those men while I was away, and I told her to close the shop. I came up with a whole new vision for myself. All of those times I wanted to call you, I was either busy renovating the shop or deep in meditation to facilitate my transformation. I didn't want to create a vision with you working there, and then I felt guilty for excluding you."

I laughed, half-joking, "No, why would I ever think that? But I'm really relieved that we're okay. Although I'm not sure you should have accepted my apology so quickly, considering what I said."

"Nonsense, Anna. You have more than suffered, promised a path that was taken back."

It suddenly dawned on me that the High Priestess dream was gone.

Lucas was still talking. "You know, Anna, we are all human. Well, some of us more than others, but you know!

Now, tell me, what do you think? Is this not also so fabulous?"

"Oh, it is! I must say, this whole devotion to light thing really works for you, not that the goth thing didn't, but you seem happier now!"

"Haha! I am! Of course, I was devastated about Isis, but I knew that I had two options: let grief consume me and pull me in deeper or use this as a learning opportunity and seek my own light, independent of the one Isis had always shown me."

"Well, I am glad to see you thriving, my friend!"

"Now, to get down to things," Lucas said, ushering me towards the back, "You, my dear, are in dire need of a reading, and I am here to help!"

I chuckled and followed him to the back. As I stepped into the reading room, where he normally gave his spooky readings, I was again shocked to see the stark changes. The large dark oak desk with Victorian charm had been replaced by a modern glass and chrome version. The dark walls were now a subtle lilac, and crystal lamps lit the room. In the four corners, normally draped in the dark crushed velvet, stood four large amethyst geodes.

"Sit, my dear," Lucas beckoned, pointing to the white leather chair across from the table.

I did as I was told and totally felt the same excitement I had all those months ago when I first came here by chance. However, what was dark, gothic, and witchy was replaced with light, modern, and ethereal.

He smiled and glanced around, "We switched it up a little here, too. Your room, sweetie, it's gone. I made it into a blending room for my Egyptian oils."

"A lot has shifted, I think, and it's beautiful," I said.

"So, your reading..."

"Yes, and I have my questions and—"

"—No need. I already have an idea of what they are."

"Oh, well then, you certainly put in the work and service, as Isis always said!"

"Yes, and don't worry, my dear, there will be gladiators and pirates and opportunities for your heart to be stolen in the future. Well, not the gladiators and pirates, but you know what I mean!" I forgot he could intuit thoughts as well and had just done that to me.

He continued on, "Yes, I think love is a little more present than it previously was; let us explore this."

Oh, my day suddenly improved, and my spirit lifted. I said nothing and waited for Lucas to say his prayer of protection, and gave a message of grace to the spirits that were present. Then, he pulled out a gold box from underneath his desk and opened it. In it sat two decks of ornately decorated cards. I hadn't seen him use these before.

"New cards?" I asked.

"Yes, I found them in London."

I don't think I've seen cards like these before."

"You definitely haven't. One deck is the tarot you are used to, and the other is a deck that is connected to the Akashic Records, and they reveal your karma and much more."

"Okay, so this should be interesting. I take it we will be using them both?"

"Yes, now let's begin."

Lucas began to lay out the cards in a spread that was new to me. He flipped over the last card and read them to me.

"These first cards denote the significant lessons in life you will need to learn. The Ten of Wands shows that you will need to face the oppression and the load you carry on your back, head-on. It is draining your energy and preventing you from fully actualising who you are. However, the Six of

Wands says that you will be victorious in your endeavours as long as you pick your opponents to battle wisely. Ah, this next card, the Devil, shows that you will have to make a choice that will change the course of your life soon. Will you go with the option that brings you to light or plunges you into darkness? The Queen of Swords is shown against your sword and will demonstrate a sharp wit and an even sharper tongue. The Four of Pentacles shows me that this woman has great command of the material world. She has the ability to stand between you and the mountain you must climb if you let her continue to scheme behind the scenes. You need to watch out for her."

Her... I thought to myself, *who was that? Naomi? Lesley? The one oracle I haven't met yet? Or maybe someone else...* I shuddered at the thought.

"Now, why don't we look at the next cards?" Lucas asked, "How must you pursue your dreams next? From the Akashic Records, we have Female Transformation and also Wars and Battles."

He reshuffled the deck and laid out six cards: The Queen of Swords, The Queen of Wands, The Queen of Pentacles, The Queen of Cups, The Empress, and The Star.

I looked at the spread of cards in front of me; they were all very powerful, but I didn't think they represented me in that particular configuration. "I don't understand," I said, looking at Lucas.

"I do," said Lucas, "Each of these cards represents one of the other oracles you have found, see? The Queen of Swords represents Alice, a card that denotes judgment and knowledge unburdened by emotion and spurred on by a fighting spirit."

I took another look, and it started to come together for me. "Oh, I think so. So does that mean that the Queen of Cups would be Laura because she is compassionate and comforting?"

"Yes! Why don't you tell me about the rest?"

"Okay, the Queen of Pentacles represents a person who is down-to-earth and wants to provide for their family and take care of them, like Emilee! The Empress must be Lucinda because she was a High Priestess of Dendara, and the Empress represents motherhood, nature, and fertility. I think the Star must be Naomi because who else could it be?"

We both chuckled at this.

"So that makes the last one, the Queen of Wands, it could be Lesley because this card represents fierce focus and passion and individualism that can come off as being arrogant and self-centred. Now, Lucas, I believe this configuration is incomplete."

Lucas smiled at my observation, "You are correct, Anna. I shall turn over the last three cards now." Lucas did so slowly, first revealing The Fool, allowing me to interpret as he went.

"The Fool," I said, "denotes a certain innocence and new beginning. The Fool is a blank slate and has infinite possibilities, and with that comes optimism. The Akashic card is Curse, and then the Fear and Ego card, so I'm clearing my ego and curses.

Lucas nodded in agreement and turned over the next card. It was the High Priestess, but it was reversed. That made total sense and was a confirmation.

I sighed, "This card represents me, of course. In reverse, it means that I haven't been listening to my intuition or my gut. I've been confused and unsure when I should be informed and confident. This card is showing me who I am right now and reminding me that I can change. You know, I think it is just the kick in the pants I need! I've focused on the title, not the true role. I'm ready to release her."

"And so it is," said Lucas.

"Now, tell me about the last one." He turned over the final card, the Emperor in reverse.

"That card represents a gross abuse of power and the subversion of normal rule. This card represents the force working against us to rebuild the temples. It has limitless ambition to achieve its goals and will do so no matter the cost. Maybe I help the priestesses become high again?"

"Correct again!

Just then, all of the levity was sucked out of the room, and a cold breeze ran through the room. I swore I heard a slight laugh. Lucas shuddered and went to his deck, seemingly drawing a card because of the breeze.

It was the Tower.

Lucas addressed me in a voice that did not sound like his own, "*You are about to embark on a journey, where at the end of it, there will be a battle between the worlds of light and dark. She is coming for you. They are coming for you. You must be ready!*"

I recoiled in horror from him, "Who is? Lucas, is that you in there?"

The voice answered, "*You know not of me yet. But I know of you, Anna. Doomed from the start, it seemed, but now perhaps not. A powerful child, hidden away from sight by a mother who didn't love her and an aunt who couldn't protect her. I read your heart, Anna Harris, and it is aching to be loved. You would be wise to temper it before it leads you too far off the path... But wait, perhaps love is what you need, and what it can provide will help you on your quest... Yes... I see now. It will have a slight part to play, only slight. Be wise, Anna, and don't let love corrupt you like it did this fool and your precious Isis. Perhaps there is hope yet.*"

He shook his head and came back into his body. I looked at him, dumbfounded, but chose not to tell him what happened. We were both a little exhausted by the whole experience, so we sat very quietly for a short time until the smell of burning sage filling the air became too strong to ignore. Lucas called out for his angelic assistant.

"Lydia, dear, are you burning sage?" Lucas asked.

Lydia entered the room then and gave us a funny look. She responded, "Why yes, of course, love. Don't you like it? It is *supposed* to clear negative spirits but looks harmless to me." She cocked her head to the side and smirked at us. Her eyes were dark now, and her face distorted into a sinister grin. I gasped at her appearance.

"Oh, Anna, don't look so shocked. You knew that I was going to come back eventually."

"'I-I I don't get—" I stuttered.

"What? You don't get what? Did you think you were rid of me that easily? Hardly. I was down for a while, but I am certainly not out! Although I will admit your mentor gave me quite a run for my money."

"My mentor?'"

"Yes, I wasn't expecting her to bring out the big guns! It's too bad that they backfired on her!"

I was putting two and two together, "Wait, did this happen in Egypt?"

The force possessing Lydia snorted and laughed, *"My dear, you sure are not a bright girl."*

"What happened there? What did you do to her?"

"I didn't do anything. Isis did a big no-no and paid for it. Tell me, how is the dear?"

I couldn't take this mocking spirit anymore, so I jumped up and ran to the altar, throwing the selenite wand towards Lucas, who by now had regained his composure. Lydia, or rather the intruding spirit, began to scream as Lucas waved the wand around her and chanted the words of the sacred exorcism. In a final screech that sounded inhuman, Lydia sank to the floor and passed out.

CHAPTER 10

Monday, 9 March 2009

On my way back to the Gables, I reflected on what had happened with Lucas earlier that day. After that entity had invaded Lydia and we had forced it out, Lydia slumped to the floor. It took a few minutes after that for her to come to. She'd had no recollection of coming into the back and speaking to us. The last thing she remembered was a tall woman dressed in a long black leather trench coat and a large felt-brimmed hat looking around the shop. We thought that maybe she had something to do with it, but when Lucas and I went up front, she was gone, and the door was locked from the inside. We thought it was strange, so we looked around outside the shop to see if anyone was there of that description, and didn't find anyone.

After all of that, I decided to head back to the Sacred Traveller café to get some hot cocoa takeaway, as I needed a hot beverage to calm and centre myself. As I picked up my order from the counter, I ran into the waitress who had first served me there. Her name was Lisa, and we had developed a friendly rapport over the last few months. She had an extra spring in her step and had come over to inform me that she was engaged. I congratulated her and spent the next half hour or so chatting about her wedding plans. Usually, I would have opted out of such talk, but it was giving me hope that I hadn't felt about love in a while. Perhaps if she had found love in this town, I could, too. It had been so long since

I had gone out with anyone or had romance, and maybe it was the card reading or the hot cocoa or whatever, but I was feeling like perhaps love was going to find me soon.

I scoffed at myself. This level of optimism was not normal for me. It was most certainly the warm, sweet cocoa clouding my thoughts. Regardless, it was nice to daydream about it.

☥

It was late afternoon when I returned to the Gables. The sun was hidden by storm clouds, casting a faint shadow over the house. Once inside, I looked downstairs to see if Emilee or Lucinda, a frequent visitor, were home. I couldn't find anyone. So, I went to my room instead, putting on a comfortable pair of sweatpants and a loose-fitting T-shirt. There on my bed was an envelope with my name on it. I quickly went to open it, and it read:

Dear Anna,

I was called away to London suddenly and will be there for the next week. I have closed The Gables for visitors.

Do not worry. The Benson sisters have cancelled their private session and switched their retreat to the time of the Summer Solstice. They still want you to teach, so there's time to prepare.

Lucinda has decided to join me and take a much-needed break. Before you think anything, our leaving has nothing to do with you. I simply have some work to do, and Lucinda wants to visit a few old friends in Soho. This has been a trying time for all of us, and I think that you will find a little alone time just what you need to reconnect with your past. We will be back in about a week, and Wallis will keep you company. If you have any questions about that or anything else, please

call me.
Many blessings,
Emilee

The silent house made more sense now. I wasn't sure if I agreed with Emilee about me needing to be alone after what had happened that day, but I guessed I could always ask Laura to spend the night if I got worried. I knew that they both needed to get away, so this didn't exactly surprise me. Folding up the note again, I placed it on my nightstand and went about preparing for a cozy evening of TV with myself, filled with old movies and lots of chocolate.

I made an effort to reach out to Lucinda, Alice, and Laura and connect with them more in a way I hadn't since Isis's passing. Naomi was totally silent and had gone on a retreat to Bali—wherever that was. The rest of the time, I went through Isis's notes and prepared for the ceremonies and retreat I would lead with the ladies from Bath. I thought about Isis every day, but the pain of her absence lessened over time. I was still upset that she left so little for me explained, but those things would have to wait. My thoughts of High Priestess and leader had long been forgotten. I would carry on my work and what was required of me. I began to lean more towards my work as a psychic and oracle to help others where I could.

Tuesday, 24 March 2009

Just when I thought everything was beginning to calm and I was finding my path in life, Laura came to the Gables with sad news.

It was a Tuesday morning, and I was clearing breakfast, helping Emilee with the group of walkers who had stopped by. My goodness, they had gone through so much coffee, you would think they could run the Tor hike rather than walk it. This was a special time during the Equinox when many began their pilgrimage hikes. We should have been in Egypt or at least doing ceremonies, but it would seem the Chalice Well and other sacred sites were booked with visiting groups, so I took it as a sign for us to rest.

I heard Laura's voice, and then I heard her and Emilee whispering. When they walked into the kitchen, I knew something was wrong.

"Sit down, *ma cherie*." Emilee moved me into a kitchen chair, taking the tea towel from my hands and going to put the kettle on.

I noticed she was using the copper kettle only used for occasions of importance. Laura sat down, and she had tears in her eyes. "Anna, I just heard from my agent in North Yorkshire, the one with my forwarding details... they said a solicitor for your mum had contacted them."

I nodded.

"Sadly, your mum died eleven days ago."

My mind was blank, and I felt numb.

Emilee handed me tea with what I gathered was one of her special tinctures. I could not move. I simply sat in silence.

After a few minutes, which felt like hours, I began to speak. My eyes filled with tears. I'd left it too late.

"How?" I said simply.

"She was in hospice. They said cancer. It was found recently, and then she only had a few weeks."

"She was alone?"

"They said not. They said she was supported by a whole hospice team, and the solicitor I spoke with said she had requested that no one be told. Not even you, hence the reason they never reached out. She wanted to leave this world and was ready."

"What was the date?"

"It was in March, on Friday the 13th, very early in the morning."

I let out a sob. While I'd been crying and mourning over Isis, my own mother had been in pain and suffering in a hospice, of all places. My grief and guilt were overwhelming, and my shame that my two friends were here with me, hearing this sad and cruel story, was beyond anything I had known.

"What happened to her?"

"They cremated her, and the solicitor wants to know what you would wish to do with her."

I stood up like Bambi, my legs wobbly, and I just made it to the door. I don't know what made me say it, but all of a sudden, it was clear. I turned around and looked at both of them. Emilee was crying into her lace handkerchief. I saw no judgment from them, just love.

"I bring her home, I will bring her home," I responded, looking around. "Here to Glastonbury."

Laura stood and came over to me, holding me as I let my sobs come out.

"We will bring her home. Tomorrow, you and I will go and collect her."

☥

Laura took care of everything for the travel to York. She arranged the appointment with the solicitor, booked the train tickets and even took care of the hotel in city center York. Emilee helped me to pack my bag and discreetly let everyone know of my bereavement. What would my friends think? Who lets this happen to their own mother?

☥

The next morning, Laura and I were bundled into the private car she had hired and were en route to the train station in London to catch our train at 10:30 a.m. from King's Cross station. I had offered to drive, but Laura would not hear of it, saying that we would be too distracted and besides, my car needed repairs. She was not willing to chance it.

We arrived early afternoon. It was so bizarre as we walked the short journey to the hotel. I felt like I'd stepped into an old version of myself when York had been a favourite city to shop and explore.

We were to be staying at the Dean's Court Hotel, a red brick Victorian building right in the centre, and an easy location from which we could see the famous York Minster Church. Laura had made conversation all the way on the train, and I could not remember a thing she said.

"Anna, did you hear me?"

"I'm sorry, Laura, I'm in another world."

She hugged me, letting me know she understood.

"I was saying the solicitor confirmed that our appointment is at 4:00 p.m. and that we can go by car with someone from their office to your mum's home tomorrow, in the morning, to see what you wish to do with the house."

I simply nodded.

"Now, why don't we leave our bags and go to Betty's for some afternoon tea?"

I smiled. Betty's tearoom was a magical place that I'd visited as a child. High tea with sandwiches, cakes, and scones. Yes, that would be most welcome. Laura checked us in, and we left our bags with reception. Within no time, we were bustling through the narrow, cobbled streets. Laura stopped outside a small bakery, and I was most surprised.

"Laura, Betty's is down there. The big café on the corner."

She smiled, winked, and pointed up to the sign. Well, that was a surprise. A small, quaint version was here in a building that looked like it had been built hundreds of years ago.

"This is Secret Betty's," she smiled and whisked me inside.

We went past the small retail area and the rows of cakes and the tins of fine coffee and teas, and to the back, where we climbed the small staircase that opened up into two rooms with eight tables in each room.

The windows were white sash windows with the subtle décor and elegant furnishings. I felt just like Elizabeth Bennett and wondered if this would have been a place she and her sisters would have visited for tea.

The waitress approached us with a welcome smile and seated us near the window, from which I could see all the people going about their business below. Her white lace-edged apron was pristine, and I felt rather special as she helped me choose an elegant rose petal tea with lemon and the shrimp sandwich. She did not even blink when I asked for the chips with mayonnaise. Laura ordered full high tea with the works.

For a moment, I forgot why we were here, as happy memories of being in York flooded back. The hot summers, the street music, and the cold, snowy winters and Christmas markets. Laura and I swapped our top ten things to do in York and were most surprised to have so many matches. I wondered how, in those years, we had never met in a social way. We had been to many of the same events. I had only known her as my kind Land Lady, only meeting when I gave her my monthly rent check.

My mother came to mind, and I was aware she was

sitting with us. Laura must have also sensed it.

"Lottie, is that you?" she whispered, and I nodded to say she was with us.

I wanted to ask questions or see if Laura could channel a message, but as soon as she was acknowledged, she was gone.

"She will come back," Laura assured me as she paid the bill and checked her watch to ensure we had time to make our appointment.

We left and once again navigated the streets as locals, reaching Shambles Street in a few minutes. This ancient and spooky street had old buildings on either side of coloured bricks and mullion windows with small doorways, and some even looked as if they were leaning, ready to fall into the street. This street was said to date back to the 1100s, and as we walked past the buildings, I saw many ghosts coming to stare at us.

I was in no mood to clear spirits, so I slipped my arm into Laura's and made haste to our destination.

We arrived at a small building at the end of the street with a very grand black door and a large lion's head for the door knocker. I reached up and gave it three taps. The windows were on either side with closed curtains, and as I looked up, I could see a further three floors above. The brass, highly polished sign simply read: *Dudleim and Co.*

Not your average solicitors. I looked at Laura to see if I should knock again when the door was unlocked and then opened. There stood an elderly man in a formal black suit with a grey-striped waistcoat and a red carnation on his lapel.

"Miss Anna, do come in, and you must be Ms. Laura. I am Mr. Dudleim."

We nodded and followed him into what could only be

described as a Victorian sitting room with small velvet sofas, heavy flock wallpaper, and vintage lamps. Then, we went up a flight of stairs to an office with large oak wooden furniture and dark green leather chairs.

He invited us to sit and began to open paper files that he had retrieved from a large mahogany credenza.

I placed his age at around 70 or older. Not a single piece of modern technology was on the desk. No computer or mobile phone. I wondered how long this poor man had been trapped in this timeline. But then again, perhaps he was happy.

He looked at me and smiled. "I'm most happy, my dear. I live in a simpler time."

I blushed. Of course I would have to have a psychic solicitor.

He muttered away and scanned the documents through his thick lensed glasses.

"Okay, Okay. I have it, yes."

"Yes, I'll tell them."

It suddenly dawned on me that he was having a conversation with some type of ghost. Either that, or he was mad.

"Don't think that Anna," I heard my mother's voice. *"Mr. Dudleim has come here specially."*

So, this was going to be interesting.

I watched as she sat down in the chair in the corner and smiled at us all.

I felt uncomfortable but decided to wait and see.

Mr. Dudleim began to explain the will. The gentleman cleared his throat and began to speak.

"Everything will come to you now, Anna. Your mother's bank accounts, the house, and everything she owned. Tomorrow, my assistant Jenny will collect you from the hotel and take you over. You can give her the instructions on what it is you want us to do. Here are the deeds, now in your name, and the list of bank accounts with all the numbers you need to call. It appears your mother took care of all the business before her passing. The only thing missing, she said, was that she did not have an address for you."

"About her passing..." I was terrified to ask.

"It was quick, and I felt no pain." My mother stood and walked over.

Mr. Dudleim stayed quiet as he apparently could see and hear her.

"I wanted to reach out and call you."

"I know, but I had a sense of this when you left for Glastonbury. My life flashed before me, and I called Laura to ask her to watch over you."

I saw Laura bite her lip. She could hear as well.

"You told her where I had gone?"

She nodded, "I promised to watch over you. If I had known she was ill, I would have insisted you visit."

Then, Mother was gone again.

Now, back to the papers. Mr. Dudleim was certainly not phased by this situation. In fact, he seemed most matter-of-fact and at ease with having a ghost with us.

"Now we have this for you, Anna." He held up a key.

"If you go upstairs to the next floor and locate box 88, the contents are yours. We will stay here."

I left the room and followed his instructions to climb the small staircase that tilted to the left. I opened the door to a room full of what looked to be safety deposit boxes. Around 200 of them, and just a table and chair sat in the corner. The room was secure with a full alarm system and metal bars on the windows that told me this room contained things of value.

I found box 88 and opened it. There inside was a paper folder, and when I opened it up, I could see a set of birth certificates. Mine, my mother's, and my aunt's, then a few others dating back to the 1800s, and one in a foreign language. There was a leather-bound book, and when I opened it, I could see it was a ledger of some sort, with names, addresses, and notes. None of it made sense as these were locations in London, Paris, and, I think, Germany.

I was closing the box when I felt something stick at the back, so I slid my hand all the way to the back. I felt a line of plastic; it was heavy. As I pulled it forward, I was surprised to see 10 large gold coins, all with strange stamps, protected by a see-through wallet.

I took the paperwork but decided to leave the coins, as for some reason, I felt they should stay in this safe place... at least until I had taken care of all my mother's business.

I made my way back down the stairs. Mr. Dudleim had all my papers in order and was explaining the house to Laura and handing her the keys.

"Just paperwork, but I left a few things in the box I should like to keep it for a while. Do I pay you to rent the box now?" I asked.

He shook his head. "No, my dear, the box was willed to you."

"I don't understand."

"Many of the old families in Europe paid for our services 50 to 100 years in advance, and we work to serve and support them. Your box was originally purchased by your ancestors in 1688."

He pointed to the image above the fireplace.

"The Templar Crest," said Laura.

It was the symbol from the gold coins, and I could now see why I had left them. They were not to be moved.

"Yes, I am from a long line of Templar Knights with an oath to serve. This office has been here for nearly 600 years, watching over the aristocratic families and their secrets. We have offices all over the world."

"My mother had social ambitions, but she was not an aristocrat, Mr. Dudleim."

He smiled and sighed.

"You have much to learn, Miss Anna. Now, ladies, if you will excuse me, I have a train to catch to London and a morning flight to Geneva. Jenny will be there to collect you in the morning. Here is her number again and my card."

I took them politely.

Laura and I left the office a little stunned and found ourselves walking into an old-worldy pub nearby.

I ordered our glasses of red wine and took them over to a table in the corner.

"Templar Knights. Laura, what is that?"

"The Templars were a society of noblemen who swore an oath to protect all that is holy and sacred. My late husband David was one in a past life. He met a very sad end in 1307 when the French king ordered them killed on Friday the 13th. It was said that the order had died out, but over the years, they have come to the rescue of many a priestess and priest of Isis. They now reside in secret, and it is said that those who are protected by them or carry their seal are worth their weight in gold."

"Did the Templars have their own gold?"

"Oh yes... crazy valuable and not just for the gold itself but what it can buy. David left me a coin that had been passed down through his family generations. A very, very small one, but he always said if I needed help and saw the Templar sign or Fleur de Lys image, that I should present the coin, and the simple image alone would ensure my safety."

I did not share with Laura that I now had 10 large coins that I'd left in the box, and I wondered why my mother had not sold them to fund a grander life.

☥

I hardly slept that night, but the next morning I felt I was nearing the end of the tunnel. Just a visit to my old home and then back on the 2 p.m. train to London so I could sleep in my own bed that night.

Jenny met us in reception. A young woman dressed extremely well in a tailored red dress suit, smart high heels, and a designer purse.

She took a moment to take me in, dressed in flat shoes and torn jeans, and I expect I was not the normal client. She must be used to the super-wealthy and immaculate.

Thank goodness Laura looked like the cover of Majesty Magazine.

The car was waiting, and we walked out to be presented with a chauffeur-driven vintage Rolls-Royce. I'd only seen these in weddings and was most surprised.

"Company car," she said, and we all climbed into the back, where the four seats faced each other. Yes, Laura was totally where she should be, and Jenny seemed not to care about my appearance.

"Now, these are all the details on the house and list of belongings that your mother had. It really depends on what you wish to do, but I can take care of anything you need." She passed me more documents.

"Did she leave any of her personal clothes I need to go through?" The reality was catching up with me as I was about to enter a home I had left many years ago.

Jenny shook her head, "No, we took care of all of that

for her."

"You helped her?"

"Yes, as soon as she had the diagnosis from the hospital, she reached out and had a precise life plan of her dos and don'ts."

"Did she mention me?"

Jenny smiled, "Yes, often, and she was very strong and stern in her request that we not contact you. She said you were in training and not to be burdened or distracted."

"Did a woman called Isis ever contact you or her?"

She shook her head, but something told me there had been some contact.

☥

We arrived at the house and let ourselves in. To my surprise, the house was empty. Gone were all traces of my childhood. Laura and Jenny stood in the kitchen as I wandered into the sterile environment.

I went upstairs and toward my bedroom, which was all cleared out; there was not a single trace of my early life. Part of me wanted to be angry, but I was more relieved. I had my memories; they would have to do.

I went into my parents' room and there was one piece of furniture, a table next to the window. I felt a sob rise in my throat as I reached it and was able to reach out and touch the small golden urn that sat in the center.

I felt Laura behind me, and she put her arm around me.

"Well, well, Lottie. Here you are, my dear," she said.

Next to the urn was the photo album I remember and a framed photo of me with my mother and father when I was about three. Then next to it was a large cream heavy paper envelope with my name upon it. I couldn't open it, but knew a time would come.

"Time to go, my love" was all Laura had to say, and I nodded.

I placed the items in my bag and gently picked up the urn, carefully placing it into the box it had been transported in.

Then we walked downstairs, where I thanked Jenny for all that she had done.

"What do you want to do with the house?"

"Sell it, sell everything, please, and post me a check. The office should have my current address now," I handed her the keys.

I looked at the urn, then at Laura.

"This life here is gone, and I have all I need with me. Let's take her home for the next adventure."

"Absolutely, and if we get going, we should make the earlier train." Laura looked like a weight had been lifted.

The angels were with us that afternoon, and we arrived back in London just after 4 p.m. and were able to avoid rush hour traffic to be home back in the Gables just before 7 p.m.

Emilee was awaiting us with a home-cooked meal. While she and Laura set the table, I ran upstairs with my bags and carefully placed my mother on one of the shelves next to my favourite crystals, with the family framed photo next to it. It seemed a little morbid, but I wanted her to share part of my new life and be a witness. When it was time for her to go, I knew she would tell me the place and time.

CHAPTER 11

Tuesday, 16 June 2009

We were now just days away from the Summer solstice. Everyone was buzzing with excitement, no one more than I. Naomi had returned earlier in the morning and was resting up before we all met to discuss details. Apparently, the event planned by the Benson sisters had become a bigger gathering than expected, and over fifty people had signed up and were attending. All of our group had been invited to participate at some level. Naomi would be a guest speaker, Alice and Laura would host at the Chalice Well, but I was asked to present on Priestesses and the Akashic Records, and to host a ceremony on the land just behind Chalice Well. The Benson sisters were devoted to Isis and the priestesses. I had spiritually read for them many times, and I knew they at least trusted me.

I had waited so long for this—so long to connect to my sisters of the past and to connect to myself, too.

Friday, 19 June 2009

Solstice eve, as I like to call it, arrived swiftly, and we all congregated around Emilee's kitchen table at the Gables in the morning. Emilee had salvaged some chairs from the Sanctuary, lending a homier feel to the setting and ensuring there was enough seating for everyone, albeit a bit snug.

My heart ached, and I felt the loss of Isis in so many ways, which was made more obvious now that we didn't have access to the Sanctuary. I found myself saying, "Do you remember when?" so many times I had to stop and reframe.

I felt I had had so little time, but in other ways, it was perfect. While I may have the advanced spiritual gifts, I still felt I needed a master to guide me. I had been tempted to reach out to the three women who had become the guardians of the Sanctuary, wanting to invite them to join us or perhaps meet in the gardens. However, something inside me insisted that no, that chapter was closed, and a new path had begun.

I consulted with the Druidesses, who now came frequently to visit the Gables, and Wallis the cat would often alert me to their presence. My heart always felt happy when they were close.

"Anna, your time is rising, and you must be patient.

"In ancient times, it took years, not days, to achieve our growth and potential.

"You are now building your own temple every day, and Isis was a part of that, but she is not your journey nor your destination. She is a guide for that moment in time."

I was truly grateful to spend these moments, and it inspired me to write more and more. By now, I had around 200 pages on my computer in a document. One day, I would do something with these words. I often wondered who the girl was all those months ago. She seemed like a character in a book, not me.

As we all sat, Emilee's phone rang. It was Naomi. We listened as she spoke on speaker as it appeared she was in the car.

"So this is the order of ceremony I gave to the Benson sisters," said Naomi, ever efficient. I had allowed her to run the show. A battle was not worth it.

"My driver is currently bringing me back this afternoon, and I will be opening the event tonight at the assembly rooms with Lucinda, and then tomorrow, Alice and Laura will be there opening the blessing in the Chalice Well at 8 a.m. sharp. Then the group have their own lunch and teaching in the Abbey before the ceremony at the Tor with Anna."

"What about Sunday?" asked Lucinda.

"Nothing planned as yet," was the reply.

"Where is Lucas?" asked Alice.

"Oh, his diary is full of readings all weekend, and I heard his shop did more turnover selling crystals yesterday than before," said Naomi.

"So let's get to work," Emilee said directly. She had little patience for the back-and-forth.

She stood up.

"And yes, here are your payments for speaking," said Emilee, handing around a white envelope containing a very welcome sum of cash. I was paying rent to Emilee and not having as many sessions as before, so I was truly grateful. My mother's house was still not sold, and I wondered about cashing a gold coin, but that felt disrespectful.

"Now, ladies, can we all tune into our intention for this weekend?" said Alice. "Naomi, please join us in our prayer."

I suddenly realised that while I had been thinking about how to spend my money, I had missed an opportunity to bring the group together in a focus. Simple mistake, but a little wake-up call to the confirmation that I was simply one of the group.

Alice spoke...

"We welcome all our dear sisters and brothers to this sacred ground.

"May their travels be full of ease and grace

"May their hearts be open and healed
"May their souls rise to their highest potential
"May we honour them and ourselves as a group and use our gifts for the highest good.
"Namaste"'

"Thank you, Alice, that was beautiful," I told her.

"Your turn next, young lady," she whispered.

I nodded and blushed a little.

"Shall I come over tonight, Naomi, to help with anything?" I asked her.

"No, no need, Anna. Lucinda and I have it all covered, but you could come and watch." Her response was curt and sharp.

"I'll be there," Lucinda chimed into the conversation.

"I'll report to Alice how it went, and then she can update you. Just remember to be at the field behind the Chalice Well, facing the Tor at 4 p.m. tomorrow for your priestess visioning and Akashic attunement session."

I knew Naomi was annoyed that the Benson sisters had requested me to do the ritual. But I had been the one all those months ago who had held their hands and taken them both through the regression and remembering their connection to Philae temple and the High Priestess of Isis during their past lives.

"Oh yes," Naomi jumped up as her other phone rang, "Thanks, everyone, I have to go, much love." And she hung up.

Whatever, I shrugged at Emilee.

She began clearing our teacups, and as she moved over to the sink, she nodded for me to join her.

Lucinda, Alice, and Laura were in deep conversation about the various people in the group who were staying at Laura's and had requested healings in the following week.

Many people were staying longer than the retreat. I could always tell when Emilee had gossip to share, so I leaned in.

"It's about Naomi and her new man," Emilee whispered. "She met him on a flight back to London last month, and they are in constant connection."

"Her boyfriend?" I was surprised.

"No, just a lover," Emilee shrugged.

"Is that the same?"

"No, no, not at all. His name is Francisco, and he told her he is a shaman and he is from Brazil. He was on her retreat in Bali."

"A shaman?"

"Yes, he does the plant medicines, among other things."

"You met him?" I whispered.

"No," she said, "but I tuned into him as I did a coffee reading for Naomi recently, and it was most powerful."

Emilee hardly did tea and coffee cup readings, but when she did, she was always correct.

"But I think he's more of a black magician."

"How so?"

"Well, he asked her for money for an investment property, but she said she met him on the flight in business class. He took her to dinner last week, and his credit cards did not work. Oh, and she's blinded by his love and devotion." She carried on... and I had a brief vision.

I couldn't help myself as I saw a whole past life in France with a wealthy older version of Naomi being deceived by her younger love infatuation.

"He told her he would help with the Egypt sacred journey business and would bring people, and they could lead trips together."

"How do you know so much?"

"I listen," she shrugged to the words between her words.

"When she's staying here, sometimes when you are in your room, we pour a little wine and talk."

At first, I thought he could be her chosen one, but then I saw her faxing him some of the Egypt business documents before she left for London, and I think, ma chere, that you should have known about this."

"Mmm... thanks, Emilee," I squeezed her arm gently.

"Let's leave this for the moment. Maybe the time and place to deal with this is not too far away." I knew her heart was true, and I could always trust her, unlike some of my spiritual sisters, it would seem.

The afternoon was very chaotic at the Gables, so I decided to walk into town, as I figured I had nothing to do until the following day. I wanted to sit in the Abbey for some inspiration.

Of course, the Abbey was busy; the sun was shining, and the families were queuing to venture inside. I wandered past Lucas's shop to see it full of tourists and a line at the cash register. I guess he had been working the money spells. I thought about taking a small table at the outside café. I could borrow some cards and make the afternoon pay, but that didn't appeal either.

I saw Laura across the road and called out to her. She was on a mission, however, and moving very quickly down the street, where she disappeared down the side road.

I ran to catch up to her and was surprised as I turned down the alley where she was waiting for me.

"Quickly, Anna, don't let them see us," and she pulled my arm and opened a large old wooden door.

"The Magdalene Chapel? Seriously, Laura, why are you here?"

"It's a long story," she said. Moving behind me, she locked the door.

"I sometimes come here as a guardian, and I display the flowers," she smiled.

"You dark horse, you never said."

"Well, it's been my secret a long time, but I knew everyone would want to come if I told. You won't tell?"

"No, our secret. Now, would you like me to go?" I offered.

"Anna," she said, standing back. "You know that's thoughtful. What's come over you? The old Anna would be asking a million questions."

"I'm not sure. I just feel this stillness and calm, and it is as if tomorrow has come and gone."

I thought she was about to speak, but she smiled and began to move vases and open the beautiful bouquets that were on the side table.

As she arranged them, she began to sing.

Give me oil in my lamp keep it burning
Give me oil in my lamp
I pray give me oil in my lamp
keep it burning keep it burning till the break of day.
Sing hosanna sing hosanna

It was a song I had heard in Sunday school, but suddenly, I was in a vision.

The chapel was a cave, and women were huddled, consoling each other. Another woman enters, and she holds a small lamp made of stone.

"They will soon be here," she tells them, and she rolls out blankets and straw and then brings a small platter of food.

I hear noises, and I see three women enter, but they do not speak. I can't see their faces.

"You will be safe here, far from harm and far from

ridicule," the woman tells them.

"Now rest," and she hands them the lamp and leaves.

It was a very powerful moment, and then I was back in the garden of the chapel, and it is present time, but I am relieved to see my druidess friends. They are all standing in front of me. A vision within a vision—something deeper and much more profound.

"Anna, beware, a dark force has returned and haunts us this solstice eve."

"But where? What can I do?"

"Find your friends and protect them."

I looked at my watch. I realised it was mid-afternoon, and in only a few hours, the retreat gathering would be starting.

"Anna, dear one, it's time to go."

I began to hear Laura's voice calling me, and I looked at my watch, and it's now 3:45 p.m.

"I just had a vision, Laura. I saw women in a cave, like they were hiding, and then the Druidesses came and told me that we are in danger."

"Nonsense," she said, shaking her head. "We have divine protection. We can go to watch the opening with Naomi and Lucinda at 5 p.m. if that would make you feel better."

"Of course, but that's not for an hour. Why don't we go get a snack and a cup of tea?"

Friday, 19 June 2009, 5 p.m.

Laura and I arrived late at the assembly rooms, just after 5 p.m. Every seat was taken, and we managed to squeeze onto a bench at the back.

The Benson sisters were welcoming everyone, and I could hear a voice behind the front door. It was Naomi.

She was on her phone and laughing, totally distracted from holding space for the opening.

"No, I'll be there tomorrow, darling."

"I'm not needed after I deliver my magic tonight, and yes, you are my focus."

It must be the new man, and I was a witness to something the universe wanted me to know.

"Look," she continued. "I'll meet you and listen to what Lesley has to say tomorrow, and we can plan the trip to Egypt."

What? Lesley and her and the black magician going to Egypt? My stomach felt sick. Emilee's teacup wisdom felt right on point and correct.

I was about to confront her when Lucinda stepped onto the stage and began to channel a message from the goddess.

Naomi was still not on the stage, and I realised that others could hear her laughing during Lucinda's presentation. Once again, poor Lucinda—her gifts not respected.

The women around me began to tut tut and look at each other, rolling their eyes.

Finally, Naomi ended her call and came into view as Lucinda was finishing, and in true star style, she began to wave and smile and greet people as if royalty had arrived.

Lucinda ended her presentation, and I knew she was going to ask for questions, but no one was paying attention while this entrance was happening.

As Naomi made her way onto the stage, Lucas crept in and managed to squeeze himself onto our ledge at the back.

"What did I miss?"

"What didn't you miss?" laughed Laura.

"Something's wrong, Lucas," I said, looking at him.

He scanned the room.

"I can feel it, but I don't know what it is," he responded.

"It's the Tower at work, I know it," I said. I can see those tarot cards in my mind.

"Shh," said Laura. "She's starting."

"My dear friends, I'm so happy to be here." We became silent as Naomi began to talk.

Normally, Naomi would start with a blessing and her gratitude and bring forward the spirit energies to wrap us all in the most beautiful light, but instead, she talked for twenty minutes about herself and her achievements.

I could see the Benson sisters looking at each other, and one of them quietly stood up, made her way to the back, and knelt down in front of me.

"Anna, what is this? We didn't ask for a Naomi ego show. We wanted a blessing, and she said she would share insight on the spirit world and bring through medium messages."

"Oh, I'm sure she's just warming up. Trust her, I'm sure it's okay," I responded.

"But she's already halfway through her time," the sister answered, tapping her watch.

"Of course, then when I had my TV show..." Naomi continued, and she was giving figures that I knew were not true; she never had a hit TV show in the USA, and she never had a best-selling book on the New York Times bestseller list. Yes, she did well in her career, but not like this. I was waiting for her to say she had an Oscar, and I would know she had lost her mind.

Four people from the front abruptly got up and turned to leave. Naomi suddenly realised the crowd was not with her. She looked and smiled at Lucinda, who was sitting back, not engaging in her friend's ego or her rescue.

"Okay, so let's see if we can contact the dead relatives waiting to talk to you." She changed her message.

Oh lord, it was a train wreck.

"Now I'm seeing your mother. She's here wishing to talk to you," she pointed to and spoke to a woman in the front row.

"What does she want to tell me?" the woman asked.

"She says she was so proud of you at her passing and loves you."

The woman looked around and called out to an older woman at the end of the aisle.

"Mum, when did you pass?"

The crowd let out a gasp.

And Naomi's face fell.

This was so unexpected that Lucas even let out a gasp. "She's lost the plot, or is she possessed?" he whispered.

"What can we do?" I looked over at Laura.

She looked straight at me.

"What can you do, Anna? What are you called to do?"

That was all I needed.

I stood up and made my way to the front.

The room was in silence, and you could have heard a pin drop.

I smiled at Naomi.

I thought she would have scolded me, but I saw the energy shift, and we were back in Egypt on the Giza plateau in front of the pyramids.

A crowd had gathered, and we were giving oracle messages.

"You see us." I stood next to her and took her hand.

"Yes," she gasped as she saw the vision.

"We have done this for over 2000 years, and we can do it again."

She nodded at me, and I smiled over to the Benson sisters.

I could see they were now quite excited. One thing they

did love was the karma drama.

I took a deep breath and allowed my energy to take command of the room.

"Ladies and gentlemen, friends, there is a dark force of energy around us, and it is closing our third eyes, and the veil is our test."

I could see a few people nodding. I looked at a woman in the front row and remembered her. She had been a healer, tried and burnt in the witch trials in England. We had cleared this for her many months ago.

"Do you sense this, Charlotte?"

Delighted I had remembered her name, she nodded.

"Yes, I sensed a disturbance when we entered this place." I could see her confidence rising, knowing she had been correct.

"Then we should clear the energy," I spoke to everyone.

"Do you agree?"

More people began to nod, and I called for Lucas and Laura to join us at the front and for Lucinda to burn the sage.

It only took moments, but just having the five of us working together felt so powerful. I knew in that moment we were meant to work together like this in the future.

"Thank you, my friends. Now, Naomi, shall we continue?"

I looked at the door and began to see the spirits of the families gently floating towards us.

"This is how you see them."

"Yes," she whispered back.

"Although it's been a while since I have seen this many and so clearly."

"Then let's get busy, Naomi. This is the real showtime." I squeezed her hand and went to sit in support on the edge of the stage.

"Now, my friends, I have a lady here with her puppy. It's a poodle called Bluebell. She's looking for her son. She says she is sorry she passed before you could reach her, and she saw you in your seat in the aeroplane when you were heading to visit her in the hospital after her fall."

A young man stood up, and his face was streaming tears. "That's my mum. She passed a few months back, and I never made it in time. My flight was delayed leaving Paris, and I knew while we were in the air she had passed into spirit."

Naomi nodded, slowed her pace of voice, bringing through the most beautiful compassion, and gave him a few more confirmations.

I felt her energy surge, and she continued on for nearly two hours until every spirit had had the time they needed with their earth-bound loved ones. So much healing was created in the group and the room.

I stayed the whole time by the side of the platform, nodding and providing tissues and hugs as each relative expressed their grief and joy. It felt as if time had stopped, and we were in another reality. But all the time I was holding space from the wings, Naomi was centre stage, and I would have assumed she was in charge, but perhaps it was something else.

As she closed the energy portals down and the veils between the worlds closed, I saw my work was complete, and I sensed I was shifting a gear in my purpose and journey.

After the session ended, we all watched as the Benson sisters and group left to go for dinner, and when the room was empty, Lucinda called us into a circle.

"How's everyone feeling?" she asked.

"Exhausted," said Naomi, "but relieved. I don't know

what happened. I can't seem to remember getting on the stage, but I do remember when my mind went blank, and I started to say ridiculous things."

I was about to tell her what I had heard but a voice in my head said no, wait till the retreat has ended and find the time.

"Well, let's leave this for now, shall we?" Laura said. "Time to rest before tomorrow."

I nodded. "I'll be there at 4 p.m."

"I'll be there with you," Naomi smiled and squeezed my hand.

☥

The next morning, I chose to rest and respond to texts. My phone was flooded with eighteen messages from group attendees requesting sessions, so I spent the next few days scheduling them in, including phone sessions for after they returned home. I also received several emails from people interested in teachings and spiritual development.

Just before 4 p.m., I arrived at the Chalice Well, where the group was already gathering. Naomi arrived, and I was glad to see that she was in full priestess dress. I wore my white outfit meant for Egypt but now seemed the time to show it to the world.

I saw so many kind faces arriving and was delighted to see Lucas, Laura, Alice, Lucinda, and Emilee all arriving together.

I felt the presence of the druidesses, and I wished for a moment for Isis to be with us. Naomi read my mind.

"Isis would have loved this," she said. "Do you feel her with us?"

Naomi looked around. "No, I thought she would, but she's not here."

'Time for you to do your work, my dear," said Alice, looking at me.

I smiled and took my place.

I talked about the Temple of Philae, our past lives there, and how my journey had led me to Glastonbury.

I felt the Druidesses so strong—all six of them had joined me—and they channelled their messages through me.

I looked out to the group and saw a number of them also seeing these Druidesses and recognizing them. I had thought I was going to be focused on Egypt, but no, the group energy had shifted that. *'Priestess inclusive of all the ages'* was the only message that came to me.

Once the channel was complete, I did another unusual thing for me. I asked if anyone had questions. Hands shot up, and I found myself answering so many questions on spirituality and psychic development. Things a year ago I barely understood, but now here I was fully fluent in the language of spooky stuff.

As the sun began to set, I was able to stop and allow the Benson sisters to take center stage again, guide the meditation, and lead the group out of the Chalice Well and to the next destination.

When it was over, they all began making their way up to the Tor, and I watched as the druidesses guided them in energy.

I was not inclined to go, and neither were my friends.

"I think our work is complete," said Emilee.

We all agreed.

"With them, yes, but not with each other," said Lucas.

"Did anyone get a message?" asked Lucinda.

"About the 8th of August, the 88?" said Laura.

"Yes, I got that," I said.

We looked at each other.

"I just got the 88 gathering," said Naomi.

"Did anyone get anything more?"

They shook their heads and then looked at me.

"Someone did," said Alice.

I nodded.

"Yes, I did."

"I was told by one of the Druidesses to call a gathering of us on the 8-8, here in this place.

"Lucas, you are to bring the box of gifts Isis left us, and in September, we are all to go to Egypt."

"But that's only a few months," said Laura.

"We can't do that. It takes more planning."

"Nonsense," said Naomi.

"We will call the agent tomorrow."

"We will?" I looked at her.

"Yes," she said. "Their office is open on Sundays as their weekend is Friday and Saturday."

"And you and I will plan this."

"Yes, who else?" she shrugged.

I was a little confused as I could hear her conversation with Francisco in my head on replay, and I was not about to forget the Lesley reference.

"Okay, let's meet tomorrow morning," I replied.

"Wonderful, now everyone get your passports ready. Egypt, here we come." Naomi was in full spirit.

"Now, Lucas, call the Italian restaurant to see if we can get a table for seven of us; I'm in the mood for pasta, my treat."

Her phone began to ring.

"Oh, I'll call him later," and she put her phone away.

Something had shifted. I was not sure what.

The following morning, I had a strange text from Naomi:

Sorry, Anna, I have to leave for London, but I called the agent in Cairo to say we would be there as a group in September. Thanks so much for helping on Friday night xx

And that was it. I decided to place it to one side and wait out her "side business" and took matters into my own hands. I went online and created invites for the 88 gathering.

Dear soul friends,

I invite you to a ceremony of remembering and celebrating the spiritual gateways we have stepped through and the new ones we are about to find.

Please join me at the sacred space behind the Chalice Well at 11 a.m. on the 8th of August.

Please RSVP to me directly.

Your loving sister,
Anna

I printed up the invite on white paper, and Emilee helped me to fold them into the white cards edged with gold I had found in a stationery store in Bath.

I hand-addressed them, and Emilee hand-delivered them and sent an image via text to Naomi.

Within a day, I had responses. Lucinda, Laura, and Lucas all called, and I had a text from Naomi and Alice. Naomi asked if she could bring guests, and I was about to text no when my curiosity took over, and I sent an "of course" message.

CHAPTER 12

Thursday, 8 August 2009

The morning arrived, and I felt sick to my stomach. I had hoped the Druidesses or Isis would have come into my dreams, but no, nothing.

Emilee knocked on my door around 8 a.m.

"I brought you some tea, ma chere."

"Oh, Emilee," I sat up in bed.

"You didn't have to do that."

"No, I know, but today is a big day for you, and I want you to remember it as a blessing and nothing else."

She laid down the tray and kissed my forehead.

I saw us again back in Salem, Massachusetts in happier times. Emilee had been my mother and was tried as a witch unfairly.

I was her young daughter, and her husband—my past life father—had abandoned us.

"Emilee, you never had children this life."

Her eyes filled.

"I did once have a baby, but I miscarried, and I saw that it was my fate not to be a mother. I was very young, and it was in my travelling days. Interestingly, it was with a young man I met in Cairo."

"An Egyptian?" I questioned her.

"Non, non, he was from Spain. We had met in Barcelona, and I followed him to Cairo."

"It was many years ago. We travelled for a few months, and he left, and I was supposed to follow him to Argentina, but my grandmother became sick, so I came back to France."

"A few weeks later, I found out I was pregnant, but he never responded to the forwarding address I had been given by him."

"I was heartbroken, and it was only a matter of days before I began to feel something was wrong."

"The hospital did scans, and the baby was not growing. The next day, I went into labour, and my baby was not to be. No, no Mother's Day for me."

My heart felt her pain, but I was not sure what to do.

"But you are a perfect mother energy, and I know my life is better by you being here," I said.

"See?" she said, wiping her eyes. "Today is better already."

She left the room, and I reflected upon her story. I tried to see if this was a past life, but nothing came. Maybe healing could happen in Egypt.

As the gathering started at 11 am. I did not want to make any timing mistakes. I had made sure I was super early. Even Alice was surprised as she opened the private gate to the sacred space for me, and I saw her smile as I laid out everything for the ceremony.

Lucas also arrived early. He struggled up the pathway with the heavy mahogany box Isis had left us.

"You still have not looked into it?" I asked.

"No, not even tuned into it, I swear," he said, crossing his heart.

"I trust you, Lucas. I know I would not have been able to resist," I laughed.

I watched as my friends joined us. Alice and Laura hugged and laughed when they saw each other in the same shirts. "Remember when Isis made us buy these in the Luxor market?"

"All three of us had to have the same style and colour."

More reminders that everyone had had a time in Egypt with Isis, but not me. But these were happy memories, so not to be forgotten. We were nearly all there when I saw Naomi's car arriving.

"Well, I guess we will wait." It was now 11 a.m., and I had wanted to start on time, but I smiled and held myself in patience and grace.

Just after 11 a.m., I was surprised to see three women walking towards us. Naomi, of course, but I didn't recognise the woman next to her, and the other looked familiar, but I couldn't place her. Oh, my goddess, it was Lesley! Her blonde hair was a deeper golden shade and longer than I remembered. The full face of makeup she was wearing told me she had prepared for this day and wanted to make an impression.

"Anna, I'm so sorry," Naomi gushed as she crossed right through the circle and hugged me.

"This is my dear friend, Gina from London," she said, introducing us.

"Welcome, Gina," I responded. Gina was not how I had imagined. She was petite like Naomi, her hair a rich black but with a striking silver-grey flash across her widow's peak. She held out her hand, delicate with the perfect French manicure.

"And you know me," Lesley said, interrupting.

"Of course, welcome back."

"Not welcome home," Lesley replied.

"Welcome, everyone," I smiled at her.

I chose to rise above this mischief and, like Friday night, I was not to be unnerved.

I looked at Emilee. She smirked and winked at me as if to say, "*Chere,* you can do this."

"Where are the scrolls and scarabs, Anna?" Naomi called out.

I ignored her.

"Now, everyone, please create the circle," I said.

Everyone moved into place, and I began to channel.

"Dear sacred land of magical wisdom

I welcome my friends here today on this Lionsgate day, a portal day when time and dimensions shift.

We remember our dear friend Isis, and I know she is watching over us.

For many thousands of years, we made our vows and promises to be here together, and we all know that we are here to support each other.

Now, everyone, we will have a minute of silence to go within and connect to the land and remember our friend, mentor, teacher, and sister."

The minute seemed to last forever as I felt everyone judging me or questioning me.

Then a thought came to mind. *Who cared, and why was my ego concerned with everyone else?*

Once the prayer was over, I called for everyone to open their eyes.

"Now maybe you can sit, it will be comfortable for the sharing."

"But the grass is damp," Lesley complained.

"No problem. Just stand, my dear," said Lucinda.

It was clear I had the support of the women as they looked at Lesley.

"Here," I said and threw a blanket over to her. "Use this."

Not expecting my kindness, she shuffled in an uncomfortable way, and everyone created a place for her to sit down. I walked towards Lucas, and he stood up.

He turned to me, and now that he was standing in front

of me, I felt safe and protected.

"Now, shall we?" He pointed to the mahogany box.

I nodded, and we both began to open the large box from both sides.

We lifted off the lid, and there I could see different bundles of cream linen on the top, wrapped with a ribbon with each of our names.

There was also a page of instructions that Lucas held up and began to read.

Dear beloveds,

If this box is now open, you are only weeks from your Egypt trip. I trust that Naomi and Anna have arranged the journey that will be the start of a whole new chapter of sisterhood and brotherhood.

Lucas, will you please hand out each of the treasures to my friends, so they may open them in front of the group?

Please know they are all to make the trip to Egypt to remind them of their sacred promise and, through the oracle wisdom, find their truth and clear the karmic path. It is time to restore the Temple.

With love ever and always,
Isis

I thought I would start to cry as Lucas began to lift each gift out and present it to its owner, but no tears came, only a sense of peace.

They were small parcels, and he read out the names. He then handed them to me, and I handed them to each recipient.

"To Alice." Alice opened hers slowly.

"It's very light. Ah, it is a pendant. It is an Isis cartouche with her sacred symbols, not her name, but a prayer," she said.

"Next, to Emilee..."

"Ah, I have a pendant, too, and mine is the pomegranate in gold," Emilee replied.

"Lucinda, here you are."

Lucinda's hands were shaking as she opened hers, and she nearly dropped her pendant. "Another pendant—this time, a small hourglass."

"Ah, the sands of Giza," called out Laura. "Isis had that made many trips ago."

"For you, Laura."

"I'm thinking these are all her pendants," she said. There was a delicate gold pendant of a heart with a rose inside for Laura.

"Now, Anna."

I opened mine gently, and it was a pendant with a beautiful gold box with a tiny key attached.

And for Lesley, it was a locket, and she opened it, and it had a small dagger image on one side and a piece of silk on the other.

"Thank you," her voice, for once, was genuine.

"Now, for Gina."

How was Gina included here? I was surprised, but then of course, Isis had already planned this in some magical way.

Lucas handed her a large envelope, and inside was a white silk scarf and a white card with a handwritten note that she read aloud.

My dear friend, how long has it been? Here are the instructions to follow the day the group leaves for Egypt and not before.

"Thank you, Anna," she smiled. "Isis once told me I would come back for the gathering and hold space here in Glastonbury when you all travelled. I asked Naomi. I hope that was okay."

"Of course," I smiled at her.

Lucas handed a parcel to Naomi and took his out last.

They looked at each other and said, "Together."

We all watched as they opened theirs.

"The wings of Horus?" Naomi asked, peering at his.

"No," he shook his head. "It's Ma'at. And yours?"

"Well. I already knew it." She smiled, and in her hand was a large golden ankh.

I had to fight back my disappointment.

A small box and key, and here my friend had the magnificent golden ankh that Isis had always worn.

But I would be professional and rise above.

"Now, everyone, let us rise and celebrate your gift," Lucas said. He held up a small package that looked like instructions of some sort and handed them to Naomi.

She looked over to me and held them up to say that Isis had handed over the journey details and then pushed them into her bag.

Naomi then spoke to say that the Egypt trip was officially open, but my mind was elsewhere.

The vision that came was overwhelming. I was at the Sphinx, and the sky was blood red.

It flashed in and then out of my mind. I didn't want this to distract, so I decided it was time to close the ceremony.

"Maybe we wait until we reach Egypt before we wear them all together, but now it's time to close the sacred circle," I said and started to place my new treasure back into the package it had arrived in.

"Now, let's gather everything. I know Emilee has created

a divine lunch, and I'm so excited to meet you properly, Gina, and of course, welcome our dear Lesley back," I called out.

Well, this was a different outcome than I had planned, but all the same, the journey had been called, and the game was at play. I stopped myself in mid-thought. Why would I think this was a game?

We returned to the Gables, and I was comforted that everyone was in high spirits. I made my attempts to have a conversation with Lesley, but it was mainly one-sided as she detailed her accomplishments and rather unprofessionally named the celebrities with whom she had been giving psychic readings. She detailed their lives like a walking, talking scandal magazine. Gina, however, was such a lovely person, and she rescued me by asking me to show her the gardens. We sat in silence on the bench, and Wallis came and sat and purred in her lap.

No visions came of her and I in past lives, but the word of sisters came to me. She patted my hand as if she had heard this too and simply smiled.

"I know. I feel like sisters, also. Another time we will chat... our time will come," she said. I felt she could be trusted and, in time, we would be great friends.

CHAPTER 13

Thursday, 10 September 2009

It was nearly time to go to Egypt. We had just under a week to go, and I was already in a panic.

"Packed already?" I heard a voice behind me. It was Lucinda.

I turned to address her, "Yeah, I'm just really excited, and I also don't want to accidentally forget anything. You know, if I'm packed early, then I have time to pick anything up that I forgot!"

Lucinda walked into my room and sat on the edge of my bed, saying, "And did you forget anything?"

"No, not as far as I can tell. My tickets are downstairs with the others, and my passport is on my nightstand over there." I was still pacing like I had had too much caffeine.

"Good, good. Listen, Anna, we need to talk about something."

Lucinda's serious tone had me worried, "Okay, what about?"

Lucinda turned to pull something out from behind her back and held a gold gift bag out to me. "Here," she said, "Isis wanted you to have this for your travels."

I took the bag from her and opened it, finding a beautiful white pashmina scarf. I gasped. It was Isis's, and she wore it all the time. I'd seen her wear it in all of the pictures from the Egypt trip.

Lucinda explained, "Once we reach the Temple of Isis at Philae, Anna, you will find your colour and your true connection. But in the meantime, carry this with you and in moments of uncertainty and fear, remember the courageous woman who wore it." She said the word "fear" very slowly, and we both looked at each other. No words needed to be said; I knew what she meant.

"In those moments," she continued, "place this scarf around you and see Isis with you, and you will always be protected."

I nodded, "Thank you."

"Now, I'll leave you to finish packing." Lucinda got up and left the room.

I stood there clutching the scarf; it felt so soft and was the purest white I had ever seen. It was hardly a good colour for me, but then this was a whole new chapter, so perhaps I could reinvent myself again.

Catching a glimpse of my reflection in the long mirror, I smiled at it, recognising and acknowledging the massive changes that had taken place in me since arriving in Glastonbury. I wasn't the same person anymore—I was me, but so much more.

The sound of a car door slamming distracted me. I looked out the window and saw Naomi walking up the drive. She must have snuck out when we weren't paying attention. Oh, our glamorous and celebrity psychic! She was hot on the heels of appearances in London and had just signed a book deal to write about her work as a psychic medium. We were so proud of her. The bad and toxic relationship with her evil ex-husband and then the cycle happening once again recently with the shaman-scheming boyfriend might have jaded some people towards her, but to all of us, she was our Wonder Woman. Underneath, there were moments of vulnerability she rarely showed. Like me, she had also changed in the past months for the better, finally coming into her own power. After our ceremony on the 88, she had confided in me that she had been bewitched by the shaman Francisco. He had been trying to steal our Egypt agent and connections for the private access tours into the sacred sites. It had been Lesley who had raised the alarm about him. I had the opportunity to forgive her, and I was glad to have taken it, but something in me sensed he was not fully gone from the picture.

Today, it would appear, was not one of those days as I heard the back door open and her high heels clattering across the old wooden floor. Her steps sounded hurried, and I heard them coming up the stairs and towards my room. She appeared in the doorway a moment later, looking somewhat dishevelled.

Naomi looked around my room a moment before, saying, "Oh, good, you're packed already."

I raised my eyebrow, confused, "Yes, I thought I would get a jump on things."

Naomi also looked confused, "Well... um, then I guess you already know," she fished an envelope out of her purse, "Here are your tickets. You leave tomorrow for Paris, and do not worry, I can take over your booked clients this week."

I was completely taken aback, "Paris? What? Do you mean Egypt, but in a week?"

Naomi sighed, looking annoyed, "No, I mean Paris, France, tomorrow. Did Lucinda not tell you?"

"Tell me what? I'm supposed to go to Egypt if you haven't forgotten. Why would I go to France so close to that? I know that I was upset about that photo, but I hardly think it needs to be addressed before the trip."

"Anna, I'm not sending you to Paris to research that photograph, although you should bring it with you, along with Isis's box. I've been talking with the Contessa, and she insists that you come and see her before the Egypt trip."

"Why?"

"She says that she can pick up where Isis left off and give you more answers and insight."

The dread that I had started to feel about having to take a detour melted away. I could do with some answers. I recalled the tarot cards with Lucas, it was foretold that I would be meeting a formidable woman, and the Contessa was it.

A thought struck me that threatened to bring back the dread, "Will I still make it to Egypt in time?"

"You should be on time," said Naomi, "I told the Contessa that she was not to keep you longer than necessary. However, I'm not sure how much she was paying attention to my instructions. That woman lives in a world of her own and seldom works well with others. But she knows many of the secrets of the sacred scrolls and scarabs and the Halls of Amenti, so I suppose that is something."

I could sense some tension. "Why do I get the feeling that you don't like her?"

"It's not a matter of like or dislike. I just don't completely trust her. She is one of Isis's oldest friends, but she was also always the most difficult to deal with. The Contessa was one of the only people I knew who could disarm Isis and make her second-guess herself. I would hate for her to do the same to you. Besides, I'm cross she never acknowledged Isis' passing or her funeral."

"I can hold my own, Naomi. Besides, unlike Isis, she is going to give me answers."

"Yes, but you have to wonder why she is so readily available to do so when Isis wasn't. I know Isis probably kept a few too many secrets to herself, but she also knew that everything has a proper time to be revealed."

"Or maybe she is just better at deciding that kind of stuff. Isis left me with very little in terms of instructions and information. If the Contessa can fill in those blanks, I don't see why that is bad. Plus, if you are so worried about what she will say, why are you sending me off to her?"

Naomi rolled her eyes, "You never go against a request of the Contessa. It isn't my preference. I personally think you should be here with us getting ready, but it's out of my hands."

"Hey, this is a good thing, Naomi, even if it's getting close to Egypt. I know you think that Isis was perfect, but the fact is, she wasn't. Whether you want to admit it or not, she failed me in some ways. In other ways, she was an amazing mentor, but I need a mentor now, even if it is just for a few days, to tell me what I need to know."

Naomi looked offended at my words but held her opinions to herself instead, saying, "Well, in any case, I think I should come with you, just in case."

"In case of what? No. You need to be here with the others, and I need to go see the Contessa. She is not going to be fully open with me if you are hovering, policing her words. You keep saying that I'm not ready, but you aren't giving me a chance to go out on my own and get ready. I'm putting my foot down. I need to go to Paris alone."

CHAPTER 14

Friday, 11 September 2009, early morning
Paris

It had been a hectic evening preparing for my additional Paris adventure, and I prayed for a nice dream to keep me from becoming too frenzied by it all. No such luck. I was still awake at 1 a.m. and had to be up at 4 a.m. to finish gathering my things to be out the door by 4:30. My taxi didn't arrive until almost twenty minutes after that, making me late for the airport. I prayed that the druidesses who inhabited the Tor would get us there in time.

The ride was not as pleasant as I would have liked, either. It was dark and raining, and as we drove past the Gables, the Chalice Well, and then down past the High Street. I could see there were no signs of life, and all was still. Only the streetlights created a golden shimmer on the shadow-cobbled streets. It was as if I were leaving or fleeing, and I wondered if I would even return after this new adventure, or how it would be for me then.

London Heathrow Airport was something I had never encountered before. Naomi had gone over every step with me, like how to claim my tickets at the counter, check my luggage, and get through security. She had even put a veiled curse over my bag of scrolls and scarabs and the red box belonging to Isis. I had left behind my books, including those from Alice.

Woe to anyone who touched those sacred objects. Luckily, the queues were short, and I got to my gate just in time for final boarding.

I was sat in a window seat next to a little girl and her mother, who fell asleep almost immediately. The little girl, dressed in a princess gown, turned to me excitedly and asked, "Are you going to Disneyland, too?"

I chuckled at this and replied, "No, but I am guessing you are? Dressed like that, I'm guessing you must be a princess!"

The little girl squealed excitedly at my words, "Oh, you think? I'm not a princess, but I want to meet one! Have you ever met any princesses?"

I thought about it for a moment and decided to tell her, "Well, no, not a princess. But, I have met a queen, two, in fact maybe three!"

That set the little girl off with a million questions, and for the rest of the flight, I quietly told her stories of Cleopatra, Anne Boleyn, and Elizabeth I, Anne's happy, content, successful daughter. Happy to have the distraction and use my creative skills, I gave the children's version of these women, as it was too early for Halloween.

☥

When I arrived in Paris, to my surprise and delight, I found a driver holding a board with my name on it, waiting at the arrivals gate.

"Bonjour, Mademoiselle Harris. I hope you had a good flight! Please allow me to take your bags and follow me! I have strict instructions to take you straight to the Contessa. She is waiting and does not like it when we are late!"

It was not long before we were driving past all the

famous landmarks, like the Arc de Triomphe, the Louvre, and, of course, the Eiffel Tower. I know it may be cliché, but it truly was an amazing sight to behold. It was amazing that not a few hours ago, I had been in Glastonbury and now, I was here in the City of Lights.

☥

We arrived at a very posh-looking area with ornate buildings, black railing, and manicured trees and shrubs tucked in the doorways. The street sign read "Avenue Montaigne," and I instantly recognised it as the epicentre for all things fashion. As we drove down the street, all of the major fashion houses came into view, like Dior, Louis Vuitton, and Chanel. Impossibly gorgeous women walked down the street, draped in designer clothes and stomping around in glossy designer boots. Just like in Naomi's magazines, her castoffs were in my treasure pile in my bedroom.

As we passed, I could not help but think about my mother and wonder about her time here. All I had was a picture from the red box of her and Isis, but I knew there was a secret in these streets.

Suddenly, we took a sharp turn up a side street to a slightly secluded and tree-lined area up a hill. As the chauffeur came up the crest of the hill, I could see the Eiffel Tower plain as day, even more beautiful from this vantage point than when we had driven by it. I found myself staring and almost missed that we had stopped in front of our destination: the Contessa's home. I suppose I should say that it was less of a home and more of a small hotel in terms of size. The façade was classic 18th-century French architecture, still reminiscent of the grandiose and excessive maximalist adornment that the pre-revolution French aristocracy was prone to.

The chauffeur then got out of the front and came round to open my door for me. Just then, another man with dark black hair, dressed in a full butler's suit, opened the front door. He briskly motioned to someone just beyond the door, and a young attendant came rushing out and collected my bags from the chauffeur, tipping his head to me and blushing before rushing back inside. The man at the door made a 'tsk tsk' sound at him before turning back to me and offering a polite smile and an outstretched arm. I gathered I should approach him and did so with haste. Up close, I could see that the man's hair was not quite all black, and there was grey at his temples. He had grey-blue eyes with slight wrinkles around them and lines on his forehead and around his mouth. If I had to guess, I would say he was in his forties or fifties.

"Bonjour, Mademoiselle Harris," he said in a thick French accent, "My name is André, the head of the household and personal butler to the Contessa. I trust your journey was comfortable?"

"Oh yes," I replied, "I was sat next to the most wonderful mother and daughter, who talked my ear off about Disneyland. It was adorable!"

André made a face that suggested his disdain for children or Disney or both, but quickly recovered, saying, "Ah, how charming. I will make sure to put you in first class for your trip to Cairo so you will have more peace. Now, normally, I would show you to your room to let you wash the travel off. However, the Contessa insists that you meet with her right away in the parlour. So, please, if you will follow me?"

He opened the door to the grand foyer and escorted me to an open metal elevator. Once inside, we travelled up two floors and out into a long gallery. He sped to the double doors at the end of the hall, and I had to run to keep up. He knocked thrice and opened the doors, motioning me to enter. I walked through the door into a brightly lit antechamber with marble floors, light pink wainscoted walls with gilt details and romantic frescos painted on the ceiling. Just ahead of me was a dark garnet-coloured velvet curtain, hiding the room that lay beyond it.

Suddenly, I heard a stirring from beyond the curtain, and a strong, commanding female voice spoke, *"Vous pouvez entrer, s'il vous plait?"* I walked cautiously over to the curtain and took a deep breath, attempting to quell my nerves. I hesitated to pull the gold thread cord a moment too long because the voice again called out:

"Entrez, immédiatement!"

This shook me from my daze, and as confidently as I could, I drew back the curtain and walked in. It took a moment for my eyes to adjust as the room was very dimly lit. But when they did, I could see a magnificent display of hand-painted dark floral wallpaper, parquet floors, gas lamps, and 19th-century velvet furniture. Everything was draped in colours of red, black, and expensive gold. There were several marble columns and display boxes throughout the room, which had a variety of curious objects. It felt more like a room in a museum than in someone's home.

I got so distracted by the scene in front of me that I barely noticed the owner of the voice that had beckoned me in, who loudly cleared her throat and said in a heavy French accent, "Are you hard of hearing or something? Or did you just forget all of those etiquette lessons your mother taught you?"

I snapped my head in her direction at the mention of my mum, "I... uh... *oui*... no... I-I-I mean, I haven't forgotten.

I just got distracted by all of your amazing curios!" I said, gesturing around the room.

The woman looked around from her spot at the large oak table she was sitting at, "Pfff, flattery will get you nowhere, Mademoiselle Harris. Now, in case it was not apparent, I am Contessa Francine Derux."

"Nice to meet you," I said as I rushed over to her and extended my hand, which she declined to take. "Oh, uh, I'm Anna! Anna Harris...but you knew that already..." I trailed off, feeling awkward.

After a pregnant pause, I sat down, not sure what else she would want me to do. She held my gaze as I did and didn't scold me, so I figured that was the next step. Her stern gaze dared me to look away, but I couldn't help but flick my eyes slightly around the area. Thus, I gleaned more awareness of my hostess and her private chambers, like the tufted crimson silk armchairs we were sitting in and the small fire burning in the stone fireplace just next to the table. It cast strange shadows onto the Contessa and table between us, and I could swear I saw the form of an ibis in them. Had my spirit friends followed me? Upon further inspection, I could see the Contessa was smartly dressed in a vintage designer burgundy wool suit with gold buttons and a vertical striped cotton button-down shirt with a three-strand necklace of pearls placed delicately around her neck. Her hair was cut, or rather carved, into a precise bob shape and was a distinct pure white in colour.

Suddenly, she broke the silence and asked, "Well? Are you going to keep me waiting all day?"

I gave her a confused look.

"The box! The box of the oracles' most treasured scrolls and scarabs?"

"Oh, I, yes, um, the box," I looked around, realising the

attendant had taken the bag that contained it.

As if on cue, André floated in, taking great care to present me with the very bag I needed. I could swear his hands were shaking ever so slightly as he handed it to me, and two beads of sweat were forming on his brow. His rigid French finery training refused to let him show his true state of being—that of a man nervous to handle such important artefacts. "Thank you," I said sheepishly. André only nodded and went off to take his position behind the Contessa. I could feel the Contessa's eyes on me as I rummaged around my bag for the box.

"Tsk, tsk, Anna, you must be more mindful of where you keep that," the Contessa said admonishingly.

"My apologies, Contessa. I am still a bit frazzled from my travels."

"Oh, is that all? I will have André bring us some tea and a—"

The thought died in her mouth as I gingerly placed the box on the table between us. Her tough façade was also crumbling, as her stern look was slowly replaced with one of awe and reverence. She began to reach out her beautifully manicured hand as if to touch the box, but then snatched it back. Then, she went to say something but thought better of it. I had only been in the presence of this woman for a few minutes, and already I could tell she was usually never this unsure.

André, for his part, regained his composure quickly and sprang into action, pulling out a lace veil from some unseen trunk behind the Contessa and draping it over her, partially obscuring her face. This seemed to do the trick, and I could hear a slight sigh of relief from her. André then briefly exited the room and escorted in a veiled woman, who sat down to the left of the Contessa without a word, only sharing a nod with her.

I wanted to bring some ceremony to the moment, so I paused and placed my hands on the box to ask its permission. "Now we have fourteen pieces, just awaiting the last scroll and scar..."

The Contessa then turned back to me and interrupted me, "Open it!" she commanded.

The whole situation was beginning to feel incredibly bizarre because I could tell that the Contessa and the veiled woman were cloaked in order to shield themselves from the contents of the box. However, my curiosity got the best of me, so I obliged and opened the box, revealing all the scrolls and scarabs we had collected. Both women let out a gasp and leaned back in their chairs as if to put slightly more distance between them and the box. As I closed the box, André again swooped in and placed a white linen cloth over the box as the two women began to chant in a strange language I had not heard of before. It sounded like a mix of Egyptian, Arabic, French, Greek, and German. They rocked back and forth in their chairs, fervently chanting.

Unexpectedly, I was hit with hazy visions of sandy hills, and I worried I was being forced back into the terrible nightmares I'd had, but it shifted.

Instead, I saw what looked like a small group of people getting into a boat, wearing strange clothes that looked Egyptian, combined with something else. It then shifted to them landing on a shoreline in the dead of night, transporting what looked like an injured person on a makeshift gurney. Little lights shone around their necks, and as they moved far beyond me towards the horizon, all I could see were those little lights bobbing up and down.

My vision shifted to the group making camp in the desert the next day, all looking worn and tired. They were taking turns going in and out of a tent with food and wet cloths. For a split second, my vision became clear, and I saw Isis and the Contessa talking outside the tent before everything went black.

As I returned to the scene in front of me, I could see the Contessa slumped over slightly in her chair, her veil now removed, and the other woman, also unveiled, fanning the Contessa as André hurried to the side table with tea, scones, and finger sandwiches. Just as he finished placing everything on the table, the Contessa woke and stood up immediately, closing the distance between herself and the box, hovering excitedly above it. I worried about what would happen should she touch it, and I reached over to retrieve the box.

The Contessa shot me a look that compelled me to remove my hands from the box and shrink in my seat. I felt her dark crimson presence invading my very essence. She was aura-shifting with me, a term Lucinda used when someone wished to dominate the energy field of another. I held strong and, with some gentle breathing, was able to stay focused and grounded. Then, I stood up and did the same to her, letting my aura swirl brilliant gold and white streaks in hers. A calm expression spread across her face, and all the tension she was carrying in her muscles loosened. She closed her eyes and smiled, feeling my energy. I looked at her now and smiled. I had sensed her energy and read her heart. It was golden. *Oh, how she reminds me of Isis, so strong and determined,* I thought. *Just French,* I inwardly chuckled.

The Contessa opened her eyes and began to chuckle as she realised she had been discovered and bested, "*Ah, ma chère soeur.* I suppose I should explain!"

The other woman in the room, whom I had all but forgotten about, piped in, "*Oui, tout de suite, s'il vous plait!*" Now able to see her more clearly, she reminded me of a younger Emilee, ever the fashionista with kind eyes and a bright smile.

The Contessa looked over to her and back at me, saying, "Oh, yes, how rude of me, Anna, this is my granddaughter, Alexandria. She is my protégé and an exemplary student of the French psychic practices and Akashic Records!"

Alexandria walked over to us with her arm outstretched and took my hand, greeting me with a big smile, "Oh, it is wonderful to meet you, Anna! I was so excited to hear you were stopping by to see us before Egypt. I can't wait to go!"

I returned her smile, "Thank you, you too! I didn't know you would be joining us. Glad to have you with us!"

The Contessa piped in, "We will both be attending. This will be Alexandria's first. I'm glad she will have someone about her age to experience this with."

Alexandria rolled her eyes, "Grandmama, please, you embarrass me!" Her mood then shifted to one more sombre, saying, "And Anna, my condolences on the loss of your mentor, Isis. I only spent a short time with her this lifetime, but I remember her well. She was incredible. You must have felt a great emptiness when she passed. Please let me know if you need anything from me!"

Tears shone in the corner of my eyes as I grasped her hand and, in a relatively steady voice, said, "Thank you, Alexandria. I appreciate the sentiment! You are so kind!" At that moment, I felt an instant bond with her that I knew had spanned many lifetimes, or at least I assumed, since I had not seen most of them.

"And don't let Grandmama intimidate you; you know why you're here, and in time, you'll know who you are."

I wondered for a moment if this was Alexandria speaking or a channel speaking through her. I motioned back for a moment, and she also.

Alexandria and I laughed at our seriousness and turned back to the Contessa, who had returned to her seat and begun sipping her tea. Amused, she looked up at us, saying, "Are you two sparrows done? Please, come and sit. Enjoy your tea and accompaniments!"

Alexandria winked at me and joined me at the side table, immediately loading up her plate with cucumber sandwiches and a large scone. I sat down and made my own plate. "No meat?" I joked with Alexandria as we sat down.

She shook her head, "No. I am an acute empath. From a young child, I felt it was like torture to eat a dead animal. I find the vegetables don't have quite the same effect!

The Contessa piped in, "That is why she came to live here with me, to learn about and understand her gifts."

"I see, I see," I said in between bites.

"Now, Grandmama, you are avoiding telling us what just happened. Why did you react to the box like that?"

The Contessa put her teacup down, sighed, and went into an explanation. "Anna, let me explain our veils. There are several reasons. The first being all the negative presences following you lately. I wanted to make sure that the box would be safe and its contents incorruptible in this new space, so I performed a ceremony of cleansing and protection. The second is, admittedly, my fault, bad karma from a past life. I was worried the box would reinitiate a curse on me and, by proxy, my granddaughter. Luckily, my granddaughter has been spared, but I fear I should still be careful around them for now."

I nodded along and mulled over her words a moment before responding, "Does this have anything to do with those hazy visions of a group of refugees being on a boat and traversing the desert?"

The Contessa leaned in, intrigued, "You saw those,

too? You are a most powerful oracle, I see. Can you tell me anything about what you saw or sensed?"

I closed my eyes and tried to remember every detail. There was something preventing me from fully going back into a regression to see more clearly, so I did my best and said, "Well, the vision wasn't super clear, and what I could see was from a distance. However, it looked like a group of ancient people fleeing their land, if I had to guess, and I saw their journey to a new land in search of refuge. They weren't Egyptian... but I must imagine they were... oh, they were Atlantean!"

"Yes, I believe they were. What else did you see?"

"They went to Egypt to try and find sanctuary. There was a sick person they were caring for, and you were there with... oh my god, yes, it was Isis and my mother!" I opened my eyes.

The Contessa let out a heavy sigh. After a long pause, she tried to speak but seemed lost for words.

"Naomi told me that your mother had passed. I offer my condolences to you."

I thought on it for a second and responded, "How did you know her?"

"I found a photograph. I mean, Isis was there, and you were there, and the two of you were also in a picture of a fashion show together in the '70s with my mother? Could you please explain that?"

"Yes, your mother and I used to run in the same circles in Paris before she moved back to England and met your father. We also knew each other back in the time of Atlantis. I had thought she would follow a path like Isis, as she had great potential and psychic gifts, but she made a firm vow to never take them on.

I lost track of her until recently, when we began to

be aware of you. Lucinda called me about the photo you found, and then Naomi and Lucinda sent me an image of you, which made me think. Then I saw Lottie in you the moment you entered the room today. Tell me, Anna, do you see anything karmic?"

"I wish I could, Contessa. But just now when I tried, something blocked me. I could maybe push through it if I tried hard enough, but I don't think it would be wise. Whatever happened back then, we must not be ready to see it. I suspect the cause of your karmic imbalance will reveal itself in due time when it is right."

The Contessa nodded, "A very astute and wise bit of guidance I would expect from an oracle. Most impressive, Anna, you seem to have a flair for this role! Now, why don't we put this subject to rest for now and discuss the contents of your box of scrolls and scarabs."

I furrowed my brow. I had so many more questions for her about my mother, like how they met. However, I could tell the Contessa wished to move on.

I brought the box closer to me onto my lap and opened it once more, half bracing for another strong reaction from her. When I got none, I said, "Well, like I said, I don't have all of them, but we have a good start to bringing all the scrolls and scarabs together."

"Which ones do you have?" the Contessa asked.

"Just about all of them," I replied.

"We have the Scroll and Scarab of Creation, Death and Resurrection, Magic and Prophecy, and Truth and Integrity."

I pointed to each in turn. Her eyes grew wider, and I could swear I saw an etheric hand reaching out to touch them.

"Then we have the Scroll and Scarab of Goddess and Fertility, Protection, and The Records of Life."

"So, seven scrolls and seven scarabs, oui?"

"Yes, that is correct."

"Wonderful. Hopefully, we can help you add to your collection," she said. Then, looking at her watch, she continued, "Oh, is that the time? Supper will be in just an hour or so. Why don't we retire to the Lilac Room for some brandy?"

Alexandria spoke up, "Grandmama, are you sure that is wise? Perhaps you want to rest a bit?"

"Oh, nonsense, Alexandria, I am not an old woman; I am fine," Alexandria gave her a look.

"Okay, I am a little bit old, but my bones don't ache yet." The Contessa got up with great agility and briskly walked towards the door, calling for me as she went, "Come, Anna, keep up, and don't forget the box and your other belongings!" In a flash, she was at the door, and for sure, she also had the speed of Isis.

We stepped into the new room, and I was immediately overwhelmed with beautiful opulence. The walls were decked with shiny lilac silk painted with lighter lilac cherry blossoms. The ornate furniture was upholstered with the same cherry blossom pattern but in different shades of lilac and violet. The large, gold, crystal chandelier in the centre of the room reflected and refracted light off the walls, giving everyone and everything a purply hue. Delicate crystal vases and lamps filled the room, and a large bookcase stood on the far side, stuffed to the brim with old leather-bound books. I walked over to the window and saw a beautiful walled garden with a bench, a small pond, and a weeping willow tree. I imagined myself going to sit on that bench, under that tree, and writing the next great novel of my generation.

I again lost myself in the magic of the room and failed to see that the Contessa was attempting to get my attention, "Anna? Anna? *'Elleuu,* Earth to Anna!" she called.

I shook my head and looked over in her direction to find her sat down in a large periwinkle silk armchair by the window with a puzzled look on her face. "Oh, a thousand apologies, Contessa!" I said with an awkward curtsey.

The Contessa laughed at this, "There is no need for that, *ma rêvasseur.* I should be bowing to you! Now, now, *s'il vous plait,* sit!" She gestured to the chair opposite her.

As I sat down, Alexandria came into the room and announced, "André will have supper for us at half past six. In the interim, could I interest you both in a brandy?"

"Brandy, for me—neat, of course, *ma poupette!*" replied the Contessa.

"I think I will do the same, Grandmama. Anna, and for you?" Alexandria asked.

"Oh, uh, same, please, thank you!"

Alexandria went about quickly preparing the drinks, bringing them over on a silver tray, and sat down with us. Each small goblet, made of a light purple-coloured crystal with silver filigree, was teeming with brandy. We each took a glass and clinked them lightly against one another in mutual acknowledgment and celebration. Then, both women took healthy gulps without any hesitation while I choked down my small sip—it was like nasty medicine.

Alexandra noticed and chuckled, "I take it you don't often drink brandy neat?"

"What? Of course, I do!" I paused and laughed, "Okay, not so much. But, when in the Contessa's home, I will!"

"That is the spirit, Anna!" The Contessa exclaimed, raising her glass before taking another large gulp, "You know, I always find my best visions arise from a healthy dose of brandy. The gods have ambrosia, and I have my brandy. This one was blessed by a group of Benedictine nuns, so as holy as one can wish!"

I had heard this from Naomi before, but hers was Malbec wine. I guessed I would follow her eventually, but certainly not with this brandy stuff. It was best saved for Christmas cakes.

"Grandmama, of course you think your visions are better after you've gotten drunk! I swear, Anna, this woman will be the death of me!"

"Well, Alexandria, your grandmother may have a point! The Oracles of Delphi used vapours to enhance their visions, and some indigenous people use peyote in their practices too, just to name a few!"

The Contessa smiled, "Ah, I knew I would like this girl!"

Alexandra playfully rolled her eyes, "Or she is just trying to get into your good graces?"

"Well, it is working! Flattery will get you everywhere, *ma rêvasseur!*"

"Contessa," I said, "what does that mean?"

"*Ma rêvasseur?* It means 'my daydreamer,' Anna. You always seem to be in some far-off place. I hope you will share that place with us in time."

"Yes, and maybe even beyond that," I answered.

"Beyond?" She paused to watch for my reaction.

"You have seen the Oracle of Atlantis, have you not, *oui* or *non?*" She tilted her head as if making conversation, but this was hardly small talk. As I was now sure my Glastonbury sisters had already updated her behind my back, I decided to simply be open.

"Uh, yes and no, I am not sure. Do you know much about her?"

"Only that she was a powerful being who served the Temple of the Children of Light and interpreted their wisdom."

"The Children of Light?"

"*Oui.* Thirty-two of them would descend from the Halls

of Amenti to impart their wisdom to us mortals. Specifically, four groups of eight went to each corner of the earth: the North, East, South, and West. For 900 years at a time, they would spread their knowledge and wisdom, taking the forms of the people they were living among. Then, at the end of that time, they would return to the Halls of Amenti and rest for 100 years. Thus, the cycle continued like that for thousands of years. The Children of Light who came to Atlantis were the West. You see, the Atlanteans were a unique people. They were the most adept at taking the teachings of the Children of Light and applying them. On top of that, Atlanteans could live for many years, allowing the Children of Light to not have to switch bodies during their 900 years on Earth. In fact, the Atlanteans became a favourite of the beings in the Halls of Amenti, who went as far as sending one of the Lords, Horlet, to take up physical residence in Atlantis."

"Oh, wow!" I exclaimed, "So, what does the Oracle of Atlantis have to do with all of that, and the Temple at Philae for that matter?"

"Well, as I said, she wrote down the teachings and wisdom of the Children of Light and was their caretaker when they were on Earth. It is said that after Atlantis's destruction, she saved many of these writings. I have witnessed this myself to be true!"

"Like in a vision?"

"Um, yes, like in a vision. Her writings eventually became the scrolls in your box. In fact, the first High Priestess of Isis, and leader of the Sacred Eight that recreated Philae Temple around 300 BC, was a descendant of the Oracle of Atlantis."

"Really? Isis had Atlantean blood in her?"

"Well, yes, at least initially. Very few Atlanteans escaped the flood. Eventually, they assimilated into the Egyptian people and culture, as well as many other indigenous cultures. So, Atlantis and the Oracles of Egypt are closely linked. As the potential leader within our group, it is important you know our origins."

"I see. Thank you, Contessa. It is so refreshing to get a straight answer from someone!"

The Contessa laughed, "You wouldn't be speaking ill of your former mentor, would you?"

My face went white, "I... I-I, no..."

"It is alright. I have known Isis for a long while, and she has always been one for the cryptic and obscure. Personally, I find little value in that. While you are here, I will try to answer every question you have as best I can. You deserve answers!"

I let out a huge breath I hadn't realised I'd been holding. To hear the Contessa say that gave me such relief and made me think that perhaps I really could get mastery of this and perhaps lead the Egypt trip with some authority and wisdom. I was about to ask more about the Halls of Amenti, as I suddenly remembered my call from Egypt those many months ago.

But just then, André came into the room and rang a bell, indicating dinner was soon to be ready.

"That's the dressing bell. Time to change." Alexandria smiled.

Content with my day's conversations with the Contessa, I rose from my seat, and Alexandria led me to my room. It resembled a hotel suite more than a simple guest room. After refreshing myself and changing, I returned at the sound of the next bell to savour a delightful five-course meal with two women who made me feel more at home than I had in a long time. Later that night, as I pulled the plush goose-down comforter over myself in my suite, I smiled and drifted into a dreamless, worry-free sleep.

Chapter 15

Saturday 12 September 2009, 7:30 a.m.

I awoke to a soft rapping at my door. It was André with a cart of breakfast treats. He went over to the small table on the other side of my room and set up a lavish breakfast spread of fresh orange juice, coffee, Danishes, croissants, and all manner of other delicious treats. I got up, put on my robe, and joined André at the table.

As he finished setting up, he handed me an envelope, saying, "For you, from the Contessa. Please, read it immediately. Merci!"

I took the envelope from him. It was made of metallic woven paper and sealed with a wax stamp of the strange symbol I had seen, but was unsure where or when. "Thank you, André."

"Will there be anything else, Mademoiselle Harris?"

"Oh no, I think you have everything covered here with breakfast, thank you!"

"As you wish!" André nodded and promptly turned on his heel and exited.

Not wanting to forget the card, amidst what was about to be my breakfast indulgence, I opened the envelope, and the card inside read:

Bonjour, ma rêvasseur!

Please be downstairs in the front parlour at 8:20 a.m. There, you will meet Alexandria, who will take you to visit the Louvre. The car leaves at 8:30 a.m. on the dot, so do not

be late! I will join you for dinner in town later in the evening. Have a wonderful day!
— C.

I was happy to go to the Louvre; it was one of the places I'd most hoped to visit. Plus, this would give me another chance to get to know Alexandria. It might be nice to have a friend my own age on this trip!

☥

We were in the car and on our way promptly at 8:30 a.m. Alexandria ended up being very forthcoming and talkative, giving me an oral history of the city as we drove. Suddenly, the car entered a roundabout, and I saw a high statue with a fountain. I was immediately hit with a wave of nausea and dizziness.

I hereby condemn... I hereby condemn...

Those words kept invading my mind, and then, I heard a crowd cheering loudly:

Liberté! Liberté!

It was so loud I had to cover my ears, and I doubled over in my seat.

"Anna," I heard Alexandria say, "Anna, do not worry, we are almost there. Just hang on a little longer, and you will be safe! Just a little longer!"

Then Naomi's words were in my head, *Not everything is as it seems, Anna. Let go of your judgment and simply observe. You will soon have Paris under your spell again.* Once again, she talked in riddles.

But just as suddenly as it came on, the sick feeling left me, and my mind was quiet. Alexandria helped me sit up and pointed out my window—we had arrived at the Louvre.

☥

Once inside the museum and less our outerwear at the coat check, I got a better look at Alexandria's attire as she went to talk to one of the officials. She was endlessly chic in her black cashmere turtleneck, grey and black tweed pencil skirt, and designer black leather pumps. My shabby bargain bin black flats, cuffed black jeans, and ruby red fisherman's sweater looked laughable next to her. I may as well have written "British tourist oaf" on my forehead.

Alexandria sauntered back over to me and smiled, "Okay, we are all set; they will let us have free rein to roam for the next hour until the museum opens. By the way, I like your ensemble. Cuffed jeans and chunky sweaters are very *en vogue* right now!"

I blushed at the compliment, "Oh, thank you! I didn't think I could hold a candle next to your fabulous look!"

She waved her hand, "Tut, tut. This outfit is safe and boring. I am not one to go out of my comfort zone. I live in black, grey, and navy. Now, shall we?"

I followed her along across the atrium to a smaller corridor.

Not wanting to walk in silence, I asked her, "So, where did you learn English? You speak with a perfect British accent."

"Oh, my tutors growing up always taught me that way. Same with the boarding schools I went to. Grandmama thought it would be better for me when I went to Oxford, so everyone would be able to understand me clearly and I could blend in."

"I see. Your grandmother is very keen on keeping up appearances, isn't she?"

"Yes, and no. She just wants to make sure that we don't

draw too much attention to ourselves. It's a safety thing, I suppose."

I nodded, wondering what they would need to be kept safe from.

Alexandra continued, "You know, the museum comes alive with many ghosts after the night has fallen, and this can be distracting! Hence, we visit in the daylight."

"Do you see ghosts?" I asked.

"*Ma oui,* of course," she smiled. "Don't you?"

"Oh, yes, I see them, and I think they see me!"

We smiled at each other, and I saw Alexandria in a grey satin dress with tears and rips in the bottom, her head covered with a white cloth cap. But I saw fear on her face.

She stopped and looked at me, "Yes, that was my voice you heard when you passed the circle with the obelisk. Perhaps I will explain another time. Now let's begin."

She escorted me into a corridor area, and all I could see were the deep walls of stone. I felt like I was stepping back into an underground chamber.

"We are well beneath the city, and there are many tunnels," she explained.

"Tunnels? But what were they for?"

"To escape, to hide, and to reach our mystery schools. We had to hide for many lifetimes."

"You were once a High Priestess connected to Isis, weren't you?"

"Yes, I was many things, and when Isis came to Paris a few times that I met with her, we remembered those lives. I may look young, but I am very, very old."

"Look!" she pointed, and there in front of me stood a perfect Sphinx—the regal head and calm expression. I walked over and had to stop myself from touching it.

"You are here to remember, and this Sphinx marks the doorway that we must honour as it is the guardian to the

Hall of Records that lies hereafter."

I nodded, "Then I thank this Sphinx, most high and regal, and may all that come to pass be." *Strange words,* I thought, but then again, this was a strange and unusual place.

"Now let us go meet some friends and look at the beautiful things we once owned!" Alexandria said, grabbing my arm and guiding me along.

I was silent and enthralled by all I saw and remembered from the images of books I had read, but now this was real. I was stopped in my tracks and stood silent. In front of me was a statue of a man with legs crossed and a papyrus in his lap. Alexandria stood next to me, silent and watching.

"I remember him," I whispered.

"Me too," she replied. "He was in Karnak Temple and wrote everything we said and did. At the entrance to the Temple of Sekhmet."

"Yes, but why?" I asked.

"So we would know and remember! Yes, and there was a School of Scribes, and every morning, they would wake at dawn and sit rigid until called to the secret places in the temple. Do you remember the silk banners flowing and incense in the air?"

"Yes, like smoke and mirrors hiding everyone's secrets!"

"These scribes sent the messages and had such power; I could feel myself being held captive by his eyes.

"They saw everything and said nothing, but what they wrote could decide a person's fate. It was said they wrote directly into the Akashic Records. They recorded the energy into the scroll with the spells and curses. These were live scribes. The Akashic librarians were also live scribes. For some reason, I see them sometimes silenced, as if their tongues were removed. A cruel yet privileged role. 'Speak no evil' comes to mind."

Alexandria turned to me and, in a quiet voice, asked, "Can we give him back his voice, perhaps, and set him free?"

I nodded, and as we stood in silence, I began to hear Alexandria utter words like an incantation. "Return his voice, return his wisdom, and release his soul bound by the secrets of others, and so it is," she breathed.

Once she was finished, I felt lighter, and I was sure his statue had begun to smile. I began to see that a statue or image could bind a soul to the work they were performing. Alexandria read my mind. "Anna, be aware that if you lend your image to a cause, it's a contract."

An image of a book cover with my image flashed in front of me; better to choose a character.

"Now, we must move quickly, as we have begun to shift the energy and magic. They will hear us, and we have much work still to do!"

I shook my head and laughed, "But of course, a priestess's work is never done! Lead the way!"

We went to several other exhibits throughout the morning, and with each scribe statue I saw, I said a prayer. They had long been held for the messages and scriptures they had written and could be free, I felt. It was so rewarding to do good work like this without any of the expectations of others or a paying client in front of me. Alexandria was easy to work with and get along with, as if this had been so in many past lives, and I wondered if she would think about moving to Glastonbury.

In the last corridor, I began to smell the strong scent of wood around me and wondered if it was a perfume of some sort, but no, in glass cases stood the sarcophagus of a beautiful woman, standing in a row with dark black hair and piercing eyes. At first, I thought these were statues, but then I realised they were coffins. Face after face, I walked along and began to feel unwell as I passed each one.

"Can we sit a moment?" I looked at Alexandria.

"Of course," she nodded, placing a hand on my shoulder, "Anna, you are white as a sheet!"

I felt a great sadness well up inside me, and at any moment, I thought I would cry.

"Is it the mummification process?" she asked.

"No, it's these sister souls. They have been trapped here for probably thousands of years, missing valuable lifetimes."

Slowly, my vision shifted, and I began to see the ghosts as they had been in their lifetimes.

As I noticed them, they slowly began to notice me.

I was transported to another time and began to have a vision of them in other lifetimes.

"Can you help us? Can you help us, Anna?" The voices echoed around me.

"How can I help?" I asked.

"Are you talking to me?" asked Alexandria.

"No, no, Alexandria. I'm communicating with them," I said, pointing to three women close together.

"They are all from the same family, and they have been ghosts here ever since they arrived in Paris," I said.

"They were cursed by something very powerful, and they walk the halls waiting for someone with greater magic."

"Is that you?" Alexandria whispered. "Anna, I think this is it. Remember, you have the oracle gift, and in ancient times, the oracle's role was also to settle the disputes of karma and the soul."

"I'm not sure, but if we sit quietly and listen to them, they may help us to unlock the souls."

Alexandria took a sharp intake of breath.

"I see them, and now I hear them," she said.

"All of them?"

"No, just a few, but they have the same message."

"They are bound to these boxes and now to this place, and they keep talking about the year 1822," I said.

"That was the year the Dendara zodiac was removed at the request of the French King," she said.

"Do you think this has a connection?"

"Possibly, I feel many of them trapped here were guardians of its wisdom."

"Then we must go to the zodiac."

"How quickly can we reach it?"

Alexandria was swift off the mark and already ahead of me.

I kept up, nearly out of breath.

When she stopped, I looked around and felt an energy above me. My eyes rolled towards the ceiling, and there she was—perfectly placed into the ceiling of the oval room with benches placed around the space against the walls, so one could gaze up and take in her magnificence.

The vision was the same as I had seen in Emilee's secret room in Glastonbury, but nothing had prepared me for this energy.

"It's a stargate."

"Yes, Anna, like a cosmic portal."

I began to see the records and curses placed around the removal.

"It belongs in Egypt," I whispered.

"Yes, I believe it does," she said.

"I have been to this room many times over the years, but I have never seen or felt the energy like this."

She began staring at her hands. "Is it me, or am I starting

to see sparkles?"

"It's the energy particles... I sometimes get them when I do healings."

"I think the presence of you and I is creating a vortex and unlocking the energy."

"Perhaps we can release the women in the other room with its power."

I chose to sit opposite, and I began to recite the ancient words quietly. I hardly knew what I was saying, but I knew it had to do with the unravelling of all the contracts created before, and something significant had happened during the move to France from Egypt.

This was a darker magic than I had expected, an older power that had worked with the explorers. They had no idea what they had done. I began to see the Scroll and Scarab of Death and Resurrection floating in front of me.

I began to touch the energy like I was touching a TV screen, and words and letters were lighting up. They then created a portal of light, like a gateway between the worlds. I was suddenly made aware of the prophecy I had learnt about when I first came to Glastonbury. I pointed out a small section to Alexandria.

"During the time of Cleopatra VII, she and Isis both had baby girls. They were to be the next oracles and temple leaders before Egypt fell to Rome."

Alexandria's eyes grew wide. "Those baby girls were Naomi and me," I continued.

I thought of Naomi and received her telepathic blessing, so I activated the symbols that foretold our path and birthright.

As I did this, Alexandria mouthed over to me. "They are here."

I looked around and began to see the spirits of the

women slowly moving towards us, and as each one passed, they smiled and bowed their heads. We sat for at least thirty minutes, and I took out my journal as if to sketch, but I was making a note of the messages they were sending me. Each one disappeared into the zodiac and back to the spirit realms, and as they departed, each had a beautiful word or blessing for us. I thought I knew some of them, but in that moment, none of that mattered—only that they found the light.

Once they finished, I felt still and calm and was ready for food and grounding. Alexandria led me to a member's lounge where we would be private and well taken care of.

I wondered how much it cost to be a patron here. Alexandria read my mind.

"A lot," she whispered. "If Grandmama were here, you would have a director running down the stairs to welcome us."

Once our tea was poured, I began to ask Alexandria about the removal of the zodiac from Egypt.

"It is said that they used gunpowder to try to break the sandstone zodiac free. It was commissioned by the King in 1822, so that's the date and timeline," she said and shook her head.

I felt a surge of fear, and I now understood. "When they broke it free, it opened up the portal to many other realms, and the oracles had seen this, and they had placed curses on those who disturbed this powerful piece."

"Well, it was removed during Napoleon's visits and occupation. He had many artefacts brought back to Paris. Even though the Louvre takes beautiful care, I feel there is something we still do not understand. It is like the Rosetta stone and the theft of other Egyptian treasures. It would seem these pirates did not understand the power of the ancient wisdom. I pray these pieces are returned home one day, but who knows the future."

"Well, you do, Anna. That's your job now," and Alexandria laughed. "But do not think harshly of these museums. Something tells me they were spread around the world to stop them all from falling into the hands of another higher power who may not have been of the light."

"We saw the future and were trained, Anna. We saw this many times, but as oracles, we were often helpless."

"Our past lives tell the tale."

"Do you remember anything?" I asked her.

"Oh, yes," she nodded. "Very vividly. I had always wondered why ancient history fascinated me, especially Egypt and Greece. As a small child, I would visit the exhibits, as my family home was only a few streets away. I have so many copies of books from the gift shop, and it was there I unlocked my gift as the oracle."

"In a gift shop?" I laughed.

"Yes. I was about 12 years old and wandering around, and suddenly, I passed a mirror and saw a reflection of myself. My brown hair was raven black, and my skin was olive. I wore a Greek white robe, and when I went to the book section on ancient Greece, I opened a book, and there was an image that looked just like me. The book was communicating to me to confirm who and what I was. My visions became more intense, and it was then that my mother took me to visit the Contessa. I had been shielded from her as a small child. Your mentor, Isis, was also there. As a child, my parents had never discussed my gifts, as my mother felt it would be a curse. But when it was obvious, she took me to Grandmama, and Isis knew at once."

"Isis helped me unlock my gifts and see myself training in the Temple of Delphi. Delphi was famous in ancient times and had a whole school dedicated to the teachings of The Goddess and The Oracles. Isis had been my teacher in a past life for both of us. Egypt and Greece had many schools linked throughout history. Isis stayed as my mentor for a few weeks, and we would walk these halls of the Louvre, but she never interacted with the statues, and nothing ever came to life as it did today with you."

I felt a breeze and noticed that someone was opening a window, and the sun was streaming through. I looked around the lounge as if I was hoping to see Isis appear. If I could see the ghosts of Egyptian priestesses, then why not see Isis?

"Do you miss her?" Alexandria must have read my mind.

"Yes, so much, and more so when I am on a journey such as this. I always had her to go to with my visions and stories, and she always helped me to put them into perspective."

"Anna, I wanted to share something I did not tell my grandmamma. Isis called me while she was in Egypt. She was most afraid but would not tell me why; she just said that when the time came, I would come to Egypt and fulfill my initiations, and it would be with a woman called Anna. I promised her I would, and now I am seeing why."

Suddenly, I remembered the doll from the Christmas tree. It was Alexandria. Her fate was already connected to our group. Emilee knew, and Isis knew, and most likely the others, but something said she was more than a friend; she truly felt like family.

I thanked Alexandria for sharing, "If Isis trusts us, I know we will be fine."

"A wise lady," she replied, and we both sighed, but it felt so good to talk about her without the tears.

"She will come back when you need her, not when you want her," said Alexandria.

"I guess so, and if she's not here, then it means I'm doing okay."

"Yes, now let's go to the gift shop. You must have a souvenir from your visit."

The gift shop was a highlight. I bought a book with all the images and postcards for memories. I was stopped in my tracks when I saw what looked to be a very old drawing of the Dendara zodiac. "What is that?" I pointed.

"Ah, that is the image from Vivant Denon." I picked up the image and added it to my collection.

I looked at the jewellery but held back as I felt it should be bought in Egypt. And, of course, I would have Naomi find me the perfect piece at the best price.

When we were at the exit, I felt such sadness and wished I had more time with Alexandria. I had a feeling she and I would be great friends.

"This is where I leave you, Anna. I have to go back in and meet with one of the curators who takes care of Grandmama's exhibits, then make a short trip. I hope to be back before you leave for Cairo," she said.

"Be safe and well."

She smiled and disappeared into the side corridor, and I went back to the main road where the driver was waiting.

"Perfect timing, Mademoiselle Harris," he said and opened the door.

"I will take you back to the Contessa's house, yes?"

"Yes, please."

Oh, and here is a note for you," he said.

On beautiful paper, a folded handwritten note simply read:

Dinner tonight, La Cinq restaurant, 6 pm. Contessa

Always straight to the point, but all the same, I was excited to see her and tell her of my adventure that day.

It would be like the times with Isis. I wondered if this restaurant would be super fancy, maybe no jeans.

The driver read my mind. "The Contessa is visiting with the Minister today and will meet you there, and Mademoiselle Alex just texted me to say she has sent an outfit over to the house for you."

Yes, my intuition was correct—super fancy.

☥

"Good evening, my dear." The Contessa was already seated like royalty at a table in the restaurant and seemed to be enjoying all the attention when I was escorted to the table.

"This restaurant has one of the finest chefs in the world, tres' chic."

I nodded, not sure what to do. I was overwhelmed by the sheer elegance and beauty of the room. The windows were arch-shaped and open, surrounded by thick silk drapes. Gold and cream colours created a historic appearance.

The waiter pulled out my seat whilst another placed a glass of champagne in front of me. I smoothed down my dress. The thick silk in a rose-pink tone dress, or should I say, the gown I wore, felt old yet so luxurious.

I noticed very few others around us. But they were looking over and whispering.

"Your dress is most becoming," she started.

"Yes, Alexandra sent it, but I don't think it was hers originally."

"No, this was from the House of Dior, 1950's. A famous piece, perhaps it should be in a museum, but it looks so much better on you. Alex has my collection, and she makes full use of it as she says each dress has a soul. Your mother had this piece in powder blue."

My eyes must have given me away as she patted my hand. "It's okay, no one will know."

"It's early and therefore quiet," she said. "Now, how was today?"

I took a gulp of my champagne and reminded myself to breathe and relax.

"Oh, I had the most wonderful visit, and Alexandria was amazing. I really like her."

"She is a charming young woman and so knowledgeable. Educated and kind. I'm sure she must have loved every moment growing up in this city." The Contessa's face softened as if with some sadness.

"I knew her in many lifetimes, as I am sure you did too, Anna," she said. "Paris is her home, but as a child, she really struggled with her nightmares, hence she lived in Toulouse."

"The French Revolution." My hand went to my throat. "I felt that today."

"Yes, dear, Alexandria spoke her truth. She warned the French court that darkness was coming. However, as with all royal families that are removed from the normal world, she was the one who was removed from favour."

"Then..."

"In the end, she still lost her head," I finished the Contessa's sentence.

"Oh, please forgive me. I did not mean to interrupt you."

"Naomi said you had a habit of reciting the Akashic Records back to people," she said.

"Occupational hazard, I think."

She smiled. It was now she who was gulping the

champagne, and I began to see her fragile self.

I could see she cared a great deal for her granddaughter. I wanted to ask more about the revolution, but she was now talking to the waiter and ordering everything in French. I only recognised a few words and knew we were about to have chicken.

"So, Anna, tell me all about the museum. What mysteries did you uncover?"

I began to recite my adventure with each twist and turn of the museum, describing it in as much detail as possible.

Like a dream, I lost myself in this wonderful world. Not only was the food delicious, but Contessa's company was also so interesting. I didn't have to watch my words or be careful not to offend anyone. I had a captive audience who truly appeared to support me. I explained about the priestesses who were still being held and needed to be released, and how I remembered the scribe who posed for the statue and his role in the temple. I talked about how the zodiac from Dendara came alive, and many of the curses were removed.

She made me go over every detail of the zodiac encounter. What I saw, what I felt, and what I heard. It reminded me of the times when I would visit Isis in her private room, often when she was in her nightgown. She would ask me to tell her of my adventures and discoveries. She always asked the right questions, and I found myself spilling out all the details effortlessly; I wish I could write like this. I even shared about the Scroll and Scarab of Death and Resurrection and the oracle prophecy, to which she stopped eating and put down her cutlery abruptly.

I paused as the emotion caught up with me. The Contessa was already clicking her fingers and checking with her higher senses for clarity and information.

"Then it has commenced," was all she said.

"What has commenced?" I asked her.

"Many years ago, when Isis was here, we saw a prophecy. In the prophecy, the Halls of Amenti would be revealed, and many of the sacred temples would begin to reactivate. I had forgotten that the original Dendara zodiac could be activated by powerful oracles, and that was what happened today."

"But I always thought of Alexandria and me as just Priestesses with oracle gifts."

I wondered if she knew of my failure to make the grade to attend High Priestess school this lifetime.

She shook her head.

"Anna, you both have had many roles. I'm not sure of the connection yet, but over time, one will surface to the top and lead you on."

She closed her eyes for a moment to think and then took a sip of her champagne.

"The two of you have created the start of a chain of events here in Paris, and Anna, as you work with all of the scrolls and scarabs, you become guardian to some of the great magic, and with the others on the Egypt trip, you may find many other temples and their wisdom can begin to open."

"But what do you think it's all for?" I asked.

"I am not totally sure, but I have a feeling that where we go tomorrow may shed some light."

"Tomorrow? What do we do tomorrow?" I asked.

"Tomorrow, my dear, you will spend the day with me. We go to one of my most illustrious lifetimes, and we will remember Versailles and the priestesses whom we served and the world of illusion in which we lived."

I had dreamt of visiting Versailles, but at the same time, a sense of dread came over me, and I shifted my thoughts as

I began to feel the past life connected to this had not been my favourite.

"So, until tomorrow, but my dear, you will return home now, as I have another important call to pay."

"To the minister?" I asked.

She looked at me and said nothing, and then the Contessa stood. At once, people came running. She was escorted to her driver and waved me towards a taxi.

"*Au revoir,* my dear, until tomorrow, sleep well and dream."

While I was with the Contessa, I felt energised, but as I reached the house in darkness, I simply went up to my room. It must be the champagne, as I seemed to float, not paying attention to Andre, who escorted me with a small lamp up the stairs. I thought he told me the time we would be leaving, but it was as if timelines of the past were moving, and deja vu was at work. I felt a sluggish energy come over me like a wave. I knew what this was and that a dream of great insight would be in store for me.

Chapter 16

Sunday, 13 September 2009

I dreamt I was in a dark tunnel, cold stone and damp. The smell of grass and the sense that I was standing in mud. I was afraid to go through the tunnel but knew I could not stand still. I could hear voices.

It's your role. You created this, and my mother and I set it in motion. You may not be Queen of France, but you have all the power; your children are of noble and royal birth.

It was the Contessa speaking with two women.

One said nothing, but something I knew was that she was connected to a very dark craft. I thought she saw me. I began to look around and could see I was underneath a bridge, and I did all I could to scramble up the side of the embankment and hide to see more clearly. Yes, there the three stood, and next to them, two carriages.

"You promised me the High Priestess position in the Temple of Isis."

"It's not that easy. Another oracle has been seen at Court, and she works with a favourite of the King."

"The oracle from the house of Courtesan," the Contessa replied.

The one with the scarred face.

"Yes, she is now within the walls of Versailles."

"They say she has great powers but is hidden away—her face always hidden."

"Then they must both perish."

"Then you must go to the temple tonight and set a

petition."

"I know the priestess there—she worked for my mother," said the Contessa.

"Be most careful," the other woman spoke.

"You watch your place, Madame Voison," the Contessa was becoming frustrated. "You are here for our bidding and poisons. Nothing more."

They all leave, and I find myself in a new surrounding, with glass, candlelight, and mirrors.

I'm in a white silk nightgown and wandering the halls of a palace.

I'm looking for my mother and my family, but there are so many doors and rooms.

I am drawn to a room, and again, there is the Contessa.

I am seeing the Contessa, speaking with a woman about it being her turn. The woman is unhappy about this and begs the Contessa to reconsider, saying she wants to live her life and not be tied down. The Contessa reminds her that it is her sworn duty to take on the mantle and that this will be the last time. Ah, yes, she is talking to Lucinda, and it seems strange to me, as I thought the Contessa was trying to be the high priestess. It was a trick. I did not know how or why, but I knew this was wrong.

"You know the magic, and I've heard you have access to a powerful oracle."

Lucinda pauses. "Yes, she is in Paris, an old woman."

"The scarred woman?" the Contessa tests her.

"No, she died, and now I mainly work alone." I think she is lying.

"You should join me and my friends."

"No," Lucinda tells her. "I could never—I know you consult with Madame Voison. I know what you have all done. The dark magic, the potions, and those precious souls. You

have woven a dark path and will pay the price."

"I never pay the price," the Contessa responds in a dark voice. "I have plenty that will pay it for me."

"They were unwanted children and part of a cause and effect. Children of lost women, children who would face pain and hardship."

"I do the bidding of Madame Montspan. Nothing more." The Contessa walks away.

I tried to call out, but my voice and body were frozen.

The dream began to shift, and now I was in a room with gilded furniture and people in painted faces. The men wore more than the women. It was strange; I felt I was at a costume party.

I tried to find Lucinda, but instead, the dancing started. It was so terrifying as I was grabbed at, pushed, and swirled by these macabre characters. Some of the faces I thought I knew, but it was so surreal that I found myself praying to be released from this curse. I found myself beginning to scream. This had turned into a nightmare.

"Mademoiselle Harris."

The knock at the door was soft, and the voice was female. I looked at my bed. The pillows and the duvet were all in a mess, and when I looked in the mirror, so was my hair. I could feel the flashbacks of the nightmare. The whole crazy succession, I thought I had seen my mother and Isis and the Contessa, but it was all a blur.

One thing I did remember was that this "Mantle of Isis" may not be my dream scenario.

"Enter," I called out.

A young woman entered whom I had not seen before. She smiled, but her eyes grew wide as she looked around the room.

"No worry, here have some coffee," she said.

I finished the cup quickly, hoping it was espresso to wake me up.

"I am Marie. Please, mademoiselle, go shower quickly. Do not wash your hair."

I did as she asked, and when I emerged a few minutes later, she had laid a breakfast. She had the dressing table set, and another maid was pressing my clothes. The rose-pink dress that had been lying on the floor was being carefully steamed and hung back into a protective bag.

Marie smiled at me, handed me another coffee, and motioned for me to sit at the dressing table.

"You go to Versailles," she said as she sat me down, applied spray to my hair, and began to blow-dry it.

I nodded while munching on a chocolate croissant and drinking my coffee.

"*Tres bien.*" I glanced over at the bed and my luggage and at the wardrobe where I had left my scrolls, scarabs, and precious artifacts for Egypt. Everything was tipped onto the floor. Luckily, the scroll and scarab box, while upside down, was not open. It did not make sense. I was not that drunk from champagne.

"You are most safe, Mademoiselle Anna. My mother and hers, also," she nodded to the other maid, "they served in this house."

As she mentioned their mothers, mothers in service, something felt familiar.

"This house, it has many secrets and many of those who visit have these dreams." She pointed to the dishevelled bed.

"We, Louisa and I, we know what to do." I looked at the other maid and noticed a small ankh on a chain around her neck.

"We know." She stressed the word "know" and pointed

to my belongings.

"And you can fix this sad story, Marie?" I laughed.

"Oh, yes. Easy," she smiled.

In five minutes, she had transformed my hair from a haystack to a beautiful, sleek ponytail and was now going through my makeup bag and tutting while applying. "You need to go shopping, I think."

"I think," I nodded, but when she had finished, I had to say I was most impressed.

Meanwhile, the other maid was holding my lavender water-pressed clothes, which I quickly slipped into.

It was nothing short of a miracle as the two of them made my bed and helped me as I packed my bag. As I stood in the doorway and caught my reflection, I had to say it was a transformation.

"We will finish everything."

"I just don't know," I stuttered, going into my purse as I felt I should tip them.

"No, no," said Marie. "Always and forever remember, as Eeses taught us."

I smiled at her pronunciation of Isis.

She unbuttoned her collar and reached for a golden chain around her neck that held a small golden ankh upon it.

"She is always with us, Isis, yes."

"Bien oui, she is," I smiled, reached out, and held her hand. I nodded to Louisa and then left the angels to work.

"Now I must fly," I smiled, and with that, I ran out of the room.

Downstairs, I felt like time had stopped. I caught sight of myself in the mirrors, and it was as if I were floating in the air. Something looked different. I was not sure if it was my hair or the chic scarf that Louisa had wrapped around the damaged handle of my bag, but this was certainly not Anna

Harris Yorkshire style. This was the new Paris version.

I reached the door and could see the driver standing with a kind smile and opening the door to a large and impressive black car.

Inside, the Contessa sat and, to my surprise, looked remarkably different.

Gone were her chic suits and pearls, and instead, expensive-looking cropped jeans, flat shoes, a multi-coloured jacket, and a bright scarf.

Of course, I noticed her bag on the seat, which probably cost more than I made in a year.

She pulled down her big black sunglasses.

"Yes, my dear, I'm not as old as I looked when you arrived."

"We are tourists today," she laughed.

Perhaps today would not be as scary as I thought. "Is Alexandria able to join us?"

"*Non, Chérie,* she has a very important job to do today."

☥

We were soon off and sailing through the French countryside, and I could not believe how beautiful it was.

For the first twenty minutes, we sat in silence.

I watched as the Contessa sat back in her seat, looking out of the window.

I thought she was sleeping, but no, she was mouthing words I could barely hear, and those I did hear made no sense whatsoever.

Every so often, she would swirl her fingers as if she was waving an invisible magical wand.

"We are not far now, madame," the driver said, and for some reason, my stomach began to churn.

I hope it was not the chocolate croissants I had stuffed

my face with. Three of them, to the horror of Marie, but then she was totally slim and thin and not like me.

I placed my hand on my stomach as it began to gurgle.

The Contessa laughed.

"Ah, so you feel the outer circle, do you?"

"Like Glastonbury," I nodded.

I remembered my first trip and how the outer and inner rings create a vortex circle of energy around a city or location that engages with those of us who have worked the energies before.

"They know you're coming now," smiled the Contessa as she removed her sunglasses.

'Who knows?" I whispered.

"Just they..."

I thought perhaps that I should share my dream.

"It's not time for your thoughts or premonitions, and I'm guessing you dreamt last night," she said, reading my mind.

I blushed once again. Here we were, where everyone knew something about me.

It felt a little like the first time I had visited Glastonbury, the sights and sounds of nature. We felt so far away from Paris, and I wondered if there was any connection between the two locations.

☥

As we entered the main driveway, I was overwhelmed by the magnificent sight of towering, beautiful, pristine buildings with manicured gardens. But we did not drive to the regular car park that was signed and open to tourists. Instead, we took a detour to another entrance. Perhaps the service entrance, I thought. I looked over to the Contessa, expecting to see an Akashic image of a past life in which she wore a serving girl outfit. But it was the total opposite. My image showed her in crimson velvet, white hair piled high with rows of pearls and jewels. Perhaps this was a secret entrance.

We drove to a very discreet and hidden doorway. The car slowly stopped, and the Contessa smiled at me.

"Showtime," she whispered. Obviously, she and Naomi had attended the same school.

"My dear Contessa." A small man in a linen cream suit with a pale blue shirt came out to greet us.

They both hugged each other, and I wondered if this was her brother. A rapid French conversation took place, which, of course, I understood nothing of until the Contessa turned to me and said my name.

"Anna, this is Jules. He is a dear old friend from past and present lives."

He stepped forward to greet me, and as usual, I saw many of his faces and past life costumes present themselves in my vision.

"What can you see? What can you see?" He was like a child. "I was told you would be visiting. The Contessa has spoken to many of us about your famous gifts."

I looked at the Contessa, and she glared at Jules. "Only in passing, Anna. It was nothing," she said, shrugging it off. But all the same, I wondered who they were.

"You are the famous oracle, Mademoiselle Anna. You know the secrets, and you can tell the stories."

I wanted to laugh, as this was not who I expected to encounter here. He began to be very animated, and I wondered if we would be simply visiting here and staying in the doorway. I looked over his shoulder into the corridor behind him. Yes, indeed, there was work to be done.

"Jules was a famous French king but totally spoiled and childlike."

"Mind you, don't lose your head," she spoke to him abruptly. She was losing patience with him.

"I was, yes. This is true, and now I am home and am one of the curators of the very special things here." He looked directly at me as he emphasised the word special.

"The Sun King," I found myself saying, and they both looked at each other. I don't know what came over me, but I walked close to him and took his face in my hands to study. "Yes, very spoilt indeed, but look what you created, my dear Louis."

"Yes, dear Louis XIV." I felt a voice not my own coming over me.

Jules began to jump up and down in excitement. But something told me that the story today may not be a glamorous historical projection, but something more dark and sinister.

"She is wise for sure, but let us see what else she knows," the Contessa whispered to Jules.

Another person arrived and broke the spell. She handed us passes and waved her hand for us all to enter.

Once again, the Contessa and Jules began to talk in French, and we were escorted in through another side door. It was as if we were finding our way through rooms and corridors. I walked with the young woman in silence in front of the Contessa and Jules as she unlocked each door. It was obvious this was not part of the tourist route.

I found myself in a state of remembering, and I felt like a small child playing a game of hide and seek. Once we reached what felt like the back of the palace, she smiled at me, handed the large set of keys to Jules, and then disappeared. There we stood, the three of us. All nervous about what was to be revealed.

"Are we going to the gardens?" I asked. They both looked at each other.

"Yes, that will be our first stop to see the magnificent panorama," Jules replied.

"I remember," I said, and suddenly I was in another world, and it was as if we were all young again, making our way through the doors and walls till we emerged at a side door and came out into the light. For a moment, I lost who I was and fell into another reality.

The image before me I had seen in my dreams the previous night.

It was breathtaking, and I ran out ahead and stood on the top steps.

I began to see that everything was similar but had changed.

The gardens had different trees, and I felt a sadness in my heart. That was not there... I pointed to various sections. And we could run over there... The landscape was the same, but the plan had changed.

"They extended things, Anna, and it is now built for tourists. But I remember, like you, that it was magnificent," said the Contessa.

Her face changed, and I saw that she was the woman from the night before in my dream, and I found myself stepping back. I was having confused visions. The Contessa in the crimson dress, and now this shadow woman of my dream, I shook my head, trying to create clarity.

Jules recognised the signs at once.

"Anna, it's not as it looked. That was another time, and you are both very different now."

"But in my dream, I saw her."

Jules and the Contessa looked at each other in concern.

"What did you see, my dear?" The Contessa was soft in her tone. She also began to shake and look vulnerable.

All I could say was, "The garden," and then the dream began to flood back to me.

"Perhaps we go inside," said Jules, and he took me by the hand and led me inside. Now I felt like the lost child.

"My Osiris Priest friend," I looked at him and saw an Egypt connection and smiled. This palace of Versailles was indeed its own vortex. My visions were fast but confusing.

"Yes, Anna, I was a man-child in those French days and a priest in the ancient Egyptian times, and we can find out more later."

Jules came very close to me as we walked back into the corridors of the palace. The Contessa marched ahead.

"But this has been a story that has haunted Versailles for many lifetimes," he whispered and pointed back to the garden and then the palace... and has held the Contessa in a karmic limbo. Perhaps we can help her and set her free." He held his finger to his lips and shook his head so that I would say nothing.

Then he bolted out in front and was the one to watch as he wove through the rooms at speed.

He quickly escorted us to a small sitting room with beautiful furniture and lamps. The extravagance was surreal. His knowledge and understanding of the rooms, the décor, and the purpose they served was outstanding.

"I use this for my VIP guests," Jules declared as he motioned for us to sit on the grand chairs.

"I escort the dignitaries and celebrities. You would not believe how many of them have a past life remembering of the years and ages here."

"Perhaps one time, Anna, you can come back and help them. We could hold a salon like the old days and have candles and mystery." He began to be excited and wave his hands around again.

"Jules," the Contessa was very sharp. "This is not the time. We came here to visit..." she smiled at me, "...and do the work. Anna leaves for Egypt soon, and we do not have time for these parades of ego."

Jules scowled at her once again, like a petulant child, but he winked at me. "We will talk," he mouthed to me, and I nodded.

"Well then, we will need sustenance, ladies," he said.

He rang a button, and tea was served a few moments later.

The Contessa sat nervously and almost dropped her cup and saucer as it was handed to her. She studied the China pattern, and I do believe I saw Jules smirking when it was brought into the room. Somehow, he was taunting her with this. What odd and strange people they were.

"The spirits are with us," was all she could say as she stared at the delicate cup as if it were to break at any moment.

The Contessa was strong and quickly composed herself, placing the focus over to me.

"Anna, we are all friends and safe. Perhaps you would care to share your thoughts or visions. Before Jules sells your soul again to the nouveau riche, perhaps he should witness your abilities."

I smiled; this was not like the times I channeled for Isis and Naomi, but they did make it feel safe and asked me questions.

This, I felt, was my examination.

I placed down my tea and sat with poise like my mother had taught me. Straight back and ankles crossed. I took a deep breath in and closed my eyes.

"We are all children, and we run through the palaces like this, but I think it was in Paris, like the Louvre yesterday.

"Yes, we are children of nobles. Families in favour at the time, and the Royals are our friends, and you, Jules, are a Prince, and we talk of the ancient days, and our teachers fill our minds with talk of ancient Egypt, Greece, and Rome.

"Of course, your lessons, Jules, are different to ours, and

the Contessa is my older sister then. We females have lessons on how to walk, talk, and charm. Sometimes, we have magic lessons, but I am not sure what they mean. I am classed as too young to share in the secrets.

"My older sister goes to other lessons, and she will not share the secrets, for these are advanced magic, and she is very secretive. This lifetime is so lavish, and I am confused about who is who, as life at court means a never-ending swirl of people."

"Do you remember our household, Anna?" the Contessa's voice spoke, but she seemed so far away.

"Yes, when I was a young child, we visited and stayed at the Palace, yet we have a large house somewhere in Paris.

"Yes, we live in a house not far from where the Louvre is now, and all the time, there are horses and carriages. I have two older sisters and a younger brother. Our mother is always at the balls and parties, and our father is some sort of minister. Our mother is a friend of the Queen, and she sometimes disappears at all times of day and night at the call of her Majesty.

"The Queen, I think she is called Anne, has the curse of miscarriage and has many conspirators plot against her. Our mother goes to advise and protect her. When she does, our father steps into a quiet room and becomes very agitated, and we are told to tell no one."

"Do you see what happens to me in that past life?" the Contessa asked in a quiet voice I can hardly hear.

"Yes, it is very clear. I am a little older, and you are now wearing more grown-up clothes. They say it's your time to shine, and you are to be prepared for court life. One day, you go to the Palace with our mother. You are older than the prince. But he is more about my age. My other sister and brother stay with me in the Paris house.

"I am seeing you and our mother talking, and she tells

the story of how the Queen was told a child of great wisdom and insight would be soon born that could guide the leader of France to the new golden age.

"Royal children born around this time should be very protected, as they had great gifts. Our mother in that past life was responsible for the survival of this child. That is you, Jules. It is as if she kept away the ghosts, and the Queen is most grateful.

"The Queen knows of the mystic and psychic worlds and does not fear them; however, her husband, the current king, and the men of the court do.

"As the Queen has had many miscarriages, she now believes that the birth, survival, and rise to power of her son, the dauphin, will be the result of our mother's work and her magical coven.

"This is what my father fears the most. He has been a protector of our family but knows as our mother and family grow closer to the royals, our fate could be doomed. But he cannot stop our mother. She is hungry now for the power and riches promised to her.

"Our mother tells you, Contessa, that you have her gifts, and the Queen is most insistent that you grow up close to her son and help guide him in the future.

"She tells you that you are a chosen child also but does not mention me or our brother and sister. As time moves on, the King does die, and there is a political struggle between the Queen's household and that of the ministers.

"The Queen keeps our mother close, but there are those who would see our mother fall, and then our father is mysteriously poisoned and very sick. He cannot move and is unable to protect us. I think he is my friend Tom from North Yorkshire, the landowner who helped me when I lost my job.

Then, our home in Paris is burnt mysteriously; it would seem our family name has already been cursed."

I pause as if a darkness and sadness have washed through me.

"What happens to you, Anna?" This time, I hear the kind voice of Jules.

"I am a young girl, around thirteen at this time, and standing in the house. It is barely standing up. Father, brother, and our other sister have perished in the fire.

"I see myself in the broken mirror which hangs by a mantle ledge, and I see my reflection, and my face is scarred, and it would seem this all happened while my elder sister and my mother were in Court, myself and our family and servants were in the house. Only I survived from the family, as I had been downstairs in the kitchen at the time. Luckily, the house servants made it out alive.

"I see our cook holding my hand and trying to take me with her. She has wrapped my head in bandages and placed a heavy salve for healing.

"She whispers to me not to trust anyone, and she wishes she could take me with her. She tells me my mother is coming for me, and she has sent word to the palace but can interfere no more.

"I love her so much, as my mother never pays attention to me, and this woman has always been there when my family was not, even when I had the bad dreams. I dreamt of many bad and dark things and of ancient times. She has understood this since I was a little girl.

"The other servants pull her away, and I am left there in my white cotton nightgown and one of my father's coats. I look a mess, and all is in chaos.

"I'm only thirteen years old and have no one."

At this point, I want to come back out. I have seen enough, and nothing seems relevant today. I open my eyes, not wanting to look further.

"I guess I must die. There is no help for that child. I

don't think she will be rescued," I offer to them.

"Anna, please. I know it appears really bad, but you must carry on. We need you to find certain secrets of the past," the Contessa tells me.

"What secrets? I am not for hire, you know, for your games."

"No, no," Jules's tone is very soothing. "We do not mean this as it appears. We, too, have seen the fire, but not a great deal after that. Please, Anna, we feel there is something more you have to see for us, please."

I take a deep breath in again and look at them both and notice they are both on the edge of their seats, so this past life must have something of importance. *I must be careful of what I feel I want to share.* I close my eyes again.

"Okay.

"I am back in the house just after the fire when someone has given me an old coat of my father's, and I don't look like the wealthy child I was a few days ago. I am watching as the servants leave, and I go out into the street to await my mother and sister.

"The cook, I adore—she is Isis. She is also leaving, but she suddenly stops, and I think she is coming back to get me, but no, she places a book in my hand, a small black leather-bound book. "Never, ever show this to anyone." She looks at me straight, places her hands on my head, and begins to chant words. "Not even your mother or sister, promise me." I place the small leather-bound book into the pocket of the coat. She leaves, and I am alone, still in the crazy noise of the street.

"My pain seems to fall away, and the salve for the burns on my face is beginning to work, and I find a small doorstop to sit down in and rest. I hear shouting as the guards from the Palace that belong to the Queen arrive.

"The Palace has been alerted to the fire, and my mother, who holds power at Court, has sent them back to seek

something or someone. At last, I am to be rescued. An officer comes over to me. I know him in this life. He was in my class at school. He is very kind but does not see who I am. Ah, yes, my name is Jeanne. I tell him who I am, but they keep asking me where the cook is, so I tell them she is gone. I shouted to them my name, and they said, 'No, all of this family is dead.' I tell them my name again, and they say, 'No, all dead.' They walk away.

"I can't believe this. My family had gone in the fire, and my mother and sister have now left me a child in the street with nothing. I look around, but our neighbours are all hiding behind their doors as they have been told that our home was cursed by a witch, and that they will face the same fate if they help me. I begin to feel like I am sinking away. Looking at my home, burnt and ready to fall away. I hide back in the corner of the doorway. I can see a small carriage at the end of the street, and I am sure it belongs to our household. My head hurts, and my eyes cannot see clearly, but I swear I can see my mother and sister looking out, and just as I begin to believe they have seen me, they drive away.

"I begin to pray to God. I am lost.

"Hours later, I feel a hand on my shoulder, and I turn to see a young woman. She wears a full hooded cape, but something is familiar.

"I know her as I have seen her pass many times in carriages, and she works at the theatre.

"Not a place for us, my father would say. She wraps me in another cape and takes me towards a carriage, and a valet picks me up and places me inside with such care. And my mind goes blank."

I come out of the trance, and my respect for the Contessa is gone.

"You left me there and my siblings to die in that house. Why?"

"Anna, this is as far as we have been able to see. My heart is broken, and I beg your forgiveness. But please, that time is gone, and we need to focus on that book and that cook who was Isis in that timeline."

"I do not think I should tell any more. This has no relevance to me or my work in Egypt. Perhaps we can rest a short time and then tour the gardens."

They both looked at each other. An emotion came over me, and in that moment, I was simply motivated by spite.

I had not been prepared for such anger and resentment.

I could feel everything in me begin to turn to rage.

I reached over towards the tea and poured a cup. I knew the china disturbed the Contessa, so I was deliberate and began to comment on how beautiful the pattern was.

The Contessa knew I was challenging her. I smiled my false grin and waited for her next move.

Then the Contessa said something very strange.

"Anna, tell me what the cook, the one from the kitchen, looked like. I know you said she was Isis, but how was she dressed?" A simple request, so why not?

I closed my eyes, prepared to tell her I could not see, and suddenly it was Isis. It was my mentor, my teacher.

I let out a huge sob, "It's Isis. She loved me, and she had to leave me." The teacup fell out of my hands and broke. I didn't know what to apologise for first, the broken china or my behaviour.

"Oh, I am sorry," my lip began to tremble.

"No, it is perfect," Jules reached down to rescue the china. "The curse is lifting, and dear Isis is back with us."

"Yes, Anna," said the Contessa, "that was a different time, and we had very different roles." "Now the secrets can reveal a missing part of the puzzle for Egypt."

I am curious now. I, too, for some reason, know that Egypt is linked to this, but have no idea how or why. I sat up straight, and for the first time, I could feel a power racing up and down my spine.

I had been timid since I reached Paris, and now, like I was going through an initiation, I had the opportunity to shrink away and hide or to take the situation on and solve this karmic mystery.

One thing was for sure now: the Contessa did not treat me like some simple young novice.

She passed me some water, took off her jacket, and calmly put her voice recorder on the table.

"*Si vous plait,* if you please... You have shown us what we know, and now we look to you to reveal the rest." I simply nodded.

As Naomi would say, it's show and tell time.

I readjusted myself in the seat and, eyes wide open, I looked around the room. My eyes had adjusted to see the past life, like a movie overlay.

"That chaise is restored, I see. It used to have green velvet on the seat. The green goes with the lion's head on the legs." I smiled, knowing I was beginning to intrigue my audience.

"Well, yes," Jules began to stutter. "It was from the time of Louis XIV and passed through the family."

"Yes, it used to sit in the window and was a gift from Austria and prized by the Queen of the time."

He looked at the Contessa, and she smiled, "She's very good," he said.

"I know, as we were promised," she replied.

Then I closed my eyes and went into the Akashic Records trance again.

"So I'm seeing Isis leave me in the street. I'm an orphan child now that my father is dead, and my mother and sister have left me in the street. It is around 1653.

"Isis, the cook, has given me a black book that I hide in

the pocket of my coat, and I'm now seeing my mother and sister leaving. I fall back into a street doorway.

"A young woman in a hooded cape descends from a carriage, and with the help of a valet, they place me safely into the back of the carriage, and we drive into the night. They take me to a safe place on the other side of Paris, and I'm placed in a room in the attic.

"The timeline moves forward, and the vision is clearer now than before.

"Darkness falls, and for many days and nights, I sleep in a small room in a home which I feel is near to the theatre. I don't leave my room, and I hear women chattering and laughter outside, but no one enters my room except the young woman to wash my wounds and feed me.

"I have seen her before... yes, she is Alexandria. I feel safe with her. Due to my wounds, they give me medicine daily... a herbal remedy. It helps me heal and sleep, but at the same time, my dreams are vivid, and I recall many things of interest. The young woman Alexandria then brings parchment, and she scribes my dreams every morning.

"I cry for my family, but she tells me to forget them, that they, the women of this house, are now my family.

"I ask her about the black book, and she tells me it is safe and that no one else has touched it. She tells me at the right time, she will return it to me. She tells me that they had been looking for me and that a great psychic connected to magic had told the madam of the house to find me, as it would bring great fortune to the house.

"The timeline shifts, and it is a few years later. I am a young woman. I can leave the room and am dressed as a servant. I serve drinks during the daytime in the various parlours, and while I can listen, I am told never to speak or look directly at anyone. There is great talk about the young king and the royal court. I always pause when this happens in

case I hear word of my mother or sister. This is a house with a scandalous reputation. The women here are actresses and singers, and some are courtesans.

"I still live in the attic rooms, and my door is locked after dark when the house is open to visitors, and I am safe. Sometimes, on busy nights, I am now allowed to assist the servants. I feel safe as none of the visiting gentlemen, and sometimes ladies will look at me. My scars are slightly hidden, but still, my face is not beholding any beauty. Sometimes, when delivering trays of food or drink, they will often throw a coin at me.

"'Poor girl,' they look at me in repulsion.

"But I don't care. Each pity coin I save is for my escape.

"The women of the house are so kind. They make their own rules, and the lady who runs the house always has a kind word for me; however, she never stays too long in my company as I think my face disturbs her.

"I have learnt another skill of value; I know secrets, and the information about people's thoughts comes to me. Some of the women find that kindness and coin will buy my time and loosen my tongue.

"I know it has always been a lonely life for me, but I have a collection of coins, and it is my dream to run away and live near the ocean.

"The black book has been returned to me in a box very safe, and I cannot bring myself to look at this. Alexandria tells me the women are afraid of it, and the gossip of the witchcraft of my family creates both allure and fear of me. However, the Madam of the house knows that she can use the myth about me to lure curiosity among the wealthy and protect us from those who would try to take our money and bribe us for protection.

"One day, I am cleaning the front parlour and notice her just watching me from a doorway."

"'I know you, Jeanne,' she said, 'This was not the life meant for you.'

"'Perhaps it is or is not, but I'm grateful to be safe,' is my answer. Oh, I see her. She is Natasha, my old boss who stole from me way back before I went to Glastonbury.

"Sometimes I visit my old home just to stand and remember. A seamstress from the theatre has created me a whole costume that masks my face so I can go out in public and I visit my old home. It has still never been rebuilt, as many say it was still cursed and that the woman who lived there is really a witch who frequents the new court being built at Versailles, and she and her daughter create potions and spells for the new King.

"One day, I am standing when a carriage arrives. Two women, my mother and sister, get out and have their servants go into the broken-down house as if they are searching for something. Something within me tells me it is the black book. It is not me they look for.

"I am dressed in my special robes, and I decide to go past them, even daring to ask for some small coin.

"They look through me in disgust, and the coach driver cracks his whip in my direction to let me know that I would be next. So that was the moment the bond was broken. I owe them nothing, and I send a curse their way.

"I am so angry, but something inside me switches, and I see them in other lifetimes, young and old, and sometimes men or women. Their neglect has opened up a dark gift within me.

"I return to the sidelines again in the doorway that gave me sanctuary as a child. I stay to observe and to listen.

"I tell you it's nearby, my sister protests... the book of the cook.

"'Nothing,' their servants shake their heads. They tell her it's not safe. They have searched many times, but the book is

gone. It's my book they search for.

"Then we are done. We are fallen. I can hear them going back to the carriage. The King needs magic, and we have failed. I move to walk past on the other side and can see their faces.

"'No, Mother, I will think of something,' the daughter promises. The mother, my mother, nods and encourages her, but something tells me her days are numbered.

"I return to the safe house, and in my room, I notice that a pack of cards with a red ribbon wrapped around them has been laid on my bed. At the time, I'm not sure what they are, but as I see them now, I see they are tarot cards.

"One evening, an older woman knocks and asks if I received the gift, and she teaches me how to use the cards and to tell fortunes. She encourages me to open up the black book, and to spite my mother, I do, and here I find all the incantations and symbols which belong to ancient times.

"At first, I believed this was the book of my mother, but no, it is the book of the cook, as it has her name inscribed as well as a few others I do not know, and this leads me to believe that it was she who gave the wisdom to my mother for her to use. My mother is a fraud. It was the cook who had the gift, and now I know it has passed to me.

"Everything begins to fall into place, but I have no time. I needed to perfect my craft to bring more wealth and protection into my world.

"The woman who gave me the cards often visits my room, and I do card readings for her. My goodness. It's Lucas! But he is a female. Each time she comes now, she leaves a gift of lace and fancy food and even begins to help me with my hair and some makeup that hides my scars. So now I'm given a better room with a private parlour, and guests are brought to me so that patrons can be given insight and messages.

"I often work with a veil, and over time, my famed services are one of the highlights of the Paris society at the time.

"The Madam who runs the house is very protective of me and never allows me to make private visits outside the house, but every so often, I will be allowed to go to the theatre or the ballet. I'm always covered so as to never reveal who I am, but everyone knows me as the Angel. I can see the future and the past and, therefore, am one of the most sought-after.

"One day, a veiled woman comes to visit me, and she is heartbroken. Her latest conquest has been seduced by another woman, who is of nobler birth, and she is about to lose her place at court. She asks about the cards and if I know how to make spells.

"She tells me how much she admires me and that only I can save her. The witch at Court, I think it's my sister, is now making everyone's life difficult since her mother has died and that she has beguiled the King with stories of his past lives. I ask her why it is so important to be at Court, and she tells me of another world where everyone is happy, loved, and beautiful. I want to be in this world and tell her I will weave this love and relationship spell if she can arrange for me to visit this utopia.

"She leaves, and I hear nothing, as with many, they came and once they have found their desires and questions answered, they leave. To them, I am simply a woman in a veil with an insight into the other worlds. Some never even asked my name.

"But one day, fate deals another hand."

I am feeling my energy falling. This is the longest vision I have held, but I know that if I don't find out what happens to us and to the book, it will haunt me, and I do not wish another night like last.

"One day, a very fine carriage arrives with four horses and full livery, and a very grand lady descends, and the whole house is woken. Fine ladies never visit in the daylight, as it would tarnish their reputation. They would send a servant to procure an appointment. Our house is a forbidden world, a

fallen temple. One of our elders comes banging on my door as this lady has asked for me. Apparently, I had done a reading and love ritual for her, and she demands my counsel. I am to be brought into her presence. This lady certainly has power.

"I find out very quickly, while I am being dressed in something finer than usual, that she did find her suitor. He did choose her and took her to Court where she caught the eye of the King and is now currently one of his favoured mistresses. As soon as I am brought into her presence, it is the veiled woman, but now she wears no disguise. I know her—I think it's Lucinda. I remember her. We did a blood curse removal and a love contract creation; yes, she had paid me triple that day, enough for a new dress and parasol. My best spell has worked, but now I was being packed up and to be presented at Court.

"I look closer to see who she is. The woman, oh my goodness, yes, certainly it's Lucinda. She is so gracious. She fusses over me and tells me to bring only what I need. All I take is my book, tarot cards, and purse of coin. She tells me that we are leaving and she has rooms for me at Versailles. I can feel the room swirl as I'll be going to the place of heaven in the sun.

"Lucinda smiles at Natasha, the madam in charge of the house. She hands her a healthy purse of gold and tells her we will not be needing anything and that all has been taken care of. Alexandria waves from a window, and I mouth, I will return, and she will be next to join us. She looks sad, as if this were her dream. I do really believe I will return for her; after all, she rescued me. But something in my heart tells me that this may not be so.

"Lucinda is most correct. We arrive at the courtyard, and I'm quickly ushered in like today. It looks to be a similar entrance, hidden and secret, and taken upstairs to a set of three rooms. Here, I am presented with two maids, and I'm

scrubbed and perfumed and re-dressed.

"The women already know about the scars on my face and go to great lengths to cover and disguise me with makeup and hair and a lace veil. Lucinda comes to me, and she says not to worry and that, for now, I will remain hidden. She hopes my services will be my priority to help her.

"She sends the maids away and sits with me in confidence to tell me about her life and how, even though she lives the dream, she is also at the mercy of the King and the woman who currently has his confidence. While she may share his bedroom, this other woman has a great insight and power.

"I realise now that I am simply here to be used for my insight and psychic wisdom. I can look to the gardens and the sun, just not go into them. I can vaguely remember my childhood when our family was in favour when I was free. How different my reality is now.

"Lucinda allows me to watch or spy on others from the window. I report my insight. They have no idea, not even my own sister, who I now realise is part of her scheme and now the King's Oracle.

"And that's how it started. I would watch the Contessa, my sister, from a window as she was in that timeline. She knows magic is being worked behind her back, but has no idea who it is. Her scarred sister was held in the rooms above... a prisoner held in great luxury but also great sadness. Even Lucinda denies I exist. I'm simply a myth."

I began to shake and realised I had gone far enough.

"That's enough." I opened my eyes, and the Contessa sat in tears.

"Anna, I am so sorry. You were my sister, and I abandoned you."

"I had a dream last night. I saw you in the red dress, and you had two women taken away in the carriages," I said.

The Contessa looked at Jules.

"Yes, I had that dream, also," she said. "It happened a few weeks ago."

"It was Lucinda and me," I challenged her.

"Yes, I had you both removed from court, and your fates were sealed." She looked away from me.

She made a gesture to show that we had not lived.

"I saw you and her in the dream but was not aware of where you came from or how you fit into the story until you arrived, and then I read the Akashic Records with my Akashic Librarian here in Paris. That is who I went to see last night. The minister is our Librarian and Oracle of Paris."

She continued. "Anna, you were to be the oracle, and I was really an apprentice, living by my wits at a time of fear and revolution. Isis, in that lifetime, had told our mother it was to be me, but when you were born, we knew it was you, yet we stayed in denial. Isis was a priestess of the Isis Temple in Paris, a temple that still resides near Notre Dame. Then, she was part of a whole Mystery School our mother wished to be part of, and Isis was kept as the cook so she could watch over me, but really, she was watching over you."

A total façade.

"Many years ago, Isis and I shared the vision once, but neither of us could recall the purpose or what was in the black book. You are the only one, Anna, ever to have mentioned its existence."

"This is why Lucinda would not come to Paris with me," I said. Everything was clicking.

"Yes, we met many years ago in Paris, and it's safe to say that it did not go well," the Contessa responded.

"Lucinda is one of the most skilled sorceresses we have ever had connected to us, both light and dark."

"She then visited with Isis and Naomi, but she found

her past life karma was very disturbing, and she created quite the disruption. It ended badly, hence she has never returned to me. Isis and Naomi also kept their distance, and your name was never brought up until the passing of Isis, when your friend Emilee called me... only out of courtesy and because she is French. She heard about your mother's photo and then urged Naomi and Lucinda to send your photo."

"And the others—Alice, Lucas, and Laura—they never visited?" I asked.

"*Non*... those friends never visit. None of them trust me. We all know we have had many lives together and shared secrets, now I hope that can be repaired. I have carried the sins of this time for many years now. I think it may have started earlier, but this is the last recall at the Court of Louis and Versailles."

She looked down at the floor, and my heart opened, and I felt compassion.

"Then let me help you," and I rushed over, and kneeling down, I placed my hands on her knees and smiled up at her.

I turned to Jules; suddenly, everything was becoming clear.

"Where is the Hall of Mirrors?"

He was speechless.

"What does this have to do with the Hall of Mirrors?" the Contessa asked.

"It's a curse, a curse that's sat in this palace for 350 years. Now, quickly, where is my black book? And don't lie to me, Jules. I know it's here. I feel it talking. It belonged to Isis and was left to me, so I expect it to be returned. I am its guardian."

He was not used to being addressed like this, but all the same, he knew the rules by which we played and, for this lifetime, wished to stay on the timeline of light.

He led us to a small room, a library, very private, and there in a large glass case upon the table sat a number of black books. I wanted to say spell books, but I knew they were spell catchers. There were brass symbols, wands, and crystals, and even some old coins. I would remember those for later.

"Those ones catch and clear the curses," I said, pointing to the two in the corner.

"Really?" he said, "We thought they were poems and prayers."

"Same thing," I shrugged. "We were skilled in all acts of exorcism and clearing curses, you know... it was not just the church that could do this." I looked over at a mirror. There I was, veil over my face and dressed in dark purple silk. Yes, I must have become quite the threat. I saw Jeanne clearly looking back at me and my scars. I felt them there on my own face, still.

"Now open this, please; we have no time," I urged him.

He did not need to be convinced and slowly opened up the lid, and there she was, my black book. The leather was worn and faded, but I knew it at once. I placed my left hand over her, and the incantations came back.

After reciting the words, I gently picked her up and opened the book to the page of its choice.

Of course, there on the page, in black handwritten ink, was the image of the ankh, and that's all I needed.

"I will be needing this for Egypt," I informed him, "and then perhaps it may, and I say, may, be returned to you."

I thought alarms were going to sound and he would be angry, but Jules simply smiled. "Then you will return and share your secrets."

I smiled at him. "I just may, I just may."

"And now, my dear sister, slash Contessa, we have some clearing to do."

"The Hall of Mirrors, before the tourists arrive for the noon tour," Jules informed me. It was 11.11. I had all the time I needed.

☥

We raced through the rooms and corridors until we reached a large wooden door.

Jules spoke to the security guards and assured us we would have a private thirty minutes.

As we entered the room, the Contessa and I began to get very hot and flushed.

Who on earth was I to be here in this moment, ordering my way around and dictating? I caught a flash of a woman on the steps of an old temple, and the image really scared me. I heard the whisper of a woman's voice. *"It is I, Arsinoe, do what needs to be done."* I shook my head. That was a weird name.

I held the black book in my hands and felt the energy begin to move through me.

I looked around the room, and the whole space was beginning to fill with light.

I asked the Contessa to stand in the middle of the room, and I began to walk around her in a clockwise direction.

Shadows began to emerge in the mirrors, some the faces of beautiful women and children, some of men and war, and even in the corners, I saw the faces of evil. I saw once again those faces in the cloaks and of the priests of Unal. I saw the story of myself, the girl with the scarred face, and of Lucinda and I, and the fate we met. We were cast out as witches and had paid a price.

"You summoned them all! I let out a gasp of surprise." I could not help myself, and I looked to Jules, and he knew enough to stand back against the doorway.

The Contessa knelt down, a woman so broken in guilt. "I did some really wicked things," she said in a small voice.

I began to see the stories like mini videos playing on each of the mirrors and the reflections of her in her past lives.

"These are your mirrors," and suddenly, I understood the true meaning of this room.

This was a room of deep magic and sorcerers. It reflected all the illusions and what needed to be seen. But it took powerful magic to summon all the Records, and I began to see why they were calling me the oracle. I was the one summoning the past lives. I was the one standing between this soul and her atonement. Some mirrors stayed with a grey mist, and I assumed they were unimportant.

I summoned the energy of the Scroll of Truth and Integrity and that of Magic and Prophecy, although that one would not open for me. I switched it out for the Records of Life. Ethereally, I began to adjust the energy of the room to align with the higher power of the scrolls and scarabs.

I opened the black book and began to recite from a page titled "Gateway of Amenti."

As I recited, the Contessa began to curl into a ball and rock, distressed, but she had started this, and now I must finish it.

"Set me free," she gasped, and I saw she was losing energy fast. "Anna, I beg you, please set me free. My dreams are my nightmares. They fill my day and night."

I stopped and opened the book to another page, and of course, it told me what to do. It was not written in words but in symbols. While I could not read them, I understood them. It was as if it were an ancient, unknown language.

I began to call upon the spirits and the karmic energies to show the lives and lessons.

I turned and began to walk counterclockwise.

"Compassion, forgiveness, love, peace, liberty, tranquility," the words began to spill out from me. Even strange languages came forward.

"Release, clear, free, forgive. Wisdom, understanding, knowledge."

As I made my way softly around the circle, my words began to whisper, and her energy began to soften.

The images began to dissolve, and I heard the Contessa begin to gasp for air.

Her voice returned, and finally, she stood up.

She turned to me and smiled, and then I watched in amazement as she opened her arms and began to chant and then sing in a tone I had never heard before. Her voice rose and vibrated around the room, and I knew at once she was clearing the energies of every panel, and this was going out across the palace, the gardens, Paris, and the world.

With the voice of an angel... moving through the mirrors and the crystals... with a sound that opened the heart.

She then became silent and turned to me.

"Anna, thank you. You saved me. I have been locked in this prison since 1678. I followed a dark path, and now I am returned to the light. Dear girl, thank you."

"For some reason, I felt it had been my duty, and I was bound to do this like it had been pre-planned, but how could that be? We had never met."

"Thank you, dear child, and now let me introduce my true self."

"My name is Francine, dear friend, and I'm so glad to meet you again this lifetime."

We were stopped from our reunion by a loud banging on the door,

"Time's up," said the Contessa, and we rushed over and, in a very tourist manner, walked out and past the waiting crowd.

Jules, ever the diplomat, looked at the awaiting Chinese group.

"Opera singer," he smiled. They all nodded and began clapping.

"Lunch ladies," our friendly guide and gatekeeper had returned; she smiled at me and gestured for us to follow.

We were escorted back to the room, and lunch was served buffet-style on a side table. I was so hungry, but was aware of how Jules stood observing me, and as he looked at me, I knew he was going to ask for the black book.

"Mademoiselle Anna, this black book is the property of the Palace and museum. I can't simply hand it over to a young woman who knows witchcraft, even though she saved my friend."

He nodded over the Contessa. I knew on some level he was correct, but all the same, this book was wasted in a glass box and a back room.

I walked over to him to hand it back when it suddenly fell out of my hand onto the floor.

I felt a presence in the room and knew a spirit was to blame. A page fell out.

"Mon Dieu." He jumped up and down and began to wail about the relic being damaged. "Se desole." I bent down and picked both pieces up and placed them into his hands, but quickly he handed them back to me as if they burnt his hands.

I held the book and the parchment and realised the loose page was not from the book.

"No, this has been an added page," I said, and opened the book to show it was a different paper.

"This book has passed through many masters' hands," said Jules. "Never has it had a loose page. Everyone, even the Vatican people, has inspected it."

"What about the man from the Cairo Museum?" The Contessa had found her voice and made her way to us.

"He mentioned the hidden pages. He warned us of a time when the book would begin to talk. Perhaps it is because of Anna," she said.

Jules was not amused, as this appeared to give me more claim to the book.

"Anna, what is on the page?" she asked. I held it up, and to my surprise, I saw words and images like I had seen before beginning to appear as I held it to the light.

"I have seen them on the scrolls and scarabs. This book has the wisdom to set our sisters and brothers free. It's not a book of just knowledge; it's a Book of Keys. If this book can set one of us free from the curses of past lives, perhaps it can help us clear the temples and pyramids to restore the balance we all seek."

"This book is the wisdom passed from temple to temple from the Halls of Amenti. I need to take the book to Egypt to meet the man who called me in Glastonbury. He is the keeper of the Amenti Scrolls and Scarabs, and this book has the keys to decode them all."

"Like the Rosetta stone, perhaps?" Suddenly, Jules seemed in a more favourable mood.

"But of course," the Contessa said.

"It is part of the puzzle, and we will solve this together." She smiled and reached over and took my hand and squeezed it. "I was unsure before, but now I know I will come with you, and I have already signed up Alexandria to go."

"But many of my friends, not really your friends, will be there," I said.

"Then I will call Naomi and insist that I join for the love of Isis. Can you sense her?' she asked.

I knew what she meant. Isis was in the room, and suddenly, I could smell the floral scent of lilies.

"Of course," I nodded. I then realised she had been here since we arrived.

We finished lunch and waited while Jules spoke with the other curators and explained it was at the insistence of the Contessa. It suddenly dawned on me that she may be the current owner but needed me to verify and confirm its purpose. I felt a little like I had been tricked.

"You own the black book." I looked at her.

"Yes, my family acquired it after the war. The Germans had taken many precious things from our vault in Paris. Our family did what we had to do to acquire it back. It never reached Berlin and Hitler; as we said, it was of no value and an old diary of a late grandmother who was cursed and mad. The curator at the time was more easily seduced by our art collections; some are here for safekeeping."

"So they stayed here in plain sight all through the war."

I felt a little sick as she began to point to other pieces of art and objects in the room.

I found myself standing looking at a striking picture of a lake and country house. "Where is this from?"

"Germany, I think. My aunt's house, very wealthy, Jewish, but sadly died in the war."

I felt I had seen the image before but could not place it. It must be from a film.

Jules handed me a linen velvet-lined pouch. I promised I would keep the book safe.

I prayed I could keep this promise. After all, in my experience, you never know what's really coming next.

We left soon after, as the Contessa had a headache, and I wanted to get back to my room and look at the scrolls, scarabs, and the book in private. So much of a mystery to solve, and now I would arrive triumphant in Cairo. This was quite the puzzle box, and even though I could not see how they fit together, it was strange that I was no longer afraid.

☥

On our trip home, the Contessa took a call from Alexandria. They spoke in French, thinking I understood nothing. I heard the words chamber, floral panel, Orient Express, and c'est magnifique. Oui tre bien.

The Contessa seemed most pleased, and she heaved a huge sigh of relief. She relaxed and closed her eyes to rest.

☥

Soon we were back in the busy city. Cars and lorries moved, and people were everywhere. It felt good to be back in a normal reality. I could understand why people favoured this day trip. But maybe not my version.

"That was Alexandria, my granddaughter, excited for Egypt." The Contessa finally spoke.

"She's meeting us back at your home?" I asked.

"*Certamaint,* I will see to the travel plans to Cairo myself once we arrive at the house."

"I will attend to business and fly the day after you."

"Yes, last night she went on board the Orient Express. Yes, the famous train."

"It will soon be closing to be refurbished, so she has gone to retrieve more of what is ours."

"What is ours?" I was intrigued.

"Yes, what is ours. We hid things on the train for many, many years and used the train to carry secrets to our brothers and sisters. Many of the famous things you now see in museums were hidden in vaults belonging to us."

"But who are the us?" I asked.

"You will see in time," was all that she would say.

"How long till we reach home?" the Contessa asked the driver.

"Around 45 minutes, Madam."

"Perfect." She pressed a button to bring up a screen between the driver and us.

"Now sit back, my dear, and allow me to tell my story."

"Many years ago, before you were even a thought, our whole world was in a situation of light and dark. For our past lives, we have always managed to return to the times in history when the eternal battle of the soul is about to consume us. We have protected the ancient wisdom and the spells and curses. Your box of scrolls and scarabs was one such collection of relics. The Egyptians obtained their wisdom from a rare tribe that had once settled on their lands when their homeland was destroyed."

"These people... like founders? Like the Children of Light."

She smiled. "Yes, the founders, that is well put. They came first."

"They shared a level of consciousness that we, as humans, are only starting to remember. Our souls..." she pointed to herself and to me, "...we are bound to this history."

"And those priests of Unal, they are also?" I was having trouble breathing.

"Anna, when you first began reading the scrolls in Glastonbury, Isis called me. She told me a magic had been opened, and we did not have time. The scrolls and scarabs open the portals and chambers across Egypt. Moving the energy to bring about a New Age."

"However, we have known about certain missing pieces. During the Russian Revolution and World War II, many relics went missing. They had been held by various families across Europe who were followers and protectors of 'us.' However, many were weak and surrendered what they had in exchange for their lives."

"One of the scrolls and scarabs was hidden, and at one point, we actually thought it had been stolen by Hitler. He took one of the carriages from the Orient Express that we used to use and signed the Treaty of Armistice in 1940 to take control in France, and then had the carriage burnt. We thought all was lost. As it happens, this particular carriage had been used during a treaty against Germany in 1918, and he had been warned of supernatural powers and that many of the Mystery Schools were working against him. He sought us out for revenge and actually had a list of families rumoured to be part of a mystical school, and my family's name was at the top."

"Luckily, we had friends such as Coco Chanel and Dimitri who would hide our secrets and work with us. Dimitri, a royal Russian count, was present at the end of Rasputin's life. They were double agents working between the worlds."

I felt a cold shudder at the mention of his name.

She went on with her story as if I knew all the characters, but I did not know their names. All the same, it felt most familiar.

So I sat back and listened to her.

"But let me back up," she said. "It started in 1905 in Russia. The monk Rasputin had been able to persuade the Russian Tsarina to loan him a scroll and a scarab for himself and his followers. The Russian imperial family had guarded it for decades, and he said he could heal her son with it.

"He never returned it and used it to conjure something most dark. The Romanov family lost their protection. They never realised the power that had been entrusted to them. They lost their way and then their lives."

"Why would a Russian queen have a scroll and scarab

of... oh, yes, it was the Light and Shadow set? I can see it. How did they have this?"

"Because Catherine the Great had stolen it. It was said to be kept in her famous Amber room, in her palace."

"That room was another Hall of Mirrors? I whispered.

The Contessa smiled and nodded. "Anna, you are probably already seeing a timeline in history that was never fully uncovered."

I was hearing the words like a history lesson, but at the same time, this timeline stirred something deep within me. This period of World War II made me feel sick, and I began to see a train and a small child, but nothing more.

I tuned back into the Contessa's story and began to see young people enjoying a party and engaging in a life of challenge, yet so exciting. My oracle channel opened to the Akashic Records.

"They worked in the light, a lightworker group, you may say. They were part of our secret society." I closed my eyes.

I saw them happy, laughing, and drinking wine. "But they are standing on a patio looking out. This can't be correct. They are looking out over the pyramids."

"Part of a secret society..." she interjected. "Dimitri had to come to London and then Cairo after the death of Rasputin. He stayed in the Mena House lodge, and he made his recovery. Both he and Coco Chanel were priests of a time long ago in Atlantis, and in their own way, they worked behind the illusions of the rich and famous to help others."

"Dimitri was part of the famous Romanov family, and Coco, well, she knew those high in Nazi Germany as well as the British Prime Minister. Ah, yes, a very interesting group of people."

I could not stop watching them as if I was already there. "Were they all part of our sacred group?"

"No," she replied. "Not really. We were all part of various soul groups, and we worked in karmic pods, you could say. But many were part of the Atlantis Mystery Schools. Some of us were tangled in the group of Rasputin, but they were also spies at the time of Rasputin's death. Dimitri took the artifact, the Scroll, and the Scarab of Light and Shadow back from him and hid them for us on the Orient Express."

"...and they travelled ever since," I said.

"Yes," she smiled. "Until now. Now they are coming home."

My visions were becoming stronger. This was such a tangled web.

I kept the information to myself. I had seen some familiar faces in these visions, and I wondered which side they really worked with.

"But what does this have to do with Egypt and us as priestesses and oracles?" I asked.

"Well, it all started in Egypt and at the fall of the temples around 33 BC. Much was displaced and lost. This led to the Age of Pisces, and now we are reaching a new age. You, Anna, have brought so much back together. Isis knew this, but we still don't know what it is all for. I guess in Egypt, we will find our answers."

Suddenly, the car pulled to a stop, and as I got out, I smiled and felt at ease with the Contessa.

"No, my dear. The prophecy is started, and the spirits are awakening. Anna, you have opened a timeline of energy, and as soon as you opened the red box of Isis, you took on her mission as well as your own. I know it has been a short time of your remembering, but please know you have spent lifetimes preparing for this. A Golden Age. Your soul can start to be truly free."

Her phone rang.

"*Oui oui,* okay, okay," was all she said.

"Alex is held up. She says we can all meet tomorrow. Now I have to go to a meeting. See yourself into the house, and Andre will assist you."

I smiled, not sure what she meant, but as in all things, I left it to trust and went inside the house, freshened up, and then, after a few hours of making notes in my journal, came downstairs to see if food was available.

I realised the staff knew my every move when Maria appeared at the bottom of the stairs and pointed to a door where it was set for dinner for one. She said nothing and simply smiled.

Indeed, I was hungry, and the beautiful lounge facing the street beckoned. Andre seated me.

"Mademoiselle Anna, the Contessa called to say she will see you early in the morning, before your flight at 6:30 a.m. But for now, she wishes for you to relax and enjoy. Chef prepared you something simple, yet French."

As if they had already known, a table was laden with a plate of steak frites and small cakes for dessert and a glass of champagne. Well, this was Paris, after all. It would be rude not to.

Monday, 14 September 2009, 6:00 a.m.

The next morning, I was so happy to visit the Contessa and Alexandria before going to the airport. Leaving the safe space of my room was difficult, as I did not know what would be next.

I had my bags and had made sure to pack the red box, scroll, and scarab box, and the black Book of Keys—I had decided to name it—very securely in my hand luggage. There was a knock at the door, and breakfast was on a trolley for me to enjoy while packing. I wondered if I could manage to stuff two more delicious chocolate croissants into my bag. Perhaps not.

☥

At 6:30 a.m., I was escorted to the Contessa's private room, surprised that she would receive me in person so early. One never knew with this woman. I had seen so many versions of her in a few short days.

Today, the authority in her had gone, and she was sitting at her dressing table and looking into the beautiful gilt-edged mirror.

"Do you ever look into the mirror, Anna?" she asked as I stood in the middle of her bedroom, or should I say master suite.

"I try not to," I laughed. "My hair can have some scary mornings."

She chuckled and beckoned me over to come and sit beside her.

I could see myself in the three-step mirror, and I began to smooth my hair into place. Everything here was so pristine and elegant.

"When we look into this mirror, we see all the aspects of ourselves. What do you see, Anna?"

"I see you with white hair, and your skin is so luminous." Then, I looked a little further and allowed my eyes to be unfocused.

It was then that I saw the strangest thing.

On the left side, I saw a woman with long dark hair, young and fresh.

She wore pearls and grand jewels. Then on the right side, I saw another woman in the mirror, a priestess with gold makeup. Ancient, and her head was covered by a veil. She wore a large golden Ankh and then a scarab of yellow glass.

"So, who do you see, Anna?"

"I see three of you. You are as you are now but younger."

"Yes," the Contessa replied.

"Then an ancient priestess."

"Ahh. My oracle self."

"Yes, and then a young version of you with dark hair and pearls."

"Ahh, that is my witch lifetime."

"I have many other versions, but these three aspects of my soul were the most important ones." "Yesterday, you helped me to release all that no longer serves, but I have decided to keep these. One never knows what one will need."

"The witch?" I was surprised.

"Yes, the witch. This was a dark past life I have been paying for with all that have followed. I was part of the royal courts of Europe and survived on my wits and ability with light and dark magic. But you saw that yesterday, as it cost me greatly. I may need her strength in the coming weeks, but I promise I will do it for the greater good."

I was hoping she could continue when there was a knock at the door.

It was Alexandria.

"Oh, *mon dieu,*" she ran into the room, followed by Andre, who was pushing a trolley with coffee and treats. She threw her coat onto a chaise and flopped down, disturbing the perfectly laid cushions.

Alexandria was clutching a black bag.

"I ran from the station. I was stopped at the border this morning. Can you believe it?"

The Contessa dropped her hairbrush and her composure and stood up.

"Call our security... this should never happen," she shouted at Andre.

"No, no, no, Grandmama," Alexandria shook her head.

"Then they will alert everyone."

The Contessa paused.

"Andre, make investigations, but that is all."

"Now I need a brandy for my coffee."

The Contessa then walked across to her bed and smoothed out the silk. Alexandria opened the bag.

Out fell a scarab and scroll.

We all gasped, and I saw at once.

"They are the Light and Shadow," I whispered.

"Tre bien," said the Contessa, "from a vault hidden in the Orient Express."

"Right under Hitler's eyes, hidden in plain sight."

"Now, Anna, quickly bring your carry bag, and we will place them all together safely and weave a spell of protection."

I did as requested and ran to my room just as the maids were taking down my suitcase.

"I'll take this one." I retrieved my carry-on and returned just as Andre was pouring the Contessa her medicinal coffee for the morning.

I slowly placed the precious box on the table and closed my eyes.

I began to see the images from the black book appear to me, and the words fell from my mouth.

I took the scroll and scarab and placed them gently into the box, and as they all reunited, they began to communicate with each other. Like musical notes of a very high frequency, it was as if they had been silent until now. I was about to show my prowess with them as the Contessa and Alexandria watched, but the box suddenly slammed its lid closed. I tried to open it, but it seemed to have locked itself. I did not wish to look amateur, so I simply smiled and made it seem as if all of this was in order, and I slid the box back into my carry-on.

We had some time, and the Contessa encouraged me to

climb onto the bed with her and Alexandria and listen as she told some of her famous gossip stories of history. I wished I could have stayed, but it was nearly 7:30 a.m. My flight was at 10:30 a.m.

"Madam, the car is ready."

"Ah, yes, Anna, my car will take you to the airport. You must not be late. Cairo awaits you. But before you go..." She signalled Alexandria to bring a box over from the closet.

"This is for you, Anna; it is old but precious and from my personal collection."

I opened the large box.

I let out a gasp. Inside was a perfect black bag with the vintage CC.

"Coco gave this purse to my family many years ago."

"We carried secrets in these purses. They had secret compartments, these spiritual diplomatic purses. Anna, it is yours so that you remember that you are part of a sisterhood that never forgets. Open the bag," she instructed.

I gently lifted the bag from the box, and my hands ran over the golden metal strap.

I then opened it to find it had felt pockets with discreet, smaller sections.

Not exactly what I had imagined. There was not much room for all the junk I carried.

I slid my hand into one of the pockets. There was room for the scroll and scarab box to be carried within, as if the bag maker had always intended it so.

"That is eight scarabs you have now and eight scrolls." We carefully laid the box into the bag.

My heart began to race. I had the full set, and it fit perfectly.

"And I see in the centre is a space for the Book of Keys," I said.

"The Book of Keys, of course," she nodded. "I knew it

would come back to you and its purpose. For now, place everything into the bag."

"But it is very discreet," I smiled.

Once finished, we were silent, and I had to ask the question. "Contessa, before I leave, I wanted to ask about you in Cairo or the connection to the war... and also more about my mother, Lottie."

"Madame, the car, the airport." Andre looked concerned.

"Okay, I must share this with you, Anna. I will travel with you."

A few moments later, we were in the back of an airport-bound limousine, with me in my travel clothes, and her in a fancy dressing gown.

"Another story?" I smiled at the Contessa.

She took in a deep breath and hesitated as if unsure what to share or where to start.

She reached across and opened up a compartment in the middle of the seats and took out an old red tin. She showed me her images of the past, and I knew they were the same as Isis.

I truly felt like I was living in another movie. I noticed newspaper cuttings, and I saw the photo I had seen in the box belonging to Isis; it was of my mother.

I stopped her hand and said nothing.

"Ah, yes, your mother was a beautiful priestess. True to the order, she had many gifts. But then she began to have nightmares, such as you have, and she left for England. She wrote that she had fallen in love. You must know, you have her gifts and more, Anna."

She proceeded to talk about my mother in her youth. How she had come to Paris to study but was swept into the society, and how her psychic gifts had been used not for the good but more for entertainment.

I told the Contessa about my simple upbringing and

what I knew of my father. She seemed most amused. "It is strange that your mother would settle. Hers was old wealth, but lost now." She looked out of the window as if to avoid the statement.

All that she said felt true and aligned. The wealth at the end was strange, but then I knew nothing of my mother's parents, only my aunt, her sister. The Contessa never mentioned her. She continued only about my mother.

Her words swam around in my head, but at least I had someone who knew my mother and had brought me some healing, as I could relate to her now and the struggle she must have faced. I wished in that moment I had visited with her before I left for Glastonbury, as things may have been very different.

"Anna, Anna," the Contessa was sharp.

"It is time. We are here." I looked up to see we were at the departure area for drop off.

"Time...yes." I felt as if I had lost a moment of time. This was strange magic.

She handed me another envelope.

"Now," she said, "show me your passport."

I reached into my bag, and there it was with my boarding pass, which was looking sad and crumpled. Andre had taken such care with my documents and their presentation.

She took my passport, and from out of her bag, she produced a delicate leather travel wallet.

"Here," she said and placed my passport into the beautiful lining.

"Now, here are your documents. To go into your old yet new bag."

"And here is your money."

"My money?"

She lifted the flap, and there sat many notes.

"Okay, pounds, euros, and United States dollars."

"At all times, remember you have money, tickets, and passport."

"But that's not my money."

"Anna, yes, it is."

"One day, I will explain, but for now, take me at my word."

She opened her arms, and we hugged.

"I do not have much time left, my oracle friend," she whispered.

"I pray when they come, it will be swift." She muttered

The door was opened, and the driver had loaded my bags with a porter.

"Madam, I must insist. It is time for Anna to go."

"I will see you very soon." I squeezed her hand and kissed her cheek on both sides.

Suddenly, I was heading at top speed to make my flight.

I just made it before the check-in closed and was not surprised when they informed me that my seat had been changed to business class.

I was certainly arriving in style and wondered what else would happen on this magic carpet.

Paris had opened her heart and soul to me, and I would return as soon as I had completed this adventure. Or should I say sacred mission? I looked at my phone, which had been silent for the past few days. I was just about to switch it off for take-off when three texts appeared from Naomi.

I'll send a person to collect you at the airport. See you at the hotel. Speak to no one—only the agent. Do not let your luggage out of your sight. I repeat, do not lose the box or your head.

Okay, so she knows I'm bringing more than a few French souvenirs. Little did I know I was bringing a whole lot more than that.

CHAPTER 17

Monday, 14 September 2009

I was surprised as we touched down earlier than expected in Cairo, that cheering had started among the passengers. My first real trip anywhere, and here I was in the Middle East. I felt as if I was on the set of a movie. As I walked down the steps of the plane and stood on the tarmac, I felt a tremor in my entire body. I had heard that in past times, people knelt down and blessed the land when they reached home. I was moved to do this, but at the same time, did not wish to bring attention to myself. This certainly felt like my home, and with every part of my body and soul, I knew this. My psychic vision returned to confirm this as I was transported back to an ancient time, seeing sand and ancient structures, and only began to move when prompted by the stewardess who was escorting the business passengers to the bus that would take us to the terminal. She smiled at me, and her eyes told me she had been a priestess before and knew to share a helping hand.

The terminal was busy and a little confusing. I knew many of my friends would already be at the hotel, and I wish I had been a part of that, but as I was learning, mine would sometimes be a lonely road. I wished Isis were with me. It felt like a lifetime, even though it had been a few days away from Glastonbury. I walked along the escalator to the terminal, glad to arrive but all the same overwhelmed, as I had not expected the afternoon heat.

I was surprised to see a woman standing with my name on a board, so I walked over, and we shook hands.

"Good afternoon, Miss Anna. I am Rashida. I'm now working with the travel agent, so I am your group's assistant at the hotel and guide for the tour." Rashida began to guide me through the terminal, making small talk. As we approached immigration, we paused and I began to fill the form she handed to me. I pulled out my pen from my bag. It had small ankhs stamped on it and we both looked at each other and one word... Isis... came to mind. I know she thought it too.

Rashida then hesitated, not sure how to address the subject.

"Anna, I am so sorry for your loss. I know Isis recently passed. I met her by chance when she was here in December. I helped her and Naomi leave Cairo. Isis was also a friend of my mentor, Mr. Imran. May the Gods bless him. He also died most recently. He was a curator at the Cairo Museum."

"Oh, I'm sorry. I think I spoke to him last Christmas."

I reached out to her and told her I was sorry for her loss. But at the same time my heart fell as I realised that I now had no-one to ask about the Scrolls of Amenti.

"Rashida, did Mr. Imran perhaps mention me?

She shook her head, and she seemed to avoid looking at me and skipped story to story. I simply nodded, and she carried on with her task at hand.

"I have many jobs, but today, we need to make you comfortable. Tomorrow we will go to the museum, but this afternoon and evening you should rest. I think many of your friends are here as I have been busy with arrivals from your group since yesterday. Now, your passport, please. Let's get you a visa stamp and your luggage, and we shall be on our way."

With that, she took care of everything, and I simply followed behind her, clutching my hand luggage and praying I would not be stopped and my precious scrolls and scarabs disturbed. Once we collected my suitcase, I discreetly opened it and slid my new purse and treasures inside.

As we walked out of the airport into a sea of families awaiting loved ones, our driver pulled up to the curb and within a few moments I was bundled into the car and we were on our way. The trip to the hotel was effortless, and along the way, Rashida pointed out the landmarks and the chaos of the traffic.

"You are staying at the famous Mena House hotel. One of Cairo's finest and historic," she stated.

"I have heard it was once a famous lodge to the rich and famous, yes, with many secrets!" I remarked. But then I caught sight of the Pyramids, and my heart stopped. We were so close, perhaps I dare say too close.

She smiled and pointed as the gateway opened and the car arrived. As I left the car and walked towards the main entrance, looking up at the large glass ornate chandelier above the arrival canopy made of dark wood—totally vintage, I saw many ghosts and stories unfolding. I may not have the restful sleep I was hoping for. Rashida smiled and pointed for me to walk the steps up to the main doors.

"Anna, my darling!" I heard a familiar voice and turned to see Naomi. She looked like a movie star. Her hair was jet black and cut so sharp and severe that she was ancient Egypt personified. Dressed in luxury of silk with an exquisite golden scarf. She patted her hair.

"Groomed by the magician on-site," she whispered. "You can't get this type of shine even in London." Then she took a step back and looked at me.

"Yes, well, we have to deal with this situation," she said,

pointing to my torn jeans and blouse, which I had splattered with my airline meal. Naomi snapped her fingers, and my luggage was already moving up the stairs.

"Is anyone else here with you?" I asked.

Naomi nodded. "No, but they will see you later for dinner." Oh, and give Rashida your passport. She will return it tomorrow." I smiled as I handed it to her. She looked at Naomi, and no words were needed as she sped off towards the reception to check me in.

The lobby featured lavish carved wooden ceilings, brass-embossed doors, and mother-of-pearl inlay. I stood in the centre, simply twirling around taking in the richness of the vintage features. It was so beautiful.

"And I just heard the Contessa was most impressed with you and will also be joining us later. Come, I will take you to your room," Naomi continued. Heading up the grand staircase, I followed obediently.

"Francine... sorry, the Contessa," I corrected myself. "She is definitely coming to Egypt?"

"Yes, and I want to know everything that has transpired in Paris. By the way, you are sharing with me while we are here for the first few nights. We managed to get some of the rooms in the original wing. It has hosted our people since the 1880's."

I felt very uneasy when she said the words "our people." I wondered who were our people?

"Are there ghosts?" I looked at her.

"Hundreds," she replied.

We got into the small elevator, and she pressed the button to go to the second floor. I'm not claustrophobic, but the elevator shook, and I was glad once the door opened, and I could see a long, carpeted hallway.

"The Contessa is in the suite opposite us with a view to

die for, as it overlooks the Great Pyramid. We, my dear, are in here, just opposite," she said.

Naomi used her key to open what was an unusually large white door, and I felt as though I were in an Agatha Christie novel. The room was very grand and large, but you could see how the bedroom had aged. The linens were crisp and white, and it was so cute to see the two small twin beds.

"Now, I don't ever share." She was smoothing her hair to greater perfection in the vintage mirror, when she paused.

"I know," I nodded. "What prompted this?"

"Well, it's said that many energies move from the pyramids each night. Like screaming mummies. It's no joke, Anna. Yes, sometimes these spirits do scream. The Contessa thinks if we are both together, I can protect you," she said.

"And the others? And since when has the Contessa been in charge?"

She did not answer my question.

"So you know, we are gathering at the pool restaurant at 7 p.m., so that gives you a little time to rest. It's nearly 5 p.m. now."

"I'll take a shower and be ready, for sure." I was determined to be perfect priestess material.

"Good. Well, I'm off to the garden for tea. I will let you rest," Naomi said.

As she reached the door, she turned and looked me up and down.

"What are you wearing tonight, Anna?"

I looked down at my outfit. "I didn't have the time to shop in Paris. I have my ceremony dresses."

I looked at my sorry shoes. I wished the Contessa had given me the money at the beginning of my few days in Paris. I had no idea where to shop in Cairo.

"No, I don't think so," she smiled, pointing to my sorry

outfit. "Here, I picked these out for you in London."

She opened up the wardrobe, and there was a long dress in royal blue with an assortment of soft cotton tops and pants, a few days' worth of dresses, some sandals with jewels, and some white tennis shoes... and a plastic bag of new makeup from duty-free sat on the dresser.

"For me?"

"Yes, for you, and tie your hair back. This is a very special hotel, and we need to have the full team on show. We can go to the gift shop later and see if we can find other creations, although I am not sure my nerves can stand it."

The thought of Naomi shopping for clothes in a gift shop almost made me laugh out loud, but for now, I simply nodded.

As she walked out the door, she stopped as if she was not sure what to say.

"Three nights we are here. That's all the time you have to prepare, Anna. And I still want to hear all about Paris."

I was not sure what I was preparing for, but just the tone of her words made me fearful. All the same, I couldn't wait to share my Paris adventures.

Once she had gone, I set about unpacking my bags. My suitcase was loaded with my treasures and newly acquired gift shop purchases from Paris.

I decided not to show them to Naomi just yet and carefully placed everything away. I placed the sacred box with scrolls and scarab at the back of the wardrobe and put the black book on top. I placed Isis's red box in my empty suitcase, and in the hotel safe, locked away my wallet and envelope of cash. As I made sure everything was in place, I found myself wondering how long I would need to keep this secret stash hidden. All these pieces were increasingly becoming both a challenge and a burden as the scrolls and scarabs seemed to be communicating with each other. Then

I took my shower and set about making myself presentable for the evening.

☥

Just before 6:45 p.m., I took a long look in the mirror and saw no weird and strange version of myself, so perhaps no past- life issues would surface, and I could be just regular Anna Harris. Naomi certainly had good taste. I smoothed the silk gown and twirled in front of the mirror before leaving. As I closed the door and looked down the hall to see how far the elevator was, to my surprise, the large white door of the room opposite opened, and there was Naomi.

Naomi arrived in another soft, white chiffon gown. She wore even more lavish gold jewellery and looked like an Egyptian queen.

"Anna, this is perfect timing. Look at what I found in the gift shop!" she smiled at me, twirling in her new outfit. Yes, this must be a magical shop I would have to visit.

"Will you walk over with me to dinner?"

"I would have come back earlier but I wanted you to rest, so I used the Contessa's room to change. She messaged to say she will be with us tomorrow."

"The scrolls and scarabs?" she whispered.

"Yes, they are totally safe, and I think as you'll be sharing with me, all will be doubly protected."

Her manner was very relaxed, and I wondered why. She had sounded concerned when I arrived but now did not appear to have a care in the world.

"Now," she whispered as we walked, "Tell me about Paris!"

I found myself giving her a brief but exciting overview of The Louvre, the fancy hotel restaurant, the Contessa's house, and the trip to Versailles. I left out the part about the Contessa's spiritual clearing in the Hall of Mirrors.

As we reached the end of the corridor, she stopped and pointed to the stairs. This was to my relief, as I could feel that the elevator was certainly haunted and to be avoided.

"Yes, I shared the box with the scarabs and scrolls. The Contessa was most pleased. She even gave me her collection, the Scroll and Scarab of Light and Shadow, so now we have the full set," I whispered, linking her arm like we were sharing secrets.

Naomi's eyes grew large, and she stopped on the staircase. I stood above her. "We have them all?"

All I could do was smile and nod—it felt very empowering to stand above her.

Again, I wasn't so sure whether I wanted to share the information about my morning meeting or that the Contessa had given me such generous gifts, and the black book was still a mystery.

It seemed strange not to share everything, but I almost felt like I was caught between the Contessa and Naomi. Perhaps there was a past life story. As empowered as I now felt, I was sure I could look at it on my own.

☥

Walking through the gardens in the early evening was like being in a movie. The smell of the night jasmine hung in the air. I was hypnotised by the lanterns swinging in the gentle breeze, guiding us towards an outdoor terrace with beautifully laid tables with white tablecloths and candlelight. As we entered the restaurant patio, I could hear chattering voices and laughter. The waiters moved swiftly between tables, all in their white jackets and black trousers, smart uniforms.

Naomi held my hand and gave it a short squeeze, "You're here, Anna, you're really here."

I found myself lost for words as I followed her towards a large table at the furthest corner of the restaurant patio. At the table were a few of my friends. All beautifully dressed, their faces glowing as the sun was setting and sending rays of gold and amber across the gardens.

As they noticed Naomi, the chatter stopped, and a very smart older gentleman, the Maitre d, rushed over.

"Madame Naomi, you came back."

"Yes, Mr. Ahmed, I have," she said in her most English lady gracious voice.

She turned to me. "Mr. Ahmed has been taking care of us for more than ten years," she whispered to me. "He was a favourite of Isis."

He extended his hand and smiled at me. "Madame Eeses, she was a great lady."

My heart began to race as I had just realised tonight should have been very different with her here, but in that moment, I also had a past life recognition. As he shook my hand, my mind flashed, and he felt most familiar. He was shown to me in ancient Egyptian costume. Black kohl eyes and a very distinct golden armband with a snake upon it, with a hawk above. I had seen this before when visiting with my friend Lucas. The snake and hawk were the signs of the Priests of Edfu.

He said nothing and simply smiled at me.

Other waiters ran forward and lifted back our chairs. Now I felt like I was living in a dream.

It was then I saw sister smiles. Laura and Lucinda stood to hug and welcome me. The table was a circle, and around it were several empty chairs. Naomi and I sat close together with our backs to the restaurant looking out across the gardens.

Naomi signalled to the waiter, and plates of unusual

food began to reach us.

"Hummus and pita bread are delicious flavours of the Middle East," Lucinda whispered.

I was most surprised to see her hand me a glass of wine. "It's Egyptian wine, Anna," she said, "just a little, though, for you."

"Wine has always been ceremonial," Laura ventured. She was on the other side of Lucinda. She reached across and squeezed my hand. "Love to you, precious," she mouthed, and I nodded and smiled. I took a sip, and the delicious red liquid ran through my taste buds. As I closed my eyes, I was aware of a whole different sensation compared to visiting the village pub back home.

Naomi already had her glass, which she raised. "Ladies, we have a new friend with us all the way from Paris. Please all say hello to our new sister and granddaughter of the famous Contessa." Naomi smiled over to Alexandria as she approached the table and sat down.

"Bonjour," she smiled sweetly. "I think I already know you all. I just need to put names on faces. Anna shared how you are now the most wonderful friends. I hope we can all be friends, too."

She was so gracious, and I watched her smile at us all with pure kindness.

"Welcome, I'm Lucinda, and I was with Anna in North Yorkshire, where she read her first tarot cards." Lucinda reached across and shook her hand.

"And I'm Laura, a dear friend and also from North Yorkshire, but I'm living in Glastonbury full time now. I bought a farmhouse with views that soothe the soul. And you are welcome anytime."

"I agree, Anna, these are beautiful ladies," Alexandria smiled at me.

Alexandria held her hand out across the table, and I outstretched mine.

"I flew through Istanbul and arrived just after you."

"Grandmama business?" I asked.

Shc simply nodded.

"Is your Grandmama well?" asked Laura.

"She is most well and even better now that she knows this work is taking place, as she's waited a long time," Alexandria replied.

Naomi smiled but said nothing.

I felt as if tonight was about opening doors of conversation but nothing in-depth.

A voice came out from behind me, and a woman stepped into the light.

I knew that voice, and I knew that face—it was Lesley.

"Surprised, Anna? Yes, me too, but Naomi invited me and Isis always intended to include me. In the past few months, I've been back in Cairo doing my own research for my new book, so I offered to be the money, tickets, and passport fixer person."

"Tour guide Lesley," I mouthed to Naomi as Lesley went about her meet-and-greet around the table.

"She's really good at it," Naomi whispered back and shrugged.

Lesley went over to Alexandria and hugged her. "I have what we need."

I couldn't help but feel that Lesley was using this to assert some kind of authority, but I was not going to rise to this.

"They let you have it?" Alexandra responded.

"Of course, Alex, you know I can find anything in this city, and the museum is all arranged. Your grandmother will be thrilled when she arrives."

"You can thank me later, Anna," Lesley announced without even looking at me.

Lesley breezed around the table and hugged Naomi. She was dressed in cargo pants and a vest top. Her hair and style had changed, but not her high-handed manner. "Sorry, ladies, no time to change."

"No worries," said Naomi, reaching down to pull a beautiful silk sheer scarf from her bag. She arranged it around Lesley until she looked fine dining.

"Is there room for more?" I heard a man's voice behind me.

"Lucas!" I jumped from my seat and saw him walking towards us, linking arms with Alice. I felt such a relief to see them both.

My stomach, of course, distracted me as it began to grumble, and I prayed dinner would start soon as the bread and wine were not going to suffice. I wondered why we were not looking at a menu. My thoughts were going into judgment when I noticed a woman walking across the grass. At first, I thought she was a ghost as I could only see light and her silhouette. But as she came closer, I felt tears coming to me.

It was Emilee. Like I had never seen her before.

The waiters rushed to lift out her chair and bring her wine. She pointed to be near to me.

She smiled and spoke words of Arabic, and I found myself totally enchanted by her confidence. She smiled at everyone as she sat down and introduced herself to Alexandria and then the table relaxed, and everyone seemed to know their place. Everyone chattered like long-lost friends. Somehow, it was not that way for me. Once again, I was on the outside looking in.

Naomi joked and spoke with such kindness even to

Lesley, although she did speak to her like a child. "Lesley, really... did you not have time to change... tut tut?" She shook her head.

"I'm dressed fine; it's my temple raider look," she said. "And anyway, no one looks at me. Naomi, it's all eyes on you." She laughed the critique off and winked at me.

This was a new side to Lesley. I looked at Laura and Lucinda, who shook their heads.

Naomi looked at me. I held my hands up and looked at her for sense in the matter.

"Exorcism," she whispered. "I have a good friend in Rome, a Catholic priest, no less. He came to London, and you remember my friend Gina? Well, she persuaded Lesley to visit. She certainly got a shock."

My eyes grew wide in shock.

Naomi just smiled. "His work, well, what can I say? It does wonders for the soul, hence we could have her come back to Glastonbury and now to Egypt."

I was about to ask for more information when I noticed that dinner was arriving. Apparently, that had all been pre-ordered. Maybe this would be an easier trip for me if I let others make the decisions.

"Now, before we eat," spoke Naomi, holding out her hands. We all joined our hands, and I thought we would be praying.

"Our Lady Isis is with us in spirit. She brought us together with one heart."

Everyone repeated the one heart. I realised they had all been in this circle before and in other lifetimes. My visions of faces and places began to swirl around me. I was about to speak, but food distracted me.

The main course had arrived—a delicious variety of chicken with vegetables and spice with perfect rice. This was a special moment of vision that no one else was aware of. Normally, I would be bursting to share, but my heart said wait. In that moment, I was able to focus, control my vision, and stay in my body. Finally, I was beginning to see how I could balance my gifts. I started to eat and relax. Yes, it was a beautiful evening, and I wanted to enjoy every moment.

The night sky soon became midnight blue, and the moon hung in an ocean of stars. Our dessert arrived, and I wondered if Naomi was going to make any announcements or perhaps she would ask me to speak. I had been rehearsing since my flight this morning.

I am Anna, the oracle priestess, and I am here to fulfil my destiny of bringing back the sisterhood with the ancient scrolls and scarabs. I could hear the voice in my head.

Well, perhaps I should stand. My mind and my ego wandered. "Are we doing more of the sharing, Naomi?"

"Maybe later," she shrugged.

"But I want to tell everyone—" I said.

She stopped me. "Anna, soon enough, maybe tomorrow."

As everyone finished and the table was cleared, I saw Naomi check her watch.

"Ladies and Lucas, it is time."

Time for what? I was unsure.

Everyone stopped talking and turned away to look into the night sky.

It was not great for my speech, but in a moment, I understood why. In the distance, I could see lights starting. Suddenly, I could see the outline of the Great Pyramid. The lights shone to reveal its perfect structure.

The colours changed, and it took my breath away to see the distinct lines and size. How it was built was unfathomable. It was odd... I had seen this magnificent sight on my arrival but had not dared to look too closely.

I leaned over to ask Lucinda a question and realised everyone at the table was held in a trance, totally focused on this wonder of the world. I had been distracted with my ego and thoughts and was missing a valuable moment. It registered that maybe I had not mastered my life balance.

Or had I? Something held me back from losing myself to the energy, and Alice and her soft voice came into my mind. *Remember, the Great Pyramid is a star chamber full of secret dimensions and other worlds.*

I looked around the group.

Lucinda and Laura had their eyes closed, and I could see they were already on the Giza plateau, floating in the energy.

Naomi stared without blinking, taking soft, deep breaths as if she were drawing information and insight.

Alexandria had her eyes open and smiling as if she had climbed a mountain and was taking in the reality.

Alice had her eyes closed, her mouth moving, and her hands doing mudras. Perhaps she was communicating with the spirits.

Lucas stood behind his chair, staring deep into the distance, while Emilee sat, eyes closed, deeply breathing.

Lesley stared at the Pyramid, and I felt a nervousness wash over her. Naomi must have noticed, too, as she broke her trance and reached her hand over to touch Lesley's.

"We will be okay this time," Naomi whispered to Lesley. They held hands, and I saw a sister connection and a past life connection that was so strong.

Naomi nodded to Lesley, who looked around nervously and began whispering to her, and then I caught her eye.

I had never seen this side of Lesley before. She had always been so strong, and I had in a way feared her, but in this moment, she was like an innocent child.

Lucinda reached over and tapped her hand.

"Shhh," she scolded Lesley.

Wow, she reminded me of my mother.

Ahh, I see a past life appearing, I thought, and as Naomi read my mind, she looked directly at me and shook her head.

"Sorry," I whispered, and then I decided to stop thinking and enjoy the moment.

I closed my eyes, and then, what felt like a second later, Laura was tapping my shoulder. Everyone else was moving around the table now, and the light show across the Pyramids had ended.

"Anna, did you fall asleep?"

"Oops, must be the wine." I smiled, hoping Naomi would not hear me.

Naomi, of course, did not miss a trick. "I think I will retire now," she said, "and I'll take Anna with me."

"As you wish," I nodded and smiled at her.

Yes, I was now emotional and sleepy. What was in that Egyptian wine?

"Good night, everyone," we shouted out to the table. Everyone was sharing their pyramid visions and seemed in another world.

"Oh, before you go, ladies, everyone, please listen," Lesley said, standing up and addressing the table.

"We have a visit to the Cairo Museum in the morning, so gather after breakfast in the main lobby."

"Tour director alert," Laura called out, pointing to Lesley.

"All room issues, travel problems, and tour options, please see me in the garden room 211." Lesley was most official, and I had to say I was impressed.

"Bring cameras and purses for shopping, ladies," she continued, "and Anna, do not bring the box. You know the one. But can you take a photo of it and what it holds?"

I nodded, not understanding how she knew, but I was sure all would be revealed in time.

"Yes, everyone, no relics tomorrow, only souvenirs. Remember, the museum and the mummies like to connect with sacred things; they are still alive in some shape or form."

"Oh, and one last thing: your small Egyptian pounds for tipping. Anyone needing a bank, please come see me. We also have the Bank of Naomi. She carries most currencies."

"We are all merchant Priestesses and leave a trail of wealth, "said Laura. "Once these pathways were filled with gold, and we honour that wealth as we go." She thanked Lesley, and the meeting was ended.

Lesley sat down, and Naomi and I walked slowly from the table.

"What about the bill? Do we need to pay?"

"No, it is taken care of," smiled Naomi as I turned and watched as Lesley called to the waiter for the bill. "Isis took care of many things before she passed, and this tour is paid for in many ways from the sacred tour account," Naomi informed me.

"Oh yes, she is very generous and kind. I wondered how the rest of the group were paying for this."

"Well, everyone paid a donation, and our tour was paid for by Isis. The Contessa paid for your entire Paris trip."

I felt embarrassed that I had simply been handed tickets and schedules and had never thought to check on how they were being funded. Maybe I needed to review my merchant priestess role.

"But Lesley, I don't understand."

"You will, over time," she smiled.

"Each of us around that table has a unique gift and purpose. Only when we work together do we unlock the spiritual and Oracle gifts and the story of our souls."

"So around the table are any of them Oracles from Egypt? I know Alice is."

"Think, Anna... you already know the answer."

She was right. I did. I had known it even as I had left the table. They were all Oracles. Oracles of ancient times. Perhaps this was why it had not been revealed straight away to me. I knew that on some level I knew them, but for now, it was all I could do to walk back to the bedroom. But who were the High Priestesses or even the Queens? I had to laugh at myself. Why couldn't I wonder who was a serving girl or a working girl like me? I was always looking for the higher station.

☥

We reached the bedroom, and the first thing I did was take photos of the box with the scrolls and scarabs with my phone. I laid them out on my white scarf and proceeded to take the images. For some reason, I knew this was more important.

Naomi was already in the bathroom. I knew with her beauty routine, I'd be lucky to make it in to brush my teeth. I quickly pulled on my PJs and hung up the blue silk gown; it was perhaps the most beautiful dress I had ever owned. I took out my journal, and on one page, I wrote each of the names of everyone who had been present and began to write keywords or things I had been aware of that evening. Their energy when the Pyramid was lit up was most interesting. Some looked quite at home, others in awe, and some looked like it was a great challenge for them to face. I was going to work with the scrolls and scarabs, but I knew Naomi might come out at any moment. I quickly put them away, back into the wardrobe, and closed the doors.

"Anna, I am done in here," she said as she walked out, looking like perfection. Her hair and skin were in perfect condition. I would be so lucky to ever look like that.

I hopped out of bed and ran to the bathroom. I was cleaning my makeup off when I looked in the mirror, and my face began to change.

It was bizarre as I saw myself as a young boy. My hair was black and tied in a braid on the top of my head. My scalp was shaved around this, and I wore gold earrings. My eyes were large and dark and lined with kohl, like Mr. Ahmed's. I had to blink to bring myself back, and I wondered if this was a spirit guide or maybe me, from a past life.

I was sneaking some of Naomi's face cream onto my skin. I prayed she would not notice; she has so many creams. I looked in the mirror again and saw the young boy; this time, he was holding out a ring. It was a large blue lapis stone wrapped in gold with a small gold serpent running over the top and what looked like a crest or seal. It was as if he were standing now in the mirror and bringing me a message. I was not sure but found myself telepathically telling the young boy I would help where I could.

At that, he disappeared, and I heard the wind at the window. This was a very strange hotel, and I wondered if I would make it through the night. Naomi may be demanding, but for once, I was really glad she was here.

When I came out of the bathroom, she was already sleeping, and the room was dark. I crept over to my bed and climbed into the cool, crisp white sheets. I closed my eyes and began to think of my intentions for the next day. Okay, so tomorrow, the museum, and I wondered if I would meet anyone connected to the man from the phone messages all those months ago. Mr. Imran. Isis and Lucas had both mentioned him, but no one seemed to know anything. It was a never-ending jigsaw.

Already, my mind was spinning. I closed my eyes and, like a movie, began to remember the flight, the group at dinner, and now this hypnotic young boy. Perhaps he was me in a past life. His eyes kept flashing in my mind, trying to figure it all out. However, the sleep gods had another plan for me, and I began to feel myself drifting away. I could not move or feel anything.

Suddenly, I was in a deep, deep dream.

I was not sure if I was still in Egypt or back in North Yorkshire, as the dream started strangely. It began in the back room of the café where I had started my spiritual lessons all those months ago with Lucinda. She was there, and her hair was a deep, bright red with golden jewels, and her clothes were like flowing robes. I tried to speak, but I was alone in a room full of shadow ghosts. I could feel the ladies from the tarot class but not see their shape or form clearly.

Lucinda turned to me and smiled.

"Anna, it's time," she said

"You're ready now."

Again, I could not move or speak.

Lucinda turned on the music, lit another candle, and began to recite a prayer for the equinox. She used words I had never heard before, an incantation, and when she said, "Relax, and close your eyes," I was already gone.

Gone into a dream within a dream.

I found myself walking down a dark tunnel. The walls felt cold, and I was not sure if it was a cave or under a building.

It was wet, and I was hugging myself, trying to warm up, but I couldn't.

I felt as if I was walking forever. I could see a light faintly at the end of the tunnel, but it was untouchable.

I began to feel a sadness, an emotion like I was lost, and I was waiting for Lucinda's voice to bring me back, but nothing came.

I remember then seeing the tunnel begin to widen. I was in a large underground chamber with stones arranged in a circle. The light began to open up the space, allowing clear viewing. Everything was in shades of grey.

I began to see people in cloaks, all hooded, coming into the room in a circle and walking around the stones. It was as if they walked straight through me. I was invisible.

They then sat down on the stone chairs, and I could hear the incantation just as Lucinda had done. I didn't understand the words, but I knew what they meant.

I then felt a presence unlike any I'd experienced. It was heavy, as if breathing down my neck.

My legs had tried to move, and my voice tried to cry out for the spirits in white cloaks to help me, but nothing came.

I began to tremble.

The presence came nearer, and I could now see its shadow on the stone in front of me.

I could see a dark, sinister outline of the head of a dog or wolf; I was not sure.

It felt as if it were 6 feet tall.

As I turned my head to the left, I looked down to see the body of a man, but as I turned to see his face, it was the image of a dog. Black with a golden necklace, and he was wearing a cape with a hood like the others; however, it was darker and heavier.

He leaned into me, and I looked away.

I could not understand what it was that he was telling me, but one thing I did hear.

"My name is Anubis."

"Do not fear me."

"I am here to protect you. We have travelled the worlds in our universe before, and now you are home. I am here and ready. We are ready again."

He then proceeded to place a dark cloak around me, and I could feel its weight—as if it were drowning me. This cloak was too heavy, and I felt I would never be able to bear its weight.

I began to scream and call to the others in the room for help.

"Anna, it's okay."

"Anna, it's fine."

I could hear Naomi, and I woke up and sat up straight.

Naomi was sitting on the end of my bed. She put on my lamp and looked like a vision in white silk PJs. She then opened the curtain wide and cleared energy out of the open window.

She closed the window and came over to switch on the other bedside lamp, and the room was lit with a soft, amber, warm light.

"Here, have some water," she said and handed me a bottle of sparkling water. The bubbles will help.

I took a few sips, and my mouth felt so dry as if I had been walking in a desert for days.

"Now take two deep breaths and smile," she instructed.

I nodded and felt like a child, but after a scary dream such as this, I was glad not to be alone.

"Did you see him?" Her voice quizzed me.

"Anubis," she said.

"Yes," I gasped. "How did you know?"

"It's your first night. Of course, he would find you."

"I don't understand... who is he?"

"He is the God of the Underworld and works with

Osiris. Sometimes, he acts like a ferryman between the worlds. In ancient times, the priest would wear his mask, the dog's head." She demonstrated by moving her hands around her head and showing where the long jaw would be, and at once, I saw her in a past life wearing such a mask.

"Yes, you are correct... we wore the mask like a veil so that we could send souls across into the other worlds when they died, or I should correct myself, they ascended."

"Anubis connects to the star of Sirius and, while wise, can sometimes forget he is a scary energy to encounter, and he will often ask you to bargain for a favour," she said.

I looked at her and shook my head, as I did not understand.

"Okay, let me explain, but if you're feeling okay, I will climb back into my bed. It's cold, and I think his spirit, or some masculine spirit, is still with us."

I was going to mention the young boy, but perhaps I would not complicate what had already been an eventful few hours.

I watched her float around the room like an angel, ethereally drawing protection symbols upon the walls and window before she climbed back into her bed. I turned off my lamp and snuggled down into my blankets. The clock showed 1:11, so it was not yet morning.

Naomi shared her story.

"Once, I was in Cairo airport, and I was telling myself it was my last trip. I remember that we were visiting at least four times that year, and it was exhausting. Anyway, when I became aware I had left a jacket in one of the stores while shopping duty-free."

"An expensive one," I offered.

"Oh yes, very," she nodded. "I went back to the shop, but nothing was there, and no one even remembered me placing the jacket down. I was heartbroken, and as I looked around, I saw a small statue of Anubis. He had been in my dreams, my first trip also, but I had kept him at a distance. I remembered one of the wise women in the group had always told me he could be paid for safe passage or favour; I thought I would give it a try.

"I bought the statue and just promised the statue I would return on the next trip with Isis, and in return, I would like my jacket, please. I then went to the gate, and sure enough, as I checked in for the flight and went to collect my duty-free, there it was on a hanger hung over a rail, but no one knew how it had got there."

"Anubis," we both said at the same time.

"Now I know he is not there to move our shopping and clothes, but ever since then, he has opened doors and sent messages to me. Especially when going to darker energy places, he can be very protective and helpful."

"But be warned," she said.

I felt the room grow colder.

"When you make a bargain with him, it will be with your soul."

"My soul," I answered, alarmed, "but it was just a jacket."

Naomi nodded. "Maybe just a jacket, but it was what it represented. Every time I wore that jacket, more magic would occur. It took me a short while to figure out the magic with Anubis continued. So I was caught in a cycle of favour."

"Did you ever repay the favour to release yourself?" I did not wish to be trapped.

"Yes," she smiled, "but that story is for another day; I want to hear what your favour or deal was."

I just kept nodding until I realised she was asking me a question.

"So what did he say?" she asked.

"Oh, yes, he said he would protect me, and he placed a

cape around me. The cape felt so heavy—that's where I felt I was drowning. He said we had worked together before and worked between the worlds, and we would do so again. And then I ran off screaming."

I felt like a novice again.

"I'm sorry," she was laughing, not so much at me, but I began to see the humour and I began to giggle.

"And was anyone else in the dream?" she asked.

"Yes, Lucinda, at my old tarot class. She was doing an incantation, and I have to say I did not love this one. It sent me through to the other side very quickly, and I was not comfortable."

"Understandable. Lucinda is most powerful, and you know her as your mentor and the High Priestess of Dendara, but she has mastered the light and the dark, and that's all I am going to say."

I was glad Naomi left it at that, as it was now nearly 1:30 a.m., and I was beginning to feel sleepy again.

"Okay, so we will sleep, and I will create a golden veil so nothing and no one is visiting us tonight," she said.

I smiled as she turned off her lamp, and I could hear her softly calling in protection.

It felt so soothing. I snuggled back into my covers and drifted off peacefully.

CHAPTER 18

Tuesday, 15 September 2009

That next morning, I awoke to see the sun streaming down into our room. Naomi was already awake in yet another beautiful outfit.

"What time is it?" I asked, rubbing my eyes.

"Nearly nine, you sleepy head. We start in thirty minutes."

"Start what? Are we having breakfast and then going to the museum?"

"No, it's the gathering of the coven with the Contessa. I got a text a few hours ago, and you were snoring," she was sharp and in action mode.

"Can't you hear them?"

"Hear who?"

"The people of our group have been coming and going from the Contessa's room since the early hours."

"Apparently, the Contessa had arrived late last night. I'm glad I had housekeeping come up while we were at dinner. My intuition is still on point."

I think she took joy in the shock on my face and the alarm that spread over me. My first gathering and I would be late and a mess.

"Shower first," Naomi pointed to the bathroom. "And breakfast is over there, and here is your outfit," she said, holding up a beautiful lilac Egyptian dress of soft cotton with purple embroidery across the front.

"Actually, it's 8:30. We start in an hour," she smiled.

"But all the same, hurry up. And don't forget the box of scrolls and scarabs. That will be the first thing the Contessa wants to see."

It must have been Anubis who shifted the time, as I was soon ready and we were heading to the suite across the hall. I wondered what my price was for his assistance.

The door opened before we had even knocked, and we entered.

There in the room was a circle of chairs. Lesley moved about the room with her clip chart, busy writing down everyone's questions and handing back passports.

She looked at us both and shook her head.

"Always drama around you, Anna... last to arrive." She said this to me, and I noticed she dared not say it to Naomi.

I was about to say something when the Contessa called me over, "Anna, please bring that box to me."

I went over obediently, smiling to myself as I felt all eyes turn to focus upon me and the prize I had brought with me.

"Alexandria, *ma cher,* can you please assist?" Her French accent was thick, and even though she spoke low, everyone turned to stare. It was like she could cast a spell.

Alexandria stood and walked over to us. As I placed the box on the small table beside the Contessa, we looked at each other before she gently lifted the lid. I heard some gasps behind me and was surprised to see Alice standing next to me.

"You know these two pieces?" the Contessa asked. She pointed to the most recent ones I had obtained in Paris.

Alice nodded. "They are the Scroll and Scarab of the Light and Shadow."

The Contessa nodded.

Alice turned and went over to Lucinda, who was white and looked in shock. I suddenly remembered I had not shared my Paris adventure to anyone except Naomi.

"They came back, my friend Lucinda. See?" the Contessa pointed to the box. "She found them again," she said, looking over and pointing to Alexandria.

I was trying to read the Record between the Contessa and Lucinda when Alice made her way in front of me and closed the box. Its energy was beginning to circle the room, and not in a great way. "Anna, sit down; you must be exhausted, and now is not the time," she said.

"There will be the time later," Alice was sharp, and I felt myself a little thrown off balance with her words and energy.

I was glad the Contessa spoke. "Alice, there will never be a good time for that story. Now, everyone, please take your seats in the circle."

"As you wish," Alice replied, "but I think we should let our Oracle sister speak."

I felt my heart swell with energy in a way the High Priestess title never had. I was confused for a moment as it appeared a whole other timeline of history and betrayal was about to be announced, and it did not feel good.

Emilee spoke, "This must be cleared, Francine." I was stunned. It would seem she knew the Contessa on a more personal level and had addressed her by name.

"Let her speak. We all need to know the cloud of shame she carries," she continued.

This was supposed to be my chance, but before I could step forward, Lucinda had already stood up and was ready to share. It would seem she was the one they were talking about. She took a long pause and then she spoke:

"This current life, I incarnated in 1963. I did not wish to return, but my soul had another plan. I had left the planet around, and I have to say I was grateful, as that was not the most beautiful life.

"My life before this started when I was born in 1874 in

St. Petersburg. A beautiful city with such culture and wealth. My family was trusted by the Royal family, and we lived in the palaces all around Europe."

As she spoke, I felt like I was floating in a dream, and I could hear the music and the past life I had seen in Paris.

Lucinda continued, "We, my family and soul sisters and I, were guardians of many of the sacred relics of Egypt and the temples around the world." She went over to the box and opened it. "This is the Scroll and Scarab of the Light and Shadow. They had been hidden in a vault of a private collection in Russia for many years, until around 1906. Then there came a time of darkness. There was a man, a man of darkness."

I heard his name in my head: *Rasputin.*

She looked at me, "Yes, Anna, you know, and some of you in this room knew him. Isis also knew as she was in this past life with me. He was a great prophet and had great wisdom. Many of you knew him from past lives, and he has taken on many guises. He would visit our mystery school gatherings—or the spiritual salons, as Madame B liked to call them. For the history lesson, those who were not there at that time, Madame B was the great Madame Blavatsky, a spiritual channel and medium. She taught us many things and warned us of the dark times to come. She passed before he came to power. Isis never trusted him in that life. But someone did."

I looked at Lucinda. I felt it was her, and a great fear came over me.

"Anyway, the Scroll and Scarab of the Light and Shadow were stolen, and even though we did not have access to them, we were taught about their powers. With these two pieces, you gained the power over another soul's karma by holding them. You could see the past timelines and influence the future ones with war or peace.

"Once Rasputin had these two pieces, he knew wars and change were coming. I was tasked with stealing the pieces back from him, and I worked with my beloved friends to create a diversion. We had replicas made of many of the relics, and this is why certain museums around the world have some of the copies."

She looked at Lesley, "I'm sorry you were tricked into that fake scroll."

Lesley shrugged and rearranged her posture as if it did not matter, but deep inside, I knew it did.

"So we created an opportunity to visit Rasputin at the Astoria Hotel in St. Petersburg. It had opened in 1912 and was a haven of the elite. We knew he met women there, whom he said he was healing, and it was always the same room, and while he was preoccupied, we switched the pieces. However, we did not remove them. We simply hid them. Over time, it was said this room and this hotel had special powers, as many reported their dreams affected, which, of course, they would. I decided that we would return for them when it was safe.

"Once Rasputin had been killed in 1916, our soul friend who had been involved in the murder, Dimitri, fled. Then the revolution came, and we thought all was lost as we had to leave the city. Many died, including Isis. I alone had gone back to reclaim the pieces and discovered they were gone. Dimitri had taken the real ones, and they would later fall into the hands of a greater evil."

"Many years later, a rumour had started that a man in Germany was gaining power and that he had acquired great wisdom. Isis had reincarnated and was a very young girl when I met her again during the time of war. I continued my work across Europe. I was introduced to her in Germany, as her family had come to see me on a spiritual mission, as I was known as the oracle to them and other wealthy families. We knew another great war was coming, and as always, no one listened. I left Germany and worked in the French resistance. Many priests and priestesses did, and we were made aware of the plans of this dark and evil soul who would remove many innocent lives. He had come into the possession of the Scroll and Scarab of the Light and Shadow and was being taught to use them by a very powerful witch.

"His name was Adolf Hitler, and he was fascinated by anything of the ancient world and the occult. He had a whole team seeking out those of our order and even had my name on a list of people he wanted to speak with. Germany had been forced to sign a peace treaty in 1918, and when Hitler took power, he used all the relics he had acquired to guide his mission and raise Germany to the ultimate powerful nation. He saw the rise to power as it had been seen in many past civilisations. But the one thing he was not taught was that there were other scrolls and scarabs that could rebalance any energy used with darkness.

"Many in this room worked to move the other relics into safe hands, I'm sure. But these two pieces were surrounded by dark magic, and we used all our friends of influence on both sides to regain them. During those dark days, the power of Hitler was rising, the concentration camps had begun, and the battle of the souls was in full-scale war.

"Finally, our chance came when the French surrender was signed on June 21, 1940. We knew Hitler had the pieces, and with a miracle on our side, we changed them for fakes. But before we could leave, we realised we had been followed and needed to hide them in case we were searched. We had managed to smuggle them onto another train, which was connected to the famous Orient Express.

"After this switch, Hitler found his choices and decisions clouded, and he realised the pieces he had used may not be the true ones. He again consulted his spiritual advisors, who were really witches, who told him of the fakes and that the real ones had been hidden in the train in the section where he had signed the treaty. It was then he realised fate had struck as he had had the carriage destroyed to show his power, as it had been that same carriage many years ago, where Germany had been forced to sign away its power. We had tricked him. But our real pieces had been placed elsewhere and would continue on for another sixty years, travelling across Europe until a few days ago when they were rescued."

Lucinda smiled at Alexandria. "How brave to even go back to that place, that timeline we all wish we could forget."

"Oh, it was nothing... actually, it was a charming journey," Alexandria said.

Alexandria seemed to brush it away, but I felt something in my heart and my stomach that told me this timeline of war and fear was so much more.

Alexandria spoke. "The head concierge of the Orient Express, whose father is third generation, has been waiting for many years for us to show up."

"Of course he was," said Laura, who was near me. She spoke as if she had sarcasm in her voice, which was most unlike her. I began to look around the room and see a karma drama rather than a sisterhood. This was very strange, as Alexandria was the kindest and most gentle soul. Perhaps a darker tale was hidden.

Alexandria continued. "When I showed up at the train a few days ago, the concierge knew me at once as he said he had had a dream about his grandfather, and he knew the time would be soon. He knew as soon as he saw the key I brought to him. For years, they knew only of the image of the key and the location of the hidden panel and that one day, a woman would come. He showed me where the wood panel was, and I used the key, which we had kept safe. So now we've able to gather together a full set of scrolls and scarabs which has to show we are heading in a positive direction."

I was beginning to shiver for no reason when Laura came over and wrapped a soft cashmere wrap around my shoulders. She kissed my forehead as if she knew what was really going on.

"We may be facing dark times like then and we now have to start to focus on our own safety," Lucinda continued.

Everything was shifting, and it struck me I no longer needed a chaperone. I would request my own room. For the first time, I looked at Lesley and smiled, as I knew she would perhaps be my key to freedom.

Now that felt familiar. I made a mental note for later.

"So, what is the focus of this group now?" Emilee asked with her smile, looking directly at the Contessa as if to challenge her. Lucinda had finished her tale, but there had been no reaction, and I knew she had left a lot out of her story.

I wanted to shout that it was to make me the High Priestess, but I sat frozen. It was Lucas who spoke.

"We are here as Isis intended. We have a group of oracles, priests, and priestesses, and each of us has a history and past here in Egypt. And we all have history together."

"That box of scrolls and scarabs unites us in a temple and a power and alchemy we have not had in over 2000 years. Now, my sisters..." His voice changed, and I saw an image of him I had not yet seen—a masculine image—strong, powerful, and wise.

"I can sense them in the room growing in power." He pointed to the box. "I once was a guardian of a scarab and know how they talk to one another. But they have long been separated. Now it is done. We have the complete sets and will see what destiny will bring." He sat back down.

The Contessa reached over as if to take the box.

Alice then stood and walked over to the Contessa. She lifted the box right out from under her, handed it to me, and spoke, "Each of you is here to remember, and with Anna's help, I think we can find healing for our souls and those we have encountered on our paths."

I nodded and smiled around the room but was not met with much encouragement. When my eyes caught the Contessa, she did nod.

"Yes," she continued. "My dears, we have a purpose, and it is within the temples and tombs here in Egypt. In the days ahead, many of the rituals and rites will return. Now that we have the temple relics we need, we can go forward to do the work we came to do."

"There is a dark force upon this land." The voice was Lucinda's. She was in trance.

"A force dark and hidden in the shadows. It can sting when you are least ready and take from you all you are unwilling to give. Beware the scorpion."

The room began to spin, and Laura stood and began to chant. I pushed back in my chair, refusing to be swept into the energies, determined to be the observer.

Laura called in all the elements and energies as Emilee went behind Lucinda and began pulling energies and entities from her. Now there was a high priestess to be seen in action.

I realised it may be time to review my career path options.

When they had finished, I could hardly breathe. But I had learnt so much, and I began to feel my book themes and writing gifts returning.

The room became silent; I longed to get back to my journal to write notes and research.

"Now then, I think it's time for an early lunch," said Lesley. The grounded business of the day brought everyone back into focus. Lucinda looked drained, but everyone else appeared to be back to the order of the day.

Lesley went over to the Contessa and whispered to her.

I was not sure what was said, but Lesley looked more than upset and flustered.

The Contessa then stood and, like a Royal Queen to her subjects, announced that the work for the day was concluded and that we would have a free afternoon.

"You make it happen tomorrow," the Contessa hissed at her, and Lesley ran from the room in tears.

We all sat in what felt like the longest silence as I could hear Lesley on the phone outside the room. It was obvious she had gone to great lengths to secure our museum visit, and now she was being tested to see if she could pivot.

At that moment, Lesley returned and simply nodded to the Contessa.

"10 a.m. tomorrow, please be ready for the museum tour in the lobby," Lesley calmly announced and nodded to the Contessa. She then walked over to her chair, picked up her bag, and in protest left the room.

I was stunned. How could she be so businesslike when she had been treated so badly? But then I thought perhaps this was just the norm on an Egypt sacred journey. I, however, was so relieved, a rest with room service was just what I needed away from karma drama.

16 September 2009, 10 a.m.
Cairo Museum

We looked like tourists standing in the hotel lobby. I looked around and could only hear Lesley giving instructions. Over to the side, I saw Emilee at a small table in the bar area. She sipped on her mint tea and sat gazing through the window, which was covered in a curtain of small metal strands. Just behind her, I could see the Great Pyramid.

I sat down next to her and remained quiet.

She turned to me and smiled. "You would think I would be tired of this view after thousands of years and many lifetimes."

"But never," I said.

"Never ever," she smiled. "Anna, ma chere, today you created a new start for us and for the first time in many lifetimes, a wheel of destiny turned, and I am not sure where that will take us."

"We will find our way, Emilee. I don't know how, but I finally believe," I smiled at her.

She smiled, and we held hands for a moment before reality returned.

"The bus, the bus," called out Lesley, and we all followed her out with our tourist bags, water, and essentials. Lesley caught my arm and quietly said, "I arranged a meeting with Mr. Imran's assistant. Shhh, do not say anything, just get on the bus." She dismissed me, and Rashida simply nodded.

What was happening??

Once seated and counted, Lesley placed herself at the front of the bus and formally introduced Rashida.

She was such a patient, polite lady, and I wondered if she had encountered a group of spiritual seekers such as us or if she would have called us crazy.

It was not long before we were driving through the busy streets, and the cars flowed in front and around us. There seemed to be no rules for following the lanes, and we only slowed for the occasional cart with a donkey or for families crossing the road—seemingly risking their lives—as I saw no formal crossings.

Rashida gave the history of politics and religion, and we all nodded politely.

Then Lesley stepped up to give the alternative review.

"The Cairo Museum holds many of the relics of the Old and New Kingdoms of Egypt, but most of all, it hosts the collections from us all through the ages. Be aware of the areas you choose to linger in and know that ghosts are around every corner.

"Please know we only have three hours from arrival, and we will meet at the coffee shop for a short time and then all journey back. This place may have energies that need you to connect with and so be present with clear attention, and also your love. And please, of course, visit the Tutankhamun exhibit as some of my personal jewels are on loan there. Well, they were mine a few thousand years ago," she joked.

"Please have your energy shields up, as many artifacts are still below in the museum crypts, and the mummy room holds some curses." No one had mentioned mummies.

I glanced around the bus, and very few seemed to be listening as if they had heard it all before. The Contessa rolled her eyes. Only Naomi sat politely, listening and nodding.

I could tell then that she and Lesley had a great history in this country, which was very unlike England. Perhaps in a few days, I would find out their secrets. But for now, I was mentally saying my clearing energy prayer and calling in Isis's protection.

We arrived outside the museum, and I could see groups

of people and schoolchildren moving around in the gardens. This was my first time seeing the stone statues up close. I felt as if their eyes were watching me, following me as we were handed our tickets and made our way through the bag security zone into the main lobby.

The Cairo Museum was noisy, and the scent reminded me of an old library I had visited as a child. In fact, that very library held a book I had borrowed multiple times—one about Egypt and the ancient gods. I thought back to my Egypt Oracle deck, one of the first things I had bought in Glastonbury. It amazed me to realise that I had only seen these images on cards, and now, here they were—full-sized statues and pieces created thousands of years ago when these were living, breathing spiritual traditions.

Naomi came up behind me. "Isis and I would visit in the nighttime and astral travel here. The funny thing was we always bought a ticket and went through security when we could have simply floated in."

"It's good to have a ritual," I laughed with her.

I noticed a small bookshop to my left and made a mental note to perhaps visit at the end. As this was my first visit, I had decided that the books here would be more powerful and aid my research no matter how much heavier my suitcase became.

"Do we go as a tour?" asked Laura.

Rashida answered, "I will take a group around according to the historical timelines, but should you wish to follow your own path, the doors are open, and you can trust your instincts."

"Okay, everyone, remember we'll meet at the coffee shop, we leave in three hours, back to the hotel," called out Lesley. "And those wanting the escorted tour, I will be with Rash."

She did not have time to finish when everyone departed

and made their way to their own connections and lifetimes.

I looked at Rashida. She pointed to Lucas, Emilee, and Alice.

"Oh, they go to the Old Kingdom to the relics of the mother of King Khafre. It is said she still walks the Giza plateau, ordaining everything for her son. This King who built the pyramids."

"Rubbish, my dear," said Naomi.

"Naomi, please," I said sharply.

And for the first time, Naomi apologised. "Sorry, Rashida."

"It's fine," she smiled. "I know you think the aliens built them."

I felt most protective of Rashida, and in a way, I knew Isis would have defended her knowledge. We should all show this lady respect.

She nodded to me and continued. "Lesley and I, we go to the Tutankhamun exhibit. The Contessa is going mummy clearing with Lucinda."

"I see," said Naomi. "But what about Laura?" I asked.

"Oh, she will be in the Ramses section mourning a dead husband. Our Lady Sitre, did you not see the black veil she was holding this morning?" Naomi whispered.

"No," I shook my head.

"Observe and learn, Anna," Naomi said as she looked around for the rest of our group. "Alexandria must be already on the move."

"Anna, do not forget you are visiting with Mr. Imran's assistant," said Rashida in a low voice.

"Can I come?" Naomi's voice was like an excited child.

Rashida deferred to me, and I smiled slowly and nodded.

Naomi was so grateful, and I began to see that this

Egypt trip might bring me some favours.

"He is meeting us at the Akhenaten exhibit. We will leave you there and continue to the Tutankhamun displays."

I felt a shudder and a cold feeling go through me. I hid it well and let her lead us through the bustle of the tourists.

Many times, I wanted to stop, but Rashida was at full speed, and I wondered if she had also come to this place in astral travel.

She turned to me, "Yes, Anna, I do come here in my dreams. It's a most wonderful place after sunset." I saw the look on Naomi's face, and I could see she had a whole new respect for our guide and now spiritual friend. The tourists parted like the Red Sea as we moved down the centre of the museum and then began to climb the stairs to the exhibit at the back.

The Akhenaten Exhibit

We walked straight to the back of the lower floor, past the capstones and the huge stone sarcophaguses. When we reached the back, we climbed the staircase, passing the two largest statues I had ever seen of a King and his Queen.

Naomi stopped, and Rashida stood beside her.

"Your father?" asked Rashida.

"Yes, and my husband," smiled Naomi wickedly.

"Ah, Princess Sitamun," Rashida said, bowing her head to honour her.

Both women turned to me. "It was most normal to have a marriage between family members.

"Here are King Amenhotep III and Queen Tiye. Parents to Amenhotep IV, who became Akhenaten."

I could feel a vision coming, but Naomi was already pulling me up the stairs and towards a large section at the back directly behind her royal parents. The room was filled with golden burial chambers in large glass cases, and in the entrance stood a tall male statue that looked very strange. His head was very elongated, and his features very pronounced. He had a stomach that was protruding, and I wondered if it was a woman who was pregnant. To my surprise, Alexandria stood transfixed as if in a dream. Next to her stood Lesley. She paid no attention to us, and out of respect, we left her alone as she looked up into a glass case holding a white statue of what looked to be the King holding a child in his lap, kissing her.

Naomi took me to an image of the man with what looked to be his family, their hands raised to the sun. We spoke no words, and I began to understand this particular family's love and wondered what had gone wrong. Then I remembered this was the image I had seen in Alice's house and the ripped pages in the Egypt book.

Rashida, meanwhile, went over to a man who was positioning various images of ducks and flowers on the walls. I turned to look over to them and find I am unable to move. The man turned to me, and I felt an energy run straight through me. As he approached, I felt like I wanted to cry, but nothing happened, and I stood there, unsure what to do.

"Miss Anna and Miss Naomi, this is Mr. Imran's assistant, Professor," she said.

Not what either of us expected.

"Miss Anna, do you remember the call in Glastonbury? I was in the room with my mentor when he reached out to you." I couldn't place his accent, and I began to see his face shift into many guises. I had to shake myself. The professor looked to be in his late thirties. He was tall and reminded me of the warrior priests in Edfu from my visions. I was lost for words. Tall and athletic with light brown wavy hair, he seemed to carry the power of the Edfu priest but with a softer presence. I heard the name Thoth in my head and understood that his soul had always been the intellectual—a son of Thoth, the God of wisdom and knowledge.

He moved quickly to greet me, in turn, knocking over his briefcase full of papers. As we both stooped down to retrieve them, I could not help but be stunned by how attractive this man was.

Naomi was over in a flash and helping rescue the situation.

"Professor, you are not what we expected. We thought you would be an elder, but here you are, a younger man who I can't quite place in a Cairo Museum."

He began to laugh, "Yes, I have this all the time. My father was Egyptian, and my mother was English. They died in an accident when I was young, so I was raised by my grandmother in London. I then studied in America before coming here. Mr. Imran was a friend of my grandmother; hence, he was my mentor." He looked a little emotional and looked over to Rashida.

"My father passed away when I was young, and I am sorry for the loss of your mentor," I replied.

I'm not sure why I shared that, but it was as if I could share all my thoughts with this person. I noticed Rashida and Naomi looking at each other. Mr. Imran was a mystery in some way. Then, there was just a silence.

I managed to say a few words to ask the professor to explain the exhibit, when I knew full well that Naomi and Rashida were both very knowledgeable.

Being a gentleman, he obliged.

"In 1372 BC, a male child was born, and his parents were Amenhotep and Tiye. He was the second son but greatly favoured, so his father would later allow him to rule by his side after the death of his brother."

"The Oracles of Siwa had foretold the prince, then known as Amenhotep, would rule and bring forward a new age."

"Much was celebrated in Egypt when this prince succeeded in becoming King and ruled with his Queen Nefertiti."

I nodded along, knowing that this was simply a history lesson whilst I was seeing so much more.

I began to see images at the back of the room, like a large movie screen showing the royal court and the Oasis at Siwa. While I could hear his voice, I found myself moving around the glass cabinets, tracing my hands through the energy fields. I watched as the professor followed me with his eyes, calling out the exhibits as I moved past them.

I pointed to the white alabaster statue of a seated king with a child on his lap. They were kissing and showing affection.

"His beloved daughter," he nodded.

I smiled and noticed everyone had turned to stare at me. Lesley began to wander out of the exhibit with Alexandria, and Rashida turned to stand next to me.

"Most beloved," I kept repeating until Naomi came close and steered me back to the history lesson. But it was too late. I was lost in the Akashic Records.

The channel was clear.

"They left for Armana to be safe and bring back the wisdom of Atlantis. Nefertiti was of Atlantean heritage and bloodline. She was the one who had access to the scrolls and scarabs," I heard.

All was silent, and I felt as if the whole museum was coming to life.

"Where is the white stone? It should be here." I looked

around. For the first time, I felt the presence of Isis.

"We don't know a white stone," Rashida looked around. She looked nervous.

I, meanwhile, was weaving in and out of consciousness.

"It's this size and this wide, and it's white," I insisted. "Professor, do you know?"

"No, darling, not this timeline. See, there is nothing here," said Naomi as she scanned the room.

The professor looked a little flustered and came over to me. "No, not here, Anna, but I can show you where it is." His face changed, and I saw an inscription marking on his forehead; it was like an eye but not like the Egyptian ones I had seen. It was oval in shape, and the eye was in a central position. "Shall we go?" He pointed the way. "Oh, and Anna, call me Michael."

I could hear the whispers of the ancient ones in this exhibit in my head. The messages said that I was safe and to trust this person. I looked at him and smiled.

"Let's go," I said.

"Do we have time, Rashida Naomi?"

"Oh yes, plenty," she nodded. They were just as eager to see where our next adventure would take us.

We found ourselves outside the museum. To the side, there was a small set of steps leading down to a door in what appeared to be a basement. Once inside, it was a rabbit hole of corridors and rooms. I could see sets of old wooden boxes, and each room had inscriptions above the door, marking the contents' timeline within.

"Ladies, you can stay here. Anna, I'm restricted by the rules of my office, but as my mentor reached out to you, I guess I have permission to take you further inside."

People were walking all around, and we appeared to be invisible.

Michael called to an associate and asked them to escort

Naomi and Rashida to some of the side rooms.

"We have some relics and jewels of the Princess Sitamum," he smiled, and I watched as the women's faces lit up.

"You were her handmaiden," I looked at Rashida as Naomi looked on, shocked.

"You are as good as Isis said you would be," Naomi paid me the compliment. "Maybe even better."

As they were whisked away by an older gentleman who did fit a professor's description, I turned my focus to Michael.

"We have no time, Anna. We have to go unnoticed," Michael said and took my hand. I thought we were in a different time, but not to waste the moment, I ran with him.

We came to a stop at the end of what was a dark corridor.

"My room," he said. "Peace and quiet and all things magical."

He unlocked the door, and we entered. It reminded me of a room from my childhood at school. There were tables and chairs and lots of whiteboards with messages, words, and images, all of which seemed to link to one central location.

In big black letters in the centre of the board was the word ATLANTIS. Then, pages of words and messages are all over the walls with sticky notes—organised chaos.

"I have been collecting everything," he said.

"I wrote down everything about the lost continent and have been studying this from a small child, and you, Anna, you are the first one to bring a confirmation of my search."

"What is in that room?" I asked, pointing to what looked like a storage room.

He opened the door, and I looked in and turned on the light.

"There you are... I knew you would be here," the words flew out of my mouth.

I slowly walked over to a table at the back of the room. There sat a large white stone. "Where did you find this?"

He shrugged. "We have it listed here since the early 1900's and the opening of the museum."

I moved slowly towards it and felt my heart connect. It felt like home, and I began to cry softly.

I felt Isis's presence with me. "I knew you would find her," she whispered in my mind.

I did not touch the stone but ran my fingers through its energy field—she was strong and sending out the most wonderful messages. I could feel my body heat up and wondered if this was a sign; it was as if these worlds were starting to cross. I paused a few moments as my mind worked at detective speed. I could see flashes back to Glastonbury when I had first arrived.

The first scrolls and scarabs, my first visions, the ceremonies, then Isis and the other priestesses. Everything was entering my mind like computer files.

When I had collected the messages, I turned back to him.

"I knew she was here." He looked at me, not understanding.

"She's here... the Stone of Consciousness... the stone from the high altar of Atlantis."

We stood in silence.

"I was not expecting that," he said. "But I have heard the stone calling, which was why we moved it here. My mentor, Mr. Imran, would lock the door as many strange things began to happen in the museum."

"What really happened to Mr. Imran? I can't seem to get a clear answer."

"It was very strange. He had a call from Isis around

Christmas time... I was in his office, and he let me listen. My mentor was very wary of the questions she asked, but responded that he had the Scroll of Amenti and the Scarab. I had seen them only once. I was never allowed to touch them. I know they are very powerful. He kept asking about you, saying that you would have the answer, and this seemed to annoy Isis. She said you were not ready, and Mr. Imran argued that you were."

I felt like we were betraying her memory and wanted to change the subject, but at the same time, here was another mystery. My head was swimming in thoughts.

"Where are they now?" I asked.

He looked down, rather embarrassed.

"Isis and he had a bigger argument, and she was very angry. She said they all had been betrayed."

"He called Isis his love, which I thought was strange, and then she really flew into a greater rage, saying she could not help him as he had put his faith in another, and she released him of all contracts. But they had no business contracts, so I'm not sure."

"She left the call abruptly, and he soon after left the museum in such a state of depression. Then had the accident when his car crashed."

"He was killed?"

"Died yes, killed no," he replied. "A heart attack."

"And the Amenti pieces?"

"Gone. I have searched everywhere," he hung his head.

Even though I had known him for a short time, I felt this man spoke the truth.

"Michael..." I took his hand. "We will find them. I know they are close; I just can't reach them."

"Well, you have superpowers to find the stone, so I will trust you."

"Now we have work to do. I need to get back to my friends, but please secure this place as I feel eyes watching and ears listening," I said, pointing to the door.

I slowly began making my exit when I was prompted to do something. The scarf Naomi gave me in Glastonbury was still in my bag. I gently took it out and went back into the room, laying it across the top of the stone. "Always and forever," I smiled and left the room.

Once back in the classroom, I began to feel uncomfortable, and I did not really know what to say. I thought we would leave, but Michael motioned for me to sit down. We then sat in silence, not sure what to do next. I wanted to leave, but at the same time was desperate to stay and learn more. He must have sensed this and spoke first.

"Mr. Imran was the one who actually identified the Amenti pieces in a box I found. Let me explain."

"My grandmother used to talk of women like you, Anna. She said someone would visit us one day and remind us of who we truly were. I have had dreams of the white stone but never knew why. Anyway, when we were digging last year in Armana, I found a small wooden box with some relics within it. Just broken pottery. I had found it late in the day and took it back to my tent ready for inspection the next morning. But when I was in my room, I began hearing messages. My grandmother's spirit came to me, and she took me through the famous museums and pointed out many things—London, Paris, New York, and then to Cairo, where she pointed to the white stone. It used to be in the Akhenaten exhibit. She told me they were connected but never explained how.

The next morning, I took the box back to Cairo to my mentor. He discovered a false bottom in the box and there inside, sat a scroll and scarab. My mentor must have sensed something as he began calling out the names of the gods and chanting strange words such as Amenti. He closed the box and began telling me of the lady called Isis from Glastonbury, but then he started acting strangely and kept saying your name. I asked who you were. He said he did not know, but he knew you from a dream. He then told me that I should not research the Amenti pieces, but I could hold other pieces for their safety in time. I did not know what they were, but he said that the woman called Anna would know, but I should await her arrival. It all seemed so bizarre and random."

He paused.

"Anna, I have a confession. I was curious. I have friends in London, and I asked them to make inquiries. Apparently, there was an Isis in Glastonbury with a gifted psychic, Anna. I found the number in his diary for a Glastonbury Isis, and I made the call that you picked up. It was my voice, not his; I pretended to be him. I had been meaning to call many times, and then one evening, I was working and realised I was becoming obsessed over this set of relics, more than any other. I picked up the phone and dialled the number, and for some reason, the words 'I have the Scroll of Amenti' flew out of me... After that, I thought you would think it a hoax, so I wrapped everything up and hid it away. I confided in my mentor. He was furious, but he said he would make everything good and keep my secret. He took them back for safekeeping, as he said they would drive me insane. I think that he reached out to Isis in private."

"Hence her secret calls," I responded.

"When he and Isis had the angry phone call and he then died, and I thought it had ended with him. As he had passed away and no one really understood our work, I was given the keys to his office and found a box. In it were some scrolls and a scarab, along with clear instructions that the pieces were to go to Glastonbury and into Isis's care, but the Amenti pieces were nowhere to be seen."

"Isis did call me after his death, and I told her of the instructions. She said that her trusted friend, Mr. Lucas, would come. I gave up my quest once I handed the box on to Mr. Lucas as per instructions left by Mr. Imram and Isis. Then I heard she had died, and I thought the story was ended."

"That was until a few days ago when I was called by a young woman named Lesley, asking to see certain pieces in the Tutankhamun collection, and also Rashida, saying that a woman from England called Anna, connected to Isis, was visiting and would likely wish to see certain pieces also."

The story was slowly merging but made no sense. What pieces did Lesley want, and she had never shared this news? Always a mystery.

"Well, now I think I need to think all about this," I said. I wondered if this was someone I could trust. He had lied about the phone call and given confusing versions. I also wondered about the Amenti pieces, but I guess they wanted to stay hidden.

"Anna, are you taking this in?"

"Oh yes, it's a puzzle, a jigsaw," I said. "12,000 years of history or even more. Atlantis falls, and many of the secrets are lost, and over time and place throughout Egypt they were spread."

I took a deep breath. I began to see this journey appearing on his walls like sheets of paper, and the message was clear in big, fat letters: YOU WILL CLEAR THE TIMELINE.

And now that we had the set of 8 scarabs and scrolls, I was sure we had the ability to clear our souls of karma and repair the damage of some dark force left in these Egyptian temples. Greater than the force of Unal. We have temples and tombs to clear and our past lives to settle.

I would need time to process this whole map of the timeline, and I needed to start now. I took out my journal to make a few notes. I looked at my watch. There was not much time, but who knew when I would return. I needed to be the Akashic Records detective.

"These two pieces of Amenti," I said, pointing to the Amenti Scarab and Scroll words written on his whiteboard. "They have been bound by many curses and, when released, they can create a cartouche around the Consciousness Stone for protection. That is the high altar stone..." I pointed to the side room, "...that is to help the great awakening of another new and golden age. But as they are missing, I'm not sure what we do next."

I felt ten feet tall and stronger than ever.

"I will have more insight for your study, but it's nearly time to leave," I said, pointing to my watch. He smiled. "Then let's get you to the coffee shop; a plan is starting," he laughed. He pointed to the door, and we were again back in the maze of tunnels.

When we reached the entrance, I thanked Michael. He looked a little shell-shocked, as if the reality was catching up with him that someone spoke his language. I began to walk away to catch up with my friends.

Now that he had encountered our coven, he had lots to ponder over.

He called my name...

"Anna, I'm not sure what to say. This supernatural is all beyond me."

"You will learn and catch up and remember," I called back.

"I'll be here when you get back to Cairo. Goodbye for

now," he waved.

His words felt so familiar that I could not wait to be back on the bus to check out our Akashic Records, but at the same time, I was terrified.

I realised I was late, but super lucky to see our group crossing towards the exit. Naomi and Rashida were there. I had completely forgotten them. I ran over and apologised. Naomi smiled totally in bliss from the encounter she had had with the jewels she had been able to examine, as well as other rare pieces.

Rashida made our exit swift and easy, just in time to reach the bus. I had missed the coffee shop and the bookshop, but I was so excited to share with the group what we had found. I was buzzing with energy.

I was about to stop and share with the Contessa when Naomi caught my hand.

"Not yet, Anna, maybe tonight."

I nodded, knowing she was correct, and slowly slid into my seat. I could see the entrance to the museum. I wanted to remember this and create a memory so I could return to it later in my meditations.

I looked back to the museum, making note of how to astral travel back, and looked to the left and saw an engraved sign that read "Museum Library." Now, that would be worth an astral travel visit. And then I noticed a figure standing in the doorway.

Michael was outside, talking on the phone and jumping up and down. I could not understand, but I knew our visit had triggered something. Then, as if he had a telepathic connection, I could swear he looked straight at me. In fright, I sat back and pulled the curtain to hide myself.

Once we were in motion, Lesley spoke.

"Here we are heading back to the hotel, everyone, and

we have dinner in one of the private rooms this evening. Everyone has an invitation in their rooms, and for you..." she pointed to me.

"Here you are, Anna," she handed me a room key card. The Contessa has asked you to be moved to your own private room next to hers."

I looked at Naomi, who shrugged and smiled.

☥

When we arrived upstairs, I saw my new room was to the left in the corridor, which meant I had a pyramid view.

"Well, you are honoured," said Naomi. She opened the door to our twin room and started to help me pack.

I said nothing and simply continued adding all my personal effects into a large laundry bag and emptying the safe when I heard a quiet knock at the door.

It was Lucas. He moved slowly towards me, not saying a word. Luckily, Naomi was in the bathroom. He pointed to the box of scrolls and scarabs.

"I think it may need safekeeping, my darling girl," he whispered.

I nodded, and without thinking, just knowing, I handed over the box. He was swift and left, not even rousing Naomi's attention.

"What did Lucas want?" She strolled back into the bedroom. Now I swear she had X-ray vision.

"Just checking... You know Lucas. Seeing if we needed help with luggage," I shrugged.

Once everything was ready to move, I crossed the corridor and opened the door, shocked by the size of the room. I entered a large living room, and to the left was an even larger bedroom with a huge golden disc behind the bed. The living area led out to a balcony, and I could see I was in the end room as the balcony was across the corner.

The balcony was so close to the Pyramids that I felt I could touch them.

"Well, look here," said Naomi as she entered behind me.

"You know I never asked for this, really Naomi. I can swap with you. I'm probably safer over there where I was."

"No, no, this was meant to be. I am just not sure why, but we will get to the core of it sooner than later. I am curious now," she said.

"With that, I will say my goodbye and pick you up at 7 p.m. Bring the box of scrolls and scarabs but be discreet."

Oh, no, how would I tell her I had given it to Lucas?

"Maybe tonight, it may not be the right time. I am so tired," I replied.

"As you wish," I could see her mind calculating and finally agreeing.

I nodded, and she did, too.

Once in the room, I began to hang up my clothes and set out everything once again. This wardrobe must have hosted the finest clothes, probably haute couture, and here I was, hanging dresses from the airport and hotel gift shops.

Dinner was a fun and lively event. We were in a private room, and everyone was full of energy and their stories from the museum.

"So I could not believe they had placed the Lapis necklace on display with the feather fan again," I could hear Lesley from the end of the table...

Lucas was arguing with her about their rights and defending the protection of the museums.

"But it's my belongings," Lesley responded.

For the first time in a few days, I began to relax. Nothing was needed from me, and as I looked around the table, I saw everyone as if a family had sat down to dinner.

Today, we had all activated various timelines of ancient

Egypt's history. I knew that was for a reason. At the moment, I was distracted and as I looked around, I could still see the traces of everyone's past lives swirling around them. Different costumes but always the same soul.

When the teas and coffees had been served, the Contessa asked that the table be cleared and the room be free of hotel staff, and then she went to lock the door.

Everyone looked around, not knowing what to expect.

"Anna, will you join me and bring the scroll and scarab box from your room?" she commanded.

I looked at Lucas.

"Toilet break for me. I'll come out with you, Anna," he said, knowing he could race back to his room in the garden and save me any explanations.

I walked slowly back to my room and chose to retrieve the black Book of Keys and freshened up to return in perfect timing, as he passed me the box. For the first time, the box did not feel so heavy or draining.

"Have you been clearing them?"

He smiled. "That's my job. Now, go be the shining star."

We walked back into the room and placed them on the table in front of the Contessa.

Laura, who was sat next to the Contessa, stood up and exchanged seats with me. I hugged her before sitting down. "I found it hard to leave the museum today. There are so many happy memories." Her eyes were red, and I knew she had shed many tears. "My darling Seti was waiting for me."

"Not so much in the mummy room; it was shocking today," said Lucinda. "When will they ever learn and place these powerful beings into a sacred shrine they deserve?"

"Another time for that, my dear," said the Contessa. "Now, Anna, please share with us what you discovered today."

I looked around the large table, and of course, this was not a speech I had prepared for.

"Ladies and gentleman." I smiled at Lucas, who winked back as if to say, "You have this covered." As I did, my mind spun to his shop in Glastonbury.

I nearly fell from my track of thought as images of tarot cards began to come into my mind. The Empress, the Star, and oh no, the Tower. I thought to return to this later, but for now, I began laying out the scarabs and scrolls.

For some reason, I felt the Amenti pieces joining my aura. It was as if they were already in my hands, just invisible. I could not work out the link. I looked at Naomi, and she knew my thought… should I reveal what I have been shown in the museum? My intuition said not yet.

"So, everyone, we now have eight scarabs, which will open sacred doors, portals, and energies that we need on the sacred journey. Matching them with the eight scrolls will give us the spells and incantations we need to clear the binding curses and contracts. And then there is this."

I retrieved from my bag the black Book of Keys.

"Apparently, this was mine many lifetimes ago, and I found it in Paris. This Book of Keys contains the details of the scarabs and scrolls, as well as details of a secret society and, I believe, some of the wisdom lost from the fall of Atlantis."

Everyone leaned in close. You could hear a pin drop.

"Clever girl," Emilee smiled, and I saw she knew this book already. She looked at the Contessa as if a high stake was at play in an "I told you so" moment.

I continued, "I believe that we have never all been together as a group on this Earth plane in a calm and harmonious way. Each time we have returned in numbers, there has been a dark force that has sabotaged us and created karma with others here at the table and in the timelines we have lived in. Some of you here will remember the red boxes.

"This is how we used to track our lives with images and historical artifacts. But as many of you will find on this trip, like myself, your oracle sight will return, and you will see the Akashic Records as they were—are—and it could well be that we may not need the red boxes in the future.

"We are Children of the Light," I smiled around the room, "and we have carried these curses for too long."

I had no idea where the words were channelling from, and at first, I thought it was Isis, but it felt like it was another power, familiar but not fully apparent.

"Each day of this trip will be a new storyline, and while glorious for some, a heartbreak or challenge for others. But in the end, we will restore what once was our sacred mission above all. To protect and free the temples to higher consciousness."

Lesley held her hand up.

"Yes?" What on earth did she want?

"Anna, if it would please you, I have the itinerary." She held up several sheets on which I could see a day-by-day visit list.

"Excellent," I nodded. After all, she had played a part in my new room, so perhaps this could be to my advantage to keep her close.

"Please hand them out... everyone, please review your connections."

"While we are awaiting these, can I ask about the sacred eight? I thought that this was the focus, but now we are a group of 10 and 11 if you count Rashida," said Lesley.

"It was originally eight, but as it comes to me now, these were small groups that could achieve a single mission. We have a number of temples to clear in a short space of time, and we need a group such as this with varied gifts and not necessarily set to a number. Each of you has a clue, a story, and a gift to share with the group. Some of you have not yet revealed who you truly are."

It was then that Isis arrived, and I began to feel her presence.

I felt the channelled words of Isis begin to come through me.

"The wisdom of the scrolls and scarabs can clear the energy, activating the sacred portals and setting the karma free for each of you who had an oracle past.

"The goal is to clear all that no longer serves and for us to establish a sacred teaching in each temple and bring each oracle to wholeness from their past and with each other.

"This will carry on the legacy and teaching of Isis."

I stopped and took a long drink of water.

"Oh, my goodness, Anna, I felt Isis," said Emilee.

"I saw Isis," said Alice.

"It was Isis," I said. "I will have to watch my step."

"But who was that at first? Was it you?" asked Lucinda.

"I am not sure. I think it was a woman, and she will come to me in a dream, I guess," I responded.

"Well, everyone, I'm tired," Alice announced. Her energy was much depleted, and I felt concern for her.

The Contessa decided to close the circle.

"Now, Lesley, can you lead the orientation for tomorrow?" she commanded and waved her hand. I stood up and wrapped everything away, nodding to Lucas our pact of sharing. He came over and began to help.

Lesley went through all the details of the trip as apparently, we were now to fly to Luxor.

I was not really listening as I glanced through the list of tombs and temples. It seemed that only after those were cleared, would we work in the Pyramids and Sphinx. Lucas stood close to me, silent, just pointing to certain places as I wrapped up the sets. Although it sounded vague, I was beginning to form a plan of what went where and who could do what. Perhaps this was the game to play?

I was beginning to see the scarabs and scrolls I needed to work more with, and the pages from the Book of Keys I needed to study. I wished we had more time to prepare.

CHAPTER 19

Thursday, 17 September 2009

I was awake at 5 a.m., and even though Lesley had informed us we would be leaving after breakfast at 9 a.m., I was afraid to go back to sleep. I felt as if spirits were entering and weaving in my dreams, and even though I called on all the angels and Anubis, nothing seemed to bring a calm, restful feeling.

I went out onto the balcony and could feel the presence of Isis. She appeared to be sitting in a chair in the corner. Was I still in my dream?

I went back into my room, boiled the kettle to make coffee, and then intended to sip it while watching the magnificent pyramids and the sunrise. To my surprise, when I went back out, she was still there.

"Anna, there is something you must know. Over there beside the Pyramids and Sphinx there lived a royal family who had a great curse bestowed upon them," she said.

I pulled up a chair and wrapped myself in the blanket that was there. I looked across Giza Plateau and began to see the outline of a royal enclosure and temple. Isis told me to close my eyes, and when I did, I was transported back to a dream of a timeline I felt I knew yet had no recollection of.

I felt like I was in a temple, but it also felt like a palace. It had rooms and corridors, and I could see many people moving around, which made me fearful.

I came into a central courtyard and saw what looked like a royal family talking and giving orders to scribes.

To my surprise, I saw Lesley leaning over what looked to be the young man of great importance.

"Does my lady wish this?"

"I know of nothing else we can do," she replied. "We need the power of my mother's ancestors. They held the power over Unal, and we can do so again."

"Look, the general has sent spies." Lesley is talking to a young man who looks like the young boy from the mirror, but I can't be sure. "We do not have much time," she says, holding her hand to her stomach. I see she is pregnant.

"My lord Tutankhamun, please listen. I have consulted with the Oracle of the Sphinx. She tells me there is no other way."

"Show me this oracle."

I see Alexandria enter from the side chamber. She's much, much older, but still a great beauty.

The royal couple smile at her.

"Tell us what you saw, oracle."

Alexandria hesitates. She is not sure if she is safe.

"My lord, I was oracle to your father." Again, she hesitates. "Amenhotep IV." She does not use the Akhenaten name. "I was sister to your Mother Nefertiti, my lady. I came back to serve you in this new age as foretold."

"Danger will follow you while you follow the new religion."

"Make time to summon the true power of Amenti in the way of your parents."

"Allow me to summon the Priests of Unal," Alexandria pleads. "Once they rise, the dark ones will fall, and we will worship the one true Aten again."

She holds out her hands, and I see the Scarab and Scroll of Death and Resurrection.

I felt a dark energy fall across the room.

"Then so be it," the young King announces. "The moon

will fully rise tomorrow, and it will be the time to perform the ritual."

I want to go over to stop them, as I know they will summon dark and evil forces.

But Isis is there with me in the vision. She pulls back my arm. "No, it is not time; you must watch more."

The timeline shifts, and I see everyone standing around a high altar in front of the Sphinx. Incense is burning, and I can hear the chants of priests in the distance calling forward the Gods.

"It must be now, my love, to protect us all."

I watch as Alexandria recites the Scroll of Death and Resurrection with the scarab, her voice louder and louder.

She then draws a symbol in the sand, which I know as it is in my Book of Keys. Then, as she throws what looks to be small white stones into the symbol, dark and shadowy figures arise. These are the creatures that have haunted my dreams and caused fear to my soul.

"See, they will make us immortal," cries Lesley. "We will overcome those against us."

One of the creatures approaches her—there are now seven of them—and points to her stomach.

It is then I realise that the death of her child or children she carries is the price for the resurrection.

"You did not tell of this price," the young king is furious. "Send them back," he orders.

I realised I had also seen him before in my Glastonbury dream, arguing with the Queen. Now I see it is definitely the young boy from the mirror in the room I shared with Naomi. He wears the serpent ring.

"I cannot, my lord," weeps Alexandria. "They were summoned at your command, and now they will work the worlds in which we live."

The young King now sees me. He comes to me and stands in front of me.

"Heal this, Anna," he whispers and again holds out the turquoise ring. I take its energy, and he begins to fade.

I watch as Lesley falls to the ground and goes into labour. It's so sad. I want to go to help her, but suddenly, the Unal priests sense me, and they turn, and I feel myself now screaming.

A hand touches my shoulder, I turn, and it is Naomi. Isis is gone, and the sun is rising.

"Anna, it's okay. I saw them, too."

She is still in her nightgown, and I hand another blanket to her.

"Naomi, what have we opened?"

"I'm not sure," she whispers, "but perhaps we will know very soon."

We look out across the Giza Plateau as the sun rises past the Great Pyramid, casting light into our world. For this moment, all is calm.

For the longest time, we simply sat in silence.

Then, the deepest grief descended on us both.

Naomi took my hand, and her eyes were filled with tears.

"Has she gone?" she croaked.

"I think she has, but I know the eternal Isis energy is with us. She flowed through the Queens and High priestesses, but yes, our friend, our mentor, she is gone, home, and star-bound."

Cairo Airport

Rashida was waiting with the agent at the airport, and it was hilarious to watch as we made our way through the crowds to the first-class check-in. The Contessa had refused to stand in line and literally ordered the baggage area to a standstill.

None of us said a word, and I watched Lesley calmly talk to the agents while Rashida translated.

With great ease, we were escorted through the security and into a private lounge.

Emilee sat next to me as we awaited boarding, and Lucinda handed me a coffee and sat on the other side.

"What on earth?" I whispered. "I thought Naomi was high maintenance."

"Ah, non, you have seen nothing," giggled Emilee.

"She is famous for her displays; she has tamed many a dark magician."

"A dark magician indeed." I was intrigued.

Lucinda smiled and said nothing but opened her journal and began to sip her herbal tea.

"See, think of the Priests of Edfu, the ones who make you feel they are your twin flame. Do you remember them from your clients in Glastonbury?"

I nodded and leaned in closer. I had encountered many of those cursed ones over the past year and the tangled relationships I had cleared.

"Well, some of them had various ways with the ladies; they had a way with the words and the eyes that would hypnotise you, and you would fall into a love spell." I could sense Lucinda was uncomfortable, but Emilee could not stop.

"You would hear their voice in your head, you would dream about them, and before you knew it, you would be at their beck and call."

"Was it real love?" I had asked her.

"Non, non, totally fake," said Emilee. "It was used to

gather secrets or to lure a poor priestess to her shame at the times of the festival."

"Did it happen to you, Emilee, this lifetime?" I asked.

"Very nearly. I was visiting London in a hotel for a spiritual seminar about love and relationships. There was this man who spoke the words of love and how we should create love relationships and speak in a love language. It was totally staged, and there were scents of candles everywhere and sounds of soft music. I understood from my days in France, the moods and movements of love. I watched as, one by one, the women became entranced with this man.

"By chance, Isis had been visiting her 'special' VIP clients in London and had invited herself to the hotel to meet me after the event, and we would travel back to Glastonbury. She always knew when mischief was happening, that wise one. I was surprised to see her sitting in the lobby scanning us all as we left the seminar when it finished. The man who had been teaching us was trying to escort all the ladies to the sofas around the bar. He then went to the bar to order celebration wine, as he called it, and I watched as Isis went over to him slowly, pulled back her platinum hair, whispered something to him, and then looked at the women awaiting him. There was a stillness in the place. I was not sure what she said, but I know she referenced a past life to him and reminded him of a sacred oath."

"She knew him?"

"Yes, apparently, he had come to Glastonbury many years ago, insecure and asking for help. He stayed for three days and had multiple sessions with Isis that had helped him find his way back to his priest connections. The next day, the bank called as his check had bounced... totally out of order. Now, here he was, and she was aware of the vulnerability he was exploiting."

"So what happened?"

"Well, there were about nine women sitting, and I introduced her to them. They were curious, and she offered to do a divine feminine blessing for love while they awaited their drinks.

"Well, Isis began to perform an undoing spell ritual and called on the Priestesses of Isis to release an energy to allow all to be well and good."

"She did the blessings to create a timeline where we all imagined the women happy and with loving partners and being honoured."

"But does that not create karma?" I asked.

"No, it gives them a path as their free will has been compromised," said Lucinda.

"Anyway, he had just arrived with several bottles of wine and was filling their glasses, ready to make a toast, when another woman walked in, sat at the bar, and waved to him. Like he was hypnotized, he finished pouring wine and said he would be a moment and went over to her.

"She was a magician too, and within a few minutes, we watched as she had him laughing and paying her attention. He was caught between the two sections and pondering his prey. It was then I suddenly awoke from my spell from earlier in the day. Yes, he had used a love spell on us.

"I began to use a prayer of sister light and remembered this had been a role for me in the ancient times. Slowly, the women finished their wine and began talking about what to do for dinner plans. The new woman at the bar had placed her hand on his arm, and just like that, the charm, the web around us all was broken. I'm sure she was in league with Isis. I know she smiled at her, and they acknowledged each other at some point. The women then finished their wine, gathered their bags and headed out the door, shouting to him, *Bye, love you, friend, thanks for the wine.* Isis and I began to giggle as a few moments later, a new man arrived to take this magician sister to dinner. The dark magician was left alone with a bill for five bottles of good wine and no option for his evening of lust or anyone to do his bidding and become a high-paying client for his love medicine."

"This is why I create the love potions to offer protection," Emilee concluded.

"But what does the Contessa have to do with this?" I asked.

Lucinda leaned in and whispered, "To do with this whole situation today? That lady wrote the book of the darker path and ensnarement and has lived it many times."

"Now watch and learn, Anna. Airports are amazing places to learn the art of magic and illusion," she said.

Wow. I was totally taken aback, and perhaps my world was too sheltered. I was about to open my eyes.

However, once again, I was only able to jot down messages in my journal when we had boarded our flight. I fell asleep on the plane.

Before I knew it, we were in a whole new world, Luxor.

☥

Luxor was stunning as our bus moved through the streets away from the modern world and the airport to a city with less chaos than Cairo.

It was bizarre to see how the modern buildings and shops had grown around the ancient temples, but I smiled to myself as this eclectic mix seemed to work. Taxis and cars followed by donkeys and carts. All of life was here to be seen.

We slowly turned down a curved road, and there she was, still and silent—the Nile River.

On one side, busy with life in Luxor and across the

river, the West Bank was still sleeping; this is where the gods resided, for sure.

We arrived at our hotel as Lesley gave the historical overview.

"The Winter Palace was built in 1905 and used by Lord Carnarvon and Agatha Christie. This world-renowned hotel has hosted the rich, royal, and famous for over 100 years."

All I could see were the beautiful trees and blossoms and the balconies with shutters on the windows.

I had loved our Cairo home, but this held a charm and nostalgia of another time.

We were instructed to rest for the afternoon before our gathering later in the evening.

☥

Our rooms did not disappoint. Although again, they were old-world with strange plumbing, the character of the palace had captured my heart. I lay down on the crisp white bed linen, drifted off to sleep, and found myself without dreams or any disturbance for the first time in a while.

When I awoke, I could see the sun high in the sky across the Nile on the other side outside my window. I was excited to see it set in a few hours. Laura had said it was putting the kings and queens to bed, but for now, it could wait. It was a time to explore, and I was hungry. I went to my bathroom to freshen up when I saw a note pushed under my door:

We knocked, but you must be sleeping. Dinner at 7 p.m. at the pool outdoor restaurant.

Love, Naomi and Lucas

I checked my watch, and it was only around 4 p.m., so I

had time to explore and maybe check out another gift shop. I had some money, so why not?

The hotel corridors were long and silent. They stretched as far as I could see, and I wondered if I were in a dream and the only one staying there. Ahead, I heard voices, and I could see Laura with Alice. I ran to catch up with them.

"We thought you were sleeping," said Laura.

"Yes, I lost time as soon as I reached the room."

"Agatha used to say that!" laughed Alice.

"Agatha? You knew her?"

"Oh yes, she was part of a group of women I would visit in London in my past life days; she was a wise old bird, and she always knew secrets."

"She would talk of this hotel and how she had inspiration for many of her novels and stories. She was a priestess once, you know. Oh, she had many past lives, and at our meetings, we would perform a séance and then have tea."

I was stunned, and Laura softly took my arm and began to guide me towards the reception area.

"I think we will take some tea, Alice, don't you think?" I was still imagining and lost in the vision of Agatha Christie in a séance, and trying to work out how Alice had known her in this past life.

Sitting with these two elder ladies was so refreshing. Emilee and Lucinda had their black-magic stories, and now I was back in 1910, when these two women would meet and share psychic readings and spiritual gossip.

For sunset, I was back in my room, and as the rays faded, I changed clothes for dinner.

I wore my beautiful blue silk dress again that evening. I felt like royalty as I glided towards the pool area through the gardens. The jasmine and nighttime scents filled the air, and a soft breeze made me think about the stories of the Arabian nights.

You could not fail to see or hear our table. Everyone else had dressed for dinner and was busy ordering from drinks menus and swapping stories or dreams of the day.

I took a seat next to Emilee. I glanced around the table at two empty chairs.

"Emilee," I pointed over.

"The Contessa and Alexandria."

"What happened?" I asked.

"I am not sure," she whispered, "but maybe later we can go to her and see if they are okay. Perhaps they have their meal in the room."

"I thought I heard them arguing on the flight, but they were in the business class seats too far to eavesdrop," Laura said.

"Oh, I didn't notice. I guess I was snoring. I had an early start today," I laughed.

"Isis?" she asked, and I smiled.

"She will stay in Cairo perhaps to hold the gates open. She came, I think, to many of us in her own way last night."

"Well, let's eat and see what happens after dinner," said Emilee.

I was halfway through dessert when I saw Alexandria approach the table. She looked as if she had been crying, and as she reached the end of the table, she burst into tears.

She looked at me across the table. "She needs you, Anna, Grandmama..." and handed a key down across everyone.

The table fell silent as I nodded. "I will come with you," said Emilee. "I know her room. It is near mine. Sometimes, a translation can help, and I have my potion at hand."

I was grateful, as I was not sure what the Contessa wanted or how I could help.

We arrived at her suite and knocked gently. We let

ourselves into this beautiful suite with lavish décor and a sense of royalty about it.

"In here," a soft voice called. We entered the bedroom, which was softly lit by the lamps.

I looked at Emilee, who was walking softly behind me.

"Contessa, it's Anna... are you okay? I have Emilee here with me. Can we come in?" I had no idea who or what we would find.

The Contessa began to speak softly in French, and it was as if she was gasping for breath.

Emilee rushed to her with her potion tincture and placed it into her water glass, and I stood silent in the corner of the suite.

The Contessa was in bed in a white lace nightgown. Her silver hair hung softly around her face, bare of any makeup. She looked like I had remembered the final days of Isis, and I was shocked.

"Anna, come closer. I'm just having a panic attack; my nerves in Egypt always fail me," she beckoned me.

"Come closer and let me look at you. In this light, I see your mother in you; of course, she was much more slender," she stopped herself, "but she never had your gifts."

I moved closer and sat on the side of the bed. Emilee smiled and let me know she would be waiting in the living room area of the suite.

"I'm afraid you will leave, and I will have to do this all myself now Isis has gone. I do not have her insight or protection, and Lucinda seems possessed, and I know Lesley would trade me for relics and museum pieces."

She was rambling in fear.

"All this is maybe true," I said, "but you have me and Alexandria, and I know Lucas can be counted on, as can Emilee. I will not leave you." I leaned in and hugged her.

"Oh, Mon Dieu," said Emilee. "My goodness, I have something here for you, my lady." Emilee was obviously listening and was more powerful around this lady than I had realised.

She came to the bedside, knelt down and gave a small glass of alcohol to the Contessa that looked like it came from the minibar rather than her medicine bag. I saw past lives and how they had transpired before.

Tudor times, I thought, and I smiled to see such kind tenderness.

"There is so much to do," the Contessa began. "And we will do this in time," I reassured her. Remember, we have all the scarabs and scrolls, the Book of Keys, and the Scarab and Scroll of Amenti are on the way." I stopped as she turned to look at me. Now she was fully present and alert.

"The Scarab and the Scroll of Amenti... that was just a legend. You have them?" The Contessa was sharp and frail no more.

"No, I just learnt about them, but I feel their energy." I looked at Emilee. Obviously, the strong drink had woken the Contessa's spirit.

"But you don't have them? I ask you again, please," she said.

"No, I only know of them," I said softly.

"Ah, okay, well, so you don't have them, I think that will be enough." She began to wave us away without so much as a thank you.

"Emilee, you may all go," and she waved her hand to release us.

"As you wish," said Emilee, and she looked at me as if to say nothing.

Once we were through the door and it was closed, she pulled me across the hall out of the Contessa's hearing.

"But you know where those pieces are."

Emilee had been the first to welcome me to Glastonbury. I could not hide anything from her.

"Yes, I have seen them in a vision and experienced them, and no, they are not with me."

"Who else knows?" she quizzed me.

"Obviously, the Professor, Rashida, and Naomi, perhaps, but I am not sure. Isis came looking for them in Cairo with Naomi and Lucas, but then she passed. Mr. Imran, who had them died, and I don't know how to ask about them without creating some sort of drama."

"Then tell no one else," she warned me. And there is where it all started again... the Contessa, Emilee, and the secrets. I wished Isis were here.

Chapter 20

Friday, 18 September
Valley of the Kings and Queens and Hatshepsut

We had boarded our bus early, and most people looked half-asleep, but I was surprised to see the Contessa in full strength. Interestingly enough, she had requested that Lucas sit across from her on the bus, and Lesley was relegated to a back seat. It would appear the bus had a hierarchy.

As we passed through the streets and over the bridge crossing the Nile, I felt a sense of sadness in my heart, but I wasn't sure why. We were leaving a vibrant, bustling city, and ahead I saw blue sky with mountains of shimmering rocks... majestic and serene. But then it occurred to me that we were about to visit one of the world's most famous graveyards.

Something felt familiar, but I was not having any 3rd-eye visions.

I sat back in my seat and decided to just relax, as I knew something dark could be looming around any corner.

The bus stopped, and Lesley called out her command to bring water and protection. "Today, we visit with all our relatives who are still present in the bardo realms, those worlds between ours and the next lives," Lesley announced.

It looked strange, as if we were in a large car park in the middle of nowhere.

I could see some small vendors ahead with scarves and statues. But we had been given strict instructions to avoid becoming lost in the trading vortex. It was all a blur as we stepped out into the brightest sunlight I had ever seen. It was already 9 a.m., and I could feel the god Ra's glare upon me.

I looked over at Naomi, all in black. She looked like she was going into a battle, with black cargo pants, a tight black vest top, and a fancy neckerchief. Her hair was swept up, perfectly framing her large-rimmed black sunglasses and signature red lips. Around her waist, she wore a thin black silk scarf. She looked as if she were about to face a titan.

I looked around the rest of the group. Priestesses in plain sight dressed as regular tourists.

"Let's move, everyone," Naomi raised her voice, and we all moved in formation, like a military sequence. We left the car park in an orderly fashion, and Rashida held up her white umbrella with golden Ankh symbols for us to follow.

Everything was sand and stone that reflected the clear blue sky.

Silent and filled with foreboding.

We made our way through the security gates and towards the map of the tombs, which revealed how deeply they were cut into the rock and how they looked like an ant hive.

I could see energy running through the tunnels and hear the voices of the builders. The reverence was woven into a team of individuals dedicated to creating the most magnificent chamber of ascension for their Kings for the afterlife.

These were not graves; they were stargates to other worlds.

We all gathered at the main entrance and took the tourist shuttles to the central location where others were also beginning their tours. Even this early, walking would have been foolish, as the heat was so intense.

As we walked towards the tomb openings, it felt bizarre to see other timelines. I kept seeing the processions of official mourners in ancient times and could smell the incense in the air. When I blinked, I saw they were really just small groups of tourists who were very distinct by their nationality and tour leader.

We were each given a ticket to access three tombs of our choice, along with a time to meet up. I stared at mine for the longest time, not understanding how to choose. When I finally looked around—no one was with me—they had all wandered off. My legs were like jelly. I noticed Rashida had gone to the coffee shop; she seemed a million miles away and focused on her phone.

I decided that just being here was enough, and if I walked around and maybe looked into a few entrances, I would be safe. I willed my legs to move, and I felt like I was floating.

I chose to look into the first tomb without a crowd.

It belonged to Ramses III. The handwritten plaque was simple. I showed my ticket to the Egyptian man who stood at the entrance. He smiled and nodded as he took a small hole punch and left a small hole in the corner.

I wandered in slowly and began to see the beautiful images; I was not afraid. This was very peaceful. On either side of me, I could see and feel the images of King Ramses and his priests as if they were offering me blessings and purification. The colour and detail were unbelievable, and I felt they were sharing a story with me.

As I made my way to the end of the tunnel, I felt a little lightheaded. I stopped at the wooden gate and took a deep breath. Then, for some unknown reason, I began to blow deep, long breaths as if to give life to the place. Nothing ahead could be seen, but I felt the spirit still present and watching me. Maybe not the wisest move, as now I was dizzy and a little overwhelmed, and again told myself I could go back to the coffee shop and sit with Rashida.

Dehydration, I'm sure.

I reached into my bag for my water and had to steady myself as I looked back down into the darkness. There was nothing there, but all the same, I could feel the presence of a spirit.

"Oracle."

I turned. *Who was that?* I felt it might be the King's spirit, and even though this place was still and quiet, I knew this King was not at rest.

"Oracle."

I heard other voices coming now, and as I turned, I could see a group of tourists descending towards me. I turned fully to avoid being in their way, and it was as if I were invisible. I gently pushed my way past when a small woman with white-blonde hair and the bluest eyes caught my arm.

"You woke him in Paris in the Louvre, and now you have brought him home. Ramses III is home. He has seen you; he has seen you," she said.

"I'm sorry, who?" I asked.

She looked at me blankly, smiled, and said something I did not understand in German.

I decided it was time to leave.

Just then, a spirit moved past me.

"ORACLE."

I began to run, run back out into the light.

I think that's enough tombs for me... back to the temples.

I was about to turn back towards the group meet-up point when I saw Naomi making haste towards the back of the complex.

She caught my interest, and I decided to follow her.

Alice and Laura called out to her. As she passed them, she made no contact as if in another dimension.

I waved to them and ran ahead to catch her.

I thought I had lost her when suddenly, I saw her small frame climbing a ladder that seemed to disappear into the rock formation.

My legs found their speed, and before I knew it, I was on the ladder and climbing high into a tomb located safely away from the rest.

As I reached the entrance, I could not see anyone—not even the guards. All I could see was a small plaque with the words, *Thutmose III.*

I took a deep breath in and walked through the small entrance. *Who was this?*

Inside, it was cool but well-lit. I could smell rose and jasmine and hear some type of chanting or singing.

The sound was gentle and soft, almost like a lullaby.

The singing was becoming louder, and I knew then for certain that it was Naomi.

I came to the entrance of a new chamber and entered slowly.

I walked slowly and quietly, preparing my best surprise face in case I came across Naomi and she thought I had been following her.

On the walls were elaborate images of people and small sketches telling stories. Very different to the tomb I had just visited with its colour and high-profile etchings. This tomb felt older, with much to teach.

In the centre of the room was a large, lidded sarcophagus. It was magnificent, and I could feel it was almost alive.

Hypnotically, I wandered into the room and towards the singing, and as I walked around, I suddenly saw Naomi sitting cross-legged on the floor at the top of the sarcophagus.

She wore the black scarf upon her head as a veil, the one she had worn earlier around her waist, and her eyes were focused on the images carved into this massive stone chamber.

She did not see or hear me. She was in another realm. Her hand clutched the gold ankh she wore that was gifted to her by Isis.

Her singing slowly faded, and once she had concluded her ceremony, she looked at me.

I stood still and quiet.

Naomi was powerful, but in this setting, she was supernatural.

"You heard the call," she said.

"I saw you climb the ladder and was curious."

"Yes, like I was once. Then I came upon this holy shrine and have been singing to the mummies ever since," she said in a hushed tone.

"Singing?"

"Yes," she laughed softly. "There are many souls bound here through many ages, and I sing to them—it calms them."

"Can we not cross them over?" I asked.

"Sadly, no, they are bound here for many reasons beyond the power of you and I."

It felt heavy, but as I knew nothing about this world, I did not dare to offer insight or a solution.

"But Naomi, this feels more than a tomb. I was just in one, and this is different."

"Yes, dear Anna, it is."

"This is a portal and temple to the goddess Ma'at, a karmic stargate," she said.

"Ma'at with the feather, yes, that's the one."

She nodded. "Okay, let me explain, but before I do, let me finish my work."

She sat up in a kneeling position with her hands placed on the stone and began to take deep breaths, blowing into the stone sarcophagus. Then she let out a loud OM sound, and after a bow and Namaste, she swung back to me.

"I knew I had to come here today," she said. "I had a dream last night, and Thutmose told me the Halls of Amenti had been opened. I thought it may have to do with the visit to the museum, but I think there is more to know. Please, Anna, come look at this."

I knew she was trying to be upbeat, but her lip trembled, and her eyes filled with tears.

We went over to a wall with small images, but I could clearly see the goddess Ma'at. In front of her stood many images of what I took to be soldiers or slaves.

"Before King Thutmose III passed, he begged forgiveness of the goddess for the souls that had died under his rule; he was the grandfather of Thutmose IV, the one who created the Dream Stele at the Sphinx. The name Thutmose means 'son of Thoth,' so the rituals would have been handed down through the sons of Thoth. Thutmose III knew what he was facing, and he feared this; he feared his karma in the afterlife."

"He had a dream?" I asked.

"No, no, that was Thutmose IV. He had the dream when he fell asleep at the Sphinx Dream Stele at the Pyramids."

She paused, as she clearly knew her story, just not sure how to share it. Something just came over me, and I placed my hand near the wall.

"No touch," said a man's voice from out of the darkness.

I turned to see a guardian, an old Egyptian man in the traditional Galabeya dress.

"No touching." I smiled and realised he was a guardian and teacher. And I was here to learn.

"Naomi, Thutmose IV already knew about the Dream Stele as he was a soul contracted to carry on the 'dream.' The dream was the entrance to the Halls of Amenti."

"I see from the Akashic Records that Thutmose III also had a dream, and he had consulted with an oracle who told him his fate should he not repent his sins against others," I said.

"But would he listen? I think not."

I turned around, and there stood Alexandria.

"I was the Oracle for Hatshepsut," she said. Chills ran through my body.

"She was a wise and gracious Queen and stepmother to Thutmose, who had realised the power of the scarabs and scrolls. She actually collected two of the sets. She had the Records of Life and the Truth and Integrity sets."

"All four pieces?" asked Naomi.

"Yes," nodded Alexandria, "and she used my gifts to decipher these. Hence, she had the power to rule. She shared the wisdom in a letter that was memorised by Thutmose III and then fell into the hands of Thutmose IV."

"And then it continued to the Amenhotep III times," said Naomi. "I remember the story of the magical pieces that was only ever shared with those of royal blood."

"The Princess," I said.

The story was coming into place.

"Yes," said Naomi. "I was his daughter, Sitamun, but also his oracle. My brother would be Amenhotep IV or, as he became later, Akhenaten."

I was trying to listen to this family and friends reunion, but I could not draw myself away from the walls and the images. Even though they were simple, I began to see the Akashic Records as they had been.

"This part tells of the new golden age of prosperity and

that the new world would rise," I said.

"That would be the prophecy of the timeline of Tutankhamun," said Naomi.

I watched as Lesley, Lucinda, and Emilee entered the chamber.

"We had the Scarab and Scroll of Death and Resurrection at that time." She continued

I tried to clear my head as I began to see how these precious pieces that I had been given guardianship of had been stolen and misused many times, totally going against the purpose for which they were created and designed.

I reached into my bag, took out the black book, and allowed it to fall open. There on the page were the figures that matched the walls.

I had felt them beginning to whisper messages to me the moment I entered this tomb, and now I knew why.

"We must make a circle," I said.

I saw Lesley's eyes grow wide as she moved over towards me, but Lucinda was already in the temple flow and pulled her between herself and Emilee. Naomi and Alexandria stood on either side of me. Out of the corner of my eye, I saw a shadow move.

"She is with us," I said.

"Who?" asked Naomi.

"It's Hatshepsut," said Alexandria, and she bowed, "Welcome, my Queen."

Lucinda took in a deep breath, and I watched as the spirit of a female entered her body.

"You have awoken my slumber, my beloved friend," she spoke to Alexandria, *"and who is this sorceress?"* she asked, pointing to me.

I began to feel the room shake as if darker forces were entering the room.

"You are the one who summoned me."

I nodded. I was not afraid anymore.

I felt the book's energy, and I could feel the text coming out of it and around me.

"He was in darkness, and Thutmose III tried to summon the priests of Unal. They were called to protect him. He used them to see. I was co-regent with him." She pointed to the wall with all the stick figures.

"We had held them safe in their dark chamber for many years. After my death, he took over, and he and his lineage would set them free. They did this evil, and he paid the price. Many of you oracles here showed these kings the way. This continued into your timeline with the golden one, Tutankhamun." She pointed at Lesley.

"Be aware of your words," said Lesley, who was now in front of Lucinda. I could see a dark cape and evil energy had taken over her being.

Although Lesley threatened Lucinda, I could see that she would not harm her.

"You have no knowledge. You have no power," the Queen said, and I watched as she floated out of Lucinda's body and into the darkness of the chambers below.

I was aware that more of our group were joining us.

Alice and Laura came through the tunnel out of breath but in full force.

Following them were the Contessa and Lucas.

"What on earth?" Alice looked angry, and she went over to the elder guardian, gave him instructions, and handed him some money.

"The door will be closed," she announced. They both looked at Lesley.

"What is this nonsense?" Laura pointed to Lucinda, who was slumped on the floor.

Lucas and the Contessa were busy laying out a cloth with the Scroll and Scarab of the Records of Life."

I moved over to them as Lesley began to circle the group.

Emilee looked away and Naomi tried to stare her down. Alexandria bowed her head, and like a snake, Lesley began to move around us, whispering secrets and our fears. Even though I was a few feet away from her, I began to see the snakes on the walls and know that this chamber had so much more potential—it was a map to something greater. This was a starting point.

I prayed to Isis to give me the strength.

"Lucinda," I called out, "you have the power to cleanse this."

Emilee looked at her, "Yes, we do."

"Lucinda has no power here," Lesley laughed. She held a dark presence within her,

"I will take those now," she said, coming close towards the Contessa, but before she could, Emilee threw holy water over her from her special Lourdes bottle, and Lucinda began reciting words.

Lesley began to curl up in a ball on the floor as the women walked around her. The old man guardian sat holding space in the corner. "Child" was all he said.

Curses flowed, and I found myself between Lucas and the Contessa, moving the scarab and scroll in various directions and reciting the words I did not understand.

The energy seemed to flow into the room as if it was clearing and releasing as it moved around.

Slowly, the energy of the room began to clear, and I knew what to do.

"Ladies, a circle," called Lucas.

We all sat down in the corner where I could see the

images of the goddess Ma'at on the wall.

"We need to look at the Akashic Records," I announced.

We looked around at each other, and Lucinda recited the words to create a sacred circle. I began to speak, this time with my eyes open.

"I see a throne room and a traveller from a faraway land. His face looks different, and he has a scroll with strange markings."

"They are Atlantean," Naomi spoke up as her usual self.

"It warns of the Scorpion Queen," I continued.

"I have read this scroll before for my Queen Hatshepsut. This is why she feared Thutmose III. He had read from the scroll," Alexandria announced.

"Then will you read this again?" I asked. She nodded and closed her eyes.

"It is said that there was an ancient entity known as the Scorpion Queen, said to have been around before the great dynasties of Egypt, who created beings so powerful that they could win any war and conquer any land. She was said to be integral to Egypt becoming so great and mighty. If a Pharaoh chose, they could request to enter a secret tomb or temple dedicated to her and her Priests of Unal that only the oracles knew about the locations."

She stopped.

"This part I did not know, but this was my fate," she said.

I began to remember the vision of Tutankhamun from the previous day, and I thought of the Egypt book with the torn pages.

"Please continue so we can break this curse," I said. She opened her eyes.

"I cannot, Anna. You must break this, please." At that moment, I saw in Alexandria a young and vulnerable priestess who had served many masters for many lives.

I held her hand, and my heart felt so heavy.

I felt Alice move closer to me, and she whispered.

"Anna, you saw Alexandra's fate. She was damned by the actions of others. Bring her back to us and set her free."

I nodded and continued the story. This time, my eyes were open.

"Once there in the sacred chamber, the ruler would bring an oracle to offer up as a sacrifice to the Scorpion Queen in a ritual. The Queen would then appear through the body of a priestess, kill the oracle, and offer the oracle's soul to the service of her Priests of Unal, giving this power to the Pharaoh. This would lead the Pharaoh to victory over any enemy and guarantee a prosperous kingdom under their rule. However, the Scorpion Queen warned that this would come at a great karmic and spiritual price, making them an enemy of Ma'at. Thus, Ma'at called out the Scorpion Queen for infecting the souls of the rulers who called upon her and preventing them from reaching the afterlife. I see Alexandria as an innocent being taken to the chamber and sacrificed, but not with the knowledge of Hatshepsut."

"The curse trickled down into the time of Tutankhamun," said Laura, looking at Lesley. To my surprise, she was white and huddled, with Naomi holding her in her arms, and the old man was now guarding her.

"Hatshepsut did not know, Alexandria. She was blindsided. She thought you had abandoned her." I reassured her.

"I would never." She looked over at her grandmother for comfort, but the Contessa was in a deep trance.

"They buried your body in the desert, and you were bound to ferry the souls to the afterworld."

"Here," I said, "hold these in your hands."

I placed the Records of Life Scroll and Scarab into her

palms. I knelt in front of her and, for some reason, called Lesley to assist.

Lucinda gave me a strange look, but Naomi nodded.

"Lesley, you tried to call on these during your reign as a Queen," I said. "Now, you must set yourself free."

"They are too powerful." Lesley shook her head.

"They took your children," said Lucinda softly.

Everyone was now seeing the timeline where we had been caught.

We all came close, and I began to recite the words to unbind the curse and release those affected by it.

I began to see an image from the Book of Keys and remembered something written on the page and began to recite it.

"I hereby move all that is not of the Earth to the realms from which it was created. Release the soul from the promise of war and power. Restore their sight to purity and release these pieces from the energy of harm they do."

"Death is but a transition, a movement to another dimension, and resurrection is the eternal life of ascension. I hereby remove the evil of pain, confusion, and suffering and transform them into illumination."

I felt the wind run through us as if a door had opened, and then all was still.

I looked around at us all.

This had been the first morning, and I wondered what lay ahead of us all.

Slowly, we all rose, and Lucas gathered the Records of Life Scroll and Scarab and placed them carefully away. I nodded to acknowledge his integrity with this task of holding them all. I would be too afraid to hold them all now.

Emilee was making her way around the group with the offer of her grounding tincture.

The elder guardian was gone, and I began to sense other tourists approaching. Their chatter echoed a warning that it was time to leave.

Then, before I knew it, we were climbing down the steep ladder and back into the valley.

The Contessa had been first out of the chamber, and I watched as she rushed down the hill with Lucas towards Rashida. They were having a conversation, and Rashida was nodding and pointing to her watch.

Lucas ran back to us.

"The Contessa has a private entrance booked to the tomb of Tutankhamun," he gasped.

"When?" asked Lesley. I saw her eyes fill with tears.

"Thirty minutes," he called out and ran back to her.

"Well, that's a turn up," said Alice.

"Laura, do you want to go?" she turned to her old friend.

But Laura was a million miles away.

I went to her and touched her hand.

"He's here and waiting for me," she said.

"Who?" I enquired.

"Seti I," and she began to wander to a closed tomb marked with a KV17 identification.

"Is this open? I still have some stamp left on my ticket."

"No, it's not ready, but Anna, can you help me remote view this and remember?"

"Of course," I said. Let's find a safe place. We have time." I led her towards the back of the tourist shelter next to the coffee shop, where it was quiet, and we would not be disturbed.

Within a moment, Naomi joined us.

"And?" I questioned her. I was not sure why she had joined us.

"Ladies, I am a priestess of the goddess Nephthys, the

goddess of the afterlife. I can gain safe passage through the veils of all these tombs."

Now the black veil made sense, and I saw her in an ancient time dressed all in black and gold, leading the processions of grief and directing the sealing of the tombs.

"You sealed the tombs and placed the scarab stamps in place." I could see it clearly.

"Yes," she laughed, "and left the curses for those who dared to cross us."

I sat between both ladies and closed my eyes. No one paid attention as we simply looked like English tourists unable to be out in the sun. I directed my vision towards the entrance of KV17 and began to guide us in our astral bodies towards the opening.

"Naomi, if you will now say the words of prayer to allow safe passage, and Laura, please declare yourself to the guardians of this tomb."

I felt them complete their work telepathically, and I looked into the chamber.

"It's dark and very peaceful. The entrance is steep, and we must enter with care. To my left, I see a carved round ring holding a scarab and an image of the Pharaoh. He wishes you to hold this, Laura, to remember when you placed your hand upon it and promised your love to stay with him."

Laura squeezed my hand. "Tell me more of what you see," she urged.

"Now I see you, Naomi. Ah, you are addressing the King's soul and preparing him."

I began to describe the walls with the images, and although everything was covered with a thin, dark veil of energy, the messages and prayers were still strong. Although disturbed and looted, this tomb's energy was still intact.

"How do I look?" Naomi asked, as always, focused on

her image.

"Beautiful. You have a terracotta dress with animal markings, and from your elbow hangs the symbols of the Ankh and the Osiris symbol... then fans and feathers... then rows of lapis and gold around your neck."

"But now it's switching to Laura."

"Oh, Laura, you were his beloved, trusted friend, his oracle, too."

"Now I see a priest guiding the King's soul."

"The King is now making his way through the stargates, and it's as if we all acted out those roles in times gone past."

"Wow, it's..."

"What is it?" Naomi asked.

"The ceiling is a map to the stars and stargates," I said.

"Each God is depicted with red circle markings, like constellations and stars in the sky.

"The main chamber is navy blue with gold, like a calendar with times and dates.

"We stayed here for several days, and we mourned and re-recounted the story of his death. And now I see a woman coming forward; I don't know her. She was the true love of this King, and she welcomes us all."

"Ahh, this had been so confusing for me," said Laura. "I had so much love for him, but I was confused... was this man my husband, my son? Now I see I was the oracle for him."

"And the woman is Om Seti," said Naomi. "I read a book about her life as an English woman whose past life memory recalls her being a great love of Seti I."

"Is he there? Can you see him?" asked Laura.

"No, the woman is shaking her head," I replied.

"I bring a warning," said Naomi. She was now channelling the spirit of Om Seti.

"In the depths of my Temple lies an even darker gate.

Find this, my oracle friends, in my temple."

I felt the energy shift, and we stopped in silence.

Naomi appeared free of the spirit of Om Seti that had entered her.

I watched as her energy floated. "I saw a lion so clearly painted into the ceiling; he has red marks. They are stars going down his back," I continued.

"A Lionsgate," said Naomi.

Then I saw the Om Seti woman going down into a shaft, way into the lower chambers, and I felt it was time to leave.

Slowly, we began to bring our energy back, just in time to see Alice waving to us, indicating that it was time to leave the underworld and return to the land of the living.

☥

We walked out into the blinding light. It was a little after 11 a.m., and I already felt the heat draining my energy. It was time to visit Tutankhamun.

We walked over to the entrance of a tiny area. I had been expecting a full-size museum spectacle, but a pale stone brick entrance opened with a metal gate and a hand-painted sign that read *Tut-ankh-Amun.*

"That's not right," I said to Lucas, standing beside me.

"Do you want to rewrite it, Anna?" Lesley was next to me and had entirely transformed.

She wore a beautiful scarf of yellow shades that was covered in scarabs and ancient jewels. "My treasure, it's from Hermes," she smiled, patting it.

"What should the sign read?" I asked.

"*Tut ankh Aten.* That was the true faith until he was brought back to the Priests of Amun, and the battle of the souls commenced."

"Anna, it is time, come meet my family." She tugged my

arm, and we descended the steep, small staircase.

As we all reached the bottom of the stairs, I heard the noise of the gateway above us close and lock, and I could see the eyes of the elder guardian peering down at us.

He lifted his finger to his lips. "Shh," he smiled, and I nodded.

We all entered a tiny chamber with hand-painted images; they almost looked like characters and were very different from those the artisans carved in the first tomb.

This tomb had a feeling of urgency, as if it was a façade. Something did not feel totally authentic.

I walked over to the rail where everyone else was standing, and to my surprise, there was a full-size sarcophagus and, lying there inside, a full-size mummy protected by a glass case.

I felt my breath blown away. This was a real mummy. The glass protected him, and at first, I thought he would feel sad and morbid, but now this felt like a release and transformation.

The Contessa had also transformed, and she was now wearing a scarf of animal print cloth to signify her position as a high priest.

Lucas held his hands out, holding the Records of Life scroll and scarab.

Naomi and Emilee stood with Lesley as if she were a grieving widow, and I stood alone. Laura and Alice began a cleansing ritual, and Alexandria stood with her hands above her head, calling in all the spirit energies of the afterlife.

Lucinda then moved into the centre and began to channel.

"Oh, Aten O Aten..."

"Turn thy face upon this body...

"... make him sound and strong in the underworld.

"The eye of no man whatsoever must see it, for it is a thing of abomination for any man to know it. Hide it, hide it again so it may remain hidden in the Temple."

The Contessa then began to let her voice make a sound, and we all joined her in an Om.

I was then aware of the young man from the mirror standing next to me.

We shifted into another dimension.

"Is it you, my young friend from Cairo?" I asked.

"Yes, it is I. I have been trapped here for many years, awaiting the doorways to be opened and reset.

"The Records of Life trapped me in this unholy place. I have waited for decades, defending my tomb against robbers. Then there was one who came, and he was part of the expedition I knew would finally find others to set me free, and my story could be told."

"I do not understand," I replied.

"Remember what you saw in the other tombs... the images on the walls?" he asked.

I nodded.

"They were channels from the oracles and Record Keepers of the afterlife. The warnings and the tests, the stories of our souls.

"They were also our fears, and I was buried with mine. But see on the walls here in my tomb no real stories are told," he said.

"When the archaeologists came in your last century, there was one of them, a young man. You know his grandson. You just met him."

"The man from the museum, Michael? Yes, I met him."

"Yes, his family had the bloodline to open the doorways. I stood back and allowed them to discover the stairs in 1923."

"I have been awaiting this man's family and the oracles

to free me again."

"So there were curses?" I asked.

He nodded and pointed to Lesley and Alexandria.

"Forgive me, my beloved one," he pointed at Lesley. But she could not hear him.

"She now walks a dark and light path; she plays the game still, but her heart can find its healing, I pray," he said.

He looked back at me, and suddenly, I realised this was also the young man who had argued with the Queen in my dreams.

He smiled as I began to pull more of the jigsaw together.

"The game, you must tell me. You were playing the game with Nefertiti, but what is the game?"

He shook his head to say not now.

"Now I must go." He held out the turquoise ring again, and I reached out and took its energy.

"This is my amulet of protection for you and my thanks," and then he was gone.

I returned to reality and could see that the ceremony was ending.

The Contessa had stopped toning, and we began to depart in silence.

Alexandria walked close to me. She said nothing, just took my hand; sometimes silence speaks volumes.

Once outside, I was struck by the bright colours, as if I had been hidden for thousands of years and finally resurrected myself.

"Time for lunch, I think," said Emilee, assisting the group with water and rescue remedy, helping them pack away their dark veils and costumes of grief into their bags for another day.

Lunch was a sombre affair at a local family restaurant next to where they had workshops to make the famous alabaster vases and replicas of the ancient statues.

I had a little chicken with rice and then wandered out to the garden, where I sat on the grass to watch the tour buses arrive for the statue-making demonstrations.

I could see a skinny, tiny kitten not far from me, with fur of golden orange and white stripes.

A little girl was playing with her, chatting and singing in Arabic. I smiled at her and watched as she fed small scraps of meat to the kitten and then gathered her up and held her, rocking her like a baby.

"Did you see the King?" she asked, looking at me.

"Your English is very good," I said.

"I speak Arabic and English and am learning French," she responded, "and I am only eight."

"That's more than me! You are very clever. Now, who is the King?" I asked.

"He comes to the garden sometimes and complains about how there is not enough gold, and they are too slow in making his precious things for his special trip."

"Is he mean?" I asked.

"No, not to me," she shook her head. "But to them." She pointed out to the fields behind.

My gaze shifted, and I began seeing a whole temple before me, with rows of workshops and beautiful statues and coffins inlaid with gold and precious stones.

Priests roamed around offering blessings to the Gods. This was their place, the workshops that created everything for the afterlife.

I could see the Priestesses over to the side reciting and learning rituals from *The Book of the Dead*. The walls had symbols, and I knew I had seen some in my black book.

They were not Egyptian symbols, but more like swirls and text I did not know. This was a whole complex dedicated to the afterlife, a world between the worlds.

I could see all this activity, and at the same time, hear the song the little girl was singing to the kitten.

I shook my head, and the little girl stood up before me.

"He says he has left something for you in the shop," she said, pointing to a door at the end of the house courtyard. I could just make out that this must be her family's other little business.

"Okay, well, it was so lovely to meet you. I will go check it out." I held out my hand to shake hers.

She laughed as she extended her hand.

"So lovely, so lovely," she giggled. She snuggled the kitten close, whispered in her ear, and went about her day.

When I reached the small shop, I was surprised to see Naomi sitting on a high stool, looking into the glass cabinet. She saw my reflection in the mirror on the wall and called out to me.

"Anna, you have got to see this."

I moved over and looked into the cabinet. Gold and silver chains and pendants with the heads of the Gods.

"This work is excellent," she smiled and nodded to the young man behind the desk.

Then she began pointing and asking to see all number of pieces.

"Do you see anything, Anna?" she asked.

The young man was busy typing numbers into his calculator and showing her the price and weight of each piece. A strange way to shop, but a whole new learning experience.

"Well, let me see." I had not spent any of my Contessa money, so a treat was in order.

"Did you leave me anything?" I laughed.

She had four necklaces, three rings, and five bracelets all on simultaneously.

"I have something for you, lady." He went to the cabinet's bottom drawer and pulled out a long box. Opening it, he revealed some truly old antique pieces made of hammered metals. "From my family's workshop," he pointed to another part of the house.

"Oh, oh, oh," Naomi squealed. "This is like the jewels in the museum." She removed all her pieces and started picking up the shiny new things.

The man smiled, and I knew he was used to this reaction, which was probably part of the show-and-tell.

These are special prices, and he began to write numbers onto paper as Naomi held the various pieces she was drawn to.

I was most surprised, however, when he ever so sweetly pointed to my left hand.

Maybe this was one of those dark, mysterious magician experiences.

"No ring?"

"No ring," I laughed.

"One will be there soon," and he nodded.

Naomi laughed out loud and then turned to me.

"Oh, Anna, I'm sorry that was not kind."

"Well, it was true, though," and I waved it away.

"Try this on that other hand," he said.

He held out a beautiful ring, and I realised it was the same turquoise colour as the one Tutankhamun had shown me.

"Is it lapis or turquoise?" Naomi asked.

"Turquoise with gold running into it." He offered it to me again before she could get her hands on it.

I took it and placed it on my right-hand ring finger.

It was a perfect fit.

"Oh, Anna, that's beautiful. How did I miss that?" asked Naomi.

"Because it is not for you, lady. It is for her," the salesman insisted.

"Yes, it is for me." I just kept staring; it was so beautiful.

"Okay, okay, how much?" Naomi, it seems, was excellent at the haggle.

"Set price for you. It is an 18-karat gold ring set with the rare stone."

His eyes looked straight into mine, and it made me shiver. Naomi was not used to being sidelined.

"Okay, you come back to her later. Now focus on me," she ordered as he raised his eyebrows.

She went back to picking out exactly what she wanted with super speed.

"This, this, and this," she said.

"This piece is a replica of a Princess Sitamun necklace..." She paused for dramatic effect. "And I'm going to wear it now."

Then, without asking, she opened up her wallet and began placing pound notes on the tabletop, counting them out as if to say, *'This is what I'm giving you, and I'm not asking.'*

"Does that cover it?" He nodded, looking very happy. He wrapped everything up, gave her a receipt, and slid the cash into a drawer below.

"Now, lady, does this please you?" He returned his attention to me.

The young man had faded, and Tutankhamun was in his place.

I could hear him clearly. I looked around, and the shop was still the same.

"Yes, this pleases me, sir," I nodded.

"Good," he said. "Now take it and be well."

I was confused; I had to pay.

I blinked—the young king was gone, and the salesman was writing my receipt.

"Oh, I have to give you money. You didn't say how much."

"No matter," he smiled. "She paid for you."

He pointed to Naomi, who was standing in the doorway, showing Lucinda her treasure.

"Thank you." I left the ring on my finger and began to tell my legs to move, trying to convince myself I was not under a spell.

"Naomi, that is too kind."

"Nonsense, I was feeling generous, and now I have my royal piece thanks to you."

She patted her gold and purple necklace, and I have to admit she looked even more like royalty than before.

"Time to go," shouted Lesley, and we followed out of the restaurant and towards the bus.

I saw the little girl with her kitten on the wall and held up my hand to show that the mission was complete. She smiled and gave me a thumbs-up.

Yes, for sure, this had been a magical lunch.

The Temple of Hatshepsut

Once we boarded the bus to leave, Lesley was now back in her own body, counting heads and telling everyone we would have around thirty minutes until we reached the temple of Queen Hatshepsut.

Rashida was counting ticket monies and using her phone to call ahead.

The bus wove through the snake-like road past small

homes in fields of crops with lonely donkeys. You would think we had gone back to 2000 years ago.

We arrived at the gateway to the complex, and I began to scan the area as Rashida told the history. There was no green here, just sand and stone.

I looked out across the desolate area with little in the way of structures and life. I saw spirits floating across the sand dunes and hawks flying overhead.

"I stayed with them once, the Carters," said Lucinda, standing beside me.

"Howard Carter was one of us who tried to preserve the temples and had a dream of prophecy in Armana in his early days. He sought us out, and we told him to beware of the curses. He had a past life in the court of Akhenaten and remembered the scarabs and scrolls. That was what he really sought when he discovered the tomb of Tutankhamun."

"So now he is a guardian, bound in spirit to walk these mountains and tombs and never to rest." I was shocked by my insight and words.

"I felt pity for him, but in the end, he had been warned," Lucinda shrugged and walked to the front of the group.

I could feel Alice staring at me. I guessed we had work to do. She pointed to the front of the tourist trolley shuttle. We jumped in together, and the trolley bus ride took us to the temple entrance.

It was magnificent and not as I had expected. Pale ivory stone that almost appeared rose quartz-like as the blazing sun and blue sky brought it into focus.

The stairs rose through the three floors of the open temple that looked to have been built into the mountainside. I counted the columns and saw a distinct difference between the left and right sides.

I knew where I had to be, front and centre, and on the

top floor towards the back, but clouds swirled around the stairs in my vision.

"Pay no attention," said Laura. "They are the energy re-enactments of 1997 when the massacre and the shooting of the tourists occurred. I will work with the energy here." I saw tears in her eyes as she walked slowly across the white stone slabs, saying prayers and gently moving through the souls still lingering.

I fell back a little to stand next to Lesley. She asked me what I saw.

I shrugged my shoulders, and then I was presented with two side-by-side visions.

I saw the tourists, the families, and then those who acted in terror.

At first, I was shocked by the vision, but then I was guided to look deeper.

I watched as Lucas joined Laura, and I could see them both healing and clearing souls who had lost their lives during the terror attack.

I looked at Lucinda, who was moving to the left side and going towards the second floor, and what looked to be a section dedicated to Hathor. Emilee followed her. They were in a totally different timeline and dimension from me and the others.

Then, below us, down to the right side in the far corner, I watched Naomi and the Contessa walk towards a small shrine. "Anubis," whispered Alice next to me. I could see now that this Temple's function was to do with Death and Resurrection.

The Hathor side to the left was for the priestesses and priests performing the life ritual. On the right with Anubis, who was the ferryman between the worlds, stood the section for the afterlife ritual.

And so Alice and I, with Lesley and Alexandria, began to climb up the stairs toward the top floor. Rashida followed us, just holding back and watching everything.

I wanted to run towards the top, but with everything going on, I felt a sense of ceremony. We reached the top floor, and Alexandria led us to the back, where we all stood at a wooden railing. It was mid-afternoon, and the sun was so hot and very few tourists were around. The guard looked at Alexandria and bowed.

He spoke something in Arabic that I did not understand.

"He tells her she comes here in his dream, and the lady is awaiting her," said Rashida.

"Ah, I had wondered why she had followed us. Always in the shadows but always present."

Alexandria smiled, placed her hands on the rail and began to whisper words.

Lesley stood behind me.

Alexandria closed her eyes and began to speak.

"She is here, Queen Hatshepsut, and she welcomes us."

I could only see the shadow, but I felt the presence so strong like I had in the tomb.

"She tells me that the work has started. By releasing the Scarab and Scroll of the Records of Life in the Valley of the Kings, the Stargates, the spirits bound by the Scorpion Queen, can be released and taken into the afterworld. The Scorpion Queen has held many of them prisoner to do her bidding here on this Earth plane. This has sent the world into karmic war and suffering for the last two thousand years after the fall of Cleopatra VII. Now, the curve and spiral are changing, and the work that will continue in the following days will release many. She tells you all to use the gifts and tools you have been given, and the ancient books are now open and there for you, Anna, to read.

"But she also gives a warning that to use the power for yourself, will create a tower from which you will damn yourself and your friends, so step wisely and do not be seduced by the forces not yet seen.

"Those who have gone before you have left the clues. You must follow your heart to find them."

"The Book of Keys," I spoke the words into the chamber. I looked up and around.

I realised that each member of our small group now had their own channelling with Queen Hatshepsut.

Each of us received a blessing or maybe forgiveness.

"Anna," whispered Lucas. He was now at my side and handed me the Death and Resurrection scarab and scroll.

I stood and offered them to the Queen and sent the energy through her chamber, suddenly realising that her chamber had a tunnel that led right into the Valley of the Kings.

"She thanks you for completing the ritual!" Alexandria nodded to the scarab and scroll. "The Queen says now that they have linked to the Records of Life and unity of the temples can be created."

"... and set to infinity," I replied.

I drew the infinity symbol in the air and began to see it weaving these two sets together—such alchemy.

Once we were all complete, I made a promise to return, and I knew then my soul had another safe home should I need to hide. This was a place of sanctuary.

As we were leaving, I felt something pull me back.

"Anna, please, I have one more role for you."

I realised it was Queen Hatshepsut herself. So vivid and real.

"Please walk with me," she said, and I watched as she joined me.

Her dress was a deep shade of pink.

Her skin was bronzed by the sun, and her hair was much different, as it was dark yet had stands of red and gold. I watched the others go ahead of me, and I slowly fell behind.

"Dear Oracle, I have two tasks for you."

"Command as you wish, my Queen," I responded.

"Please come."

She took my hand, and we walked down the staircase, then the next, turning left.

We walked towards the temple wall towards the alcove covered in ancient art. I searched the wall for the clues.

There I found her image, and like many of the images, her face had some damage, but as she waved her hand, all the images became perfect again, and I saw a clear picture and the story she wished to share.

I pointed to the woman on the wall who also wore the clothes of a King.

"For protection and leadership."

"And you're pregnant?" I pointed to another version, and she smiled.

"Your daughter... but where is the child?" I enquired.

She nodded to acknowledge my question, and then I saw tears.

"But I sense her," I said.

She nodded again, and at that moment, I saw Alexandria wander past, lost in a dream.

I called out her name, but she heard nothing, so I ran over to her.

"Alex, Alex."

For some reason, I wanted to use a short name as she felt almost like a sister now, not just a soul friend. She turned to run back to me and took my hands.

"Anna, everyone went to the coffee shop... Anna, I feel I

am missing something."

"I have it here... please come."

I led her over and could see Hatshepsut waiting.

I moved to Alexandria and just brushed my hand across her forehead.

"Do you see her?"

Alexandria's eyes opened so wide, and she bowed down.

"My Queen."

"No, no," the Queen gathered her in her arms.

"You are my child, my daughter, my dear one. I have been waiting."

I watched as they embraced and created a healing. Alexandria was more than her Oracle. She had been family and not just any family. She was of royal blood and lineage.

☥

I decided to go to the coffee shop. I could still see Lucinda and Emilee on the next level up in the Hathor Temple. Standing at the edge looking out, I could see they were deep in ritual and in the healing they knew how to do.

"Don't you want to visit me?"

I heard a male voice behind me and turned to see Anubis.

Tall, strong, and jet black, wearing a royal blue and gold wrap priest robe, his face shifting from a man to a jackal.

I followed him over to a small shrine with a metal gate. Clearly, this was the sacred place where they held the ritual and ceremony for the afterlife.

"It is not my time, is it?" I gasped.

"No, but I wish to share with you what has happened before."

"Death?" I was concerned.

"Yes and no. In ancient times, we always had an oracle present; they could be male or female, and they would channel the messages from the valley," he said.

"How so?" I asked.

"This realm is between the worlds of life and death, and because of the powerful rituals, the energy was very magnetic, and sometimes you were unsure if you were in this world or the next."

"We were not meant to see into the afterworld?" I asked.

"We could see, just not be in that realm," he answered. *"That was the role of the oracle."*

I looked around and was surprised to see various timelines of battles in the physical and spiritual realms all at play simultaneously.

I took a step towards Anubis for safety and covered my eyes. I had seen a war zone playing out in this location for the last 2000 years. It was brutal and frightening, and now I understood the particular ritual from this tomb. The clear message was we should not be in these realms too long.

"This temple was not meant as a tomb but was built as a sanctuary between the worlds, and Queen Hatshepsut was a guardian. She was a priestess trained in the spiritual arts and the game of the soul," he said, and my whole body shivered.

This game I had heard of already, and now again today. The one that Queen Nefertiti and Tutankhamun had been arguing about all those months before in my dream.

"Tell me about the game, please."

"I cannot, but soon you will connect to someone who has successfully played the game, the only one to my knowledge."

As quickly as he was present, he was then gone, and I looked around to see Naomi waving a red scarf, which meant we were leaving.

I ran and caught up with them all and walked alongside

Alexandria.

She said nothing but took my hand and squeezed it.

"Thank you, Anna, it was *trés incroyable*... incredible."

"Remember those from the Louvre, the souls we saved?"

I nodded.

"They were here. They are helping now with the realms of the souls caught between worlds."

"Did they tell you anything else?"

She shook her head. That felt good. I had a strange feeling that to share everything would begin to distort the picture and I needed clear focus.

Valley of the Queens—Nefertari's Tomb

I was hoping we would be returning to the hotel. It was already nearly 3 p.m. when the bus turned left, and we began to drive further into the mountain area, not towards the Nile River. Few others ventured here, or followed this path, it seemed, as I saw no other buses or cars.

Lesley announced we were near the Valley of the Queens; I was totally surprised, as it had not been on the schedule. But hey, we were here; why would we not visit the Queens?

As we left the bus, no vendors or other tourists were around. All was empty and still.

Rashida left to find the tickets.

I looked around the group and was surprised to see Emilee smoothing out her dress, applying oils to her wrists, and then fussing with everyone to create a procession.

She even adjusted the Contessa's scarf and began to inspect Naomi.

Lucinda slowly moved up next to me.

"Are we about to have a parade?" I whispered.

"No," she laughed.

"We are about to visit the Queen Nefertari."

Apparently, you needed a special ticket and could only stay a short time in the tomb due to how precious and delicate it was.

Once Emilee had everyone in line at the entrance, she turned to us. It was as if she had grown in height and stature.

"You are about to enter one of the most holy and royal realms. This chamber hosts her most royal majesty, Queen Nefertari. Most beloved Queen of Rameses II, daughter of Isis and sister of Ma'at. She who stands most beautiful and just, she who commands the heavens on Earth."

A beautiful speech. I was almost afraid of who we would find. But we all followed her as she moved into the tomb, slowly uttering the various mantras, stopping at the gateways to show respect.

I was a few people back in the queue and could not quite see, but when Emilee stopped under the gateway of Isis marked by an image of a Goddess with outstretched wings on the wall that spanned across the top of the tunnel that sloped down, I turned to feel the presence of two goddesses with me.

I looked in front of me, and the two images of Neith and Serket were on the walls.

One had what looked like a cartouche with no writing within it, and the other had a scorpion upon her head.

Neith spoke first.

"Come, child, come to our sacred sanctuary."

I followed my friends, but I was now distracted by these two goddesses.

Emilee was leading them through a challenging teaching and pointing out the story of Nefertari, and it was at that point I realised she had been the oracle to this great

Queen.

Rashida had not been permitted to guide us in the tomb, so we were very much left to our own devices.

Emilee had gathered everyone into a circle, and Lucas had brought out a sacred scarab and scroll.

They were the ones of Magic and Prophecy. I then realised this was not a tomb like those in the Valley of the Kings.

As I stood back, I saw the energy beginning to swirl into the chamber. The figures and images on the walls seemed almost lifelike, and I watched as a high priest shifted from the wall to stand with me.

"The Queen has been waiting."

He gestured towards the left side of the chamber and turned to face the wall. There, on the upper level of the text, was an image of a woman who I took to be Nefertari. She was dressed in white with a crown on her head.

She was seated at a table as if enjoying afternoon tea, but on the table was the game, the Senet. I had seen it in my Egypt Oracle deck, but never as powerful as this image. The ten pieces were placed like a chess game, but I couldn't see her opponent.

Her left hand was outstretched, meaning she was playing from her heart and her feet were planted firmly on the ground to show a powerful message of control.

She was holding what looked to be a fan in her right hand, but I felt it looked more like a wand ready to cast a spell of a royal decree.

"You found my secret, young oracle," I heard a woman's voice behind me.

"This is the game?" I pointed to it.

I quietly reached into my bag, pulled out the black book, and opened it to a random page. There was a flat grid with three rows of ten boxes. Small markings were on four boxes, but there were no pieces to play with.

I held the image up towards her. She smiled and then pointed to the walls with all the depictions and images.

"*There was the Book of the Afterlife,*" she said, pointing to the walls.

"*And then there was the game, a game with the Gods,*" I said telepathically, as I had just noticed that Emilee was in full honour and prayer, and my little visit with her precious Queen would have surely disrupted this. The Queen nodded and smiled.

I wanted to ask more, but suddenly, she was gone, and I found myself slowly moving near Lucas, who still held the Magic and Prophecy Scroll and Scarab. But I could not reach him as he was at the front with Emilee.

Even though this was a tomb, it was a sacred place, and I decided to participate in the initiation ritual that Emilee was hosting. Out of respect, I stood at the back of the queue as we were each presented with the image of the Queen on the wall. Emilee poured the energy of the Queen into our hands, and then held our hands up to mimic the wall.

Once the ritual of life, rather than death, was complete, we were allowed to wander, and I began to take pictures to help me remember. I stood for the longest time, trying to decipher the figures and the characters. Who had they been? And who were they now? Then, a thought came.

"The game is still in play," I said out loud.

I let out a gasp, and the Contessa shushed me.

The others sat down and prepared themselves for silent meditation for the remaining minutes we had left.

But I needed to leave and made my way past Emilee, who caught my arm.

"She came to you, my mistress, yes," she whispered.

I nodded.

"And she showed you the game, perhaps?"

I could not find the words, so I simply nodded.

Then something came over me.

"Emilee, it's still in play, or it's been reawakened."

Emilee was no longer all smiles and joy—I had triggered a memory of her past lives.

"We must go," she said, looking around at the others and touching their shoulders to bring them back present and ready to leave.

"Anna, sit with me on the bus back to the hotel, please," she said.

I nodded and walked back up the stairs to the daylight, where Rashida was arguing with a guard.

Something had happened, and we obviously had outstayed our welcome.

Lucas came out of the tomb, followed by Emilee, leaving last as she had to close the chamber and the portals; otherwise, who knew where we would be that evening in our astral travels?

We boarded the bus swiftly, and in a moment, everything changed as Lesley began handing out gifts of statues and scarves throughout the bus. Apparently, she had connected with some of the local artisans and bought their treasures for us all. I looked at their stalls, old and unkept. I gathered that they had very few visitors; however, this was a much more powerful place than the Valley of the Kings.

I was handed a beautiful stone square with a hand-carved image of Nefertari, who was seated on her throne, and the goddess Ma'at was kneeling in front of her with her wings spread, offering allegiance to the Queen.

Emilee sat in the seats across the row from me in the back of the bus. She pointed to the stone plate in my hands.

"My mistress was a kind and just woman. I saw my past

life again today, though not clearly. "Anna, would you open the Records so perhaps I can see more?"

"Of course," I smiled, and I closed my eyes and held her hand, and she closed hers.

"I see us. We are in the temple once again, and I am her oracle. This was such a happy life for me, Anna."

"Then stay, Emilee," I told her. "Stay in this beautiful love and light."

I looked at my watch. It would be at least another hour before we were home, so I simply closed my eyes and held space for her as she travelled to a very happy time.

☥

That evening, I was so exhausted that the thought of dinner and conversation felt draining, and I wanted to go back and study the Book of Keys. It had, without doubt, helped me today, and I realised it was not to be read front to back but instead to be used like an oracle to ask questions or to transmit insight.

I also felt it was important to remember, so I began to journal, and I began to create a list of the scrolls and scarabs and their locations, thinking I might need this later. I would have added the details into the book if it were not so precious. Maybe I should start Volume 2.

I would allow it to guide me. I began to look through various pages to gather information. But as soon as I climbed into bed, my mind had other intentions, and I fell into a deep sleep and dreamt.

I am a small child and playing in the street with friends. My mother often checks on me, yet I see no other grown-ups. I never feel scared. My father is a policeman. He takes bad people away. I am wearing my blue dress, the one I wore the day he died.

Suddenly, I find myself in a warehouse and see my father. He's alone, but he cannot hear me. His partner, his friend, lies unconscious, and I try to wake him, but I have no response. I'm now running towards my father, but the floor is again like sand, and I'm standing in a large Egyptian temple or palace. There are so many rooms. My father appears and is in the costume like a palace guard. He is running to a small stone building just outside the palace.

I run after him, but a woman stops me and stands behind me. "You can't stop this."

"Anna, all that is, will be done."

"No, I have to help." I run to the stone building and see it has three small rooms. I can hear him,

"Oracle, please tell me what is to be done."

"You cannot save him," she tells him, her face now covered by a veil.

The assassination has already occurred; save the others and the children, as this queen may not be merciful."

My father rises but does not see me.

I go before the oracle.

"Who is he trying to save?" I ask her.

"Ramses III," she replies.

"But why?"

"His wife, Queen Tiye, seeks power for her son Pentawere and has summoned the dark Gods. She prayed to Set, and this led her to the Scorpion Queen. She is now possessed and will not stop till her son is ruler."

I turned to run.

"It is his destiny to protect you and the others."

I stopped and turned. She had removed her veil, and it was then I realised she was my mother, younger like the Lottie I had seen in the images in the red box of Isis.

"I will save him and the others."

I run back to the palace, but I am too late. The palace is in a frenzy of fear. The pharaoh lies dead, and the Queen stands over him. His throat is slit, and blood is everywhere.

I hear the same cackling behind me and realise it's the same voice that has been following me throughout the last year. The Scorpion Queen. Although I can't see her face, I know her.

My father and the other guards are fighting those loyal to the Queen.

I face the Scorpion Queen, and she tells me she has been searching for me, and it is as if the picture stops in slow motion.

I see my father walking towards us, and he has a sharp sword with a crystal.

The Queen addresses him.

"Let us have this girl who will serve us as our new oracle. You will serve me and my son. You see, we have the Power of the priests of Unal."

"You have an oracle!" I shout to the Scorpion Queen, who laughs behind me, and she holds up the oracle's veil stained with blood. My mother is dead.

My father lunges at her as she disappears to smoke, and the Priests of Unal descend upon him.

I find myself again in the warehouse. My father lies there. He's not breathing, and I realise he's dead.

I hear a voice in my head. "Anna, run, leave this place. He can only protect you so far. The veils are now thin, and she will find you."

I woke up suddenly and checked the time—it was midnight. I looked out of my window to the west.

"I will find out the answers. I know you hide secrets, but I will find the truth," I said out loud.

I then fell into deep relaxation and a sense of calm I had not felt before.

CHAPTER 21

Saturday, 19 September
Karnak Temple

At breakfast, I could see Naomi watching me out of the corner of her eye. I wanted to tell her about my dream and connections to Ramses III, but something held me back. I just wanted to sit with this puzzle piece. It was so random, and no one in the group had mentioned this king or timeline to my memory. I decided to let it go for now.

As we boarded the bus, I watched as Naomi moved into the front-row seats across from the Contessa. I realised now that on each bus trip, certain people moved into specific seats and next to key people. It was like a foreshadowing of the karma to come. Lesley and Rashida had been relegated to the third row, and I sat behind them. Thus today, I knew the Contessa must have something to share.

But she sat motionless and said nothing. Her head was covered with a blue shawl and dark sunglasses.

Today, we visited Karnak, which, from what I understood, was a political temple or a royal palace. So, this could be my free day as a tourist.

The other ladies chatted, and I paid no attention as I opened my journal and wrote in big letters the words: KARNAK TEMPLE

The bus pulled to a halt, and we all began to disembark. The vendors paid no attention until Naomi entered at the end in her white silk dress and red shawl with delicate gold embroidery.

Our guide walked slowly with the Contessa, who looked straight ahead and focused on the temple without wavering. Even when Rashida offered her a ticket, she shook her head as if to let everyone know she was already in a sacred space and not to be bothered.

We began walking towards the entrance. It was lined on each side with the large seated Ram statues.

"Khnum, the mighty guardian," was all Rashida said.

I sensed their judgmental gaze as if they were awakening rudely, and their eyes fixated upon us.

After crossing a small security gate, the high temple walls, yellow and bright against the blue sky, could be seen ahead. Each side had four perfectly straight grooves carved into it like shelves, which I assumed would have hosted statues. Above were small cut-out squares to allow light to enter the temple at various times of day. In the middle was a narrow walkway with no gate, although in my vision, I could see a large wooden door that was closed each night to protect those who lived within the security of this powerful building.

We moved into the first courtyard and were drawn to what appeared to be a large stone cube just in the middle. It reminded me of the sacred white stone I had seen with Professor Michael in the Cairo Museum.

Rashida was about to talk about the time period and the various pharaohs when everyone gathered around the stone. I was not following the protocol. My mind was wandering back to Michael and pondering whether I should reach out to tell him about this world wonder and my insight when Lucas nudged me to pay attention. The women began to lift their scarfs like veils over their heads, and I knew this must be a type of ritual.

The Contessa began to chant, and all the others were

silent and closed their eyes. As I closed my eyes and touched the stone, I felt like I was in a dream. I could see people moving around. This was not like a temple just for prayer; this was an active and lively space.

Within the bustling scene, priests bore scrolls while people of diverse cultures mingled, each attending to their daily affairs. I looked up behind me and saw that various cube holes in the temple walls gave light and shadow to various parts of the temple, and of course, this was a clock that signified who or what was able to cross through the temple. Perfect timing, it would seem, as I was made aware of a very powerful group of priests that moved through. All the other priest groups hid as they passed me.

I looked at their robes, their heads shaved, and the kohl around their eyes. Some of them even nodded and smiled at me. They appeared to be still residing here, living in another dimension, and going about their business. There were very distinct symbols on their heads... two thick black lines joined from the front at the third eye to the back of their skulls.

"Anna, come on," said Lucinda. The ritual had ended, and I wondered which timeline I was in.

"Lucinda, I saw them, the priests and scribes." I nodded and pointed to where I had seen them.

"Ah, how did they look?" she winked at me.

"Busy, crazy busy, but I thought everything would move at a slow pace here."

"No, not here. This was a working and vibrant place," she said.

"I worked just over there in that chamber," Laura whispered.

"We worked to protect the royal children and therefore watched over all those who entered."

She bit her lip, and Alice was quickly by her side.

"No need, no need today," she whispered, "Come, my dear, let me escort you through the hypostyle hall."

Up ahead was a narrow walkway and large temple walls. As we entered, I was amazed at the courtyard, which was filled with large, thick columns nearly 70 feet tall and covered with Egyptian images. The gods were depicted with animals, along with hieroglyphics... messages left behind to teach us and let us remember our past.

We walked forward, and I could see the towering columns above me. I kept seeing various silk flags and banners hanging throughout the temple as if to signify certain high-ranking families, and it came to me that people here may have had a hierarchy.

I wanted to stop and marvel at the columns, but I could see that the others did not wish to wait. I was like the outsider following their mission, as I was pulled to other directions when all I wanted to do was explore. I looked at Lesley, and she held her finger to her lips. She came over to me.

"These are the sacred halls where everyone and everything is listening. Behind each column is a blind spot, and above are the areas where we are being watched."

I felt the hairs on the back of my neck begin to rise.

Rashida stopped and beckoned us all to gather to the side, away from the tourists pouring through the centre row. I looked over at Laura. She was now sitting on one of the column edges, just rocking and holding herself. She stared out into the distance, lost in a trance.

"It's always a hard place for her," said Lucinda as she rested her hand on my shoulder.

Alice was sitting with her, and Naomi stood before her, reciting something that sounded like an ancient prayer. As I watched, Naomi looked over to me and nodded, beckoning me to come over. I looked at the Contessa; she looked straight at me and smiled. She appeared more like her usual self. It dawned on me that she had used her energy and her ritual of silence to gain us entry to the spiritual plane while Rashida bought entry to the physical one.

Over the recent months, I had learnt to watch for signs of what was occurring and what was not, and not to judge too easily from an earthbound dimension. I moved over to where the women were sitting.

"It's just the heat," said Naomi as a guard passed. Alice was giving Laura water.

I knelt down and began to feel the presence of the children. "Were there children here?" I looked at Laura.

"Yes, yes, there were," said Laura. "My children."

My heart began to feel such pity, "But you were a priestess."

"And I was a royal queen."

"And they took your children. Two girls and a boy. I saw them—they were young."

"The boy was nine, and the girls were twins," said Alice.

"Gifts from the gods," Laura began to shake.

I could see the children running in and out of the columns, the nursemaids laughing and playing.

"My last chance at children, and ever since, I have been cursed because I cursed him."

I knew in an instant what had happened. "You were one of the priestesses who made the curse with Sekhmet."

At this, Naomi stood up. "Laura, it is time. You cannot carry this anymore. Anna is here, and she will help us clear this."

For a moment, I was taken aback. Naomi's deferral to me to clear this felt like an honour and an upgrade in my position, but rather than wonder and sabotage myself, I simply nodded and told them I would do what I could.

"Everyone... we go to the shrine," said Naomi.

I expected the Contessa to move first, but no, it was Alice. I watched her turn and go across the hall diagonally, taking us all to what appeared to be a derelict area, which seemed remote. There were no other people around. No tourists or guards were near.

Before long, we had reached a small temple with an inner chamber that housed a small stone altar that felt all too familiar. The main door was locked.

Alice stepped forward. She took command and pulled a blood-red silk scarf from her bag. "Light the fire," she commanded of Naomi, and I watched as Naomi lit a small candlewick in a glass bottle of oil and placed it upon the altar.

Alice then began to chant, and I watched as the guard, who appeared from nowhere, bowed his head and opened the metal door. Alice motioned to Lucas, who stood nearby, following everything she said and did. He then gently turned and, from his bag, brought out a set of scrolls and scarabs. He went over and knelt down in front of Alice, offering them up to her.

"Truth and Integrity, my lady," he said, and she smiled and took them.

We all waited while she whispered words I did not understand into them and then blew on them. She then proceeded into the chamber, and Lucas motioned for us to follow.

Our guide, Rashida, must have paid the guard well, as it was so easy for us to perform the ceremony. But then, as he looked at Laura, I also saw fear on his face, and he quickly disappeared from view. We all entered the chamber, which had a small main room with what appeared to be two side rooms. In front of us stood a statue, which I recognised as Ptah, but it was missing his head. Rashida motioned for us to enter one by one, and another guard who had appeared stepped forward with incense. As I looked closer, I saw them as the priests with the two black lines on their heads.

Once we were cleansed by the incense in front of Ptah, we moved to the room on the right and filed into the small, long, and narrow chamber. I was one of the last, as the energy was beyond intense. When I did make it into the chamber, I saw a statue and an image I would never forget. There, standing eight feet tall in ebony black stone, was the statue of the goddess Sekhmet. Naomi was laying flowers at her feet, and Laura crouched in the corner, weeping. Alexandria was near the front and held out her hand to me.

"Anna, come here, sit down and tell us the vision. We need to heal this for our sister."

I did as was asked and sat down to the side of the statue, but for some reason, I did not dare sit with my back to the statue. Everyone else knelt down, and the room was silent.

"Laura, come to the center, my dear," said Alice.

Laura knelt down, her eyes full of tears. She could not seem to look directly at the statue, which I swear now had red eyes and a face of a lioness that moved. I closed my eyes and was transported back in time.

"It is nighttime, and the priestesses of Sekhmet are handing over their place to hold the fire burning. This connects the sacred sisterhood. The fire here in this shrine never dies. It's guarded around the clock.

"Word has come that there are issues with the oracles; those who speak from the Gods. There is a battle for the souls within the temple. Many rituals are performed, and curses are written. I see a political battle of good and evil. But I cannot work out who is at fault. This feels familiar. There are many whispers, and I see boats moving back and forth across the Nile River, bringing news from another palace. It's from the place we now call Medina Habu Temple on the West Bank.

"Now it is morning, and I see Laura... and yes, she is a beautiful majesty and a beloved wife of the Pharaoh. He has many loves, but his children with her are his favourite, especially as she has a son and twin girls. This is such a positive omen. But dark forces are gathering. They overshadow the priestesses of Sekhmet, and they begin to do blood rituals. This temple was corrupted.

"Laura goes to the priestesses of Sekhmet for guidance as she feels threatened by the other wives of the pharaoh, and believes her children are at risk. She performs a great ritual and curse to keep these children safe, and in this very temple, she calls on Sekhmet for protection."

"I promised, if she would keep the souls of my children safe and that they would rule, I would do her bidding," sobbed Laura. "And do her bidding I did. I spied on the other wives and carried back the stories to my husband. I rose to power at the expense of others. Many women and children were lost or removed from the temple. It was a cold and dark time, and before long, no children were running in the halls. My family was powerful but alone and lost. I am so ashamed. She promised me everything, and now..."

"I do not believe this was Mother Sekhmet," Lucinda said, interrupting her.

My voice began to tremble. I remembered my dream.

"You were tricked, Laura. This is not the work of Sekhmet, but of darker forces. This was a witch at work. I saw this in my dream last night. I saw what you did and know it was not you," I said.

"I saw the death of the Pharaoh Rameses III at your hand, and your son's rise to power, and I saw the death of an oracle," I said.

You could have heard a pin drop as the women went very silent. I was going to continue the story when Alice began to speak. She was in a deep trance, and her eyelids fluttered.

"For many years, the queens and women of royal position came to my temple here.

"For I have carried the mantel of Sekhmet for many years.

"We were created like the karmic board, with seven statues in a circle. We were the highest Council of Oracles to settle disputes and were, therefore, very revered.

"When our sisterhood walked through this temple, even the Pharaoh would stop and acknowledge us. But after many years, our power grew weak, and we found ourselves ignored and criticised as a new power was rising. The Scorpion... she poisoned our hearts. It was she who tricked you, Laura. She, the Scorpion who played on your fears and led you to dark corners to whisper a plot to move you and your children into powerful positions."

Alice had stopped speaking and was now in front of the statue. She seemed to merge with the statue, and slowly, she moved behind. She stood with her back to the statue, and I watched as she tilted her head back and began to speak to the wall. Her voice began to vibrate around the small chamber. Lucas then stepped forward and went beside her. He handed the scroll and scarab to her.

"Oracle, use this," he said. "The Scroll and Scarab of Truth and Integrity."

Alice nodded and turned in front of the statue, holding the pieces up to the Sekhmet. Then she turned to face us and held them out in front of her as she spoke. I watched as her face took on that of the lioness.

"Oracles of Egypt, you once again come before me and my council from the stars. You seek forgiveness for acts and curses created many, many years ago. There is a dark force that follows you from the shadows. The scrolls and scarabs you

seek are all available to you now, and your purpose in this land is to restore them to the sacred places again.

"The Scorpion has risen again, and she means to control these relics for herself. She will use all her magic and alchemy to trick you into trusting her again.

"Do not just look for answers in the past, but open your third eyes to the future.

"The end of this age will soon be upon us, and a new age of Aquarius must start.

"The scrolls and scarabs can lead the way to the great healing and restore many of the gifts lost to the priestesses of Isis over the years. Then, the temples can be restored.

"I, Mother Sekhmet, am presenting to you the Scarab and Scroll of Truth and Integrity.

"This is a wise choice, as this is the balance of this temple. A balance that has been challenged many times.

"Come forward to my image," she said.

Laura stepped forward.

"Laura, I call on the Council of Sekhmet and the justice of Ma'at to stand before you." I watched as the women all began to stand. Lucas now sat still in a crossed-leg position at the base of the statue, as I had seen in the scribe statues in the Louvre Museum in Paris.

"Laura, open your heart and release the pain and suffering, the loss of children, and the curse of never bearing or holding a child. I restore your life and power to the sacral energy, and the healing can begin."

Laura began to cry. She knelt in front of the statue and gently placed her left hand on her heart and her right hand on top of the flowers Naomi had laid at the feet of Sekhmet's statue.

She then took a deep breath, turned, and looked at us all.

"Dear sisters, I know what I did. I created a curse, a curse to rule over the birth choices of others in this temple... to rise as the pharaoh's favourite and have my children rule. I thought I did this for their safety as this was not a safe place, and many plots were created between the women here. The harem conspiracy was our story and fate.

"In the end, however, my children were all poisoned or doomed to death, and I was lost. I wandered out to the Nile and drowned myself. For lifetimes and now this lifetime, I have had many miscarriages. Many years ago, I stopped bleeding, and my doctors told me I would never have a child, and this again broke my heart. I was only twenty-eight years old.

"I succeeded in so many things, but my ultimate goal was to be a mother. My life has not been fulfilled, and now it is beyond too late."

Alice stepped back into the circle, and Naomi and Lucinda gently walked Laura back to sit down. I had never thought about why she had never had children, and now, obviously, it was too late. Alice came out of trance and began to do the ritual and offering to the statue, and I felt a divine energy flow around this small room and was moved to speak.

"I hereby call forward the honour of the Gods.

That they may speak in truth, and we may act with honour and integrity.

This temple is the holder of strength and wisdom that have been lost in lies and deception.

May this now be healed and the divinity of this sacred space be restored."

The chamber became silent as I saw the timelines shift and how this shrine had been a powerful location for working between the worlds. Something struck me that a whole other temple site was behind this shrine of Sekhmet.

Something very dark indeed. But there was no time for this. We were being ushered out, and I was trying to make mental notes for my journal while Alice performed a closing ritual.

As we left, I retrieved my journal and began to jot down the words. I could see the others looking at me, but no, I needed to document and be the scribe; otherwise, we would all forget.

"It's okay, I had my voice recorder," whispered Naomi to me. "I hope that's okay. Anna, I'll give this to you as I think your book is beginning to come through, and you should tell our story. I always thought I would write this, but no, this is your purpose," she smiled.

"I will help," Lucas said, coming over to us and holding my hand.

I had a flash of my dream and remembered my father and mother. I still had to clear this story. I wanted to run to Laura and tell her she had also been responsible for the murder of my mother and father in a past life and that I had been placed at risk... that she had summoned the Priests of Unal and worked with the Scorpion Queen, but as I looked at her with her head hung down in shame, I felt nothing but compassion. I wondered if the dream was really true. But maybe that was me trying to avoid something.

I could see everyone was ready to leave, but I knew our work was not yet finished. So I walked over to her.

"Oh, Anna, I am afraid I opened up a dark energy," she said.

I was reminded of how kind Laura had been, in truth, a catalyst for my spiritual awakening. Like a fairy godmother giving me a place to stay in her Yorkshire home when my home was flooded and supporting me after news of my mother's death. She felt more like a caring family member than my birth parents.

"Laura, that was another time, but I have to ask you something," I said. I was distracted by the noises of the guards arguing over the money share of our visit. I looked around the group, and they were all smiling except Laura. She looked distracted, like she wanted to go back inside the shrine for some reason.

"Everyone, it is time to go," said Naomi, and they all began to move quickly.

All except Laura and me. Laura seemed in a trance and turned around. I watched as she went back to the shrine, and I followed her. The guards said nothing but simply unlocked the doors again. I watched as she went to the Sekhmet statue and placed her hands together in prayer.

"Se al et an ke shan," she whispered. Then, with her left hand, she touched her third eye and knelt down to touch the foot placed forward on the statue. "Thank you, my sister," she said, then turned and saw me standing.

"Laura, what is behind this shrine?"

Laura went over and placed her hand on the back wall. She looked at me, and her eyes were wide, like in a trance. "The Priests of Amun held a secret sanctuary located behind this wall, but it was not for the God Amun but for the worship of Set." Her voice was hissing.

She began pulling her hands as if she were bound and being pulled into the wall.

"Anna, help! Stop this," she cried out.

I was helpless. I watched as she struggled, and I began to see that she, like others before and after her, had been drawn to the dark side of Set and other dark energies. Sekhmet was the gatekeeper and the protection. She was the guardian. I could not reach Laura and began to panic. I saw Laura shift into her past life. This was a test in the game. I felt the presence of another in the room. I turned and looked at her.

I had seen her in a vision, but could not remember when. Her eyes flashed gold, which reminded me of Cleopatra, but she was different.

"Tell them what you see," she commanded.

"You are in the game." Her voice grew louder. *"Play your hand, girl."*

"If this is the game, I demand justice," I called out. "I play my soul for her soul. I offer forgiveness for the loss of an oracle, my mother, and a guardian my father."

"Lord Set, you held power over this temple and allowed the darkness to enter from this portal. I place karma at your doorway and on your priests. This woman is an innocent and seeks atonement, and as an oracle, I lay this at your door."

Laura froze as if the energies of Set had been shocked to have been seen. I turned back to see the gold-eyed woman, but she was gone. At that moment, I saw Lucas race back into the chamber and hand me a scroll and scarab.

"Protection, Anna, use them," he said, his voice hoarse from running.

I held the Scroll and Scarab of Protection in my hands and remembered a symbol from the black book. It was a triangle with a circle within it. I began to draw the symbol in the air with the scroll and scarab, and Lucas began to recite a verse from the Bible.

"The LORD is my shepherd. I shall not be in want. He restores my soul. He guides me in paths of righteousness for his name's sake. Even though I walk through the valley of the shadow of death, I will fear no evil, for you are with me; your rod and your staff, they comfort me."

I watched as the binding cords began to dissolve around Laura's hands, and she was able to step back. Slowly, my actions ended, and Lucas and I stood looking at each other. I saw us back in ancient times, more ancient than Egypt. We had done this work before. Lucinda appeared at the chamber door entrance.

"Anna, hurry, we must go," she insisted.

I felt slightly blind as we walked out of the small temple shrine, the sun was so bright now.

"We will carry on and catch you up," announced Lucas. "Tell everyone to meet for the purification before the Holy of Holies." Lucinda nodded and began to run back to the group.

I felt like I was in slow motion. I had played my soul for hers. On one hand, I had my work ahead of me, but watching Laura slowly slide down the wall outside the shrine, I questioned myself for all my lifetimes. Should I stay and return to her or carry on? What had I truly played, but at the same time, what had I healed?

Suddenly, Laura's eyes met mine. She smiled and nodded, and it was clear she was free. I turned back to the path, grabbed Lucas by the hand, and we ran forward to meet the group.

I ran, hoping to escape the game I was now contracted to. That scared me more. We walked as a group now, to the large lake in the center of the temple that was supposed to purify us. Rashida had rejoined us.

"I have to say, Lucinda, it does not look too healthy today, and I'm hoping we don't have to drink from this again," the Contessa complained.

"No," Lucinda smiled, "the lake only purifies and clears our hearts and thoughts."

The Contessa smiled at Lesley and beckoned to Lucas. "It's our time," she smiled at them.

Lesley nodded and stepped in front of us. Lucas came forward, and they joined hands. I saw them as friends, priests, and priestesses connected to each other in this temple, both students and teachers. This was now the Tutankhamun timeline, and it was something calmer and gentler than we had just experienced.

"Ladies," spoke Lucas, "please create your word of sacred intention and then raise your hand and draw the word onto the water." We all stood, and in silence, we traced the words.

"Now call out your word."

I could hear all the positive words, such as love, peace, and harmony. My word was grace. This was perhaps not such a scary place after all.

"Now to the Sacred Mother Scarab. We will walk around her for the blessings of the divine mother," said the Contessa. She seemed to have come awake and was not hiding in the shadows.

I turned to see a large stone scarab placed on a stone altar with tourists walking around, and we joined the formation. Laura was suddenly behind me and full of energy... a total surprise... after her ordeal.

"We go around for good luck, seven times for marriage and nine times for pregnancy, just in case that's your wish," she winked at me.

I walked slowly. I did not even have a boyfriend, so I did not wish to burden the scarab with the heavy-lifting task of shifting me out of my spinster destiny.

"Now that is complete, can we stop before our Holy of Holies visit?" said Naomi, pointing to the small coffee shop.

Everyone agreed.

"And we can see the obelisk to start the activation from the coffee shop," she called out as she plopped down in a chair and ordered a mint tea.

Spiritual multi-tasking was perfectly demonstrated here.

We all sat down and ordered an array of drinks. The poor waiter was confused by the tea order, but I was used to this by now.

"The tea with the mint?"

"No, English tea."

"With the mint?"

"No, with the milk."

This could go on for days, so I looked at Rashida. She spoke in Arabic to instruct that we wanted black tea with sides of lemon, mint, and milk.

Once the tea had arrived, Naomi pointed up the obelisk. "Queen Hatshepsut created this famous landmark. She was a powerful ruler and had full knowledge of the Akashic Records and how to work with the powerful ley lines. Many of the pharaohs created these as living records, but also to mark the power points of energy. And now many of them are located around the world. Located in places connected to major times in history."

"Like historic markers?" asked Alexandria.

"Yes," she nodded, "to help us remember."

The others asked many questions, and I simply looked up, stared, and marvelled at how something so tall could have been created from one piece of stone all those thousands of years ago.

At that moment, I was taken to a vision of the past and saw many scribes sitting in front of this stone column. As I saw the light hitting the stone, it began to vibrate. I looked across the lake, and to my surprise, more priests in white were walking towards us.

"Did you see that?" I whispered to Lucinda, sitting next to me.

She shook her head.

Naomi continued to talk about the famous obelisks in London, Paris, and New York. Lesley shared how she was able to see the one in New York. The Contessa shared about the one in Paris, and Alice went into detail about the one in London. I watched as the Contessa was about to tell another story, but she was distracted by something.

"*Yallah, yallah,*" called out the Contessa. "We must hurry—the sun will fade." I looked up to see some very strange dark clouds that had appeared out of nowhere. I was also struck that coming from the far side of the lake was a procession of priests. I walked quickly and caught up to the Contessa.

"Do you see them?" she asked quietly.

"I saw the scribe priests," I answered.

"Yes, very good. They walked from Luxor temple this morning and are now coming with us to reconnect the holy chamber."

We moved back to the hypostyle hall, and I thought we were returning to the original large white stone when the Contessa turned right. We all lined up behind her. We moved slowly and silently towards what looked like another shrine and stone altar right in the center of the complex. We entered the stone chamber and circled around the holy of holies. This time, Naomi called out a high-pitched sound. It was as if the whole temple stopped in time and began to vibrate. The Contessa waved her hand, and from nowhere, two private guards appeared from the side with a red rope to section off this part as a private stand and to seal the shrine from tourists.

Lucinda looked at me and smiled. She pointed to Contessa and said, "She certainly has friends in high places."

As we walked into this small shrine, there was a large opening at the back and a large stone altar that was rectangular in shape. The energy of the stone was so powerful that I began to sway. Everyone took their places, making a circle around the altar.

The Contessa began to speak quickly, and I was unsure of the words. I saw her then as a female in a white robe and tall headdress. One hand held a tall golden staff, and the other hand she had placed onto the altar. I reached my hand out to do the same.

"No, Anna," called Lucinda, but it was too late, and my hand was now locked onto the stone surface.

I tried to move to lift it, but the force was like a magnet. For a moment, I began to panic.

Everyone was staring at me. But the ritual had started. I was doing so well, and now I would be in trouble. But before I could let that thought settle, I found myself flying all over Egypt.

I was at the Pyramids of Giza.

Now Philae, now Edfu.

I could hear lots of voices, and I felt like I was drowning. So many voices and many prayers and chants. A voice came through me.

"Philae is falling. The end is coming. Rome is marching, and even the Alexandrian army cannot save us. The oracles are hiding, and the inner sanctums of the temples are being looted and burnt."

I was sobbing, as was Naomi. I broke from my trance and grabbed back my hand. I felt as though fire had passed through me. I looked around the circle and was surprised to see our guide, Rashida, had joined our circle.

"Anna, put your hand back in place, and Lucas, bring forward the Scarab and Scroll of Light and Shadow," commanded Alice.

I did as she asked, and all eyes stared at me.

"The Book of Keys." The Contessa held out her hand, and although my soul said no, I reached into my bag and placed it on the altar.

At this, an electrical current ran through the chamber, and I saw it run to the obelisks and the large white stone at the entrance.

Then, I watched as Lesley placed both her hands upon the altar. This seemed to create a new, even more powerful energy.

"I call forward the ancestors of my birth," she called out.

"My mother Nefertiti and my father Akhenaten... the ones of true faith. Through the Scroll and Scarab of Light and Shadow, I renounce the curse that holds my soul, which had held me bound and shattered the truth and integrity of this temple. May all the lines be restored from when we removed them to find the new promised land. May they now be returned."

"It's working," said Emilee. As we thought, the ley lines were being repaired.

"Lucinda, I will link to Luxor, and you bring forward Dendara," Lesley called.

"I bring Abydos," called Laura.

"I have Edfu," said Naomi.

"And I have Kom Ombo," called Lucas.

"Hatshepsut Temple is coming through me," said Alexandria.

"I now have Abu Simbel," said Emilee.

"I have Karnak," called the Contessa.

"I have Philae," I called.

"Alice, can you assist to Giza?" I looked for Alice, but for some reason, she had gone to a higher plane and dimension. I knew she could run these lines to the Pyramids and the Sphinx. But for some reason, she would not or could not. I looked at Lucas.

"She will have a reason." I looked at the Contessa. She said nothing. But I knew she was not happy.

For many moments, we held our space, running the energy, and many of the timelines flashed in front of me. I tried to link the Pyramids and Sphinx, but instead, the face of a lion rose in front of me and shouted.

"It is forbidden. How dare you!"

I almost fell over. I could not make sense of this. I had performed all that was asked of me, and now I was being blocked.

I then saw the image I had been dreading since we arrived—the fall of Philae. I realised this had also opened the story to this chamber and our group of Oracles. I feared that the fall would happen again and that I would be responsible. That was my true fear, and what I felt was my darkness, and I wondered how I could find the light.

I stopped running energy and held back as everyone else reconnected. It was as if I could feel and sense everything. Was I the only one who saw danger? Time stood still, and I began to see the true corruption of this temple. Many Akashic Records were open. But one theme stood out clearer and louder than anything else. I was then aware of another powerful energy. A Queen's energy had entered the chamber. Tall, slim, and beautiful, I knew her from my dream. She was the woman who argued with the young man in the desert.

She smiled as she walked towards me. *"Greetings, dear Anna."*

"You are Nefertiti."

She smiled.

"What is it we are really doing here?" I asked.

She pointed to our group. I nodded.

"Ah, this is a re-enactment of another time," she responded.

"How so?" I asked.

"Let me tell you... During the reign of Amenhotep III, Egypt lived in a golden age. He and his wife were great rulers and created many cities that will be discovered during your lifetime. They had their son Amenhotep IV, and as a young man, he would wander through these temple sites and speak with the elders and the wisdom keepers.

"He had a sister, Princess Sitamun, and you see her here. You know her as Naomi. He and his sister would visit with the oracles and study their prophecies. The Priests of Amun ruled here. They were the true protectors but could be corrupted."

She pointed outside, and I saw the priests who had smiled at me on my arrival. Now, their eyes were black, and they looked at me with anger.

"One prophecy was that a royal princess would emerge, and Amenhotep IV could build a golden age with her. I was from lands not far away, you had to travel through the land you now know as the holy lands, and my family or tribe had visited many islands throughout the Mediterranean. It was said we were descended from the original Atlanteans, and ours was a strong bloodline of both warrior and ascended consciousness. When I met the young Amenhotep, I knew he was the one for me.

"Ours was a love match, and we created many ceremonies to the gods to ask for guidance. We had a vision one night during the festivals when we called the oracles to help channel the future. You see them here." She pointed to Emilee, Lucinda, and Alice.

"But Thebes, now Luxor, was becoming an ever-dangerous place. My husband and I began to fashion ourselves in a very new and different way, and this caused many disagreements, especially when he changed his name to Akhenaten. A High Priest of Amun was aware of this, and he foresaw danger; he did a deal with those of the darkness who commanded the

Brothers of Set. You encountered them at the shrine of Sekhmet. We did not know how he achieved this, but we suspect he used many of our scrolls and scarabs.

"One day, we found a scorpion nest in the chambers of our children, and we knew we had a curse on our relationship only to have female children. We sought the advice of the Oracle of Siwa."

"And you were told to go forth into the desert, where the sun shines so high it turns the sand to crystalline and would also turn you all to luminous light," I said.

"Yes," she smiled. *"You remember. Siwa was the original temple for the oracles and their wisdom. We had a sacred temple to Amun that was not corrupted. Our Amun Priests stayed true.*

"So," she continued. *"We sent out scouts, and they came back with the location of Armana. We began to build a city of Light. Many of those here in Karnak Temple turned against us, and there was great sorrow when we left."*

"It was the same as the fall of Atlantis," I said. *"Those who left and those who were left behind."*

She nodded.

"A grave mistake on all pathways. We created a utopia for our family but forgot about our sacred promise to the land of Egypt and the mother Nile. The Gods brought a great vengeance. For years, the temples fell into chaos. The High priest of Amun," she pointed to the Contessa, who had commanded the rituals.

"But as she began to lose power, the oracles, Alice, Emilee and Lucinda, were forced to cast spells as rituals. Before long, the dark forces had gathered a great army. They came to our golden city, and a war was staged. The children and I were brought back to Luxor, and my husband's fate was a tragic one. By this time, my husband did have a son; His mother

was a priestess of Isis but not of royal blood. My daughter Ankhesenamun, who would be his wife, was of highborn lineage, and we struck a deal that if we returned and followed the old religion, they would let us live." She pointed to Lesley.

"When we returned, the temples were in chaos, and many of the vaults of gold and food had been looted. Many of the priestesses and oracles had lost their way and had either gone insane or died at the hands of those in power who had not resonated with their messages. I took to ruling for a while to bring balance and sent messages to all the temples and the high priestesses to support me. No responses ever came back.

"I decided to pray to the goddess Sekhmet, and in my time, we had a whole row of her statues in a larger complex than you see now. I was shown to connect to the scrolls and scarabs you have in your collection. Truth and Integrity were the first ones to be restored. We were unaware it had been used against others to reveal their secrets. The Oracle..." she pointed to the Emilee, "...had visited me in my chambers in secret one night, and she told me of a great game that many of the queens had played and that if I could collect all the pieces, it would recreate such a power my family would be safe. I tried, but sadly, I sought to include my daughter and son-in-law.

"We were persuaded to enlist the High Priest of Amun and unleash the Priests of Unal back into our world to have power against the Priests and the army that waited at our door. When we reenacted the ceremony of the temple stone as you are doing here, it was filled with darkness. My daughter, the one you see as your friend Lesley, conjured up something so powerful and dark it overtook her and took the lives of her children. She is now forever bound to walk in lives of light and shadow, she faced this trial many times in her lives and faces it again here now," she said.

"So, what can we do now? I want to help," I said.

"Set my family free, Anna." Then she left.

I began to see the lines of broken energy running through the high altar stone and then I moved behind each person, gently repositioning their hands to affect the change. As I re-took my place, I saw the faces of the past, and I knew that adjusting each one had a major effect on the karma they carried. I looked at Alice as she held the Scroll and Scarab of the Truth and Integrity. I saw again how this had been taken from her in the past.

I watched as all the souls linked to this fate lifted up like floating ghosts. A karmic constellation. I felt the presence of the woman from the shrine of Sekhmet behind me.

"Anna, speak the words."

Telepathically, I began.

"Oh, Isis Lady of Light, I ask thee be present. Oh, Ma'at, our sister of judgement, allow these souls to see their actions in a dream. Father Osiris, grant us all safe passage and may our contracts to brother Set be released. That golden age has passed, as many others have, and another timeline is approaching. Let us complete this work."

I began to see the ghost-like images fade like sand falling away. I had no idea we were all linked in this timeline. How had I not seen this with Isis? She must have known. But perhaps not. I heard the woman behind me utter her prayer and then disappear. As I looked up, I was back in my normal reality. The woman was gone. Now, it was returned and restored. Finally, I felt it could be finished. But it felt all too easy.

I watched as everyone calmed their energy, and I checked that the links to this ancient temple transmitter were rewired and restored. I looked at Naomi; it was as if she knew, and I watched as she drew an infinity symbol in the air above the altar to protect the portal. Then, I gathered my book. No one said anything. It was strange, no closing ritual, as we all seemed in our own worlds. I wondered what everyone else had seen or felt, but I knew I had done what was required of me. Without a word, I left the shrine and sat on the wall outside.

"We will be returning to the bus now," Rashida said, and without a word, everyone began to leave.

"I will stay with Anna," said Naomi, and she sat down with me. I did not look at the other women, but as they left, Lucinda winked at me, and even Lesley nodded.

Naomi looked at Rashida and smiled. "I will bring Anna back. She and I are quite safe."

"Anna, let's take a walk." She linked arms with me.

We walked out past the obelisk and the lake.

"You saw the end, didn't you?" she asked.

"The temples falling... yes, I did. But I thought that was clear and forgotten once you and Isis had been reunited. I saw many things in that moment. That stone, that chamber, and altar, it was so powerful. I am almost afraid that in reuniting the temples, we may have caused more harm than good."

Naomi motioned to sit down. "Here, Anna," she said. We were safe and alone.

"I shall explain this place," she began. "Many of the temples have holy altars. Remember Edfu and Philae?"

Like I could forget. "Yes," I said.

"They were places where the high priests and priestesses spoke to the gods. The stone we just touched, the altar here, it connected them all," she said.

"Like an ancient telephone," I laughed.

"Yes, this was why this was such a powerful political temple. The high priest and priestess knew everyone's secrets because the oracles had access to the information. They would open and close the portals as they saw fit, or in later times as they were commanded. The oracles were here many lifetimes ago. The last oracle here was helpless to support the other temples when the Romans began moving into the sanctuaries."

I felt a shiver as she said the last oracle. I wondered if that had been the woman in the Sekhmet chamber who had helped me with Laura and the one who had just stood behind me. I got a "yes" response in my body.

"During the time of Cleopatra?" I asked.

Naomi nodded.

I thought about sharing my Nefertiti story but decided to wait. Today, we had started a chain of reconnection from the Akhenaten timeline, but in my heart, I knew it was not so simple with many obstacles in our way. But I reminded myself I had waited all my life for the opportunity to return to this. If I was in the game like these Queens, I needed to understand the rules.

"Did I ruin the altar experience?" I was genuinely sorry.

"Absolutely not." Naomi shook her head. "You confirmed what we had always wondered about—that the temples were all linked somehow."

"Yes, and the Oracles of Egypt talked to each other," I offered. "But I also heard what I thought to be the high priests and priestesses."

She laughed. "Yes, you did, but that did not mean that they communicated with each other. They communicate directly with you. The oracles did, telepathically, and we knew everyone's business. This is what secured our future. It kept us all safe."

"And what do you know of the purpose of the scarabs and scrolls now?" I whispered.

I could still hear the mantra in my head that perhaps someone was listening.

"I know they are sacred, and we all lived in harmony for a while as they were spread across the kingdom and watched over by the most holy and respected. It is said they came from the Oracle of Atlantis and were brought to Egypt to recreate the ancient and magical Atlantean realm. Powerful tools and teachings could give someone the power of life and death. Together, they create an energy capable of amazing things. I want to show you something, Anna."

She reached into her bag and began to search around.

"My coin. I'm sure I brought it with me... it's been with me everywhere. It's from the Ptolemy family and buys me safe passage anywhere in Egypt." She reached into her bag.

"No! It's gone!"

"Are you sure? Check the bag again," I said.

"No, it's always in this pouch... it's my medicine."

Of course Naomi would have currency as a medicine.

"I rarely remove it from the bag, so I never thought to check.

"That coin, Anna. I was told by the healer who gave it to me 'to pay the ferryman'—whatever that means. To barter for one soul or another. Anna, did you barter for a soul?"

I nodded... "Mine for Laura." Her eyes were wide.

We looked at each other, and we instantly knew what it meant. Either the coin was spent, or I still owed the Priest of Set. With that, Naomi and I began a swift return to the hotel.

☥

The Winter Palace felt like a safe fortress as we raced up the steps, and as Naomi ran to find Lesley, I departed and went to my room. I lifted my suitcase and began to go through my belongings. I was afraid that perhaps I was missing something. Did we have a thief? I hoped not. Something told me it was only a matter of time before whoever this was would return and try to claim what was most sacred and holy to me and all the oracles.

I closed the suitcase slowly as everything seemed to be in order, put everything away, and freshened up. But I could not settle and so made my way towards the room where the Contessa was staying. I could already hear the hysteria, and I knew I was not about to make things any better. To my surprise, Lucas was heading down the corridor.

"Anna, Anna, over here," he beckoned me. Laura is having a re-birthing with Lucinda, Emily, and the Contessa."

"That does not sound fun." I was alarmed. Poor Laura. The sweetest one among us.

"No, it's not. They are taking her soul back to the original source to release all the curses of the years. Maybe best to leave them for a while."

"But we may want to talk about Alice," he said.

"She's been out by the swimming pool since we got back, and I am not sure why..."

"Let's go," I said. It was not like Alice to lose composure. I was also confused by her behaviour at the high altar. I would have thought the Pyramids and Sphinx were integral at this time, but she had resisted.

We hurried down the stairs to the outdoor area. We passed Lesley and Naomi having tea on the terrace. Naomi looked very distressed as Lesley tried to pacify her. This coin obviously had great significance.

I slowly walked past and heard the conversation thread about the theft Naomi was sure had happened with her ancient coin. They both stopped abruptly when they saw me. Lesley smiled as if there was no issue, but once again, another secret was stirring.

"Anna, we leave at 6 p.m. today. It's now nearly 3 p.m.," Lesley called out.

I looked at Lucas. “I don’t suppose we can have some late lunch at the same time? My coffee shop sandwich really did not hit the spot.”

He laughed. “It never does. Okay, you go find her, and I’ll get the table and order.”

We both set off searching for our target, and I found Alice sitting on the grass. She was easy to spot, sitting alone with a faraway gaze.

“Alice.” I sat down next to her.

“I could not make the link, Anna. I could not bring the Pyramids and Sphinx into focus. I saw the large face of the lion, and I suddenly felt myself sinking. I promised Isis I would be strong, but I am ashamed that I could not hold the line and energy. Anna, I think I failed again. I lost Oracle sisters before, and I prayed this time would be different.”

“I saw the losses, and the lion, too,” I said.

“You saw it? You never said...”

“I know; I was afraid, too. Alice, I have seen so many things so far and have been unable to share them.”

She smiled and took my hand. “Of course you have, my dear. Now, we must work out what step to take next. Did the Queen Nefertiti come to you today?” She turned to look at me directly.

I nodded. “Nefertiti, yes, she told me the story of her rise and fall.”

“So sad,” she shook her head.

“But not too sad. She was a very clever one, and for all the time we were in Armana in the new city, she was in contact with Thebes and the High Priest of Amun. She had been warned by the Oracles of Karnak that the new city that Akhenaten was creating may not be sustainable, so she worked both worlds.”

“She thought that was the game to play,” I said.

"Anna, do you remember her famous bust of her in the Berlin museum in Germany?"

I nodded.

"Well, there were two made. One was in Armana and the other in Karnak Temple. They worked like a telephone and would come alive in her image, and she could speak into the one in Armana, and the High Priest of Amun would hear her message in his chambers. But this was dark magic, and when the army arrived, the general brought the bust statue back to her in Armana. He had the power over her. That was one of the deciding factors why she came back with the royal children. She did not want anyone to know her motives or actions. The busts were buried and discovered many years ago. Every time I see them, I am reminded of their true purpose and what they cost us," Alice said.

"So if you sensed she was present, were you fearful?" I asked.

She replied, nodding. "This was a powerful timeline, and Nefertiti was a master of playing both sides of the battle for survival. I think the Pyramids and Sphinx will open, but not until we as a group are stable and many things have cleared. I just came past the Contessa's room, and it certainly was not stable."

"Alice, I thought I saw the Contessa as the High Priest of Amun. Was I correct? But she showed no emotion or connection to that today."

"Well, either she is hiding it, or you are being tricked." Her response shocked me.

I was not often wrong, but reading this incorrectly could mean facing a massive failure on my part by bringing it into our circle.

"Yes, I have been avoiding that drama," she nodded. I was relieved she did not pick up on more.

"So, will you join Lucas and me for something to eat? He was concerned for you and came to find me."

She smiled. "Of course."

We made our way to the table where Lucas had laid a banquet, lentil soups, pots of tea, French fries and pita bread.

He smiled at Alice, "For once, let's look after you. I feel a few days of crazy coming, and my tarot cards say as much."

"Alice, tonight is Luxor Temple." Lucas was looking at her with fear on his face.

"Yes, but he won't come when we are in the group," she replied.

"Who won't come?" I asked.

There was a long pause as if they did not know how to break the news.

"Alexander," she looked at me. "That's also why I wish to keep a very low profile in this next temple."

"Luxor was the temple where Alexander the Great took his initiation and had his vision moment where he saw himself as a living God."

"But that's not good. Will he not challenge you, Alice?" I was alarmed.

"No," she said. "For I have the blessing of Seshat and Thoth. They reside in Luxor Temple, and they will protect us, especially you and me, Anna. Seshat was one of the Atlantean Oracles and Akashic Records readers."

I wanted to listen, but Lucas was already tapping his watch.

"Ladies, it's 4:30 p.m. We need to prepare, and I want to do a tarot reading for myself before we go."

Luxor Temple at Sunset

I was amazed at how the light changed on the temple

walls of Luxor around sunset. Rashida secured us a private visit to the Luxor temple that evening. As we stood for a group photo at the temple entrance, I could see the sun slowly moving, ready to leave us for the day.

I then understood what it was like to see the sun fall behind the mountain range and how the ancient Egyptians saw this as the afterworld, hence the Valley of the Kings and Queens being stationed on that western side where Ra, the Sun God, went to sleep.

The last of the visitors were leaving, and we moved slowly towards the large entrance statues. As the sunset lights hit them, I felt them waking and stirring. It was a similar building to Karnak, but the walls looked higher. The temple was guarded by large statues of Pharaohs that looked 60 feet tall. Massive and intimidating. I looked behind us further back into the distance and turned to Naomi.

"But this would have been the main entrance," I said, pointing across from us to the area leading to the temple, where a few small sphinx-posed ram statues of the god Khnum sat.

She smiled, and Emilee came over. "You remember, Anna," she said.

"Yes," Naomi nodded. "That over there was the sacred path to Karnak."

"We stayed here in this Temple of Luxor to prepare, and then each morning at sunrise, we made the procession to the Karnak Temple and then returned home at sunset."

I felt a beautiful calmness come over me and knew I had nothing to fear in this temple. We all made our way slowly and silently into the first section of the temple. Lucas was in the front, and just seeing him enter this temple, I could see an elegant and gracious priest. He turned to me and smiled.

"Is this not the most beautiful? My tarot card today was

the Star." He was pure radiant light.

The walls were now fading into the dark with the pink light, and the electrical lights were beginning to come on, which allowed us to make our way safely, but I tried to remember how this must have been in ancient times with oil lamps. I felt I was in a magical dream and began to see the temple restore itself in front of me.

We were about to walk forward into the main corridor from the small courtyard, moving past a large, seated statue of a man on the right side of the entryway. I heard a loud voice saying, "Stop," and I turned to see who had joined the group.

But no one was speaking.

"Stop." The voice boomed out again.

I was looking around when my gaze fell back upon an enormous statue of what I now assumed was a pharaoh sitting to my right. I looked up at his face and swore his eyes were alive, looking down at me. Rashida came up next to me.

"Ramses II, a great Pharaoh and King," she said, pointing to the large statue.

I moved around in front of him and stood looking up into his eyes. I thought they blinked, and I remember feeling this energy before.

"*Use the key child*" was the next message.

"*Unlock the secret*" was the following one.

"*They are awaiting you.*"

Lucas came behind me with Laura.

"Anna, what is it?"

"He spoke," I whispered.

"What did Ramses say?" Laura asked.

"He told me to find the secret and to use the key, and they are awaiting me," I replied.

"I know a secret," said Emilee. She came over to us, raised her hand towards the statue, then put her hands together and began to pray. Her mouth moved, but we heard no words.

"It is now unlocked for you, Anna. You may go around the back of the statue."

I hardly understood what she meant.

"Lucas, you will need the torch," she said, "and Laura, hold the gateway open, please, by standing in front of the statue."

I followed her around the statue, still unable to understand, as all I could see was a stone wall.

"Lucas, shine the torch upon the back of the statue," Emilee called.

He did as asked, and there, to my surprise, were the most exquisite carved reliefs of Thoth and Seshat.

Standing facing each other and standing at least six feet tall, these masters revealed themselves. Emilee beckoned for me to stand and climb onto the rock at the base and place both my hands upon their feet. Seshat stood wearing her robe of animal print with the star above her head. She looked down at me and smiled.

"We have been waiting for you, dear one."

She held a staff in her hand, and Emilee came over and began to reach up and gently touch her feet. It was as if she was full of light.

"We have to sometimes wake them up," she laughed, pointing to the image across from Seshat.

Thoth, displayed as an ibis with his pen in hand, took down the sacred message and brought it forward from the Seshat. And right then and there, on the high wall next to us, sat the baboon and ibis, my protectors from my dream.

"You see," Emilee pointed, "they worked together in

balance. Her the channel, and he the scribe. Now, Lucas, come and stand under Thoth, and Anna, stand under Seshat. I know it's a tight squeeze, but we are family, remember."

"Now, Anna, it is time," she said, taking both my hands and placing them on the statue near the feet. "Oh, Lady Seshat and my Lord Thoth receive this initiate with love and grace. Open with her the realms that cannot be seen or heard and allow her to channel the messages from the children of light. Her words be sacred, and her thoughts be pure. And so it is."

I had closed my eyes, but I could see the images of many others standing with this mastery and alchemy. It was as if I could see from the beginning of time and even glimpse the future.

"Are you seeing, Anna?" whispered Emilee.

"Now you, Lucas."

She recited the same words, and I watched as he transformed into pure light.

"Yes, I'm seeing, and it's amazing. I see everything, a true priest of Thoth."

"Then my work tonight is complete," she laughed.

She began to say a loud OM sound, and then I felt myself complete and stood back. I was not too steady and had to catch my balance. I turned to leave the small area back into the temple courtyard, and at the side stood Lucinda.

"Isis knew it. We all knew it," she said.

"Knew what?" I quizzed.

Lucinda held out her hand to help me down and led me into an amazing open courtyard in the center of the temple. As we stood in the center, I began to feel the whole courtyard fill with the energy of priests and priestesses.

"You see them?" she asked.

"I do. They are so beautiful."

"Yes, we were," the Contessa said, joining us. Then Alice and Laura. Lesley stood on the other side, and Emilee was nearby.

Naomi and Lucas now stood in the centre, and Alexandria performed a ceremony around them. First, she had them face each other and hold hands. Then she walked clockwise around them. Everyone stood still and waited until she welcomed us forward. We then made a circle around the three of them.

Alexandria took from her pocket a small bottle of oil and, taking her left index finger went from person to person placing the oil delicately onto their third eye. "Slowly breathe, my friends. Take in the activation."

She smiled as she reached me. "Your sacred time is coming."

Then she moved to Naomi and Lucas and began first to do some unbinding ritual, and I began to see all their lives where they had been married, brother, sister, father, mother, and even enemies.

"You two are soul mates bound on this Earth plane," said Alexandria.

"Your lives have started and ended together. Now you are both free."

I watched as they looked at each other, and there was such love and compassion, but also a deep understanding and a friendship that I had never experienced with another person. I had thought soul mates were star-crossed lovers of destiny, but now I witnessed something far more beautiful. The ceremony ended, and we all stood back and looked up at the stars, who were now beginning to join us.

"What was this place?" I looked at Lucinda. She smiled at me.

Lucinda spoke, "In our ancient times, Luxor Temple

was a sacred space of sacred union and the worlds and realms for magic. We were called upon by the gods and the kings at the same time, and we kept everything in balance. But not everyone could be here; it was so special and a true place of heaven on Earth. Here, we lost the darkness and only felt the light. Here, we were untouchable."

I took a deep breath in.

Untouchable, what must that be like?

I began to see the ghosts dancing. I could smell the incense and found myself captivated by this sense of love and beauty.

"We have awoken the spirits again, Anna," said Lucinda.

"The true union of the Halls of Amenti. The re-balancing has started from our work in Glastonbury, and the balance will be created again."

"I don't understand," I said. Once again, I was the novice.

"Well, this is the work of the ages we have been creating, and Isis and I spent many hours here trying to activate the union. We blessed this place and brought many initiates through, but no one was ever stopped and summoned by Ramses. He always let them pass by, but you, who put the scrolls and scarabs back together again, have begun to add links to the whole story. He seems to trust you."

"It's not just about rebuilding one temple; it's about us all having a chance to remember. All these spirits are dancing; they are linked to our spiritual aspects, and their magic lives on when we remember. This was part of the wisdom of the Halls of Amenti—the doorways to the Earth plane and the afterlife."

"You remembering means we remember." Lucinda took my hand, and we held hands as everyone took a moment to be present in the joy.

When we finished, Rashida said we had thirty minutes of free time to explore. Alice moved towards me and whispered, "Come with me." She led me by the hand to a small inner chamber at the back of the temple, which was about the size of the Holy of Holies in Karnak, but it had an entrance and an exit. It was as if you went through this space to something greater. But I could not sense which was the entry or exit.

This part of the temple felt very familiar.

"Where is the altar, the crystal?" I asked.

"There was a white stone here like the one in the Cairo Museum, the Atlantis one. This linked the temples and allowed us to communicate across Atlantis," Alice paused.

"Anna, you are in a trance? What are you talking about? What white stone?"

I fell silent.

"No one ever talked about this. Anna, what do you know?"

Again, I could not speak.

"Alexander the Great talked of this, and I know the Oracle of Siwa had the power to connect to a sacred white stone. It was said this particular temple humbled Alexander like no other. After his visit, he seemed to have a new respect for the religion and spirituality of Egypt," she said.

"Can you recreate this, Anna?" The Contessa was near me. I wondered how long she had been standing there listening. Something about her request made me uneasy, but Alice seemed okay with her being there, so why should I worry?

"Yes," I said, reaching into my bag and bringing out the black book.

Without any prompting, the rest of the group had found us. I looked at the chamber, black from the soot of fires, and

I began to send the light into the chamber. I was flicking through the book when, to my surprise, Lesley stood beside me, reached into her bag, pulled out a white scarf, and held up a small torch to allow me to read the pages. Alice placed the scarf gently around my shoulders. I turned to a page with many infinity symbols and began to weave them into the air, drawing them into the walls.

"To be the symbols of love and hope, may the sacred union return between ourselves and our souls and may the grace be with us."

Naomi then signalled for us all to join hands and began the chant with the AHH sound. It echoed through the entire chamber, and I closed my eyes and began to see the history of this temple. I saw how it had been in times of grace and beauty, what had happened as the Romans and warriors moved into this area, and finally, how it had been used as housing for the poor before it was cleared and opened to tourists.

And now sacred souls were dancing again. Not souls locked in a halfway-to-heaven space but in a chamber where we could all visit in our astral sleep and celebrate the energy. Then, there was silence as the group sat down and went into meditation.

But not for me. Alice stood up slowly and beckoned. She had one more place for me to visit.

"Now, Anna, one last place for you to visit," she whispered, pointing to an open-air area at the back of the temple. "Surely, you knew this was more than just a place of pillars. This was the education area and living library," she said.

"I'm sorry, what? The living library? But there are no shelves for books."

"No," she said, "a living library. It was started by the

Greeks when they came with Alexander the Great. Wise ones would sit here in this area and channel messages from the Gods."

"Like the inner sanctum?"

"Yes, and then we came to know Serapis Bey, the guardian of this sacred area."

"Like my oracle cards, Ascended Master?"

"Yes, he was a scholar and a teacher. Sit with the energy awhile. I'm going to get the others moving before they become too blissful and ask to stay the night."

I sat very still. It was dark, and I was alone, but I felt no fear.

I was then aware of a man's voice. It was softer and gentler than before.

"We were waiting for you to come," he said, *"but you must have heard this many times of late."*

"I have..." I smiled, "yet it keeps me focused. In a journey when I have no idea how to move forward, this keeps giving me courage and hope."

"Well, thank you. I am here to answer your questions."

"I can ask anything? Will you show yourself? Who are you?" I quizzed him.

"I will remain in the shadows for now," he answered.

"What am I doing? What are we here for?"

"Many things, and I think you are slowly seeing that a chain of events was created in Glastonbury."

"You know of Glastonbury?"

"I do. Your mentor and friend Isis would come and spend many hours with me," he said.

"I miss her," I said.

"She is with you, with us all. Write the sequence of events, Anna. Write the diary," he said. "Start with the ceremony in Glastonbury when you first put the scrolls and scarabs into

the box. They began to reconnect, and when all sixteen pieces were placed in sequence, it sent a message through all the sacred sites in Egypt. It began to wake us all up—we have been asleep for 2000 years. We need to be awoken as many will visit, and they seek to remember and hear who they truly are. Our statues and temples were once living and breathing, but when the temples fell, we retreated and went into a slumber. Your past life mother, Cleopatra knew this. She was helpless and promised to bring the karmic order back one day. When she first rose to power, her first duty was to ride to the major temples to offer rituals, honour the Gods, and reconnect. She took this trip with her sister Arsinoe, a great priestess and Oracle. However, their unity was broken over time, and the invasion by Rome would forever seal the fate."

I felt a heart connection with Cleopatra, but when he said her sister's name. My head spun, and my hands tingled. I had heard that name before. I didn't know her story, but she felt significant.

"But with you and your friends, she can do this again," he continued.

"But that's not my role, is it? My purpose? I don't follow Cleopatra?" I was suddenly back in my body and, for once, alarmed.

"No, no, that is the role of many, but you, my dear, hold the keys to re-open the energy. You will visit many more sacred temples and be mindful of all you open and close. There is one who is close on your heels."

"The Scorpion Queen," I whispered. "Yes, I feel her."

"Yes," he responded. *"She seeks to close the portals and not allow you to open anymore."*

"Is she evil?" I whispered, afraid she might be listening.

"Some would say she wishes to hold the power for herself. She seduces many. But you and your group, when in union, are

a mighty force. She still holds power over the priests of Unal through the energy of Lord Set. Many have sought their power, and they hide in the dark shadows of our temples, corrupting the soul. Like you saw today, the power of Set still lives in dark corners. In these areas of darkness, she feasts."

"So there is a lot more that my friends and I can do?"

"Certainly. You, Anna, are becoming a key master."

"I don't know what that means," I said.

"You just had your initiation with Thoth and Seshat, yes?"

I nodded.

"They master the Halls of Amenti and the Akashic Records of the soul. They have given you this gift. The Book of Keys came back to you. It means you have unlocked your past life and spiritual gifts and are unlocking them for others. It is your spiritual heritage, your lineage, like physical keys to doorways and energy. Imagine that you are surrounded by many rooms. Each has a doorway to insight and information. As an oracle, you would have known how to access this."

"I can do that now," I said.

"Yes, and in time, you will unlock for others, starting with your friends. They have all been called here on the purpose of the soul, and in certain locations and times to come, they will have more access. You will help them understand how to use their sacred keys. Remember how you were shown to unlock and use the keys of Thoth and Seshat? Emilee is also a key master."

"Yes, yes, I placed my hands and heart into the space and just reached out. It can't be that easy... and Emilee did most of the work. Don't I have to run around, burn a candle and recant sacred texts?" I asked.

He laughed gently. *"You could, but this is a great deal of work; a pure intention and a few words can suffice."*

I wished Isis were here. She would know what to do. I looked up to the stars above and held my hands up. "I miss you," I whispered.

"She is here. She is with you, but this is not her work; it is yours," he said.

"Anna," I could hear someone calling my name.

It was Rashida.

"Anna, what are you doing here in the dark? Are you okay?"

"Yes, I'm sorry. Just needed a quiet place."

"I'll let the others know we are ready," she said.

"I must go," I said in a quiet voice. "I'm so glad we met. Perhaps we will meet again."

"Perhaps," he said.

"Perhaps on another trip," I offered.

"Perhaps."

I remembered Naomi's commitments and was not sure I could offer my life to endless journeys.

"Anna, you will bring many people; for each of them, an experience is awaiting, and in turn, you will fulfil your role and purpose. My karma is bound here. Maybe you will help me be free in time."

"Inshallah," I said, "God willing."

I prepared to go. I was sad to leave my new friend.

"But please... you know my name. I do not know yours."

He paused.

"Alexander, Alexander of Macedon," he said.

I was a little shocked, as I had suspected he might be connected to this man, but now here he was and in such a place of calm respect. Not at all like the person Alice had described from her past life—the one who had sought power, calling for the murder of many oracles.

"Well, Alexander, we will see what the Gods bring."

And with that, I left.

I was sad to leave this corner of peace and stillness. To be with this version of Alexander was a calming change to the karmic stories and drama.

I joined the group at the entrance, where Lesley was counting smiling faces. Alice was smiling at me and beckoned me over. "How was your visit?"

"Oh, it was wonderful. I felt like I had a healing in many ways."

I turned to look at the road leaving the temple, a road towards Karnak. It was broken and old, but suddenly, it was as if the lights had gone on, and I saw the row of Sphinx illumined. The path was cleared, and I was walking with a group of others. We were walking towards the town and enroute to Karnak. I looked at Lucinda and Laura. Alice and Emilee had joined us.

"We see it too, my dear," said Alice.

"The trail has opened, and what you are seeing is the future."

"I see us with new people. We are on a sacred trip like this."

"More hearts opening and souls awakening," said Lucas, joining us.

"It's real," said Emilee. "It's happening merci to the gods, and Anna, you will bring them home for the Opet festival that can once again be re-enacted. The festival that we rejoiced in, that linked the Temples of Egypt."

I turned and nodded.

"I'll bring them home." I felt this sacred promise with my entire soul. I had no idea how, but I would bring them all home. The Oracles of Egypt would remember, and the priests and priestesses would know. For some reason, my eyes filled, and I wanted to cry. I turned away, and behind me stood the

Contessa. She placed her hands on my shoulders. I stood very still, but I wanted to run and hide. It was as if she was placing a mantle upon my shoulders that felt heavy—a little too heavy.

☥

As we walked through the Winter Palace hotel lobby, I was weary and wanted to go to bed, but Naomi insisted that I join them in the garden for drinks and snacks.

"Anna, the night Jasmine is awake and waiting."

I smiled and followed.

We all sat at the table and ordered drinks. I decided a celebration was in order and so asked for red wine. Sitting in the gardens of the Winter Palace sipping wine was a long way from Yorkshire. No one that I grew up with would even believe where I was. My mother, I'm sure, would have been proud.

To the lifestyles of the rich and famous.

I sat very quietly, just observing the others. Naomi, Alice, and Lucinda were laughing with Emilee. Alexandria was in deep conversation with Lucas, who was reading her palms. Laura and Lesley were sharing images from their photos on their cameras. The Contessa had retired.

Around 9 p.m., I made my excuses. I knew tomorrow would be a long day with two powerful temples to visit. Something told me that my trip to Luxor had been the calm before the storm. This, I felt, was all about to get very interesting.

I made my way down the corridors. They were wide, and the doors and ceiling looked like they had been made for giants. I began to see others moving around and realised that they were spirits dressed in costumes of old. I felt very strange, so I quickly stepped into my room and double-locked my door.

CHAPTER 22

Sunday, 20 September
Dendara Temple

I awoke really early. It was a relief, as I did not want to be the one everyone was waiting for. Apparently, our bus had to leave in a convoy at 7 a.m.

"Nothing to fear," said Lesley, as it was the security afforded to all the tourists.

Those who had stayed up late made their way onto the bus slowly and looked a little fragile, and even Naomi was not looking her typical glamourous self.

Luxor Temple had been hypnotic, and I wondered if the Priests and Priestesses of Luxor held celebrations each evening as we all slept. It had felt that way, and now perhaps our group was feeling the aftereffects. A spiritual hangover? Or was it the Egyptian wine?

"Party time, princess," I said, standing in line, all fresh-faced, showered, and groomed.

Naomi pulled down her dark sunglasses to reveal her bloodshot eyes.

"You would think," her voice was hoarse.

"Laura had a full psychic attack last night, and it took me, Lucas, and Lucinda to clear it. A very nasty little entity. We sent it back to the museum, and I will deal with it later."

She nodded to Lucinda, who was boarding and covered, or should I say veiled from head to foot, in baggy clothes and scarves. Lucas appeared unshaven and was still wearing last night's clothes. He carried a hotel pillow and quilt.

"Here, Lucas," said Lesley, handing him a bag from the hotel gift shop.

"Thanks, Lesley," he said. "I appreciate it."

Laura was last to appear, and she looked clear and refreshed. She came over to me. "Anna... last night," she said, as if she were apologising.

"We won't talk of this," I smiled. Isis once told me that one person in the group sometimes takes the "hit" for everyone else.

"And look at you—you look amazing," I said.

"Maybe on the outside. That's my boarding school training. As a child, I was taught how to cope with very little sleep. I feel I've been on alert all my life."

Then she hugged me, "I am so glad you're here," she said.

Laura was my elder, and I respected her very much. But it was as if she was on a rejuvenation program and felt like a best friend. Did she have a spiritual secret to turn back time?

Finally, everyone had boarded the bus, and those who worked the night shift went to the back, where they made up their bus beds and closed the blinds.

"Lesley, my dear, thirty minutes before Dendara, please," shouted Naomi.

"Okey dokey," Lesley shouted back. "Give me two minutes for Rashida to go over the plan for the day."

She made a very quick announcement for safety, asked if anyone needed water, and gave us the expected arrival time. Rashida gave the outline of the day and then silence descended among us. I put on my headphones and turned my music to new-age calm. Within a few minutes, I, too, was asleep.

"Welcome, everyone," called out Lesley on the microphone. "We are now passing the inner rings of Dendara temple. Our Hathor friends are awaiting our arrival and I'm asking that everyone make themselves presentable and ready. We have only a short time in this temple, so please make the most of the visit."

"Anna, can you come forward, please? Alexandria also, thank you."

We moved forward to the front of the bus, and Lesley handed me a letter.

"You had better sit down," said Alexandria.

"Okay," I smiled. I opened up the white envelope and inside was a cream piece of card with a handwritten note.

Darling Anna,

If you are reading this, then I'm not with you...

Oh no, I looked to the bottom of the note and there in gold lettering was her name: *Isis.*

I took in a deep breath.

If you are reading this, then I am not with you, but the journey continues on.

This card is written for Dendara.

Part of your birth story and heritage.

Know that Alexandria knows this Temple well. It was she who brought our attention to the crypts many years ago when I did a past-life regression with her. Though she has never visited in person, please trust her.

This is a temple of love, joy, and also sorrow.

Be aware that this temple has hidden doors and walls.

Look to Lucinda like a sister, and she will open up the main chamber. Please support her in any way you can.

Together, you can lead them through, and this will be our home again.

All my love,
Isis

I thought I was going to sob out loud.

"I know she is with us, just not getting off the bus in the regular way," I said and folded the card away, biting my lip.

"You are to lead us, please, Alexandria, and if we can carry Lucinda, she will open up the energies. That is, if she is okay from last night, and we will see how the rest goes."

Alexandria nodded and smiled.

I looked over at the Contessa. Her eyes were closed, but something told me she was already in the temple energetically. Emilee and Alice sat behind her, chatting away and sharing remedies and essential oils.

I brought my attention back to Alexandria.

"Remember the Louvre?" she asked.

I had almost forgotten; it felt so long ago. "Yes, the zodiac we worked with. That was from here?"

"Yes," she nodded. "You knew what to do then. You're a natural, Anna."

"I pray," I sighed and went back to my seat and closed my eyes.

☥

Our night shift was beginning to stir in the back when Lesley made her announcement that we were not far away. I hoped they were wide awake and ready.

The bus pulled into the small car park, and from there, I could see one other large coach and a minivan from the convoy. Compared to Karnak, it felt almost deserted. We all disembarked, and I made my way towards Rashida and Lesley. While Rashida went to get the tickets, Lesley gave the trip protocol.

"Everyone, gather around. We have a two-hour visit here, and Alexandria and Anna will facilitate the work we do. Once they finish, you will have free time."

Everyone nodded, but then the focus shifted as Naomi, Lucas, and Lucinda began to disembark. I had expected them to be trailing and complaining, but no.

Lucas appeared first in a full, white Galabeya dress. He had now shaved and looked pristine. It's amazing what an electric razor, facial wipes, and a spritz of one of Emilee's elixirs could do.

Lucinda had shed her layers to reveal a beautiful white gown. Her hair was piled high, and she wore golden cuff bracelets and a white chiffon scarf draped across her shoulders.

Of course, Naomi was last and did not disappoint. She wore a full red silk dress trimmed with gold ankh symbols, full black kohl makeup, and a commanding look. If I hadn't known better, I would have taken pictures. I closed my eyes and made a mental note, as I knew this should surely be written into a book.

My book, yes, I would keep the Isis note and journal key points.

I felt a shiver run through me.

Isis had asked me many times to share the stories. I knew as I opened more sacred doors, I would have my work and my stories to accompany hers.

Our intrepid trio made it off the bus and stood in front of our group. I watched as Emilee and Alice exchanged glances. I looked for the Contessa. "Where is your grandmama?" I asked Alexandria. She shook her head. "She never enters this temple. She says she prefers to be a protector and her role is that of guardian."

I looked at our group and sensed this would be something other than a gentle and peaceful experience.

"Shields up, everyone," said Laura, and we all knew what that meant.

Alexandria was first. "Friends, please walk with me to the temple of Dendara," she said, and we all followed. "Here were once lavish gardens and ponds and the most beautiful creations in statue form."

As we neared the entrance, a stone doorway with no doors, she pointed over to the high walls and whispered as if to open the doorways. It was strange. There were supposed to be large wooden doors, always locked and protecting. I was at the back of the group, still musing over the doors, when I realised I was separate from the group. They all followed Alexandria in silence.

Up ahead was a very impressive temple. Tall columns loomed with large heads depicting Hathor. I tried to imagine what this temple must have looked like in ancient times, with vivid colour standing in an oasis of beauty.

We all stopped mid-way as Alexandria described the temple in greater detail. But I could see most of us were already floating inside the temple. When she finished, she turned, and we walked side by side towards the majestic columns. The statue's faces towered above us, and I expected to enter at the front when Alexandria shook her head.

"First, the purification and the blessings."

Of course. I pretended to know as I caught up to her.

We walked down the side wall to the right, but I was drawn to a relief of a woman and a child drawn into the wall.

"Yes, she was here, ma cere," said Emilee.

"Cleopatra, with her son Caesarean, your past life mother and brother, Anna."

"Oh, I feel her, but I can't see her in my dreams or visions," I whispered.

As soon as Emilee revealed this, I had expected to see a

woman with green eyes, but nothing came.

We stopped at the higher wall to the right and climbed onto the step. As we looked over, it looked like the sacred lake from Karnak, but without water. It had the same bricks placed like steps going down, which would have assisted you into the water.

Naomi stepped forward.

"Oh, waters of purification and blood, be alive with our light. May we be cleansed and worthy of stepping forward into this temple."

She then took a spray bottle from her bag and began to go from person to person, spritzing over the head with a beautiful rose-scented spray. She nodded to Alexandria and then retreated to the back. Alexandria moved forward, turning left and walking towards a small chamber temple at the back.

"We will receive the blessing of Isis," I heard myself call out.

"Very good," said Alexandria. "Yes, Hathor was the main goddess here, but this was a private shrine dedicated to the priestesses of Isis. They watched over the temple and guarded the back entrance."

"They were protectors?" I asked.

"Yes," she replied.

I watched as Alice and Laura took their places outside the temple, guarding the doorways and access route.

We all filed in, and I took my place in the centre of the back wall. Behind me, an image of a goddess was engraved into the wall. Often, Rashida waited outside, but today, she walked into our small, gathered circle and handed me a lit stick of incense.

"Are we allowed?" I leaned in and whispered.

"From one of the guards and guardians," she smiled. "I

was surprised also, Anna. They rarely acknowledge this, but today it feels like the gods are with us."

I waited until everyone was in position, then I handed the incense to Lesley, who was standing next to me. I had expected her to scold me, but instead, she took it and bowed her head to me and the circle. I cleared my throat, and a thought popped into my head. I pictured the image of the Ankh, and that's all it took. I brought my hands together in prayer.

"Oh, Mother Isis,

Hear us all, and we ask for your blessing in this holy shrine. We are travellers, but in our hearts, we are oracles, priests, and priestesses. We hold your space in sacredness within our hearts so that we may be worthy of shining your light. Oh, Mother Isis, open the doors of the ancient realms and allow us to see through the veils into the true nature of this sacred space."

I then made the sound of Om, and everyone joined me. The sound carried through the chamber, and I felt like it was calling to all the energies.

We finished our ceremony. As I went around the circle, I looked each person in the eye. I could see that this had touched many, as they had begun to remember when times in this temple had been gentler and kinder.

Everyone except Lucinda. Tears streamed down her face, and I was unsure what to do or say. But she had been a high priestess here before, and now it was time to restore all that had been taken. I stepped forward and stood in front of her.

"Lucinda, it is time," I told her.

"In lifetimes before, we did not acknowledge your gifts," I said loud enough for everyone to hear but without a declaration. "You were the gift, and now I ask you with the divine will of Isis and Hathor to remember and surrender to your true identity here in this temple without fear."

She let out a loud sigh and stopped the sobbing that I knew was rising within her.

"Lucinda, no more tears. We need you to do the work you came to do. Restore the temple. Restore our home. Restore this sacred place for them all to come home. Lucinda, for 2000 years, we have been kept at the doorway, a doorway I now see was broken, smashed, and burnt after you left. I have the keys you need, but these walls need your sacred soul."

Naomi was standing next to her and squeezed her hand.

"It's time, my sister," she whispered.

Lucinda took in a deep breath and smiled.

"Well, then," she said, "Follow me."

She walked out of the chamber, and I saw the light catching her hair. She nodded to the ladies who had guarded the Temple.

"It's time we go home," she said.

As we left the small shrine, she led us to the wall at the back of the temple. There in the middle of the wall was the large Hathor head, and to each side, it showed a procession of kings and queens leading off.

Lucinda began to chant and blow energy towards this, and then it was as if she were turning the energy like a wheel to open a portal with her hands. I was suddenly aware that energy was now streaming into the temple, and I realised she was starting to bring it back to life. It was the rear of the temple that held the powerful doorway.

"Now we can enter," she said.

Rashida sprang into action, moving in front of us as we made our way to the front entrance of the temple. She handed the tickets to the guards and paid the tipping money so we would not be disturbed.

We lined up behind Lucinda; Emilee stood beside her with Laura, Lucas, and Naomi behind her, protecting her. I followed up with Alice and Alexandria. Holding sacred space at the back was Lesley. I realised then the Contessa was on the bus weaving a protection across the entire temple.

As we walked into the temple, the columns stood tall and were covered in the most amazing hieroglyphics. I almost felt dizzy, but as I watched Lucinda begin her walk towards the chamber at the back, I grounded myself and focused. I thought we would go straight into the chamber, but she paused at the entrance way and knelt down gently. She motioned with her hand for us to stay back before she went into the chamber. She stood very still in the center, and I knew she was connecting to some ancient wisdom. But something stopped her, and to my and everyone else's surprise, she turned.

"Anna, quickly," she summoned me. "They tell me three curses remain that were placed here when I last left."

I did not wish to draw attention to myself as this was Lucinda's moment, but suddenly, I remembered the scarabs and scrolls. I turned to Lucas to see if he had brought a selection today. He was already prepared and handed over exactly what I needed.

I looked down and saw one scarab and one scroll. "I hereby invoke the power of the Scroll and Scarab of Creation," I said.

Lucinda held out her hands, and I placed the scarab into one and the scroll in the other.

I whispered to her, "This was mine, gifted to me by you, but it comes from my lineage and connection with Cleopatra. It was removed and cursed when you left the temple." The curses were around chastity, obedience, and power."

Lucinda looked delighted to see this, and I saw that she was already remembering her last past life here, when she had been stripped of her power. With these pieces, she could redeem herself. She waved to call us all into the chamber in a circle. We stood in a line facing her.

"I, Lucinda, High priestess of Hathor and daughter of Ra and Nut, call this Temple to divine order. Three curses lie here in these walls. Curses that would create the vows of chastity, poverty, and obedience. I challenge them in front of the Council of Oracles and sacred ones."

She looked at all of us.

"Will you swear to break the binding of chastity to allow us to love with our hearts, minds, and bodies?"

"Yes," we all said in unison.

"Will you swear to break the binding of poverty? We will have abundance and wealth of mind, body, and soul."

In unison, we all said, "We do."

"Will you swear to break the binding of obedience? We are in service and no longer servants to the masters of the dark."

"Yes," we all said in unison.

"And so it is, my brother and sisters. May it now be restored and order brought forward in this Temple of Light," she smiled.

I felt an energy swirl around us all. I could now see Lucinda in her true self.

"The Temple is open," whispered Lucinda. "We can enter the crypt."

"The crypt... what?" I stuttered.

"No time," she said. "She is coming—hurry."

"Who is coming?" I trailed after her.

But by now, Lucinda was on her way.

Laura was already weaving a cloaking spell, and Rashida

was catching up to Lucinda with the rest of the group and turning left. We all followed, trusting the process.

Lucinda stopped at a corner where a guard stood, and she instructed him to lift the grid. To my surprise, she began to climb down into a small tunnel.

"Only our group," Lucinda said to the guard and motioned for us all to follow.

We all filed down the tiny shaft and into a long corridor chamber that was only one person's width apart. There seemed to be two chambers joined in the middle.

We did as she said.

Naomi stood with her back to the wall on one side, facing into the group and Lucas to the other. It was as if they were holding the energy of the chamber. I could also see he was holding a new set of scrolls and scarabs out for Lucinda, and as she took them, he whispered their names.

Then, we all took our places along the wall facing into the chamber. The stone wall felt old, and as I leaned back, it was as if it connected to me.

"Deep breathing, everyone," said Lucinda as she stood in the middle of the corridor, one foot on either side.

She called to the ancient ones to acknowledge the scroll and scarab of Goddess and Fertility.

"Mother Hathor, hear my prayer. I have brought before you the initiates of true heart to receive the blessing of the kundalini life force. That their Ka, Ba, and Khat be reconnected and rebirthed into the new consciousness."

She then moved like she was floating down the corridor towards Naomi. Standing in front of her, she started the initiation by placing energy from the scarab into the various chakras in our bodies and drawing symbols. Then, she touched the ankle, hip, third eye, and crown lightly with the scroll.

Once complete, she moved to the next initiate. I wanted to open my eyes and watch but was too scared.

"Anna, it's your time," Lucinda said as she reached me.

I kept deep breathing and nodded my head. I heard her words, and they were like nothing I had heard before. It was almost like a hissing sound, and my body vibrated. I felt this tremendous rush of energy and heat.

My head began to spin when she reached my crown chakra, and it was like my hair had static and was rising. My body vibrated in a way I had never experienced. My breathing became low and shallow. I felt Lucinda touch my ankle and hip, sending the energy higher and higher. I could hear the noises I was making—primal and guttural. But they would not stop, and I felt myself slip into pure energy, no physical form.

When my initiation had ended, I felt myself slowly softening into the wall and relaxing. I looked down at those who had gone through the initiation before me. Everyone looked in a state of bliss, smiling and breathing gently. I thought I saw Naomi looking at me, and I quickly closed my eyes again.

Before long, Lucinda must have finished the initiations as she was back in the middle again and giving praise to Mother Hathor, Nut, and Isis. Once she had completed the ritual, we stood in silence for a minute before Lucinda spoke.

"Now we all make our ascension. Creation within us all has been activated, and we move towards the birth, death, and resurrection chambers."

It was quite the scramble for us all to climb out, and to my relief, there was Rashida with a pile of our bags. The guard gave us a helping hand and began laughing.

"What's he laughing at?" I asked Naomi in front of me.

"Oh, he is getting some of the kundalini energy, and

you, lady, were above and beyond the call of duty in there. I want you to teach me in private," she whispered.

"Well, I never," I heard Laura giggling.

"Well, you just did," said Lesley, "Now, where did Lucinda go?"

I went to follow when Naomi said, "Anna, wait a little. Lesley also has karma to clear in this temple with Lucinda. Let's see if she can. Stay close."

Lucinda was far down the corridor to a staircase. It was narrow, and I noticed how the stones were rising, blending unlike clear-cut steps; they looked so worn, like they had been walked on a million times. They felt alive, taking us to the higher floors and chambers in this temple. We moved quickly along the corridors. They were now dark and narrow. We then turned and entered the sacred chambers. The first had the image of a pregnant woman drawn on the ceiling.

"Our birthing chamber," announced Laura.

We stood still, and I began to see the images of the past. I saw sacred ceremonies with women as midwives welcoming children into the world with grace and prayer. I had noticed on the walls of the staircase that priestesses were carrying small stools, and I realised they were birthing stools. I watched as various members of the group performed prayers and rituals.

"The women giving birth were so honoured and supported," said Laura, and she smiled at Lucinda.

Then we moved to the next chamber, and I felt some grief. When I looked upwards, I knew why. Here was the chamber with a female stretched out as if she was being laid to rest. I began to see the women creating funeral rites. I saw the body of a young female in the center of the chamber. My vision shifted into the past life. A priestess was there reciting from the Book of the Dead, and I saw Emilee place a white cloth over the body. Only then did I realise I was seeing the body of Lesley, and as I did, I refocused out of the vision and looked over at her. She was shaking in the corner.

"Alice, Emilee, quickly," I said, pointing in Lesley's direction.

They rushed over, and I noticed Lucinda did nothing. Lesley was shaking.

This soul was bound here over time and a part still remains. We can free what was bound here to create a new dawn for this soul.

I heard the words in my head. I looked at Alexandria, and she shook her head.

"Not me. I was here at a different time."

"Lesley left herself open to the darker forces, and they were the ones who bound her after Lucinda left the temple and was not here to protect us," said Alice.

I was seeing the story again—the betrayal—but now I was seeing what had happened to the temple after Lucinda had left. Emilee sensed I was about to read the Akashic Records and motioned for us all to sit together.

I began to channel,

"The Roman soldiers came and took all that was sacred. Once Cleopatra was gone, Egypt was a province, and Octavius ordered us under Rome's control. They made a prison of this place. Priests and priestesses were abused, and torture was a game. The Priests of Unal that Lesley brought forward when she was a priestess here and also at Edfu, could not be controlled. Lesley may have opened the gateway, but they were bound to a darker energy. The Scorpion Queen was their puppet master. But no one knew... how could they?

"There is a very powerful guard. He knows the names of magic. I see him in the temple, and he is weaving the spell that would start 2000 years of witch naming. He stands at the

high altar and calls forward such dark forces. He is placing the curse upon the sacred herbs and the potions that helped the birth process for women. He orders that the birth stools be broken and burnt. The sacred linens burnt, and the oils. Into the fire, he throws the papyrus of the medicines used by the priestesses.

"These earth medicine women... he curses that they will be hunted down and abused. They will face the wrath of men in the future. They will be outlawed and set to roam the earth like a gypsy. He will return only to see this cycle continue. I have seen him before. He was at the Salem witch trials and spread the word across America and Europe. I saw him—his eyes haunt me. Rasputin. He was a son of Set.

"He placed this darkness on the Scroll and Scarab of the Goddess and Fertility and violated many at the high altar. The protection was gone, and many of our brothers and sisters took their own lives. You, Lesley, took your own life. You have been trying to reclaim it ever since."

Lucinda knelt down and held Lesley's hands. Naomi stood behind her.

"Lesley, allow me to help you reclaim the fragments of your soul. Release yourself from this timeline and seek forgiveness from the high priestesses Mother Hathor and Mother Isis. Lesley, it is time. You have carried this for over 2000 years. Rejoin the sisters and claim your true place."

"But I'm afraid," she said. Lucinda stood back and sighed; I could see she was afraid of failing again.

Naomi stepped to her side and knelt down to hug her. "Lesley, my sister, Lesley, my family. You came here to do this healing."

Naomi pointed to Lucinda, who now stood in front of them looking even more regal than before. "She is ready, and so are you."

Lucinda remained motionless. "It is her free will, but I am here, present and will not leave. I will not waiver. I am here," she said.

Lesley took a deep breath and knelt before her.

"Oh, High Priestess, true sister of Mother Hathor and Mother Isis. I hereby renounce all the words I used and the sacred vows I created that have caused harm and sadness. I renounce my claim over the Priests of Unal and for all crimes committed that would harm the divine sisterhood and brotherhood of Light. I stand before you humbly and ask for my divine lineage to be restored."

I saw Lucinda hold Lesley's hand and smile.

"Let us go to the Chapel of Ascension."

She gently walked with Lesley to the rooftop, and we followed.

☥

After being in the dark rooms, I had to blink. We gathered in an open rooftop chamber, the faces of the Hathors smiling upon us from the pillars around us. Lucinda stood in the centre with Lesley, and the rest of us stood around.

"Dear brother and sisters, we welcome home this dear beloved. She has been lost in the lifetimes, trying, I know, to find her way home."

"It's time," said Lesley. Emilee reached into her pocket and brought out a small bottle of Egyptian oil.

"The rose and jasmine," she said, handing it to Lucinda.

Lucinda poured a small amount into her hands and handed the bottle back. She then rubbed her hands together, and Lesley stood before her, her hands stretched open.

"I welcome you home, dear child. You are safe, you are loved."

Lucinda then pressed her hand gently to Lesley's hands.

She then placed Lesley's hands crossed across her heart. She anointed her feet and then her third eye. I could smell the sweet perfume, and it was as if all of us were receiving the blessings.

"And so it is," said Lucinda, smiling as Lesley fell into her arms, sobbing.

We all slowly departed and began moving down the sloping corridors. I felt I could hear the priestess's chants again, and I knew that the Scarab and Scroll of Creation were still at work in the high altar chamber below, recreating what was required. Alexandria caught up with me.

"Anna, before we go, do you not wish to see the true zodiac?"

"Of course, how could I have forgotten?" She moved swiftly, pulling me through the temple until we entered a chamber where soot was still on the walls and ceiling.

"Look up," she said.

I did, and at once, I felt like I was back in the Louvre, only this time, this was a portal to the astrological worlds.

"Shall we open it?" Alexandria was excited.

"No, I think we just marvel at her beauty."

I was unsure, but I felt like something was following us. I was becoming aware that we were opening many new energies and restoring those cursed or damaged.

"Let's leave this portal to rest for now, I feel we will work with her another time," I said, waving my hand across to cloak its power and purpose.

"As you wish," Alexandria replied. But something caught my attention before we left. In the corner, I saw an Oracle spirit. She was alone, drawing images on papyrus. She was the woman from Karnak but a younger version of herself. Her eyes shone gold.

"Do you see her?" I asked Alexandria.

"Who? It's just us," she replied.

The Oracle turned and smiled at me and held her finger to her lips. I smiled and nodded. Telepathically, she began to communicate with me.

"The time is coming, Anna, and each step you are closer to restoring our order—the order of the Oracle."

"Do you wish to leave?" I spoke out loud, and although Alexandria did not see her, she understood what was happening.

"I can free you, dear one," I said. She shook her head.

"I know, but now they will come, the other oracles, we will help them restore their psychic sight as you once did for us all."

"But I don't know who 'all' is," I replied.

"You will soon... you will."

With that, she folded her papyrus, stood up, walked through the wall, and disappeared.

"Time to go," I said, looking at Alexandria.

We literally ran down the corridor and out of the temple.

"Are we last?" I said breathlessly as we ran towards the bus. "No," replied Alexandria. "See? Lucinda is last. She is closing up the doorways and dimensions until we return."

And there she was, and for some reason, I saw her with others—other women who had worn the mantle of the High priestess of Hathor in this Temple. I knew then they would be returning in person and in dream time, and I knew they would find home and sanctuary.

Abydos Temple

After Dendara, I was sure that I would be able to rest. I was confident the priests of Osiris would be gentle souls, and as far as I knew, all we were there to do was view an image of the much-famed Flower of Life symbol.

I looked into my lunch box and was grateful that I had eaten a large breakfast. It looked like our lunch items were not holding up well in the heat.

I looked around the bus, and everyone was sleeping. Naomi was at the back doing private readings. Love and money, love and money. I could hear her in my mind. We may be spiritually advanced but when it came to seeing the future, even I was curious. Perhaps I should ask her for a reading on the way back... yes, love and money.

Or why not ask Lucas?

I decided to go visit with him and catch up.

As I stood up and made my way over to his seat, I was struck by how he was sitting... eyes open and tears streaming down his face.

I looked at Lucinda as I passed her; she was out and sleeping, making cute snoring sounds. Alice caught my glance, and I motioned that I was going over to Lucas. She nodded, and something told me she knew what was going on.

We had so much space on the coach as it was a large 50-seater, but I guess we needed this with the ghosts we carried.

I sat in the two seats across from Lucas, who was sitting at the window, and I reached across and touched his arm.

"Lucas," I said gently, but his arm was cold, and I became quite alarmed.

Alice had moved into the seat behind him and was holding her hands up to the seat against his back to create a protection.

"Anna," he whispered. "I don't think I can tell you, but perhaps I can show you."

I nodded, alarmed and intrigued.

"Do you want me to clear the story in the Records?"

I could feel pains all over my body, and I knew something terrible must have happened to Lucas.

I took a deep breath and began to tune in.

I was aware that a stillness had come over the coach and that others had heard the call and were shifting in their seats. I looked out into the centre of the bus from the aisle and could see that the others were around us, also ready to listen. I moved into the seat next to him and closed my eyes.

"I see us in Egypt, flying through the sky, and it's miles of desert. We land in a temple in the middle of nowhere, but the kings are long gone, and all that is there are several priests. But it's not what it should be. Why are they hiding? I see them trying to perform rituals to protect and seal the various energies around the temple. This is not just a temple; it's a crypt of souls and a stargate.

"These priests are protectors. I see Lucas, I see Laura, and I see Lesley. It appears the three of you work with others, but I hear screaming in the halls, and yet I feel the peace in the gardens. This is a very weird dichotomy, like the energy has been turned upside down and fractured. This was once a beautiful, gentle place with great healing. Now, I'm shown a stargate with several portals to the other worlds. It is broken and separated from all the other temples, and there is such a sadness—a total feeling of violation. The other priests walk around with no purpose. They meditate all day to the gods, but there is no connection. This temple is dead and dying."

At this point, Lucas let out a large sob and began to shake.

"I see a King arrive. He is from Upper Egypt and into Nubia. He has heard that a great Oracle resides here, and he needs him to open the gateways of the darkness. His name is

Nectanebo II, the last true Egyptian Pharaoh. He is here to capture Lucas. I don't see him betrayed, but he has sacrificed himself and walked willingly to the King and his entourage outside the temple. The King is not allowed to enter for some reason. I see Laura and Lesley creating circles of light that forbid him from coming forward, but they know they cannot hold him for long. Lucas is bound by his hands and neck, with his robes removed. He now wears a loincloth. He holds back the tears and follows his chariot. The King knows that by taking him from this temple, he will have power again one day. But for now, he needs him to be his oracle and channel information on how to defeat his enemies.

"They take Lucas to what appears to be an inner chamber or cave. It's large and has white limestone walls. But soon, the King does not trust him and abandons him. Lucas brings messages to warn him, but he doesn't wish to listen. Lucas warns that a Greek prince will take the land of Egypt.

"He is kept there for many years as if he is going mad. He had aged so much, and the people come and visit, and he answers their questions in exchange for food and water. All his sacred ceremony has been removed, and he calls out to the Lord Osiris, but no one answers, and he is in despair. Sometimes people do not visit, and he is on the brink of starvation. I can't see why he does not leave, then yes, I see. He is chained by the ankle like a wild animal.

"One day, a wealthy family visits with food and offerings, but he gives them an answer they do not wish to hear. He tells them they may lose their fortune if they do not tend to the lands and the community. The father does not listen; instead, he tells the family to throw the black stones at the priest. Some strike him, but most land in his enclosure.

"One of the daughters takes pity on the priest, and she comes to visit and tells him her family has not listened and

has fallen to poverty, but she has taken heed and has brought herself and her small brother, and they are hiding nearby in a smaller cave. They have created a small home and they bring food, and the young brother is allowed to spend time with Lucas. One day, the young boy picks up one of the black stones, and he writes his name on the wall.

"Lucas springs to life and begins to write symbols and words on the walls. He has been tormented by his dreams ever since he arrived and has had no way to share his messages. Now, he has found a way to bring his messages. These are prophecies of the future. I'm seeing words and images from modern-day history.

"Lucas, my dear friend, I see the wars and floods, and you knew it all.

"The cave of the oracle has become well known, and many travel to consult with this oracle. The young woman has created a home nearby, but no one dares release Lucas in case they incur the wrath of the King. Word reaches the King of his success, and he decides to revisit him.

"One day, he returns and sees who Lucas truly is. He is cautious, as he knows he has seen his triumph and demise. Lucas is presented to him, and Lucas asks about his brothers and his family in the temple, to which the King replies they are all dead, slain by his warriors. He asks what happened to their bodies. He smiles and telepathically shows him the image of how they were murdered and their bodies broken and separated—their hearts crushed, and a dark ceremony performed to curse them. Lucas breaks down and sobs, and the King gives him a choice: The souls of his friends at the expense of the keys to the temple. As he is the last living pure priest of Osiris, his blood holds the key. He has lineage back to Atlantis and the ancient ones.

"When given freely, it provides the key to opening all the

gateways to the other worlds and commanding the dead. He will have the power of Osiris and Anubis, and can resurrect all he chooses.

"The desire to save the souls of the innocents is too great, and Lucas agrees to give his blood.

"He wants to protect the young woman, and he tells the young woman of a plan. I see clearly that the woman is Naomi. She is to leave and travel to the pyramids in Lower Egypt, as he has heard of a sanctuary there.

"He confides in her and tells her some secrets, and she and her brother leave. Naomi makes a sacred blood vow to find Lucas again and help him become the priest and Oracle again.

"Once gone, Lucas awaits the King, who returns and tricks Lucas into giving his blood into a cup that looks like a chalice or sacred cup. I have seen the symbols from this chalice before in the black Book of Souls, but I am not sure of their meaning. Lucas thinks the King will allow him to free his brothers. He gives him the words, symbols, and magic of the temple. The King deceives him and is not truthful, and once he has the wisdom he wants and leaves.

"Lucas is left alone to die and unable to set his friends and his family free. He vows to search the earth through all the temples to free them and protect them. He is bound to live each life with his karma until his vow is complete. He is cursed for leaving them, as he saw the temple's fall in a vision. In his dreams, he saw this King, and he still haunts him.

"But now I see the King's true path. He takes the wisdom to a palace and trades with a woman who resides there. Her name is Olympus, mother of Alexander the Great, but this is a façade. I see now that she is the reincarnation of none other than the Scorpion Queen. She has bewitched this King."

I had to stop. It was so painful, so ugly and dark. Lucas

touched my hand, and I let go.

"I see her, and I have felt her before. She was in Glastonbury in the shop that day," he whispered. "Remember, Anna? When you came for your reading?"

I nodded, saying, "Hers is a spirit that hides in the shadows and has tormented us for many of our lifetimes. She is the Scorpion Queen." I took a deep breath and opened my eyes.

"She takes over souls."

All except Lucinda were now gathered around in the bus seats, even the Contessa. We all looked at Lucas. He sat so still, his face white and tear-stained.

"I have carried that shame for a long time, Anna. When I first came to Glastonbury, I came with a troubled heart and past. I could see things others could not, and my dreams had demons. I came to find Isis, as I was told she would have the answers to help me. She saw who I was as soon as I walked through the door. She saw a similar past life temple story to you, Anna ... not in such great detail, but she said the temple was Abydos."

"She saw the shame and the blame that had been left at my door. The innocents I had left behind. The Lord Anubis often came to me with prophecy and warning, but I was content with a comfortable life. I began to tell those who visited what they wished to hear in my psychic readings. I felt like a puppet and a fraud. I hid in the shadows as entertainment. Isis helped me to find my truth and my origins, and even helped me with the deposit for the shop and sent clients to me. She was my mentor and saviour. She loved the Temple of Abydos and often commented on how it was one of the most powerful because of the stargates. We talked many times about the old days and past lives. She knew many had been bound to this temple and given their lives or had their lives taken. She told me of a dark portal deep within the temple, but never shared its location. So I promised her I would return one day and clear this. Until now, I have never been able to. But today, Anna, when you touched my hand..."

His voice paused, and I was sure he was about to speak about something deep in his soul.

"I had hope, Isis was supposed to heal this with me when we came here at Christmas. On previous trips she always got sick or the roads were blocked, so the last trip she promised me that we would do the work to clear my karma for good. However, in the days before the visit was scheduled, she became distant and focused on the work she shared with Naomi. Always the work and rarely the person. Which is why I left them, to be honest, but today, Anna, you have shown me you can help me. I am not sure how, but I need soul release from this sacred place. It has such a hold over me."

I nodded and began to tune into the Akashic Record.

"Lucas, my friend, close your eyes and journey with me."

He nodded and let his head rest back, and I watched as a stream of light energy began to flow around him.

"Now, my friend, I want to imagine you are going back to a garden of paradise. Going back to your soul's home, where you are perfect and created by love."

I was not sure where this place was, but it felt like the best place to guide him for healing.

"Now, Lucas, see your guardian angels or spirit guides coming forward and making a circle of light around you."

I watched as he nodded his head and smiled.

"Now feel their energy and hear their whispers... this has been closed since this past life tragedy, but now it is time to return to your own temple."

"I see stars, Anna. I think I'm going home."

"What do you feel?" I asked.

"Wisdom, love, and compassion. I'm with my star family and my cosmic friends now."

"Then hold space and feel the love."

He nodded, and I became aware of such a beautiful sensation. We sat in silence, and I even closed my eyes to feel into the exquisite energy.

"I'm complete Anna," he whispered.

I began to lead him gently back to the present reality. He opened his eyes and looked so peaceful. I was about to reassure him that all would be well. However, I was suddenly pushed back in my seat by the energy force field that had hit the bus like a wave. Our conversation was broken by something distracting, and we lost the moment. I was taken over by such a force. Not darkness... I tried to look, but nothing came to me.

"The first gate," said the Contessa into the microphone. "Quickly, everyone, take your seats. I think we are about to meet a karmic story that we all share."

I looked at Naomi, who had moved into the seat across from Lucas and I.

"The gateways to Abydos reached well outside the temple. Remember the seven rings around the Tor in Glastonbury?" she whispered to us.

I nodded.

"This bridge and statue mark the first gate," she said.

So, time to leave the Akashic Records for now. I nodded and moved back to my original seat.

We all sat in silence, although I could not help but look out of the window, smile, and wave to the children standing in the doorways. Their smiles were bright and innocent.

We turned towards the temple and parked outside what looked like a large, outdoor coffee shop in an oasis garden. A simple hand-painted sign, ABYDOS TEMPLE, with an arrow pointed the way behind the coffee shop to the sacred site.

We were just leaving the bus when I saw a small boy out of the corner of my eye. The vendors had been alerted and were beginning to run around the buses, and as I wrapped my scarf around my shoulders, they ran straight past me. It was as if I had disappeared.

While everyone was waiting for Rashida, once again, the little boy caught my eye as he sat on a wall nearby me, playing with a sistrum—a long, slender handle topped with the face of a goddess. The rattle expanded outwards, resembling the top of the ankh symbol, with strings running through the middle of metal discs.

"Hello," I smiled and sat down near him.

He looked at me, smiled, and shook the rattle three times.

"This is wonderful," I smiled, pointing to it.

"You want to buy it?" he smiled.

"How much?" It felt wrong to haggle with a child, but he looked around ten years old, so he was probably the best salesman in the family.

"It's real and very old."

"Your English is very good," I said.

"My grandfather," he pointed to a very old man sitting in the shade near the coffee shop.

The old man lifted his hand and waved.

I felt more at ease. This precious angel probably sold things for his family under the watchful, safe eye of an elder.

"Okay, let me see," I said, looking in my purse.

"I have thirty English pounds," and held it out. I knew this was a lot for a temple trinket, but I also knew this temple probably had few visitors and, therefore, less opportunity.

"I go ask," he said, handing me the rattle. Then he ran to his grandfather, taking the money with him.

Soon, he ran back and said I was to come meet his grandfather.

I went over to the old man. I knew I was beginning to be late. I could see Rashida leaving the ticket desk.

As I approached the old man, his eyes shone brightly.

"Is it she?" asked the boy.

"It is she," the grandfather nodded.

The boy began to jump up and down.

I knelt in front of the old man, and he took my hands.

"Do you want more for the rattle?" I asked.

"No, I just want to look at you. You came home. She said you would."

"Who said?"

"The lady with the green eyes."

"Oh, her, you know her."

"Yes, we are from her family," the little boy said.

"Once we were kings," the grandfather laughed. "Now we are traders."

"No," I shook my head. "You, sir, are guardians, and I'm honoured to be in your presence. In the afterlife, you will be kings again." I smiled and felt my energy run into his.

"I remember," he said. "I remember."

He muttered some words in Arabic, and the young boy sped off.

He returned soon after with a wooden ankh.

"Keep this safe," he said, and motioned for me to put it in my bag.

The old man then held out the money and motioned to the rattle. "You take the sistrum of Hathor, and I take the money. The deal is done, and the debt is paid. Our family is free."

"I don't understand; this is my first visit to Egypt," I answered him.

"But you will. Once the sacred relics of protection were taken from the temples, my ancestors vowed to help restore them, and now we have. This will give you access to great healing skills again."

He then stood up and began a full chant in a strange language. I felt a blessing on my crown, third eye chakra, and heart.

"Now, lady, go," he said.

I bent over and touched the forehead of the young boy, and his lifetimes flashed before me. It was hard to leave him, but I could see he was full of joy at his sale. I ran back to the group.

Soon, Rashida and Lesley were handing out the tickets.

I wrapped my new treasure in a scarf and placed it carefully in my bag. I wondered which scarab and scroll I would be called to use. I knew Lucas had brought a selection for this temple, but he seemed so distressed that I hated to ask.

I wondered how he was and looked for him, but he was already in action—a professional.

His white Galabeya outfit was still pristine, and his eyes bright and alert.

Laura led the way with him.

As I began walking the path towards the temple, there was something very unique, and I was unsure what to expect. We made our way slowly, and I watched as Alice stayed close to Lucas. I stayed at the back.

Lucinda was helping the Contessa, who seemed to have recovered from her journey on the bus but looked pale and shaken. She now looked like Isis had when she returned from that last trip to Egypt, and I wondered if she was shielding us and taking on the negative powers. I became distracted by this thought and wasn't paying attention, so I nearly fell into everyone when Laura stopped the group and raised her hand.

"We must greet his majesty," she announced.

I looked around, but I could not see anyone. I looked to where she was pointing, and in the corner to the left was a statue. Laura stepped forward and spoke some words of an ancient language, and then she turned.

"Seti welcomes us and allows us to pass." I saw the statue come to life and begin to talk.

"I am he

"I am he

"The oracle child may come forward

The one who sees."

It was as if the whole group had heard and, for some reason, turned to look at me.

Alice and Naomi both pointed at me.

"It is she," said Alice.

"Let her approach," the voice said.

Laura came and guided me forward. "Anna, you have nothing to be afraid of. Come closer."

I moved slowly forward until I stood between the statue and the group.

"Reveal yourself," the voice said.

"I am Anna, an oracle of these lands."

"Ahh, the land of magic," he responded. *"And why have you come?"*

"To free my friend and restore this oracle priest," I said, pointing to Lucas.

"To open the stargates and align the light and shadow."

"And how can you be trusted?" the voice responded.

"Because I have this."

I reached into my bag and pulled out the wooden ankh and the Hathor sitstrum. I did not wish to parade them to the group for some reason, so I placed them gently in front of the statue.

"And we have this." Lucas was behind me and handed me a scroll and scarab. It was the Scroll and Scarab of Creation connected to my past-life mother, Cleopatra. I held up the scarab and showed the side with the cartouche.

"Then you have returned," the voice responded. *"The prophecy has started. The children will be reunited."*

I didn't understand all that he meant.

"You may proceed," was the answer, and I placed my new treasures away and handed the scarab to Lucas.

"Be warned, they are still here," I heard him whisper as we walked away.

"Who are they?" I asked, daring not to turn around to face him.

"Unal."

I felt a chill in my entire body.

"They have ruled here since he left."

I looked over to Lucas. I held out my hand, and he took it.

"Then their time of power is over," I whispered.

"Wise words, child."

I turned again, bowed my head, and then turned to the group.

"We can enter," I said slowly to everyone, "but they are here. The priests of Unal still have control." I looked at Lucas.

His eyes filled with fear like they had on the bus.

"Anna, I pulled the tower card today," he whispered.

"Then this will be the tower to fall for Unal," I responded, and I felt Isis was with us. Naomi felt her also and came over to me.

I turned to Laura and then to Alice. "Ladies, please assist and open your temple and let this be our father's house once more."

As I said this, I was also aware that the energy of the goddess Isis was with me, stronger than ever. I was sure that Sekhmet had joined us, too. I couldn't explain it; I just felt it. I had thought this was my mentor, Isis, but no, this was a different power. I looked at Naomi.

Yes, they are here, she mouthed, nodding and smiling.

I prayed we would be divinely protected. Alice and Laura stood in the first doorway, and Rashida began to hand out the tickets. Everyone else was silent and still. Lesley and Naomi were holding hands and reciting words to each other.

"There is nothing to pay here, Naomi; you will be safe," Laura said.

Without her coin, it seemed Naomi was lost, but we will change that, I thought.

The Contessa began to cough, and I could feel her pain and wondered if she was strong enough.

"I have you protected; you have my strength," I could hear Lucinda whispering to her repeatedly.

Alexandria held her grandmother's hand. Lucas was shaking, but as he stood alone, I was aware Emilee was there giving him comfort. I moved slowly to the front of the group, and we began a solemn walk inside.

"First to the Holy of Holies," I whispered to Laura.

"Which one, my dear?" she asked. Suddenly, I saw there were seven chambers.

"The middle one." I tried to sound as if I knew what I was doing.

Laura walked into the chamber, and I could see what appeared to be a doorway carved into the wall. Images of

Gods, Goddesses, and Kings covered the walls.

I did not know what came over me, but I followed her in, knelt down in front of the doorway, and closed my eyes.

Suddenly, I was taken out into the dark night sky, floating in the stars; I could see a bright blue star ahead of me. In an instant, I knew that was my home, my home in the stars.

"Anna, Anna, wake up. We are about to begin," said Alice, now next to me.

I looked around and shook my head. No, something was wrong. The ritual was out of order.

"Where are the three chambers?" I whispered to Alice. "We must have everyone reinitiated."

"Follow me," came a voice from outside the chamber. An old woman stood there, her eyes sparkling. She was English and like a tourist, but at the same time, not.

"I am connected to Om Seti," she said, "and now a guardian of this temple. My name is Ann. Many years ago, I came to this temple and waited outside. I feared entering. One day, a young initiate visited the temple, saw me, and brought her mentor over to help me. Together, they cleared a spell and curse. The mentor was your friend Isis, and she told me that her friends would return one day and that I would help them. After I was cleared, I began to work with the spirit of Om Seti until, at last now, we could merge at the perfect time. I watched as she shape-shifted, and I recognized the woman from the Seti I tomb, the real Om Seti."

I was unsure if she was good or bad, but I felt we could trust her.

"Come," she beckoned, and like children, we followed.

She reached out and took Lucas' hand.

"Oracle, you came back. We have been waiting. Now quickly, this light will fade soon, and shadow will take over."

"She has brought the Light," Om Seti said, pointing at

me. *"This is the stargate to her home star. They offer you sanctuary, but not for long."*

Even though she was elderly, she was fast. She moved left out of the shrine and again left until we reached a small room with thick columns from floor to ceiling. The Contessa sat down on one of the columns and placed her head down. She was having trouble breathing. She raised her hand to signal she was okay, and Rashida sat nearby.

"Quickly, choose your room," she said with a hoarse voice and began to cough as if the life was being drained from her.

Om Seti motioned for me to stand with her, and there in front of me were three smaller rooms, each with a different image on the back wall. I could see clearly that they were the rooms of the gods Osiris, Isis, and Horus.

Lucas, Laura, and Alice stood in the room with Osiris.

In the Horus room were Naomi and Lesley.

In the Isis room were Lucinda and Alexandria.

Emilee faltered. She seemed uncertain, finally choosing Isis.

"Now, proceed," said Om Seti.

I went over to each room, first to Osiris.

"Oh, Father, hear my prayer. Bless these initiated with your patience and wisdom. Allow them to reclaim all of their soul that once pledged themselves to you. May they serve you again."

Next, Horus.

"Oh, Brother, bless these initiated with your courage and strength. Allow them to reclaim all of their soul that once pledged themselves here to protect this temple. May they serve this temple again."

Finally, to Isis.

As I walked to the doorway, I felt the presence of my

teacher and friend again. I could see her spirit in the Isis shrine. But I saw her as a young girl and an initiate herself. She smiled at me and then disappeared.

"Oh, Mother, feel my sacred heart send love and welcome these initiates back to their promise of the heart. Allow them to heal their hearts and bring this sacred love to others. May they serve to heal this temple again."

I turned to see Om Seti for the next direction, but she was gone. I looked for the Contessa, she also had gone, and I could see her and Rashida walking towards the entrance about to leave the temple. I assumed they were leaving. I knew we had to act quickly as many things were shifting in the timelines of the temple, and I could feel the spirits watching.

"Now quickly, the Flower of Life chamber, wherever that is," I said.

"The Osirian," smiled Laura. "I know the way," she said and darted out of the chamber, turned left, and then right across the seven chambers. At each one, she waved her hand as if she was opening a door, and I realised that this would wake the shadow, but it was the only way to start the chain of events about to happen.

I felt as though we were flying, and I was most surprised to see the Contessa rejoin us. It seemed she had returned to her normal colouring and had quite the spring in her step. But something had changed. I could not tell what, but I could certainly feel it.

We walked the cobblestoned corridor toward a gate to the outside and then out onto the sand. All I could see was blue sky. We walked around, and below us, I could see a smaller temple set deep into the earth. The energy felt so different; this was a temple of darker stone that looked in disrepair.

"Everyone, be seated," said Alice. We all sat down and overlooked the broken, derelict temple site, which surrounded a floor covered and submerged in a dark green, almost glowing water. This was the place of shadow.

"We will remote view," said Alice. "Anna, will you lead the way? Those of you harmed in this temple, know the demons are still here. They know your fear."

I opened my bag, took out the black Book of Keys, and began to draw the shapes on the page that revealed itself into the sand with my fingers.

Lucas came close and handed me a scarab and scroll.

"This is Light and Shadow, Anna," he said.

"And for you, Alice, the Death and Resurrection and the Records of Life."

I closed my eyes and allowed the vision to come through me.

"Let all be shown; let the truth rise.

"Now, everyone, we go together.

"Imagine yourself full of light.

"You are lighter and clearer in your sacred heart.

"We are now walking down the stone staircase and into the first level of the chambers.

"We move through the purification.

"Each chamber you see is a place for meditation and communication with other dimensions.

"Take your place in your sacred space.

"Now, feel yourself being lowered into the afterworld.

"You're finding yourself in the tunnels and small chambers.

"The walls have images and inscriptions of the souls of darkness.

"Osiris watches over this world. This is his domain.

"The Osirian. The world between the worlds.

"Horus, his son, guards the path to the Earth realm.

"We were once guardians of this holy place and will be so again."

I kept going with the meditation, guiding the group. Various members spoke affirmations, reversed curses, and reclaimed spiritual gifts. All was good until a dark and evil spirit began to move towards us. I felt the fear within the group.

There was a scroll in the demon's hand, and I knew it at once. It was the true Scroll of Unal. The demon was reciting the chants and drawing the symbols. And I knew them, too. As they were recited, I saw the creatures of my nightmares coming through the chambers. They looked at us with curiosity, and it was then I realised this demon was connected to the energy of the Scorpion Queen, and this was her domain.

She rushed towards us, and I held my ground, and for some reason, she could not reach me. I felt Sekhmet and Isis guarding me. Something was pulling her back. I could see a Stargate portal behind her. She was trapped here. And she had trapped these souls of Unal. The demon came to her and handed her the scroll.

I held up my hands and began to recite words, almost like a light language.

I then held up the Hathor sistrum, and the scroll began to dissolve.

I watched her retreat.

"*You are weak, Anna,*" she cried out. "*You can claim the souls of this Temple for yourself. You have called the Death and Resurrection, Records of Life and the Light and Shadow energies. But as you use each one, its power weakens. Look at your sister Naomi; her wealth has been removed. She may carry wealth in her purse, but her soul has no currency.*

"And her friend Lesley, who looks to her as a friend, but it is ego that is her desire. The beautiful Emilee. Her looks are failing, and no man will want her. She has the dark past as a witch.

"Alice is old and faded; the Contessa has no fight left and carries the karma of unimaginable things in history. Her granddaughter Alexandria knows some of the secrets and lies to you, Anna.

"You think Lucinda is a high priestess, but she can barely command herself and never a temple. Laura looks for comfort but feeds from the energy of others. Lucas is a broken, useless child.

"And you were told you were special by a weak father and miserable mother..."

"Stop!" I screamed out. "How dare you in our father's house!" I pulled out the rattle from my bag and began to shake it, evoking the names of all the gods I could think of. Alice handed me the Scroll and Scarab of the Records of Life. They came to life, and I watched as they began to bring energy from the Akashic library, which appeared to be drawing other powerful sources of Light. Michael came into my mind, and I dismissed this as a distraction. I prayed he would not ridicule or reject me.

"I'll see you very soon," she laughed and then retreated. She went through the Stargate and disappeared.

I wondered if the others had heard her cruel words, and by the looks on their faces, they had.

"Let us not have her distract and destruct," I said.

"Anna, you brought forward the truth, and we heard her," said Emilee.

"Her truth, not ours. Now let's clean this house," I said.

Once we had all returned to our bodies, I asked Emilee to check that everyone was okay and Lucinda to make sure no entities had attached themselves. We all stood up to leave when I caught sight of a young man's spirit standing on the sand about 30 feet away,

"Free us, please," was the message I heard.

It was beyond hot, and I could see everyone, red in their faces, gulping water. But something more was required.

"Rashida, what is the history of this temple around 4000 BC? I am sensing the priests, the warriors who died here."

Rashida came over, and she had tears in her eyes.

"There was a legend that before the great Kings, there was a great war—in the early stages of Egypt. This was once a great city, perhaps even 12,000 years old. Many soldiers who were also priests died here, conquered by a leader with great power. However, the priests were not buried according to the correct custom. Their bodies were not laid to rest, and their souls were locked forever on this site. It was said that the kings knew of this, and they would conjure their souls to fight their battles. We do not know how they knew, but it was said that the King-maker Scroll contained this wisdom and informed the kings in exchange for their power. It was said that the last king to use this power was Alexander the Great, but the scroll was destroyed in the fire of the Library of Alexandria. Queen Cleopatra did not have access to it for Julius Caesar or Mark Anthony, so the souls of the priests remain in limbo."

"Then we free them," I said, calling for our group to gather and hold hands. "The Scroll of Unal will have no power over them. The King's List of names holds this karma. It is connected to the King-maker Scroll. It's time to sever and dissolve the cords that bind."

"Then we must go," said Laura, and led us to a wall of

cartouches... the King's List. I moved my hands across the energy of the wall, speaking Light language.

I began to see the spirits of warriors and priests shifting slowly and making ready to leave this place between the worlds. I called upon the group to assist me and help our brothers. I passed the Death and Resurrection and Records of Life Scroll around, followed by the scarab, and everyone placed blessings or clearing into each cartouche. Many souls from the temple began to pass us by, each nodding and following his brother and his enemy. Many battles had left many scars, but as they found the light, the fight was over, and they were ready for the afterlife.

We all remained silent, each person remembering their own interpretation and sense of journey. Then I called Lucas to stand in front of me.

"Oh, Brother of Light, long have you shielded your sisters. Now it is our turn to shield you with love. Let the power of Unal be released from your soul."

Each of the women began to stream light towards him, and I watched as the records of his soul began to shift and recalibrate.

Finally, Naomi went to him and, placing her arms around him, allowed him to rest his head on her shoulder. Slowly, he released what was left of the pain from this temple and, for a strange reason, began to laugh. It was not the reaction I expected, but I could see the perfect message for us all: he was healing, just like us.

Rashida checked her watch to tell us the bus was ready, and it was time to go.

Slowly, we made our way out, but not before I had the chance to visit my star chamber and make a promise to visit again. I watched each one of the group go to the various other chambers, and I made a mental note of each one.

Something told me we would be visiting here again. I felt so strong again in the middle chamber.

"You feel at home in here," said the Contessa as she stood in the doorway of the room I was standing in.

"Through that doorway, that Stargate was my home. It's a blue-white star, and the beings are talking to me," I responded.

"Then it is true. Isis said you would know what to do when you brought her home," she said.

"This is her home?" I asked, pointing to the stone wall.

"Yes," the Contessa nodded.

Part of me felt sad. As we left, I could feel a little of Isis with us. I knew it would not be long before she left us for good. At least I knew where she was going and perhaps how I could reach her.

"I am ever so glad that all cleared," I told Alice and Naomi. "Now we can relax."

Naomi and Alice looked at each other.

"We saw her, too," said Naomi.

Alice nodded. "Then it has started."

"What's started?" I asked. "I banished her with my energy and dissolved the scroll of Unal."

"Maybe from Abydos," said Alice. "But she's gone into the world of the inner cities and will be ready for you, I'm sure, in the next few days."

"You must watch your thoughts and dreams, Anna," warned Lucinda.

"She knows," were the last words I remembered.

I felt a sickness go through my body, and by the time we reached the bus, I had a temperature and, within minutes, had fallen into a deep sleep and trance.

Chapter 23

Monday, 21 September 2009
Luxor

I didn't remember the journey back to Luxor from Abydos. I do remember Lucinda and Lucas helping me to my room and saying prayers. I slept more soundly than I remember in a while. I awoke early to the 5 a.m. call to prayer coming from the local mosque, and to my surprise, Alice was asleep, snoring on the small sofa in my room.

I went to the bathroom, and this must have awakened her.

"I'm so sorry, Alice, but it's 5 a.m. What are you doing?" I asked.

"Oh, it's okay. Emilee will be here soon. We all took shifts sleeping and protecting you." She yawned and rubbed her eyes.

I felt so bad that everyone was giving up precious sleep for me. There really was no need.

"But Alice, why? We got back, and I went straight to sleep, but that's not alarming."

Alice avoided my question, and I was about to push on this when I heard the bedroom door open. It was Emilee, with a room-service trolley full of hot coffee, tea, juice, and light, fluffy croissants.

"It is early, but remember, we pack, and we head to the boat. My favourite to be on the Nile," she said.

Alice cheered to the sound of tea, and I realised I had

not eaten since the dreaded lunch box the previous day.

"The boat is awaiting us at 10 a.m.," said Emilee. She came over, checked my temperature, and smiled.

"Did Naomi switch the boat?" asked Alice.

"Yes, she did, and we have our own boat for four nights."

Our own boat. Now I was excited also.

"Yes, it is smaller, with eight rooms, but we can stop when we want and how we want."

"Early tomorrow morning, we will sail and reach Edfu Temple mid-morning," said Alice.

Now that did not sound so great, but a private boat? Apparently, Naomi's credit cards were still working, or maybe it was the Contessa. I was still determined to find her coin and, with that, began to ask Emilee and Alice about their experiences and thoughts of the previous day. But they were making a quick exit, taking their drinks and croissants, both avoiding why I needed protection.

It was 9 a.m. when Naomi knocked at my door, and I was still in PJs.

"Anna, get dressed, we leave soon."

"Chop chop... I'm not dealing with this," she pointed to my room with clothes and bags, a total mess. Nothing like packing to get you grounded.

☥

The boat was amazing as we entered from the narrow platform of the dock, and the crew greeted us with warm hand towels and hibiscus tea. Our bags were carried to our rooms, and some of us were sharing except for Naomi, Lucas, the Contessa, Rashida, and Lesley. I was sharing with Alexandria, which I thought was perfect. Even though we were not moving yet, something about being on the Nile and the gentle floating motion made my heart so happy.

After checking into our room, Alexandria and I set about to explore the boat. Some of the group were going shopping in Luxor as Naomi had declared this a free day. She had a list of activities, including in-room massage, meditation, perfumes, and the market.

Alexandria and I decided on the evening market visit and claimed our places up on the deck to relax on the lounge chairs. I even brought out my laptop and began to write.

"You're writing, I see," said the Contessa as she swept by us, veiled from head to toe in case the sun should burn her.

"Mais oui grandmama," said Alexandria, "and she's writing about us," she giggled.

"Oh, make me younger," the Contessa laughed.

"And me in love," said Alexandria.

"I shall see," I laughed.

"'Living on the Nile—The Lives and Loves of the Priestesses of Avalon.' How's that for a title?"

"Excellent," said the Contessa. "A best-seller, I am sure."

It felt so good just to relax and let the day drift by.

At 5 p.m., we all gathered on the deck for teatime and sunset. It was magical watching the Nile at night as the sun fell behind the Valley of the Kings, and the remaining red light turned the water a certain shade. Once the sun was gone, the night lights brought a whole new perspective.

After a light evening meal, a few of us gathered to leave the boat to explore the Luxor market. "But it's so late, will anything be open?" I asked.

"Yes, that's the adventure," said Lesley.

So Lesley, Rashida, Emilee, Lucas, Alexandria, and I ventured out into the night in the small taxi bus the boat steward had secured for us. They parked in the car park next to Luxor temple, and I could almost hear the whispers luring me back to visit. I found myself making a promise to return. I guess Naomi was correct. I was now making deals with my soul. I looked at her, talking to the driver with strict instructions about when to pick us back up. I looked back at the temple.

"Alexander, if you are there, bring the coin back to my friend, and I will return to you next year."

There it was official—a deal had been offered.

Luxor Market

We entered a very small and busy street. It was so crowded, it seemed like it could have been midday. All the stalls were filled with scarves, bags, and trinkets—all the things tourists in Egypt can't live without.

"We only stay one hour..." said Rashida, "...so do not be late. Be back at the entrance."

"After that, you become a pumpkin," said Lesley, and she disappeared into the crowds.

"We should stay together," said Alexandria, and I realised we were suddenly alone.

"Let's not go too far," I said, and suddenly felt a little afraid.

We ventured past each of the storefronts and were surrounded by smiles and compliments. Each one looked like a hidden mystery. I hoped not to find any of the forbidden experiences or magicians.

We stopped at a store on the right with the most beautiful golden statues in the window. Rows of glass bottles in many colours created a striking array of magical light.

"Oh look... it is like the museum goddesses," said Alexandria.

"This one, I think, is the one for us," I whispered, afraid that the other shopkeepers would descend and distract us, and we opened the door.

We stepped into what appeared to be a very small store. On the walls were shelves of statues, perfume bottles, and jewellery. The shop display cases were dark brown with glass. I peered inside at the various objects that did not look to have been touched for fifty years.

"Isis, Nephthys, Hathor," Alexandria was naming and pointing to the statues.

"Very good, *habibi*," the voice of a man came out from behind a curtain. "This is the work of my family."

"It's beautiful," we both said in unison.

"Who would you like to see first?" he asked.

"We have not got long," I said to Alexandria.

She shrugged. "Then I speed shop," she smiled.

"This Isis and that Isis and this Hathor," she kept pointing, and he kept smiling and bringing forward various pieces and adding the number on the calculator.

"Oh, and that Osiris and that Anubis."

"Alex, how will we carry this?" I asked, alarmed.

"Oh, we will ship," she was shopping as if she had taken a drug of some sort.

It was at that point I was aware of the incense and the look of the man's eyes staring into hers.

"And this one," he smiled, taking down a very large Bastet cat.

"Oh yes, I have to have that."

"Stop!" I held up my hand as I saw the numbers on the calculator reaching into the 1000's rather than the 100's.

I did not know where it came from, but I placed my hand on the countertop and looked deep into the man's eyes.

"*Habibi,* please look at me," I smiled. I felt an energy stir within me. An energy of protection and power.

"She does not need all of these treasures, do you not think?" I smiled and looked at the man very intensely.

His eyes widened, "You are the woman with the green eyes."

He was shocked, and in stepping back, he dropped the calculator, which broke into several pieces.

I just kept looking at him and shaking my head.

"But Anna," Alexandria stamped her foot, and I saw a whole timeline of us in 1888, my younger, impatient sister. But it was just a flash and nothing more.

"No, my sister, we can select one thing, maybe two."

So the spell was now dissolved, and I could see he was angry that he had broken his precious math machine, and he had taken down half the shop he thought we would buy. The silence was broken by the laughter of an older man who came from the back shop area. He looked about 100 years old and smiled with twinkling eyes. His hair was grey and thin. He wore a striped Galabeya dress and a small, crocheted hat.

"My son, my son. She is the gifted one I warned you of," he chuckled.

"Your ego and greed," he said, pointing to the array of merchandise everywhere.

"And you, my lady, you have the skill to see and defeat the magician."

"I do not see magic tricks," I responded with a smile.

"No, but you see the game at play."

"In ancient times, the Kings and Queens would have to play the game of the magician with the gods for safe access."

"This is the game," he pointed to the glass cabinet.

"The Senet," said Alexandria, coming out of the spell.

"I have seen that in images of Nefertari. She plays the game in her tomb," I said.

The old man smiled. “Yes, she plays opposite the Scorpion Goddess to keep her distracted.”

“Learn how to play, ladies, and you will fulfil your destiny.”

“You are sisters, yes?” he asked.

“Only in soul,” I replied.

“Give me your left hands.” We both held out our left hands, and he turned them palms upwards.

“See,” he said, pointing to our lines in our palms. “Same line here and same line there.”

“I never thought to look at that,” I shrugged.

He then held both our hands and closed his eyes.

“Your blood is her blood. Your timeline was split and broken. One of you went to faraway place, and they tried to separate you both, but you are bound by the promise of the oracle. Her blood is your blood,” he repeated as he opened his eyes.

“My vision does not see anything,” I whispered to him.

He smiled. “It will when the time comes.” He let go of our hands.

“Choose your item each,” he pointed at the statues. “I sense your friend’s approach.”

I pointed at the Nephthys in gold and Alexandria at the golden Isis. They were the same size and certainly portable.

“Wrap them, my son,” the old man ordered.

“How much?” I reached into my bag.

“You say,” he smiled.

I looked in my bag and saw I had the envelope from the Contessa. When I heard shopping, it seemed appropriate to bring some of her magical money. It contained various currencies, and I noticed a few 50-pound notes. I pulled out two and handed them over. The man smiled and said something in Arabic to his son. His son nodded and lifted up a flat plate with crystals, scarabs, and all sorts of mini trinkets.

"Choose a gift each."

Alexandria reached for a small Ankh, and I, for some reason, did the same.

"Treasures," his son said.

"Don't look at me with those eyes," Alexandria laughed.

"No, my lady," he said, looking down.

"We'd best go, Alex." She nodded and did a little jump up and down to shake off the last of the spell.

We were about to leave when Naomi opened the door and her eyes grew wide with delight.

"Naomi, we don't have time," I steered her back toward the door.

"I have something for you, my new friend." The father went into the cabinet on the wall with all the glass perfume bottles.

"For you," he said, holding up an exquisite pink and purple glass bottle—it was so delicate. "You will return?"

She smiled and I could read her mind. Naomi knew that if she accepted this gift and made a promise to return, her fate could be sealed.

"I may," she smiled, "but just in case, let me leave some offering for the bottle."

He paid no attention and simply wrapped the bottle with care and handed it to her.

With just as much care and ceremony, she reached for her purse and opened it.

"Anna, my coin is back."

She held up an old, large coin stamped with what looked to be an ancient king.

The old man held his hand to her. "May I see?" She hesitated, but then she placed it in his palm.

The old man studied it and smiled. "It is Alexander the Great—very powerful and beautiful."

Naomi smiled, took the perfume bottle, and placed it into her bag. The old man then handed her back the coin.

"The debt has been paid, and the contract is now in place," he said. "Not for you but for her."

He pointed to me, and I shivered. Naomi and Alexandria looked at me, and I shook my head to say, "Not here, not now."

Then I smiled at the father and son, aware that we may be late and needed to wrap this up and get back to the group. "Thank you, friends. Next year, I will be back."

"*Inshalla,*" the old man said, "and may I still be here."

CHAPTER 24

Tuesday, 22 September, Equinox
Edfu Temple

Early morning, we set sail going south towards the Upper Nile region. The boat engine woke me, but all was very calm and peaceful. I turned over and carried on sleeping.

It was a quiet morning; however, it was a different story as we passed through the Esna lock, with vendors in boats chasing us, laden with tablecloths and Egyptian scarves. Apparently, all boats underwent this rite of passage, remaining stationary for around 30 minutes as they waited in the lock before being lifted into the next stretch of the Nile.

There was quite a commotion as we watched a cruise boat on the opposite side of the lock, heading in the other direction. Vendors crowded along the dock, throwing their goods in plastic bags up onto the upper deck. Tourists would pick their items, tossing back the money in the same bags along with any unwanted goods. The shouts and haggling grew so loud that it drew everyone from their cabins, and even those of us having breakfast ventured out to watch.

The Contessa complained about the noise, but Lucas had had an amazing time buying many things and precisely throwing the money back to the grateful vendors. He shrugged and smiled as I helped him sort and fold everything.

"I can sell this all in my shop," he said. That was fair enough, but I could see the compassion in his eyes, as he knew many risked their lives selling in this way just to support their families. Still, I wondered how many suitcases he would need to carry it all. But we were stopped from having that discussion when Naomi announced that we were an hour away from Edfu, our next stop.

This was the temple visit I had been dreading—the time had come to return to Edfu Temple, and it also happened to be the day of the Equinox, a powerful day for energy shifts.

I had gone to sleep that night after our shopping initiation, imagining how Edfu Temple would be. Would I know the chambers, or would they know me? I rehearsed so many things in my mind. I wondered what was real and what was imagination. When I had first come to Glastonbury and met Isis and Naomi, I had never imagined that I would be the key to unlocking a very sad and destructive time in our Oracle history. A time when the balance between the male and female temples was broken, and when the young male priests would be initiated through pain and fear.

As we gathered on the boat's deck, ready to leave, Lesley went to each person and pointed to their bags and backpacks.

"Anna, do you really need that bag for this trip? It will only be a short visit."

"Well, I have my water and my journal and a few pieces that may be needed for this particular temple." I looked at her very matter-of-factly. Maybe my green eyes were shining again. But no, nothing worked on Lesley. She was above the magic tricks.

Naomi came over.

"Take nothing but yourself," she said, handing me a small bag that looked like a purse with a long cord.

"Here, put in a little cash and your phone if you must, and wear it around your neck. There is a small place on the back for your special pieces, and your black book will fit. Lucas has the only scroll and scarab that we need, and that is the ones of Protection, and I shall be the one to use them," she said.

"Keep both hands free—you don't want to lose your balance in this temple."

As Rashida walked us up the walkway ahead, I could see many carriages and horses lined up, awaiting us.

"Chariots," said Lucas from behind me. "Anna, I'll ride with you."

I was so glad he did, as the horses began to race in the streets of the town, and I began to see the carriages shapeshifting.

Suddenly, the shops and cafes were gone, and all I could see was sand and the Nile.

The carriages became chariots, and the men riding in them looked like priests but wore golden vests and animal skins. They held spears, and I could see they were warriors. They feared nothing and no one. These Priests of Horus, at this time, had their hearts closed and their egos on full display. I looked over to Lucas and watched as he took on their form, and I wondered if I should be afraid.

As we neared the temple, I began to feel cold and tremble.

Lucas took my hand, "Anna, we have to end this battle."

"End this battle?"

"Yes," he said. For too long, this temple took our hearts and trapped our souls, and now it's time to release all our fears. You helped me in Abydos, and I'm going to help you all today."

I began to feel some relief, but only just. The horses drew to a stop, and I could see the towering temple ahead. We gathered as a group before slowly following Lesley and Rashida. Lesley stopped before the entrance and turned to Naomi and Lucinda.

"Ladies," she said, and beckoned them to come forward.

They moved into position. Naomi had been the Oracle of Edfu, and Lucinda was the High Priestess of Dendara, so their lineage was the highest here. Naomi took Lesley by her hand.

"We will do this for Isis," she said, and Lesley nodded.

"But before you do... Anna will vouch for me as I have work to do, also." It was the voice of the Contessa.

The Contessa then joined them and turned to the group. "I was once a high priest here and will perform the honours again."

It was strange to see her now in the body of a man wearing the robes and animal skin. Everyone was unsure, and Lucinda looked most alarmed. They all turned to look at me.

"I see her, I mean him," I stuttered. "She... He holds the mantle of Lord Horus."

The Contessa bowed to me, "With thanks," she said.

"Mine was a forgotten rule, a time before the time of famous kings and queens. In my time, this was a temple of balance, and then another greater temple was built. This is the temple you see today. The Greeks and then the Romans honoured us, but they did not know the true power of this place or its intention. Today, we will remember the true faith of Horus."

With that, she turned and slowly walked towards the temple. We followed at her pace, and I could now see why we had started late afternoon to be free of the tourists, as the place looked deserted.

The Contessa started to walk towards the entrance when Naomi stopped her.

"Contessa, with respect, we must do the blessings to Hathor and Isis." I could see the towering temple ahead, far taller than anything I had seen in Luxor and Karnak. But to the left sat a small temple that reminded me of the shrine to Isis in Dendara temple.

"This shrine you see to the left is the Temple of Birth. This is where the priestesses would bring the young priests, and for ten days they would stay with them, preparing them to step into the temple and be received," Naomi said.

It was strange, but the Contessa nodded and bowed to her knowledge. Lucas stood close by me, honouring his promise.

"Many young boys would be sad to leave the nurturing, as many were not ready," Lucas said.

"You were ready," I said to him. "You had no fear."

He nodded and stepped forward. "Hold the group, please. I would like to share something," he called out, and everyone turned and gathered around him.

"Here in this shrine, I was brought when I was a young boy who had been nurtured and raised in Philae Temple. I had waited for this day when I would be presented to the Temple of Edfu and the mighty Horus, and I could serve my King. For the days of preparation, I was purified and given the sacred rites. I could recite the prayers of the god and goddess, and I knew the story of how Horus defeated his uncle, Set. I was ready to help defeat the enemies of my King in this life and the afterlife."

"I remember when I walked through the main gate, I did not look back. But I wish I had, for I would have carried that last look of my mother forever. Life in this Temple was very different from what I knew from my early years in Philae Temple. The military style was the order of the day, and we lived and prayed by the cycles of the sun and the moon. If you missed training, you were punished, and we grew to learn through fear and not love. I never saw love in this temple except for when the time of the 13-day festival of the union occurred. That became my favourite time when the priestesses from Dendara and sometimes Philae would visit, and the temple energy would be filled with love and celebration."

It was then that I began to see his fate, and I lifted my hand to cover my gasp. Lucas looked at me.

"Yes, I was initiated in the chambers within the walls. I was taught the secrets of the darker alchemy, and yes, I faced the Unal trials, and I failed. Somewhere within this temple, I lost my heart and was discarded. It was then that I left the temple to follow Naomi the Oracle when the High Priest took his revenge on her and Philae Temple. I had followed her father, the previous High Priest. So today, with your help, I come to claim my place again as a Priest of Horus and protect you all."

I saw the sadness on his face.

I stepped forward. "Then today, we claim back all that was ours and leave what no longer serves. Please tune in to your intention."

Everyone took a moment, and Alice looked over at me and smiled. She pointed to the towering temple. I nodded.

"Then we begin," said the Contessa, and our journey in Edfu began.

As we entered the main complex, I was taken by surprise. The relief on the outside was the clearest image I had yet seen. Rashida walked with us and simply pointed out the key pieces with short sentences and one or two words, so we did not draw attention to ourselves.

As we entered the first gateway into the large courtyard, I watched as the Contessa took her place at the front again. As everyone filed behind her, I saw who in our group had been a priest here at one time and who had not. It was clear many had connections to this temple, and I wondered who I had been, but nothing came to mind.

We first arrived at two large Horus statues standing on the side of the next gateway.

The Contessa performed a sacred rite.

"I place the heart of Horus back into his chest," she announced. She stood before one of the large hawks, and you could see where, physically, a large piece of the stone had been cut away, where his heart would have been.

I was not sure why or how, but it appeared very symbolic. The others took turns to also add their prayers and forgiveness to the statue. Then we moved through the temple and stood in a large section with towering columns similar to the hypostyle hall in Karnak. I looked up to the black ceiling, which had yet to be cleaned and refreshed. The Contessa was now standing in the centre of the avenue of columns, pointing to the high altar that lay ahead of us.

"Oh Lord Horus, welcome us home; we have come far to remember our journey here on earth. You bless us with your winged protection and insight. Let us pass and let us perform the ritual you have called us home to perform. Let us cleanse this place and reinstate the energy of the light."

I remembered Naomi's trials and story and turned to see her. She was all in black with a red scarf, very military style, but now her face had softened.

"I feel no anger in this place today," she said.

I looked at those who had belonged to this temple. The

Contessa, Lucas, Alexandria, Naomi, Lesley, and Emilee. All at various times, as I saw them in different robes but always in the service of Horus.

Except for the Contessa. She kept shapeshifting. I could not place her true lineage. Everyone stood very still, and Alice came over to stand next to me.

"Some of them were here before the time of Alexander the Great."

"Of course. You knew him," I whispered to Alice.

"Yes, he started the plans for this new temple here on this site. It was here they first brought the Scroll of Unal and, over the next 300 years, used parts of its wisdom to undo the Scroll and Scarab of Protection."

I became aware that those in our group who had worshipped here in this temple were beginning to look at each other and remember who they were, but I was more drawn to Alice.

"All is well... all is in divine order," she said.

She nodded to the group who were recalling their past lives and then we looked to Lucinda, who was using energy to heal the various ley lines around the temple. Only Laura stood alone as if acknowledging all the spirits still walking around.

"They come forward to her as she once was also an Oracle here," said Alice. "Most ancient."

"I don't see any of us with her," I said.

"Laura's soul is possibly one of the oldest here," smiled Alice. "She remembers a time of grace and divine masculine power before the corruption."

Once everyone had an understanding of why they were there, we moved slowly towards the High Altar. As we entered each section, I could see many inscriptions upon the walls. Alice walked with me and whispered wisdom.

"Alexander came here and felt the power, and he wanted to know more. The Oracle at Siwa had told him to raise a great army, and if he was to be all-powerful, he would have to conquer the Priests of Edfu. They were being corrupted by an evil force, and that force had summoned the scroll of Unal. After he had a vision in Luxor Temple, he came to the wall of scrolls over there," she pointed back to a small doorway inside the temple wall, a part of the original temple. Like a temple within a temple.

"Alexander removed all of the sacred texts and then began to describe to his key soldiers how a temple would be remade. This was around 333 BC; he never returned, however, as he lost his life, but he had passed his wisdom to his general. General Ptolemy would be the next ruler of Egypt and, over time, became the King. Each of the Ptolemy Kings was sworn to secrecy and handed the sacred texts and artifacts; they were also told the legend of the Priests of Unal, and thus for 300 years this Temple was in battle with itself, sometimes light, sometimes dark."

"Was this all given to Cleopatra?" I asked.

"Yes," Alice nodded.

"She was supposed to end the rule of the power of Unal to destroy its scroll and lineage."

"But she did not," I answered.

"No, she did not. Instead, she looked to Julius Caesar and then Mark Anthony. They knew she had an ancient power, and she used this leverage to secure their protection for her and to give her the crown."

"My friends," said Laura, "it's time."

Then we moved slowly, and I could see the room of the Holy of Holies, the high altar ahead. The stone floor was uneven, and I had to watch my steps. I began to see energy curtains at various stops. The Contessa stopped at each of these energy doors and whispered to allow us to move forward.

Then we moved until we stood in front of a middle chamber that had a large stone altar and a shrine behind. The shrine was polished stone with etchings and shone like silver. This was where the statues of the gods would be placed and where the high priest would hold the rituals. We all gathered around the high altar.

Meow, meow.

I could hear a small cat, and so I looked down. To my surprise, a tiny golden and white kitten was rubbing against my foot.

"Here, little one," I said, and bent down and picked her up and placed her upon the altar.

"Bastet," said Alexandra, taking the kitten and placing her in her arms in a scarf.

The Contessa began the ceremony. As she did, I saw Lucas reach into his bag and retrieve the Scroll and Scarab of Protection. He placed them on the altar in front of me. Everyone turned to look, and the Contessa smiled at me. She looked to Naomi, who nodded to give permission.

The Contessa cleared her voice and began.

"Oh Lord Horus, receive us with your light and protection. You who have fought the battles of darkness and guided us, we ask now that our brothers and sisters be released from the karmic cycle and battle. Release the soul this temple has claimed and restore them to their place of eternal glory."

She looked at me.

I placed both hands upon the altar.

"I now restore the energy of The Scroll and Scarab Protection," I said. "Within these walls are many secrets that have been used to hold others from their free will. Lives have been damaged, and souls corrupted. Lord Horus, I pray you allow us to clear this temple and restore our true path, to set our sisters and brother free. Unal has no power here, and I invoke the gods to allow us safe passage."

As I spoke, I could feel the wind at my back, and I knew that some evil force had reentered the temple. I could see its energy like a black cloud in my third-eye vision. Suddenly, the energy took the form of a tall, slim man with a shaven head. He wore a long black robe, and his eyes were the darkest of kohl. A Priest of Set.

He was moving swiftly towards us, and I could see the alarm on the faces of others. While they may not see him, I was sure they could feel him. Alexandria covered the kitten, and I knew I must protect the group. I looked at Lucas, and he nodded to me.

"You shall not enter here by the divine claim of Horus," I declared out loud.

"I am the Keeper of the Protection,
I am the Lord of the skies and Lord of the living,
I forbid you entrance to this holy shrine,
I forbid thee!"

It was as if a divine force had taken over my body. I was shaking, but as I held firm, I saw the energy of the dark priest rise up and turn to dust swirling around the entrance. Laura and Naomi then joined hands and stood in the doorway of the shrine. In union, they confronted the spirit.

"As oracles of this temple, we declare that you may not enter."

He had no power here. I opened my eyes, and everyone was staring at me. It became clear that we had been responsible for creating this and that we were not innocents.

"This curse that lies here was placed by oracles from this land, and as oracles, we must reverse its claim."

I watched as the dark priest took form and stood his ground outside the chamber. His face shifted many times. I called out to the spirit of the Oracles of Edfu to reveal the Akashic Record.

"We all saw this timeline of terror approaching. Laura, you saw it 3000 years ago, and Naomi, you saw it 2000 years ago."

I looked around the group as the Akashic Record began to open itself, and I watched as each of our group saw themselves cursing the divine masculine energy for the pain and suffering that the Oracles of Egypt had endured. It seemed much blame and shame had found itself a home in this temple. I began to see those curses now dissolving.

"Cleopatra was my mother in a past life, and she was not able to defend this temple, but today we have. I now release this from my lineage." I felt a presence next to me, and everyone faded as the woman with gold eyes from Karnak and Dendara stood next to me.

She appeared more clearly to me. Her black hair was in braids, and her skin was a light olive tone. She wore white robes and simple gold jewelry. She came closer, and I could smell the light fragrance of jasmine. Her eyes were painted with the distinct black kohl, and she also had symbols of ankhs painted on the palms of her hands.

"I summoned this dark presence, Anna." Her voice was soft.

"Naomi was here during my timeline. I was the royal Princess but also a great Oracle. When my sister and I went to war with each other, I sought to take her place, but she had secured great allies. I took my revenge here and have regretted it ever since."

"Arsinoe, you were bound here also," I replied.

She nodded, *"I'm still in the game, Anna."* Then she

faded.

It was as if time had stopped, and the group were still in their ritual.

"And so it is," Lucinda said.

The Contessa began to chant and then gently closed the ritual. It was then that a temple guardian came forward. I expected him to ask us to leave, but he was looking for something.

"She's here," said Alexandria.

"Ah, my baby," he said and gently retrieved his precious one.

He stroked her head and held her so gently.

"She is Eeses," he said as she purred in his hands.

"Isis," whispered Alice.

He walked away and I saw such love and compassion in his heart as he petted her and took her to safety. I knew then that Isis was watching over us, and the curse had been released. We could now clear the chambers, Arsinoe's curse, and play some aspect of the game.

"Anna, will you lead us? We need to find the initiation chamber." Naomi spoke for all to hear.

"I will do my best."

I went into a slight trance and felt myself stumbling, but I tuned with the energy and heard the voices of those still held in the chamber. I felt an energy beside me. It was Naomi.

"I know the way," she whispered. "I am not afraid anymore."

I looked over, and I could see Lesley at the back of the group, but I was so glad to see Lucas holding her hand and reassuring her. I followed Naomi through the small corridors. This place was a maze. Around the high altar room was a set of corridors, and the walls were covered in images of priests, gods, and kings all being attended by the goddesses. When we finally reached what appeared to be a dead end, Naomi turned left.

We arrived at a small chamber, and I felt a freezing-cold energy run straight through me. The chamber was a square shape, and I could feel a vortex of energy as I crossed to stand in the corner. I could see what I assumed were ancient guardians in spirit standing at a wall, and I noticed a small stone in the wall was loose, which I knew meant that these stones had been replaced over time. It looked like it was the opening for ventilation, but I could feel it was a tunnel that descended under the temple to a very dark place.

The Contessa stepped forward and began to clean the energy.

"This was an abomination," she said. "This is a holy space and place. Corrupted by ego and fear."

I stepped forward and began to read the energy records still in place.

"Once they worked in union but were divided by the masculine power," I said.

"Lucas, please come forward."

He stepped forward, and the light caught his face. I saw once again the strong and courageous priest he had been.

"I invoke the Scarab and Scroll of Protection once again."

I began to recite the messages from the scroll and was reminded that I had seen a tunnel in the Book of Keys. I asked everyone to focus on the tunnel with their light and love. I began to see the faces of the young boys and, to my surprise, some young girls. I saw them bound by curses and living half-lives both in the temple reality and in our reality. I also saw the ghosts of the Priests of Unal who had created these curses.

"I see curses in the Akashic Records," said Emilee. "Hidden curses that we have been carrying." How strange these records have been affecting us all.

"This temple was once created in harmony in my time for male and female," said the Contessa. "Losing the children to this barbaric trial caused the curses to have power as the priestesses no longer trusted the priests."

"We were all damned," said Lesley, coming forward.

"The curses I now name," said Lucinda. I saw her again with her mantle of Hathor and her power within this temple again.

Alice came over, and she held hands with Emilee.

"As a librarian, I bear witness that they are removed power in the Akashic Records."

"I call you all to witness, as this has affected all our lives." Lucinda turned to the group and beckoned them to come forward.

"Let these curses now be revealed and revoked.

"The curse of betrayal, we will now find truth and love.

"The curse of slave, we will now be of service to our highest self.

"The curse of separation, we will now find sacred union.

"The curse of greed, we will flow with abundance.

"The curses of the past 2000 years be healed and released from this holy place.

"This holy place may it be now restored, and we order it brought forward that this now be once again a Temple of Light."

Again, I felt an energy swirl around us both and then spin around the group. In that moment, I began to see where we had all been betrayed, kept as slaves and servants, and separated from love and light. No wonder none of us had a love relationship in real life. We had been trapped in this cursed box of tricks for lifetimes.

I was then aware that the energy of the dark priest who appeared to have been following us was fading, and in his place was my father.

He smiled at me. He must have been a priest in this temple. I telepathically spoke to him.

"You were here?"

He shook his head.

"I should have been, but I failed the initiations and was sent to Esna Temple, not far from here. I was angry and turned to Set. I thought darkness was my power. I was wrong. I was not subjected to the trials of this place, but I heard of them. To clear my karma, I have tried to be your protector. Now I see Lucas is your protector. I can rest."

Then he also faded, and I began to hear the voices of some tourists making their way towards us. I watched as energy began to flow out of the temple walls and around the rooms. I could hear the laughter and the love. I began to see the spirits of those held for such a long time shifting and moving to the light.

"The temple is open and cleared," whispered Lucinda, "let love find the way."

☥

As our boat left Edfu, I waved to the children, who were running alongside the barriers where the boats docked. We were to sail slowly and moor overnight a little further south, before an early start for Kom Ombo Temple the next day.

I watched the children's ancestors waving with them, and I felt a sense of relief. My fears of the darkness were shifting as I began to feel for the first time that whatever we were facing, whatever all those who had gone before had faced, could be overcome.

Naomi joined me on the deck.

"They are so adorable," she smiled and waved to the children, "they have so little but look at their smiles and spirits."

I nodded.

"How was that temple visit for you?" I asked.

"A very different visit for sure. I feel a great deal of work was performed from the Sanctuary in Glastonbury, and Isis and I and others have been clearing the chambers for years. But this time, Anna," she paused to think out her words. "This time, we managed to push forward a balance and actually manage the energy," she said.

"I know you have been resisting the high priestess title, but today, you totally acted like one."

These were amazing words of praise. I hardly knew what to say.

"You know, Naomi, I do not really know who I am anymore. One day, a priestess, another an oracle, and sometimes a silly girl. Do you think we can be many things in our lifetime from our past lifetimes?"

She nodded.

"Of course. It's in your Akashic Records. You simply need to move through your scrolls of past lives and perhaps see the significant timelines. I can understand it can be confusing for you, Anna, as you so clearly see the Akashic Records of others. I think over time, you will be able to see your own and know the difference."

"Where can I learn this skill? Can you teach me, or Alice, perhaps? She is a master librarian."

Naomi smiled.

"Kom Ombo," she leaned in and whispered.

"This Temple to Horus and Sobek has many secrets, and I know they are awaiting you to reveal them at this auspicious time over the Equinox time. In Kom Ombo tomorrow, we will light a candle in the darkness that will shine for the rest of the year."

"The medical temple?" I asked. "I looked it up online, and it had initiations, and there were images of medical instruments carved into the walls."

"It was..." she stopped.

Lesley and Lucas had just come up onto the deck, and Lucas was preparing an initiation clearing for Lesley.

"That poor girl," I shook my head.

"Nonsense," said Naomi. "She will be a great teacher one day, as her soul will be cleared and stronger if she stays the path."

I began to ponder on this. But Naomi gave me no time.

"So, Kom Ombo is famous for the crocodile initiations," she said.

"This temple is built on several energy grids and vortexes. It was said that the mind, body, and spirit were split into various systems, and the ancient Egyptians understood this.

Like a modern-day hospital, you had various areas to care for patients, such as physical systems, intensive care, birth, death, and outpatient care. In ancient times, they worked on the body, heart, soul, shadow, and everything. But to do this, they had to face the darker dimensions and death itself. The doctors and healers in this temple had to look death and fear in the face and command it to leave. Like you did today with that dark priest energy."

"Many spiritual seekers return to Kom Ombo to face their fears as they failed this initiation of the crocodile, and the rest move through as tourists. But there is a hidden layer, Anna, that Isis told me you would uncover when we visit."

"What is that?" I asked.

"Not sure, but she did leave instructions," and Naomi held out a letter.

Dear Anna,

I'm praying you are safe and by now, you will be leaving Edfu. I pray with a happy heart you will now find your way to Kom Ombo.

When you arrive at the temple, move slowly up the stairs. In front of the temple, you will see two avenues of columns.

To the left is the path to Horus, and to the right is the path to Sobek.

Please take the group to the entrance of this temple. Someone who was a Priest of Horus will step forward, someone who knows the story of the crocodile initiations. Allow them to retell the story.

Let them step forward and ask the group who wishes to join them to do so.

You, my darling, are to walk the path to Sobek, the path to the ancient records, and you are to ask the group who wishes to join you to do so.

Anyone who chooses neither path at this time will either stay on the boat or make their own path.

Allow the group of Horus to continue their journey. They will heal and clear the path of the fallen initiates.

Your path will reveal itself once you arrive at the altar at the end of the columns. I have not seen past the high altar, but I know a great sadness is hidden there behind a powerful curse. The power of Light and Shadow moves around this Temple, so be prepared.

Trust your heart, my dear girl; destiny awaits you all.

Forever, Isis

I read it out loud to Naomi.

"Then the work has started," she said, nodding over to Lucas and Lesley, who were already in preparation. I watched as he placed a scroll and scarab into her hands, but I could not read the energy from so far away.

It was as if he were coaching her through something she feared deeply.

"I will stay on the boat tomorrow," Naomi said. "I still have some heart healing from Edfu Temple to process, and the rest and sunrise will help me."

I don't know what came over me, but I leaned over and hugged her.

"Then let the next chapter begin," I smiled.

CHAPTER 25

Wednesday, 23 September 2009, Sunrise
Kom Ombo

It was early morning when we began to drift towards the embankment, and the boat came to a halt. As our boat had been moored overnight midway between the temples, we'd had a calm and restful evening. The beauty of a private boat meant we were the creators of our journey.

We assembled on the upper deck and watched as the temple of Kom Ombo came into view. I was amazed at how close it was to the Nile—literally walking distance.

"Just a walk in the park," said Alice as she came over and squeezed my hand. "Oh, and you should know, Anna, I just heard Naomi will definitely not be joining us for this."

"Nor grandmama," said Alexandria. "She has to rest and told me she will watch from the boat."

"As they wish," I said.

"Lesley, can you please gather everyone? I am leading this tour," I smiled at her.

"As you wish," she responded. "I already know where my work lies, so some of us have free will and choice, Anna."

"Yes, you do." Something told me this may not be the happy family I expected today.

We all disembarked and walked towards the entrance, where Rashida gave us tickets and told us to wait at the large stone at the temple entrance. I had a flashback to days gone by and saw that this stone was where the dignitaries visiting the temple would place their standards, statues, and tributes to demonstrate who was visiting. It also felt as if this temple had actually been built in layers and timelines—at least three timelines of temples built one on top of the other.

Sections had been repurposed, some enlightened and some corrupted. Yes, this was a powerful yet forgotten place. In front of us stood an open temple featuring five columns and two distinct sections. At the rear, I could just make out two stone altars, each adorned with ethereal statues of the gods. I was suddenly aware that many of the temple spirits were coming to life. I could see the Horus priests to my left, and to my right, a line of Sobek priests and priestesses. I was sure I could see my friend Anubis in the centre, not choosing a side. I was already lost in the energy. I shook myself back into my body. I then wondered who would step forward for Horus. I assumed Lucas and was a little shocked when Lesley stepped forward.

"Welcome to Kom Ombo, the Temple of Healers and Seekers," she said.

"I hold the ancient keys to this temple and have been its High Priest before, and I welcome you all to be present here with me."

Suddenly, I began to see the temple in my vision, seeing how it must have looked, the colour on the walls, and the hieroglyphics so visible that they seemed alive.

"May our esteemed guest from the House of Horus step forward," she said.

As I suspected, Lucas stepped forward. Ahh, I had not lost my gift. As Lucas moved forward, once again, I saw him in his priest robes, wearing his distinct symbols drawn onto his arms. Around his neck was a beautiful glass scarab made from a yellow crystal.

"I hold the energy for Lord Horus and the initiates who will walk with me today," Lucas proclaimed.

Laura pointed to the path to the left. She moved into place.

"Those who will join him," Laura continued.

I watched as Lesley and Lucinda moved to join him. I was left standing with Alexandria, Alice, and, surprisingly, Emilee. Lucas stood very still and smiled.

"Before us stand the initiates who perished in the Initiation of the Soul."

He pointed at the group of women who stood with him.

"They were all young men and women who came to heal others. But fated to a sad path."

He looked at Lesley.

She stepped forward and spoke. "I did not fail this initiation, but my fate was to send many to their death."

"For this, I now invoke the Scroll and Scarab of Light and Shadow so that we may see our way to face the trial and survive another day."

"We were trained to face our fears and not fear death. We swam in the Nile and prayed to the God Sobek for our protection. We entered the initiation chamber and swam down to the bottom, but could not find the secret entrance, and therefore, we perished and failed. Our fate was cast into the water of the Nile, as were our souls. I failed in so many ways."

I could not help myself. I moved forward and spoke.

"Today, you will not fail. Sobek and Horus watch over you as do I, and you will walk the path again. Lesley and Lucas, please guide our friends through the chamber again and out towards the initiation arena so they can reclaim their soul's wisdom and not fear the path to enlightenment."

I pointed to the chamber far over to the left, where you could see a round stone wall, which I felt was the entry point, and then to the right, a stone gateway exit to the side.

People were peering over the top of the round wall, dropping stones to see how long they took to land at the bottom of this chamber. I felt a chill. I had a flash of initiates entering and their soul brothers and sisters trying to hide the grief and loss when they did not return. The energy felt heavy—not painful, but confused and sorrowful. I could see the similar trials and lessons of Edfu again and wondered if the Priests of Unal had also left their mark here.

"Now the chamber is open to Horus; please make your way forward," said Lucas, and his party walked slowly into the Temple.

"And we ladies will walk the path of Sobek," I said and smiled. "We will remember the secrets that this temple wishes to share." My mind began to overthink. I had no idea why I was here, and if this was the dark side, I wanted to skip out and follow those with Lucas.

I moved towards the temple entrance with my small group. Emilee seemed to falter as if she were unable to break through an invisible veil. I stood with her and held her hand.

"Anna, please help me walk with the spirits that still journey here. I watched as the crocodile trials took place and saw many of this temple's cruel aspects in the search for healing."

"I have spent many of my lifetimes healing others, and I know today, with your work, Anna, my karmic record can be reviewed and recorded, and I may be released. Isis told me many times to come and heal myself here, but I was afraid. But today, perhaps... today, I can see a path for myself."

I nodded to her and watched Lesley disappear with her group down into the temple. I knew she would be sharing the story, and I also began to see spirits following. I could see them all as initiates, some strong and confident, and some fearful that their testing day had arrived.

"Come close," I said to the remaining ladies.

I watched as Anubis began to stand with us, silent and powerful. I saw such compassion in his eyes. We all stood together as I closed my eyes and began to see a timeline of the past.

"I see a time when the priests were performing rituals to hold the souls to this temple like slaves. This temple has many oracles, Akashic librarians, and even medical intuitivism. Wise and full of knowledge, many of our brothers and sisters were tricked here, made to perform miracles. Their services were sold, and they themselves were sold. The lack of respect for the healers and teachers here is so sad."

"Do you hear them, Anna?" asked Emilee.

"I do," I replied. "Do you?" She nodded.

"Then we go forward," said Alice.

"Yes," I said and moved ahead into the columned pathway.

We entered the first section, the hypostyle hall. I saw priests and priestesses moving with herbs and oils. They carried medicines and tools for healing. One carried a birthing stool. They looked surprised to see us but carried on with their work. I began to see patients being brought through and much activity as they were taken to the other passageways. We moved slowly to the first chamber. Here, I saw scribes taking the details of the patients and the medical intuitive reporting on them—what they saw, heard, and felt. It was as if they scanned people with their hands and appeared in a dream state.

The second chamber was where the record keepers sat, the Akashic librarians who spoke of the karmic debt and ancestral karma that resided. A woman sat in the corner and reported on the records of the babies to be born or those brought to the temple for examination.

The third chamber held the Oracle of Kom Ombo, who would declare this person's future and the path ahead. Everything was in a structure of help and healing. It was quite surreal, and I saw the women with me, experiencing their versions of the vision. It was as if we were walking into the dimensions of time.

Before long, we found ourselves at the altar of Sobek. It seemed so strange that this small stone block could carry such powerful energy. I ran my hands around it and watched as the energy rose out of it and around it until a statue was visible.

"Anna, you're bringing him alive," said Alice.

"*Who has awoken my slumber?*" A deep voice came from the statue that was beginning to reveal itself.

"It is I, Anna," I said, bowing my head.

I reached into my bag, took out my black book, pulled off my turquoise ring, and placed them on the altar. The statue came alive in the form of a man with a crocodile head, and I saw the ibis and baboon had joined him.

"*Then open the gates,*" and the statue pointed to the small rooms and chambers to the back, behind where we were standing.

In front of us were the chambers, and on the floor were more chambers covered by metal gates. I was surprised to see Emilee going to each one and trying to clear the energy, but nothing appeared to be working. She looked up at me.

"Anna, you have to help them. They are screaming and crying." Emilee was becoming more and more distressed.

I asked the ladies to join me at the altar, and we stood around Sobek. I then brought out my healing sistrum. For this temple, I had come prepared.

"*Ah, you have brought powerful tools,*" said the voice as I placed them into his energy field on the altar.

"Oh, Lord Sobek, will thou work with us, with my sisters and I?"

It was as if he were scanning the energy of each of us.

"You all are here of true heart, one heart, and we will work as one."

"Many are still trapped in this temple," I called out, and I caught the attention of Lucas, who was standing with his group just across the way at the altar of Horus.

Emilee made her way back over to me, "In the name of Neith, mother of Sobek, Anna, please help me. They are trapped in the world between the worlds."

"This is more than the power of Set and his league of dark lords and ladies," the voice said.

"But there is one who can set them free and she comes to us now."

I suddenly became aware of another female presence that stood next to Alice and Alexandria. Behind them, I saw a whole line of men and women, all wearing white robes and carrying tablets and pens. They began to emerge from the chambers.

"You came," a voice from behind a pillar said loudly.

Emilee stepped into the centre between the two altars. To my surprise, I saw the voice enter her crown chakra. She was no longer Emilee. She was the Goddess Seshat. She was dressed in a simple white dress, but her scarf was leopard print.

"These are my Akashic librarians, placed upon the Earth during times of great significance. They chart and scribe everything of karmic balance."

Emilee pointed to the women standing with me and all the spirits that were now joining us.

"Once, we had a great school of learning here," she continued. "But when the energies shifted, and the Ptolemy

family rebuilt our shrines, they wove spells to bind us to them and their timelines. Alexander the Great had opened the doorway for their lineage, but he was unprepared for the forces they would bring.

"They evoked a great force of darkness for the Priests of Unal to seal the portals or guard them. We were visited by a dark entity that would force the librarians to write the Records in their favour. They conjured up great forces that allowed many great battles to be won and even attracted the great Julius Caesar to our shores.

"When they had no need for him, they cast him aside. Cleopatra tried to hold her power, but all was doomed, as Cleopatra was not given the steps of the game. Her sister Arsinoe was one of us, but her short life and fate fell to the curse of the Scorpion. She was the one who had studied the game, but her sister Cleopatra did not listen. She still is held in the game, as are you, Anna."

Emilee was now moving around us, and it was as if time had stood still.

"I do not understand the game. What do you mean?" I asked. "I am simply clearing each temple and helping my friends."

Emilee continued. *"She comes in many forms, but you know her as the Scorpion Queen. The only one we know who could keep her at bay was the Queen Nefertari. She listened to me during the reign of her husband, Ramses II. In her tomb, the Akashic librarians recorded Nefertari playing the game of Senet. This was a secret message to learn, and now, Anna, you are playing the game—this game across the worlds and dimensions.*

"Some of the souls you may lose, and some of your friends may cross to the other side. But this is a warning from the Akashic Librarians who understand the Game of Souls is

in play, and like a game of chess, each party has a team. For all the souls you set free today, your energy will be depleted, and your scarabs, scrolls, and books will only guide you so far.

"Isis was only able to make it this far, and in Philae, she failed as the grief of the past was too much to bear. Even though it seems you only have a few more temples to go, the stakes are higher. Watch your thoughts and watch your step. For she knows where you are, who you are, and what you could become. You are her enemy. Make no mistake."

I felt myself slump onto the altar, and Alexandria caught me. I looked around and saw that Lucas had now moved to the crocodile initiation chamber and was reciting the prayers as each woman released their fears and regained their confidence in their abilities. Emilee was standing more at ease, and I watched as she wove the energy to free herself and her friends.

I looked at Alice. She nodded. "I know of this game, Anna. It was written on a scroll in the Alexandrian Library. The scroll was lost in the fire, and many of the oracles and librarians of Alexandria lost their lives. Those who survived ... I do not think they remembered everything."

"You mean the living books?" said Alexandria. "I know now I was one of them."

"You were, my dear," said Alice, "and we have waited a long time for you to remember."

"I just did," said Alexandria. "Anna, I don't know how you do it, but I see so much more clearly."

"It's the Scarab and Scroll of Light and Shadow," I pointed to Lucas, who was using them to release the trapped initiates. He saw me and handed them to Lesley and told her to bring them to me.

Lesley then made her way back over to us, and she placed them in my hands.

"See?" I said, holding the scroll up. "It says, 'All life shall be restored, and the gates of oneness can return.'"

"I can't see that," said Lesley. "It is just scribble and signs."

"Seriously, you can't see the words?" I responded.

"No," they all shook their heads.

"Perhaps only I can read all of these, and I think I may have written this book to translate," I said, holding up the Book of Keys.

I remember now, and like a movie screen, many visions came forward.

"No time for that," laughed Alice. "Look."

I turned to see around thirty tourists making their way into the temple towards us.

"Let's let everything rest," I said.

As we left, I watched Emilee go through each chamber, closing down the energy and vortexes. She whispered healing words to every doorway and screened area. It was as if she were fully clearing the gates never to be locked again. This was a temple where I knew my dream time would love to visit.

☥

We slowly returned to the boat, and I watched Lucas and Lesley head to the mummified crocodile museum to release their souls. Thankfully, we were so early that the vendors had not fully opened any stalls, and we moved with ease from one temple timeline to the reality of our breakfast on the boat.

The staff had kindly laid out a feast for us on the upper deck. Fruit salad and delicious sweet and savoury breads were arranged so beautifully with pots of fresh tea and coffee. The waiter in his smart red waistcoat took our hot breakfast order. When my pancakes arrived covered in fresh raspberries and whipped cream, I knew I would have to eat every delicious bite.

An hour or so later, we sailed away. I stood there up on the deck, unable to move due to the overindulgence and energy of the Temple. I found it difficult to say farewell to a place I now felt so connected to. Soon, the temple became a small dot on the horizon, and my heart felt heavy.

Naomi and the Contessa rejoined us up on deck and talked about their wonderful experience with the facial and massage treatments they received. I listened politely and was a little shocked. We had been accessing some of the great wisdom and the most powerful karmic clearing, and two of our most powerful members were at the spa.

I caught Lucinda's eye and knew she was reading my mind. She smiled and shook her head, warning me to be mindful. Then she motioned to the front of the boat, where I saw Emilee standing, arms stretched up. A hawk flew overhead. She was gently swaying, and I thought she must be singing to the spirits. I walked over to her and saw then what she was seeing.

The Nile water glistened in the sun, and I could see energy streams swirling. It was as if souls were leaving, souls that had been trapped for thousands of years. My heart felt full at this vision, but my head asked, at what cost? I took her hand, and she looked at me and smiled.

"I faced the light and shadow," she said, "and it was beautiful."

"My Queen Nefertari taught me," she whispered. "I can't wait for you to meet her properly."

"Me, too," I replied.

I looked back around at everyone; we were all bonding and laughing. The energy was so high, and we were excited for tomorrow. For this would be the day to visit Philae Temple, home to Isis and many of our past lives.

CHAPTER 26

Thursday, 24 September 2009
Philae Temple

I was in a dream within a dream. It was as if we had just left Kom Ombo, and my soul was now wandering around the temple, or was it somewhere else? I was not sure.

I saw myself walking across the courtyard of a temple that felt familiar. Darkness and death were stalking me from the side, hiding behind the columns.

Barefoot and in a simple white dress, I began to see the temple alive and awake.

It was approaching sunset, and the priestesses and priests were busy. Food and wine were being served, and I could hear the music and see those who celebrated Ra dancing by the edge of the water as he left to go to the other realms. Graceful and poised, I looked to the main temple, knowing that this was where a high priestess and her elders resided.

The ibis and baboon were not far away, like guardians between the dream dimensions.

I was floating and felt the energy of the spirits move through me.

One of the spirits stopped. "You should not be here," she hissed. It was Naomi.

Then she disappeared.

I stood still at the water's edge and began to see the sunset. A dark cloud drifted across the temple, and I could see a faint moon in the distance.

I felt the ground begin to shake. I turned and watched

as a young woman ran from the temple, her clothes torn and blood on her face.

Across the courtyard, the dark shadows began to move into the hearts and souls of this temple. I had felt this before but could not place it, perhaps from a far more ancient time.

I could hear things breaking and people running.

Now, it looked as if soldiers were arriving. Swords moving and people falling.

I could see ahead several priestesses trying to move a large stone across the temple gateway entrance, but I already knew it was too late.

"Anna, there is nothing you can do," a voice came from behind me.

It was Isis.

I tried to scream, but nothing came from my throat. I looked at her and ran to the temple door to help them seal the chamber, but the soldiers were already in place, and these brave women never stood a chance.

I ran through the first hall and to the back, but my fears were confirmed.

There they lay, the Oracle of the Temple, the elders and priestesses, all on the floor, soaked with blood.

Then I saw her, and at last, I could scream. Isis, our Isis, my Isis, slumped over the altar with many wounds on her body. She was gone. It made no sense. She had been protecting the temple. She was needed to hold the balance and the sacred Nile.

I don't know what came over me, but I entered the chamber and began to weave a curse.

I was so angry.

"I call forward Osiris and Ra to witness this evil and abomination. May all those who struck a blow and held open the doorways carry this karma from this day forward. This darkness from Unal will not prevail. I stand. I call for justice

and offer my service to anyone who will avenge us."

I was not sure if it was me, my soul, or another force, but I knew this curse would be powerful. I was simply re-enacting it and making it live again.

I was shaking, not knowing where to go next, when I felt a familiar presence and looked up to see Cleopatra. The baboon and ibis were with her, and they were all witnessing my work.

"You are weaving a powerful curse, child," she said.

I still could not speak, but was aware of another woman who stood behind her. They looked similar.

"You see her?"

I nodded. "Yes, we have met."

"My sister Arsinoe."

"Anna, once I cast a powerful curse, and it rebounded upon me." Cleopatra continued, "My sister warned me, and I betrayed her. I tried to play the game to save us and undo the harm I had created with the Romans, but no, my ego overtook me, and I thought I was all-powerful."

"I lost," she looked around us at the bodies of the priests and priestesses.

"This was the fate of us all."

The woman behind her, obviously younger and not so lavishly adorned, stepped forward.

Arsinoe smiled at me and held out her hand. I felt such comfort knowing that this woman had been with me, protecting and, at times, guiding me on this journey through Egypt.

"Anna, you and your friends can make this right. I foresaw this terrible scene. I had a vision of this temple over 2000 years ago and saw the blood and the fate of Isis, but no one believed me, least of all my sister. I was sent away to a powerful temple called Ephesus. Bound by the oracle curse and doomed to wait. It was your birth that started all of this."

"My birth?" I shook my head.

"Yes, when Cleopatra had the girl child, you, she was supposed to be Julius Caesar's oracle. She had the gift of our family line.

"I have that gift like you, Anna. What happened to me in that life had happened to you in other lives. This is our fate."

I wanted to know more.

But like any dream, they were suddenly gone, and I found myself sitting up in bed in silence, shaking in fear, unable to grasp my part in this story and curse.

When I finally pulled myself around, I dressed in my white clothes, laid out the night before, anointed myself with rose oil, took my bag, and quietly crept out of the room to avoid disturbing Alexandria. I saw it was well before sunrise, around 4:30 a.m. The Nile was still, but I was more alive and, for some reason, not afraid. How long that would last, I could not say. Soon the others would be gathering, as we were to visit early, at 5.30 a.m., before the temple was open to the public at 8 a.m. I found myself a chair up on the deck and sat in prayer and meditation. I would be prepared for all that came my way today.

Despite the early hour, everyone was excited, chattering, and hugging as we gathered up on deck to make our pilgrimage to the temple. For many, it was their personal link to Isis, the goddess, and Isis, the mentor, who had guided us and helped us to heal in various and magical ways.

It took no time for our bus to arrive at the location where we would board a small boat to make a short sail to the temple located on a small island nearby.

I could hear the voices of my friends, but I chose to tune everything out and stay focused. The Contessa shushed us all like a schoolteacher, reminding us of the reason we were here.

And so we walked down the jetty way and boarded the small boat silently, simply nodding and using small torches to guide the way into the boat.

"Now the journey of Philae can begin," Naomi said, and at the other end of the boat, I heard the sound of a singing bowl being struck. We all sat down in silence.

The Contessa recited a prayer of safety, and I saw her throw a coin into the water to pay the ferryman for safe passage. She then asked us to remain in silence and gaze out across the Nile, and Rashida asked the boat captain to set our course. We were all having a peaceful moment when the Contessa announced she would channel and had a message from Isis.

"My beloveds, we arrive today with one heart. This is my temple and my island. I have watched over all of your past lives, and now I fly like a white dove above you. But know this: we were once betrayed, and one among you is responsible for that curse. One among you who can call the darkness back, so be aware and walk with care."

Rather than a message of love and light, we were all shocked by this warning. I looked over to Naomi, and she shook her head, and then I looked to Lucinda, who looked shocked and alarmed. But then I remembered my dream, and in that moment, a great fear came over me. What if it was me—my birth, over two thousand years ago—that had caused this chain of events? I felt scared and alone, and I began to think everyone was looking at me and judging me.

We soon arrived. It seemed so strange to arrive in the darkness, but it also felt like a veil of protection. I heard a whisper, "Remember, we left in the dark." I looked and saw no one speaking.

As we left the boat and walked onto the Island, I could see everyone supporting each other. There were whispers of, "Hold on, I have your hand."

"Take care; it's still quite dark."

"I can support you. Lean on me."

"We go to the Dream Chamber first," said Lesley, and pointed to the temple ahead and nodded to the Contessa.

I could make out who was who in the shadows and clearly see Lucas helping everyone. It was as if we had turned back time to an ancient timeline, as I could only see the outline of faces that appeared to change into past-life versions.

Very slowly, we began to move across the courtyard, Lucas and Rashida guiding us with flashlights. It was strange that no one took control, and no one assumed the role of High Priestess of Philae.

I knew then that the honour would always remain with my friend and mentor, Isis.

"Come closer, everyone, into the main temple," Lucinda said. But I could not help but stop and look at the heavens and stars above. "Look, it's Venus," whispered Laura next to me.

I followed as we walked up the small steps into a dimly lit area in the center of the temple. The Holy of Holies room was up ahead with its high altar visible, and I wondered why we had not gone straight to this. I could see ghosts swirling around, and I was relieved when we stopped in the chamber outside.

"Now, everyone, find a comfortable place," said Lucinda.

We all spread out, sitting on the floor and leaning against the columns.

"Now close your eyes, my dears," said the Contessa, "for

this is the place where our secrets will be revealed in this Dream Chamber."

I simply left my body. I began to float around, and although I could hear the voice of the Contessa in the distance, the spirits were taking me to a whole new realm of information and understanding. I watched as a spirit that I sensed was my mentor, Isis, came and began to show me what she had seen here. I was seeing a famine and drought. Pain and suffering. The records of Egypt from the Akashic and Oracle realms were being revealed to me. But like a deep dream, I could not fully make them out or even try to understand. One thing I knew was that Isis had also seen this, and she knew that it might happen again. She had failed to complete something on her last trip, and therefore, it was a task set for me, but I knew I could not do this alone.

"And now, my dears, it is time to return to your bodies and bring back your unique Philae Temple story and your true connection to Isis and the Priestesses." The Contessa closed the meditation.

Suddenly, my dream was present with me again. I opened my eyes and could see the blood on the high altar, and I was weaving my curse. I wanted to claim it back and tell everyone of what I had seen the night before.

As I looked around, the light was starting to come into the chamber. I saw that everyone was calm and appeared to have had a positive experience.

But I certainly did not feel like that. So I stood up as if to give a speech, but Naomi came over to me.

"Anna, we can talk about this on the cruise boat when we return," whispered Naomi.

"Yes," I said, and then I could not help myself.

"But did you see her, Isis, and where she fell?" I pointed to the high altar.

Naomi looked around, then directly at me, and took my

hand. She was shaking.

"Yes, I did, and when we were here last, Isis did have a fall in the same place. Something dark got to her, Anna, and I pray it is still not here."

"Then we have work to do," I said.

"Yes," she nodded, "but not here. This is not to be shared yet."

Out of the corner of my eye, I could see the others watching our exchange.

I wondered if they had seen her, too.

"Now the sun is rising; we must go to greet her," said Laura, and we all began to file out of the temple. As I looked at us all, we seemed to be shimmering with light.

It was much lighter now, and I began to see the temple in her true beauty.

Rashida came over to me, and Lesley followed her.

"Anna, we now have over one hour before the boats and the tourists arrive," said Rashida.

"And you are to have this. I was instructed to give it after the Dream Chamber meditation was completed," said Lesley, handing me another white envelope with what I knew was direction from Isis; I read it in a whisper to Lesley and Rashida. They both nodded, understanding the locations where they would take me.

Anna,

You have made it so far now.

Honour the sun rising and give thanks to the Nile.

Request purification, then create the initiation of the Priest and Priestess of Philae.

Then, once again, walk through the Lionsgate and bring all home to me.

We will then release all that needs to be cleared.

Use your wisdom and the scarab and scroll of your choice,

and I pray you have chosen wisely.
Restore all that asks.
Then, move to the dance and gather those of Hathor to offer gratitude.
We will need all the souls of the priestesses for the journey ahead. Call on your brother and sisters, as each has a key to this temple, and all are needed.

Always and forever,
Isis

We made our way out of the temple. Day was breaking, and the sky was becoming lighter.

"Now, everyone quickly," called Alice, and she stepped forward. "Let us greet the sunrise," she said, and we all followed.

We all walked in a procession down towards the edge of the temple that overlooked the Nile and stood in a line looking out across the water.

The sun was just beginning to rise as we lifted our hands above our heads to create the sun salutation yoga pose. Lucas had tried to teach me in Glastonbury, but I always fell over, yet today, I was so overcome with a sense of ritual that it came effortlessly. We performed the movement three times.

Today was the day we would rise with the light. When we finished for some reason, I was overcome with a sense of grief. I began to sob and crouch down.

"Anna, you cannot break down in tears in this temple," said Lucinda, leaning over me.

"Leave her alone," snapped Emilee.

"Attention, again," Laura tutted.

"Leave her be. Let's go visit the temple," Naomi announced.

People began leaving the line or stopping to look into

their bags, and the sense of ceremony was lost.

"Then it has begun," said Alice with tears in her eyes.

"What has begun?" said Alexandria, who sat near her.

"What Isis feared most," said Alice, "that we would turn on each other. This temple still carries the shame and pain."

"Isis knew this," said the Contessa. "Her death ended the reign of the Egyptian Kings and Queens."

"But this had started long ago." I was getting up to my feet as Lesley handed me a tissue.

"Do you see when it began, Anna?" she asked.

"I don't see yet, only death and drought, but it was a cycle over 4000 years ago that played out in history, and we were all part of this."

Half the group stood, and the other sat when Lucas stepped forward.

"Ladies, I wish to present something to you and remind you of what happened here. I do not care if you were here then, but use your oracle gifts and tune in with me. We must clear this before we re-enter this holy place." He pointed up towards the Dream Chamber and high altar.

I knew he was right, and I looked at Naomi, who had stopped in her tracks and was listening.

She nodded, "I think this is what Isis would have wanted," she said.

Lucas looked at Rashida. "As you wish. We still have time until the tourists arrive."

Lucas came and sat beside me, beckoning everyone to gather and sit back down. He then faced me and took my hands.

"Anna and everyone, I want to share with you what happened that night."

I turned to look at him.

"Everyone, come sit close," said Naomi, and we all gathered closer.

"Now, ladies, please look up and face this temple. You have the light behind you, and the sun is rising. Look to this sacred place."

We all turned and sat with our backs to the wall and the water.

"Now, please stand, turn around and look to your right out to the water and those wooden posts. Once, this temple was not in this location. It was far over to the right, where just a few stone doorways and wood parts show out of the water."

I felt calm for the first time since we arrived as I remembered that this temple had been moved. I began to see how it had been at one time and felt the love that drifted across the water.

Lucas continued, "But these temple stones, statues, and columns remember, and they hold onto the secrets, and every one of you was initiated in this order of Isis at some point."

I took a moment to glance and began to see everyone's faces. Yes, we had all been initiated here at some point, even Rashida.

"The Order of Isis. We were initiated in the teachings of the divine goddess, and it was not just a person in a past life; this was a soul-connected group." He paused.

Then Lucas took a deep breath and began to speak again. His words echoed around us.

"It is 48 BC, and news of the fires at Alexandria reached the Temple of Philae quicker than anyone had expected. The Oracle of Philae had seen the fears and heard the screams of the other oracles in the sacred fires weeks before it had happened. No one believed her, and she had retreated to the back of the temple. They had sent a small group of priestesses to Dendara temple to see what their oracle had seen, but when they reached it, they found it under siege with a Roman garrison positioned around it.

"Isis had been consulted, but she was unsure of what to do. For the first time in her reign as the High Priestess, she was questioning her decisions. She knew that if the Library of Alexandria fell, Cleopatra would look to Philae Temple for its relics and scrolls to consult.

"Philae temple had been the protector of the scrolls and their copies for many years, and the wisdom had been hidden and concealed from everyone except the highly initiated. Many had tried to make copies, and indeed, Isis and the priestesses had made copies of the spells. However, they always made sure that a certain key element was missing so that a forgery could always be spotted. During the reign of the great kings of the Old Kingdom, these had been used to summon great energies and secrets; hence, the pyramids were created. But at the end of the reign of Pepi II, 2052 BC, Egypt fell into civil war and over a century of darkness. Many of the relics were brought to the area around Philae for safekeeping.

"The Cult of Isis was known to possess the magic of invisibility in plain sight. They knew many spiritual arts, and it was said they could travel by moving in the shadows. And that's how they stayed a protected group, veiled to those who could not see and did not know of the magic. This was until the times of Alexander the Great, who exposed many of them, as he sought to take their secrets. However, he learnt that he could be more powerful if he worked with them and gave them sanctuary, and so he was responsible for the physical creation of the temples being built from 333BC through the Ptolemy family, who followed him as rulers of Egypt.

"These Greeks were not of Egyptian lineage but integrated the sacred rites of the Egyptian gods and goddesses into their dynasty.

"It was said one of the last true Egyptian kings who ruled was a man called Nectanebu II, a King who caused my demise, and had possession of many scrolls and scarabs. However, he was bewitched by Alexander the Great's mother, Olympias. It was said that Nectanebu and Olympia conspired to create their own Mystery School to link Egypt and Greece's wisdom and raise Alexander in the new ways of their beliefs. Some people thought he was their son. The Oracle of Siwa had prophesied that Alexander the Great was the golden child who would conquer many nations. But some in Egypt were jealous of this Greek connection, and Nectanebu was deceived by those close to him.

"When his reign ended, the kings that followed him could not hold power. But the prophecy was fulfilled when Alexander took Egypt for himself. It was said that the Oracle of Siwa told Alexander that his lineage would rule for 333 years, and Alexander thought he himself to be immortal. Alas, this was not so. His reign ended early, and Egypt was passed to the Ptolemy general, who would proclaim himself a King and thus his family dynasty was started. He was the ancestor of Cleopatra VII, the last of the Ptolemy line to really rule over Egypt.

"In 47BC, a dark force spread through the land when Cleopatra and her sister Arsinoe found themselves on opposite sides. Arsinoe had raised an army in Alexandria and captured Julius Caesar, but he had escaped. Arsinoe was an oracle and had spent much of her life in the temples, and it was said she had trained in Siwa and the Pyramids. She saw many things and had always shared them with her father and sister. But now she was imprisoned and would later be banished.

Cleopatra would solidify her relationship with Julius Caesar as she bore him children and declared him a living god in Egypt. She believed he could protect her position and lands.

"After the death of Julius Caesar, many dark omens visited the land of Egypt, and when Cleopatra called for protection, very little was forthcoming. The religious orders of priests and priestesses had been weakened. After the Alexandria fire, the Romans became a greater force around Egypt's temples. Isis called for Philae to be protected and closed the entrance gates. No more ceremonies outside of the temple, and no more tributes and visits were allowed. Of course, that created discord, and the temple became out of balance. The festivals ended, and children who had once played and created together began to compete and fight within themselves.

"The priestess initiations had been delayed due to the Priestess of Ceremony and Priestess of the Initiation having created an ongoing argument about who would lead the process now. Isis wanted the young boys initiated like the girls, and this caused great unrest with their birth mothers, who wanted them initiated first with the god Horus. Isis claimed she could initiate for any of the gods and goddesses. After all, she had the power of the earth and heavens.

"This would cause the rebellion; messages would be passed around, and whispers would be shared in the halls at night. There was disruption once again throughout Egypt, as there had been after Pepi II, during the Akhenaten timeline, and after Nectanebu II. Then came the news of the war with Rome and Caesar's successor Octavius. A great battle was fought at sea, and the oracles of the temples foretold in secret messages, Cleopatra's and Mark Anthony's death. They saw Rome marching in and the temples burning.

"This should have been kept secret, but it swept through the temples like a lightning strike. The hawks were dispatched and brought the papyrus messages; however, not all messages were for peace. The oracles tried to communicate through the high altar in Karnak, but again, the Romans had swept through, taking control.

"The factions began to plot, and a group of priestesses with ties to the temple of Edfu and Horus's High Priest began to receive messages. The High Priest was a man of a darker heart and knew there was a chance for the priests to rule as governors of their regions—if they commanded the secrets. He summoned the dark forces known as the Priests of Unal to visit Philae. He made a deal with his soul. These had once been Priests of Horus, but the Edfu trials had corrupted their souls. They sat dormant until summoned.

"He knew that the Priests of Unal were on their way to capture the scrolls and scarabs that the Oracle of Edfu, you Naomi, had spoken of, and he had to be prepared. Those in league with him in Philae were told to place a piece of red silk upon their quarters, and the Unal Priests would pass by. The priests were looking for Isis. For once she fell, the High Priest of Edfu could work with those he trusted to bring order and work with the Romans for his own gain. He would be a leader. He had also made a sacred blood oath to Set and was simply pretending to be Horus."

Lucas paused, but I already knew what was coming.

"In the weeks that followed, news eventually reached the Temple of Philae that Cleopatra had taken her life, but the temple already knew, as the Oracle had come forward with her fate in earlier days. Philae was silent for seven days, and Isis performed all the high-altar rituals. She ordered everyone to their chambers. They all took provisions, and those who could care for the sick and elderly, and those who cared for the children, took them to the places they thought they would be safe. The ferryman was given seven coins and told not to visit the island or take anyone to or from the island. He took with him a few trusted priestesses and an Oracle. I was with them for protection. I had abandoned my allegiance to Edfu, pledging to serve my Goddess Isis. The ferryman was to return with us before sunset on the eighth day.

"But the priestesses faithful to Edfu, who were tricked by the energy of Set, could wait no longer. On the seventh night, they went to the entrance gate and unlocked it. They placed the red silks around their quarters and told those they trusted to hide and be silent that night after sunset prayers until sunrise.

"The Priests of Unal came fast. Their boat floated into place silently, and they climbed out in dark cloaks with short swords dipped in poison. Once, they had been children in this temple, nurtured and loved, but now their souls were corrupted by vile and evil. They already knew the temple layout as these priests had been born here and had played here as children before they left Philae for Edfu. The spirits of Unal now owned their souls. Dark and dead. Just simply moving. They stole silently into the temple and headed for the high altar.

"Now, Isis knew they were coming. She did not fear them and was sure they would not strike a chosen goddess down. On the previous day, in secret, she had already dispatched her most trusted priestesses with the secrets, scarabs, and scrolls, and they had stolen away before sunset to protect the important documents. She told them to return a few days later when all would be healed, and the temple could rise again. She did not believe the words of her elders that all could fall.

"This, however, had left Isis vulnerable, but her Oracle assured her that the dark ones would not cross the threshold, and they would remember the Isis who had watched them being born.

Once the ritual was over for the evening, Isis and the Oracle smiled, and the Oracle left the high altar to place the oils and symbols on the sacred shelves. She did not hear the priests approaching and had her back turned when they stole into the sacred place.

"Isis faced the priests and was surprised as they looked upon her, taking down their hoods and revealing their faces. Each one she had held as a baby. Each one she had kissed, blessed, and loved. But now their faces were twisted, and their eyes were blank. Their shaved heads and evil glare showed no sense of love or connection. It was as if each one had a demon in his heart.

"One by one, they descended upon her. Their daggers flew into her. The poison went through her... until she was lifeless and lying on the floor with her eyes still open. The oracle had raced back to save her and began to scream. The dagger turned upon her.

"The temple began to stir as the priestesses and children poured out of their rooms towards the high altar. They could see Isis lying on the floor in the entranceway. They began to scream and run towards her, but the priests flew through them, taking their lives. They preyed on the innocents with no remorse, subjecting them to horrific humiliations and levels of abuse. Some of the priestesses simply walked out into the water and drowned themselves, as they had watched these evil ones harming babies and children, unable to do anything. Powerless, they ignored their teachings, believing the gods had forsaken them.

"Those who knew to stay safe in their rooms could hear the screams of the others, and they held each other tight, not daring to breathe and not daring to step out to save another. Those with the gift of sentience and feeling simply rocked as if they were being driven mad. It would be a full eight hours before the screams, shouting, and crying stopped.

"At daybreak, those who had survived ventured out slowly. Bodies were everywhere. The priestesses who remained faced the worst fate and were cursed ever since for not defending the sisterhood and temple. The priests had gone, and all that was left was the shame and pain. Life was never the same, and those who remained had to clear what had been left behind. They have carried the shame, blame, and guilt ever since. The sacred temple was shattered forever."

Lucas hung his head.

"When we returned on that eighth day..." but he stopped, unable to speak.

Alexandria sat down next to him and held his hand. "Shall I continue?" she smiled at him, and he nodded and gently kissed her forehead.

"When we returned, the temple was in great mourning. There were priestesses who had survived, many of them beaten and wounded, but they had survived. They were trying to give those who had perished a funeral rite of passage, but there were many. I still have nightmares about this." She tried to stop her tears, but we could all feel the emotion. "Those little ones with such potential, such innocence, so pure." She hung her head.

"Alexandria, my darling, continue." The Contessa was so gentle and supportive, just like I had seen her in Paris.

"The priestesses aligned to Set had fled, as they believed they were to go to the Temple of Edfu to be celebrated. What fate fell on them is unknown, but I think it was a dark one. Those who remained set about clearing the temple and trying to wash away the blood. The apprentice of the Oracle came forward. She admitted she had hidden, but it was by the order of the Oracle as she was told that someone needed to carry on the story."

She looked at me, and suddenly it was clear to me, so I stepped forward. Now I understood how and why I knew what had happened. I continued the story.

"As the apprentice of the Oracle, I was just a young child. I listened to her every day when I brought her food and water. I watched her rituals and listened when she told

Isis that the dark ones were coming, but Isis did not believe. She even feared it was those close to her in the temple who conspired against her. That evil night, I tried to help the others. I tried to move the doorways closed, but was told to hide. The Oracle knew who I really was.

"I was hidden in a corner, simply listening, and refused to speak. I heard the plotting, but Isis dismissed me when I told her. The Daughters of Set, as they became, thought I had no gifts and that I was simply a servant to the oracle. At that point, my gifts had not been revealed, nor had my birthright and lineage to Cleopatra. When they went to escape after the massacre, they left behind all those who could not serve their cause, and so I was left behind. I stayed and helped the others clear and honour what was left of our temple, and then we prepared to leave." I reached my hand out to Alexandria.

"We survived, didn't we?" I said.

She nodded, and this told me to continue.

"Once we had buried our sisters and brothers, the small group that we were left the island. We covered ourselves in simple clothes and evoked the ritual of protection and invisibility. All that we had were a few of our personal treasures and statues. We travelled as simply as we could. But we had friends along the way, and we rejoined the priestess group that had left, taking the scrolls and scarabs for safekeeping, and who were in hiding. They knew we were coming, and so a group of around twenty of us who had survived set off to travel up the Nile.

"When we reached the area now known as Cairo, we were taken in by a tribe looking for lands to settle, and we all travelled west to what you now call the Holy Lands. We lived with those people for many years, sharing our stories and hiding in plain sight. We passed on our wisdom and became part of the ancient mystery schools. We led everyday lives, taking husbands and having children. Many of us travelled and taught the secrets of the Isis wisdom and had many amazing students. Jeshua and Mary would carry on many of the traditions."

"Yes, Anna." Lucinda stepped forward. "We carried on the lines of sacred wisdom so that it would not be forgotten. Some of us were in the Coptic area when the family came to hide after Bethlehem. Mother Mary carried a rare blood lineage and had a connection to Isis from her ancestors. The Goddess Isis did not just touch those in Egypt; she connected with many who sought higher wisdom. She was the life force of energy rather than the force of life energy."

"That was 2000 years ago," said Alice, "and I wonder, are we now ready to step forward again?"

"But don't you need a high priestess?" asked Lesley.

"No," said Lucinda. "We need an oracle, a teacher who remembers. The Oracles of Egypt knew the ritual, and we need to be reminded. Many here have been High Priestesses, and I am not sure we wish to take on that mantle again, but we do wish to serve. I believe you, Anna my friend, can help us remember."

Finally, I had found my place. I was an Oracle, and I knew exactly what to do.

Lesley handed me a letter, "I have this letter from Isis, but something tells me you do not need it. She is with us on some level. I'll put it in my bag for safekeeping."

I smiled, nodding in agreement. I held my hand out to Rashida. This was my place and my work. "Rashida, be my guide, please, navigate the places I need to go. Lucas, we need to start the creation again."

He smiled, reached into his backpack, and pulled out the box with all the scrolls and scarabs.

I walked over and selected the Scroll and Scarab of Creation. I held them in my hands and felt the messages running through me.

"First, we need water for purification," I said.

I wondered if we should wait while everyone found their balance, but it was as if everyone had been awaiting the command. Rashida began to walk through the temple to the right-hand side and then towards the back, and the area where the steps led down to the water's edge. We stood in an archway, and Alice pulled a small glass bottle from the Chalice Well from her bag. She handed it to Lucas and motioned for him to go to the water's edge and retrieve the Nile water. We all stood back, as who knew if a crocodile would visit.

When he returned, I handed the scroll and scarab to Alice.

Lucas handed the bottle to me, and I held it in my hands. I saw a vision begin of an ancient time when the young priestesses and priests were brought to the water's edge to give gratitude for the Nile and the life that it brought to them. I placed the bottle down, and Alice handed me back the scroll and scarab.

"I invite and evoke the Scarab and Scroll of Creation.

May they rise within these sacred waters and align within us all.

In this moment, we are purified by the Nile as she is the mother of all."

My attention was drawn to Lesley, and I realised how she had tried to warn Isis about that impending evil, but Isis had not seen her. In the end, Lesley had fallen to her death trying to protect the temple, and no one had noticed.

"I see that you tried," I said, nodding to her. She knew at once that I had seen and that she could now be cleansed and released from the curse of betrayal.

I poured the water back into the Nile as everyone repeated the words:

"We are purified by the Nile, and she is the mother of all."

I watched as one by one, everyone said their prayer and then stood back, awaiting the next part of the ritual.

"I now invite and invoke the Scarab and Scroll of Creation for all those held and bound to this land. May they be released and follow their soul's paths to their next afterlife and soul journey. May they find their peace."

Everyone replied, "May they find their peace."

Naomi stepped by my side and performed a blessing from the ancient ones.

"Oh mother, oh father, open your arms and hearts to hold these souls and all that is held in sadness within them. They suffered here, and I call on your blessing that they will suffer no more."

"Rashida, where would the initiation take place? I am not thinking the high altar, but seeing that smaller temple structure over there."

"Yes, this is correct, and where Isis would conduct the initiations."

I suddenly remembered that this was a sketch from my Book of Keys.

"Over there." I pointed to what looked like a chapel similar to the one on the roof of Dendara, but much, much bigger. We had come past this before to stand to look over the Nile, but now it felt as if this holy place was awake and waiting. I saw Naomi wink at me, and suddenly, we were on the move.

Before we entered, I asked everyone to stand for a moment and reflect on their connection to our beloved Isis, our friend and mentor. "Now, please enter with an open heart and walk with a friend," I called out, and as if they already knew my thoughts, they began to enter.

First came Lucinda and Emilee, followed by Alice

and Laura holding hands. Then Lesley and Naomi walked together, with Alexandria and the Contessa next in line. Rashida and Lucas followed, and for some interesting reason, I was last, alone. However, I felt sure that Isis was with me. For some reason, she felt different.

Everyone then gathered in a circle, all facing inward and joining hands. For a moment, I remembered the ceremony held in Glastonbury, where my ego had caused disruption within our group, and I felt all was lost. But today, of all days, I had to hold the circle. I closed my eyes and felt the energy of Isis, but it was not my mentor. It was the goddess who moved into me.

"My beloveds, you are here.

"Once again, in our much-loved home.

"Our sanctuary.

"I welcome you all as if you never left.

"You are here once again to sing the songs of joy and take on the covenant of the sisters and brothers we came to be.

"I stand before you to offer the initiation of the Ankh, the Key of Life."

I moved to the centre of the circle and began to stand in front of each initiate. I don't quite remember what happened, but it was different for each person. I imagined the Ankh symbol moving into the blue like the cosmic sky. Isis is now blessing each of our chalices and saying a blessing for us. Now imagine you are taking a sip from your chalice before you hand it to the person on your left. Use your imagination to pass each chalice and watch as it floats to the left as you receive from the right. Take the sip and pass it on."

It was as if time had stopped, and this endless stream of chalices started to move. I saw the symbol of the Ankh on each of them. This became a circle of giving and receiving of love and trust. Lucas played a clown as he pretended almost to drop his. The Contessa scolded him, and people laughed.

"Once again, one heart," I said, signaling that it was time to end the ritual.

"You are now purified and hold the sacred water and key of life. We will now move through the Lion's Gate to complete your full initiation."

I looked to Rashida, and she nodded and led us out of the temple and back into the courtyard.

I began to see the swirling silks and smell the incense.

Lucinda walked close to me. "I am sensing an energy wishes to talk," she said, and I looked over to see shadows on the right.

I was tempted to walk up the stairs through the Lions Gate to the high altar, but something stopped me.

"Anna," I could hear my name being called.

"What's that?" I pointed to a large, round stone disc with hieroglyphics upon it.

"That is the ancient texts and a stargate," said Alice.

"See, it is guarded by God Ptah." Laura pointed to a figure upon a column facing towards the stone.

Rashida stood on the stairs, unsure how to move, as everyone gathered around me.

"This stargate has been compromised," said the Contessa. "See the dark energy moving through this."

I began to see the figures of female spirits holding it closed, as they had for many years. Emilee stepped in front of the group.

"This is a stargate also connected to Karnak Temple and was used during the times of Nefertiti to carry messages to the temples."

"But she was struck down." And so I began to have a vision.

"After the fall of Akhenaten, the remaining royal family

was brought back to Luxor, and Nefertiti was acting ruler, but this was not her; she was acting under a curse," I said.

"Yes, Anna," I heard a voice. I felt the presence of Nefertiti and then saw her spirit beside me. It was as if time had stopped, and we began to have a telepathic conversation.

"When my husband was murdered, I surrendered up many of the scarabs and scrolls and returned to Luxor in a trance. We have been trapped between the worlds ever since. This is the work of the Scorpion Queen. She said she was the true oracle, and she persuaded my family to pursue the Aten. She created great temples with us and promised us we would resurrect Atlantis again. We assumed that she came from that ancient world."

At the mention of Atlantis, I felt a shiver going through me.

"The Scorpion Queen had lied. She was not the true Oracle of Atlantis. We eventually knew that, but after I passed, I tried, but I could not play her game in the afterworld."

Again, the game they spoke of.

"I was unable to free my family and my lineage, and sadly, my family and their children were cursed not to live. This stargate is a portal for new children to pass through, yes, to the stars, and those of us close to Isis guard this, watching over new Children of Light who are being born onto the planet."

"Anna," Nefertiti smiled. "We remember the times when your soul came."

"What would you have me do?" I asked her.

"Play her game and then set us free. Restore the Children of light."

"Can I do this here? Did Isis know this?"

"Not here, and yes, Isis knew, but she was not strong enough in the end, and said another would come. One who knew the game and had the command of the scrolls and scarabs."

"I am learning the game, and I promise, as I have all my family here with me."

"Make sure you can trust them," she warned me.

"Now, the chamber awaits you. Go quickly, as I feel darkness is following you."

"Quickly, we must perform the ritual," I said, and we all ran to the stairs and past the two statues of the lions.

"Left foot first, ladies, for it is closer to the heart and will lead us with light," said Lucas, and we all entered the dream chamber, slowly moving to the Holy of Holies and the high altar.

"Let me open the doors," whispered Emilee.

She smiled at me, and I was sure I had seen a shadow of Arsinoe next to her.

"As you wish," and I watched her move back through to where we had started that morning and through the chambers to the high altar.

"Everyone, please gather," I said, and Alexandria stood beside me.

I smiled and nodded for her to continue.

"Place your left hand on the altar." All did as she requested.

Lucas had opened up the box of scrolls and scarabs, and I placed those of Creation into the centre. I placed the other seven around them. When the sequence was complete, I nodded to Alexandria and took my place in the circle.

Alexandria then began the sacred prayer.

"I call back the divine goddess of magic, I call back our oracle sight, and I call the order of divine protection."

"Dear Isis, hear my prayer.

"Awake, awake, awake

"Awake in peace
"Lady of peace
"Rise thou in peace
"Rise thou in beauty
"Goddess of life
"Beautiful in heaven
"Heaven is in peace
"Earth is in peace
"O goddess
"Daughter of Nut
"Daughter of Geb
"Beloved of Osiris
"Mother of Horus
"Goddess rich in names
"All praise to you
"All praise to you
"I adore you
"I adore you
"Lady Isis"

With each word of prayer, I could feel her voice rising higher and higher. When she had finished, she turned to me.

"Anna, now is your time. You did not finish your initiation when the temple fell. You would have followed the oracle who died here. Your birthright gave you the sight."

I took a deep breath, let my hands sweep the scrolls and scarabs, and began to see so many visions.

"So many things I see. Look, everyone."

Everyone held their palms up towards the altar, and I began to see their faces change.

"We had been friends, family, and each other's enemy over many lives, but today, for this moment, we are oracles."

I wished I had a mirror to see myself in my past oracle life, but I trusted that that would come one day. Here, we were oracles again.

When I was complete, I looked to my left and saw Alice.

"Now, dear friend, please will you complete the ritual, Alice?" said Alexandria.

I noticed that Alice's eyes had tears as if she were staring across the room. I felt the presence of another woman, but was unsure.

"I would be honoured," she said, and we switched places.

"Oh, Mother Isis, we come here before you with open hearts, sacred hearts.

"We have loved and lost and know the feelings of pain and grief.

"Let us once again return to the order of light and restore this holy temple to a place of grace.

"We now weave a layer of light and evoke the Book of Keys to return all destroyed to order.

"Now, everyone, take your hand from the altar and place the blessing into your third eye, throat, and heart."

It was as if we had reconnected with something old and ancient.

"The ritual is complete; may we now give thanks." I heard a voice in my head.

It was as if a heavy weight had lifted, and we all smiled again.

"Now, to the Temple of Hathor, and let us give thanks to bring back the celebration," said Lucinda. She waved her scarf above her head and began to chant and sing.

Rashida looked a little alarmed, but you could not help but feel the joy streaming into the quiet, holy place.

Everyone left the temple and went to the left to another chapel. Alexandria seemed to linger in the Dream Chamber, so I decided to stay back.

"Alexandria, you okay?" She looked a little faint, and I worried it was all too much. Strange, though, considering that in her past lives, she had fought against some of the worst evil in history.

"My love is here, my soul twin flame," she said.

"I'm sorry, your who?" I had never known Alexandria talk of a relationship.

"Come, Anna," she said.

She led me through a small chamber, and I could see on the walls the relief of a royal and a priestess leading each other.

"After Cleopatra took her initiations, she visited with the Oracle of Siwa, and she had a great change of heart. She was then just a royal princess at that time. But the oracle gave her some insight, which she took literally; we never knew what was said.

"In the beginning, Cleopatra came to visit Philae with her sister Arsinoe, who was both a royal Princess and an oracle. Arsinoe and I had a powerful connection. In this temple, the elders proclaimed us soul sisters. She was initiated into the full rites as a priestess, and we planned a happy life together. Arsinoe, although younger, was totally devoted to the Goddess Isis. She understood the ways of the temple, and I told her a great lion was about to rise and take Egypt deeper and deeper into an unknown world. Arsinoe saw this as I did, and we tried to warn Cleopatra. But we were young, and I was still in my oracle training. Arsinoe left and returned to Cairo and Alexandria. I continued on in my training, watching over the birth of Naomi and seeing how she was taken to Edfu. I was here when they brought you as a baby to be hidden here in the temple, the oracle daughter of Cleopatra and Julius Caesar."

"And Arsinoe?" I asked.

"She died. She was first banished by Julius Caesar and sent to Ephesus. She was murdered on the call of Cleopatra, her sister. The order was completed by Mark Anthony."

I was aware that Arsinoe was then with us and realised she had not been just following me and protecting me, but also watching over Alexandria. After her death, I removed myself from service and another, your mentor Laura, took my place."

I slipped down in the chamber. My mentor, a mother from my past life—the one with the green eyes who had protected me so many times—had murdered her own sister. I felt a stab in my stomach, and I doubled over. I was soon aware that Laura and Alice had returned to the chamber and had sat down with us.

"Where is everyone now?" Alexandria did not wish to gather everyone for this.

"They are still dancing," said Laura.

"We don't have much time," said Alice.

I stood up but stumbled. I felt like I was leaving my body. The pain was intense.

"Let me look," Alexandria knelt down with me. Laura sat behind me, and Alice was joined by Arsinoe who, I could see, was holding a small bowl with strange-looking liquid.

"It's a dagger with scorpion venom," Alexandria said as she placed her hand on my stomach.

I was now lying flat on my back, but my soul had lifted out, and I watched the whole scene like a movie from above.

"Pull it out, the dagger, pull it out!" screamed Laura.

"No, we need to push it through her," Alexandria was determined.

Alice said nothing but took the bowl of liquid from Arsinoe and poured it into a water bottle. She then chanted over the liquid as it swirled. Arsinoe said nothing, but I suddenly saw this had also been her fate: a poisoned dagger, and no one had saved her. The Scorpion Queen had been the puppet master of her death.

Arsinoe then looked to Alexandria, nodded to her, and then was gone.

Alexandria began to speak in a language I had never heard, and I started to see spirits coming out from the side rooms of the temple. A dark cloud began to descend towards us.

"Your soul will not pass the first gate, Anna; I will not allow this," she said.

She began to dissolve the dagger, and the venom ran through my body. Alice removed my sandals and began to pour the water at my feet, and I watched the venom travel towards the water, where it began to disappear.

I began to swim back to my body. I felt a sense of great clearing, and now I knew that this had been the fate of Arsinoe, who did not have the love and support she needed or had been promised. I hoped I could help her clear this when we met again.

Very slowly, I was able to stand, and with support, we walked slowly out into the daylight to join the others. As we made our way back, I could hear chanting. I watched as a few of our group swirled with their scarves, laughed, and sang. I could see the temple had the stone heads of Hathor, and I could even make out the symbols of the rattle like the one I had.

"Let them enjoy while they can, for she is watching you and awaits you. Remember, you are still in the game."

The voice came from nowhere and left me cold. It was time to leave. I walked slowly back to the coffee shop.

I noticed that time had vanished, and the first boats of tourists had started to arrive. The lake that had been so still and reflected the rays of the morning sun was now full of waves as the small boats cut through the water. It was like a magical spell had been broken.

I walked towards the coffee shop and sat in a chair. It felt good to feel the breeze. The Contessa was already seated close to the water with her back to me. She turned around and we looked at each other. She said nothing, but from behind her large sunglasses and wide-brimmed sun hat, she was clearly working on something in another dimension.

Rashida had just started asking us to make our way back to the entrance when Lucas held up his bag and patted it to signal that he had all our precious relics. Thank goodness I had trusted him.

I had quite forgotten them. People seemed to get the telepathic message and quickly gathered, and soon we were back on board the boat and headed back to the mainland.

☥

"One stop, please, before we leave the lake," said Rashida. I wondered where on earth we could be stopping. In the middle of this water, there was nothing that I could see.

"Here," she said gently, and we stopped just outside a smaller island and what looked like an arch of stone. Everything else was underwater.

"This was our true home," she said to everyone, and she pulled out a bag of rose petals from her bag and threw them into the water. We all gently stood, and I began to see the true Philae again. The heart of Isis was beating again.

Philae Market

We made our way swiftly from the boat to the bus, and I smiled in humour at the erratic shopping experiences tourists were having, with shopkeepers chasing them with scarves and T-shirts. The stores arranged on either side of the car park had all the things we had seen before, but this was Philae, and I wanted to pay my respects with some cash.

"Twenty minutes shopping," Rashida called out.

With that, our group disappeared into the various stalls and crowds of shopkeepers.

I found myself alone.

"Anna, Anna." I heard a voice and there stood Lesley at the entrance to a scarf store.

I did not wish to be lost alone and followed her inside.

"Good price, ladies," the shop owner kept saying, and I wondered how long it had been since he had made his last sale. I was aware that tourism could be unstable in a country with such a rich history. On the other hand, Lesley was thriving and had already struck a deal for ten scarves.

I watched as she negotiated back and forth. Finally, she pulled out an American 100-dollar bill, and his eyes began to shine like stars. Three times, she took it back and forth while expertly pulling the specific colours and patterns of pashmina scarves she wanted. She inspected each one with an expert eye, rejecting the ones with a slight fade or pull in the fabric. As she was nearly finished, she looked at the man.

"This is my friend. She needs a scarf also. A gift, perhaps."

"I have money," I spoke up, opening my purse, excited to choose.

"Well, I'm done. That's the souvenirs taken care of," said Lesley. "Hurry up and choose if you're getting one."

In that moment, the energy shifted. Maybe not. I smiled and put my purse away. Lesley gathered her ten scarves and handed money to the shopkeeper. We could hear our guide calling that it was time to leave, so we began to walk to the entrance. I had scarves already—no need for more. I was simply hoping we were invisible to the crowds of vendors outside.

As I was leaving, I heard the man call to me.

"But you have not chosen your scarf."

I turned to look at him.

"Oh, I'm good," I smiled. Lesley was gone. Friends we may be, but she would always look out for herself.

"Choose, please, my friend."

This was a first, and the shopkeeper placed his hands together in a prayer and bowed his head.

"Choose."

I looked around the rails of colours. They were exquisite. Reds, blues, greens, purples, and all the shades of the rainbow. My eyes fell to the end of the rail, and there was a beautiful golden yellow. It was not my usual shade of clothing, but something called out to me. I also pointed to the pink one and a pale blue, and the shopkeeper walked over, gently removed it from the rail, and held it out to me. As soon as it was in my hands, I saw myself in another memory. Another world.

"What is your name, my dear lady?" he asked.

"Anna," I answered.

"Well, my dear, meeting you was a joy; perhaps we will see you here again. You brought great blessings to my family and friends. We were told that darker days may be coming, but do not be afraid, for Isis and her followers will return."

I clutched at the scarves and could hear my name, with a few others being called out. I reached into my bag and pulled out my money.

He shook his head, so I gently placed the thirty pounds on the small table where his Isis statue stood. I smiled, said nothing, and ran back to the bus, the scarves in my hand. My heart was racing as we pulled out and left to go back to the boat, and I prayed I would be able to rest. This morning had been an odyssey.

CHAPTER 27

Thursday, 24 September 2009
Back to the Boat

We all boarded the boat in high spirits, ready for breakfast, but Naomi was staring at me and came over. As I tried to walk past her, still holding my scarves, she reached out and caught my arm.

"You saw her, didn't you?" she whispered.

I was not prepared to share.

"I saw many people... Isis, Nefertiti, Arsinoe, and I felt Cleopatra there, but I am not sure what you mean by her. And maybe I think the Scorpion Queen is making herself known." I felt a stab in my stomach.

"Then meet me in my cabin at 2 p.m. sharp," she said.

I just kept nodding and slowly pulling my arm back, then hurried to my cabin. It was now 9:30 a.m. I was hungry, but I also knew I needed to sleep.

☥

I just caught the end of lunch. Thankfully, Alexandria had woken me; otherwise, I think I would have missed the rest of the day. I sat at the table with the others and noticed everyone was resting and writing in journals.

"Alice has had to have a doctor come. Laura is with her now," said Alexandria.

"Did you notice anything while she was in the temple?" Emilee asked me.

I stayed silent, just shaking my head.

"Are you still meeting with Naomi later today?" Lesley looked up from her journal.

I guess everyone knew my comings and goings today.

"Yes, I'll go over to Her Highness soon," I said, and began to feast on the warm lentil soup our server had thoughtfully brought up for me.

☥

Just before 2 p.m., I went to Naomi's cabin and knocked. Laura opened the door, and to my surprise, there sat Naomi, Lucas, Lucinda, and Alice. I was glad to see Alice was well, but I also wondered why these people had asked to see me.

"Anna, sit," said Naomi, pouring me some mint tea.

"We are the only ones who have encountered the Scorpion Queen before, to our knowledge. Although the others know of her, we in this room have come to realise we were part of a past life in which she did have a personal impact on our lives and perhaps yours."

I knew I didn't really know her origins, and so I wanted to hear the truth. How else would I know how to play the game? I nodded and stayed silent. I slid into a small chair and smiled at everyone to show I was ready and open to whatever they wished to share.

"Then I will begin," Naomi said.

"There was a time when the gods walked among us in the world, especially in Egypt. Beings not yet ascendant to their full power, they were present at a time when the boundaries between our physical world and that of the cosmic soul were not so harsh. Information between the Halls of Amenti flowed freely to us by way of its ambassadors, the Children of Light. These immortal beings would manifest themselves in human bodies and walk among us, spreading the light and wisdom of the Seeds of Life, the source of our metaphysical and spiritual knowledge.

"The Children of the Light were welcomed by all in the world like the gods we now only see as statues, and they helped usher in a time of prosperity and intellectual advancement. I should note that despite their immortality, they were not infallible beings and often fell victim to the faults of man if they were away from their celestial bodies too long. One such fault, so seemingly inconsequential at the time, would lead to their demise and throw the world out of balance for thousands of years to come."

"Are these the Children of Light that Nefertiti told me of, and I think Laura mentioned them once? Sorry to interrupt," I said.

"Don't be sorry, Anna," said Lucas. "It's a good omen that you are aware of them."

"But still, I'm sorry, Naomi; please continue," I said.

"The Children of the Light, of which there were thirty-two, always sent eight of themselves to each of the four corners of the earth, ensuring that they could properly spread their light and wisdom to everyone. One set of eight always travelled to the West, to a region that would house Atlantis. The people there were in tune with their metaphysical selves and uniquely adept at applying the teachings of the eight.

"Thus, one of the most powerful Lords of Amenti, the Dweller, named Horlet, who had also become enamoured with these people, created a great civilisation for them, erecting an ornate temple on the island of Unal and establishing the twelve united kingdoms of Atlantis. He was a way-shower and a key master. The Atlanteans showed great reverence and respect for their teachings, which many other people around the world did not. Not long after the

Children of the Light descended to Earth for the first time, these eight Children of the Light made Atlantis their home, leaving only on occasion to fulfil their obligations to the other people in the world.

"It became apparent that these eight favoured Atlantis above all other people, bestowing them with powerful crystals that, it was said, led them to live for hundreds of years. They were also bestowed with magic that helped them reach new spiritual and technological heights, far above that of any other people on Earth. The Eight even chose to be born in Atlantean bodies when they returned to Earth from Amenti after their 100-year periods of spiritual convergence with the Flower of Life and the seeds of universal creation. This continued for many thousands of years.

"As the Atlanteans called them, the eight, or the Sacred Eight, would be born to Atlantean bodies, spend 900 years teaching man and spreading light, leave for the Halls of Amenti, and return to them 100 years later. While the Sacred Eight did not see any harm in their favouritism, it would become apparent as they were about to end their tenth cycle and return to their celestial bodies in the Halls of Amenti.

"As the cycle was nearing a close, Atlantis experienced an intense spiritual sickness due to the growing selfishness and arrogance that comes with being favoured by such powerful beings. Atlanteans were abusing the power of the crystals, and that led to the people becoming out of balance with themselves, leading to the spiritual sickness that ended up killing over one-third of their population. This led to the pulling away of the surviving elite of the twelve united kingdoms from the rest of Atlantis and doubling down their efforts to protect themselves and their wealth.

"Each kingdom elected a member, an anointed one who sought resources from the King of the Twelve. They would become a powerful council. The King of Twelve was the ruler of all twelve kingdoms in Atlantis, but he could wield power only with this council on his side. The King, worried about another sickness sweeping through and killing more people, declined to give them funds from the royal reserves. He had already lost his wife to the last sickness and wanted to make sure those left in the royal family had the resources to survive it if they were to fall ill. The council then attempted to pass a measure taxing the elite class to pay for the projects they needed to help the rest of the people. The anointed Council of Twelve strongly objected to this and pressured the King to strike it down.

"This led to rising tensions between the elites and the non-elites, who started to talk about getting rid of the King and the anointed council. It got so bad that elites hoarded crystals and used them to build powerful defenses that would put those who sought to steal from them or harm them in a torturous spiritual stasis for years. These tactics put even more people out of balance and spurred the non-elites on, prompting them to regularly protest in the capital city outside of the King's palace.

"This all came to a head when the celebrations for the end of the tenth cycle began. A year-long celebration was filled with parades, parties, and games to usher the Sacred Eight back to the Halls of Amenti, where they would reunite with their celestial bodies and converge with the Seed of Life. On the inaugural day of the celebrations, the King came out to the city streets to officially start the ceremony and was met with an angry crowd of protesters. One of the King's advisors, frightened that the crowd would mob them, used his crystal to try to subdue the protesters, but instead killed several who were standing in the front. Before anyone could stop it, the mob rushed the King and his advisors, killing them all.

"Unfortunately, this did not lead to the change in government, as the non-elites had hoped. Instead, power just went to the King's daughter, a young, intelligent woman who, at the time, had been serving as one of the Sacred Eight's handmaidens. This was an honour only given to women of the most prominent families in Atlantis. She stepped up and promised to make sweeping changes to save the people she was sworn to care for. The new Queen did, in fact, attempt these changes; she dipped into the royal reserves and diverted the money for the Sacred Eight celebrations to fund housing projects and set up food programs for those most affected by the disasters. However, with much of Atlantis's industries still affected by the damage from the protests and the lack of workforce due to the sickness, there was no way to replenish the royal reserves, which ran out only after a few months.

"The Queen had no choice but to tax the elites, who rebelled against her and did everything they could to keep her and the royal guard from obtaining their wealth. The Queen knew that if she didn't find another way, the elites would fully turn on her and most likely remove her from the throne and replace her with someone who would protect them. The elected council could not help her, as they, too, had no alternative options to turn their economy around. So, the Queen turned to the Sacred Eight, who were only a month away from leaving for the next one hundred years. She knew of the Sacred Eight's long-held affection for Atlantis and pleaded with them to stay and help her fix the place they loved so much. The Sacred Eight said they would do all they could to help but could not stay longer without causing imbalance.

"The Queen accused them of not doing what they

promised, saying it was their job to help humans and give them wisdom and knowledge to better their lives. She told them that there must be some alternative food source or method of production that could save Atlantis, but that they were unwilling to share. The Sacred Eight, again, said that they would do all they could to find a solution in the next month, but that if one were not found, Atlantis would have to figure it out on their own or wait 100 years until they returned.

"This sparked even more fear in the Queen, as she knew that the 100-year period always led to more unrest and uncertainty in Atlantis. The previous 100-year absence had led to the prior royal family being removed and her family replacing them. She knew that this time would be different; that Atlantis would not survive the one-hundred-year absence of the Sacred Eight. So, the Queen travelled to the island of Unal and broke into Horlet's temple, which was then in a chamber in spiritual stasis. She came across a series of Emerald Tablets detailing a ritual that could be performed with eight others to bind the Sacred Eight to Earth and give her control over them. It seemed that Horlet had toyed with the idea of doing this to the Sacred Eight at one point, as he was a lover of Atlantis, but had abandoned that notion for some reason.

"So then, the Queen copied the ritual down onto a piece of papyrus and gathered eight of her most trusted advisors and secretly prepared over the next month with them to force the Sacred Eight to stay on Earth. This would secure her throne, and she believed she could learn their secrets and become immortal herself. She studied everything she could from Horlet's Temple. In these Emerald Tablets as well as other sacred texts, she discovered dark, powerful wisdom she would choose to use in a corrupt way.

"When the day of their departure came, the Eight were preparing to enter the spiritual chambers that would allow them to leave their human body and enter their celestial one in Amenti. As was customary, the Queen would send them off to the Halls of Amenti by placing offerings on their bodies before closing their chambers, which she did. But when the time came for her to close the chambers, she instead revealed her plan. She brought out her eight advisors, who had been transformed into gaunt, grim-looking, monstrous creatures during the month of preparation, barely recognisable as humans. The Queen commanded them to remove the Eight from their chambers and stand them in a line, which no ordinary human could do. She then recited an incantation in their own cosmic language, blocking their access to Amenti. Try as they might, the Sacred Eight could not break free from the beings' grasp and, with one more utterance, were spiritually bound to them, making it impossible for them to return to Amenti.

"The Queen named these beings that she had created, the Priests of Unal, the spiritual opposites of the Children of Light, and she created a Scroll of Unal, which she used to control and invoke them. They were the Children of Dark. They had human forms but could freely move between cosmic planes, taking that energy from the Sacred Eight. The priests were under her control, and the Sacred Eight could do nothing to free themselves so long as she had control. Their cosmic fate was now subject to her will. They were her prisoners. The Queen offered them the chance to return to the Halls of Amenti if they saved Atlantis, but the Sacred Eight refused. They said they could not help Atlantis now and that the Queen had doomed them all by attempting to save her people in this way.

"It was then that Horlet, of Atlantis, arose from his sleep

and, upon seeing what she had done, ordered the Seven Lords of Space-Time to destroy Atlantis. Horlet had seen Atlantis declining for some time, but this abomination the Queen had created had gone too far. The Seven Lords shifted the earth around them and caused the sea to rise up around Atlantis, but one place stayed protected. The Queen knew that Horlet would not have his own temple destroyed, so she, along with the Priests of Unal and the Sacred Eight, fled to the island, narrowly escaping the destruction of Atlantis.

"Therefore, at the Dweller's temple, Horlet summoned the Queen. He confronted the Queen and demanded that she release the Sacred Eight from her grasp so they could return to the Seeds of Life and restore balance. The Queen refused, saying she would only do so if Horlet commanded the Lords of Space-Time to restore Atlantis and its people to a peaceful and prosperous state. Horlet said he would not grant such a request to someone who had greatly abused his gifts to man. The Queen then begged him to reconsider, stating that it was not her people's fault, that it was hers, and that he could exact whatever punishment he saw fit on her if he allowed the rest of Atlantis to return.

"Horlet refused again, stating that her actions were the culmination of generations of spiritual imbalance and abuse of the Children of Light's gifts. Enraged, the Queen threatened to eradicate the Sacred Eight if he did not grant her request. At that, Horlet laughed and told her she could only bind them to Earth. She could not destroy them. Not completely. He tells her one more time to release them, saying that his only offer in return will be to let her live out the rest of her life in exile, a generous deal, considering the rest of her people suffered a much worse fate for a far less severe crime. The Queen refused again, saying that if he did not restore Atlantis, she would use the Sacred Eight to build a new one.

"Horlet tells her it will never work and states that if she does not release them, she will not be released either. He then binds her spirit to Earth, as she did to the Eight, forcing her to reincarnate every time she dies, just like the Eight will have to do now, until such a time she decides to release them. She balks at this, stating she will live an eternity on Earth if she has to in order to exact revenge on the beings that destroyed her home. With that, Horlet departs, returning to his chamber, hoping that the Queen will reconsider in her next life.

"The Queen then wandered the world for 200 years, dragging the Sacred Eight along with her, poisoning the people's minds wherever she went, showing them the dangers of trusting the Children of the Light. The Priests of Unal followed her and did her evil bidding. The people of the world began to call her the Scorpion Queen as she infected whatever she touched with a vile poison of hateful ideas. Over several lifetimes, the sacred ones forget that they were Children of Light. The only things left are scrolls from their past lives containing the wisdom of the Halls of Amenti, and scarabs created to help decipher them. The Scorpion Queen never forgets, though, and never fully reincarnates. The combination of her new dark powers and Atlantean heritage allows her to live on in the shadows and shapeshift into other people's bodies that she chooses. She and her Priests of Unal spend the next thousands of years tracking down each Child of Light in each new reincarnation to exact as much cosmic torture as they can on them, filling their past lives with trauma that they are unable to resolve, distracting them from who they truly are and making them play her in a dangerous game.

"And so, the cycle of abuse continues, and it will

continue until the Sacred thirty-two can reclaim their Light, free the others, and enter the Halls of Amenti to restore balance to the world and usher in a new era of peace and prosperity."

I sat very still as the new information washed over me.

"Can I ask questions?" I whispered.

"Yes, of course," said Naomi.

"Are the sacred eight the same as the sacred eight who created Philae?"

"No," said Laura, "but you will find the eight is often a number of balance and ritual. So very often, it is used when bringing forth something of power."

This story explained so many things. Why had I been so focused on the "sacred eight" concept? I wondered if I had been distracted. Maybe this was a red herring sent to distract me.

"So are we to find the Amenti Atlantis ones?" Lord, as if I did not have enough to do.

"We don't think so," said Lucas, shaking his head.

"We think," said Lucinda, "that the scrolls and scarabs can re-create the Children of Light in the Great Pyramid and set their souls free. But you, Anna, need to know how to play the game to protect them. Every major Queen we know over history has come against the Scorpion Queen at some time, and only one that we know of ever managed to play her at this game and have her line continue."

"Nefertari," said Laura. "I once knew Seti I, the father of her husband Ramses II. Nefertari was the skilled queen who encountered the Scorpion Queen and played the game against her for many years in life and the afterlife."

"So why did Hatshepsut, Nefertiti, and Cleopatra fail? They were rulers in their own right, much more powerful."

"*She failed because of vanity*," I heard a voice and turned around.

No one else seemed to hear the voice. In the doorway stood Alexandria. Lucinda stood up and went over to her; it was obvious she was in a trance.

"*She never listened, and she was my sister,*" her voice hissed at us.

"Who was your sister?" Lucinda asked gently. I held my breath.

"*Cleopatra.*"

"Full possession, I see," whispered Lucinda as she gently guided her to sit down.

Alexandria held herself like royalty as she moved into the room and sat down, her face shadowed by another spirit that had taken over her body.

"*You all sit here, planning to take on these forces. You have no idea who they are,*" the entity said.

I looked at her eyes, motionless, with eyelids flickering. I moved from my seat closer to her and sat on the floor.

"Then why don't you tell us, Arsinoe?" I said softly. This was a very different spirit from the one that had followed us previously, but I guessed there was anger hidden within, just waiting to show itself.

I saw the others looking around at each other, wondering who or what this was. She looked down at me and lifted my chin to look at my face, and continued her story.

"*My niece,*" she smiled, "*you have the gift your mother craved. My sister, beautiful, powerful, and educated... She was born to rule but had to share the throne with my brother... She was told she had to rule through a man. I had the gifts like you and was destined to be a great Oracle. My sister ruined that chance when she brought Julius Caesar into our world and into her bedchamber. She granted him the rights of a king and watched as our temples grew weak at the will of Rome. She changed the rituals of the temples that had kept them safe for 2000 years.*"

"How was that so?" Laura spoke, her voice calm and patient.

Arsinoe continued, "*When we were young, we were taught in the library of Alexandria. We found a scroll that detailed the game of the immortals, and it taught us about the rituals of a time we had no history of. Cleopatra memorised this, and then, before I could fully study it, she burnt it. That burning would cause a curse to be placed on our family. Now, Julius Caesar was fascinated by the ancient world of Atlantis, and Cleopatra promised him she would recreate the magic. Magic and alchemy that had at one time belonged to Alexander the Great.*"

"Yes," said Alice. She was frail and struggled with her words. "Today, I met with my past and was shown a vision of the game Alexander the Great tried to play, but he was outplayed, as the Oracle of Siwa had warned him, if he ventured too far. But he had sealed his fate with the abuse and murder of the Oracles of Alexandria."

I had a flash of him visiting the Oracle of Siwa.

Alexandria glared at Alice, and I watched as her life force and colour drained.

"Please continue, princess," I sought to distract her.

"*But Cleopatra sought to align with the darkness to bring protection and greater power.*"

I was not too sure of this, but I allowed her to continue.

"*I went to visit the Oracle of Siwa without my sister's knowledge,*" Arsinoe continued.

I began to see the vision.

"*You see it, child.*" She looked down at me again.

I nodded.

"*Then continue,*" she smiled.

"I'm seeing you and a group of other women. You're riding out to the desert, and you come to an oasis. It's very lush and probably not as it is now. You create a camp outside the temple of Amun and offer rituals to the gods. You know that they will protect you. You await a sign, and you will know when to enter the temple.

"You wait for three days and three nights until you see a large scarab beetle cross the doorway, and this is the sign. You enter alone, and you are still a very young woman. I suspect this is before your sister becomes Queen. There are eight oracles, but only one true one. You are tested, and you succeed. This true oracle is male, and he whispers to you. I am not sure what he whispers, but I see your face, shocked by the task you must face. You keep saying, 'But she's my sister,' and shaking your head. He tells you that this is the time of the wounds. Then you return with your group to Alexandria. But you can't tell your sister your secret. Before you know it, she has been declared a Queen, and you are pushed aside.

"You could warn her, but you choose to stay silent. You begin to plot, and you visit the temples. You and the other oracles have the same message. Caesar must not be allowed power."

Arsinoe then spoke. "*And we nearly defeated him. I was tasked with an army, and the temples and priests were with me. We drove him from Alexandria, and my army defeated him at one point. He escaped and never forgave me. After this, my sister did not trust me. I was sent away to Rome to be detained at the discretion of this great leader. I was abused on all levels and defiled, which took my soul to a very dark place.*

"*Finally, I was sent to a temple in Ephesus—the Temple of Artemis. Those who worshipped here tried to protect me, but orders had been given that the temples were aligned to my cause. Word had spread through the Priestesses of Isis, and many knew of my sacred oaths and gifts. Sadly, I was murdered on the steps, and it sent a message throughout our world that even those of pure intent could be dismissed and murdered. Did I curse my sister and you, poor child? Yes, absolutely. I called to all the Gods. After this, as the temples soon fell, I became the forgotten and broken initiate who would be the last true Oracle of Egypt.*

"While this was all occurring, the fall of Edfu and Philae was playing out. After mine and Cleopatra's deaths, not many survived, and many of the holy women fell to the same fate as me when given into the brutal hands of Rome. Mark Antony had allowed the legions to flow through our lands. He was weak and, in the end, powerless. He was supposed to be the next Horus, a protector, and all he did was open the doors to the pain and suffering of the priests and priestesses."

You could hear a pin drop in the room as everyone sat silently.

"Are we here to break the cycle?" I asked.

"*I know not,*" she answered.

"Do you know how to play the game?"

"I started to learn my fate was to guide my sister and work together, but I think the knowledge was in the scriptures Cleopatra burnt."

Then she took a deep breath, and I watched as Arsinoe floated up out of the body she had possessed, and Alexandria looked around in shock.

"Was I sleepwalking again?" She looked around the room like a lost child.

Naomi nodded, and Laura handed her some water.

"So, who knew the full game?" asked Lucas.

"Only one Queen," said Alice. "Nefertari."

"So, how can I channel Nefertari? Can we do it here?" I

looked at the others.

"No," said Naomi, "we must go to where she is still Queen."

"Tomorrow, we go to Abu Simbel."

CHAPTER 28

Friday, 25 September 2009
Abu Simbel—Temple of the Oracles

We boarded the bus very early that morning. No one spoke as we settled into our seats and prepared for the 3-hour drive. Thank goodness the boat did not mind us bringing pillows, but I think they would have refused the quilts. I settled into my seat and watched as Lesley did the headcount and handed bottled water to everyone.

"Are you okay?" she asked, touching my shoulder with compassion and gentleness. "I am so glad to get off that boat, but it seems the bus is not much better," she laughed.

"I think so. I can't see much happening today, so perhaps we can all rest." I wasn't too sure what to share with her.

"I'm not so sure," she whispered, looking up and back across the passengers.

Emilee was sitting behind me, and I could hear her talking.

"We will be all connected again, ma chérie," she said, reaching out and squeezing Lesley's hand.

Soon, we were off driving through the desert; it looked so remote I wondered why anyone would dare to make the trip.

We arrived just before 9 a.m. Interestingly enough, quite a few buses were parked. We all disembarked and followed Rashida out towards the lake and through the main entry point.

As we approached the lake, we stopped, and I felt my legs go to lead. For a moment, I could not move.

We gathered in a circle for Rashida to give the orientation, but to my surprise, Naomi stood in the centre and began to tell the journey of the oracle.

"Many years ago, this lake was known as a magical place and portal to other dimensions. We would gather for the festival and bless the sacred waters. Many did not know the secrets that lay beneath. But a great King did; Ramses II was a wise and powerful leader. He supported the oracles in his time and the priestesses of Ma'at and Seshat. His favoured Queen, Nefertari, was most honoured for her insight and wisdom.

"Around 1265 BC, he built temples on the small islands, and these were areas where we the Oracles would live in peace and bring forward information from the other worlds. By day, it is a stunning lake of still and calm water, but at night, the portals would open, and the inner worlds and dimensions would become visible. Over time, this has changed, but for now, let us remember the glorious days. I want you to know that the Ramses II empire stretched from here all the way to the Mediterranean Sea. He was powerful, yet he allowed himself to be guided by women who sat behind his throne. Sadly, over time, other rulers did not follow the course and example he set, and by 42 BC, the lineage was completely broken. After this, the oracles, who were once respected and looked after by the temples that resided on those islands you see in the distance, were forgotten. When our temples fell, the oracles were ignored, and they starved to death in lonely places.

"This temple we are about to enter was the key; however, it was moved around 1967 to this new location. So, while the outside does not look to the true direction and connection of the small islands and portals, the magic remains inside. You only have to look with your heart."

"But my friends, today is not one for sorrow," Emilee stepped forward.

"It is my belief this portal will today be rejoined. As we walk through this temple, please be mindful that although things may not be as they were, the energy lines still remain. I thank our sister Naomi, but this was my temple. I was a trusted handmaiden and the Oracle to the Queen Nefertari. This is a place connected to my soul. I was in Oracle training here for many years. The oracles who lived on these islands may have been forgotten, but they are not entirely lost."

I could now see and feel them, and the energy ran through my body like electricity.

Naomi smiled around the group.

"This is a temple where we were acknowledged and even worshipped. The oracles here guided the justice and karma to the afterlife. Ramses II and his father, Seti I, were our protectors. Here, we were safe, and our work was at its finest."

That was a relief. So far, many of the temples and tombs had been witness to death and destruction. Our powers and insight were ignored and disrespected, but here was a place where we could be at ease—I hoped.

"We shall continue," the Contessa stepped in front of the group, and we all began to follow around the lake at a gentle pace.

We came around the bend, and I let out a gasp. I could see the four massive statues, and the high pillars took my breath away. My heart was beating fast, and I knew that I knew this place.

"We will first go to honour our lady," Emilee called.

"Our lady?" I looked at Lesley, "Does she mean Isis?"

"No, silly. Nefertari. Is that not why you're here?" She winked once at me. Again, nothing was a secret.

It seemed odd to walk past the large temple first, and I put my head down as I feared the wrath of the King and the Gods who appeared to be staring down at me.

We made our way to a smaller temple with male and female statues, and the gatekeepers opened the door to let us enter. No other tourists were here as they were too distracted by the grandeur of the Ramses temple. Everyone moved around slowly, and I felt a sense of calm and beauty; the smells of oils and the feeling of safety washed over me. I decided to make a note in my journal and sat down in a corner. My vision took over, and I saw that a beautiful woman was approaching me. Dressed in white, she looked familiar, but by her costume, I could see she was royal and so much more.

"*She said you would come,*" she spoke, and we engaged in our telepathic connection.

"*Who?*" I asked. "*I don't understand.*"

She sat beside me and whispered, "*She, the woman with the white hair and the name of Isis.*"

"*What did she say?*" I asked.

"*She said you would come and free us from the curse of the Scorpion Queen and create the ritual again to join the temple to the islands and restore the connection to the other temples.*"

"*What was the curse?*" I asked.

"*Separation—and the gateways were closed.*"

"*Did this happen during your reign?*"

"*She tried, but no, it was much later, during the time of another great queen. I held her by having the game replayed in my tomb in the Valley of the Queens every night, keeping her at bay for many years. But eventually, my tomb could not hold the balance after the reign of Alexander the Great, and for 300 years, a struggle continued. Finally, with Cleopatra, we had hope; with you, Anna, as her daughter, we had hope. However, once she died, we lost track of you, also."*

"What must I do? I have been trying to understand the game."

"It is like the game of Senet. Two players, thirty places, and ten counters. It is a battle of wits and words."

Suddenly, I was transported back to the Valley of Queens, and we were walking into the tomb.

"Is this your tomb? I think I remember."

"Yes," she said, *"I had this built to honour all the gods and the afterlife, and it was to also connect to the legends of Atlantis."*

"This is a Hall of Amenti," I smiled, *"and you're Nefertari."*

"Clever girl."

"Now, watch how I play," and there I could see a Queen sitting playing the game. At various times, the images from the walls came forward, and I could see the living energy.

"Now, hold up your hands to the walls like me."

I did as she asked, and the messages began to flow back to me.

"*Good work, Anna. I see and feel them also,*" she smiled.

"These are scripts taken from the Emerald Tablets and Pyramid Texts. They are in Saqqara near the pyramids. I held the wisdom for my family for so long and was instructed by your other oracle friends in my time as Queen. We also guarded the Scroll and Scarab of Amenti, but they were stolen. You need to find it. You will all remember today how you all worked as a group. Anna, know that you were here before and worshipped the Gods that still reside here."

I shifted my vision, and I suddenly saw many of our group here at the time of her burial. We were not sad. We understood how important this chamber was. I could see Naomi, Alice, Laura, and Lucinda all standing around her coffin, being lifted into a final resting place. The Contessa and Alexandria were reading the rites of the Book of the Dead. Lucas was with the priests, preparing the seals to place on the chamber. Lesley and Emilee were mourning as family members of royalty.

"*Where is Isis?*"

"*Do you not see?*" she smiled.

I looked and saw that Isis was a High priestess. Then where was I? I slowly saw myself dressed as a priestess in the robes of Seshat.

"*But we worked all together. What happened?*"

"*Your friends forgot the promise. I did battle while you all went on with your lives, and it has taken over 3000 years to bring you all back together again. I am a Child of Light but am limited, and so you, Anna, must carry on, as the energy at my tomb is fading somewhat, and the Scorpion Queen is in a physical body again.*"

"*So tell me what to do?*"

"*You will know, you will know,*" was her response.

And then she was gone.

☥

"Anna, Anna, are you okay?" It was Lucas.

"I'm fine, just a daydream."

"Come, the others have gone to the main temple. We should go."

He helped me to my feet, and as we stepped outside, Lucinda and Laura were waiting.

"There's no time," Laura said, "We have to reach the temple."

'Why?" I asked.

"Look," she said.

And there she was, the woman in red robes with her small group making their way towards the temple. They looked to be carrying sistrums like mine from Abydos, and some had drums. They stopped at the lake's edge, and I knew the woman in red was about to perform a ceremony.

Something told me this was not right. We raced through a stone wall section set between the temples.

"Laura, wait, we must close the portal door to the Nefertari Temple," I called.

"But, Anna, we do not have the time."

"Yes, we do," said Lucas.

I could see Naomi and Lesley waving from the main temple entrance, but I knew this must be done first. I placed my hand against the wall and whispered an incantation. I began to see how these portals had worked and the line of energy that had linked the high altars and shrines.

I saw the Scorpion Queen when she sent the Priests of Unal in the form of soldiers to break the energy and the link between us. It had been them who had closed the doors and connections to the Oracles on the islands. They had destroyed the boats and those who protected the Oracles. So I called on the giant statues outside the Ramses Temple and summoned them to life. I could feel the energy running through my soul, creating a new link to the smaller temple where the statues looked alive.

"I can see them coming to life," Lucas exclaimed.

"I do, too," said Emilee.

"They are the guardians between the worlds, and they have been frozen in time, but now they are moving."

We watched as their energy began moving towards us.

"We must move also," Lucinda said adamantly.

As we ran towards the entrance, I looked back to see

the stone guardians moving toward the group at the water's edge. It was then that I saw a huge wind begin to form, a swirling of sand moving towards them. As I ran into the temple for shelter, I saw the group turning around with the other tourists and heading back to the car park and their buses for shelter.

As I entered the temple doors, we were greeted by Rashida, Lesley, and the guard on duty. As the sand was coming at speed towards us, they were closing the doors. I knew what to do next. I moved slowly into the temple and noticed the columns. They were high and majestic, opening a portal to another world. At the end of the temple, I could see four seated statues of gods in a small room, and there stood Emilee, Alice, the Contessa, and Alexandria, saying prayers and sending them energy.

I arrived with Lucas, Laura, and Lucinda beside me. Naomi, I could see, was praying to a wall that showed an image of what looked to be a King on a chariot going to battle before she disappeared into another chamber.

Emilee turned to Lucas.

"Do you have as I requested?" she asked, smiling.

He nodded and handed her a scroll and scarab.

"Magic and Prophecy, as you requested."

Everyone then stood with their backs to the columns and began looking up to the roof. They were re-gridding the energy in the temple. I turned and looked at the main doors where Lesley whispered spells of protection. The wind was still raging, and no one was entering. Rashida was in the doorway, standing with one of the guards. No other tourists were present. We were alone.

Emilee turned her back to the four statues and looked at me. "This temple is now open, and you are to be prepared for your initiation. Come with me, Anna."

"This way, Anna," a voice called out, and I saw it was the Queen Nefertari again pointing to an entrance to an outer chamber. From there, I could see a passageway to two smaller, narrower rooms. In front of me stood the Queen and also Emilee.

"Which place is yours, my dear?" Emilee asked.

"That one," and I pointed to the one furthest away.

"Very good," she smiled and bowed to the Queen.

I walked slowly past the first chamber and looking in, I saw Naomi in stillness, meditating on a ledge in the middle of the back wall. She looked like a living statue, and I was glad I had chosen the other chamber.

Emilee and the Queen led me over, and I walked inside.

"It is time, Anna," was all they said.

"Time to take your place in the chamber where all our oracles were initiated."

I moved slowly into the chamber and towards the back wall. It was lit with golden light and still had the images carved into the walls. I could read the images and messages, and they talked about the holy wisdom in these two chambers. I sat down, placed myself into a meditation pose, and felt a column of light surrounding me. I closed my eyes but could hear a familiar woman's voice. I opened my eyes, and there was Isis. Moving slowly, she walked gently towards me.

"Beautiful dear oracle," she spoke.

"I love you, and always and forever, I am here with you, beloved one."

I wanted to cry, but I knew this would be a powerful initiation, and I was ready; I knew I was ready.

Emilee stood behind her, reciting the prayer.

"This justice of Ma'at

"The wisdom of Seshat

"The courage of Nephthys

"The love of Isis

"I restore to you the grace that you may pass this to others.

"And so it is."

I repeated the prayer, "And so it is," and felt myself turn to light. The whole room, including her, became a blur. I felt the blessings and her love. I missed her so much, but I knew much work could now be done with these sacred keys and codes settling onto my soul.

I continued my breathing until I felt her presence leave, and the chamber returned to normal. There was an eerie silence, and I knew the wind must have faded, and it was time to go. I stood up and saw Emilee coming in to assist me.

"The temple is now realigned. It is time to go, Anna," she whispered.

I nodded and followed her out, glancing back at the four seated statues at the back of the temple. I could feel their energy pulling me close. "I didn't have time to say hello," I whispered back to her. "I must do an offering."

She smiled, "Then you will need these," she said, handing me the Scroll and Scarab of Magic and Prophecy.

She then led me towards the four gods and presented me to them using a strange language.

I stood silently before the chamber and held onto the wooden gate, looking into the small chamber where they sat. There were four stone statues with various shaped heads and crowns. Suddenly, their eyes opened, and they were alive.

Emilee spoke.

"Oh fathers

Ramses, Ptah, Ra Horaky, Amon

Hear thy humble prayer. Shield her from the darkness of

the land and help her free the souls of our friends so that we may be reunited to the eternal light."

I began to hear them speak as if they were giving me personal messages.

"Welcome, Anna child, our daughter of Magi. We acknowledge your presence and grant you the sacred keys of the elements of Earth."

I felt the elements of earth, water, fire, and air rushing around me. I held up the scarab and felt the words of the scroll being transmitted to them, restoring their magic and giving them the gift of prophecy. Then, all was silent and still. I felt Emilee leave, but I could not move for some reason.

"What do they know?" the Contessa asked behind me. I watched them close their eyes, and I was surprised that she, of all people, would interrupt my sacred moment. I wondered if she sought to sabotage me.

"I am not sure, but something is different."

"How so?" the Contessa pressed me.

I shrugged my shoulders and shook my head. All I could hear were their whispers to each other, and something told me this was not to be shared.

As we walked out of the temple, the sun was shining, and the visitors were beginning to be given access to the temples once again. The four enormous statues of the King, and our protectors, were silent and sleeping once more.

"Did you recover the four elements from the Gods?" Emilee whispered to me as we slowly walked out of the temple.

"Yes, how do you know? I felt them... I think I recovered them."

"The Akashic Records showed they were once stolen

from our oracle friends, but now they can be restored," she replied.

"How will I use them?" I asked.

"When the time comes... my Queen will show you," she whispered. She was short of breath, and I put my arm around her to support her.

"Quickly and quietly," said Rashida, and Lesley pointed the way to the exit.

I looked back towards the smaller temple of Nefertari. I saw the group with the woman in the red outfit. It was strange. They were talking and taking photos. Their tools of ceremony lay on the ground. I found myself staring, and suddenly, one of them looked straight at me.

"I see you," I heard her voice.

The voice made me shiver, and I quickly handed the scroll and scarab I had been holding back to Lucas. I continued to stare, willing the Scorpion Queen to show herself; then it would all be over. I was exhausted with the game of cat and mouse. But they remained in tourist mode, laughing with the guards, pretending to open the door with a large Ankh key.

Naomi saw me staring.

"They have no power here," she said, "Come, let's go."

"Naomi, have you heard the word Magi before?" Her eyes grew wide, and she grabbed my arm.

"Do not say that word."

"Why?"

"Just don't say that word. It's sacred and also a conjuring word."

"Okay, okay."

I pulled my arm away and caught up to Alice. Naomi still stared at me, and I was beyond uncomfortable.

Alice looked at me and smiled, "Come, Anna, I'm

exhausted of the spiritual duty."

We turned right, and I tried to walk at a quicker pace to leave. But even though I tried, I was much slower.

Lucas caught up with us. He was wearing his hat and scarf as his face had been growing redder from the sun. The sun was burning now and rising high in the clear blue sky.

"Let's get to the vendors. I feel an urge to buy scarves," urged Lucinda.

We all followed and came across the row of stalls selling the statues, scarves, and trinkets.

Naomi was most generous, buying and paying double. I watched as word spread through the stores that tourists with cash had arrived.

Before long, every stall was bustling, and even more tourists appeared, making it seem like a sales day. This vendor market was very different from others we had encountered. People smiled, and I watched as they helped each other like a community. It was a relief to shift back into tourist mode, and I looked and saw our group in high spirits.

"Did Naomi just cast an abundance spell?" I asked and watched her telling Lesley about her newfound money miracles.

"I think so. She's even better than any of us," laughed Emilee, who was also watching them. "She used her magic. I think I will try to steal it for a potion."

"Well, since my coin returned, my goodness, my investments..." She was stopped mid-flow by a very joyful Emilee.

"Now, Anna, I think I just spotted something for you," Emilee squealed. Everyone stopped and turned to see the new shiny thing she had found.

"What?" I looked around and wondered what she could have found for me that I did not already have.

She pointed to a pale cream cloth dress trimmed with cream satin in the front; it was as wide as it was long.

"Nooooooooooo, not that dress. It is like a smock. Like from a biblical storytime. That's the dress you wear to ride a donkey in the desert."

I burst out laughing. "No, absolutely not... can't I have the sexy belly dancer costume?" I pointed to a red and gold elaborate costume that looked straight out of Arabian Nights.

"No, Anna, definitely not," she shook her head.

"This dress, this dress... well, it's your wedding dress. *Chere*... we must buy it."

Oh, Lord, help me. What could she mean?

CHAPTER 29

Saturday, 26 September 2009
Back to Cairo

The terminal was busy and full of activity as we arrived back in Cairo from Aswan. The agents in their suits were waiting for our arrival with bouquets of flowers and delightful smiles. They handed them over to each of us and loaded our luggage onto the trolleys as we trailed behind. I had to smile as I saw Naomi and the Contessa, each with two trollies, while the rest of us were three to a single trolley. Maybe Naomi would share some of her clothes if I wore that hideous "wedding dress." Oh, the shame was unthinkable.

I had tried it on in the room for Alexandria, and she laughed so hard that she fell off the bed. To my dismay, she had made so much noise that Lucinda and Emilee knocked and came into the room.

"Oh, *Ma chérie*," said Emilee as she looked at me, and Lucinda shook her head. "Perhaps Naomi has a scarf to brighten this."

"Lord, she would need a quilt cover to hide it," laughed Lucinda.

"All she needs now is a donkey and a stable, and we have the start of the new nativity story."

"Not funny," I snapped as I looked in the mirror. I prayed there was no story or past life connected to this, and it was simply Lucinda having fun.

But that memory I decided to hide away for now. I set my focus on the agents who moved at speed, and we were quickly herded back on another bus enroute through the crazy roads to our home for the next few days.

It was a relief to be back at the Mena House Hotel.

I smiled as Naomi handed me my room key, “You’re in the garden rooms now, safe from the wicked witches and ghosts,” she said.

She winked, and we both knew it was a relief to be in the regular rooms and not back in the haunted housing.

“Ladies and Lucas, can I please have your attention?” called Lesley, and we followed her into the lobby bar.

I watched as the poor porters struggled with all of the luggage, and thankfully, Rashida was expertly tagging everything.

“We now have our final few days in Cairo,” said Lesley.

“I was just informed by the agent that the Great Pyramid will be available for our private visit tomorrow morning at 6 a.m. and that the Great Sphinx will be available from 4 p.m., and yes, I’m afraid it’s all in the same day.”

I looked around at the group.

“So soon?” said Alice. “I’m so tired.” She was pale and looked very weak.

“I’m so sorry,” said Lesley. “It appears some important leaders are coming to visit over the next week, and the Great Pyramid may be closed for security after our visit. Not even the Contessa can change that.” She looked at Lucinda and Emilee.

“Ladies, can you offer healing, perhaps?”

“Of course,” nodded Lucinda.

“I think we know what this means,” said the Contessa from a far corner of the room. We have less than twenty-four hours in which to prepare and complete the work we came to do.”

I did not know what to think. Perhaps Naomi and

the Contessa would be creating a mighty storm of energy, as I felt as if my part was complete. Maybe not the game Nefertari had talked about, but surely my work at Philae and Abu Simbel had opened up enough doors and portals. The Scorpion woman was still in the south, for sure. We were safe here.

"Then I suggest we meet tonight at 6 p.m. in the Room of Souls," said Naomi, looking at Lucas, who looked a little in shock.

"But Naomi... the last time..." he protested.

"Shh, we will meet in the Room of Souls. The Contessa will arrange it with Lesley, as she can call the manager. So please gather back here in the lobby at 5:50 p.m., and you will be guided to the room."

"As you wish," said the Contessa. "Lesley, come here, child. We have much to prepare."

I watched as Lesley looked at Naomi like she had won a major award. The Contessa had never really uttered a kind word to her the whole trip, except for "Get me this" and "Get me that."

"Now, everyone rest, please," said Lesley. She then wandered off like a puppy after the Contessa, who was staying in the spooky suites upstairs with pyramid views.

I looked at my watch. It was only 1:30 p.m. Perhaps I would have a late lunch and pool time.

We all walked to the garden rooms. My luggage was already delivered, so I decided to shower and take a short nap. With the dark curtains drawn and the cool air-conditioning on, I found a calm and stillness that had escaped me for the past few days. Soon, I was in a deep sleep.

Symbols floated on past me, and everything I tried to grasp onto slipped away. Dark shadows swirled around me, and the faces of the women with whom I had travelled the past few days came into my awareness. I felt like an observer, yet each time I tried to move, it was as if I were glued to the bed. It was as though time had come to a standstill. The sun was setting, and the others were wandering silently, but I remained near the back, watching. I could not see, but I knew there were three doorways. But were they physical or etheric in my imagination?

I was in a trance. I could see the women, but it was as if I were invisible. I moved to the front; all the while, the sky was growing darker and darker. I moved in front of the Sphinx, edging toward the walk between the paws, standing in front of a large altar stone.

Ahead, I could see and feel the Dream Stele calling me—the famous carved stone with hieroglyphics. I reached out my hands towards the high altar stone and touched it. It was deep red granite, cold to the touch. I found myself floating up and standing behind the altar with my back to the head of the Sphinx. Then I moved further back towards the Dream Stele.

I climbed up onto the step that was at its base, stretching out my hands in front of me. I could see and feel energy rising up into my body. Suddenly, my mouth opened, and I began to speak with strange sounds and words. As my chanting began, I saw the women stop what they were doing and focus on me.

More words and sacred chants began to come from my mouth, and the women gathered in a circle. Then, as if they read my mind, they began to sound the note of A.

AAAAAAAAAA... the sound rose around me and seemed to fill the air. My body was shaking, and the ground began to move. Higher and higher, the sound rose, and then I saw the woman dressed in red from Abu Simbel walking towards me, her eyes black as coal. She held a large black scarab in her hand, and I could see the white markings. She appeared to be chanting and reading its inscription. Behind her, I could see the ghosts of the Priests of Unal. They were bound to her. This was the Scarab of Unal that was created at the same time as its scroll, and I was not sure my whole box of scrolls and scarabs could defeat this darkness. This was an evil alchemy that she was creating.

☥

I awoke suddenly to a banging on my door, not sure what time it was or even where I was.

It was Laura and Alexandria.

"Anna, it's nearly 4 p.m.," said Laura, and she came in and turned on my lights.

"Oh, I was lost in a dream. I don't know where I was... at the Sphinx, I think."

I lost my balance and slid back on the bed.

"As we thought," said Alexandria.

"Grandmama has opened the Room of Souls but said she would wait till 6 p.m."

"But she never waits," I said.

"It's okay, Anna. Now go have a shower—quickly," said Laura as she ordered some immediate room service and, to my surprise, began making my bed.

☥

By 5:45 p.m., we were ready and walking back to the main hotel, the palace. I watched as Lesley greeted us at the main staircase and whispered the instructions of where we were to go.

Apparently, you needed special permission to visit this room as it was of historic value. Of course, the Contessa could open more doors and had made it happen. I smiled around at this group of people I knew as friends and family. Yes, we had our issues, but then again, who didn't? And this spiritual family had some of the worst past-life battle scars. I was sensing that this was the time we would be reviewing this past life karma and I wondered which temple it stemmed from. Time to be totally clear before the Great Pyramid visit.

"Anna, this may be a modern-day hotel now, but she still has her secrets," said Naomi, standing behind me. "It was built in 1886, and that was when many of the great hotels around the world were not just vacation destinations, but strategic meeting places."

"A hotel with secrets?" I asked.

I turned to Naomi, "And you had secrets, too."

She did not wish to catch my eye, but I was in full view of the Akashic Records now and beginning to understand what had to be done.

I saw the hotel manager walk over as we all hesitated at the stairs.

"I believe you have requested our Mena room?" he said in a disturbing and somewhat hypnotic voice.

"Yes, why?' Laura looked at him and asked, "Is there a problem?"

"No, no," he said, looking at our group.

"We were told it was ready. Maybe you could escort us?" she smiled.

The hotel manager moved quickly, and we all followed behind. "This room is not often used," he muttered. We will be building soon and..."

"It will be demolished," said Laura.

"Yes, sadly," he nodded.

"Then we have work to do," I said, looking at Lucas. He held up his bag with the scrolls and scarabs, and I patted my bag to signal that I had the Book of Keys. I also had brought my Hathor sistrum. I was not sure it could clear demons, but it was worth a try.

Laura caught up with me.

"Anna, I get a sense I'm going home," she said.

"And it's not Yorkshire?" I asked.

"No, it's not. It's many miles away, and it is a home we have long forgotten with wisdom we have hidden."

We came to an abrupt stop. The double doors before us felt strangely familiar, as though I had seen them before. The door was already unlocked, and the manager bowed his head but did not enter. We entered the room. It was not what I had expected. The old wood panels on the walls and the low lighting gave it an eerie feeling. The carpet was dark brown and red with patterns and swirls. It looked like sacred geometry. One could see this room had housed many meetings and celebrations over the years, and who would have thought it had an etheric portal leading onto the Giza plateau?

The Contessa stood up to greet us. "This room is similar in size to that of the King's Chamber in the Great Pyramid," she said.

The chairs were stationed in a rectangular shape, into four sections of three. I was impressed that the Contessa had ordered the chairs laid out in a similar configuration.

"Are we awaiting anyone else?" asked Lesley, still with her clipboard in her hands and awaiting the approval of the Contessa, who smiled at her. I looked around, and yes, everyone was here.

"Well done, my dear. This is perfect." She congratulated Lesley, who beamed around the room.

"I'll lock the door," said Lucas, and I noticed his skin was still red and irritated. Yes, we were all beginning to fade, and I prayed that the twenty-four hours would come and go quickly.

The Contessa looked at Naomi and summoned her

over. Naomi whispered something to her and pointed at various chairs, and the Contessa nodded.

"Anna, will you please choose your seat?" she asked, pointing to all the chairs.

It felt like musical chairs, and I moved around slowly. I saw the room change as if it now had stone walls. I went over to the smaller side, where there were three seats across. This felt strong and stable, and I was drawn to sit in the corner. I hesitated, then went to sit down, and I shifted and sat in the middle seat.

I happened to look across, and to my surprise, Naomi and the Contessa were holding hands, not daring to look. When they saw me sit, they looked more relaxed, and Naomi came over and sat in the corner seat on my right, where I had intended to go.

"Wow, a close call," she said, "You nearly took my seat."

"Your seat?" I whispered.

"Yes, I always hold the right-hand corner. This is the realm to the darker chambers and where the mischief elements occur. It's said snakes and scorpions can rise through this part of the chamber."

"No, I'll take the safer seat," I smiled.

She held her hand over her mouth to stop laughing. "Oh, Anna, you're hysterical. Do you really think any of this is safe?" Her eyes had a red glow, and I wondered if perhaps I had chosen unwisely.

"Ladies, please," said the Contessa. "This is a serious moment."

We both sat up straight and focused.

"Now, Lucas," prompted the Contessa.

He sat in the same spot on the opposite side, facing me. "To hold for you, Anna," he smiled.

"Now Lesley..." She sat next to Lucas in the corner to the

far left of me.

"To hold the door closed, and I'll be the last person in," she said.

I was beginning to see that at each of these chairs were our roles and positions in the Great Pyramid, similar to when we had visited Kom Ombo and chosen our places and pathways to walk.

Next, Alice slowly moved to the other side of Lucas on the corner. "Not my normal place, but I feel safer here, and it is time for someone else to hold that position."

"Now Alexandria..."

She walked over and sat to my left. "I'm here for you, Anna," she said.

"Lucinda and Emilee, please choose," said the Contessa, and without thinking, they chose the middle seats in the centre of the longer sides. Lucinda to my right, and Emilee to the left.

"Everyone else, please," said the Contessa as she sat between Alexandria and Emilee, followed by Laura, who sat between Alice and Lucinda. There were two gaps between Lucinda and Naomi, and Lesley and Emilee. But I was sure it would work out.

Laura pulled her chair closer to Alice as it was obvious she was in pain again. It crossed my mind that this was what may have happened to Isis.

"Now, Lucas, did you bring the scarabs and scrolls?" asked the Contessa.

He nodded, and I wondered if this were the actual ceremony we would be performing or if it would be the dress rehearsal.

Lucas placed a large white cloth on the floor in the centre, and around it, we placed the scrolls and scarabs in the shape of a flower with the sistrum and the Book of Keys in front of me. The others lit tea lights, and then it would seem all eyes were upon me.

"Oh, I forgot," said Naomi, placing her old coin in the centre.

"To pay the ferryman," she said.

"Now, Anna, your back is against the sarcophagus," said the Contessa.

"It's time to begin the ritual of clearing the Records."

I then relaxed in my chair and allowed the channel of information to come forward. I called on everyone to close their eyes, hear the words, feel the motion, see the visions, and know the truth. I could hear a muttering around the room as we all settled into place. For a moment, I wondered what I was supposed to do, my ego doubting, when I felt a hand upon my shoulder and a presence sit down next to me. At first, I thought it would be Isis, but no, it was Arsinoe.

"Anna, this is your time; you have come further than anyone in this group has before, further than your beloved Isis was able to."

Now, I felt I could let go and really trust. She was not at all like the energy we had encountered on the boat. She was more protective and calm. I began to channel.

"Many thousands of years ago, there was a young King Pepi II born in 2288 BC. He worshipped the sun and watched over the Pyramids and the Well of Souls from his palace every day and night. He had possession of many sacred pieces that the elders from Atlantis had brought. Relics saved from the floods. This location, where the Mena House Hotel now sits, is where he kept many of the secrets that the trusted priests and priestesses used. He coveted the famous sacred eight scrolls and scarabs of the Oracles brought from Atlantis. It was known that they could be used to create great temples, and Pepi had sought this power for himself.

"Working with the Scorpion Queen, he sought ascension and eternal life. He did, however, sell his soul to the Scorpion to gain them. He brought forward the words for his tomb from the Emerald Tablets, and after his death, Egypt was left in civil war, death, and drought. He stole these Records to give him everlasting life, and as Oracles of Egypt, we have returned life after life to clear this and bring forth healing forces and information of Light. He had curses woven into these lands of Khemit.

"With one heart, we return these true sacred scrolls and scarabs to their original state and remove all curses, contracts, and vows from their Akashic Records. These are our scrolls and scarabs. Each of these belonged to its own sacred temple, and many of you here in the room today were their guardian, scribe, and activator. Please know that as we recreate these temple connections, we all intend to respond and work together harmoniously."

I wondered if I should stop and take questions but was taken over by a higher energy and began to lead a meditation.

"Now let me lead you back in time, to a time out of time when life was magical.

"The air was crisp and clean, and all was in balance in our world. The sky was blue, and the sun and the moon always brought light into our world. The Earth was vibrant, plants and trees grew, and we all had purpose and community.

"Allow yourself to take this journey to the Temple of the Oracle, a tall temple created from energy and crystal. Shining bright and sending a pulse of love to all.

"As you make your way into this temple, you have a sense of home, of belonging. This is a safe space where you remember who you truly are and your purpose as a messenger at this time. As we sit now in this circle, we can project ourselves into this sacred space and create our soul connection. See the Temple of the Oracles as they once were."

I began to sense many others in the room and opened my eyes. Everyone was in a deep state, but I could see each of the storylines of pain and suffering, like timelines, behind each one. Sometimes, the lines crossed.

I saw the timelines of history. I was lost in what seemed to be a streaming room of information. It appeared as if it was too vast, so I simply allowed the timelines to swirl and merge. It was as if I began to see us all at various times as the oracles we were and currently are. In that moment, I understood why I was here. This was more than a temple; it was about understanding who we truly were.

As that realisation came, I began to see the figures of the past coming forward. Famous faces, important faces. They had all come here searching for the truth and purpose of the Children of the Light and the Mystery School. I saw those who had lost their way and those who were so brave they had faced the trials. I stopped momentarily, thinking I saw my parents or at least my mother. Perhaps I had ancestors who had visited this room. I saw the lights begin to flicker, and the room had become colder. I knew it was time to end the session, knowing that it would be re-enacted for some reason only twelve hours from now in the Great Pyramid.

"And very slowly, everyone, please, it is time to come back to your bodies and into the light."

I saw everyone gently coming back very slowly, but something told me that a negative force was present. I looked at Naomi, and she nodded towards Lucinda. Lucinda was red in the face and glaring at the Contessa.

"You left them to die; you took the relics and left them to die."

The Contessa refused to look at her.

"Hold her still, Naomi," said Laura. "We don't need this drama."

"It's not the time," Naomi replied, almost in a whisper.

"If you do not heal this now, that timeline will cause us all to fail," said the voice of Alice. She looked stronger.

"Should I look in the Records?" I asked Alexandria, but she was already crying.

"She needs to know," said Lucas. "Anna needs to know."

"No, no..." The Contessa was also in a state of distress.

"I can only hold the door closed and protect this circle for so long," said Lucas.

"I was a young girl then," said the Contessa. "This serves no purpose now."

"You are the only one here apart from Isis, who lived in your current incarnation in that time. You were both born in 1929."

"All of us were born after that," said Alice. "I was born in 1946, and Laura in 1948."

"We were children ourselves, and our parents had very little power, not like the 1890s," said the Contessa, looking at Lucinda.

"You and the Mystery School took away the relics in St. Petersburg. They were supposed to protect us all, and they were sold to Rasputin by your family," Lucinda hissed.

"He was dark and evil," said Lucinda, "I told him to take the Imperial family away to safety, but his protection of the Queen was lost in an evil seduction he had created to gain power over her. We knew we all had to escape the nightmare that was coming, then Count Dimitri and his friends killed him, and we all fell into a battle again."

Like history in Paris and Egypt, I could see it clearly, time following time. Another cursed family set to lead and bring forward a golden era that failed and paid a heavy price.

"But what is everyone hiding, please?" I had never felt so alone in the room.

Laura came over to me, knelt in front of me, smiled, and gently took my hands.

"She has to remember her last incarnation. We cannot take her into the chambers not knowing, or she will be blindsided," said Laura.

"Anna, my darling, do you trust me? We are going back to Germany," Laura said to me. I looked around the room, and far to the corner, I was sure I had seen Isis in the shadows.

"I will stay with you," said Laura. She nodded to Alexandria, and they swapped seats. She sat down to my left. I closed my eyes and began to channel.

"Germany, I'm not sure. Okay, it's coming through. It's late 1935, and we live, I think, in a place called Frankfurt. I live with a wealthy family, and we have a piano. My mother's name is Elsa. We are rich, and our family is very respected. I'm young, maybe three or four years old, but I'm bright for my age. I tell my mother of my nightmares, but she tells me it's nonsense and not real. I see that she's alarmed but will not speak of why.

"I go for special lessons with a few other children, and my family attends many parties. I'm too young to go... Oh, Contessa, I see you and Isis as very young and beautifully dressed girls. Everyone speaks different languages, but it's a very magical group. You're all very young. Then, things change, and my nightmares grow more intense. The parties cease to happen. It's nearly winter. I visit my mother in her bedroom and see that she is most upset. I see her in a silk pink robe with lace. She is frantically pacing and shouting to the maid. She keeps saying, 'We should have left' and 'the fate of her family'—the curse is following her.

"She shouts about how my two brothers had been sent away to school, and my three sisters are already in society elsewhere in Europe. She carries such guilt and confusion. She has so many regrets."

"What was your birth story, Anna?" I could hear the Contessa in the distance.

"I was born on a date that the wise woman my mother consulted said would be profound. I was conceived in Paris at the time of a great eclipse. My parents only had two witnesses to my birth. A nurse, oh, that's you, Alexandria, and a priest. We were a wealthy family, and for some reason, my birth was kept a secret unless you were a trusted ally. My parents feared too much attention, and they decided that I should be removed from the notoriety of our society.

"More people are coming into focus. My mother does not want to leave me. Oh, Emilee, I see that's you. And Lucinda, you are a wise woman who gives advice to her—a best friend. Now I'm all alone. My mother is leaving, and she tells me she will see me soon. I'm left with nannies, and soon, other families move into our large home. I keep asking when we will leave, but now everyone is afraid. Laura, you are with me—I think a nanny—our money is running low, and we are afraid.

"One day, we are in the nursery, and we hear a banging at the door. We run to hide down the back stairs. I'm dressed in one of the coats from the other families and blended in, hidden in plain sight. Laura is so afraid. The other families tell the police that the rich family has gone. I think they are police, but they look evil and very angry.

"I can hear the families talking and looking at us. They begin to argue, and Laura promises we will leave once she gets word to the station master. If we can make it to the train station, we can board a train, and we will be rescued and on our way to safety aboard the Orient Express.

"One of the mothers in the house comes over to me and strokes my hair. I tell her that soon, the evil ones will come back for them and that she and her loved ones should all leave. I am so young, I don't understand how I could even have used this term. Laura sends word to the stationmaster that it is time. He is trusted. We will use the last of our money, a magical gold coin with the Templar crest on it, as this is safer and more valuable than banknotes to bribe our way to freedom. That night, a man and a woman arrive, sent by the stationmaster, and Laura tells me we are leaving.

The couple comes to our rooms. I follow them and see they are in the nursery at my toy boxes and loading what look like old relics from hidden compartments into saddlebags. The man sees me and is surprised. The woman tells him not to be distracted and that she knows my mother. I think she is you, Lesley. Laura now enters and pleads with them to take us. They promise and tell us we are being watched. They say they will come back at dawn. The stationmaster has arranged everything. Laura gives them a gold coin and says, 'It's our last.' It is becoming light, and a dark force descends upon the city. The children downstairs tell me that people like me are being hunted. The word hunted seems strange to me, but by now, Laura is most frantic. Apparently, I was on a list of gifted and coveted children. I hear the mothers talking with a priest... no, it's a Rabbi in the kitchen. The couple returns, and we leave the house. We make our way to Frankfurt train station with the couple, but we had been followed. The couple disappears—they say they are going for tickets—and Laura and I are alone.

"We wait, but they do not return. Laura and I try to leave the station, but we are greeted by German officers and escorted to the trains on the far side of the station. I see a stationmaster hurry over, pretending we are his family and leaving for another train location. It's Lucas! They don't believe him, and then there is a disruption, like an explosion with a firing of guns. People scatter, screaming, and Lucas dies. I see in the distance those who could have helped us. I see the man and woman across the station with the saddlebags. I am not sure they see us, but they are getting on another train.

"Laura and I run to find shelter, but the soldiers pull us over to a carriage used for cargo, not people, and insist we get on, so we board the train. As we enter the carriage, I see faces and people from our neighbourhood that I recognise. They look desperate. Soldiers with dogs are everywhere, and Laura and I hide with the others. Our butcher, our mail collector... but now they tell us they are having to leave because of their religion. Before we know it, the train is leaving. People on the train are kind. However, it is hard with no food or bathroom, and people are getting sick. The journey feels endless.

"Alice, I see you staring at me across the carriage. You have your daughter, Naomi. You are hiding her as well. You tell us to sit with you. You tell Laura that they are looking for young girls like us; you point to Naomi and me. Alice asks what Laura knows. She has been told to protect me, but never really understood why.

"Alice asks if she is my mother, and Laura looks at me and tells her, sadly, no. Then she tells her my family name. Alice asks her to bring me over closer, and she asks for my date of birth. She tells Laura she knows of our family, and Laura and I feel safe now to sit with them. They have prepared for the trip and share their food and water in secret. Naomi, it seems, already saw this fate.

"Alice tells the story of how the dark man in Berlin is

searching for those who see the future. She looks at Naomi... you are in your early teens. She tells us she is part of the group connected with our family and has been in hiding. Many of our special friends' homes have been raided, and many valuable pieces of art, books, and artefacts have been taken to Berlin. Alice and Naomi also had passage to the Orient Express, but they were also betrayed. Hence, they were now hiding on the refugee trains.

"Laura asks Alice what she thinks will happen to the children. She explains that we were targets for our gifts and our minds. The women decide to rest. The day is so long, but I snuggle next to Naomi. She reminds me of my sisters. It's only when they think that I am asleep that Alice wakes Laura to tell her the real story.

"She begins to whisper a story I have seen in my nightmares. A man is searching for the Oracle of the bloodline, Laura whispers, and she looks at me. If he finds any of them, it is said he can control many dark forces, as they will play the game for him. He knows that if he plays the game, his rule could continue. He was ready to call dark forces and had already had many psychics tell him secrets of Egyptian magic. He had gained the trust of several members of a secret society. It is said that he had even planned a victory in the headquarters of this society in St. Petersburg at the Astoria Hotel, where it was said Rasputin stayed and hid documents and relics.

"We travel for two nights and days. My heart knows my family is looking for me. I can see my mother sending word to many important people and pleading with a very rich and politically connected family in Paris. Money and expensive art are being handed over for my safe return. Lots of wealth. She's selling everything, and in my vision, I see her prepared to work for the Germans if she has to. I am not sure where my brothers and sisters are. But no one can find me.

It appears many in our carriage have come together, and they let us know a secret that they plan to escape.

"The next day, the train stopped, and I see men running—all with guns. Some people in our carriage are trying to escape, and many do flee, but in the gunfire, a stray bullet comes through the open doorway and hits the side of my leg. Now, there are only a few people left in our carriage. In our carriage, the women who stayed gather and appear to weave magic around Naomi and me. They will not leave me, even though they know the carriage is heading to the camps of evil.

"Singing songs of the old country, they gather and call on Alice. It appears she is a great healer. She prays over me. I am getting weaker and weaker. I saw her eyes, sad and clear, as she saw who I was. I am passing... leaving my body as I lose a lot of blood. The women cannot hold me; they know it will not be long before we reach the camp. Now, I am floating like an angel above them all, leaving my body, which is taking its last breaths.

"I hear them promise that we will all meet again, and I feel the carriage slowing. Alice has medicine. She gives each woman a small dose, including Naomi and herself, and I watch as they fall asleep. Laura gently places a pillow over me, and I feel an unconditional love as I drift away... she takes the last drop.

"I am not sure if I'm dreaming. I can still see my body, yet I'm flying above, now watching as the carriage door opens and the guards see all of us lying there looking as though asleep. They realise that we all lie dead. I am in spirit, but I watch them. One of them comes over to Alice and looks at an image on a paper. He sees that those they have been ordered to find are now here dead and that they will be blamed."

I begin to sob, and I open my eyes. The room is still and silent.

"Please, everyone, open your eyes," Laura instructs them.

For a moment, I was not sure what to do. Then, I felt Arsinoe's presence again.

"Come to circle, Anna," she whispered, then disappeared.

"Quickly, everyone, clear the floor," I ordered, and everyone moved into action.

I stepped into the middle, picked up my Book of Keys, and stood in the middle of the scroll and scarab circle and turned to each of them.

"Naomi, my friend, step forward. I thank you for your kindness."

"Laura, thank you for my gentle release."

"Alice, thank you for your wisdom."

"Emilee and Lucinda, bless you both."

"Lucas, you tried, and I love you for that."

"Lesley, you were faced with a choice. My fate was sealed, I'm sure, and risking yourself would have changed nothing."

"I didn't last that long in the war," said Lucinda. "I was captured working for the resistance, and I was lost at the end of the war when they thought I was a collaborator." She touched her head, and I saw a flash of her beautiful hair gone, and the shame and abuse she was subjected to.

"I was lost and alone in the ghetto. My fate was sealed in the death camps," said Alexandria.

Lesley stepped forward. She looked so humble. "I thought we all had time, but when the disruption started, I was waiting for you on the train. I saw your train leave and made no attempt to help. I left and went to Paris to find your mother and deliver the relics." Her voice was low, and she looked ready to cry.

Emilee came over and stood behind her. "She found me, but we were captured and did not survive. We tried to help the resistance and used every piece of wealth we had. We lost everything," she said.

"I think we all met fate and crossed in that timeline." I looked around the room. "We all paid a price."

"Well, maybe not everyone," said Naomi, and we all looked at the Contessa.

There was a long silence.

"Isis was my friend, and she was sent to England to a boarding school. My family stayed in Paris and gathered wealth, and we worked with many to free people and to conceal people during the war," she defended herself.

The Contessa came over and stood in front of me. "Anna, one day I will share the story of your family, but for today, we have to move past this. This is not the time or place," she said, casting a glance at Lucinda.

I wanted to trust her, but as I looked around the group, I saw the price we had all paid for such a terrible time. There would be a time to forgive, but maybe not forget.

"I think they need the room." I could sense the manager moving up the stairs.

"Yes, it's getting cold. Let's leave," said Alice.

Very quickly, we moved everything. Lucas and Naomi scrambled to retrieve the scrolls and scarabs into the box, and as the manager knocked and entered, it was obvious there was nothing more to be seen.

"Tomorrow in the lobby at 5 a.m., everyone. The Pyramids await us," Lesley did not need to say anymore.

We knew our places, just perhaps not what was to come.

CHAPTER 30

Sunday, 27 September 2009
The Great Pyramid

I was unable to sleep. I pondered everything I had seen in the previous evening's ceremony. I kept having flashbacks of the train station in Frankfurt, and even though I had gone to bed exhausted, nothing was sending me to a restful slumber.

By 3 a.m., I figured that if I was to fall asleep, I would be out for the count and certainly miss my wake-up alarm. I decided that the best option was to get ready and be prepared, and then I could wait in the lobby, perhaps even sit and meditate.

As I slowly walked back to the main entrance of the hotel via the beautiful gardens, I took in the scents of the night jasmine and the vision of stars in the sky. All was calm and still, and I wondered how long that would last. Suddenly, an uneasy feeling came over me, like someone was walking behind me.

"I'm with you," I heard a deep, masculine voice.

"Anubis," I whispered, afraid to turn, but quickened my step.

"Very good, Anna, my friend. Now hurry; it's not safe to be out here alone; there are many energies of ill intent."

I did not need warning again, so I ran up to the main hotel and through the security door.

The night porter was sitting in the lobby entrance, his hand holding his head as he nodded in and out of sleep. I held up my bag, and he smiled and waved me through. No one was in reception, and the lamps were dimly lit, casting shadows upon the walls.

I crossed over to the open bar and lounge area, and to my surprise, Lesley and Naomi were already sitting with pots of hot tea, simply staring out of the window towards the pyramids. I crept up and sat at the next table. They said nothing, but Naomi acknowledged me and simply reached across and squeezed my hand. Lesley was motionless, with tears streaming down her face. I decided not to interfere and to simply sit in silence, so I leaned back and rested my eyes.

I must have dozed off, as when I woke and checked my watch, it was 4:30 a.m. Naomi and Lesley were whispering; the crying had obviously stopped. Lesley looked at me.

"We stayed and watched you sleep. You know you snore," she smiled.

"I couldn't sleep in my room, but I guess here works," I replied.

"Are you okay?" I asked Lesley. "I wondered if the meeting last night had upset you, the one in that spooky room."

"No, well, yes, that was difficult, but..." she stopped, and her lip trembled.

She looked at Naomi.

"Once Lesley and I were initiates," Naomi responded, pointing to the Great Pyramid. "In ancient times, you entered the tunnels in the pyramids and climbed to the initiation chambers without any support, just your faith. We went through all the trials and saw the hidden messages, but failed the final initiation," she continued.

"How so?" I asked.

"We are not sure, but when Isis read our Akashic Records before you arrived to Glastonbury, she saw one of us slipping and the other falling—falling to our deaths,"

Naomi answered.

"I slipped," said Lesley, "and then you fell because of me. I can still see the fall in my dreams, and I caused us to fail."

"Can I look?" I asked.

"But why?" Naomi questioned.

"Something does not seem correct," I shrugged. "It's worth a try."

"Okay." They both looked at each other and nodded, and Naomi signalled to the night porter for more tea and coffee.

"They will all be here soon, so better get it started," she said.

I gently touched each of them on the hand, closed my eyes, and began to channel.

"It is daylight, and in front of the Pyramid are schools of priests and priestesses. Each day, you train with various teachers who lead you through the trials.

"No food or water; it is like you live on fresh air.

"My goodness, Giza looks so lush, so different.

"Anyway, you practice in smaller pyramids in confined spaces with no air and special breathing practices.

"There is taming of snakes and scorpions and reciting of prayers that you have learnt by heart."

"I could never have managed these, but you both did.

"Now is the time you both trained for the initiation ceremony. I see you, Lesley, going first, and it's like you sit in the upright tunnel and ease yourself up with no robes or ladders. It's like you defy gravity.

"Lower down the tunnel, I see you, Naomi. You believe Lesley has made it to the chambers, and a rock falls, so you think it's the signal to start your ascent. I see that as you move up the shaft, the prayers you recite create symbols and lights within the walls.

"Oh no, Lesley, you have not quite made the final ascent. You're distracted. You hear something.

"You don't see the energy that's coming from the chamber below... it's a really creepy creature. It has sensed your fear, crawled up from the chamber below, and is following you. It can walk on the walls, and now it's above you. It is the one throwing rocks to trick Naomi.

"Lesley, you look up and see it, and it pushes you.

"Lesley, you were pushed, and then you fell, and Naomi, you tried to catch her, but you both tumbled."

I stopped and opened my eyes. They both sat in a state of shock. I looked over at the pyramids.

"But you won't fail today. Not on my watch. Now, let's clear this. Please, left hands on your hearts."

Both women did so obediently.

"Please repeat: I hereby understand that there are forces within these mighty pyramids that I do not yet fully understand. However, I have been trained and taught not to fear the unknown, and I now release my soul from any thoughts of failure. What happened was in divine time, and I hereby now recall all of my ancient wisdom blocked from that timeline and claim my divine right to access and reside in the great chambers for my initiation. And so it is."

Both women followed and repeated my every word.

At the end of the decree, my energy felt so strong. It was as if my true self was emerging. My mentor Isis had awakened me, but now it was me, remembering myself.

"I'm remembering the training," said Naomi.

"And me, too," said Lesley.

"Here, Anna, hold our hands so you can access the Records also," said Naomi.

"But it's your training," I shook my head, "your gifts."

"No," they both said in unison as we all joined hands. They both looked at me and said, "Ours now."

Now I knew why I had been awake. It was to become aware of their training records and understand the protocol for the Great Pyramid. I had been thinking Alice would guide me, but something in my heart told me she might be too weak.

It was just after 5 a.m. when the others gathered, and Lesley went into tour guide mode. I took out my journal, flicked through my Book of Keys, and wrote down a few pointers of the ritual as I remembered them.

At 5:30 a.m., we were on the bus. Taking a bus across the street twenty yards seemed strange, but this was the security requirement. Nobody seemed to mind. Just jobs to do. Even though I had been staring at the pyramids, standing before them and seeing how large the stones were, it was now real and even more breathtaking. It seemed strange that no other tourists were present. It was just our group, along with Rashida and the guards, who were to open the Great Pyramid for us.

Our bus parked right outside the Great Pyramid, and we disembarked in silence. I felt like I was floating as I followed everyone up the steps of the entrance. I was slowly beginning to understand the energy and power of this place. I watched as the guards handed Alice a key. The wonder of the world apparently still had an actual padlock on the gated entrance.

Alice smiled and looked at me. "Anna, please come here," she said. "Next time, you will lead, but today, I will open the gateways, and if you follow me, you will learn."

Alice had once been a guardian of the secrets here and a master, so I was honoured she would teach me.

"Lesley, come here, my dear." Her voice was powerful, but I could already sense her weakness.

Lesley moved slowly towards her.

"You will be last in, holding the doors of darkness closed. We need your strength today," she said, taking her hand.

"You see them waiting?" she asked.

"I know them," nodded Lesley, "and I know what to do. They won't catch me again. Naomi will be in front of me."

I glanced at Lucas, and he came over to us.

"I have left the scrolls and scarabs in the layout we used last night in my room on my bed, but I have the Scroll and Scarab of Creation and Protection with me," he said, patting his pockets, and I was relieved. Something told me that ritual had a space and place, but sometimes we need to make adjustments.

I patted the pocket on the side of my trousers to show I had the Book of Keys. Everything else I had left in my room, hidden underneath one of my pashmina scarves.

"Good call," whispered Lesley.

"Good, then we will begin," said Alice.

"Everyone, line up in the place that resonates."

"I will make the climb but remain outside the chamber," said Rashida.

I nodded.

Everyone shuffled around Alice: me, then the Contessa, then Lucinda, Laura, Emilee, Lucas, Alexandria, and finally, Naomi, Rashida, and Lesley. We made our way through the carved tunnel lit by a few lamps. Then we turned to see the small metal ladder that would allow us to step onto what was known as the gallery, the shaft that climbed up to the chambers. I looked at the shaft leading down into the basement.

"No, Anna, do not look there yet," said the Contessa behind me. "It must stay sealed."

"If we are ready," said Alice. She appeared to have regained her strength, but I was not sure how long that would last, so I set my intention to send her as much healing energy as I could.

She stepped onto the metal 3-step ladder, then pulled herself onto the flat wooden-slat ladder and held onto the two wooden bars for support. "Like this, Anna. Use your arms to pull yourself up," she whispered.

"Wait, I need to take my shoes off," I answered. "I need to be barefoot."

She looked at me and smiled as I slipped off my shoes and placed them onto a small ledge.

"Well, well, you may not need any guidance. Now let's go."

We all slowly began the ascent, and I just kept looking forward, breathing slowly. Looking behind, I could see us all in a line, following along and taking care.

"Akul akul akul"

Alice softly sang the word like a mantra, and I began to join the melody. Soon, everyone joined the chant, and I remembered Isis using this. She had explained it was to call the ancient ones. I had a flashback to us all in Glastonbury, which seemed so long ago.

We reached the halfway point and turned to climb another ladder. I could see Lesley all the way at the end, clearing energy and placing protection all around us.

The climb continued, and I could see the priests of the past watching us as if floating around the walls. They studied us and whispered to each other, curious to see who had summoned them.

When we reached the top, we climbed the final few bars, and ahead was a narrow shaft way. I watched Alice say a spell to unlock the small tunnel, and crouching down, we all followed her, crawling on our knees and moving into the large rectangular stone chamber.

As my eyes adjusted to the light, I felt strange. Everywhere we had gone so far, we had seen images and hieroglyphics, vivid storylines left as clues, but here was nothing.

At the back, I saw the sarcophagus and paid attention as

Alice went behind it to whisper into all the walls to open up the other dimensions. She then moved back to her corner, the place she had chosen for herself the night before. She sat down and pointed for me to take my place.

Everyone sat in their designated place, and I watched as Laura tended to Alice, who had used nearly all of her life force to get us to this point. Then she took her place.

Finally, Lesley entered, and she sat next to the tunnel entrance. I could now see why she would be our perfect guardian and gatekeeper. Alexandria was to my left, and Naomi to my right. I could feel their support. It wasn't until Naomi leaned over and whispered that the reality hit me.

"Anna, you're on... it's show time."

I took a deep breath and asked everyone to access their hearts and bring their energy into balance.

It gave me a moment to think. But before I could, the energy took over...

"Everyone, please say with me, *OM...*"

"Ommmmmmmmm..."

We chanted in union, and then I remembered Isis, and the ceremony we had once held in the Sanctuary for a private group. And so I began to summon the ancient ones. I sang what sounded like a melody.

Netjer Amun Ra
Netjer Nut
Netjer Geb
Netjer Osiris
Netjer Isis
Netjer Horus
Netjer Hator
Netjer Nepthys
Netjer Set
Netjer Sekhmet
Netjer Ptah

Netjer Thoth
Netjer Seshat
Netjer Anubis

With each calling, I felt my energy rise as I could hear the words echoing into the ceiling and around the chamber.

"I now invite each of you to declare yourself by name and what you wish to bring to this circle."

"I am Anna. I bring peace."

"I am Alexandria. I bring love."

"I am Emilee. I bring gratitude."

"I am Laura. I bring strength."

"I am Lesley. I bring protection."

"I am Lucas. I bring healing."

"I am Alice. I bring wisdom."

"I am Francoise. I bring knowledge."

"I am Lucinda. I bring kindness."

"I am Naomi. I bring joy."

"I will now build the violet flame in the centre of the room. Please focus on this light; see that it is purple, red, pink, and white. This is the energy of transmutation and transformation.

"Now, everyone, please place your left hand on your heart, and with your right hand, move it towards the fire. You are now releasing anything that no longer serves you."

I watched as everyone began clearing into the imaginary Violet Flame.

"Now, everyone, I will call forth the guardians of this chamber," and I started to mutter words I had never heard before. I began to see hooded figures enter the chamber. I heard the message, *We are the Elohim.*

They then walked clockwise around the circle, creating a wave of electric blue energy that rose high into the ceiling. As they passed, I could just about see their faces. They passed by one by one, and then one stopped and looked at me, lifting their hood. It was my mentor, Isis. She simply smiled and carried on past.

I then stood and called for everyone else to stand and receive the initiation of the Elohim, the wise ones. I watched as golden discs of energy flowed from these Masters' hands into all of us until we all stood in illumination. Then, they simply faded into the walls of the chamber, and our ritual continued.

The most exquisite energy flowed through me, and I began to see the messages and symbols illuminated on the walls. I could see that everyone else was seeing and sensing the wisdom.

"This is the wisdom of Atlantis, and you, as Oracles, are being invited to read the messages and visions of what is to come for your work and spiritual service."

Everyone began to turn to the walls, holding up their hands to capture streams of energy. Some were even creating mudras with their hands as if pulling in strands of consciousness. I went to the back wall. I was not translating messages; I was hearing them. I placed my forehead against the cold stone wall, and it was as if I could see through it—it was transparent.

What appeared to be two large Anubis statues had come to life and stared back at me.

"*From where do you come*?" they asked, coming closer.

"*I come from the stars*" was the message I gave them. This seemed to work, and they lifted a veil to their side of the wall.

Just past them, I was surprised to see a large open chamber.

"*What am I to do*?" I began to communicate telepathically with them.

"Align this chamber and join it to the temples you know,

then realign the energy with the Halls of Amenti at the Sphinx," they responded and pointed to our group. *"Your Oracles are locating what they must do personally."*

I watched as everyone moved around, gathering the energy and messages that were now streaming into the chamber. By some miracle, they all moved in unison and never seemed to clash with anyone else. Except for Alice—she had gone back to sitting in the corner.

"Can you help her?" I asked.

"She is making her way home to us," they replied.

"No, not yet, no, she has so much to teach me," I pleaded.

"Your teachers are everywhere. She is not the only one, and she has work to do. She knows this." I looked back at Alice, who was smiling at me.

"A few more weeks, Anna," she telepathically called to me. *"Then tell them I will join them willingly."*

I relayed the message, trying not to become emotional.

"We will finish the journey tonight at the Sphinx," I told the guardians.

"The journey has just started, Oracle. The gateway of souls is opening again. The Children of Light are becoming more present. Your Oracle work can continue in the future, and they will be aligned to Atlantis again. The sacred game will play until the prophecy is fulfilled. It is time to weave everything together."

Then, I watched as they began to retreat, and the veil closed. I wanted to ask more, but they were gone. So I went and stood at the sarcophagus and waited for the group to finish.

Everyone seemed to sense the energy subsiding, and they all returned to their places—all except the Contessa and Lesley, who stood in the centre facing each other with arms above their heads. They then placed their hands palm to palm. I had not seen this ritual before, but I respectfully waited for them to finish.

"Everyone, please gather," I said, signaling them to stand around the sarcophagus. Lucas joined me and handed me the Scroll and Scarab of Creation. He held the Protection pieces.

Once again, I began to speak in a strange language, weaving the energies of the scroll and scarab across the empty chamber until visions of all the temples that we had cleared began to surface. I began to see all the scrolls and scarabs being joined in a pattern swirling around the room. It was as if I could hear their voices and see the rituals again.

"Quickly," said Lesley. "I feel something moving on the staircase."

I had not expected this, so I began to finish my work, seeing the records of the temples intertwining with these sacred relics again and unbinding the curses and spells from the previous owners over thousands of years. I did what I could, but I knew something was missing. Perhaps I could dream back into it later.

"Everyone, please seal this chamber with an *Om*."

I watched as everyone began, and I could see blue light coming from their mouths and moving around the chamber. I could feel the wisdom of my Book of Keys streaming out, and then suddenly, I was distracted by what I thought was a large black object flying towards me and smashing into the wall behind me. I could hear Rashida arguing outside the chamber with someone.

Very quickly, I ran to the walls, as I had seen Alice do when she opened them. I was now closing them, and as I looked down, I saw the broken object was gone. Everyone else went back into tourist mode. I waited inside the chamber, and soon I heard steps coming through the tunnel.

"The rudeness of that lady and her friends," said Rashida. She came over to me. "I was waiting in the last part of the gallery, and they started coming up the chamber," she said.

"But it was private," said Naomi.

"I think they bribed the guards," said Rashida.

"Where are they now?" the Contessa asked.

"Gone, waiting outside, I told them a group was coming down, and there was nowhere to pass, then I came to warn you all."

"Then we must leave," said the Contessa. "Anna, are you complete?"

"Most complete and ready for the next move," I nodded and handed the Scroll and Scarab of Creation to Lucas. I knew something was still missing, but now was not the time to second-guess. We had done as best as we could.

It took forever to leave, as we virtually had to carry Alice slowly back down. Lucas was a hero—so gentle, kind, and patient. When we reached the tunnel exit, I couldn't see the other group.

"Where did the group go?" I asked a guard.

"Down, down the shaft." He pointed to the place I had considered when we arrived.

I had a terrible feeling they had gone to the Dark Well of Souls underneath the Pyramid, which meant they were working in the darker realms while we were opening up portals. I did not need to ask who they were, as I knew this was the Scorpion Queen at work, and it would appear that she was ready to play. The game had really started.

We boarded our bus, and as I looked around, I could not see any other cars or vans, so this group must have wandered into the complex. But our work was done, and I was ready to rest.

☥

Back safely at the hotel, we all met up again for breakfast at the restaurant around the pool. Only Alice was missing. She had gone straight to her room, and people were taking turns checking on her.

As I looked around the table, I saw a more aligned group than ever. Food was being shared, coffee was being poured, and laughter was abundant. It was hard to believe we had just been to work in one of the most powerful and sacred places on the planet.

I continued to see everyone still retrieving their messages from the King's Chamber, and it suddenly dawned on me that we had been in a Hall of Amenti, but without the Amenti Scroll and Scarab. That was what was missing. That was the key, but I was not sure I had time on this trip to find them.

I sat silently as I began to see flashes of a very vague past life, which was right in front of me to review. It was a time when we gathered together to share great wisdom and relayed it to others. The only message I received was that this was the true purpose of an Oracle temple. As quickly as the vision came in, it slipped away. Perhaps later, after the Sphinx visit, more would surface, but for now, I had to have another chocolate croissant.

"Everyone, I am going to rest and see that Alice is okay," said Lesley. "We will meet at 5 p.m. for the Sphinx visit this afternoon."

"Is she okay?" I asked.

"She will be. We have a doctor there now. He says dehydration, but we know better."

"I'll stay with her in her room," said Laura.

After everyone had gone, I ordered more coffee. I had never had so much coffee in my life.

Lucinda approached me and signalled to the waiter for another cup.

"Have you ever?" I smiled and lifted my cup.

"In ancient times, we would drink coffee or cacao after a great ceremony," she said. "It's from the earth, and it's grounding... well, maybe not Nescafé."

We laughed. It felt good to share time with my friend, and she had been the one who had started my whole spiritual journey. I was about to express my gratitude when Lucinda spoke.

"How are you, Anna, really? I can't imagine the burden this trip must be, and in just over a year, you go from novice to holding ceremony in one of the most powerful places on the planet," she said.

"But I am not alone, Lucinda. I've thankfully had so much help," I replied. "Isis shows up from time to time, and the Queens... Nefertari, Cleopatra, Hatshepsut, and I know Nefertiti is never far away, and Arsinoe was the last true Oracle of Egypt, and I know she has been my guide. Oh, and Anubis is my protector."

She looked a little taken aback, and I realised how little I had really shared. I had taken for granted that everyone else was receiving the same messages and counsel.

"But something is troubling me, Lucinda. I would appreciate your help. I had a dream the other night, and I think it was a prophecy."

"Go on," she said. I described the dream at the Sphinx and then told her about my vision in the tomb with Nefertari and the game of Senet.

"I think the Scorpion Queen now has the Scroll of Unal, and she has, I am sure, a black scarab of darkness that goes with it."

"Are you sure, Anna? A black scarab? Are you sure it was not like obsidian? That can be a protector."

"No, it was dark energy, like not from this world," I assured her.

Lucinda was most concerned.

"Yes, I'm totally sure. When I looked at all the scrolls and scarabs and placed them around the Book of Keys, they all aligned. The black scarab was blocking them... a dark curse from a dark time, and I think it came back today to sabotage me in the King's Chamber."

"So what do we do next?" asked Lucinda. "There is not a moment to waste, and we came to do this work for sure. Perhaps we look into the Records for this curse to understand once and for all what happened."

I shook my head.

"I don't think it is that easy, and I can't help feeling something or someone is listening in," I said.

"Seriously? Why would you say that?" Lucinda replied.

"Since Philae, it is as if we have been followed, and they are waiting. I think, waiting for us to go into the Records and then trapping us."

"How can anyone trap you in the Akashic Records?" She shook her head.

"Very easily," a voice came from behind us—it was Alice.

"Alice, please sit down." I pulled out a chair. She had more colour but still looked very tired.

"Alice, what do you know of the black scarab and the..."

"The Scroll of Unal," she finished for Lucinda.

"Yes, you know of this."

"Yes, it was a real scroll and scarab. I know that it was hidden in the Alexandria library. It was said that all the great leaders sought these pieces. Some even said it came from a warrior race in the stars. The Unal Scarab was made of a material not of this planet.

"In Atlantis, it was said there was a great Temple like a City of Light, and each room contained a certain magic and wisdom. There was a dark chamber deep within, and the Atlanteans knew its energy was not of this world. Guarded by brave priests for many years, it was safe. But then came the times of change; like everything, the crypt was opened. The Scarab of Unal, as we knew it, the black scarab, came from that place, and the scroll taught its history and purpose. If it has presented itself to you, Anna, then you have been chosen to work with its energy."

"But I can't," I said, shocked. "I don't do darkness."

"It's just powerful energy; how it is used is what matters, Anna. I think you have been chosen. We can't tell you what to do, but it would seem you have been given all the tools... more than Isis had."

I nodded and thought about all the tools: the scarabs and scrolls, the Book of Keys, the sistrum, and the turquoise ring. My mind was buzzing.

"I think I need to go rest and prepare, and maybe there will be no more coffee today," I said.

Alice took my hand as I stood up.

"Anna, our timeline is short. I think we opened up a chamber of Amenti this morning, and you have given us all our oracle sight again. The Sphinx is the gateway and has been closed for over 2000 years. Think about your intentions."

I nodded and then hugged them both. I was tempted to ask about the Amenti Scroll and Scarab, but I was already on overload.

As I walked back to my room, I had a strong sense I was being watched. I checked the time; I still had a few hours but needed to prepare.

As I entered my room, I felt a sense of calm. The maid

had been to visit, but something more. There on the desk was a glass bottle of perfume with the word "rose" written on it. Next to it was a large, old coin with a woman's head upon it.

A handwritten note:

Dear Anna, today you will need this pure rose oil to summon the Priestesses of Isis and a coin of Cleopatra to pay the ferryman. Love.

I was not sure who had left it, but I did know what to do with it.

The Sphinx at Sunset

The afternoon passed so quickly that I did not dare take a nap. Instead, I sat on my bed with the Book of Keys, trying to find some insight. Nothing was coming to me, so I knocked on Lucas's room and asked if I could borrow the scrolls and scarabs for insight.

He was reluctant as he handed them over and insisted they be back in his possession before we went to the Sphinx. I would have assumed he would have known I needed them, but then it struck me that Isis and Naomi had not had access to the full set when they had last been here.

It took only a few moments to realise then that perhaps no one had reached this far, and no one had recorded the ritual. I shook my head. "No, I have a special bag. I'll bring them in that and give it to you to hold for me."

As it would now appear, I had no guidance to gain from him. I would have to create this from instinct. I, therefore, cleansed my hands with some rose oil, anointed myself, and set to work clearing the scarabs and scrolls of non-serving energy. I restored them by using the rattle and chose to wear my turquoise ring, for some reason, singing to them—soft songs like nursery rhymes. I had not thought about my childhood in a long time, and since my dream about my father and seeing my mother with the Contessa and Isis in the photos, I had conveniently pushed any thoughts or curiosity away. I wondered what my mother would think if she knew the life I was leading, if she was watching over me from the other side.

I was packing my bag and anointing myself again with rose oil when there was a knock on the door, and I opened it to find Lucinda waiting for me.

"I know I'm early, and I can see you are in preparation," she said.

"Yes, I am trying to connect to the energies and read the signs, but not much is coming."

"Here, read this, perhaps," she said, handing me another white envelope with a card written by Isis.

Dear Anna,

Oh, blessed day this is if you have reached the Sphinx. I tried to make it to the altar this time with you; however, too many obstacles were in my way. I cannot give you any guidance as I have not held a ceremony or ritual for the Halls of Amenti within the Sphinx paws myself in this way.

Use all of your tools, and remember that the altar is a gateway, and you must find the key. This will unlock the Halls of Amenti and fully restore the gifts and psychic sight of the oracles with you. They, in turn, will unlock the gifts of others, and our Mystery School connected to the Children of Light will be restored again. My love is with you, one heart, one love,

Always and forever,
Isis

I couldn't help it, but the tears came, and my grief was overwhelming. Lucinda sat totally still, allowing me to let my emotions surface, and went to the desk to make some tea.

As I cleared my tears and pulled myself together, I continued to place all the scarabs and scrolls into the bag that the Contessa had given me, with all the pouches and compartments. I placed my book and rattle with the rose oil. As I laid them carefully, I felt something in the base of the bag. I pulled it out, and to my surprise, it was the pendant with the box and key Isis had left for me. I took it out of the bag, put it on, and turned to show Lucinda. She smiled as she lifted her necklace, and I could see she was wearing hers.

"You know, Isis had been searching for you for a long time," she finally said.

I shook my head. "But we didn't know each other when we met; it was all by chance."

Lucinda smiled and sat down in the chair at the desk.

"Anna, your mother and Isis knew each other. I met your mother in York a few times to update her on how you were doing once you arrived in Glastonbury."

"But she and I were estranged."

"Yes, but not for the reasons you think. Your mother had some of your gifts from her mother's family."

"I don't know much about my family from her side except my aunt."

I was still in shock and wondered if this was a tactic to throw me off guard. This timing was very distracting.

"No, I am sure Isis would have told me." I was positive.

"She wanted to, I think," Lucinda shrugged, "but they all decided it was better to see how far you could go with your gifts."

"Who is 'we'?"

"Well, Isis, me, Naomi, the Contessa, and Lucas."

I felt a total betrayal and quickly finished packing my bag and sat down.

"So, why was my mother never in contact?" I asked.

"I don't know."

"She preferred to stay away, perhaps," Lucinda said.

"Well, this will have to wait. I checked my watch. It's just after 5 o'clock. We should be on our way."

"Aren't you going to ask questions?" asked Lucinda.

"No," I shook my head. "No, I have work to do, and my mother's distractions will not help in any way. Now, are you ready?" I looked at her, swirled my golden pashmina scarf around my shoulders, and walked towards the door. I picked up my purse, and I watched Lucinda's eyes blink like she was seeing and not believing. Obviously, she had been wrapped in her storytelling.

"Yes, it is mine, vintage Chanel. Paris opened many new adventures for me." I patted the bag.

Lucinda nodded and followed.

I was angry, but I was hopeful and intrigued to find out who my family really was. Then, a thought struck me: Why was Lucinda causing trouble again?

As we left the bus, the sun had started its descent. Once again, the Giza Plateau was empty, and we were the only visitors with two Egyptian inspectors. Today, to my surprise, they handed me the key to open the locked gate, and very soon, we were all streaming into the area.

Rashida smiled and nodded to me to tell me we had free rein to explore and connect to the energy. She sat with the inspectors to distract them, and I watched them walk out of sight. Lucas stood next to me, and I handed him my bag. The energy here felt very different, but I did feel much safer.

"Just in time," he joked. He looked a little bizarre holding my bag, but he patted it like an old friend and mouthed, "But it's Chanel, I love it." I smiled and tried not to laugh.

The Sphinx stood high and magnificent, and we all began to walk around clockwise as a group. We moved slowly.

"First, we will open the space and guide the energy in silence," I said, and we set off in a procession.

"Can everyone create a grid of protective energy?"

Scanning the energy, we began pointing to sections we felt were open and where there were energy portals. No one spoke, but everyone appeared to hear the messages. We must have looked strange to the inspectors as we weaved energy, but I was sure they had seen many more things stranger than us.

We came to a stop in front of the Sphinx, which towered in front of us. I could feel its eyes looking down upon me, judging to see if I was good enough to enter.

"Now we will enter the Sphinx paws and stand at the high altar," my voice was calm and clear.

I held up my hands with my turquoise ring on full display.

Everyone gathered and, by instinct, knew what to do. Lucas opened my bag and handed the rattle to Naomi next to me, and she began to walk around, clearing everyone's energy field. Then, he handed the rose oil to Lesley, and she began going through the group, placing a drop into their hands and anointing them on the third eye with another drop.

He handed me the coin, and I began following Lesley, pressing the coin gently into each person's palm. "This will allow you all to pay the ferryman for safe passage as we take the journey into the Halls of Amenti."

Finally, Lucas took out the black Book of Keys and gave it to me. I laid it into the centre of the altar and began laying each of the scarabs and scrolls around in a circle so that it looked like a sun with the scarab and scroll as the rays. I was about to name them all when suddenly I heard the noise of shouting again.

I looked out of the circle and saw that the women who had tried disrupting the Abu Simbel visit were once again asking for access. I presumed they were also the ones from that morning in the Great Pyramid.

Thankfully, the inspectors were not having any of this.

However, it was too late to stop the darker forces from breaking through the protection line. The women walked away, but had given a window of time to open up a dimensional door. That had been their purpose.

There she was in her full strength, the Scorpion Queen, followed by her priests of Unal.

The rest of our group seemed to be motionless, and it appeared that only I could see them. It seemed I was powerless. Everyone else was frozen. For a moment, I thought the Contessa could see them, but then she froze, and it seemed she, too, was held under their spell.

"*You will be needing this*," she hissed. The Scorpion Queen held up the black scarab, and one of her priests opened up a scroll with red blood ink on it. I knew this was the cursed Unal Scroll that had held many of us bound over lifetimes. These were the evil forces from Unal.

I tried to call Lucinda for help, but my voice was out.

The Queen came towards me and pushed my energy out of my body, and I could see the group all standing, waiting.

"*They can't hear or see us*," she laughed and pushed me again.

"Anna, your body may carry on, but I have come for your soul."

"No!" I shouted, and in my rage, I pushed her back. The priests began swirling around me, uttering words of damnation, and I was totally outnumbered.

At that point, I saw a flash of energy, and there beside me were Nefertari, Nefertiti, Hatshepsut, Arsinoe, and Cleopatra. I did not know if they were real or not.

"You are not enough," the Scorpion Queen mocked us.

"But this is," said Nefertari, and she held out a crystal dagger in her hand. *"Anna, remember the elements. They will keep you safe."*

I took in a deep breath and called the energy of the water to swirl around me for protection and act as a barrier.

Anubis appeared, along with the baboon and ibis. He took hold of the dagger from Nefertari.

"Quickly, Anna, read the scroll," he said, snatching the Unal Scroll and throwing it to me while slaying the priest who had been trying to read it with the dagger.

I quickly read it while the battle of energies continued and saw that it was a scroll of slavery to darker forces. I grounded myself in the Earth so as not to be swept away, my feet deep in the sand below me.

I saw how the priests and priestesses of Isis had been held by a soul contract to forget their true soul intention and to follow a path of confusion and self-doubt. A covenant to remove the sight of the Oracle and to hold the Children of Light who walked upon the planet in silence. So much on one single, powerful piece of papyrus.

The Queens and Princess who had come to support me began to create a distraction, and they opened energy to battle with the Unal Priests. Nefertari swirled around the Scorpion Queen, taunting her as she must have done over the years to stay in the game.

I quickly ran to my book, opened it, and began to recite words from the Book of Keys and draw symbols as I undid each of these curses. I sent them on the wind around the priests.

I recited them all three times and invoked each scarab in turn from its scroll.

"Oh, Scarab of Protection, open up a portal of energy for us to step forth into our new age.

"Oh, Scarab of Truth and Integrity, find my sacred words to release us from these curses.

"Oh, Scarab of Death and Resurrection, may all that does not serve, dissolve, and the light of love be restored.

"Oh, Scarab of Creation, allow a new dawn to be born on our souls.

"Oh, Scarab of Magic and Prophecy, let me weave the alchemy of freedom.

"Oh, Scarab of Light and Shadow, cast away your veil for us to see.

"Oh, Scarab of Goddess and Fertility, may we plant seeds of wisdom and hope.

"Oh, Scarab of The Records of Life, may this new day show a new plan for the Children of Light on this Earth plane."

As the words came through, they began to create an energy swirl of fire. Suddenly, the red ink scroll set itself alight with a purple flame, and I reached over and grabbed the black scarab. I visualized the blue light of the Elohim around it, and it seemed to fracture. I began to see I was crushing it with my hands.

The battle, however, continued, and I watched Nefertari,

Arsinoe, and Cleopatra grow weaker and weaker. Nefertari and Hatshepsut lay injured on the ground. Then, something came over me, and I took the crystal dagger from Anubis's hand. I held it high above my head and began to recite the 23rd Psalm in my mind towards them:

"The LORD is my shepherd; I shall not want. He maketh me to lie down in green pastures: he leadeth me beside the still waters. He restoreth my soul: he leadeth me in the paths of righteousness for his name's sake.

"Yeah, though I walk through the valley of the shadow of death, I will fear no evil: for thou art with me; thy rod and thy staff they comfort me."

"Thou preparest a table before me in the presence of mine enemies: thou anoints my head with oil; my cup runneth over."

"Surely goodness and mercy shall follow me all the days of my life: and I will dwell in the house of the LORD forever. Adonai Adonai Adonai."

As I said the words, I saw the Elohim come through the Dream Stele. I had no idea how I remembered this verse, but it appeared to work. The Elohim began to flow through our group, and I swear I saw Isis, but she looked more ethereal. The priests began to stumble, and I could feel myself growing in power. The Scorpion Queen began to contort and fade. I made my way over and held up the dagger.

"Anna, her heart, take her heart," called Nefertari.

"No, for if I take her heart, she shall take mine. Defeat is your prize today, oh Queen. You have no power here," I said. With everything I had, I summoned the winds to carry her away. Her priests lay dazed and confused as if they had been awoken from a long sleep.

I looked at Lucas. He had awoken to my reality, seeing all that I saw. To my surprise, he appeared to know these priests. He greeted them, helping them, and I saw the lives of priests, soldiers, and gladiators. Their fight was over for today. I smiled at my friend. He would, in the future, guide many souls of men. He nodded to let me know he heard me.

"*They must go,*" he said, and I watched them wander into the boats around the Sphinx and on the sacred blue waters. I watched them float away back into the desert.

"*Anna, we must return to the circle, but please know this is your destiny. You will face her many times in your life. This started many years ago when we were living in Atlantis,*" said Arsinoe.

"*I think I am remembering,*" I said.

"*Good, now let us rejoin the others. We are here to help,*" she smiled. Suddenly, back in the group, we were joined by all the Queens, surrounding us and protecting us.

Then, Lucas and I were back in the group, but time had stopped around us. Slowly, everyone began to stir, and everything was moving again. It would seem only Lucas and I had witnessed this battle of souls.

I began to clear the energy of all the scrolls and scarabs and then invited everyone to come and sit beside the altar. I sat on the Dream Stele. The Queens guarded the altar. The magnificent sun was now setting, and I could feel the rays bathing the Sphinx in light. I gathered our group close. I became aware of my pendant, and as I looked around, everyone was wearing theirs. How special. I knew then Isis was with us.

"Our high altar is protected." I pointed to the Queens and watched the faces of everyone now able to see these amazing women, now our protectors. They, too, now knew the Scorpion Queen was gone. I realized that this was my karma—to face her and the Priests of Unal.

While some of them had conjured a connection in past lives, they all had their own pathways and purpose to find. I had cleared the way today and fought with my demons, and so it was now my role to guide everyone to the next step.

"It's time, my friends, for us to visit the Halls of Amenti.

"Very gently, everyone, close your eyes.

"Be comfortable and breathe gently.

"Take your left hand, middle three fingers, and gently press them to your third eye chakra.

"Now to your lips and now your heart and begin to see the sacred heart opening.

"We will now imagine we are moving towards the dream stele, and as it opens like a door, we are greeted by Lord Thoth and Lady Seshat.

"They lead us down into the chambers below, and we see Lord Anubis on the boat, who will take us to the Temple of the Oracle and the rooms we may discover."

I watched as all of our energies began to drift in and down under the Sphinx.

"Now, we board the boat and hand over our coin, and the boat moves gently across the water and into the cavern.

"Slowly ahead, we see the light, and we begin to see the temple standing, waiting for us to enter again.

"I will guide you and initiate you into every room where you may assist and guide others.

"I call forth the sacred eight scarabs and scrolls.

"Each set will lead us to their room of origin, and we will reactivate them.

"First, we call forward the Scroll and Scarab of Creation. As we do, see yourself moving into this room. You see the cosmic blueprints and energy swirling all around. Feel the magic of the healing qualities in this room.

"Secondly, we move to the temple room of Truth and Integrity—the all-knowing sense and feeling. You know what is in alignment now and can speak with high truth.

"Thirdly, we enter the room of Magic and Alchemy. From here, your gifts of alchemy return. You are a magician and can see energy as it forms to create new wonders in our world.

"The fourth is Records of Life. Here, you can see the books, scrolls, and even the living books that bring wisdom from the past and open doorways and portals to the future.

"The fifth is the room of Death and Resurrection. To hold the power of death and rebirth is the bridge to life. This knowledge was often misunderstood by the greatest of civilisations. Bring peace to this world, and the only thing to die will be fear.

"The sixth holds the energy of the Goddess and Fertility. Here on Earth, we choose to be born from the goddess and then return to this Earth. Understand how to honour the Earth. The goddess energy moves in swirls and draws you to her.

"The seventh is the room of Light and Shadow. Beware of the light and dark in this room. You must open your hearts and observe. This way, the dark will not fear you. You may see those of your past lives, those who have wronged you, or whom you have wronged. This is a time to see all in balance.

"The eighth room holds the Keys of Protection for you to use on your sacred journey. This is the true room of the spiritual warrior who uses energy for the Light rather than as a weapon of power.

"As you breathe in this sacred wisdom, you begin to see the geometry of the temple and the stargates opening to other temples that we have visited."

When I opened my eyes, I saw everyone in a deep trance. Some had their hands outstretched as if they were pulling stands of energy, and others created mudras and symbols with their hands. Others had their heads tipped back as if they were receiving information downloads, and others were creating uploads.

Everyone was working in unison. Everyone in their sacred place, each at the right time. Now, I could see my work and mission clearly. It came to me that I was not meant to be a high priestess organising others into their worlds, but to hold a sacred space to provide an energy source from which they could work. I was suddenly aware there was someone in the sacred chamber with me. I closed my eyes again. I could see Isis walking towards me.

"You are a master of keys, Anna. You gave everyone the keys they needed to succeed in the work that they came to do. You held no power over them. You simply opened doorways for them all to be the Oracles of Egypt and all the other worlds and dimensions. Your love can open up the gift of the oracle. Use this energy and power wisely, and remember, I love you always. I gave you all gifts that you will all use in time," she said, pointing out the pendants she had left us when she had died.

"Oh, my goodness, Isis, I didn't see this," I said.

She laughed.

They all made sense now.

"I collected each gateway in a pendant that leads to the Halls of Amenti."

"But what of the Scroll and Scarab of Amenti?" I asked.

She smiled. *"They will come to you, but not yet. Then the work will be completed."*

That was the step my body could not master. I had thought the work was complete today, but it seemed this was the beginning of my quest.

Then I saw everyone in the dimensions of Amenti, under the Sphinx, weaving and working.

I shifted my awareness back into the chamber to look

for Isis. She turned and began to make her way to the back of the chamber, and I knew then that I may never see her again.

But then I noticed she was not alone. Another four women walked with her: Hatshepsut, Nefertiti, Nefertari, and Cleopatra. Arsinoe was standing with me.

"*I will walk with you, Anna. My role is your role. We can walk in dreamtime as I share with you all I know.*" Then she faded.

It was time for me to complete the ceremony, so I opened my eyes and guided the others back through the temple and back to the reality of life.

"Now, everyone, take a breath; on the count of three, breathe gently, relax, and open your eyes."

I felt my energy pull back into the chamber between the Sphinx's paws, and all I could see were calm, smiling faces.

"How long was I gone?" I whispered to Lucinda, who sat to my right.

"Long enough," she laughed.

"Thank you, dear Anna. I have not been able to return to my original Earth home in thousands of years, and you created this miracle," said Laura.

I looked at the others, wary that I had not created a seamless ritual and meditation.

"But is everyone back in their bodies?" asked Lesley. I glanced around. "Each of you has unique gifts and messages, and all are equal, and I'm honoured we could open the doors for this."

"We?" asked Emilee.

"Isis," I smiled and touched my pendant.

Everyone smiled and, in unison, said, "Yes, Isis." They touched theirs.

We gathered our belongings and took time for photos. Alexandria had an instant camera and took many photos that would help us remember such a powerful day. I helped

Lucas recover all my treasures and put them safely away in the bag.

"Now I know you are ready, Anna," he said. "But I have a plan for them," I replied. And whispered the plan.

We all slowly made our way back to the inspectors and Rashida, then onwards towards our awaiting transport back to the hotel. The sun was gone and it was becoming darker, and I could feel the hotel calling us home for sanctuary.

"So what do we do now, Anna?" asked the Contessa. She pointed to my bag.

"Well, I will return some of these pieces to the museum tomorrow. Lucas and I have selected a few for our sisters in Glastonbury. Some will be stored with your family in Paris. After this, I'm not sure. I have many stories to write and remember, and I guess they all have temples to create and their sacred work." I pointed out to our group.

We reached the hotel, and it seemed everyone wanted to relax, so we went to the lobby bar, ordered drinks, and took in all that we had experienced. Everyone began to write in their journals and whisper to each other.

Lucas came over and pointed to my bag that carried our relics and joined me as I sat at a corner table. As he skillfully divided the scrolls and scarabs into various groups, I suddenly saw that this had been his role many times.

"Lucas, please document everything and help it reach its correct guardian and home. But the book, sistrum, ring, and coin are mine." I smiled as he was already handing them over. He nodded, and no words needed to be said. We knew perhaps that our journey with the Scorpion Queen was not over, as it would seem we were the only ones to witness the battle. And we both knew neither was ready to address that next chapter for now.

CHAPTER 31

Sunday, 27 September 2009
Mena House Hotel

Giza Plateau was once again empty of tourists, and the spirits of the ancient ones could return to their sacred ritual. We were finishing our drinks in the bar, and everyone was thinking about dinner plans. No group plan had been decided. I wondered if I should share what had happened but realized that was my ego wanting to exert itself. The story would come at the right time and in the perfect setting. For now, it was a secret for Lucas and I to keep. He had taken my bag back with him to clear the energy of the relics and prepare them for their next journey.

Naomi came over.

"Anna, would you join me for dinner? There are things to explain." I was exhausted. But she was my friend, so I pointed to the restaurant in the main hotel overlooking the pyramids.

"Thirty minutes?"

She nodded and told me she would get us a table, and I ran back to my room to change.

☥

I decided to wear my blue silk dress, and Naomi was impressed, as she was still in her Sphinx tourist outfit when I arrived. She already had a corner table in the main restaurant, and it looked like she had been writing notes, probably trying to remind herself of what she wanted to say to me.

"Let's have a nice dinner, and you can bring me up to speed with everything later, perhaps?" I said before she had a chance to speak.

Naomi was totally taken aback but looked relieved and put away her journal.

"One more full day, and we'll be flying back to London, so I guess we have time," she said, waving the waiter over and ordering a very expensive bottle of wine.

"Celebration?" she laughed.

I lasted only an hour at dinner. As soon as I finished my meal and half glass of wine, I began to yawn, so I said goodnight, and Naomi went to join the rest of the group, who had arrived and were eating appetisers at another table across the room.

I saw her hug Lucas, Laura, and Emilee, pass compliments to Alexandria and Alice, and even joke with Lesley and Lucinda. Obviously, the Contessa had retired early. Flashes of the Akashic Records revealed the past lives they had been linked to. How had I not seen this connection before? They had been hidden from me in many ways. But seriously, in this moment, why did it even matter?

I made it back to my room, quickly changed, and climbed into bed.

Lucas must have returned my bag, as it was sitting on the desk. I picked it up and checked; no scrolls or scarabs remained; there was only the rose oil with my sacred pieces, the book, coin, and rattle, in their place. The Ankh from Abydos was on my nightstand, and I placed my turquoise ring beside it for protection.

I wanted to sleep, and although I feared the Scorpion

Queen would return at some point, I knew I could deal with her much better with a few hours of rest. I closed my eyes and drifted away.

I found myself standing in the middle of nowhere. I could see sand, and I felt like I was sinking. I tried to pull my feet out and could see green palm trees and what looked to be an oasis up ahead.

The area was lush, and I felt refreshed as I placed my hands into the cold water.

Not too far away, I could see stone buildings, perhaps a temple. I was not sure.

A cone-like tower appeared with small lookout holes and a small wooden entrance door.

The whole place was deserted—no people, no animals.

I made my way to the building, where I could see beautiful planets and water features. This was a place of great stillness and peace.

"I knew that you would find your way, my child," a woman's voice said, and I turned around to see her green eyes looking intently at me.

"Cleopatra," I gasped.

"Anna, I have waited such a long time, unable to share this wisdom.

"Go over now to the door and open it. I did once as a young woman, and now it's your turn."

I did not know if I could trust her, not after all that had transpired in Egypt so far. But she had come to my rescue many times in my dreams in Glastonbury and as a past-life mother. I prayed she would not steer me into danger.

I walked to the door and pushed it gently open.

"What do you wish to know?" A woman's voice was coming from inside the cone building.

"Hello, hello!" I called out.

"What do you wish to know?"

I decided to go through the door, not sure what I would find.

The room was round. It had two staircases built into the walls that led up to small doorways I assumed were other rooms on higher levels. The main room was empty, containing only a circle of stones and some small stools. I looked up and could see at the top of the building was a smaller round hole where you could see the sky. I looked for the woman, but I could not see her.

"What do you wish to know?"

I looked around, and there, through another open doorway built into the wall, was a smaller room with several steps built into the wall. On the top step sat an older woman with white hair wearing Egyptian robes. It looked like she was floating in mid-air.

"I am Anna," I said as I walked towards the doorway.

"Are you sure?" she asked.

I stopped to think, but it seemed the words were already moving out of my mouth.

"No, I am not sure. I want to know who I am," I replied.

She said nothing but slowly walked down the steps.

"He asked me that question once."

"Who?"

"Your friend Alexander of Macedon and many others over the years. Even she did." She pointed to the entrance, but Cleopatra was nowhere in sight.

"He was not 'The Great' at the time of visiting me, but he understood many powerful magical spells. He had been mentored by the best teachers in Egypt and Greece. I shared with him images of his past lives and karma."

"From Atlantis?" I asked.

"Yes. Well done," she said.

"I told him..."

I could already see it.

"You can see," she smiled.

"You are the Oracle of Siwa. I think I have been waiting to meet you," I said.

"Then you should know who you are."

She spoke in riddles, but I was not afraid.

"Come sit. Pull up a stool, and we can sit together."

She came out of the smaller room into the central chamber. She pointed to the hole in the top of the room. "From there, we can gain access to the elements and stars."

"Do you receive messages from the stars?" I asked, and she nodded.

"Did you know I would be coming?"

She nodded. "The scrolls had given the prophecy. We still keep many scrolls here; they may interest you."

She pointed to another door on our level that had magically opened itself to us. "You can go through," she said.

I opened the door and found myself in another chamber, its high stone walls lined with bookcases. I could feel a cool breeze, as at the end of the chamber was an opening to an oasis.

"Where is this?" I asked.

"Alexandria, the Library. Don't you remember?"

I was in the dream, going deeper into another dream.

I could see the scrolls and ancient papers, maps, and charts.

I was drawn to a particular part of the room at the back that overlooked the oasis with large screens of wood around it to give it privacy. It felt like a vault or safe room where secrets were kept... a private room with scrolls laid out on a table in the centre. It was strange. I could still see back to the Siwa location, and I knew that this was miles away from Alexandria. But all the same, it felt so real. I looked at the scrolls.

"What does the scroll say?" the woman asked. She now stood with me, watching over my shoulder.

I began to trace the letters and symbols with my hands. "I am not sure, but they talk of boats and prophecy."

"Close your eyes, Anna, and read the scrolls."

I did as she asked, and there in front of me, I began to see a whole new world.

"I am seeing structures and homes built a little like in Siwa. But they have a crystal content to the walls, and there are symbols everywhere. Rooms and tunnels and houses all seem to flow together. Very ancient, and it even looks a little like it is on another planet."

"Find yourself, Anna," she said.

"I am walking up the cobblestone path, and houses are on either side. I wear robes and a high hat with a veil that covers my face. It's strange because I do not seem to leave my home very often. It is as if I am always hidden."

"Are you alone?"

"Not really. I have a protector with me, and there are others like me. We form some sort of council.

"I can see people looking out of their windows, but no one is allowed out on this particular day, but it appears I am. Ah, no, I'm not. I am in a nonphysical form, invisible to others."

"What are you seeking?" she asked.

"I am seeking confirmation of something by floating through the streets, and now I am standing at the ocean's edge, high up and looking out to sea. My hands are reading the elements and energy around me. They are coming by sea, bringing new thoughts and disease."

"What happens next? And who are they?" she asked.

"Outsiders, warriors, I think, and then I go back to the temple where I live. We live in a very remote part of the country. I think it's an island. When I look out of the window, I see hills and oceans and even mountains. The energy is so strong, but it is pure.

"We live very simply, and I am here in the temple, and there are others like me. We are apprentices, and we seek information for our mentor. We all feel female, but I can't be sure. It's not like the men and women we are in current time. I have my own room, and we have others who bring us food and take care of our protection," I said.

"What is your purpose?"

"I seek wisdom, and it is my role to gather the energy and knowledge from the towns and villages. I read the signs of the natural kingdom. I meditate or remote-view into the local area and then relay all the information I have seen. Then, our mentor will prepare a message or channel, and she will give that to the leaders.

"They have not been happy with us lately, as our messages talk of the invasion. We talk about keeping things to the old ways and not meddling in natural forces. The new leaders are creating solutions, but they are so fear-based that it is feeding a negative energy into the ground. Our mentor tells us she must seek out the wisdom of the great mountain. It's a large crystalline grid that resides in the area now known as the Bermuda Triangle. It's a portal between the worlds.

"But she never returns, and many leave our sacred order. They were afraid. There are only four of us now, and this is an issue, as our limited number offers fewer answers when we receive messages than when we were a larger group. When we all do the remote viewing, this often brings other messages to give perspectives. We have begun to argue, and it's not a harmonious time. Our messages are no longer as pure, as we

are losing the trust. We wait for another leader, but no one comes. We hear that the land is becoming more challenged, and outsiders have begun to visit.

"Families of mixed blood types are being created, and the specific Atlantean bloodline is becoming less and less. Our blood is not of this world and carries specific energies. As oracles, we are confused by this, as, on the one hand, we become more human and earth-based, but on the other, our gifts are diluted.

"One night, I think it is an equinox; we lie in the dream chamber and look out at the night sky. I see we have eight stone and crystal beds, but only four are occupied now. We all begin to channel and see that invaders are indeed coming closer to our shores, and many of our high priests and priestesses will be leaving soon for other lands in order to survive and share the wisdom. We also see that darkness has been released upon the whole planet. This is a dark force that holds our mentor captive. We descend into deep fear.

"The next few days, we are visited by many leaders, and some listen to us, and some do not. We know that we must also leave and go out into the world. I am now seeing us reach the areas where the boats are leaving. I can't stop crying, but our choice has been made. My other three sisters all leave on separate boats. I am now being shown a map, and the Earth looks very different, but I think one goes to North America, entering through the area of New York. One through Tulum in Mexico. One through Cornwall in England.

"I am moving in through Morocco and following the waterways across Northern Africa until I reach Egypt. I come to make my home in Siwa. Some of the order who left when our leader disappeared have joined me. We work with the temples, training the oracles. They come to Siwa for lessons and activations. We live for such a long time. We train priests

and priestesses. They give me the name of Wadjet, and I am acknowledged as being in direct connection to the great God Amun.

"I can contact my sisters in my dreams, but otherwise, it is a very sad existence, always at risk of the wrath of others seeking power. I long to find my mentor, but I fear she is long gone. My life force is fading, so I train another to take my place. When my time is complete, I hand over to another. They carry on the work until I can return. This has been the way for over 4000 years."

I close the scrolls and move back into the central room of the stone circle. I turn to look around but the woman is gone. I look around, and I am alone.

Slowly, the memories fade, and I am left with what feels like an emptiness—a sad ache in my heart. I watch as I slowly come out of the dream. It is like I am sleepwalking. I suddenly understood that my work here had started, and I was not in a dream, but the dream lived on through me.

My role is to support the remembrance—this was why the Scorpion Queen sought my soul and not my death. She wanted my body to carry on with the existence as before, before my gifts had shown themselves. I shake myself awake and find myself back in my room. Strange... it's still only 10 p.m. For the first time in a few days, I open my computer and begin to write and don't stop until I look over and see it's 3 a.m. At least I have my 10,000 words.

Monday, 28 September 2009
The Museum

It was 8 a.m., and I had to drag myself out of bed and then joined everyone for breakfast. I was still feeling like I was in a dream, so I simply made small conversation and nibbled on toast. Most of the group were taking a rest or shopping day, and I had left messages asking the Contessa to see if she and I could meet at 3 p.m. in the upstairs members' bar that I knew she had access to. It was private enough. I felt we had unfinished business and today would be my last opportunity for a while. I desperately wanted to share my Siwa and Atlantis dream with everyone, but for now, I just wanted to process it myself.

After breakfast, I looked at Naomi. I mouthed "museum," and she understood.

"Michael," she smiled and mouthed back. I blushed. I had texted him earlier that morning to say I was stopping by and needed him to take care of some relics for me. I also wanted to press him on the Amenti pieces.

His response was super casual. Just an "Okay, see you later any time."

Maybe he was not to be my Prince Charming.

I silently left the table as everyone chatted about their shopping excursion. I smiled as I gathered my bag and listened to the remarks of the table, which were focused on the task of sacred shopping and the ceremony of exotic oils and perfumes.

Lucas came over and discreetly handed me a box with the scrolls and scarabs I was to take to the museum. "Bring back the Glastonbury and Paris pieces," he said, and I nodded.

As I was about to leave the restaurant, Lesley handed me a note.

Dear Anna, please come to my suite at 3 p.m. I feel we need some privacy.

Kindly,
Francine

I nodded to her and smiled. She had not been the demon drama I had expected, and perhaps we could be friends.

"I'll be at the oils and then carpets," remarked Lucinda.

"I did oils last time, but if we are going to the oil place that does the massage, I would be interested," said Lesley.

"No, no," called Lucas down the table. "Remember that poor girl who got the peppermint massage and was red and sore for three days?"

"Ohhh, then maybe not *that* place," Lesley laughed. She started to tell the tale.

I decided it was time to leave. Another forbidden experience story was about to unfold.

☥

I reached the hotel lobby door, and the concierge was hot on my heels.

"Limousine, Miss."

"No, thank you," I smiled. "I'll just grab a taxi from the street."

"But madam, that's not safe."

"I'm okay." I smiled and made my way out of the door towards the street.

It was crazy busy, but I needed to do this alone. *Fearless* was my word for the day. After the fast pace of the last few days and knowing that the group was shopping and spending money, I knew no one would notice me or ask about my whereabouts.

I made my way out of the security gate and took a deep breath. I went towards the queue of cars waiting to serve the tourists. I popped my head into one.

"Cairo Museum, please."

"Yes, yes, very good. I know it."

The taxi was damaged on all sides, with missing floorboards in some areas, and cardboard was taped across it.

I paid no attention. I felt safe and invisible.

Traffic was crazy, but we made it to the museum safe and sound, as my driver knew all the shortcuts.

"100 Egyptian pounds, please," he said.

I opened my purse, gave him 150, and asked him to be back in two hours. He smiled as if I had given him gold.

I entered the museum and went to buy my ticket when I saw Michael outside the library, where he had been the day we visited. He waved and came over.

"Have you been waiting for me?" I smiled.

"No, Naomi called me when you left, and you do not need to go through security with precious artifacts." He pointed to my bag.

"Of course she did," I felt myself blush.

I assumed he would help me to buy my ticket.

"No, Anna, come with me," he said, opening the gate and waving to security. I was escorted towards the side of the museum. "Let's walk back to my office."

"I can't believe it has been all those months since I called you," he said.

"And you came, and now that you have finished your tour, you are back again."

"I know, and I wish it had been sooner, but we had some issues bringing all these little treasures together." I held up the box, and his eyes grew wide.

"That's the set of eight?"

I nodded, "Yes, all of them."

"And the work, was it satisfactory?"

"Yes, the work was completed. We held the ritual at the Sphinx and the ceremony at the Great Pyramid."

He took a giant sigh of relief. I wondered how much I could share with him.

"Since I was a child, my grandmother told me they were returning. I just did not believe it." He spoke with such gentle sincerity—I could feel his heart was pure.

"Now, please come this way."

We made our way down to the back of the museum and then through a side door. It was interesting that the old rooms above us were filled with glass cases and tourists, while the rooms below were like a hospital, with rooms, machines, and various types of equipment.

"Everything is studied, and all the details noted. Many scientists from all over the world have visited. They bring things for us to examine. Many of the Egyptian treasures have been spread across the world without an understanding of what they are really for or just how powerful."

I smiled and lifted my bag.

"But no, nothing like you have in there," he said, smiling back.

"In here, please," and I was shown to a tiny office at the back. It was very quiet and private.

I hoped and prayed I could trust Michael, but I did not have much choice at this stage. He had laid out a table with candles and a cloth with various symbols upon it. He locked the door. I turned around and smiled, and for some reason, I felt safe and knew that we had performed this ritual before in a past life.

He nodded. "Anna, I remember this as well."

I opened my bag and took out the box and laid each scroll from left to right out upon the cloth, and then underneath, I laid the matching scarab. I placed the sistrum and the Book of Keys in the front to align perfectly. He then took out a blue silk scarf and placed it over himself. It had markings similar to those in the Atlantis room in my dream the previous night.

"Where did that come from?" I said, pointing to the robe.

"My family. I found it in the attic in my grandmother's London home. At first, I thought it was for magic tricks, but then..." he stopped.

"The Magi, perhaps?" I asked, and I smiled as I started to work. He nodded, afraid to say more.

He held his finger to his lips. "Another time we will share that story, but to invoke their wisdom... well, here may not be the best place."

I smiled, and a shiver ran through my soul. Here was someone who knew the wisdom, yet no ego guided him to elaborate. I moved my hands over each scroll and scarab with my hands like they were precious jewels, and the words and incantations came easily. Once I had worked through them, Michael went over them, blessing each one with the power and words of the Light. It seemed so interesting to be performing this while in an office.

When we had finished, I felt as if the final part of the puzzle had been completed. It seemed strange that it would be here, but then, it may have needed Michaels's special scarf.

"So, what will you have me do with all of this?" he asked.

I did not know quite what to say, so I changed the subject. "Oh, look. Here is a note from Lucas. He is their true guardian, after all."

To those who hold possession, know that we all share the caretaker role.

Anna is to keep the Book of Keys.

The Cairo Museum will watch over the Scarabs and Scrolls of Protection and Death and Resurrection with those of Truth and Integrity and Light and Shadow.

Glastonbury will protect the Magic and Prophecy and Records of Life safe in the hands of Laura and Alice.

Creation and Goddess and Fertility Scrolls and Scarabs will travel to Paris with the Contessa.

"Now, I wish to introduce you to something special," he said. "Let me gather up the scrolls and scarabs you wish to leave."

I did as requested and handed him the scarabs and scrolls I was leaving in his care. Leaving them was so hard, but I knew they had work to do. I carefully placed them into his hands and watched as he placed them into a velvet-lined box and then locked them away in a large wardrobe. I placed the remaining pieces into my box.

He unlocked a safe and brought out another small wooden box, similar to mine but smaller. He opened it. They reminded me of the dream.

"Where did you find them?" I asked.

"So, you know, a few days back. I was moving something from my mentor, Mr. Imran, from another archaeological dig that he did a few years back. Well, this box was in the container. He must have hidden them for some reason, so I tested the sand from around the box, and I now know they came from... the desert to the west of us," said Michael. "A place called..."

"Siwa. These are the Amenti ones," I finished his sentence.

I wanted to cry. I knew they were mine from long ago. I picked them up and held them to my heart.

Michael leaned in close to me, "Are they talking?"

I began to blush. He was a little too close. "They are singing," I said.

Suddenly, I was aware of others, and they were humming the same tune as the Amenti pieces.

"And now you are among friends, see?" he said.

I turned, and there stood a group of five, and they all had their hands in prayer.

"Ms. Anna, may I present the guardians of the museum. They all remember their past lives in Atlantis, too."

Everyone looked familiar, like old friends. I had no hesitation in feeling at ease and comfortable. Something told me my precious treasure would be safe here and well-protected.

I began to shake and felt myself sink down into a chair at the neat desk by the door. I just needed a moment. They looked at Michael, smiling at me without a word, and retreated out of the door.

To ground myself, I began to take deep breaths, and then I placed the scroll and scarab in front of me to gain connection. I bowed my head and closed my eyes.

Many, many visions began to return to me, like when I began my oracle training in Atlantis and how I was schooled in the Temple of Light. I saw how life was and how magical and connected everyone was. Slowly, I was able to connect to my true lineage and see how I had been connected to everyone. I already knew the sad ending to my last past life, so it was uplifting to be presented with how it all began and a time of true enlightenment and connected consciousness.

It felt like hours that I was connected, but to the rest of the world, it was a matter of minutes. I suddenly sat back, opened my eyes, and began to share the visions of us leaving and those who had to stay behind. I was aware of many other messages and Akashic Records, but decided to wait until I was in private to recall the rest.

After my vision, I announced that it was time to leave. It was so hard.

Michael returned the Amenti pieces to their box and locked them away. "Just till you need them," he assured me. "There is talk of a new Museum in Cairo in the coming years, so we will find an amazing place to exhibit these treasures, and perhaps we may even have an Atlantis exhibit. Maybe with your white Atlantis stone."

I was not sure the world was ready for that. We left the office. I hoped he would show me more, so we had more time together, but it looked like we were heading for the exit.

As we walked the corridor, a man pushed past us.

"Sorry, I'm in a hurry," he said in an American accent.

"Who is that?" I whispered to Michael.

"Oh, he's one of the professors from the Met Museum in New York. The old professor had a distinguished yet slightly dishevelled appearance, with a head full of wild, wispy white hair. His thick, round spectacles rested precariously on the bridge of his nose, magnifying his sharp but slightly weary eyes. His attire was unmistakably old-fashioned: a tweed jacket with elbow patches, a buttoned-up vest, and a slightly wrinkled dress shirt with an outdated tie. He looked as if he had spent decades lost in the depths of dusty museums.

"He's been here for weeks trying to figure out the hieroglyphs of something very old. It came from Dendera, and the Americans have first option to examine... let's follow."

Despite his hurry, the man was still trying to open the door when we reached him.

"Professor, this is my friend Anna, who has made interesting studies of the Priestess temples."

"I heard that someone had arrived with an amazing

discovery," I said, looking at Michael, my new crush and superhero.

The professor nodded as if under a spell, and the door magically opened. We entered the room. I looked back at Michael and watched as the professor began explaining what they had found.

On the table were a sword, a bowl, and some scarabs. They reminded me of something I'd seen in a vision in Glastonbury.

"It dates back many years, and we cannot trace the metals or materials used," he said.

He seemed to accept my validation for being there, so why not take a look? I removed the pendant Isis had gifted me and held it above them, and I began to see unique swirls of energy forming around the outside. Is she a professor?!" he exclaimed, and Michael shrugged, "Kind of, but very liberal studies."

I had a vision of an amazing pyramid of glass and a procession of Kings in the streets, but I thought perhaps I should save that for another time. I simply smiled.

"And those relics were found in a desert crypt outside of Dendara Temple. We think they are ceremonial pieces, but they were stored in an old wooden box for some reason." He pointed to another table.

I went over to examine the pieces. As I looked down, tears came to my eyes.

"Do you know what these are?" Michael asked.

"I have studied the hieroglyph, but I cannot find who or what their name was, and if it was a Queen or Princess. It must have been someone important and powerful. The jewels, the gold, and the detail are quite elaborate." The professor continued to talk, but I was hardly listening.

I ran my hand across the table and the silk robe, the

chain with the crystals and the large Ankh, the beautiful comb, the golden cuffs, and the sandals.

I began to explain what I saw.

"These were the robes of the most High Priestess of Dendara. She was directly connected to Queen Cleopatra VII, and I would date them around 48 BC. They belonged to the last true High Priestess of Hathor. When she was removed in disgrace from the temple, her signatures were placed in a box like this and stored in the temple. You can see where the cartouche has been removed, but here, ah, yes." I moved a piece of gold that resembled a locket. I felt both Michael and the professor take in deep breaths, and I prayed it would not break. I pointed to the cartouche of Cleopatra.

"Another step closer to finding her," the professor said. He was jumping up and down as I pointed to the other parts of the relics that he should study.

He asked me how I knew and why they would be in an old box, hidden and not in an elaborate coffin.

"Maybe the high priestess or a trusted friend kept them somewhere safe until she could claim them later, or perhaps a Roman hid them and wanted to steal them..." I shrugged, knowing they belonged to my friend Lucinda. I desperately wanted to take them with me and return them to her.

"Either way, please treat them with the utmost respect and love, as these are things of great power and beauty, and who knows, this lady may come back to claim them sometime from the spirit world. Until then, they are safe with you, but I will take a picture, if you please."

"Perhaps one day I will share her story with you. I'm writing a book," I winked at Michael, and this time, he blushed.

"Thank you, I can't wait to hear more, Anna," he said. "I will have our team review this with great enlightenment, and perhaps you will visit us again with your stories. I feel there is much room for collaboration, and we are all linked by something so much greater and powerful than ourselves." He had found his voice and professional composure.

The professor, meanwhile, was moving at speed around the room, gathering notes and books to start his study in more detail. We left him to this.

I held up my phone to take the images. "No," Michael shook his head. "I have something better for your private memory." He went to a desk drawer and held up an instant camera. "My grandmother uses these all the time and stores them..."

"...In a red box," I was now finishing his sentences. Perhaps there was something more than a professional connection in our future path.

He smiled and began to take the photo images, handing them over. As I stood watching them develop, I knew my friends would welcome them into our red box collection tonight.

Speaking of time, I realised that it had gone by so fast and wondered if my driver would still be waiting.

It was time for farewells, and it crossed my mind that I might just stop by the perfume store to see what elixirs and potions the ladies had found.

"Anna, I'll walk you out," Michael said, steering me to the door. The professor was totally engrossed with the new information, and he simply ignored us.

As we walked, I knew Michael wanted to ask me some questions.

"You can ask, and yes, I just read your mind," I smiled.

"Anna, how do you know all this?"

"I'm known as an Oracle and spiritual channel," I replied.

"Like in ancient times."

"Somewhat," I said, smiling, but something told me that he knew more than he was sharing.

"Perhaps we can have a drink and talk this over sometime." He held out a card with his contact details. "So you don't forget me, and you can call me directly anytime."

"I would like that," I smiled and accepted the card that he was holding out to me. "But now I have to get back to my friends. We leave tomorrow afternoon."

For the longest moment, I stood there. I tried to move, but I looked deep into his eyes and felt a sense of kindness, hope, and something I could not describe. A deep connection of friendship and trust. I smiled, but the words would not come.

He looked uncomfortable, and I saw his face change. I knew then that a past life remembrance was stirring, perhaps for us both.

"I hope to," was all he said. He pointed to the exit door, and with that, I left.

☥

As I left the museum, I felt a sense of relief. I had placed four sets in a safe place and saw that the Atlantis altar and the Siwa Amenti Scroll and Scarab were protected in the haven that was this museum with guardians I felt I could trust.

I walked out to the sunshine and out of the museum gate. I watched as all of Cairo moved around me, and the buses passed by. Was I invisible? In the world but not of it? I was lost in a moment. I walked to the area where my driver had dropped me. Thankfully, my taxi was still nearby.

I smiled, waved, and made my way over to him.

The driver looked relieved. As I stepped into his

battered, broken taxi, he looked at me and announced, "Mena house?"

"Yes, my good man." I addressed him like the gentleman from Paris, and this was my limousine.

Back at the Hotel

I arrived at the hotel, and the driver hesitated at the gateway, so I asked the driver to drop me off outside. I didn't ask how much the fare was. I simply handed him 300 Egyptian pounds. He smiled, and I saw that this meant much to him.

He looked over to the pyramids and sighed.

"Do you ever visit the pyramids?" I asked as I began to depart the car.

"Yes, I go with my friends once a year, and we bless the land and say our sacred prayers. Perhaps they heard mine," he said, holding up the cash.

☥

Thankfully, it was still lunchtime, so I raced upstairs to the restaurant. Mr. Ahmed was there, seating guests at their tables. "Mr. Ahmed, are any of our group here?"

"No, madam. They left after breakfast, but can I seat you at the window?"

"Of course," I smiled, and he led the way.

"I'll just take a club sandwich and English tea," I told the waiter and sat back to marvel at the view. This was an incredible last day to have lunch served overlooking the Great Pyramid, without the creepy visitors.

I was finishing up and checking my watch. It was just after 2 p.m., so perhaps I could have a nap before my meeting with the Contessa. I thought I should make a list of questions and was reaching for my bag and journal.

"Excuse me, Miss Anna, we have someone to see you," said the waiter.

It was Michael.

He came over to the table and was so apologetic. I wondered if I had left something as he carried a large bag from the museum gift shop.

"Please sit, Michael. Did I forget something?" I asked.

"Oh no, but I wanted to share something with you, and it did not feel like the right time at the museum."

I asked the waiter to bring more tea.

"Well," he began, "the people you met this morning, the ones who prayed at the door."

"Yes, the people from the museum... they seemed really nice."

"Yes, well, we all belong to a very private ancient society."

"Well, I don't know if this will surprise you, but we have been linked through the ages, and it seems we are always reincarnating back together at the perfect time."

"Actually, in the early 1900's, many of us were here in this very hotel."

Hmm, perhaps I had underestimated his awareness of the mystical and strange.

"My parents' families were here and would join the adventurers, as my grandmother called them. The stories they told were passed on through the generations. Many of my ancestors died in the wars, and when my parents died, I was sent to my grandmother in England. She has a large house near the British Museum and was a patron, which is why I have an interest in all things old and strange. Sadly, she died a few years back, leaving everything she owned to me, and I don't get to visit the house much, but it's still there. She insisted it be maintained after her death. Nothing moved or changed; it was just dusted every month. My room is still the same, I think. But when she died, she left a red box and insisted in her Will that I take it on my travels with me. I never understood why, I think, until today when you mentioned it. Have you seen something like this before?"

He reached down for the small red box he had been carrying in the carrier bag.

"It's their secrets," I whispered. I poured some tea into his china cup and added lemon and a small amount of sugar. He looked at me strangely, as if wondering how I knew his tea order.

"Oh yes, you're psychic," he smiled, but it felt like it was something more.

Michael continued, "But one of the things I took out from it was this."

He opened the box and began to take out images of old photos in sepia, like the ones you see from olden times. I saw dates written on the back.

"Look, do you see these faces ever in your dreams or visions?"

I looked carefully.

"Yes, I see her, and I saw those two people were at the museum today."

And this one... he paused and held up an image of a group of people. They appeared as smartly dressed European couples visiting Egypt, exuding an air of refinement and adventure. The gentlemen were impeccably tailored, wearing crisp linen or lightweight wool suits in pale shades of beige.

The ladies are equally well turned out in long, flowing dresses of white or pastel cotton and linen, adorned with delicate lace and embroidery. Their silhouettes were Victorian, with cinched waists and structured bodices. I searched their faces to see if anyone felt familiar.

"Wow, that looks like me, and that looks like you." He nodded and just stared at me. As soon as I said it, I wanted to take it back.

He turned the photos over.

Honeymoon 1909–stopped over in Cairo en route from India.

I was in shock. Here was a past life and a relationship. But was this my honeymoon? I dared not ask any more. I handed the photo back quickly, as if it was burning my hands.

"My grandmother had photos and records of everyone she brought here to Cairo, and I think you're meant to have this, Anna, for your memory and safekeeping. Perhaps we will look into this when you have more time." I wanted to look then and there, but it would have to wait as I began to hear loud voices and laughter, and I knew my friends had returned and were heading over to us. So I slid the picture towards me and put it in my bag for safekeeping.

Michael nervously looked towards the entrance, gathered everything up back into the box, and began to make his exit.

"I think we will meet again, Anna." He touched my hand and shook it, and I felt such an electric shock. The universe was certainly playing tricks with me.

And just like that, he was gone.

I had no time to really think, so I quickly put away the photo that he had left and turned to focus on the ladies.

They all arrived, and the ordering of drinks and lunch began. Shopping treasures lay everywhere. Scarves, papyrus, oils, statues, and then the jewellery came out, along with gossip and laughter.

I sat back, calm and in no rush, just amused by the spiritual circus before me.

I was not sure if my work in Egypt was complete, but for now, I was not feeling any fear.

Naomi came over and sat with me. "Did I just see Michael leaving? Any news to share?"

I nodded. "But not here; I will tell you later."

"Aren't you visiting with the Contessa? It is nearly 3 p.m.," said Emilee.

It would seem that my days were not my own.

"Now, everyone, remember it's our celebration dinner tonight in the private dining area...," said Lesley, "...and you all have your travel plans detailed in your room."

I took it as my time to leave. It was time to visit with the lady I knew might have all the answers I sought, but I was dreading having a conversation with.

I said my goodbyes and made my way to her suite. I knocked on the door, and it opened. It was Alexandria.

"Grandmama's a little weak, but she wants to see you."

As I entered the bedroom, I had a flashback of Isis, frail and in her nightdress.

"I'm leaving for Paris in the very early morning, my dear, but Alexandria will stay around this last day and attend the dinner tonight."

Alexandria smiled and slowly left the room to go be with the others and to give us some privacy.

"Come sit, my dear."

We sat in silence, and I knew the clock was ticking, so I opened up the conversation.

"Contessa, do we have an unfinished soul contract?"

She sighed, nothing where to begin.

"Let me tell you a story, Anna. Many years ago, Isis and I knew each other as children. Our families moved in the same circles of wealth and power. It was just as the Second World War had started, so there was a great deal of speculation and fear.

"Isis lived in London. My family was in Paris, and my parents were strong supporters of the French resistance, but my mother also knew how to play the situation to our best advantage and survive and help others."

"When the Germans came to Paris, they used one of my family's homes. My family played both sides of this evil game. Do you remember the vision you had of the family from Frankfurt?" she asked.

I nodded.

"Now, your past life mother was closely related to us, and she came with rare antiques and jewels, and she spoke of her daughter, a gifted child who was to be rescued. She thought that if she travelled alone, you would not be tracked to her. She planned to hide you in plain sight until she had dealt with your siblings and secured a safe home in Paris. She did not trust my family to assist in handling things and put all of you at risk. We were family. We tried to protect them, but in the end..."

Tears sprang from her eyes, but she continued. I was, however, not sure if this was genuine, so I just listened.

"Your past life father was killed as a sympathizer to the Jewish community. Well, sadly, your mother, she died also, not knowing if you had survived. A total tragedy. However, it would seem that one of the daughters, your past-life sister, survived the war, and then she had two daughters in England. This would be Lottie, your biological mother, and your aunt. It took many years for my family to track them, and this is how your mother came to Paris as a young woman."

I could not breathe. "You mean... I'm connected to you in both families by birth and past life?"

The Contessa nodded.

"Your mother, Lottie, grew up never feeling safe in

the world. She was surrounded by such wealth when she came to Paris, but she never had her own. She was loved and accepted in Paris, but all the same, she talked about her dreams and dark forces. Your aunt stayed in England. We had no real contact with her. Finally, your mother left us and returned to England, and it would seem she fell in love and married your father. We never heard from her until Isis called me to tell me that she had had a daughter.

"We always were watching you from the shadows. When your father passed, we wanted to connect with you, but your mother said to leave you be and that she and your aunt would protect you. That's when we created the plan for Isis to find you later in life. As it happened, Isis had been connected to Lucinda since she was a young girl. We are often alerted to children who show psychic gifts as we could protect them. So when it turned out you were both in the same part of the world, we allowed fate to take its place."

"Who knew about me?" I asked.

"My family had kept journals of the families of certain bloodlines and our connections to the mystics. Your family was said to be of a rare line and very ancient, so many connected to the Mystery School knew of you, just not where you were. Many reported seeing you in dreams."

"Isis and I, as we had for years, carried guilt about your family from Frankfurt in Germany. When we were young, we had met them all. They were our friends and family, such a beautiful family. Originally, we did not know the little girl was you, Anna, in your past life. We only knew you were the blood descendant. When Isis first met you again, she was most upset as she realized the parallels. How could she not have seen this? We had the ability to save you in that lifetime. We could have shared your gifts generations before now."

I wanted to scream. I was so angry.

"Why didn't you find her, me, the little girl?" I was a little confused. "Maybe you didn't care," I said, sarcastically.

"Anna, that was during the war; Isis and I were children. We could do nothing about the past for you, but we could affect the present."

"So, you came to Glastonbury, and Isis and Naomi began to teach you. We confided in Lucinda and shared small parts with the group, but not everything. No one knew who you truly were. When you shared the past life about Germany and the war, I knew we had parts in that puzzle, but you were the catalyst."

"So, your childhood was difficult, yet you've lived a beautiful life since," I said.

"Yes, but I have kept my family business safe and supported those from our society," she said.

"Selling private collections to the Germans," I said.

"Anna, you're not listening."

I could hear in her voice that she was frustrated, not used to being questioned, but now she was caught in this terrible past-life loop. An innocent child abandoned. Left to die. The words went around and around my head.

"What happened to the family collection from Frankfurt? My real biological mother's family. And my past life family." I sat and looked her straight in the eyes. "My inheritance, perhaps?"

I had no idea where this came from. A few years ago, it would have never crossed my mind, but as I was learning about this new world, I dared to ask.

The Contessa sat back.

"Well, some... we still have some paintings, I think," she stuttered. "They were so rare we did not wish the Nazis to have them, so we had them re-painted to hide them. Your German mother tried to bribe many with her fortune, but was seriously misled. So my family took over any of the collections she had left."

"But why did my mother not have an inheritance sent to England?"

"We tried," she said. "She believed her family was cursed by the wealth. She knew of the secret vaults and had full access to make enquiries. Did you not visit the offices in York? She did not wish to step into this world in which I live. She was afraid, but Anna, know this: she and you could have had a very different lifestyle.

"Well, I am not afraid," I snapped.

"Anna, why are you so angry?" She reached to touch my hand.

"What was the name of the child lost in the war, the so-called abandoned one?"

The Contessa stopped.

"She was called Anna."

She stopped and looked at me.

"I was Anna, and I'm Anna now. My grandmother was my past-life sister in the war, and you all left me to perish on that cold train, lost and afraid."

The Contessa sat in shock. She was beginning to understand that this was not the story I wanted to hear. Obviously, forgiveness and compassion were not my words and actions of choice.

"Your bloodline is intact, child." The Contessa was growing increasingly impatient with me.

"Why do you think you were so sought after? The true Oracles came from the rare blood group. Many of them died out. But some returned in the bloodlines. Look at Naomi. She was on Hitler's list as a child in Nazi Germany. She was hidden for years until she died on that train. That's why she came back to the parents she did, the travelers they had to move to keep her safe. Her mother was of the bloodline. But you, Anna, your line is clearer than any of us, you *enfant terrible*."

"Line of what? I am not following," I snapped.

"Because you're in your ego. You *idiote* girl. Your line is from Atlantis. Anna, you are of an Atlantean lineage. Now leave me. I am tired, and you're playing the victim. I have no time for you, *idiote idiote* girl."

One too many "sillys," and I was out of my seat. I simply left the room. I had no words.

I slammed the door behind me and ran down the stairs.

Naomi and Lucinda were walking up the stairs, as they both had rooms in the creepy original wing. They were all probably having private nighttime chats with the Contessa to review my progress and evaluate if I was acceptable.

I moved to rush past them.

Lucinda caught my arm.

"What happened? We thought you were meeting with the Contessa?" she asked.

"Anna, please stop."

I was beginning to sob, and the words would not come out.

"Naomi, I'll take her to my room. Go and get Emilee and Laura," and she put her arm around me.

"And Alice," I finally was able to find the words.

Lucinda took me to her room, which was on the opposite side of the Contessa. It was larger than the one I had been in with Naomi, with a small sitting area. Her scarves were everywhere and covered the lamps, creating a mystical and magical feel.

"Sit down over there on the sofa, and I'll get you a drink." She opened up a bottle of water and added one of Emilee's remedies.

When the others arrived, the room was full. Lucinda sat next to me with Alice and Laura on the bed and Naomi and Emilee on the chairs.

"So, where do you want to start?" asked Laura.

"Well, not me. I want to know who else knew my mother and who conspired not to tell me?" I looked at them all.

They all looked at each other awkwardly.

"Do we need Lucas?" said Naomi.

"No, this is enough," said Alice.

"Anna, what do you remember about your last incarnation?"

"Everything now," I answered, "everything I need."

The room was silent.

"The Contessa told me that my birth grandmother was the sister of the little girl."

"Then that explains why we all came back to that Germany past life in the gathering," Lucinda took my hand.

"But please know we all came back together, Anna, for this time, not then. If you had not died, then you would not be who you are now. You would be old like Isis and the Contessa, not able to do what you came to do, to reconnect our oracle friends."

Suddenly, I began to cry. Finally, I understood it made sense and could let go of the past. None of it mattered now. What mattered was what we were doing now and what we would do in the future. I had decades in front of me to work with others.

"Let me take you all on a little journey to Atlantis to see a higher perspective," said Laura to break the silence.

She was so gentle and sweet.

"There is a reason we are all here."

Laura led the meditation into the journey, taking us all back to the temple and city that were now underwater, lost to the physical world.

But this is what I saw:

First of all, I was swimming deep, deep down into the blue water.

I could breathe, and I was simply light energy.

Then, as I saw the first statues that looked like the heads of Lions, all covered in flora and fauna from the ocean, I realised I was going into the temple of Isis.

At that point, I was transported back in time to when this was a beautiful structure, and the stone was like that of Philae.

I walked the stone floor and saw the columns and statues. The high altar stood in front of me, and again, I saw the lion's head. I must walk through towards the inner sanctuary and sacred area.

As I reached the high altar, I saw two women standing, praying at the sacred stone.

I moved towards the doorway, and they both looked at me and smiled.

One flashed with golden eyes and the other with green. I knew who these women were, and they welcomed me.

"This is as far as we both can bring you, Anna. You have all the gifts to support others. To help them remember and return."

"But you will always be with me? I can call on you in my dreams and visions?" I asked.

"Sometimes, yes, but now that you are becoming a clear channel for Akashic wisdom and energy, you may not need us. This temple fell in the same way as Atlantis," said the woman with the green eyes, and I knew once again that Cleopatra was here with me.

"I held on for love and power, but did not hold the mystery schools and spiritual wisdom in the way I should have. As you

see, Alexandria, just like Atlantis, was burnt and broken over the years, and many of the sacred areas were reclaimed by the ocean."

"*Do not let the wisdom drown within you,*" said the woman, who now had golden eyes. I saw this was Arsinoe.

"*We do have a gift,*" they said, presenting me with a beautiful golden coin bearing the goddess Isis, her wings spread wide.

"*Hold this within your soul; we will watch over you wherever you travel. This will always buy you safe passage.*"

Laura spoke. "Now, ladies, it is time to return to the location and feel the energy of the boat bringing you back clear and refreshed."

Oh, how I loved Laura's calming voice. We all looked at each other.

"Anyone else in the Temple of Isis in Atlantis?" said Lucinda, and everyone put their hand up.

"Told you so," said Laura, and with that, she rose. "Now let's rest and get our glad rags on for tonight."

I wanted to tell the Contessa everything I had now seen, and that the past life did not matter, but when I reached her room, I saw the card hanging from the door handle saying she was not to be disturbed. Tomorrow, early, I would catch her, and I would make everything right. But tonight would be our celebration before the departure. I had the final scrolls and scarabs to give out. Then, back home to Glastonbury and, I prayed, a rest.

Our Final Dinner

I wandered out to the pool before dinner at 6.30 p.m. The sun was beginning to set, but I could still see the pyramids in clear view. I sat at one of the small tables and beckoned a waiter over, who lit the candle at my table.

I ordered a glass of red Egyptian wine and took in the exquisite view and the smell of the evening jasmine. I had brought my bag, which contained the last of the scrolls and scarabs, and reached into it to retrieve my journal. I continued to write notes in the candlelight.

I slowly reviewed the pictures I had obtained and closed my eyes to recall the images of the Sphinx and also the Amenti pieces. I was even brave enough to look at the old sepia picture Michael had given me. His business card was next to it, and I was so tempted to text him.

I checked my watch, and it was nearly 7 p.m., so I signed my bill, hurried back up to the hotel, and just made it in time as we all wandered into the restaurant and over to the private room we had reserved.

Alexandria was making apologies for her grandmother, saying she was resting and would be travelling very early, although she was not sure where to. I made a point of telling her I would be calling on the Contessa before we all left, as early as possible. She looked at me strangely.

"I need to make things right and whole, if you can help me?"

She smiled and nodded. "We are real family, my sister. *Très bien*. Now, shall we sit together?"

Once everyone was seated, the meal began. Everyone was in high spirits, and I began to relax for the first time in days. Lavish plates of grilled meats and vegetables appeared with the most delicious saffron rice. I was in heaven, and I have to say, totally overindulgent.

Once the meal was over, the room was cleared, and we went about discussing the trip over tea and coffee. It was interesting that Naomi stood up first and said a prayer for those who could not be with us, and that we all were aware they were on Earth or in Heaven, and that the Priests and

Priestesses of Isis would carry on with the sacred work.

I was then invited to stand and speak and share the fate of the scrolls and scarabs.

I nodded and stood up.

"We have waited for many lifetimes, and the work, yes, it does continue. So, in saying that, the Scarab and Scroll of Death and Resurrection and Protection and the Scarabs and Scrolls of Truth and Integrity and Light and Shadow, I have left in the safe hands of my friends at the Cairo Museum.

"Alexandria, please give the Scarab and Scroll of Creation and the Goddess and Fertility to the Contessa so she can hold them in Paris to connect to the energies of the Louvre." She took them and smiled, patting them and placing them into a red velvet pouch that Lucas had thoughtfully handed to her.

"Laura and Alice will take the Scarab and Scroll of Magic and Prophecy and the Records of Life back to Glastonbury, and I hope Naomi, we can take them to London at some point."

Everyone nodded and came over to Lucas to collect them, and then, after whispering words into them, he handed the scrolls and scarabs out to Laura. He had also prepared a blue velvet pouch for her. He looked a little lost when I handed him back an empty box.

"I hold the Book of Keys, and therefore, you can all bear witness to this event, and should the time come when I require them again, you will all hear my call. Lucas, I have something greater in the future for you to protect, I am sure." His face lit up, "Just stick around and wait and see."

As I sat, Naomi looked across at me approvingly, and at last, I began to see a future for all of us.

"Now, we all joined many days ago under this Egyptian moon. It is time for goodbyes and departures to new adventures," said Alice.

We all understood what she meant as she was growing frailer than ever.

"I will be leaving the Chalice Well this summer, and an apprentice will join me on my return home." I looked around to see who in the group she meant, and then back to Alice.

"It's a surprise," she smiled.

"Lucas and I are spreading our wings," announced Naomi. "We have new horizons in Europe and America."

"We will be holding the Glastonbury temple," announced Laura. "That is, me, Emilee, and Lucinda, and I think Gina will stay, also."

"I'm not sure where I will be," I said. "I'm feeling lots of things change, but I think I may have a whole new group of people to explore some other sacred sites with, around the world."

"Maybe I can travel with you," said Alexandria. I took her hand. "I would love that."

"Well, I am going to a healing Ashram in India," announced Lesley. This took everyone by surprise, especially Naomi.

"But Lesley, you said you were leaving for London."

"No, I am flying out from Cairo tomorrow evening once everyone has departed. Anna, thank you for all you have done and trusted me with. I am truly grateful, but now I am going to study with an amazing guru. She's a healer, and I know many of the priestesses follow her. I think this is as far as I can go with this group. Sorry, Naomi, but not sorry."

Naomi was speechless.

We all wished Lesley well, and I wondered how long she would last in spiritual service, but at least she had found her calling, or was it simply an escape?

We then joined hands and hearts around the table, and while we knew we might never gather as a group again, we knew the work we had created and succeeded with would last through this lifetime and the next.

My journey had only just started.

☥

I returned to my room with a full heart and a title for my book. I opened my journal. On a new page, I wrote, "*The Journey of the Initiate" by Anna Harris.*

Then, I started a new page, "*Mystical Journeys of the Oracle in Egypt.*"

I listed the locations where I would take others, then closed the book to allow it to do its magic. I promised the gods I would return, and I would meet Anubis again, and many more. The Queens and Arsinoe were only a thought away. So, I just left it up to the gods as to when and where this would happen. I really felt my work had really started.

For the first time since arriving, I fell asleep that night and did not fear my dreams.

I found myself wandering the corridors of the hotel. I was back in another time, and many people were visiting in various types of clothes. They all walked together, going towards the sacred rooms hidden from common view. It was like making a passage through time. I looked out of the windows, and all I saw was sand and a few old carriages with horses.

There was a gathering in the great room, and I made my way over to it. I knew I was still in the Mena House Hotel, just not sure where.

When I reached the room, I entered, and one of the gatekeepers escorted me to a seat near the front.

There stood a woman who introduced herself as Madame

Blavatsky, and as I listened, I understood she was teaching the Laws of energy, the new world, and what events could come to pass. She talked of wars and the power of destruction to the soul that would come from atomic energy.

She warned that a great sadness would come, but that this was the old age of Pisces and the age of the great wars. We would evolve through this, and in our future lives that we would come back into, we would find a way. She talked of a darkness that was hiding.

She honoured all the elders, priests, and priestesses in the room and thanked the Oracles who had come forward and spoken. I was aware of a man coming in and sitting next to me, and as she spoke of the Oracles, I was sure she looked straight at me. I thought I saw people I knew, but their faces kept changing.

The man beside me turned and smiled and then held my hand, and I felt safe and excited. I looked at our hands and saw our wedding bands. He was my husband. I was still unsure who he was.

The dream shifted, and I was in a dream inside of a dream.

The alarm call went off, and it was 7 a.m. Where had the night gone?

I went back into my normal world and showered. I had packed the night prior, so no drama or mischief could find me.

I left the room early and, with my suitcase, walked back to the hotel lobby to find the Contessa, but no one was around. Thankfully, I saw there was coffee and I still had time before our bus arrived for the departure. So, I went towards the lobby bar, left my suitcase at the concierge desk, and proceeded to get a coffee and wait. Oh well, no one here yet. Never mind.

Well, no one except Isis. She sat there, all in royal blue, in the corner of the bar area, simply staring up at the pyramids from the window.

She turned and beckoned me over to the table.

"I was at the gathering in the great room with Madame B," I said.

"Of course. I saw you there, Anna, with your gentleman. My, he was so handsome."

"I thought I was just in a dream."

"No, not a dream, another reality. Anna, we are bound to each other's souls from the time past, present, and future. These memories sometimes all cross for an amazing moment in time, and we once again see, feel, and hear each other. We all made a promise to be present at those times, and at 3:33 a.m. this morning, we all were."

She reached across and patted my hand. Of all the mornings, this was my favourite in a long while.

"Look at how the moon and sun have risen over our sacred home," she said, pointing out of the window.

I could see the Great Pyramid. The sun had risen, and you could still make out the shape of the moon.

"We are so blessed and fortunate," I whispered.

She smiled, and I wondered if this would be our last time doing this.

"Now, don't you have to meet with the Contessa?"

It was that last line that woke me. I looked at the clock on the nightstand. It read 07:00, and I realised I had been dreaming in multiple timelines.

I held back my tears, but they were not of sadness. I had had this perfect moment alone with Isis. I had opened the doorway to an amazing group of souls and perhaps a soulmate. I shivered—that was a dangerous thought. I quickly showered and dressed, then headed up to the main hotel and knocked on the Contessa's door.

"Enter," she said, and I pushed the door open.

There she sat, fully dressed and looking better than I had seen her all trip. All her cases were packed and stacked.

"So you look much better," I remarked.

"Better than in years," she said. "I am leaving in a few minutes and will be back in Paris this afternoon. Anna, sit down. I have something I wanted to share."

I sat down nervously on the edge of a chair and began to hear the conversation of the previous afternoon in my head.

I started to apologise when she held up her hand.

"No apology. My family has been beyond blessed, and we survived the war to be able to support the spiritual work, but I never really knew how or why it would turn out like this. I want you to know that before Isis passed, she told me she had suggested that the sacred journey part of her business be passed directly to you and Naomi. I now see that Naomi may not wish to carry on with this, but you, I am sure, can work with our agents here in Cairo, and I am sure Rashida will be willing to partner with you. I feel your work will be greater with time, money, and opportunity and I can help with that. When you return to England, I wish for you to look for a location to create a retreat centre and School of the Oracles. I will fund it and invest in you."

"My own business, a school?" I was shocked.

"Your own business. Guiding the priests and priestesses. Yes, and your own teachings as well."

"Does anyone else know?" I asked.

"No," she said, "although they may suspect. I know Isis talked the tour business situation over with Naomi, and you and her can still partner on other ventures. But Naomi has her path to fame and fortune to find."

"Also, I just heard from my curators that we still have a few pieces of art and jewellery that belonged to your maternal grandmother that I will have returned to you. There is a picture that they think may be very valuable. And there is an account still in Geneva belonging to your family, and as you appear to be the last living relative after your mother, I will have my private banker contact you with account details and keys to your vault."

Oh, my goodness. I had my own business and possibly some inheritance.

"Do you think it will be enough to buy a new car?"

She laughed.

"Maybe a fleet of cars, my dear. Now I'll be leaving in half an hour, and I have others to see. Be useful and go over and call the front desk to say I am checking out and my bags are ready for my limousine."

I nodded, made the call, and then ran back and hugged her and kissed her cheek, to her surprise and mine.

"Till our next adventure, bon voyage," and I ran out, this time not slamming the door. I needed to be in the fresh, open air. As I darted out of her room, I was surprised to see Lucinda coming towards me.

"Unfinished business?" I asked, and she nodded.

I watched as she entered and greeted the Contessa, and while the old me would have listened at the door, my senses told me to be nowhere near this healing encounter.

☥

I ventured outside the hotel to the garden area. On the grass outside sat Naomi. She was in meditation, so I sat a little distance away until she turned, acknowledged me, and beckoned me over.

"So, the last morning, this should be exciting, do you not think? All new directions," she said, not looking at me.

"I just spoke to the Contessa," I said.

"Did you agree and take on the sacred retreat and school?" She smiled and looked at me. She was the best psychic and 'eye in the sky' I had ever met.

I nodded. "I'm not sure I'm ready for this next step."

"You will be, Anna, trust me."

"And I will be the first to sign up with you when the time comes to return to Egypt, and I expect to bring my clients and students."

That vote of confidence gave me such a lift.

"But you must finish your book now."

"It's so much work," I complained.

"No, do like I do. Write a little each day, and then we will find someone to help with the editing and publishing." Her words were encouraging.

"But what if my work is not great?" Now, I sounded like a child.

"Don't worry about the writing. You can now afford to hire the best support. You, Anna, are a storyteller, and you will find gifted writers along the way to help. I also heard your guides tell me you had received some inheritance," she smiled.

"Which ones told you that?" This was a little more than accurate. Or had she been listening?

"Don't you know I'm psychic?" she said. "I know everyone's business."

"And gossip?" I laughed.

"Yes, but that I keep to myself. But seriously, Anna, don't worry about the writing; focus on creating great content. Isis asked you once to write for her, and she trusted you with the sacred trips. I am not to be trusted. I nearly sold our souls to that creepy shaman Francisco."

"I'm not sure. What if I have a creepy black magician who seduces me?"

"Well, Anna, don't be ridiculous. You are invisible to that type—they feast and feed on glamour. Now, seriously, focus on the book."

"If not for yourself, then for Isis Now..." she concluded.

"Oh no, I think I can see Lesley making her way to us. It's time to gather our brooms and fly. Let's go have breakfast. It's too early for talk of Ashrams."

☥

It was just after lunch when the bus arrived to take us to the airport. We checked our bags with the porters and began boarding, leaving our palatial exotic home to return to quaint Glastonbury. I was surprised to see the concierge running over to me.

"Ms. Anna, this was left for you." He held out a small bag that held a box and a card.

I smiled, took the package, and boarded the bus. I could see Naomi looking over, and I smiled and shrugged. I opened the card. It was from Michael at the museum.

Dear Anna,

I called by the hotel early, hoping we could talk and connect again. The front desk said they were not sure where you were, and no one was answering your room phone for me to consult with you about how I should do this. I was afraid to text or call you; I did not know quite what to say.

You have such knowledge and wisdom, and I know I can learn so much more from you. Last night, you were in a dream with me, and we were attending a group meeting of some sort. I also have this brooch of my grandmother's—it was in the red box I showed you yesterday. I saw it in the dream, so I want you to have it with my thanks and gratitude.

I am going to stay here at the Cairo Museum for now, but already, my dreams and spiritual quests are becoming a larger part of my life.

I know that you will be travelling back to Glastonbury today and may not visit Cairo anytime soon.

Anyway, I am giving a lecture at the British Museum in London in December, and it would be great if you could attend. These people are also our friends, and I hope we can show you some of the amazing things that were found with the Rosetta Stone, and we are looking for insight on other weird and wonderful discoveries. Also, it would be wonderful to spend some time exploring London, just you and me. Well, I must go. Thank you.

Safe travels,
Michael

I could feel my heart racing. I began to remember the man in the sepia photo and the man in my dream this morning. I started to think that this was the same person. I opened the small giftbox, and the brooch felt so familiar. I put it back into the bag and tucked everything away safely.

So, December it is, I thought to myself.

"You're blushing, Anna," said Naomi. "Was that a love note from the perfume salesman with some more rose oil?"

I laughed. "Of course. He asks me to come back to Egypt, and we will be soul mates. I am his Queen of the Nile."

"Oh no, not that old line," I heard the women in the back all sing out in a chorus.

We moved quickly along the road back to the airport. I was sure I would never tire of this trip, but I wondered if March next year was too soon to plan another. I moved down the bus and sat with Rashida. I thanked her for such a wonderful trip, and she smiled and held my hand. "Come home soon, my friend. Me and your museum family will be waiting."

That was all I needed hear. I smiled, hugged her, and began to share my thoughts of what our partnership could look like.

☥

We pulled into the departures area, and our airport agent and Lesley bounced into action. Once again, we were tourists, hugging Rashida. Everyone else was now thanking her for a wonderful trip.

"Energy shields up, ladies and Lucas. This is where I leave you," shouted Lesley. With that, she picked up her large duffel and bag and literally ran down the terminal to find her flight and leave us or to escape us. Anyway, she never looked back.

Everyone did their own little mudra and ritual, and I pulled my scarf around me and put on my sunglasses.

We were going back to another world—another timeline—but I knew this trip would stay with us forever.

CHAPTER 32

Monday, 17 November 2009
Return to Glastonbury

Has it been only two months since we returned? The weeks flew by.

The Gables was very busy from the moment we arrived home. Clients and our friends in town reached out to us to find out what treasures and stories we had returned with. Apparently, as we had been opening temples and tombs and clearing the past lives and curses, anyone connected to these times also had dreams and visions.

When we returned, our emails and voicemails were overloaded at both the Gables and Lucas's shop. The diary was full, and we had no downtime. Every day was a flurry of activity. Every room at the Gables was booked, and Laura had to employ two girls from the village to help out at her cottage, which we used as a sister property.

Gina had done an amazing job taking care of the Gables and had decided to stay on, renting a place in town. She helped Lucas and even took care of some spiritual readings when we were double booked, which seemed to happen more often than not.

Even Lucinda was performing sessions up at her tiny cottage. She had many of the overdue repairs done and the whole place repainted. Isis was only a memory now in this sacred place. Lucinda had framed the picture of her and Isis in Egypt that I had found in the red box. It was a perfect reminder of happy days.

Alice had officially retired when we had returned from Egypt. The journey had really taken its toll on her health, but she still lived on site at Chalice Well... "to keep the fairies company," she said.

Emilee had hired an extra housekeeper to help with the house, and thankfully, they could help with the early mornings, which meant Emilee and I were off emergency kitchen support.

I had no breakfasts with burnt toast and eggs to worry about.

Emilee had moved into her converted attic room, a beautiful sanctuary, in order to create more wonderful oils, potions, and remedy recipes.

The town seemed to take a new life and vibrancy, and so had we. It would seem we were no longer considered the witches on the hill, as local people often stopped me to say hello and ask about how I was.

Our sisterhood from Egypt tried to stay connected and I so wanted to make time to visit everyone, but it was clear we were all still processing what we had experienced in Egypt.

The Contessa was true to her promise of financial support, but I had to keep the thought of the sacred retreat school to the back of my mind, as every property was either too big, needed renovations, or was too far out of town. I had called on the Tor Druidesses to help, yet it would seem they were focused only on their work at the Tor, and their visits and connections to me grew less and less.

How I missed The Sanctuary. Naomi and Laura had approached the women on my behalf to see if they were interested in selling, but they were holding strong. It was confusing, as many of Isis's clients and students would visit there to feel the old magic, but like myself, we knew she had really gone.

In the end, I decided to park the search for the new school in my journal, focus on my work, and try to write my book.

☥

One afternoon in late November, I visited the Chalice Well. The sun was shining, but the weather was becoming colder, and the wind was crisp and icy. Alice had sent regular texts to invite me, but I only had time to visit if I was providing an initiation or teaching there. But today, something told me she wanted to see me, so I braved the cold.

"Anna, my dear one." She welcomed me with a hug and a smile. She had grown so frail in such a short space of time and even had a cane to walk.

"Anna, come sit in the gardens near the Red Lion's head." I remembered this from my first visit so long ago. We snuggled up on the bench.

"Now, I know you are busy," she said. "But Anna, are you writing? Are you remembering?"

"Yes, I am, always and every day. I have to send chapters to Naomi, and I am nearly up to the Great Pyramids visit," I told her.

"Good, good," she seemed relieved.

"You will write the book of our stories. I know you shared so much with me over the years; please know these are also your stories to tell. And you will tell them in your special way."

"Yes, Alice," I had promised everyone's stories. I hugged her but was afraid she would break.

That afternoon was so peaceful. We laughed and talked about our past year and past lives, and I told her what I had written about her memories of Egyptian times with

Alexander and the library.

"Alexander was there in Luxor, and I promised I would return for Naomi's coin."

She looked at me. "Anna, take care of bargains you enter into, no matter what the cause."

"Oh, Alice, do you still have that Akhenaten papyrus picture? I wanted to take a picture sometime to write about it."

She shook her head.

"No, apparently it fell from the wall and smashed during our trip, and my cleaning lady was unable to save it."

"I think a curse was cleared," she whispered. It was a strange piece indeed, and to this day I do not know who sent it... Now, do continue."

I continued and shared my story of Siwa, which brought her great joy and many questions. But soon I could see she was tiring, and I made an excuse to leave. As I was getting ready to leave, she walked me out.

"Alice, take care. I can come and help some more," I offered.

"My sisters are here. We are well and able," she laughed.

I had turned to look, and there they were, the Druidesses from the Tor, all in their gowns of rich colour. They waved and smiled. I was sure I saw Isis at the back, but as always, I was in a hurry to get back and didn't want to linger. I wish now I had taken time to stop, but I just kept thinking there would be a next week. I had promised Alice I would visit her the following Sunday afternoon.

☥

A few days later, to my shock, Alice had passed away while in the sanctuary of meditation. It was mid-afternoon, and the first snow had come to our town. It was Lucinda who had found her. She was in her chair, looking like she was sleeping. Her face calm, rested, and at peace. I was relieved it was not me who had found her.

She had no family that we knew of... No, that was not true. We were her family. And so the call had gone out, and in those first few days of December, everyone we knew stopped what they were doing and came home to visit Glastonbury and the Chalice Well. Another master had passed to the other side.

Monday, 21 December 2009
Ceremony at the Chapel

Alice had then been cremated as per her wishes, so there had been very little for our group to do except create a celebration for her life. We had decided it should be the December Solstice when we said our proper goodbye to her with ceremony and celebration. We just did not know where, and we assumed it would be the Chalice Well when something strange happened, and we had a sudden change of plan.

Lucinda had texted me in the morning of December 20.

"Meet me at the church of St. Patrick in the Abbey at 6 p.m. tomorrow."

"But will the Abbey be open?" was my reply.

"No, but it will be open to us. And bring the pendant Isis gave you. And spread the word."

"I thought we held the celebration at the Chalice Well?"

She did not respond. I waited for her text but decided to just go with it and trust her.

It was nearly 6 p.m. when I walked slowly up to the

entrance of the Abbey. The main doorway was closed, but ahead was a figure in a long cloak who had opened the side exit door. The walls were high and medieval, and it felt as though I was back 500 years ago. No tourists or cars were passing by. The town was still in a slumber.

I was very nervous, but I felt a little at ease as I saw it was Laura in the long cloak. She stayed very silent, only nodding and smiling.

As I stepped through into the Abbey, I could see the outline of the ruins. I could see where the stones of the old buildings were still present, and even though I had visited many times, this time was very different.

Laura came over to me, took my hand, pulled me inside, and wrapped a cape of deep red velvet around my shoulders. She then closed the large wooden door behind me. In silence, she guided me towards the small church of St. Patrick.

Most visitors walk straight past this beautiful part of the Abbey, as I had on my first visit. Today, however, this place was vivid and alive. As we entered, someone had lit candles in the small chapel, and the light bounced around the room, bringing the images in the stained glass to life. I glanced to my right at the image of Mary Magdalene drawn as if she were floating upon the wall with what looked to be deadly sins attached to her heart through baby dragons. The image tells a million stories, but I have a sense that she was taking on the issues and pain of mankind.

Inside were two rows of pews, each side facing towards the altar at the front. The small altar, a single white slab, was covered in lilies, and the fragrance filled the room. The green and cream tile in front of the altar on the floor showed Egyptian symbols, and candles were placed in a circle to represent the cycle of life. The four panels of stained-glass behind the altar told the stories of this sacred place, and

I thought I saw other timelines being revealed. On either side of the stained glass were two images of a king and queen holding Jesus and the angels. A biblical scene... but somehow, it felt familiar.

At the very front stood Lucinda, who was creating a ritual with incense. I then began to pay attention to the people in the pews. I looked at Naomi and Lucas. They also wore cloaks of velvet. Lydia sat behind them in her ceremonial robes.

"I don't understand," I whispered.

"You will, my dear," Laura moved me forward.

"Sit down," and she motioned for me to sit at one of the pews across from them near the front.

I again glanced around at the images; they all seemed to come to life and were whispering to me.

Emilee sat down in the pews behind me and was joined by Gina. I wondered why she did not sit with me.

"Anna, have patience," she leaned over as she read my thoughts.

Soon, I heard footsteps. I turned around, and to my surprise, there stood Alexandria. She was in a cloak, too. She bowed her head to Lucinda and looked at me. She checked her watch and turned to speak with Laura.

"We have time, can we wait? We're just waiting on Lesley," she said.

"Yes, but I don't think she will be here," Laura whispered.

"No, Lesley will not be here, but we are," said Naomi, "and she is with us from her prayers."

She held up the pendant Isis had gifted her with together with her gifted Ankh.

"That's what matters." I heard the voice of the Contessa from the back, and I turned to look. She stood in a dark green velvet robe and then proceeded to sit in the back row.

Alexandria squeezed my hand and went back to sit with her.

I took a breath. Tears were streaming down my face.

Emilee continued to whisper in my ear.

"Anna, our soul sisters had been meeting here in Glastonbury for many lifetimes and holding space in this chapel. This is the sacred space where the priestesses would meet and hold the ceremony of Isis. Hidden for many years, the secrets were brought here during the biblical days and have protected us ever since. However, after World War II, our kind were not allowed to meet for some reason. We had to meet at the Sanctuary or the Chalice Well.

"Since we returned from this last trip to Egypt, it appears the guardians, those who are part of the Children of the Light Society, reached out to say we have access again. Apparently, Alice received the letter the day she died and was able to share this with Lucinda, who held her during her last moments and performed the rituals of Dendara. We have waited to share what brought dear Alice to peace."

To this, I wanted to really sob, but held it hidden. Laura sat next to me and held my hand, not daring to look at me in case she lost control of her emotions as well.

As Lucinda finished her ritual, I began to hear the sound of a flute approaching. As the sound became louder, I looked behind and saw many others entering the chapel in their cloaks. Many of the women I had seen in the cafes and shops in town.

"The picture on the wall at the back is the true story of the death of Isis, which Mary Magdalene represents," whispered Laura, pointing to the image on the back wall I had first noticed on arrival.

"This is her chapel, but for now, for tonight, it is the High Altar of Philae." I looked back to the altar and suddenly saw that Alice now sat in a small golden urn next to her picture. My lip began to tremble again.

Laura handed me a tissue. She held up her pendant with the rose from Isis and proceeded to rise up and hand it to Lucinda to place on the altar.

I held mine out and walked forward to place mine with the box and key next to the one that Alice had owned with the cartouche. Emilee laid hers that showed the pomegranate. Lucinda placed her hourglass into the row. Lucas came over and placed the small dagger from Lesley as well as his winged Ma'at. Then, finally, there was Naomi with her ankh. I realised that we had all carried them through Egypt, and these would give a priest or priestess the perfect rites of passage to the next world. Each was a symbol of the ceremony I had dreamt about when Naomi and I had guided Isis through to the other world.

Laura looked at me as I retook my seat next to her and took a deep breath.

Then the flute stopped, and the women began to chant. As I looked to my right, I began to see Isis and Alice walking down the aisle, and at that, I burst into tears.

The chapel was full, and I barely held it together as I watched my friends perform the most beautiful and moving ritual.

"This is the honouring for those who also had the Druidess Initiation. Alice and Isis both followed the order," said Laura. I watched as they bowed to the altar and then turned to walk back out of the chapel.

This would be a new chapter. Now, we would begin to lift the veil. Perhaps Alice, I was sure, would appear in my dreamtime.

As I sat quietly, my thoughts began to form into ideas for teaching.

Then Lucinda began to sing, and I was transfixed.

EPILOGUE

The New Year had arrived and 2010 came with a fresh new start. After an uneventful Christmas, I returned to work at the Gables with a new perspective and a renewed commitment to teach and train others in the Psychic Arts. January was a whirlwind.

Straight after the celebration of life for Alice, Naomi and Lucas made a short trip to India to visit Lesley and return her pendant. To their surprise, she had already left. They tracked her down to Bali, living with none other than the shaman Francisco, who had charmed Naomi. They were leading kundalini tantric retreats and had a following of devotees. Goodness knows how long the guru life will last for them, but Lucas said they were happy in a weird, dysfunctional way.

In Bali, Naomi and Lucas had parted ways, as they seemed to have shifted their focus and sacred contracts with each other. Naomi went east to California, where she now lives in a beachfront home in Malibu. The new-age California market is booming, and she already has a lifestyle channel starting in the summer.

In a very strange turn of events, Lucas headed back to Europe but never got any further than Paris. He now helps the Contessa with various spiritual tasks, as he calls them, and is training with the Minister, and always seems to be visiting another European 6-star hotel. He won't share too much of his business, but it is only a matter of time before I figure it out.

Gina, to my surprise, had stepped in as an amazing healer and spiritual counselor—a wonderful complement to our tribe. She sold up her home in London and moved full-time to Glastonbury.

With Lucas and Naomi gone, Gina and I advertised for psychic readers and mediums and began to create a metaphysical hub in Lucas's shop to offer our services via phone and online video calls.

Within a week of taking a leap of faith to expand the business, my mother's house sold and I was able to actually buy the shop and make my first property investment in Glastonbury. The day I signed for the property, I had the courage to open the envelope my mother had left me.

It was strange as it was a good luck card with roses on the front and a simple message:

"*I love you*

"*I am sorry*

"*Please forgive me*

"*Thank you.*"

Then she had signed her name.

However, the large envelope also contained a fascinating document that seemed to be a family tree with dates spanning many timelines and locations around the globe. I wasn't sure what to do with it, but I knew it was of value and could be a map to explore in the future.

Then by some miracle just the next day, when Alex came to visit, we finally found a perfect house for my school, which had come on the market for sale. It was located in central Glastonbury, too perfect for words, at the edge of the Abbey. True to her word, the Contessa sent the funds to make it mine, and I promised to pay her back and make good on her loan.

It was a grand Victorian house with walled gardens, six bedrooms with ensuites, and four large rooms for sessions and classes. It even had top-floor attics that I could convert into a home for myself.

I called the new space "Amenti House."

Alexandria had stayed and helped with the new Amenti House renovations. We created an amazing library for all my books and the collection that Alice had left our school. I finally found the courage to look back through the Emerald Tablet and Scorpion book that had long been hidden in my wardrobe, but as yet, nothing new had come to me. The damaged book that I had saved from the Isis collection was stored with care, and I had promised to share the story of Akhenaten and Tutankhamun with the blessing of Nefertiti and share the truth as they had shown to me in my teachings and new book.

My priestess book was nearly complete thanks to all the Queens who visited in my dreams and to Arsinoe, who had settled with us for a while, living, it seemed, in the garden gazebo. I would sit and visit with her when I sought ancient wisdom, as she still had the knowledge of the Alexandrian library and its famous scrolls, and we even were able to access some of the so-called Dead Sea Scrolls. She is now a walking, talking holographic library that I greatly admire and treasure. Often, I see Alex with her, laughing and sharing time, so loving.

Alexandria and I grew close like sisters. It also helped me to have her as an on-call oracle and for her to be there for support to message Grandmama, the Contessa, when we needed money and additional funds. Budgets were not our strength, so we have needed a little help in the area of logistics.

As neither of us can cook, I must admit I have grown to love and appreciate the food parcels and hampers that her grandmother sends up from Marks & Spencer and Harrods in London. They are a godsend. After all, if God had meant for girls like us to cook, why would she create these food hall temples with delivery service?

Emilee often visits to help us with the accounts and check, or rather raid, the fridge for foods we have no idea what to do with, such as truffles, mushrooms, and some weirdly named cheeses from the hampers. Once a week, she will visit us, and we hand over our receipts. She relieves us of such food items in exchange for balancing our accounts and processing payments.

Emilee is naturally a gifted healer, but also a very shrewd businesswoman. She has expanded her online business in aromatics and remedies and has taken over a storefront opposite the Abbey. Here, her herbal remedies are highly sought after, and she has just started to talk about the lease of a shop in Covent Garden in London. I told her I see her going international, but she simply smiles and tells us she could never leave her sanctuary in Glastonbury. Perhaps the Contessa has extra budget for Emilee. After all, they were related in the German past life.

Speaking of the Sanctuary retreat center. Not long into the New Year, the ladies suddenly closed the Sanctuary and boarded up the property. No one is sure why. I choose to think that they were holding spiritual space while we went through our transition. But I'm not clear about its future—neither Alex nor I had a clear vision. Perhaps the building is simply sleeping, exhausted from all the work we all did while living and working there.

To my surprise, Laura stopped hosting guests and began volunteering at the Chalice Well gift shop. She said she had found her happy place and stayed connected to me as she guided some of my students around the Chalice Well Gardens and holds a monthly meditation group at Amenti House. She is coming with Lucinda and me to Egypt in March. The trip is already full with a waitlist.

As Naomi is too busy with her fame and fortune, Rashida is now my true business partner in Egypt, and Lucinda is the ceremony coordinator. Lucinda, well, she is becoming the next guardian of the Chalice Well. One of its founders appeared to her in a dream: a woman named Alice Buckton. So now, musical and goddess events are planned for the summer, as well as all things magical. She and Laura can be found in the gardens with the fairies and elemental spirits.

I see the Druidesses visiting her more and more, and Lucinda has even had custom-made gowns fashioned like theirs. She says it is for theatrical effect, but I think it's because she loves the timeline and who she becomes.

The Contessa also came through for me on a karmic level and contacted me regarding my inheritance from my birth grandmother's family.

One day in late January, a large delivery truck arrived, and a huge crate was brought into the house to be signed for. I opened the crate that had arrived in the living room with Alex, who I suspected knew of its arrival but wanted it to be a surprise. It had many words written in French and German, so she was the perfect one to translate.

It was delivered by a firm with a security guard who watched over us to make sure all was in order. It took forever to unpack as everything was sealed and boxed with great care and very efficient labelling. We even had to wear white gloves.

To our surprise, it contained photo albums, some books, and small paintings, as well as a velvet case of jewels that we would later discover to be rare and valuable, having belonged to some notorious women in history. I dare not wear them as I know their stories could pour into me, and I am not sure that would be so great.

Also, it seemed that the painting the Contessa had mentioned had already been cleaned and sent to Sotheby's in London for sale. Their appraisal had been a surprise as apparently, the painting was one of the fifteenth-century missing masters. The Contessa had decided it should go to someone who could take care of it properly, as it may look out of place next to my Egyptian papyrus and Ikea landscapes. I had to agree. Goodness knows what the insurance would have been.

And heaven knows what lies in the family vault. Next month, I fly to Geneva to meet with the Contessa and some of her advisors. Alexandri is coming for support, as I have found this all a little overwhelming.

As for Michael, well, new discoveries around Egypt started to happen after we lifted the veils on our September trip. Apparently, a whole new section had been discovered around Karnak temple, thus his December trip had to be cancelled, but he texts me often with updates, and we speak on the phone most weeks.

It now turns out he and another professor are giving a lecture about the High Priestesses of Egypt on Valentine's Day at the British Museum. I have tickets to go with Lucinda. We are staying in London for a few days at a house that Naomi has also bought. She has become a real estate queen. Naomi talks about new money, new technology, and her investments of the future. It seems her Alexander the Great coin is active and working. My abundance energy seems to be pretty active also with my good fortune, but I'm aware I may have a price to pay.

Michael also told me his friends are bringing over the relics that I had identified in the Cairo Museum just before I had left. And since they actually belonged to Lucinda, I have organized for her to view the relics in private before they go on display in the museum.

Michael has also invited me to visit his grandmother's house and tour the British Museum behind the scenes the day after the event. Who knows where that will lead? Perhaps we connect because of my skill of reading the symbols no one else seems to understand.

And yes, he is often in my dreams. When I dream about Michael, it's always the same. We meet in the Room of Souls in the Mena House, and we share the vision of the dream that could come again with our soul friends from through the ages. Isis is sometimes there but it's becoming less and less.

And finally, for now...

Friday, 12 February 2010

Last night, I dreamt I walked the Tor in the moonlight all the way to the top. The Druidesses were there and they sat with me on the bench. I watched as Isis and Alice danced past us. Their faces and energy were those of young women, at home and happy.

Suddenly, I felt a cold hand on my shoulder, and I was afraid to turn.

"*Anna, do not turn around*," the voice was that of Anubis. "*The Scroll and Scarab of Amenti have been removed, and a dark cloud is moving this way towards you from the Cairo Museum. You must warn your friends and prepare for the Children of Darkness who seek their power. Now it is time to go to Siwa and find your answers—the Priests of Amun are still of pure heart and there awaiting you with the Oracle. She will guide you next.*"

My whole body seemed to jump, and I woke from my dream and saw a text flashing from Michael.

"Hey, Beautiful, I will be leaving Cairo today and have decided to bring the Scroll and Scarab of Amenti. Let's play our new game in London like we promised. See you soon."

Why would he bring them? And what was this new game to play? And since when did he start calling me beautiful? What was he weaving?

About the Author

Amanda Romania is the visionary international bestselling author of *Return to the Temple* (Book 1 of the Divine Oracle Series), *Cosmic Connection with the Akashic Records: Awaken the Star Seed of Your Soul* and *Akashic Therapy: Healing, Clearing, and Gaining Clarity for the Records of Your Soul.* She is also the creator of the *Akashic Records Oracle Cards.*

Amanda specializes in sacred Temple work, spiritual mentorship and empowerment. As a master Akashic Record Oracle and Librarian, Amanda is able to open the veils to the mysteries of the Akashic matrix and cosmic realms and the etheric database of knowledge containing all the records of our incarnations. She is able to assist in developing our skills to further enhance all of our unique spiritual gifts, and leads us towards next generation ascension consciousness and greater understanding of true spiritual purpose.

For the past 20 years, Amanda has led tours to the world's major sacred sites including Glastonbury, Central America, Egypt, and beyond. Join her on the path of the oracle—a journey into the mystical realms to examine the past, present, future, the lives between lives, and the effects of our karmic choices on future timelines.

Amanda lives with her family in the heart of Sedona, Arizona. Learn more at **www.amandaromania.com.**

Visit us at **www.floweroflifepress.com**

www.ingramcontent.com/pod-product-compliance
Lightning Source LLC
La Vergne TN
LVHW091248110826
845146LV00001BA/1

* 9 7 9 8 9 9 8 7 8 7 0 9 6 *